GHOSTS

A Treasury of Chilling Tales Old and New

GHOSTS
A Treasury of Chilling Tales Old and New

Selected by
Marvin Kaye

With
Saralee Kaye

STATE STREET PRESS

Published by State Street Press, an imprint of Borders Group, Inc.
100 Phoenix Drive, Ann Arbor, MI 48108
All rights reserved.

State Street Press is a trademark of Borders Group, Inc.

ISBN 0681984120

10 9 8 7 6 5 4 3

Printed and bound in the United States of America
Manufactured by Edwards Brothers, Inc.

ACKNOWLEDGMENTS

"Minuke" copyright © 1950 by Nigel Kneale. Reprinted from *Tomato Cain and Other Stories* by permission of the author.

"Legal Rites" copyright © 1950 by *Weird Tales;* renewed 1977 by Isaac Asimov and Frederik Pohl. Reprinted by permission of Isaac Asimov.

"A Quartet of Strange Things": "The Vampire of Croglin Grange," "The Old Man in Yellow," "The Glowing Maggot of Doom" copyright © Bernhardt J. Hurwood 1971; "Corpse at the Inn" copyright © Bernhardt J. Hurwood 1965. Reprinted by permission, of the author.

"The Lady of Finnigan's Hearth" copyright © 1977 by Parke Godwin. All rights reserved. Reprinted from *Fantastic Stories* magazine by permission of the author.

English versions of "The Fisherman's Story" and "The Ghost of the Capuchins" copyright © 1981 by Faith Lancereau and Marvin Kaye, and reprinted by permission of the adapters.

"Who Rides with Santa Anna?" copyright © 1958 by Columbia Publications, Inc. Reprinted by permission of the author.

"Jane" copyright © 1981 by Barbara Gallow. Permission granted by the author.

"The Hounds of Hell" reprinted by permission of The Society of Authors as the literary representative of the Estate of John Masefield.

"Doorslammer" copyright © 1969 by Donald A. Wollheim. From *Two Dozen Dragon Eggs,* by arrangement with the author.

"A Gathering of Ghosts" copyright © 1981 by Craig Shaw Gardner. Permission granted by the author.

"21 Main Street No." copyright © 1981 by Ila Jerom. Permission granted by the author.

"Four Ghosts in Hamlet" copyright © 1965 by Mercury Press, Inc. Reprinted by permission of Robert P. Mills, Ltd., literary representative of the author.

"The Ghost of Sailboat Fred" copyright © 1981 by Saralee Terry. Permission granted by the author.

"The Haunting of Y-12" copyright © 1981 by Al Sarrantonio. Permission granted by the author.

"Blind Man's Buff" copyright 1929 D. Appleton & Co., renewed 1957 by H. Russell Wakefield. Permission granted by Arkham House Publishers Inc., Sauk City, Wis.

"Money Talks" copyright © 1981 by Dick Baldwin. Permission granted by the author.

"The Last Traveler" copyright © 1965 by Lowell Bair. Reprinted by permission of MCA Publishing.

"How Fear Departed From the Long Gallery" reprinted by permission of the Estate of E. F. Benson.

"Ralph" copyright © 1981 by Marvin Kaye. Reprinted from *The Possession of Immanuel Wolf and Other Improbable Tales* by permission of the author and Doubleday & Company, Inc.

Thanks to my wife, Saralee, for handling all the basic negotiations and technical demands of shaping this huge volume in a tiny amount of time.

My gratitude to Kit MacDonald and Bernhardt J. Hurwood for making available certain valuable works of ghost literature and folklore.

—M.K.

Contents

x

WARNING TO THE READER

Tales rich in atmosphere may please in moderation but—just as sweet-meats cloy if eaten wholesale—will lose luster if read overabundantly at a single sitting. The stories and verses in these pages vary greatly in mood, style, and impact, but for best effect, they ought to be consumed like chocolate marshmallow fudge: a little at a time.

For best results, take one or two just before bedtime, preferably on the stroke of twelve and with the rain slashing at the panes, the lightning splitting the firmament, and soft music on the FM interrupted by storm reports that all nearby bridges have been washed out. Taken neat under those conditions, the doses herein contained ought to have optimum results, especially if there is no one else in the house, for many occultists believe that if one thinks profoundly enough upon the spectral, some itinerant phantom will look upon that state of mind as an invitation to come in through the wall and enjoy a midnightcap. . . .

Enjoy, enjoy! And I hope you make it to daybreak.

—M.K.

Why Are Ghosts Coming Back to Life?

When I was a boy, I whiled away many lonely hours shivering with the latest issue of *Weird Tales* and other macabre magazines and comic books. Saturdays were reserved for going to the movie house across the street, where I squirmed impatiently through the latest rubber-stamped Western in order to see the featured event of the week, Universal's most recent *Frankenstein, Dracula,* or *Wolfman* film.

My taste for the ghastly did not please my family, and at school my closest friends were those who shared a similar predilection. Easily cowed then, I accepted the attitude of relatives and teachers as accurate: Fantasy fiction was not really respectable, and I would probably outgrow it.

Then one day I bought an early paper edition of *Dracula* and discovered, to my astonishment, that Bram Stoker's classic graveyard thriller was a smashing success in England and America when it appeared in print in 1897.

I wondered what was wrong with people at the turn of the century.

Today I know the people weren't at fault, the culprit was American pragmatism in the 1940s. As long as man could transfer concept into symbol, weird fiction has flourished. Yet several generations of Americans tried to turn their backs on past superstitions; where could ghosts lurk in a world flooded with fluorescence—lightning—lit by the atom?

But there was still a trickle of fantasy magazines and books being published in the mid-40s. The night side of human nature found other devious channels of expression; science-fiction soon came of age; radio thrillers stressed the unknown and inexplicable; in Hollywood, horror films were big business, and we were not far away from the advent of television, many early shows of which were supernatural in character.

Yet ghostly tales were rare in literature, and the idea of an occult novel achieving best-seller status was ludicrous as America moved into the 1950s. (Shirley Jackson's *The Haunting of Hill House* was not printed till late 1959, and one might well argue that even it is really a psychological suspense tale.)

The era of best-seller horror novels did not occur until nearly a decade later—significantly, after the assassinations of John F. and Robert Kennedy.

The funereal weekend following November 22, 1963, ushered in a new era of American national awareness. Tragedy, confrontation, and strife distinguished the presidencies of Lyndon B. Johnson and Richard Nixon.

At the same time, the spiritual conflict that spawned agnosticism, atheism, irrelevationism, and other humanistic philosophies began to work surprising face-lifts in many organized religions. Age-old canons began to become modified to contemporary needs; the form of services saw sea-changes in a desperate effort to keep straying youth in the bosom of traditional Church.

Crime, too, changed in character. It escalated, became commonplace in overcrowded cities, and organized crime assumed a quasi-respectable profile. Morality began to develop an unhealthy relativistic appearance.

America was ripe—spiritually and practically—for a rebirth of faith and its "flip side," superstition. An explosion of fundamentalism, back-to-Jesus movements, Hari Krishna, and Reverend Moon demagoguery was matched by a new interest in vampirism, satanism, demonic possession.

Why is today's crazy quilt of faiths a logical adjunct to the sudden popularity of supernatural literature?

America is no longer adolescent. The bright dreams of the Industrial Revolution and the counterthrust of labor unionism are both tarnished; our invincibility abroad has been challenged at the same time that our international and domestic motives became gravely suspect. As our country emerged from the blood-spattered '60s, the common citizen dimly began to perceive man's age-old dilemma: that we seem to be lost in a void with no guide star. Even as scientists probe beyond the old limits set on human knowledge by orthodoxy, a backlash of superstition grips Americans. Frightened youth of all ages cast about for faiths that will not crumble overnight.

The idea of an afterlife, even a hellish one, has the roots of permanency in it. It suggests a plan, an order to life; ultimately it lets believers avoid the heavy weight of self-responsibility.

In a recent interview in the Sunday magazine section of the New York *Times*, filmmaker Stanley Kubrick put it succinctly: ghost stories, no matter how dreadful, still are ultimately optimistic: they promise shape beyond Self.

For Ghosts Only

I admit to feeling mystified at the success of much of today's supernatural literature. Witchcraft, vampirism, demonic possession seem to me, at best, impossibly dated themes, incapable of making me look over my shoulder; at worst, they excuse the sociopath his culpability. The thing that really frightens me, for instance, about Blatty's priest-despoiling imp in *The Exorcist*—other than the critical acclaim accorded his embarrassingly purple prose—is that it is a premise which attempts to excuse human nature for its bloodiest actions, shunting aside guilt onto the scapegoat of the Medieval painted devil.

Ghosts alone retain their ability to make me uneasy, largely because it is not necessary to accept any concomitant religious system to believe the possibility of their existence. If man passes to another plane, it may only be because there are more aspects to our puzzle-box universe than we originally realized. Or parapsychologists may be right when they suggest that violent emotions leave an energy residue in "haunted" houses, an ash that manifests itself as magic-lantern shows of the mind.

Eyewitness accounts of meetings with ghosts abound throughout history. Even discounting the ephemera, the magnitude is remarkable. Personally, I have experienced a few odd things in my life, things which further persuade me to keep an open mind on the topic of the spectral. (See Appendix A.)

By personal preference, then, I have excluded from this collection all miscellaneous demons, witches, elder gods, invisible damned things and the like. Only ghosts appear (and vanish) in these pages . . . though an occasional Hell-sent phantom may flit by, and a pair of vampires did manage to creep past Charon. But, remember, vampires are, technically, reanimated corpses, and I have nothing against *revenants*, other than their compelling need for deodorant and dentifrice.

The stories and poems I picked represent a great variety of style, theme, and mood. I tried to choose selections that embody many viewpoints of the spectral. (One might call it a relativistic anthology aimed at defining the state of ghosthood, though that smacks of pedantry and, after all, the underlying reason for any ghost compendium is to raise goosebumps.)

A few principles guided the final choice: limitation of each author to a single story; preference given lesser-known works over familiar tales; inclusion of a few "true" accounts and occasional stories that, despite literary merit, depict some classic aspect of the folklore of ghostly behavior. Finally, I commissioned a few new stories specially for this volume.

Those who wish to continue their midnight reading, but don't know where to find first-rate ghost tales and novels, may consult Appendix D for a representative sampling of some of my personal favorites that length or familiarity excluded.

Those hardy souls who yearn to confront a spook face-to-sheet will do well to read the advice of Appendix B, and before starting out, check Appendix C, which lists the sites of more than fifty allegedly haunted houses and spots throughout nineteen American states, as well as the District of Columbia. Many of the places named are open to the public.

Now it is time to dim the lights and embark on a journey into night. But first, be sure to stop at the Prologue and read a few choice epitaphs. Since the Other World is usually reached by way of the cemetery, it is appropriate, I feel, to peruse a sampling of tombstones. For is it not written that the paths of gory lead through the grave?

MARVIN KAYE,
Manhattan, 1980.

A PROLOGUE OF LAST WORDS

Bon mots at the time of death are probably few—though H. G. Wells is reported to have snapped at an overly fussy nurse, "Get away, woman! Can't you see I'm busy dying?"—but those who survive often cannot resist a final joke at the expense of the deceased.

Here are a few of the more inventive epitaphs and parting shots I have gleaned from the annals of humorous verse and transcriptions of actual gravestone markers. (The last and longest entry was really copied from a tomb in Penobscot, Maine.)

*　　　*　　　*

Hurrah! my boys, at the Parson's fall,
For if he'd lived he'd a buried us all.

*　　　*　　　*

Within this grave doth lie
Back to back, my wife and I.
When the Last Trump the air shall fill,
If she gets up, I'll just lie still.

*　　　*　　　*

Here lies father and mother and sister and I,
We all died within one short year.
They all be buried at Wimble, except I,
For I be buried here.

*　　　*　　　*

This is the grave of Mike O'Day
Who died maintaining his right of way.
His right was clear, his will was strong,
But he's just as dead if he'd been wrong.

*　　　*　　　*

Here lies old John Porter,
Who was both 'ale and stout.
Death laid him on a bitter bier
And in Hell he hops about.

*　　　*　　　*

Here lies John Bun

Who was killed by a gun.
(His name wasn't Bun, it was Wood,
But Wood wouldn't rhyme with gun, but Bun would.)
*   *   *
Beneath this clay
Lies Arabella Young.
On the 24th of May
She finally held her tongue.
*   *   *
Here lies the body of Mary Anne Beltzer,
Who burst while drinking an Alka-Seltzer.
Called from this wide world too soon, no doubt;
She should have waited till it all fizzed out.
*   *   *
Little Willie from his mirror
Licked the mercury right off,
Thinking in his childish error,
It would cure the whooping cough.
At the funeral, his mother smartly said to Mrs. Brown:
" 'Twas a chilly day for Willie when the mercury went down!"
*   *   *
Beneath this stone, a lump of clay,
Lies Uncle Peter Daniels,
Who too early in the month of May
Took off his winter flannels.
*   *   *
Beneath these stones repose the bones
of Theodosius Grimm;
He took his beer from year to year,
and then the bier took him.
*   *   *
Here lies a poor woman,
Who always was tired;
She lived in a house,
Where help was not hired;
Her last words on earth were,
"Dear friends, I am going;
Where washing ain't done,
Nor sweeping nor sewing;
But everything there is exact to my wishes.

For where they don't eat,
There's no washing dishes;
I'll be where loud anthems will always be ringing,
But having no voice, I'll be clear of the singing;
Don't mourn for me now, don't mourn for me never,
I'm going to do nothing forever and ever."

*　　　*　　　*

But death is not always such a lark. Beethoven is said to have died shaking his fists at the lightning-split skies, Abraham Lincoln is rumored to walk the corridors of the White House whenever the country is troubled. (When does he *ever* rest?) And one obscure political terrorist in the sixteenth century penned what may be the most moving final words in English . . .

I sought for death and I found it in the womb,
I lookt for life and saw it was a shade,
I trod the earth and knew it was my tomb,
And now I die, and now I was but made;
My glass is full, and now my glass is run,
And now I live, and now my life is done.

The grave gapes, the earth yawns and the hosts of night bid you welcome. The comedy is ended.

"Minuke" *is an ugly house that one would do well to avoid. This gripping story is taken from* Tomato Cain, *the first collection of tales by* NIGEL KNEALE, *one of England's finer writers. Born in 1922 in Lancashire, Kneale studied law, changed allegiance to the theatre, acted for two years at Stratford-on-Avon and wrote in his spare time. In 1949, the British theatre was not healthy, and Kneale was advised to try writing full time. Soon after,* Tomato Cain *appeared in Great Britain and America. Science-fiction buffs know Kneale as the creator of the "Quatermass" series, the scripts of which are available in Penguin paper editions. The first of the trilogy was filmed as* The Creeping Unknown, *starring Brian Donleavy as Quatermass. It is still being shown today.*

"Minuke"
by Nigel Kneale

The estate agent kept an uncomfortable silence until we reached his car. "Frankly, I wish you hadn't got wind of that," he said. "Don't know how you did: I thought I had the whole thing carefully disposed of. Oh, please get in."

He pulled his door shut and frowned. "It puts me in a rather awkward spot. I suppose I'd better tell you all I know about that case, or you'd be suspecting me of heaven-knows-what kinds of chicanery in your own."

As we set off to see the property I was interested in, he shifted the cigarette to the side of his mouth.

"It's quite a distance, so I can tell you on the way there," he said. "We'll pass the very spot, as a matter of fact, and you can see it for yourself. Such as there is to see."

It was away back before the war (said the estate agent). At the height of the building boom. You remember how it was: ribbon development in full blast everywhere; speculative builders sticking things up almost overnight. Though at least you could get a house when you wanted it in those days.

I've always been careful in what I handle—I want you to understand that. Then one day I was handed a packet of coast-road bungalows, for letting. Put up by one of these gone-tomorrow firms, and bought by a local man. I can't say I exactly jumped for joy, but for once the things looked all right, and—business is inclined to be business.

The desirable residence you heard about stood at the end of the row. Actually, it seemed to have the best site. On a sort of natural platform, as it were, raised above road level and looking straight out over the sea. Like all the rest, it had a simple two-bedroom, lounge, living-room, kitchen, bathroom layout. Red-tiled roof, roughcast walls. Ornamental portico, garden strip all round. Sufficiently far from town, but with all conveniences.

It was taken by a man named Pritchard. Cinema projectionist, I think he was. Wife, a boy of ten or so, and a rather young daughter. Oh—and dog, one of those black, lop-eared animals. They christened the place "Minuke," M-I-N-U-K-E. My Nook. Yes, that's what I said too. And not even the miserable excuse of its being phonetically correct. Still, hardly worse than most.

Well, at the start everything seemed quite jolly. The Pritchards settled in and busied themselves with rearing a privet hedge and shoving flowers in. They'd paid the first quarter in advance, and as far as I was concerned, were out of the picture for a bit.

Then, about a fortnight after they'd moved in, I had a telephone call from Mrs. P. to say there was something odd about the kitchen tap. Apparently the thing had happened twice. The first time was when her sister was visiting them, and tried to fill the kettle: no water would come through for a long time, then suddenly squirted violently and almost soaked the woman. I gather the Pritchards hadn't really believed this—thought she was trying to find fault with their little nest—it had never happened before, and she couldn't make it happen again. Then, about a week later, it did; with Mrs. Pritchard this time. After her husband had examined the tap and could find nothing wrong with it, he decided the water supply must be faulty. So they got on to me.

I went round personally, as it was the first complaint from any of these bungalows. The tap seemed normal, and I remember asking if the schoolboy son could have been experimenting with the main stop, when Mrs. Pritchard, who had been fiddling with the tap, suddenly said: "Quick, look at this! It's off now!" They were quite cocky about its happening when I was there.

It really was odd. I turned the tap to the limit, but—not a drop! Not even the sort of gasping gurgle you hear when the supply is turned off at the main. After a couple of minutes, though, it came on. Water shot out with, I should say, about ten times normal force, as if it had been held under pressure. Then gradually it died down and ran steadily.

Both children were in the room with us until we all dodged out of the door to escape a soaking—it had splashed all over the ceiling—so they couldn't have been up to any tricks. I promised the Pritchards to have the pipes checked. Before returning to town, I called at the next two bungalows in the row: neither of the tenants had had any trouble at all with the water. I thought, well, that localized it at least.

When I reached my office there was a telephone message waiting, from Pritchard. I rang him back and he was obviously annoyed. "Look here," he said, "not ten minutes after you left, we've had something else happen! The wall of the large bedroom's cracked from top to bottom. Big pieces of plaster fell, and the bed's in a terrible mess." And then he said: "You wouldn't have got me in a jerry-built place like this if I'd known!"

I had plasterers on the job next morning, and the whole water supply to "Minuke" under examination. For about three days there was peace. The tap behaved itself, and absolutely nothing was found to be wrong. I was annoyed at what seemed to have been unnecessary expenditure. It looked as if the Pritchards were going to be difficult—and I've had my share of that type; fault-finding cranks occasionally carry eccentricity to the extent of a little private destruction, to prove their points. I was on the watch from now on.

Then it came again.

Pritchard rang me at my home, before nine in the morning. His voice sounded a bit off. Shaky.

"For God's sake can you come round here right away," he said. "Tell you about it when you get here." And then he said, almost fiercely, but quietly and close up to the mouthpiece: "There's something damned queer about this place!" Dramatizing is a typical feature of all cranks, I thought, but particularly the little mousy kind, like Pritchard.

I went to "Minuke" and found that Mrs. Pritchard was in bed, in a state of collapse. The doctor had given her a sleeping dose.

Pritchard told me a tale that was chiefly remarkable for the expression on his face as he told it.

I don't know if you're familiar with the layout of that type of bungalow? The living-room is in the front of the house, with the kitchen behind it. To get from one to the other you have to use the little hallway, through two doors. But for convenience at mealtimes, there's a serving-hatch in the wall between these rooms. A small wooden door slides up and down over the hatch-opening.

"The wife was just passing a big plate of bacon and eggs through from the kitchen," Pritchard told me, "when the hatch door came down on her wrists. I saw it and I heard her yell. I thought the cord must've snapped, so I said: 'All right, all right!' and went to pull it up because it's only a light wooden frame."

Pritchard was a funny colour, and as far as I could judge, it was genuine.

"Do you know, it wouldn't come! I got my fingers under it and heaved, but it might have weighed two hundredweight. Once it gave an inch or so, and then pressed harder. That was it—it was *pressing* down! I heard the wife groan. I said: 'Hold on!' and nipped round through the hall. When I got into the kitchen she was on the floor, fainted. And the hatch-door was hitched up as right as ninepence. That gave me a turn!" He sat down, quite deflated: it didn't appear to be put on. Still, ordinary neurotics can be almost as troublesome as out-and-out cranks.

I tested the hatch, gingerly; and, of course, the cords were sound and it ran easily.

"Possibly a bit stiff at times, being new," I said. "They're apt to jam if you're rough with them." And then: "By the way, just what were you hinting on the phone?"

He looked at me. It was warm sunlight outside, with a bus passing. Normal enough to take the mike out of Frankenstein's monster. "Never mind," he said, and gave a sheepish half-grin. "Bit of—well, funny construction in this house, though, eh?"

I'm afraid I was rather outspoken with him.

Let alone any twaddle about a month-old bungalow being haunted, I was determined to clamp down on this "jerry-building" talk. Perhaps I was beginning to have doubts myself.

I wrote straight off to the building company when I'd managed to trace them, busy developing an arterial road about three counties away. I daresay my letter was on the insinuating side: I think I asked if they had any record of difficulties in the construction of this bungalow. At any rate I got a sniffy reply by return, stating that the matter was out of their hands; in addition, their records were not available for discussion. Blind alley.

In the meantime, things at "Minuke" had worsened to a really frightening degree. I dreaded the phone ringing. One morning the two Pritchards senior awoke to find that nearly all the furniture in their bedroom had been moved about, including the bed they had been sleeping in; they had felt absolutely nothing. Food became suddenly and revoltingly decomposed. All the chimney pots had come down, not just into the garden, but to the far side of the high road, except one which appeared, pulverized, on the living-room floor. The obvious attempts of the Pritchards to keep a rational outlook had put "paid" to most of my suspicions by this time.

I managed to locate a local man who had been employed during the erection of the bungalows, as an extra hand. He had worked only on the foundations of "Minuke," but what he had to say was interesting.

They had found the going slow because of striking a layer of enormous flat stones, apparently trimmed slate, but as the site was otherwise excellent, they pressed on, using the stone as foundation where it fitted in with the plan, and laying down rubble where it didn't. The concrete skin over the rubble—my ears burned when I heard about that, I can tell you—this wretched so-called concrete had cracked, or shattered, several times. Which wasn't entirely surprising, if it had been laid as he described. The flat stones, he said, had not been seriously disturbed. A workmate had referred to them as "a giant's grave," so it was possibly an old burial mound. Norse, perhaps—those are fairly common along this coast—or even very much older.

Apart from this—I'm no diehard sceptic; I may as well confess I was beginning to admit modest theories about a poltergeist, in spite of a lack of corroborative knockings and ornament-throwing. There were two young children in the house, and the lore has it that they're often unconsciously connected with phenomena of that sort, though usually adolescents. Still, in the real-estate profession you have to be careful, and if I could see the Pritchards safely off the premises without airing these possibilities, it might be kindest to the bungalow's future.

I went to "Minuke" that afternoon.

It was certainly turning out an odd nook. I found a departing policeman on the doorstep. That morning the back door had been burst in by a hundredweight or so of soil, and Mrs. Pritchard was trying to convince herself that a practical joker had it in for them. The policeman had taken some notes, and was giving vague advice about "civil action" which showed that he was out of his depth.

Pritchard looked very tired, almost ill. "I've got leave from my job, to look after them," he said, when we were alone. I thought he was wise. He had given his wife's illness as the reason, and I was glad of that.

"I don't believe in—unnatural happenings," he said.

I agreed with him, noncommittally.

"But I'm afraid of what ideas the kids might get. They're both at impressionable ages, y'know."

I recognized the symptoms without disappointment. "You mean, you'd rather move elsewhere," I said.

He nodded. "I like the district, mind you. But what I—"

There was a report like a gun in the very room.

I found myself with both arms up to cover my face. There were tiny splinters everywhere, and a dust of fibre in the air. The door had exploded. Literally.

To hark back to constructional details, it was one of those light, hollow frame-and-plywood jobs. As you'll know, it takes considerable force to splinter plywood. Well, this was in tiny fragments. And the oddest thing was that we had felt no blast effect.

In the next room I heard their dog howling. Pritchard was as stiff as a poker.

"I felt it!" he said. "I felt this lot coming. I've got to knowing when something's likely to happen. It's all round!" Of course I began to imagine I'd sensed something too, but I doubt if I had really; my shock came with the crash. Mrs. Pritchard was in the doorway by this time with the kids behind her. He motioned them out and grabbed my arm.

"The thing is," he whispered, "I can still feel it! Stronger than ever, by God! Look, will you stay at home tonight, in case I need—well, in case things get worse? I can phone you."

On my way back I called at the town library and managed to get hold of a volume on supernatural possession and what-not. Yes, I was committed now. But the library didn't specialize in that line, and when I opened the book at home, I found it was very little help. "Vampires of southeastern Europe" type of stuff. I came across references to something the jargon called an "elemental," which I took to be a good deal more vicious and destructive than any poltergeist. A thoroughly nasty form of manifestation, if it existed. Those Norse gravestones were fitting into the picture uncomfortably well; it was fashionable in those days to be buried with all the trimmings, human sacrifice and even more unmentionable attractions.

But I read on. After half a chapter on zombies and Rumanian werewolves, the whole thing began to seem so fantastic that I turned seriously to working out methods of exploding somebody's door as a practical joke. Even a totally certifiable joker would be likelier than vampires. In no time I'd settled down with a whisky, doodling wiring diagrams, and only occasionally—like twinges of conscience—speculating on contacting the psychic investigation people.

When the phone rang I was hardly prepared for it.

It was a confused, distant voice, gabbling desperately, but I recognized it as Pritchard. "For God's sake, don't lose a second! Get here—it's all hell on earth! Can't you hear it? My God, I'm going crazy!" And in the background I thought I was able to hear something. A sort of bubbling, shushing "wah-wah" noise. Indescribable. But you hear some odd sounds on telephones at any time.

"Yes," I said, "I'll come immediately. Why don't you all leave—" But the line had gone dead.

Probably I've never moved faster. I scrambled out to the car with untied shoes flopping, though I remembered to grab a heavy stick in the hall—whatever use it was to be. I drove like fury, heart belting, straight to "Minuke," expecting to see heaven knows what.

But everything looked still and normal there. The moon was up and I could see the whole place clearly. Curtained lights in the windows. Not a sound.

I rang. After a moment Pritchard opened the door. He was quiet and seemed almost surprised to see me.

I pushed inside. "Well?" I said. "What's happened?"

"Not a thing, so far," he said. "That's why I didn't expect—"

I felt suddenly angry. "Look here," I said, "what are you playing at? Seems to me that any hoaxing round here begins a lot nearer home than you'd have me believe!" Then the penny dropped. I saw by the fright in his face that he knew something had gone wrong. That was the most horrible, sickening moment of the whole affair for me.

"Didn't you ring?" I said.

And he shook his head.

I've been in some tight spots. But there was always some concrete, actual business in hand to screw the mind safely down to. I suppose panic is when the subconscious breaks loose and everything in your head dashes screaming out. It was only just in time that I found a touch of the concrete and actual. A kiddie's paintbox on the floor, very watery.

"The children," I said. "Where are they?"

"Wife's just putting the little 'un to bed. She's been restless tonight: just wouldn't go, crying and difficult. Arthur's in the bathroom. Look here, what's happened?"

I told him, making it as short and matter-of-fact as I could. He turned ghastly.

"Better get them dressed and out of here right away," I said. "Make some excuse, not to alarm them." He'd gone before I finished speaking.

I smoked hard, trying to build up the idea of "Hoax! Hoax!" in my mind. After all, it could have been. But I knew it wasn't.

Everything looked cosy and normal. Clock ticking. Fire red and mellow. Half-empty cocoa mug on the table. The sound of the sea from beyond the road. I went through to the kitchen. The dog was there, looking up from its sleeping-basket under the sink. "Good dog," I said, and it wriggled its tail.

Pritchard came in from the hall. He jumped when he saw me.

"Getting nervy!" he said. "They won't be long. I don't know where we can go if we—well, if we have to—to leave tonight—"

"My car's outside," I told him. "I'll fix you up. Look here, did you ever 'hear things'? Odd noises?" I hadn't told him that part of the telephone call.

He looked at me so oddly I thought he was going to collapse.

"I don't know," he said. "Can you?"

"At this moment?"

I listened.

"No," I said. "The clock on the shelf. The sea. Nothing else. No."

"The sea," he said, barely whispering. "But you can't hear the sea in this kitchen!"

He was close to me in an instant. Absolutely terrified. "Yes, I have heard this before! I think we all have. I said it was the sea, so as not to frighten them. But it isn't! And I recognized it when I came in here just now. That's what made me start. It's getting louder; it does that."

He was right. Like slow breathing. It seemed to emanate from inside the walls, not at a particular spot, but everywhere. We went into the hall, then the front room; it was the same there. Mixed with it now was a sort of thin crying.

"That's Nellie," Pritchard said. "The dog: she always whimpers when it's on—too scared to howl. My God, I've never heard it as loud as this before!"

"Hurry them up, will you!" I almost shouted. He went.

The "breathing" was ghastly. Slobbering. Stertorous, I think the term is. And faster. Oh, yes, I recognized it. The background music to the phone message. My skin was pure ice.

"Come along!" I yelled. I switched on the little radio to drown the noise. The old National Programme, as it was in those days, for late dance music. Believe it or not, what came through that loudspeaker was the same vile, sighing noise, at double the volume. And when I tried to switch off, it stayed the same.

The whole bungalow was trembling. The Pritchards came running in, she carrying the little girl. "Get them into the car," I shouted. We heard glass smashing somewhere.

Above our heads there was an almighty thump. Plaster showered down.

Halfway out of the door the little girl screamed, "Nellie! Where's Nellie? Nellie, Nellie!"

"The dog!" Pritchard moaned. "Oh, curse it!" He dragged them outside. I dived for the kitchen, where I'd seen the animal, feeling a lunatic for doing it. Plaster was springing out of the walls in painful showers.

In the kitchen I found water everywhere. One tap was squirting like a fire hose. The other was missing, water belching across the window from a torn end of pipe.

"Nellie!" I called.

Then I saw the dog. It was lying near the oven, quite stiff. Round its neck was twisted a piece of painted piping with the other tap on the end.

Sheer funk got me then. The ground was moving under me. I bolted down the hall, nearly bumped into Pritchard. I yelled and shoved. I could actually feel the house at my back.

We got outside. The noise was like a dreadful snoring, with rumbles and crashes thrown in. One of the lights went out. "Nellie's run away," I said, and we all got into the car, the kids bawling. I started up. People were coming out of the other bungalows—they're pretty far apart and the din was just beginning to make itself felt. Pritchard mumbled: "We can stop now. Think it'd be safe to go back and grab some of the furniture?" As if he was at a fire; but I don't think he knew what he was doing.

"Daddy—look!" screeched the boy.

We saw it. The chimney of "Minuke" was going up in a horrible way. In the moonlight it seemed to grow, quite slowly, to about sixty feet, like a giant crooked finger. And then—burst. I heard bricks thumping down. Somewhere somebody screamed.

There was a glare like an ungodly great lightning flash. It lasted for a second or so.

Of course we were dazzled, but I thought I saw the whole of "Minuke" fall suddenly and instantaneously flat, like a swatted fly. I probably did, because that's what happened, anyway.

There isn't much more to tell.

Nobody was really hurt, and we were able to put down the whole thing to a serious electrical fault. Main fuses had blown throughout the whole district, which helped this theory out. Perhaps it was unfortunate in another respect, because a lot of people changed over to gas. And the local rag still ran a leader about "lost standards in the building trade."

There wasn't much recognizably left of "Minuke." But some of the bits were rather unusual. Knots in pipes, for instance—I buried what was left of the dog myself. Wood and brick cleanly sliced. Small quantities of completely powdered metal. The bath had been squashed flat, like tinfoil. In fact, Pritchard was lucky to land the insurance money for his furniture.

My professional problem, of course, remained. The plot where the wretched place had stood. I managed to persuade the owner it wasn't ideal for building on. Incidentally, lifting those stones might reveal something to somebody some day—but not to me, thank you!

I think my eventual solution showed a touch of wit: I let it very cheaply as a scrap-metal dump.

Well? I know I've never been able to make any sense out of it. I hate telling you all this stuff, because it must make me seem either a simpleton or a charlatan. In so far as there's any circumstantial evidence in looking at the place, you can see it in a moment or two. Here's the coast road. . . .

The car pulled up at a bare spot beyond a sparse line of bungalows. The space was marked by a straggling, tufty square of privet bushes. Inside I could see a tangle of rusting iron: springs, a car chassis, oil drums.

"The hedge keeps it from being too unsightly," said the estate agent, as we crossed to it. "See—the remains of the gate."

A few half-rotten slats dangled from an upright. One still bore part of a chrome-plated name. "MI——" and, a little farther on, "K."

"Nothing worth seeing now," he said. I peered inside. "Not that there ever was much— Look out!" I felt a violent push. In the same instant something zipped past my head and crashed against the car behind. "My God! Went right at you!" gasped the agent.

It had shattered a window of the car and gone through the open door opposite. We found it in the road beyond, sizzling on the tarmac. A heavy steel nut, white-hot.

"I don't know about you," the estate agent said, "but I'm rather in favour of getting out of here."

And we did. Quickly.

This quietly cruel tale is an exercise in atmosphere and character, and a memorable one. Most of its impact lies in what is not said. MARY WILKINS-FREEMAN lived her life in New England and at one time is said to have been secretary to Oliver Wendell Holmes. This story dates back to 1903.

The Wind in the Rose-Bush
by Mary Wilkins-Freeman

Ford Village has no railroad station, being on the other side of the river from Porter's Falls, and accessible only by the ford which gives it its name, and a ferry line.

The ferry-boat was waiting when Rebecca Flint got off the train with her bag and lunch basket. When she and her small trunk were safely embarked she sat stiff and straight and calm in the ferry-boat as it shot swiftly and smoothly across stream. There was a horse attached to a light country wagon on board, and he pawed the deck uneasily. His owner stood near, with a wary eye upon him, although he was chewing, with as dully reflective an expression as a cow. Beside Rebecca sat a woman of about her own age, who kept looking at her with furtive curiosity; her husband, short and stout and saturnine, stood near her. Rebecca paid no attention to either of them. She was tall and spare and pale, the type of a spinster, yet with rudimentary lines and expressions of matronhood. She all unconsciously held her shawl, rolled up in a canvas bag, on her left hip, as if it had been a child. She wore a settled frown of dissent at life, but it was the frown of a mother who regarded life as a froward child, rather than as an overwhelming fate.

The other woman continued staring at her; she was mildly stupid, except for an overdeveloped curiosity which made her at times sharp beyond belief. Her eyes glittered, red spots came on her flaccid cheeks; she kept opening her mouth to speak, making little abortive motions. Finally she could endure it no longer; she nudged Rebecca boldly.

"A pleasant day," said she.

Rebecca looked at her and nodded coldly.

"Yes, very," she assented.

"Have you come far?"

"I have come from Michigan."

"Oh!" said the woman, with awe. "It's a long way," she remarked presently.

"Yes, it is," replied Rebecca, conclusively.

Still the other woman was not daunted; there was something which she determined to know, possibly roused thereto by a vague sense of incongruity in the other's appearance. "It's a long ways to come and leave a family," she remarked with painful slyness.

"I ain't got any family to leave," returned Rebecca shortly.

"Then you ain't . . ."

"No, I ain't."

"Oh!" said the woman.

Rebecca looked straight ahead at the race of the river.

It was a long ferry. Finally Rebecca herself waxed unexpectedly loquacious. She turned to the other woman and inquired if she knew John Dent's widow who lived in Ford Village. "Her husband died about three years ago," said she, by way of detail.

The woman started violently. She turned pale, then she flushed; she cast a strange glance at her husband, who was regarding both women with a sort of stolid keenness.

"Yes, I guess I do," faltered the woman finally.

"Well, his first wife was my sister," said Rebecca with the air of one imparting important intelligence.

"Was she?" responded the other woman feebly. She glanced at her husband with an expression of doubt and terror, and he shook his head forbiddingly.

"I'm going to see her, and take my niece Agnes home with me," said Rebecca.

Then the woman gave such a violent start that she noticed it.

"What is the matter?" she asked.

"Nothin', I guess," replied the woman with eyes on her husband, who was slowly shaking his head like a Chinese toy.

"Is my niece sick?" asked Rebecca with quick suspicion.

"No, she ain't sick," replied the woman with alacrity, then she caught her breath again.

"She ought to have grown up real pretty, if she takes after my sister. She was a real pretty woman," Rebecca said wistfully.

"Yes, I guess she did grow up pretty," replied the woman in a trembling voice.

"What kind of a woman is the second wife?"

The woman glanced at her husband's warning face. She continued to gaze at him while she replied in a choking voice to Rebecca:

"I—guess she's a nice woman," she replied. "I—don't know, I—guess so. I—don't see much of her."

"I felt kind of hurt that John married again so quick," said Rebecca; "but I suppose he wanted his house kept, and Agnes wanted care. I wasn't so situated that I could take her when her mother died. I had my own mother to care for, and I was school-teaching. Now mother has gone, and my uncle died six months ago and left me quite a little property, and I've come for Agnes. I guess she'll be glad to go with me, though I suppose her stepmother is a good woman, and has always done for her."

The man's warning shake at his wife was fairly portentous.

"I guess so," said she.

"John always wrote that she was a beautiful woman," said Rebecca.

Then the ferry-boat grated on the shore.

John Dent's widow had sent a horse and wagon to meet her sister-in-law. When the woman and her husband went down the road, on which Rebecca in the wagon with her trunk soon passed them, she said reproachfully:

"Seems as if I'd ought to have told her, Thomas."

"Let her find it out herself," replied the man. "Don't you go to burnin' your fingers in other folks' puddin', Maria."

"Do you s'pose she'll see anything?" asked the woman with a spasmodic shudder and a terrified roll of her eyes.

"See!" returned her husband with stolid scorn. "Better be sure there's anything to see."

"Oh, Thomas, they say . . ."

"Lord, ain't you found out that what they say is mostly lies?"

"But if it should be true, and she's a nervous woman, she might be scared enough to lose her wits," said his wife, staring uneasily after Rebecca's erect figure in the wagon disappearing over the crest of the hilly road.

"Wits that so easy upset ain't worth much," declared the man. "You keep out of it, Maria."

Rebecca in the meantime rode on in the wagon, beside a flaxen-headed boy, who looked, to her understanding, not very bright. She asked him a question, and he paid no attention. She repeated it, and he responded with a bewildered and incoherent grunt. Then she let him alone, after making sure that he knew how to drive straight.

They had traveled about half a mile, passed the village square, and gone a short distance beyond, when the boy drew up with a sudden *Whoa!* before a very prosperous-looking house. It had been one of the aboriginal cottages of the vicinity, small and white, with a roof extending on one side over a piazza, and a tiny "L" jutting out in the rear, on the right hand. Now the cottage was transformed by dormer windows, a bay window on the piazzaless side, a carved railing down the front steps, and a modern hard-wood door.

"Is this John Dent's house?" asked Rebecca.

The boy was as sparing of speech as a philosopher. His only response was in flinging the reins over the horse's back, stretching out one foot to the shaft, and leaping out of the wagon, then going around to the rear for the trunk. Rebecca got out and went toward the house. Its white paint had a new gloss; its blinds were an immaculate apple green; the lawn was trimmed as smooth as velvet, and it was dotted with scrupulous groups of hydrangeas and cannas.

"I always understood that John Dent was well-to-do," Rebecca reflected comfortably. "I guess Agnes will have considerable. I've got enough, but it will come in handy for her schooling. She can have advantages."

The boy dragged the trunk up the fine gravel-walk, but before he reached the steps leading up to the piazza, for the house stood on a terrace, the front door opened and a fair, frizzled head of a very large and handsome woman appeared. She held up her black silk skirt, disclosing voluminous ruffles of starched embroidery, and waited for Rebecca. She smiled placidly, her pink, double-chinned face widened and dimpled, but her blue eyes were wary and calculating. She extended her hand as Rebecca climbed the steps.

"This is Miss Flint, I suppose," said she.

"Yes, ma'am," replied Rebecca, noticing with bewilderment a curious expression compounded of fear and defiance on the other's face.

"Your letter only arrived this morning," said Mrs. Dent, in a steady voice. Her great face was a uniform pink, and her china-blue eyes were at once aggressive and veiled with secrecy.

"Yes, I hardly thought you'd get my letter," replied Rebecca. "I felt as if I could not wait to hear from you before I came. I supposed you would be so situated that you could have me a little while without putting you out too much, from what John used to write me about his circumstances, and when I had that money so unexpected I felt as if I must come for Agnes. I suppose you will be willing to give her up. You know she's my own blood, and of course she's no relation to you, though you must have got attached to her. I know from her picture what a sweet girl she must be, and John always said she looked like her own mother, and Grace was a beautiful woman, if she was my sister."

Rebecca stopped and stared at the other woman in amazement and alarm. The great handsome blonde creature stood speechless, livid, gasping, with her hand to her heart, her lips parted in a horrible caricature of a smile.

"Are you sick!" cried Rebecca, drawing near. "Don't you want me to get you some water!"

Then Mrs. Dent recovered herself with a great effort. "It is nothing," she said. "I am subject to—spells. I am over it now. Won't you come in, Miss Flint?"

As she spoke, the beautiful deep-rose color suffused her face, her blue eyes met her visitor's with the opaqueness of turquoise—with a revelation of blue, but a concealment of all behind.

Rebecca followed her hostess in, and the boy, who had waited quiescently, climbed the steps with the trunk. But before they entered the door a strange thing happened. On the upper terrace, close to the piazza-post, grew a great rose-bush, and on it, late in the season though it was, one small red, perfect rose.

Rebecca looked at it, and the other woman extended her hand with a quick gesture. "Don't you pick that rose!" she brusquely cried.

Rebecca drew herself up with stiff dignity.

"I ain't in the habit of picking other folks' roses without leave," said she.

As Rebecca spoke she started violently, and lost sight of her resentment, for something singular happened. Suddenly the rose-bush was agitated violently as if by a gust of wind, yet it was a remarkably still day. Not a leaf of the hydrangea standing on the terrace close to the rose trembled.

"What on earth . . ." began Rebecca, then she stopped with a gasp at the sight of the other woman's face. Although a face, it gave somehow the impression of a desperately clutched hand of secrecy.

"Come in!" said she in a harsh voice, which seemed to come forth from her chest with no intervention of the organs of speech. "Come into the house. I'm getting cold out here."

"What makes that rose-bush blow so when there isn't any wind?" asked Rebecca, trembling with vague horror, yet resolute.

"I don't see as it is blowing," returned the woman calmly. And as she spoke, indeed, the bush was quiet.

"It was blowing," declared Rebecca.

"It isn't now," said Mrs. Dent. "I can't try to account for everything that blows out-of-doors. I have too much to do."

She spoke scornfully and confidently, with defiant, unflinching eyes, first on the bush, then on Rebecca, and led the way into the house.

"It looked queer," persisted Rebecca, but she followed, and also the boy with the trunk.

Rebecca entered an interior, prosperous, even elegant, according to her simple ideas. There were Brussels carpets, lace curtains, and plenty of brilliant upholstery and polished wood.

"You're real nicely situated," remarked Rebecca, after she had become a little accustomed to her new surroundings and the two women were seated at the tea-table.

Mrs. Dent stared with a hard complacency from behind her silver-plated service. "Yes, I be," said she.

"You got all the things new?" said Rebecca hesitatingly, with a jealous memory of her dead sister's bridal furnishings.

"Yes," said Mrs. Dent; "I was never one to want dead folks' things, and I had money enough of my own, so I wasn't beholden to John. I had the old duds put up at auction. They didn't bring much."

"I suppose you saved some for Agnes. She'll want some of her poor mother's things when she is grown up," said Rebecca with some indignation.

The defiant stare of Mrs. Dent's blue eyes waxed more intense. "There's a few things up garret," said she.

"She'll be likely to value them," remarked Rebecca. As she spoke she glanced at the window. "Isn't it most time for her to be coming home?" she asked.

"Most time," answered Mrs. Dent carelessly; "but when she gets over to Addie Slocum's she never knows when to come home."

"Is Addie Slocum her intimate friend?"

"Intimate as any."

"Maybe we can have her come out to see Agnes when she's living with me," said Rebecca wistfully. "I suppose she'll be likely to be homesick at first."

"Most likely," answered Mrs. Dent.

"Does she call you mother?" Rebecca asked.

"No, she calls me Aunt Emeline," replied the other woman shortly. "When did you say you were going home?"

"In about a week, I thought, if she can be ready to go so soon," answered Rebecca with a surprised look.

She reflected that she would not remain a day longer than she could help after such an inhospitable look and question.

"Oh, as far as that goes," said Mrs. Dent, "it wouldn't make any difference about her being ready. You could go home whenever you felt that you must, and she could come afterward."

"Alone?"

"Why not? She's a big girl now, and you don't have to change cars."

"My niece will go home when I do, and not travel alone; and if I can't wait here for her, in the house that used to be her mother's and my sister's home, I'll go and board somewhere," returned Rebecca with warmth.

"Oh, you can stay here as long as you want to. You're welcome," said Mrs. Dent.

Then Rebecca started. "There she is!" she declared in a trembling, exultant voice. Nobody knew how she longed to see the girl.

"She isn't as late as I thought she'd be," said Mrs. Dent, and again that curious, subtle change passed over her face, and again it settled into that stony impassiveness.

Rebecca stared at the door, waiting for it to open. "Where is she?" she asked presently.

"I guess she's stopped to take off her hat in the entry," suggested Mrs. Dent.

Rebecca waited. "Why don't she come? It can't take her all this time to take off her hat."

For answer Mrs. Dent rose with a stiff jerk and threw open the door.

"Agnes!" she called. "Agnes!" Then she turned and eyed Rebecca. "She ain't there."

"I saw her pass the window," said Rebecca in bewilderment.

"You must have been mistaken."

"I know I did," persisted Rebecca.

"You couldn't have."

"I did. I saw first a shadow go over the ceiling, then I saw her in the glass there"—she pointed to a mirror over the sideboard opposite—"and then the shadow passed the window."

"How did she look in the glass?"

"Little and light-haired, with the light hair kind of tossing over her forehead."

"You couldn't have seen her."

"Was that like Agnes?"

"Like enough; but of course you didn't see her. You've been thinking so much about her that you thought you did."

"You thought *you* did."

"I thought I saw a shadow pass the window, but I must have been mistaken. She didn't come in, or we would have seen her before now. I knew it was too early for her to get home from Addie Slocum's, anyhow."

When Rebecca went to bed Agnes had not returned. Rebecca had resolved that she would not retire until the girl came, but she was very tired, and she reasoned with herself that she was foolish. Besides, Mrs. Dent suggested that Agnes might go to the church social with Addie Slocum. When Rebecca suggested that she be sent for and told that her aunt had come, Mrs. Dent laughed meaningly.

"I guess you'll find out that a young girl ain't so ready to leave a sociable, where there's boys, to see her aunt," said she.

"She's too young," said Rebecca incredulously and indignantly.

"She's sixteen," replied Mrs. Dent; "and she's always been great for the boys."

"She's going to school four years after I get her before she thinks of boys," declared Rebecca.

"We'll see," laughed the other woman.

After Rebecca went to bed, she lay awake a long time listening for the sound of girlish laughter and a boy's voice under her window; then she fell asleep.

The next morning she was down early. Mrs. Dent, who kept no servants, was busily preparing breakfast.

"Don't Agnes help you about breakfast?" asked Rebecca.

"No, I let her lay," replied Mrs. Dent shortly.

"What time did she get home last night?"

"She didn't get home. She stayed with Addie. She often does."

"Without sending you word?"

"Oh, she knew I wouldn't worry."

"When will she be home?"

"Oh, I guess she'll be along pretty soon."

Rebecca was uneasy, but she tried to conceal it, for she knew of no good reason for uneasiness. What was there to occasion alarm in the fact of one young girl staying overnight with another? She could not eat much breakfast. Afterward she went out on the little piazza, although her hostess strove furtively to stop her.

"Why don't you go out back of the house? It's real pretty—a view over the river," she said.

"I guess I'll go out here," replied Rebecca. She had a purpose: to watch for the absent girl.

Presently Rebecca came hustling into the house through the sitting-room, into the kitchen where Mrs. Dent was cooking.

"That rose-bush!" she gasped.

Mrs. Dent turned and faced her.

"What of it?"

"It's a-blowing."

"What of it?"

"There isn't a mite of wind this morning."

Mrs. Dent turned with an inimitable toss of her fair head. "If you think I can spend my time puzzling over such nonsense as . . ." she began, but Rebecca interrupted her with a cry and a rush to the door.

"There she is now!" she cried.

She flung the door wide open, and curiously enough a breeze came in and her own gray hair tossed, and a paper blew off the table to the floor with a loud rustle, but there was nobody in sight.

"There's nobody here," Rebecca said.

She looked blankly at the other woman, who brought her rolling-pin down on a slab of pie-crust with a thud.

"I didn't hear anybody," she said calmly.

"I saw somebody pass that window!"

"You were mistaken again."

"I *know* I saw somebody."

"You couldn't have. Please shut that door."

Rebecca shut the door. She sat down beside the window and looked out on the autumnal yard, with its little curve of footpath to the kitchen door.

"What smells so strong of roses in this room?" she said presently. She sniffed hard.

"I don't smell anything but these nutmegs."

"It is not nutmeg."

"I don't smell anything else."

"Where do you suppose Agnes is?"

"Oh, perhaps she has gone over the ferry to Porter's Falls with Addie. She often does. Addie's got an aunt over there, and Addie's got a cousin, a real pretty boy."

"You suppose she's gone over there?"

"Mebbe. I shouldn't wonder."

"When should she be home?"

"Oh, not before afternoon."

Rebecca waited with all the patience she could muster. She kept reassuring herself, telling herself that it was all natural, that the other woman could not help it, but she made up her mind that if Agnes did not return that afternoon she should be sent for.

When it was four o'clock she started up with resolution. She had been furtively watching the onyx clock on the sitting-room mantel; she had timed herself. She had said that if Agnes was not home by that time she should demand that she be sent for. She rose and stood before Mrs. Dent, who looked up coolly from her embroidery.

"I've waited just as long as I'm going to," she said. "I've come 'way from Michigan to see my own sister's daughter and take her home with me. I've been here ever since yesterday—twenty-four hours—and I haven't seen her. Now I'm going to. I want her sent for."

Mrs. Dent folded her embroidery and rose.

"Well, I don't blame you," she said. "It is high time she came home. I'll go right over and get her myself."

Rebecca heaved a sigh of relief. She hardly knew what she had suspected or feared, but she knew that her position had been one of antagonism if not accusation, and she was sensible of relief.

"I wish you would," she said gratefully, and went back to her chair, while Mrs. Dent got her shawl and her little white head-tie. "I wouldn't trouble you, but I do feel as if I couldn't wait any longer to see her," she remarked apologetically.

"Oh, it ain't any trouble at all," said Mrs. Dent as she went out. "I don't blame you; you have waited long enough."

Rebecca sat at the window watching breathlessly until Mrs. Dent came stepping through the yard alone. She ran to the door and saw, hardly noticing it this time, that the rose-bush was again violently agitated, yet with no wind evident elsewhere.

"Where is she?" she cried.

Mrs. Dent laughed with stiff lips as she came up the steps over the terrace. "Girls will be girls," said she. "She's gone with Addie to Lincoln. Addie's got an uncle who's conductor on the train, and lives there, and he got 'em passes, and they're goin' to stay to Addie's Aunt Margaret's a few days. Mrs. Slocum said Agnes didn't have time to come over and ask me before the train went, but she took it on herself to say it would be all right, and . . ."

"Why hadn't she been over to tell you?" Rebecca was angry, though not suspicious. She even saw no reason for her anger.

"Oh, she was putting up grapes. She was coming over just as soon as she got the black off her hands. She heard I had company, and her hands were a sight. She was holding them over sulphur matches."

"You say she's going to stay a few days?" repeated Rebecca dazedly.

"Yes; till Thursday, Mrs. Slocum said."

"How far is Lincoln from here?"

"About fifty miles. It'll be a real treat to her. Mrs. Slocum's sister is a real nice woman."

"It is goin' to make it pretty late about my goin' home."

"If you don't feel as if you could wait, I'll get her ready and send her on just as soon as I can," Mrs. Dent said sweetly.

"I'm going to wait," said Rebecca grimly.

The two women sat down again, and Mrs. Dent took up her embroidery.

"Is there any sewing I can do for her?" Rebecca asked finally in a desperate way. "If I can get her sewing along some . . ."

Mrs. Dent arose with alacrity and fetched a mass of white from the closet. "Here," she said, "if you want to sew the lace on this nightgown. I was going to put her to it, but she'll be glad enough to get rid of it. She ought to have this and one more before she goes. I don't like to send her away without some good underclothing."

Rebecca snatched at the little white garment and sewed feverishly.

That night she wakened from a deep sleep a little after midnight and lay a minute trying to collect her faculties and explain to herself what she was listening to. At last she discovered that it was the then popular strains of "The Maiden's Prayer" floating up through the floor from the piano in the sitting-room below. She jumped up, threw a shawl over her nightgown, and hurried downstairs trembling. There was nobody in the sitting-room; the piano was silent. She ran to Mrs. Dent's bedroom and called hysterically:

"Emeline! Emeline!"

"What is it?" asked Mrs. Dent's voice from the bed. The voice was stern, but had a note of consciousness in it.

"Who—who was that playing 'The Maiden's Prayer' in the sitting-room, on the piano?"

"I didn't hear anybody."

"There was some one."

"I didn't hear anything."

"I tell you there was some one. But—*there ain't anybody there.*"

"I didn't hear anything."

"I did—somebody playing 'The Maiden's Prayer' on the piano. Has Agnes got home? I *want to know.*"

"Of course Agnes hasn't got home," answered Mrs. Dent with rising inflection. "Be you gone crazy over that girl? The last boat from Porter's Falls was in before we went to bed. Of course she ain't come."

"I heard . . ."

"You were dreaming."

"I wasn't; I was broad awake."

Rebecca went back to her chamber and kept her lamp burning all night.

The next morning her eyes upon Mrs. Dent were wary and blazing with suppressed excitement. She kept opening her mouth as if to speak, then frowning, and setting her lips hard. After breakfast she went upstairs, and came down presently with her coat and bonnet.

"Now, Emeline," she said, "I want to know where the Slocums live."

Mrs. Dent gave a strange, long, half-lidded glance at her. She was finishing her coffee.

"Why?" she asked.

"I'm going over there and find out if they have heard anything from her daughter and Agnes since they went away. I don't like what I heard last night."

"You must have been dreaming."

"It don't make any odds whether I was or not. Does she play 'The Maiden's Prayer' on the piano? I want to know."

"What if she does? She plays it a little, I believe. I don't know. She don't half play it, anyhow; she ain't got an ear."

"That wasn't half played last night. I don't like such things happening. I ain't superstitious, but I don't like it. I'm going. Where do the Slocums live?"

"You go down the road over the bridge past the old grist mill, then you turn to the left; it's the only house for half a mile. You can't miss it. It has a barn with a ship in full sail on the cupola."

"Well, I'm going. I don't feel easy."

About two hours later Rebecca returned. There were red spots on her cheeks. She looked wild. "I've been there," she said, "and there isn't a soul at home. Something *has* happened."

"What has happened?"

"I don't know. Something. I had a warning last night. There wasn't a soul there. They've been sent for to Lincoln."

"Did you see anybody to ask?" asked Mrs. Dent with thinly concealed anxiety.

"I asked the woman that lives on the turn of the road. She's stone deaf. I suppose you know. She listened while I screamed at her to know where the Slocums were, and then she said, 'Mrs. Smith don't live here.' I didn't see anybody on the road, and that's the only house. What do you suppose it means?"

"I don't suppose it means much of anything," replied Mrs. Dent coolly. "Mr. Slocum is conductor on the railroad, and he'd be away anyway, and Mrs. Slocum often goes early when he does, to spend the day with her sister in Porter's Falls. She'd be more likely to go away than Addie."

"And you don't think anything has happened?" Rebecca asked with diminishing distrust before the reasonableness of it.

"Land, no!"

Rebecca went upstairs to lay aside her coat and bonnet. But she came hurrying back with them still on.

"Who's been in my room?" she gasped. Her face was pale as ashes.

Mrs. Dent also paled as she regarded her.

"What do you mean?" she asked slowly.

"I found when I went upstairs that—little nightgown of—Agnes's on—the bed, laid out. It was—*laid out*. The sleeves were folded across the bosom, and there was that little rose between them. Emeline, what is it? Emeline, what's the matter? Oh!"

Mrs. Dent was struggling for breath in great, choking gasps. She clung to the back of a chair. Rebecca, trembling herself so she could scarcely keep on her feet, got her some water.

As soon as she recovered herself Mrs. Dent regarded her with eyes full of the strangest mixture of fear and horror and hostility.

"What do you mean talking so?" she said in a hard voice.

"It *is there.*"

"Nonsense. You threw it down and it fell that way."

"It was folded in my bureau drawer."

"It couldn't have been."

"Who picked that red rose?"

"Look at the bush," Mrs. Dent replied shortly.

Rebecca looked at her; her mouth gaped. She hurried out of the room. When she came back her eyes seemed to protrude. (She had in the meantime hastened upstairs, and come down with tottering steps, clinging to the banisters.)

"Now I want to know what all this means?" she demanded.

"What what means?"

"The rose is on the bush, and it's gone from the bed in my room! Is this house haunted, or what?"

"I don't know anything about a house being haunted. I don't believe in such things. Be you crazy?" Mrs. Dent spoke with gathering force. The color flashed back to her cheeks.

"No," said Rebecca shortly. "I ain't crazy yet, but I shall be if this keeps on much longer. I'm going to find out where that girl is before night."

Mrs. Dent eyed her.

"What be you going to do?"

"I'm going to Lincoln."

A faint triumphant smile overspread Mrs. Dent's large face.

"You can't," said she; "there ain't any train."

"No train?"

"No; there ain't any afternoon train from the Falls to Lincoln."

"Then I'm going over to the Slocums' again tonight."

However, Rebecca did not go; such a rain came up as deterred even her resolution, and she had only her best dresses with her. Then in the evening came the letter from the Michigan village which she had left nearly a week ago. It was from her cousin, a single woman, who had come to keep her house while she was away. It was a pleasant unexciting letter enough, all the first of it, and related mostly how she missed

Rebecca; how she hoped she was having pleasant weather and kept her health; and how her friend, Mrs. Greenaway, had come to stay with her since she had felt lonesome the first night in the house; how she hoped Rebecca would have no objections to this, although nothing had been said about it, since she had not realized that she might be nervous alone. The cousin was painfully conscientious, hence the letter. Rebecca smiled in spite of her disturbed mind as she read it, then her eye caught the postscript. That was in a different hand, purporting to be written by the friend, Mrs. Hannah Greenaway, informing her that the cousin had fallen down the cellar stairs and broken her hip, and was in a dangerous condition, and begging Rebecca to return at once, as she herself was rheumatic and unable to nurse her properly, and no one else could be obtained.

Rebecca looked at Mrs. Dent, who had come to her room with the letter quite late; it was half-past nine, and she had gone upstairs for the night.

"Where did this come from?" she asked.

"Mr. Amblecrom brought it," she replied.

"Who's he?"

"The postmaster. He often brings the letters that come on the late mail. He knows I ain't anybody to send. He brought yours about your coming. He said he and his wife came over on the ferry-boat with you."

"I remember him," Rebecca replied shortly. "There's bad news in this letter."

Mrs. Dent's face took on an expression of serious inquiry.

"Yes, my Cousin Harriet has fallen down the cellar stairs—they were always dangerous—and she's broken her hip, and I've got to take the first train home tomorrow."

"You don't say so. I'm dreadfully sorry."

"No, you ain't sorry!" said Rebecca, with a look as if she leaped. "You're glad. I don't know why, but you're glad. You're glad. You've wanted to get rid of me for some reason ever since I came. I don't know why. You're a strange woman. Now you've got your way, and I hope you're satisfied."

"How you talk."

Mrs. Dent spoke in a faintly injured voice, but there was a light in her eyes.

"I talk the way it is. Well, I'm going tomorrow morning, and I want you, just as soon as Agnes Dent comes home, to send her out to me.

Don't you wait for anything. You pack what clothes she's got, and don't wait even to mend them, and you buy her ticket. I'll leave money, and you send her along. She don't have to change cars. You start her off, when she gets home, on the next train!"

"Very well," replied the other woman. She had an expression of covert amusement.

"Mind you do it."

"Very well, Rebecca."

Rebecca started on her journey the next morning. When she arrived, two days later, she found her cousin in perfect health. She found, moreover, that the friend had not written the postscript in the cousin's letter. Rebecca would have returned to Ford Village the next morning, but the fatigue and nervous strain had been too much for her. She was not able to move from her bed. She had a species of low fever induced by anxiety and fatigue. But she could write, and she did, to the Slocums, and she received no answer. She also wrote to Mrs. Dent; she even sent numerous telegrams, with no response. Finally she wrote to the postmaster, and an answer arrived by the first possible mail. The letter was short, curt, and to the purpose. Mr. Amblecrom, the postmaster, was a man of few words, and especially wary as to his expressions in a letter.

"Dear madam," he wrote, "Your favour rec'ed. No Slocums in Ford's Village. All dead. Addie ten years ago, her mother two years later, her father five. House vacant. Mrs. John Dent said to have neglected stepdaughter. Girl was sick. Medicine not given. Talk of taking action. Not enough evidence. House said to be haunted. Strange sights and sounds. Your niece, Agnes Dent, died a year ago, about this time.

"Yours truly,

"THOMAS AMBLECROM."

Isaac Asimov *is one of the eight wonders of the world. Born in Russia in 1920, his first story appeared in 1939; since then, he has written well over two hundred books, most of them brilliant popularizations of contemporary scientific data and methodology. He has tried his hand at widely diverse subjects—from* The Bible *through* Shakespeare *through the risibly bawdy. But he is best known as a science fiction writer whose output includes the* Foundation *trilogy and perhaps the most astonishing tour de force in all SF,* The Naked Sun, *in which Asimov concocts an ingenious murder mystery that could only occur on an alien world, yet also manages to say quite a bit about contemporary society. (No one told him it couldn't be done.) The one type of story Asimov has eschewed is the traditional supernatural tale . . . but editor Frederik Pohl once suggested such a clever idea for a ghost story that Dr. A. succumbed. The result:* "Legal Rites," *as untraditional a ghost story as ever hath been wrought!*

Legal Rites

by Isaac Asimov and Frederik Pohl

I

Already the stars were out, though the sun had just dipped under the horizon, and the sky of the west was a blood-stuck gold behind the Sierra Nevadas.

"Hey!" squawked Russell Harley. "Come back!"

But the one-lunged motor of the old Ford was making too much noise; the driver didn't hear him. Harley cursed as he watched the old car careen along the sandy ruts on its half-flat tires. Its taillight was saying a red *no* to him. *No, you can't get away tonight; no, you'll have to stay here and fight it out.*

Harley grunted and climbed back up the porch stairs of the old wooden house. It was well made, anyhow. The stairs, though half a century old, neither creaked beneath him nor showed cracks.

Harley picked up the bags he'd dropped when he experienced his abrupt change of mind—fake leather and worn out, they were—and carted them into the house. He dumped them on a dust-jacketed sofa and looked around.

It was stifling hot, and the smell of the desert outside had permeated the room. Harley sneezed.

"Water," he said out loud. "That's what I need."

He'd prowled through every room on the ground floor before he stopped still and smote his head. Plumbing—naturally there'd be no plumbing in this hole eight miles out on the desert! A well was the best he could hope for—

If that.

It was getting dark. No electric lights either, of course. He blundered irritatedly through the dusky rooms to the back of the house. The screen door shrieked metallically as he opened it. A bucket hung by the door. He picked it up, tipped it, shook the loose sand out of it. He looked over the "back yard"—about thirty thousand visible acres of hilly sand, rock and patches of sage and flame-tipped ocotillo.

No well.

The old fool got water from somewhere, he thought savagely. Obstinately he climbed down the back steps and wandered out into the desert. Overhead the stars were blinding, a million billion of them, but the sunset was over already and he could see only hazily. The silence was murderous. Only a faint whisper of breeze over the sand, and the slither of his shoes.

He caught a glimmer of starlight from the nearest clump of sage and walked to it. There was a pool of water, caught in the angle of two enormous boulders. He stared at it doubtfully, then shrugged. It was water. It was better than nothing. He dipped the bucket in the little pool. Knowing nothing of the procedure, he filled it with a quart of loose sand as he scooped it along the bottom. When he lifted it, brimful, to his lips, he spat out the first mouthful and swore violently.

Then he used his head. He set the bucket down, waited a second for the sand grains to settle, cupped water in his hands, lifted it to his lips. . . .

Pat. HISS. Pat. HISS. Pat. HISS—

"What the hell!" Harley stood up, looked around in abrupt puzzlement. It sounded like water dripping from somewhere, onto a red-hot stove, flashing into sizzling steam. He saw nothing, only the sand and the sage and the pool of tepid, sickly water.

Pat. HISS—

Then he saw it, and his eyes bulged. Out of nowhere it was dripping, a drop a second, a sticky, dark drop that was thicker than water, that fell to the ground lazily, in slow defiance of gravity. And when it struck each drop sizzled and skittered about, and vanished. It was perhaps eight feet from him, just visible in the starlight.

And then, "Get off my land!" said the voice from nowhere.

Harley got. By the time he got to Rebel Butte three hours later, he was barely managing to walk, wishing desperately that he'd delayed long enough for one more good drink of water, despite all the fiends of hell. But he'd run the first three miles. He'd had plenty of encouragement. He remembered with a shudder how the clear desert air had taken milky shape around the incredible trickle of dampness and had advanced on him threateningly.

And when he got to the first kerosene-lighted saloon of Rebel Butte, and staggered inside, the saloonkeeper's fascinated stare at the front of his shoddy coat showed him strong evidence that he hadn't been suddenly taken with insanity, or drunk on the unaccustomed sensation of fresh desert air. All down the front of him it was, and the harder he rubbed the harder it stayed, the stickier it got. Blood!

"Whiskey!" he said in a strangled voice, tottering to the bar. He pulled a threadbare dollar bill from his pocket, flapped it onto the mahogany.

The blackjack game at the back of the room had stopped. Harley was acutely conscious of the eyes of the players, the bartender and the tall, lean man leaning on the bar. All were watching him.

The bartender broke the spell. He reached for a bottle behind him without looking at it, placed it on the counter before Harley. He poured a glass of water from a jug, set it down with a shot glass beside the bottle.

"I could of told you that would happen," he said cautiously. "Only you wouldn't of believed me. You had to meet Hank for yourself before you'd believe he was there."

Harley remembered his thirst and drained the glass of water, then poured himself a shot of the whiskey and swallowed it without waiting for the chaser to be refilled. The whiskey felt good going down, almost good enough to stop his internal shakes.

"What are you talking about?" he said finally. He twisted his body and leaned forward across the bar to partly hide the stains on his coat. The saloonkeeper laughed.

"Old Hank," he said. "I knowed who you was right away, even before Tom came back and told me where he'd took you. I knowed you was Zeb Harley's no-good nephew, come to take Harley Hall an' sell it before he was cold in the grave."

The blackjack players were still watching him, Russell Harley saw. Only the lean man farther along the bar seemed to have dismissed him. He was pouring himself another drink, quite occupied with his task.

Harley flushed. "Listen," he said, "I didn't come in here for advice. I wanted a drink. I'm paying for it. Keep your mouth out of this."

The saloonkeeper shrugged. He turned his back and walked away to the blackjack table. After a couple of seconds one of the players turned, too, and threw a card down. The others followed suit.

Harley was just getting set to swallow his pride and talk to the saloonkeeper again—he seemed to know something about what Harley'd been through, and might be helpful—when the lean man tapped his shoulder. Harley whirled and almost dropped his glass. Absorbed and jumpy, he hadn't seen him come up.

"Young man," said the lean one, "my name's Nicholls. Come along with me, sir, and we'll talk this thing over. I think we may be of service to each other."

Even the twelve-cylinder car Nicholls drove jounced like a haywagon over the sandy ruts leading to the place old Zeb had—laughingly —named "Harley Hall."

Russell Harley twisted his neck and stared at the heap of paraphernalia in the open rumble seat. "I don't like it," he complained. "I never had anything to do with ghosts. How do I know this stuff'll work?"

Nicholls smiled, "You'll have to take my word for it. I've had dealings with ghosts before. You could say that I might qualify as a ghost exterminator, if I chose."

Harley growled. "I still don't like it."

Nicholls turned a sharp look on him. "You like the prospect of owning Harley Hall, don't you? And looking for all the money your late uncle is supposed to have hidden around somewhere?" Harley shrugged. "Certainly you do," said Nicholls, returning his eyes to the road. "And with good reason. The local reports put the figure pretty high, young man."

"That's where you come in, I guess," Harley said sullenly. "I find the money—that I own anyhow—and give some of it to you. How much?"

"We'll discuss that later," Nicholls said. He smiled absently as he looked ahead.

"We'll discuss it right now!"

The smile faded from Nicholls' face. "No," he said. "We won't. I'm doing you a favor, young Harley. Remember that. In return—you'll do as I say, all the way!"

Harley digested that carefully, and it was not a pleasant meal. He waited a couple of seconds before he changed the subject.

"I was out here once when the old man was alive," he said. "He didn't say nothing about any ghost."

"Perhaps he felt you might think him—well, peculiar," Nicholls said. "And perhaps you would have. When were you here?"

"Oh, a long time ago," Harley said evasively. "But I was here a whole day, and part of the night. The old man was crazy as a coot, but he didn't keep any ghosts in the attic."

"This ghost was a friend of his," Nicholls said. "The gentleman in charge of the bar told you that, surely. Your late uncle was something of a recluse. He lived in this house a dozen miles from nowhere, came into town hardly ever, wouldn't let anyone get friendly with him. But he wasn't exactly a hermit. He had Hank for company."

"Fine company."

Nicholls inclined his head seriously. "Oh, I don't know," he said. "From all accounts, they got on well together. They played pinochle and chess—Hank's supposed to have been a great pinochle player. He was killed that way, according to the local reports. Caught somebody dealing from the bottom and shot it out with him. He lost. A bullet pierced his throat and he died quite bloodily." He turned the wheel, putting his weight into the effort, and succeeded in twisting the car out of the ruts of the "road," sent it jouncing across unmarked sand to the old frame house to which they were going.

"That," he finished as he pulled up before the porch, "accounts for the blood that accompanies his apparition."

Harley opened the door slowly and got out, looking uneasily at the battered old house. Nicholls cut the motor, got out and walked at once to the back of the car.

"Come on," he said, dragging things out of the compartment. "Give me a hand with this. I'm not going to carry this stuff all by myself."

Harley came around reluctantly, regarded the curious assortment of bundles of dried faggots, lengths of colored cord, chalk pencils, ugly little bunches of wilted weeds, bleached bones of small animals and a couple of less pleasant things without pleasure.

Pat. HISS. Pat. HISS—

"He's here!" Harley yelped. "Listen! He's someplace around here watching us."

"Ha!"

The laugh was deep, unpleasant and—bodiless. Harley looked around desperately for the tell-tale trickle of blood. And he found it; from the air it issued, just beside the car, sinking gracefully to the ground and sizzling, vanishing there.

"I'm watching you, all right," the voice said grimly. "Russell, you worthless piece of corruption, I've got no more use for you than you used to have for me. Dead or alive, this is my land! I shared it with your uncle, you young scalawag, but I won't share it with you. Get out!"

Harley's knees weakened and he tottered dizzily to the rear bumper, sat on it. "Nicholls—" he said confusedly.

"Oh, brace up," Nicholls said with irritation. He tossed a ball of gaudy twine, red and green, with curious knots tied along it, to Harley. Then he confronted the trickle of blood and made a few brisk passes in the air before it. His lips were moving silently, Harley saw, but no words came out.

There was a gasp and a chopped-off squawk from the source of the blood drops. Nicholls clapped his hands sharply, then turned to young Harley.

"Take that cord you have in your hands and stretch it around the house," he said. "All the way around, and make sure it goes right across the middle of the doors and windows. It isn't much, but it'll hold him till we can get the good stuff set up."

Harley nodded, then pointed a rigid finger at the drops of blood, now sizzling and fuming more angrily than before. "What about *that?*" he managed to get out.

Nicholls grinned complacently. "I'll hold him here till the cows come home," he said. "Get moving!"

Harley inadvertently inhaled a lungful of noxious white smoke and coughed till the tears rolled down his cheeks. When he recovered he looked at Nicholls, who was reading silently from a green leather book with dog-eared pages. He said, "Can I stop stirring this now?"

Nicholls grimaced angrily and shook his head without looking at him. He went on reading, his lips contorting over syllables that were not in any language Harley had ever heard, then snapped the book shut and wiped his brow.

"Fine," he said. "So far, so good." He stepped over to windward of the boiling pot Harley was stirring on the hob over the fireplace, peered down into it cautiously.

"That's about done," he said. "Take it off the fire and let it cool a bit."

Harley lifted it down, then squeezed his aching biceps with his left hand. The stuff was the consistency of sickly green fudge.

"Now what?" he asked.

Nicholls didn't answer. He looked up in mild surprise at the sudden squawk of triumph from outside, followed by the howling of a chill wind.

"Hank must be loose," he said casually. "He can't do us any harm, I think, but we'd better get a move on." He rummaged in the dwindled pile of junk he'd brought from the car, extracted a paintbrush. "Smear this stuff around all the windows and doors. All but the front door. For that I have something else." He pointed to what seemed to be the front axle of an old Model-T. "Leave that on the doorsill. Cold iron. You can just step over it, but Hank won't be able to pass it. It's been properly treated already with the very best thaumaturgy."

"Step over it," Harley repeated. "What would I want to step over it for? *He's* out there."

"He won't hurt you," said Nicholls. "You will carry an amulet with you—that one, there—that will keep him away. Probably he couldn't really hurt you anyhow, being a low-order ghost who can't materialize to any greater density. But just to take no chances, carry the amulet and don't stay out too long. It won't hold him off forever, not for more than half an hour. If you ever have to go out and stay for any length of time, tie that bundle of herbs around your neck." Nicholls smiled. "That's only for emergencies, though. It works on the asafoetida principle. Ghosts can't come anywhere near it—but you won't like it much yourself. It has—ah—a rather definite odor."

He leaned gingerly over the pot again, sniffing. He sneezed.

"Well, that's cool enough," he said. "Before it hardens, get moving. Start spreading the stuff upstairs—and make sure you don't miss any windows."

"What are you going to do?"

"I," said Nicholls sharply, "will be here. Start."

But he wasn't. When Harley finished his disagreeable task and came down, he called Nicholls' name, but the man was gone. Harley stepped to the door and looked out; the car was gone, too.

He shrugged. "Oh, well," he said, and began taking the dust-cloths off the furniture.

II

Somewhere within the cold, legal mind of Lawyer Turnbull, he weighed the comparative likeness of nightmare and insanity.

He stared at the plush chair facing him, noted with distinct uneasiness how the strangely weightless, strangely sourceless trickle of redness disappeared as it hit the floor, but left long, mud-ochre streaks matted on the upholstery. The sound was unpleasant, too; *Pat. HISS. Pat. HISS—*

The voice continued impatiently, "Damn your human stupidity! I may be a ghost, but heaven knows I'm not trying to haunt you. Friend, you're not that important to me. Get this—I'm here on business."

Turnbull learned that you cannot wet dry lips with a dehydrated tongue. "Legal business?"

"Sure. The fact that I was once killed by violence, and have to continue my existence on the astral plane, doesn't mean I've lost my legal rights. Does it?"

The lawyer shook his head in bafflement. He said, "This would be easier on me if you weren't invisible. Can't you do something about it?"

There was a short pause. "Well, I could materialize for a minute," the voice said. "It's hard work—damn hard, for me. There are a lot of us astral entities that can do it easy as falling out of bed, but—Well, if I have to I shall try to do it once."

There was a shimmering in the air above the armchair, and a milky, thin smoke condensed into an intangible seated figure. Turnbull took no delight in noting that, through the figure, the outlines of the chair were still hazily visible. The figure thickened. Just as the features took form— just as Turnbull's bulging eyes made out a prominent hooked nose and a crisp beard—it thinned and exploded with a soft pop.

The voice said weakly, "I didn't think I was that bad. I'm way out of practice. I guess that's the first daylight materialization I've made in seventy-five years."

The lawyer adjusted his rimless glasses and coughed. *Hell's binges*, he thought, *the worst thing about this is that I'm believing it!*

"Oh, well," he said aloud. Then he hurried on before the visitor could take offense: "Just what did you want? I'm just a small-town lawyer, you know. My business is fairly routine—"

"I know all about your business," the voice said. "You can handle my case—it's a land affair. I want to sue Russell Harley."

"Harley?" Turnbull fingered his cheek. "Any relation to Zeb Harley?"

"His nephew—and his heir, too."

Turnbull nodded. "Yes, I remember now. My wife's folks live in Rebel Butte, and I've been there. Quite a coincidence you should come to me—"

The voice laughed. "It was no coincidence," it said softly.

"Oh." Turnbull was silent for a second. Then, "I see," he said. He cast a shrewd glance at the chair. "Lawsuits cost money, Mr.—I don't think you mentioned your name?"

"Hank Jenkins," the voice prompted. "I know that. Would—let's see. Would six hundred and fifty dollars be sufficient?"

Turnbull swallowed. "I think so," he said in a relatively unemotional tone—relative to what he was thinking.

"Then suppose we call that your retainer. I happen to have cached a considerable sum of gold when I was—that is to say, before I became an astral entity. I'm quite certain it hasn't been disturbed. You will have to call it treasure trove, I guess, and give half of it to the state, but there's thirteen hundred dollars altogether."

Turnbull nodded judiciously. "Assuming we can locate your trove," he said, "I think that would be quite satisfactory." He leaned back in his chair and looked legal. His aplomb had returned.

And half an hour later he said slowly, "I'll take your case."

Judge Lawrence Gimbel had always liked his job before. But his thirteen honorable years on the bench lost their flavor for him as he grimaced wearily and reached for his gavel. This case was far too confusing for his taste.

The clerk made his speech, and the packed courtroom sat down en masse. Gimbel held a hand briefly to his eyes before he spoke.

"Is the counsel for the plaintiff ready?"

"I am, your honor." Turnbull, alone at his table, rose and bowed.

"The counsel for the defendant?"

"Ready, your honor!" Fred Wilson snapped. He looked with a hard flicker of interest at Turnbull and his solitary table, then leaned over and whispered in Russell Harley's ear. The youth nodded glumly, then shrugged.

Gimbel said, "I understand the attorneys for both sides have waived jury trial in this case of Henry Jenkins versus Russell Joseph Harley."

Both lawyers nodded. Gimbel continued, "In view of the unusual nature of this case, I imagine it will prove necessary to conduct it with a certain amount of informality. The sole purpose of this court is to arrive at the true facts at issue, and deliver a verdict in accord with the laws pertaining to these facts. I will not stand on ceremony. Nevertheless, I will not tolerate any disturbances or unnecessary irregularities. The spectators will kindly remember that they are here on privilege. Any demonstration will result in the clearing of the court."

He looked severely at the white faces that gleamed unintelligently up at him. He suppressed a sigh and he said, "The counsel for the plaintiff will begin."

Turnbull rose quickly to his feet, faced the judge.

"Your honor," he said, "we propose to show that my client, Henry Jenkins, has been deprived of his just rights by the defendant. Mr. Jenkins, by virtue of a sustained residence of more than twenty years in the house located on Route 22, eight miles north of the town of Rebel Butte, with the full knowledge of its legal owner, has acquired certain rights. In legal terminology we define these as the rights of adverse possession. The layman would call them common-law rights—squatters' rights."

Gimbel folded his hands and tried to relax. Squatters' rights—for a ghost! He sighed, but listened attentively as Turnbull went on.

"Upon the death of Zebulon Harley, the owner of the house involved —it is better known, perhaps, as Harley Hall—the defendant inherited title to the property. We do not question his right to it. But my client has an equity in Harley Hall; the right to free and full existence. The defendant has forcefully evicted my client, by means which have caused my client great mental distress, and have even endangered his very existence."

Gimbel nodded. If the case only had a precedent somewhere. . . . But it hadn't; he remembered grimly the hours he'd spent thumbing through all sorts of unlikely law books, looking for anything that might bear on the case. It had been his better judgment that he throw the case out of court outright—a judge couldn't afford to have himself laughed at, not if he were ambitious. And public laughter was about the only certainty there was to this case. But Wilson had put up such a fight that the judge's temper had taken over. He never did like Wilson, anyhow. "You may proceed with your witnesses," he said.

Turnbull nodded. To the clerk he said, "Call Henry Jenkins to the stand."

Wilson was on his feet before the clerk opened his mouth. "Objection!" he bellowed. "The so-called Henry Jenkins cannot qualify as a witness!"

"Why not?" demanded Turnbull.

"Because he's dead!"

The judge clutched his gavel with one hand, forehead with the other. He banged on the desk to quiet the courtroom.

Turnbull stood there, smiling. "Naturally," he said, "you'll have proof of that statement."

Wilson snarled. "Certainly." He referred to his brief. "The so-called Henry Jenkins is the ghost, spirit or specter of one Hank Jenkins, who prospected for gold in this territory a century ago. He was killed by a bullet through the throat from the gun of one Long Tom Cooper, and was declared legally dead on September 14, 1850. Cooper was hanged for his murder. No matter what hocus-pocus you produce for evidence to the contrary now, that status of legal death remains completely valid."

"What evidence have you of the identity of my client with this Hank Jenkins?" Turnbull asked grimly.

"Do you deny it?"

Turnbull shrugged. "I deny nothing. I'm not being cross-examined. Furthermore, the sole prerequisite of a witness is that he understand the value of an oath. Henry Jenkins was tested by John Quincy Fitzjames, professor of psychology at the University of Southern California. The results—I have Dr. Fitzjames' sworn statement of them here, which I will introduce as an exhibit—show clearly that my client's intelligence quotient is well above normal, and that a psychiatric examination discloses no important aberrations which would injure his validity as a witness. I insist that my client be allowed to testify on his own behalf."

"But he's dead!" squawked Wilson. "He's invisible right now!"

"My client," said Turnbull stiffly, "is not present just now. Undoubtedly that accounts for what you term his invisibility." He paused for the appreciative murmur that swept through the court. Things were breaking perfectly, he thought, smiling. "I have here another affidavit," he said. "It is signed by Elihu James and Terence MacRae, who respectively head the departments of physics and biology at the same university. It states that my client exhibits all the vital phenomena of life. I am prepared to call all three of my expert witnesses to the stand, if necessary."

Wilson scowled but said nothing. Judge Gimbel leaned forward.

"I don't see how it is possible for me to refuse the plaintiff the right to testify," he said. "If the three experts who prepared these reports will testify on the stand to the facts contained in them, Henry Jenkins may then take the stand."

Wilson sat down heavily. The three experts spoke briefly—and dryly. Wilson put them through only the most formal of cross-examinations.

The judge declared a brief recess. In the corridor outside, Wilson and his client lit cigarettes and looked unsympathetically at each other.

"I feel like a fool," said Russell Harley. "Bringing suit against a ghost."

"The ghost brought the suit," Wilson reminded him. "If only we'd been able to hold fire for a couple more weeks, till another judge came on the bench, I could've got this thing thrown right out of court."

"Well, why couldn't we wait?"

"Because you were in such a damn hurry!" Wilson said. "You and that idiot Nicholls—so confident that it never would come to trial."

Harley shrugged, and thought unhappily of their failure in completely exorcising the ghost of Hank Jenkins. That had been a mess. Jenkins had somehow escaped from the charmed circle they'd drawn around him, in which they'd hoped to keep him till the trial was forfeited by non-appearance.

"That's another thing," said Wilson. "Where is Nicholls?"

Harley shrugged again. "I dunno. The last I saw of him was in your office. He came around to see me right after the deputy slapped the show-cause order on me at the house. He brought me down to you—said you'd been recommended to him. Then you and him and I talked about the case for a while. He went out, after he lent me a little money to help meet your retainer. Haven't seen him since."

"I'd like to know who recommended me to him," Wilson said grimly. "I don't think he'd ever recommend anybody else. I don't like this case —and I don't much like you."

Harley growled but said nothing. He flung his cigarette away. It tasted of the garbage that hung around his neck—everything did. Nicholls had told no lies when he said Harley wouldn't much like the bundle of herbs that would ward off the ghost of old Jenkins. They smelled.

The court clerk was in the corridor, bawling something, and people were beginning to trickle back in. Harley and his attorney went with them.

When the trial had been resumed, the clerk said, "Henry Jenkins!"

Wilson was on his feet at once. He opened the door of the judge's chamber, said something in a low tone. Then he stepped back, as if to let someone through.

Pat. HISS. Pat. HISS—

There was a concerted gasp from the spectators as the weirdly appearing trickle of blood moved slowly across the open space to the witness chair. This was the ghost—the plaintiff in the most eminently absurd case in the history of jurisprudence.

"All right, Hank," Turnbull whispered. "You'll have to materialize long enough to let the clerk swear you in."

The clerk drew back nervously at the pillar of milky fog that appeared before him, vaguely humanoid in shape. A phantom hand, half transparent, reached out to touch the Bible. The clerk's voice shook as he administered the oath, and heard the response come from the heart of the cloudpillar.

The haze drifted into the witness chair, bent curiously at about hip-height, and popped into nothingness.

The judge banged his gavel wildly. The buzz of alarm that had arisen from the spectators died out.

"I'll warn you again," he declared, "that unruliness will not be tolerated. The counsel for the plaintiff may proceed."

Turnbull walked to the witness chair and addressed its emptiness.

"Your name?"

"My name is Henry Jenkins."

"Your occupation?"

There was a slight pause. "I have none. I guess you'd say I'm retired."

"Mr. Jenkins, just what connection have you with the building referred to as Harley Hall?"

"I have occupied it for ninety years."

"During this time, did you come to know the late Zebulon Harley, owner of the Hall?"

"I knew Zeb quite well."

Turnbull nodded. "When did you make his acquaintance?" he asked.

"In the spring of 1907. Zeb had just lost his wife. After that, you see, he made Harley Hall his year-round home. He became—well, more or less of a hermit. Before that we had never met, since he was only seldom at the Hall. But we became friendly then."

"How long did this friendship last?"

"Until he died last fall. I was with him when he died. I still have a few keepsakes he left me then." There was a distinct nostalgic sigh from the witness chair, which by now was literally spattered with muddy red liquid. The falling drops seemed to hesitate for a second, and their sizzling noise was muted as with a strong emotion.

Turnbull went on, "Your relations with him were good, then?"

"I'd call them excellent," the emptiness replied firmly. "Every night we sat up together. When we didn't play pinochle or chess or cribbage, we just sat and talked over the news of the day. I still have the book we used to keep records of the chess and pinochle games. Zeb made the entries himself, in his own handwriting."

Turnbull abandoned the witness for a moment. He faced the judge with a smile. "I offer in evidence," he said, "the book mentioned. Also a ring given to the plaintiff by the late Mr. Harley, and a copy of the plays of Gilbert and Sullivan. On the flyleaf of this book is inscribed, 'To Old Hank,' in Harley's own hand."

He turned again to the empty, blood-leaking witness chair.

He said, "In all your years of association, did Zebulon Harley ever ask you to leave, or to pay rent?"

"Of course not. Not Zeb!"

Turnbull nodded. "Very good," he said. "Now, just one or two more questions. Will you tell in your own words what occurred after the death of Zebulon Harley, that caused you to bring this suit?"

"Well, in January young Harley—"

"You mean Russell Joseph Harley, the defendant?"

"Yes. He arrived at Harley Hall on January fifth. I asked him to leave, which he did. On the next day he returned with another man. They placed a talisman upon the threshold of the main entrance, and soon after sealed every threshold and windowsill in the Hall with a substance which is noxious to me. These activities were accompanied by several of the most deadly spells in the Ars Magicorum. He further added an Exclusion Circle with a radius of a little over a mile, entirely surrounding the Hall."

"I see," the lawyer said. "Will you explain to the court the effects of these activities?"

"Well," the voice said thoughtfully, "it's a little hard to put in words.

I can't pass the Circle without a great expenditure of energy. Even if I did I couldn't enter the building because of the talisman and the seals."

"Could you enter by air? Through a chimney, perhaps?"

"No. The Exclusion Circle is really a sphere. I'm pretty sure the effort would destroy me."

"In effect, then, you are entirely barred from the house you have occupied for ninety years, due to the wilful acts of Russell Joseph Harley, the defendant, and an unnamed accomplice of his."

"That is correct."

Turnbull beamed. "Thank you. That's all."

He turned to Wilson, whose face had been a study in dourness throughout the entire examination. "Your witness," he said.

Wilson snapped to his feet and strode to the witness chair.

He said belligerently, "You say your name is Henry Jenkins?"

"Yes."

"That is your name now, you mean to say. What was your name before?"

"Before?" There was surprise in the voice that emanated from above the trickling blood-drops. "Before when?"

Wilson scowled. "Don't pretend ignorance," he said sharply. "Before you *died*, of course."

"Objection!" Turnbull was on his feet, glaring at Wilson. "The counsel for the defense has no right to speak of some hypothetical death of my client!"

Gimbel raised a hand wearily and cut off the words that were forming on Wilson's lips. "Objection sustained," he said. "No evidence has been presented to identify the plaintiff as the prospector who was killed in 1850—or anyone else."

Wilson's mouth twisted into a sour grimace. He continued on a lower key.

"You say, Mr. Jenkins, that you occupied Harley Hall for ninety years."

"Ninety-two years next month. The Hall wasn't built—in its present form, anyhow—until 1876, but I occupied the house that stood on the site previously."

"What did you do before then?"

"Before then?" The voice paused, then said doubtfully, "I don't remember."

"You're under oath!" Wilson flared.

The voice got firmer. "Ninety years is a long time," it said. "I don't remember."

"Let's see if I can't refresh your memory. Is it true that ninety-one years ago, in the very year in which you claim to have begun your occupancy of Harley Hall, Hank Jenkins was killed in a gun duel?"

"That may be true, if you say so. I don't remember."

"Do you remember that the shooting occurred not fifty feet from the present site of Harley Hall?"

"It may be."

"Well, then," Wilson thundered, "is it not a fact that when Hank Jenkins died by violence his ghost assumed existence? That it was then doomed to haunt the site of its slaying throughout eternity?"

The voice said evenly, "I have no knowledge of that."

"Do you deny that it is well known throughout that section that the ghost of Hank Jenkins haunts Harley Hall?"

"Objection!" shouted Turnbull. "Popular opinion is not evidence."

"Objection sustained. Strike the question from the record."

Wilson, badgered, lost his control. In a dangerously uneven voice, he said, "Perjury is a criminal offense. Mr. Jenkins, do you deny that you are the ghost of Hank Jenkins?"

The tone was surprised. "Why, certainly."

"You *are* a ghost, aren't you?"

Stiffly, "I'm an entity on the astral plane."

"That, I believe, is what is called a ghost?"

"I can't help what it's called. I've heard you called a lot of things. Is that proof?"

There was a surge of laughter from the audience. Gimbel slammed his gavel down on the bench.

"The witness," he said, "will confine himself to answering questions."

Wilson bellowed, "In spite of what you say, it's true, isn't it, that you are merely the spirit of a human being who had died through violence?"

The voice from above the blood drops retorted, "I repeat that I am an entity of the astral plane. I am not aware that I was ever a human being."

The lawyer turned an exasperated face to the bench.

"Your honor," he said, "I ask that you instruct the witness to cease playing verbal hide-and-seek. It is quite evident that the witness is a ghost, and that he is therefore the relict of some human being, ipso facto. Circumstantial evidence is strong that he is the ghost of the Hank Jenkins who was killed in 1850. But this is a non-essential point. What is definite is that he is the ghost of someone who is dead, and hence is unqualified to act as witness! I demand his testimony be stricken from the record!"

Turnbull spoke up at once. "Will the counsel for the defense quote his authority for branding my client a ghost—in the face of my client's repeated declaration that he is an entity of the astral plane? What is the legal definition of a ghost?"

Judge Gimbel smiled. "Counsel for the defense will proceed with the cross-examination," he said.

Wilson's face flushed dark purple. He mopped his brow with a large bandanna, then glared at the dropping, sizzling trickle of blood.

"Whatever you are," he said, "answer me this question. Can you pass through a wall?"

"Why, yes. Certainly." There was a definite note of surprise in the voice from nowhere. "But it isn't as easy as some people think. It definitely requires a lot of effort."

"Never mind that. You can do it?"

"Yes."

"Could you be bound by any physical means? Would handcuffs hold you? Or ropes, chains, prison walls, a hermetically sealed steel chest?"

Jenkins had no chance to answer. Turnbull, scenting danger, cut in hastily. "I object to this line of questioning. It is entirely irrelevant."

"On the contrary," Wilson cried loudly, "it bears strongly on the qualifications of the so-called Henry Jenkins as a witness! I demand that he answer the question."

Judge Gimbel said, "Objection overruled. Witness will answer the question."

The voice from the chair said superciliously, "I don't mind answering. Physical barriers mean nothing to me, by and large."

The counsel for the defense drew himself up triumphantly.

"Very good," he said with satisfaction. "*Very* good." Then to the judge, the words coming sharp and fast, "I claim, your honor, that the so-called Henry Jenkins has no legal status as a witness in court. There is clearly no value in understanding the nature of an oath if a violation of the oath can bring no punishment in its wake. The statements of a man who can perjure himself freely have no worth. I demand they be stricken from the record!"

Turnbull was at the judge's bench in two strides.

"I had anticipated that, your honor," he said quickly. "From the very nature of the case, however, it is clear that my client can be very definitely restricted in his movements—spells, pentagrams, talismans, amulets, Exclusion Circles and what-not. I have here—which I am prepared to deliver to the bailiff of the court—a list of the various methods of confining an astral entity to a restricted area for periods ranging from a few moments to all eternity. Moreover, I have also signed a bond for five thousand dollars, prior to the beginning of the trial, which I stand ready to forfeit should my client be confined and make his escape, if found guilty of any misfeasance as a witness."

Gimbel's face, which had looked startled for a second, slowly cleared. He nodded. "The court is satisfied with the statement of the counsel for the plaintiff," he declared. "There seems no doubt that the plaintiff can be penalized for any misstatements, and the motion of the defense is denied."

Wilson looked choleric, but shrugged. "All right," he said. "That will be all."

"You may step down, Mr. Jenkins," Gimbel directed, and watched in fascination as the blood-dripping column rose and floated over the floor, along the corridor, out the door.

Turnbull approached the judge's bench again. He said, "I would like to place in evidence these notes, the diary of the late Zebulon Harley. It was presented to my client by Harley himself last fall. I call particular attention to the entry for April sixth, nineteen seventeen, in which he mentions the entrance of the United States into the First World War, and records the results of a series of eleven pinochle games played with a personage identified as 'Old Hank.' With the court's permission, I will read the entry for that day, and also various other entries for the next four years. Please note the references to someone known variously as 'Jenkins,' 'Hank Jenkins,' and—in one extremely significant passage—'Old Invisible.'"

Wilson stewed silently during the slow reading of Harley's diary. There was anger on his face, but he paid close attention, and when the reading was over he leaped to his feet.

"I would like to know," he asked, "if the counsel for the plaintiff is in possession of any diaries *after* nineteen twenty?"

Turnbull shook his head. "Harley apparently never kept a diary, except during the four years represented in this."

"Then I demand that the court refuse to admit this diary as evidence on two counts," Wilson said. He raised two fingers to tick off the points. "In the first place, the evidence presented is frivolous. The few vague and unsatisfactory references to Jenkins nowhere specifically describe him as what he is—ghost, astral entity or what you will. Second, the evidence, even were the first point overlooked, concerns only the years up to nineteen twenty-one. The case concerns itself only with the supposed occupation of Harley Hall by the so-called Jenkins in the last twenty years—*since* 'twenty-one. Clearly, the evidence is therefore irrelevant."

Gimbel looked at Turnbull, who smiled calmly.

"The reference to 'Old Invisible' is far from vague," he said. "It is a definite indication of the astral character of my client. Furthermore, evidence as to the friendship of my client with the late Mr. Zebulon Harley before nineteen twenty-one is entirely relevant, as such a friendship, once established, would naturally be presumed to have continued indefinitely. Unless of course, the defense is able to present evidence to the contrary."

Judge Gimbel said, "The diary is admitted as evidence."

Turnbull said, "I rest my case."

There was a buzz of conversation in the courtroom while the judge looked over the diary, and then handed it to the clerk to be marked and entered.

Gimbel said, "The defense may open its case."

Wilson rose. To the clerk he said, "Russell Joseph Harley."

But young Harley was recalcitrant. "Nix," he said, on his feet, pointing at the witness chair. "That thing's got blood all over it! You don't expect me to sit down in that large puddle of blood, do you?"

Judge Gimbel leaned over to look at the chair. The drip-drop trickle of blood from the apparition who'd been testifying had left its mark. Muddy brown all down the front of the chair. Gimbel found himself wondering how the ghost managed to replenish its supply of the fluid, but gave it up.

"I see your point," he said. "Well, it's getting a bit late anyhow. The clerk will take away the present witness chair and replace it. In the interim, I declare the court recessed till tomorrow morning at ten o'clock."

III

Russell Harley noticed how the elevator boy's back registered repulsion and disapproval, and scowled. He was not a popular guest in the hotel, he knew well. Where he made his mistake, though, was in thinking that the noxious bundle of herbs about his neck was the cause of it. His odious personality had a lot to do with the chilly attitude of the management and his fellow guests.

He made his way to the bar, ignoring the heads that turned in surprise to follow the reeking comet-tail of his passage. He entered the red-leather-and-chromium drinking room, and stared about for Lawyer Wilson.

And blinked in surprise when he saw him. Wilson wasn't alone. In the booth with him was a tall, dark figure, with his back to Harley. The back alone was plenty for recognition. Nicholls!

Wilson had seen him. "Hello, Harley," he said, all smiles and affability in the presence of the man with the money. "Come on and sit down. Mr. Nicholls dropped in on me a little while ago, so I brought him over."

"Hello," Harley said glumly, and Nicholls nodded. The muscles of his cheeks pulsed, and he seemed under a strain, strangely uncomfortable in Harley's presence. Still there was a twinkle in the look he gave young Harley, and his voice was friendly enough—though supercilious—as he said:

"Hello, Harley. How is the trial going?"

"Ask him," said Harley, pointing a thumb at Wilson as he slid his knees under the booth's table and sat down. "He's the lawyer. He's supposed to know these things."

"Doesn't he?"

Harley shrugged and craned his neck for the waitress. "Oh, I guess so. . . . Rye and water!" He watched the girl appreciatively as she nodded and went off to the bar, then turned his attention back to Nicholls. "The trouble is," he said, "Wilson may think he knows, but I think he's all wet."

Wilson frowned. "Do you imply—" he began, but Nicholls put up a hand.

"Let's not bicker," said Nicholls. "Suppose you answer my question. I have a stake in this, and I want to know. How's the trial going?"

Wilson put on his most open-faced expression. "Frankly," he said, "not too well. I'm afraid the judge is on the other side. If you'd listened to me and stalled till another judge came along—"

"I had no time to stall," said Nicholls. "I have to be elsewhere within a few days. Even now, I should be on my way. Do you think we might lose the case?"

Harley laughed sharply. As Wilson glared at him he took his drink from the waitress' tray and swallowed it. The smile remained on his face as he listened to Wilson say smoothly:

"There is a good deal of danger, yes."

"Hum." Nicholls looked interestedly at his fingernails. "Perhaps I chose the wrong lawyer."

"Sure you did." Harley waved at the waitress, ordered another drink. "You want to know what else I think? I think you picked the wrong client, spelled s-t-o-o-g-e. I'm getting sick of this. This damn thing around my neck smells bad. How do I know it's any good, anyway? Far as I can see, it just smells bad, and that's all."

"It works," Nicholls said succinctly. "I wouldn't advise you to go without it. The late Hank Jenkins is not a very strong ghost—a strong one would tear you apart and chew up your herbs for dessert—but without the protection of what you wear about your neck, you would become a very uncomfortable human as soon as Jenkins heard you'd stopped wearing it."

He put down the glass of red wine he'd been inhaling without drinking, looked intently at Wilson. "I've put up the money in this," he said. "I had hoped you'd be able to handle the legal end. I see I'll have to do more. Now listen intently, because I have no intention of repeating this. There's an angle to this case that's got right by your blunted legal acumen. Jenkins claims to be an astral entity, which he undoubtedly is. Now, instead of trying to prove him a ghost, and legally dead, and therefore unfit to testify, which you have been doing, suppose you do this. . . ."

He went on to speak rapidly and to the point.

And when he left them a bit later, and Wilson took Harley up to his room and poured him into bed, the lawyer felt happy for the first time in days.

Russell Joseph Harley, a little hung over and a lot nervous, was called to the stand as first witness in his own behalf.

Wilson said, "Your name?"

"Russell Joseph Harley."

"You are the nephew of the late Zebulon Harley, who bequeathed the residence known as Harley Hall to you?"

"Yes."

Wilson turned to the bench. "I offer this copy of the late Mr. Zebulon Harley's will in evidence. All his possessions are left to his nephew and only living kin, the defendant."

Turnbull spoke from his desk. "The plaintiff in no way disputes the defendant's equity in Harley Hall."

Wilson continued, "You passed part of your childhood in Harley Hall, did you not, and visited it as a grown man on occasion?"

"Yes."

"At any time, has anything in the shape of a ghost, specter or astral entity manifested itself to you in Harley Hall?"

"No. I'd remember it."

"Did your late uncle ever mention any such manifestation to you?"

"Him? No."

"That's all."

Turnbull came up for the cross-examination.

"When, Mr. Harley, did you last see your uncle before his death?"

"It was in nineteen thirty-eight. In September, some time—around the tenth or eleventh of the month."

"How long a time did you spend with him?"

Harley flushed unaccountably. "Ah—just one day," he said.

"When before that did you see him?"

"Well, not since I was quite young. My parents moved to Pennsylvania in nineteen twenty."

"And since then—except for that one-day visit in nineteen thirty-eight—has any communication passed between your uncle and yourself?"

"No, I guess not. He was a rather queer duck—solitary. A little bit balmy, I think."

"Well, you're a loving nephew. But in view of what you've just said, does it sound surprising that your uncle never told you of Mr. Jenkins? He never had much chance to, did he?"

"He had a chance in nineteen thirty-eight, but he didn't," Harley said defiantly.

Turnbull shrugged. "I'm finished," he said.

Gimbel began to look bored. He had anticipated something more in the way of fireworks. He said, "Has the defense any further witnesses?"

Wilson smiled grimly. "Yes, your honor," he said. This was his big moment, and he smiled again as he said gently, "I would like to call Mr. Henry Jenkins to the stand."

In the amazed silence that followed, Judge Gimbel leaned forward. "You mean you wish to call the plaintiff as a witness for the defense?"

Serenely, "Yes, your honor."

Gimbel grimaced. "Call Henry Jenkins," he said wearily to the clerk, and sank back in his chair.

Turnbull was looking alarmed. He bit his lip, trying to decide whether to object to this astonishing procedure, but finally shrugged as the clerk bawled out the ghost's name.

Turnbull sped down the corridor, out the door. His voice was heard in the anteroom, then he returned more slowly. Behind him came the trickle of blood drops: *Pat. HISS. Pat. HISS—*

"One moment," said Gimbel, coming to life again. "I have no objection to your testifying, Mr. Jenkins, but the State should not be subjected to the needless expense of reupholstering its witness chair every time you do. Bailiff, find some sort of a rug or something to throw over the chair before Mr. Jenkins is sworn in."

A tarpaulin was hurriedly procured and adjusted to the chair; Jenkins materialized long enough to be sworn in, then sat.

"Tell me, Mr. Jenkins," he said, "just how many 'astral entities'—I believe that is what you call yourself—are there?"

"I have no way of knowing. Many billions."

"As many, in other words, as there have been human beings to die by violence?"

Turnbull rose to his feet in sudden agitation, but the ghost neatly evaded the trap. "I don't know. I only know there are billions."

The lawyer's cat-who-ate-canary smile remained undimmed. "And all these billions are constantly about us, everywhere, only remaining invisible. Is that it?"

"Oh, no. Very few remain on Earth. Of those, still fewer have anything to do with humans. Most humans are quite boring to us."

"Well, how many would you say are on Earth? A hundred thousand?"

"Even more, maybe. But that's a good guess."

Turnbull interrupted suddenly. "I would like to know the significance of these questions. I object to this whole line of questioning as being totally irrevelant."

Wilson was a study in legal dignity. He retorted, "I am trying to elicit some facts of major value, your honor. This may change the entire character of the case. I ask your patience for a moment or two."

"Counsel for the defense may continue," Gimbel said curtly.

Wilson showed his canines in a grin. He continued to the blood-dripping before him. "Now, the contention of your counsel is that the late Mr. Harley allowed an 'astral entity' to occupy his home for twenty years or more, with his full knowledge and consent. That strikes me as being entirely improbable, but shall we for the moment assume it to be the case?"

"Certainly! It's the truth."

"Then tell me, Mr. Jenkins, have you fingers?"

"Have I—what?"

"You heard me!" Wilson snapped. "Have you fingers, flesh-and-blood fingers, capable of making an imprint?"

"Why, no. I—"

Wilson rushed on. "Or have you a photograph of yourself—or specimens of your handwriting—or any sort of material identification? Have you any of these?"

The voice was definitely querulous. "What do you mean?"

Wilson's voice became harsh, menacing. "I mean, can you prove that *you* are the astral entity alleged to have occupied Zebulon Harley's home. Was it you—or was it another of the featureless, faceless, intangible unknowns—one of the hundreds of thousands of them that, by your own admission, are all over the face of the earth, rambling where they choose, not halted by any locks or bars? Can you prove that *you* are anyone in particular?"

"Your honor!" Turnbull's voice was almost a shriek as he found his feet at last. "My client's identity was never in question!"

"It is now!" roared Wilson. "The opposing counsel has presented a personage whom he styles 'Henry Jenkins.' Who is this Jenkins? What is he? Is he even an individual—or a corporate aggregation of these mysterious 'astral entities' which we are to believe are everywhere, but which we never see? If he is an individual, is he *the* individual? And how can we know that, even if he says he is? Let him produce evidence—photographs, a birth certificate, fingerprints. Let him bring in identifying witnesses who have known both ghosts, and are prepared to swear that these ghosts are the same ghost. Failing this, there is no case! Your honor, I demand the court declare an immediate judgment in favor of the defendant!"

Judge Gimbel stared at Turnbull. "Have you anything to say?" he asked. "The argument of the defense would seem to have every merit with it. Unless you can produce some sort of evidence as to the identity of your client, I have no alternative but to find for the defense."

For a moment there was a silent tableau. Wilson triumphant, Turnbull furiously frustrated.

How could you identify a ghost?

And then came the quietly amused voice from the witness chair. "This thing has gone far enough," it said above the sizzle and splatter of its own leaking blood. "I believe I can present proof that will satisfy the court."

Wilson's face fell with express-elevator speed. Turnbull held his breath, afraid to hope.

Judge Gimbel said, "You are under oath. Proceed."

There was no other sound in the courtroom as the voice said, "Mr. Harley, here, spoke of a visit to his uncle in nineteen thirty-eight. I can vouch for that. They spent a night and a day together. They weren't alone. I was there."

No one was watching Russell Harley, or they might have seen the sudden sick pallor that passed over his face.

The voice, relentless, went on. "Perhaps I shouldn't have eavesdropped as I did, but old Zeb never had any secrets from me anyhow. I listened to what they talked about. Young Harley was working for a bank in Philadelphia at the time. His first big job. He needed money, and needed it bad. There was a shortage in his department. A woman named Sally—"

"Hold on!" Wilson yelled. "This has nothing to do with your identification of yourself. Keep to the point!"

But Turnbull had begun to comprehend. He was shouting, too, almost too excited to be coherent. "Your honor, my client must be allowed to speak. If he shows knowledge of an intimate conversation between the late Mr. Harley and the defendant, it would be certain proof that he enjoyed the late Mr. Harley's confidence, and thus, Q.E.D., that he is no other than the astral entity who occupied Harley Hall for so long!"

Gimbel nodded sharply. "Let me remind counsel for the defense that this is his own witness. Mr. Jenkins, continue."

The voice began again, "As I was saying, the woman's name—"

"Shut up, damn you!" Harley yelled. He sprang upright, turned beseechingly toward the judge. "He's twisting it! Make him stop! Sure, I knew my uncle had a ghost. He's it, all right, curse his black soul! He can have the house if he wants it—I'll clear out of the whole damned state!"

He broke off into babbling and turned about wildly. Only the intervention of a marshal kept him from hurtling out of the courtroom.

Banging of the gavel and hard work by the court clerk and his staff restored order in the courtroom. When the room had returned almost to normalcy, Judge Gimbel, perspiring and annoyed, said, "As far as I am concerned, identification of the witness is complete. Has the defense any further evidence to present?"

Wilson shrugged morosely. "No, your honor."

"Counsel for the plaintiff?"

"Nothing, your honor. I rest my case."

Gimbel plowed a hand through his sparse hair and blinked. "In that case," he said, "I find for the plaintiff. An order is entered hereby that the defendant, Russell Joseph Harley, shall remove from the premises of Harley Hall all spells, pentagrams, talismans and other means of exorcism employed; that he shall cease and desist from making any attempts, of whatever nature, to evict the tenant in the future; and that Henry Jenkins, the plaintiff, shall be permitted to full use and occupancy of the premises designated as Harley Hall for the full term of his natural—ah—existence."

The gavel banged. "The case is closed."

"Don't take it so hard," said a mild voice behind Russell Harley. He whirled surlily. Nicholls was coming up the street after him from the courthouse, Wilson in tow.

Nicholls said, "You lost the case, but you've still got your life. Let me buy you a drink. In here, perhaps."

He herded them into a cocktail lounge, sat them down before they had a chance to object. He glanced at his expensive wrist watch. "I have a few minutes," he said. "Then I really must be off. It's urgent."

He hailed a barman, ordered for all. Then he looked at young Harley and smiled broadly as he dropped a bill on the counter to pay for the drinks.

"Harley," he said, "I have a motto that you would do well to remember at times like these. I'll make you a present of it, if you like."

"What is it?"

" 'The worst is yet to come.' "

Harley snarled and swallowed his drink without replying. Wilson said, "What gets me is, why didn't they come to us before the trial with that stuff about this charmingly illicit client you wished on me? We'd have had to settle out of court."

Nicholls shrugged. "They had their reasons," he said. "After all, one case of exorcism, more or less, doesn't matter. But lawsuits set precedents. You're a lawyer, of sorts, Wilson; do you see what I mean?"

"Precedents?" Wilson looked at him slackjawed for a moment; then his eyes widened.

"I see you understand me." Nicholls nodded. "From now on in this state—and by virtue of the full-faith-and-credence clause of the Constitution, in *every* state of the country—a ghost has a legal right to haunt a house!"

"Good Lord!" said Wilson. He began to laugh, not loud, but from the bottom of his chest.

Harley stared at Nicholls. "Once and for all," he whispered, "tell me —what's your angle on all this?"

Nicholls smiled again.

"Think about it a while," he said lightly. "You'll begin to understand." He sniffed his wine once more, then sat the glass down gently— And vanished.

"Smee" *is a muted little tale of a haunted house that manages to chill me more effectively than a lot of more melodramatic stories.* ALFRED M. BURRAGE, *born in Middlesex in 1889, was a British journalist, poet, and short-story writer whose work is little known in America. This is our loss, as the few fantasies of his I've read are all first-rate.*

Smee
by A. M. Burrage

"No," said Jackson, with a deprecatory smile, "I'm sorry. I don't want to upset your game. I shan't be doing that because you'll have plenty without me. But I'm not playing any games of hide-and-seek."

It was Christmas Eve, and we were a party of fourteen with just the proper leavening of youth. We had dined well; it was the season for childish games; and we were all in the mood for playing them—all, that is, except Jackson. When somebody suggested hide-and-seek there was rapturous and almost unanimous approval. His was the one dissentient voice.

It was not like Jackson to spoil sport or refuse to do as others wanted. Somebody asked him if he were feeling seedy.

"No," he answered, "I feel perfectly fit, thanks. But," he added with a smile which softened without retracting the flat refusal, "I'm not playing hide-and-seek."

One of us asked him why not. He hesitated for some seconds before replying.

"I sometimes go and stay at a house where a girl was killed through playing hide-and-seek in the dark. She didn't know the house very well. There was a servants' staircase with a door to it. When she was pursued she opened the door and jumped into what she must have thought was one of the bedrooms—and she broke her neck at the bottom of the stairs."

We all looked concerned, and Mrs. Fernley said:

"How awful! And you were there when it happened?"

Jackson shook his head very gravely.

"No," he said, "but I was there when something else happened. Something worse."

"I shouldn't have thought anything could be worse."

"This was," said Jackson, and shuddered visibly. "Or so it seemed to me."

I think he wanted to tell the story and was angling for encouragement. A few requests, which may have seemed to him to lack urgency, he affected to ignore and went off at a tangent.

"I wonder if any of you have played a game called 'Smee'? It's a great improvement on the ordinary game of hide-and-seek. The name derives from the ungrammatical colloquialism, 'It's me.' You might care to play if you're going to play a game of that sort. Let me tell you the rules.

"Every player is presented with a sheet of paper. All the sheets are blank except one, on which is written 'Smee.' Nobody knows who is 'Smee' except 'Smee' himself—or herself, as the case may be. The lights are then turned out and 'Smee' slips from the room and goes off to hide, and after an interval the other players go off in search, without knowing whom they are actually in search of. One player meeting another challenges with the word 'Smee,' and the other player, if not the one concerned, answers 'Smee.'

"The real 'Smee' makes no answer when challenged, and the second player remains quietly by him. Presently they will be discovered by a third player who, having challenged and received no answer, will link up with the first two. This goes on until all the players have formed a chain, and the last to join is marked down for a forfeit. It's a good noisy, romping game, and in a big house it often takes a long time to complete the chain. You might care to try it; and I'll pay my forfeit and smoke one of Tim's excellent cigars here by the fire, until you get tired of it."

I remarked that it sounded a good game and asked Jackson if he had played it himself.

"Yes," he answered; "I played it in the house I was telling you about."

"And *she* was there? The girl who broke—"

"No, no," Mrs. Fernley interrupted. "He told us he wasn't there when it happened."

Jackson considered.

"I don't know if she were there or not. I'm afraid she was. I know that there were thirteen of us and there ought only to have been twelve. And I'll swear that I didn't know her name, or I think I should have gone clean off my head when I heard that whisper in the dark. No, you don't catch me playing that game, or any other like it, any more. It spoilt my nerve quite a while, and I can't afford to take long holidays. Besides, it saves a lot of trouble and inconvenience to own up at once to being a coward."

Tim Vouce, the best of hosts, smiled around at us, and in that smile there was a meaning which is sometimes vulgarly expressed by the slow closing of an eye.

"There's a story coming," he announced.

"There's certainly a story of sorts," said Jackson, "but whether it's coming or not—"

He paused and shrugged his shoulders.

"Well, you're going to pay a forfeit instead of playing?"

"Please. But have a heart and let me down lightly. It's not just a sheer cussedness on my part."

"Payment in advance," said Tim, "ensures honesty and promotes good feeling. You are therefore sentenced to tell the story here and now."

And here follows Jackson's story, unrevised by me and passed on without comment to a wider public:

Some of you, I know, have run across the Sangstons. Christopher Sangston and his wife, I mean. They're distant connections of mine—at least, Violet Sangston is. About eight years ago they bought a house between the North and South Downs on the Surrey and Sussex border, and five years ago they invited me to come and spend Christmas with them.

It was a fairly old house—I couldn't say exactly of what period—and it certainly deserved the epithet "rambling." It wasn't a particularly big house, but the original architect, whoever he may have been, had not concerned himself with economising in space, and at first you could get lost in it quite easily.

Well, I went down for that Christmas, assured by Violet's letter that I knew most of my fellow-guests and that the two or three who might be strangers to me were all "lambs." Unfortunately, I'm one of the world's workers, and I couldn't get away until Christmas Eve, although the other members of the party had assembled on the preceding day. Even then I had to cut it rather fine to be there for dinner on my first night. They were all dressing when I arrived and I had to go straight to my room and waste no time. I may even have kept dinner waiting for a bit, for I was last down, and it was announced within a minute of my entering the drawing-room. There was just time to say "hullo" to everybody

I knew, to be briefly introduced to the two or three I didn't know, and then I had to give my arm to Mrs. Gorman.

I mention this as the reason why I didn't catch the name of a tall, dark, handsome girl I hadn't met before. Everything was rather hurried and I am always bad at catching people's names. She looked cold and clever and rather forbidding, the sort of girl who gives the impression of knowing all about men and the more she knows of them the less she likes them. I felt that I wasn't going to hit it off with this particular "lamb" of Violet's, but she looked interesting all the same, and I wondered who she was. I didn't ask, because I was pretty sure of hearing somebody address her by name before very long.

Unluckily, though, I was a long way off her at table, and as Mrs. Gorman was at the top of her form that night I soon forgot to worry about who she might be. Mrs. Gorman is one of the most amusing women I know, an outrageous but quite innocent flirt, with a very sprightly wit which isn't always unkind. She can think half a dozen moves ahead in conversation just as an expert can in a game of chess. We were soon sparring, or, rather, I was "covering" against the ropes, and I quite forgot to ask her in an undertone the name of the cold, proud beauty. The lady on the other side of me was a stranger, or had been until a few minutes since, and I didn't think of seeking information in that quarter.

There was a round dozen of us, including the Sangstons themselves, and we were all young or trying to be. The Sangstons themselves were the oldest members of the party, and their son Reggie, in his last year at Marlborough, must have been the youngest. When there was talk of playing games after dinner it was he who suggested "Smee." He told us how to play it just as I've described it to you.

His father chipped in as soon as we all understood what was going to be required of us.

"If there are any games of that sort going on in the house," he said, "for goodness sake be careful of the back stairs on the first floor landing. There's a door to them and I've often meant to take it down. In the dark anybody who doesn't know the house very well might think they were walking into a room. A girl actually did break her neck on those stairs about ten years ago when the Ainsties lived here."

I asked how it happened.

"Oh," said Sangston, "there was a party here one Christmas time and they were playing hide-and-seek as you propose doing. This girl was one of the hiders. She heard somebody coming, ran along the passage to get away, and opened the door of what she thought was a bedroom, evidently with the intention of hiding behind it while her pursuer went past. Unfortunately it was the door leading to the back stairs, and that staircase is at straight and almost as steep as the shaft of a pit. She was dead when they picked her up."

We all promised for our own sakes to be careful. Mrs. Gorman said that she was sure nothing could happen to her, since she was insured by three different newspapers, and her next-of-kin was a brother whose consistent ill-luck was a byword in the family. You see, none of us had known the unfortunate girl, and as the tragedy was ten years old there was no need to pull long faces about it.

Well, we started the game almost immediately after dinner. The men allowed themselves only five minutes before joining the ladies, and then young Reggie Sangston went round and assured himself that the lights were out all over the house except in the servants' quarters and in the drawing-room where we were assembled. We then got busy with twelve sheets of paper which he twisted into pellets and shook up between his hands before passing them round. Eleven of them were blank, and "Smee" was written on the twelfth. The person drawing the latter was the one who had to hide. I looked and saw that mine was a blank. A moment later out went the electric lights, and in the darkness I heard somebody get up and creep to the door.

After a minute or so somebody gave a signal and we made a rush for the door. I for one hadn't the least idea which of the party was "Smee." For five or ten minutes we were all rushing up and down passages and in and out rooms challenging one another and answering, "Smee?— Smee!"

After a bit the alarums and excursions died down, and I guessed that "Smee" was found. Eventually I found a chain of people all sitting still and holding their breath on some narrow stairs leading up to a row of attics. I hastily joined it, having challenged and been answered with silence, and presently two more stragglers arrived, each racing the other to avoid being last. Sangston was one of them, indeed it was he who was marked down for a forfeit, and after a little while he remarked in an undertone, "I think we're all here now, aren't we?"

He struck a match, looked up the shaft of the staircase, and began to count. It wasn't hard, although we just about filled the staircase, for we were sitting each a step or two one above the next, and all our heads were visible.

"... nine, ten, eleven, twelve—*thirteen*," he concluded, and then laughed. "Dash it all, that's one too many!"

The match had burnt out and he struck another and began to count. He got as far as twelve, and then uttered an exclamation.

"There *are* thirteen people here!" he exclaimed. "I haven't counted myself yet."

"Oh, nonsense!" I laughed. "You probably began with yourself, and now want to count yourself twice."

Out came his son's electric torch, giving a brighter and steadier light and we all began to count. Of course we numbered twelve. Sangston laughed.

"Well," he said, "I could have sworn I counted thirteen twice."

From halfway up the stairs came Violet Sangston's voice with a little nervous trill in it.

"I thought there was somebody sitting two steps above me. Have you moved up, Captain Ransome?"

Ransome said that he hadn't. He also said that he thought there was somebody sitting between Violet and himself. Just for a moment there was an uncomfortable Something in the air, a little cold ripple which touched us all. For that little moment it seemed to all of us, I think, that something odd and unpleasant had happened and was liable to happen again. Then we laughed at ourselves and at one another and were comfortable once more. There *were* only twelve of us, and there *could* only have been twelve of us, and there was no argument about it. Still laughing we trooped back to the drawing-room to begin again.

This time I was "Smee," and Violet Sangston ran me to earth while I was still looking for a hiding-place. That round didn't last long, and we were a chain of twelve within two or three minutes. Afterwards there was a short interval. Violet wanted a wrap fetched for her, and her husband went up to get it from her room. He was no sooner gone than Reggie pulled me by the sleeve. I saw that he was looking pale and sick.

"Quick!" he whispered, "while father's out of the way. Take me into the smoke-room and give me a brandy or a whisky or something. You know the sort of dose a fellow ought to have."

Outside the room I asked him what was the matter, but he didn't answer at first, and I thought it better to dose him first and question him afterwards. So I mixed him a pretty dark-complexioned brandy and soda which he drank at a gulp and then began to puff as if he had been running.

"I've had rather a turn," he said to me with a sheepish grin.

"What's the matter?"

"I don't know. You were 'Smee' just now, weren't you? Well, of course I didn't know who 'Smee' was, and while mother and the others ran into the west wing and found you, I turned east. There's a deep clothes cupboard in my bedroom—I'd marked it down as a good place to hide when it was my turn, and I had an idea that 'Smee' might be there. I opened the door in the dark, felt round, and touched somebody's hand. 'Smee!' I whispered, and not getting any answer I thought I had found 'Smee.'

"Well, I don't know how it was, but an odd creepy feeling came over me. I can't describe it, but I felt that something was wrong. So I turned on my electric torch and there was nobody there. Now I swear I touched a hand, and I was filling up the doorway of the cupboard at the time, so nobody could get out past me." He puffed again. "What do you make of it?" he asked.

"You imagined that you touched a hand," I answered, naturally enough.

He uttered a short laugh.

"Of course I knew you were going to say that," he said. "I must have imagined it, mustn't I?" He paused and swallowed. "I mean, it couldn't have been anything else *but* imagination, could it?"

I assured him that it couldn't, meaning what I said, and he accepted this, but rather with the philosophy of one who knows he is right but doesn't expect to be believed. We returned together to the drawing-room where, by that time, they were all waiting for us and ready to start again.

It may have been my imagination—although I'm almost sure it wasn't —but it seemed to me that all enthusiasm for the game had suddenly melted like a white frost in strong sunlight. If anybody had suggested another game I'm sure we should all have been grateful and abandoned "Smee." Only nobody did. Nobody seemed to like to. I for one, and I can speak for some of the others, too, was oppressed with the feeling that there was something wrong. I couldn't have said what I thought was wrong, indeed I didn't think about it at all, but somehow all the sparkle had gone out of the fun, and hovering over my mind like a shadow was the warning of some sixth sense which told me that there was an influence in the house which was neither sane, sound nor healthy. Why did I feel like that? Because Sangston had counted thirteen of us instead of twelve, and his son had thought he had touched somebody in an empty cupboard. No, there was more in it than just that. One would have laughed at such things in the ordinary way, and it was just that feeling of something being wrong which stopped me from laughing.

Well, we started again, and when we went in pursuit of the unknown "Smee," we were as noisy as ever, but it seemed to me that most of us were acting. Frankly, for no reason other than the one I've given you, we'd stopped enjoying the game. I had an instinct to hunt with the main pack, but after a few minutes, during which no "Smee" had been found, my instinct to play winning games and be first if possible, set me searching on my own account. And on the first floor of the west wing, following the wall which was actually the shell of the house, I blundered against a pair of human knees.

I put out my hand and touched a soft, heavy curtain. Then I knew where I was. There were tall, deeply-recessed windows with seats along the landing, and curtains over the recesses to the ground. Somebody was sitting in a corner of this window-seat behind the curtain. Aha, I had caught "Smee"! So I drew the curtain aside, stepped in, and touched the bare arm of a woman.

It was a dark night outside, and, moreover, the window was not only curtained but a blind hung down to where the bottom panes joined up with the frame. Between the curtain and the window it was as dark as the plague of Egypt. I could not have seen my hand held six inches before my face, much less the woman sitting in the corner.

"Smee?" I whispered.

I had no answer. "Smee" when challenged does not answer. So I sat down beside her, first in the field, to await the others. Then, having settled myself I leaned over to her and whispered:

"Who is it? What's your name, 'Smee'?"

And out of the darkness beside me the whisper came back: "Brenda Ford."

I didn't know the name, but because I didn't know it I guessed at once who she was. The tall, pale, dark girl was the only person in the house I didn't know by name. Ergo my companion was the tall, pale, dark girl. It seemed rather intriguing to be there with her, shut in between a heavy curtain and a window, and I rather wondered whether she was enjoying the game we were all playing. Somehow she hadn't seemed to me to be one of the romping sort. I muttered one or two commonplace questions to her and had no answer.

"Smee" is a game of silence. "Smee" and the person or persons who have found "Smee" are supposed to keep quiet to make it hard for the others. But there was nobody else about, and it occurred to me that she was playing the game a little too much to the letter. I spoke again and got no answer, and then I began to be annoyed. She was of that cold, "superior" type which affects to despise men; she didn't like me; and she was sheltering behind the rules of a game for children to be discourteous. Well, if she didn't like sitting there with me, I certainly didn't want to be sitting there with her! I half turned from her and began to hope that we should both be discovered without much more delay.

Having discovered that I didn't like being there alone with her, it was queer how soon I found myself hating it, and that for a reason very different from the one which had at first whetted my annoyance. The girl I had met for the first time before dinner, and seen diagonally across the table, had a sort of cold charm about her which had attracted while it had half angered me. For the girl who was with me, imprisoned in the opaque darkness between the curtain and the window, I felt no attraction at all. It was so very much the reverse that I should have wondered at myself if, after the first shock of the discovery that she had suddenly become repellent to me, I had no room in my mind for anything besides the consciousness that her close presence was an increasing horror to me.

It came upon me just as quickly as I've uttered the words. My flesh suddenly shrank from her as you see a strip of gelatine shrink and wither before the heat of a fire. That feeling of something being wrong had come back to me, but multiplied to an extent which turned foreboding into actual terror. I firmly believe that I should have got up and run if I had not felt that at my first movement she would have divined my intention and compelled me to stay, by some means of which I could not bear to think. The memory of having touched her bare arm made me wince and draw in my lips. I prayed that somebody else would come along soon.

My prayer was answered. Light footfalls sounded on the landing. Somebody on the other side of the curtain brushed against my knees. The curtain was drawn aside and a woman's hand fumbling in the darkness, presently rested on my shoulder. "Smee?" whispered a voice which I instantly recognised as Mrs. Gorman's.

Of course she received no answer. She came and settled down beside me with a rustle, and I can't describe the sense of relief she brought me.

"It's Tony, isn't it?" she whispered.

"Yes," I whispered back.

"You're not 'Smee' are you."

"No, she's on my other side."

She reached a hand across me, and I heard one of her nails scratch the surface of a woman's silk gown.

"Hullo, 'Smee'! How are you? *Who* are you? Oh, is it against the rules to talk? Never mind, Tony, we'll break the rules. Do you know, Tony, this game is beginning to irk me a little. I hope they're not going to run it to death by playing it all the evening. I'd like to play some game where we can all be together in the same room with a nice bright fire."

"Same here," I agreed fervently.

"Can't you suggest something when we go down? There's something rather uncanny in this particular amusement. I can't quite shed the delusion that there's somebody in this game who oughtn't to be in at all."

That was just how I had been feeling, but I didn't say so. But for my part the worst of my qualms were now gone; the arrival of Mrs. Gorman had dissipated them. We sat on talking, wondering from time to time when the rest of the party would arrive.

I don't know how long elapsed before we heard a clatter of feet on the landing and young Reggie's voice shouting, "Hullo! Hullo, there! Anybody there?"

"Yes."

"Mrs. Gorman with you?"

"Yes," I answered.

"Well, you're a nice pair! You're both forfeited. We've all been waiting for you for hours."

"Why, you haven't found 'Smee' yet," I objected.

"*You* haven't, you mean. I happen to have been 'Smee' myself."

"But 'Smee's' here with us," I cried.

"Yes," agreed Mrs. Gorman.

The curtain was stripped aside and in a moment we were blinking into the eye of Reggie's electric torch. I looked at Mrs. Gorman and then on my other side. Between me and the wall was an empty space on the window seat. I stood up at once and wished I hadn't, for I found myself sick and dizzy.

"There *was* somebody there," I maintained, "because I touched her."

"So did I," said Mrs. Gorman in a voice which had lost its steadiness. "And I don't see how she could have got up and gone without our knowing it."

Reggie uttered a queer, shaken laugh. He, too, had had an unpleasant experience that evening.

"Somebody's been playing the goat," he remarked. "Coming down?" We were not very popular when we arrived in the drawing-room. Reggie rather tactlessly gave it out that he had found us sitting on a window-seat behind a curtain. I taxed the tall, dark girl with having pretended to be "Smee" and afterwards slipping away. She denied it. After which we settled down and played other games. "Smee" was done with for the evening, and I for one was glad of it.

Some long while later, during an interval, Sangston told me, if I wanted a drink, to go into the smoke-room and help myself. I went, and he presently followed me. I could see that he was rather peeved with me, and the reason came out during the following minute or two. It seemed that, in his opinion, if I must sit out and flirt with Mrs. Gorman —in circumstances which would have been considered highly compromising in his young days—I needn't do it during a round game and keep everybody else waiting for us.

"But there was somebody else there," I protested, "somebody pretending to be 'Smee.' I believe it was that tall, dark girl, Miss Ford, although she denied it. She even whispered her name to me."

Sangston stared at me and nearly dropped his glass.

"Miss *Who?*" he shouted.

"Brenda Ford—she told me her name was."

Sangston put down his glass and laid a hand on my shoulder.

"Look here, old man," he said, "I don't mind a joke, but don't let it go too far. We don't want all the women in the house getting hysterical. Brenda Ford is the name of the girl who broke her neck on the stairs playing hide-and-seek here ten years ago."

JOHN KENDRICK BANGS *today is an undeservedly obscure American humorist. Author of a great number of delightfully ridiculous short stories and novels, including the charming* A Houseboat on the Styx *and its equally affable sequel,* The Pursuit of the Houseboat (*in which a dead Sherlock Holmes makes a premature appearance because who knew he was going to walk away alive from Reichenbach Falls?*), *Bangs was born in 1862 in Yonkers, New York, studied law at Columbia, but went instead into journalism. He edited several periodicals during his career, including* Life, Puck, *and* Harpers' Weekly. *He wrote quite a few tongue-in-cheek ghost stories, and an occasional serious one, of which the following riddle-tale is a first-rate example. Humor is not lacking in it, but it is the essentially chilly device of irony that distinguishes this curiously hysterical history.*

Thurlow's Christmas Story
by John Kendrick Bangs

I

(*Being the Statement of Henry Thurlow, Author, to George Currier, Editor of the* Idler, *a Weekly Journal of Human Interest.*)

I have always maintained, my dear Currier, that if a man wishes to be considered sane, and has any particular regard for his reputation as a truth-teller, he would better keep silent as to the singular experiences that enter into his life. I have had many such experiences myself; but I have rarely confided them in detail, or otherwise, to those about me, because I know that even the most trustful of my friends would regard them merely as the outcome of an imagination unrestrained by conscience, or of a gradually weakening mind subject to hallucinations. I know them to be true, but until Mr. Edison or some other modern wizard has invented a searchlight strong enough to lay bare the secrets of the mind and conscience of man, I cannot prove to others that they are not pure fabrications, or at least the conjurings of a diseased fancy. For instance, no man would believe me if I were to state to him the plain and indisputable fact that one night last month, on my way up to bed shortly after midnight, having been neither smoking nor drinking, I saw confronting me upon the stairs, with the moonlight streaming through the windows back of me, lighting up its face, a figure in which I recognized my very self in every form and feature. I might describe the chill of terror that struck to the very marrow of my bones, and wellnigh forced me to stagger backward down the stairs, as I noticed in the face of this confronting figure every indication of all the bad qualities which I know myself to possess, of every evil instinct which by no easy effort I have repressed heretofore, and realized that that *thing* was, as far as I knew, entirely independent of my true self, in which I hope at least the moral has made an honest fight against the immoral always. I might describe this chill, I say, as vividly as I felt it at that moment, but it would be of no use to do so, because, however realistic it might prove as a bit of description, no man would believe that the incident really happened; and yet it did happen as truly as I write, and it has happened a dozen times since, and I am certain that it will happen many times again, though I would give all that I possess to be assured that never again should that disquieting creation of mind or matter, whichever it may be, cross my path. The experience has made me afraid almost to be alone, and I have found myself unconsciously and uneasily glancing at my face in mirrors, in the plate-glass of show-windows on the shopping streets of the city, fearful lest I should find some of those evil traits which I have struggled to keep under, and have kept under so far, cropping out there where all the world, all *my* world, can see and wonder at, having known me always as a man of right doing and right feeling. Many a time in the night the thought has come to me with prostrating force, what if that thing were to be seen and recognized by others, myself and yet not my whole self, my unworthy self unrestrained and yet recognizable as Henry Thurlow.

I have also kept silent as to that strange condition of affairs which has tortured me in my sleep for the past year and a half; no one but myself has until this writing known that for that period of time I have had a continuous, logical dream-life; a life so vivid and so dreadfully real to me that I have found myself at times wondering which of the two lives I was living and which I was dreaming; a life in which that other wicked self has dominated, and forced me to a career of shame and horror; a life which, being taken up every time I sleep where it ceased with the awakening from a previous sleep, has made me fear to close my eyes in forgetfulness when others are near at hand, lest, sleeping, I shall let fall some speech that, striking on their ears, shall lead them to believe that in secret there is some wicked mystery connected with my life. It would be of no use for me to tell these things. It would merely serve to make my family and my friends uneasy about me if they were told in their awful detail, and so I have kept silent about them. To you alone, and now for the first time, have I hinted as to the troubles which have oppressed me for many days, and to you they are confided only because of the demand you have made that I explain to you the extraordinary complication in which the Christmas story sent you last week has involved me. You know that I am a man of dignity; that I am not a schoolboy and a lover of childish tricks; and knowing that, your friendship, at least, should have restrained your tongue and pen when, through the former, on Wednesday, you accused me of perpetrating a trifling, and to you excessively embarrassing, practical joke—a charge which, at the moment, I was too overcome to refute; and through the latter, on Thursday, you reiterated the accusation, coupled with a demand for an explanation of my conduct satisfactory to yourself, or my immediate resignation from the staff of the *Idler*. To explain is difficult, for I am certain that you will find the explanation too improbable for credence, but explain I must. The alternative, that of resigning from your staff, affects not only my own welfare, but that of my children, who must be provided for; and if my post with you is taken from me, then are all resources gone. I have not the courage to face dismissal, for I have not sufficient confidence in my powers to please elsewhere to make me easy in my mind, or, if I could please elsewhere, the certainty of finding the immediate employment of my talents which is necessary to me, in view of the at present overcrowded condition of the literary field.

To explain, then, my seeming jest at your expense, hopeless as it appears to be, is my task; and to do so as completely as I can, let me go back to the very beginning.

In August you informed me that you would expect me to provide, as I have heretofore been in the habit of doing, a story for the Christmas issue of the *Idler;* that a certain position in the make-up was reserved for me, and that you had already taken steps to advertise the fact that the story would appear. I undertook the commission, and upon seven different occasions set about putting the narrative into shape. I found great difficulty, however, in doing so. For some reason or other I could not concentrate my mind upon the work. No sooner would I start in on one story than a better one, in my estimation, would suggest itself to me; and all the labor expended on the story already begun would be cast aside, and the new story set in motion. Ideas were plenty enough, but to put them properly upon paper seemed beyond my powers. One story, however, I did finish; but after it had come back to me from my typewriter I read it, and was filled with consternation to discover that it was nothing more nor less than a mass of jumbled sentences, conveying no idea to the mind—a story which had seemed to me in the writing to be coherent had returned to me as a mere bit of incoherence—formless, without ideas—a bit of raving. It was then that I went to you and told you, as you remember, that I was worn out, and needed a month of absolute rest, which you granted. I left my work wholly, and went into the wilderness, where I could be entirely free from everything suggesting labor, and where no summons back to town could reach me. I fished and hunted. I slept; and although, as I have already said, in my sleep I found myself leading a life that was not only not to my taste, but horrible to me in many particulars, I was able at the end of my vacation to come back to town greatly refreshed, and, as far as my feelings went, ready to undertake any amount of work. For two or three days after my return I was busy with other things. On the fourth day after my arrival you came to me, and said that the story must be finished at the very latest by October 15th, and I assured you that you should have it by that time. That night I set about it. I mapped it out, incident by incident, and before starting up to bed had actually written some twelve or fifteen hundred words of the opening chapter—it was to be told in four chapters. When I had gone thus far I experienced a slight return of one of my nervous chills, and, on consulting my watch, discovered that it was after midnight, which was a sufficient explanation of my nervousness: I was merely tired. I arranged my manuscripts on my table so that I might easily take up the work the following morning. I locked up the windows and doors, turned out the lights, and proceeded upstairs to my room.

It was then that I first came face to face with myself—that other self, in which I recognized, developed to the full, every bit of my capacity for an evil life.

Conceive of the situation if you can. Imagine the horror of it, and then ask yourself if it was likely that when next morning came I could by any possibility bring myself to my work-table in fit condition to prepare for you anything at all worthy of publication in the *Idler*. I tried. I implore you to believe that I did not hold lightly the responsibilities of the commission you had intrusted to my hands. You must know that if any of your writers has a full appreciation of the difficulties which are strewn along the path of an editor, I, who have myself had an editorial experience, have it, and so would not, in the nature of things, do anything to add to your troubles. You cannot but believe that I have made an honest effort to fulfil my promise to you. But it was useless, and for a week after that visitation was it useless for me to attempt the work. At the end of the week I felt better, and again I started in, and the story developed satisfactorily until—*it* came again. That figure which was my own figure, that face which was the evil counterpart of my own countenance, again rose up before me, and once more was I plunged into hopelessness.

Thus matters went on until the 14th day of October, when I received your peremptory message that the story must be forthcoming the following day. Needless to tell you that it was not forthcoming; but what I must tell you, since you do not know it, is that on the evening of the 15th day of October a strange thing happened to me, and in the narration of that incident, which I almost despair of your believing, lies my explanation of the discovery of October 16th, which has placed my position with you in peril.

At half-past seven o'clock on the evening of October 15th I was sitting in my library trying to write. I was alone. My wife and children had gone away on a visit to Massachusetts for a week. I had just finished my cigar, and had taken my pen in hand, when my front-door bell rang. Our maid, who is usually prompt in answering summonses of this nature, apparently did not hear the bell, for she did not respond to its clanging. Again the bell rang, and still did it remain unanswered, until finally, at the third ringing, I went to the door myself. On opening it I saw standing before me a man of, I should say, fifty odd years of age, tall, slender, pale-faced, and clad in sombre black. He was entirely unknown to me. I had never seen him before, but he had about him such an air of pleasantness and wholesomeness that I instinctively felt glad to see him, without knowing why or whence he had come.

"Does Mr. Thurlow live here?" he asked.

You must excuse me for going into what may seem to you to be petty details, but by a perfectly circumstantial account of all that happened that evening alone can I hope to give a semblance of truth to my story, and that it must be truthful I realize as painfully as you do.

"I am Mr. Thurlow," I replied.

"Henry Thurlow, the author?" he said, with a surprised look upon his face.

"Yes," said I; and then, impelled by the strange appearance of surprise on the man's countenance, I added, "don't I look like an author?"

He laughed and candidly admitted that I was not the kind of looking man he had expected to find from reading my books, and then he entered the house in response to my invitation that he do so. I ushered him into my library, and, after asking him to be seated, inquired as to his business with me.

His answer was gratifying at least. He replied that he had been a reader of my writings for a number of years, and that for some time past he had had a great desire, not to say curiosity, to meet me and tell me how much he had enjoyed certain of my stories.

"I'm a great devourer of books, Mr. Thurlow," he said, "and I have taken the keenest delight in reading your verses and humorous sketches. I may go further, and say to you that you have helped me over many a hard place in my life by your work. At times when I have felt myself worn out with my business, or face to face with some knotty problem in my career, I have found much relief in picking up and reading your books at random. They have helped me to forget my weariness or my knotty problems for the time being; and today, finding myself in this town, I resolved to call upon you this evening and thank you for all that you have done for me."

Thereupon we became involved in a general discussion of literary men and their works, and I found that my visitor certainly did have a pretty thorough knowledge of what has been produced by the writers of today. I was quite won over to him by his simplicity, as well as attracted to him by his kindly opinion of my own efforts, and I did my best to entertain him, showing him a few of my little literary treasures in the way of autograph letters, photographs, and presentation copies of well-known books from the authors themselves. From this we drifted naturally and easily into a talk on the methods of work adopted by literary men. He asked me many questions as to my own methods; and when I had in a measure outlined to him the manner of life which I had adopted, telling him of my days at home, how little detail office-work I had, he seemed much interested with the picture—indeed, I painted the picture of my daily routine in almost too perfect colors, for, when I had finished, he observed quietly that I appeared to him to lead the ideal life, and added that he supposed I knew very little unhappiness.

The remark recalled to me the dreadful reality, that through some perversity of fate I was doomed to visitations of an uncanny order which were practically destroying my usefulness in my profession and my sole financial resource.

"Well," I replied, as my mind reverted to the unpleasant predicament in which I found myself, "I can't say that I know little unhappiness. As a matter of fact, I know a great deal of that undesirable thing. At the present moment I am very much embarrassed through my absolute inability to fulfil a contract into which I have entered, and which should have been filled this morning. I was due today with a Christmas story. The presses are waiting for it, and I am utterly unable to write it."

He appeared deeply concerned at the confession. I had hoped, indeed, that he might be sufficiently concerned to take his departure, that I might make one more effort to write the promised story. His solicitude, however, showed itself in another way. Instead of leaving me, he ventured the hope that he might aid me.

"What kind of a story is it to be?" he asked.

"Oh, the usual ghostly tale," I said, "with a dash of the Christmas flavor thrown in here and there to make it suitable to the season."

"Ah," he observed. "And you find your vein worked out?"

It was a direct and perhaps an impertinent question; but I thought it best to answer it, and to answer it as well without giving him any clew as to the real facts. I could not very well take an entire stranger into my confidence, and describe to him the extraordinary encounters I was having with an uncanny other self. He would not have believed the truth, hence I told him an untruth, and assented to his proposition.

"Yes," I replied, "the vein is worked out. I have written ghost stories for years now, serious and comic, and I am today at the end of my tether—compelled to move forward and yet held back."

"That accounts for it," he said, simply. "When I first saw you tonight at the door I could not believe that the author who had provided me with so much merriment could be so pale and worn and seemingly mirthless. Pardon me, Mr. Thurlow, for my lack of consideration when I told you that you did not appear as I had expected to find you."

I smiled my forgiveness, and he continued:

"It may be," he said, with a show of hesitation—"it may be that I have come not altogether inopportunely. Perhaps I can help you."

I smiled again. "I should be most grateful if you could," I said.

"But you doubt my ability to do so?" he put in. "Oh—well—yes—of course you do; and why shouldn't you? Nevertheless, I have noticed this: At times when I have been baffled in my work a mere hint from another, from one who knew nothing of my work, has carried me on to a solution of my problem. I have read most of your writings, and I have thought over some of them many a time, and I have even had ideas for stories, which, in my own conceit, I have imagined were good enough for you, and I have wished that I possessed your facility with the pen that I might make of them myself what I thought you would make of them had they been ideas of your own."

The old gentleman's pallid face reddened as he said this, and while I was hopeless as to anything of value resulting from his ideas, I could not resist the temptation to hear what he had to say further, his manner was so deliciously simple, and his desire to aid me so manifest. He rattled on with suggestions for a half-hour. Some of them were good, but none were new. Some were irresistibly funny, and did me good because they made me laugh, and I hadn't laughed naturally for a period so long that it made me shudder to think of it, fearing lest I should forget how to be mirthful. Finally I grew tired of his persistence, and, with a very ill-concealed impatience, told him plainly that I could do nothing with his suggestions, thanking him, however, for the spirit of kindliness which had prompted him to offer them. He appeared somewhat hurt, but immediately desisted, and when nine o'clock came he rose up to go. As he walked to the door he seemed to be undergoing some mental struggle, to which, with a sudden resolve, he finally succumbed, for, after having picked up his hat and stick and donned his overcoat, he turned to me and said:

"Mr. Thurlow, I don't want to offend you. On the contrary, it is my dearest wish to assist you. You have helped me, as I have told you. Why may I not help you?"

"I assure you, sir—" I began, when he interrupted me.

"One moment, please," he said, putting his hand into the inside pocket of his black coat and extracting from it an envelope addressed to me. "Let me finish: it is the whim of one who has an affection for you. For ten years I have secretly been at work myself on a story. It is a short one, but it has seemed good to me. I had a double object in seeking you out tonight. I wanted not only to see you, but to read my story to you. No one knows that I have written it; I had intended it as a surprise to my—to my friends. I had hoped to have it published somewhere, and I had come here to seek your advice in the matter. It is a story which I have written and rewritten and rewritten time and time again in my leisure moments during the ten years past, as I have told you. It is not likely that I shall ever write another. I am proud of having done it, but I should be prouder yet if it—if it could in some way help you. I leave it with you, sir, to print or to destroy; and if you print it, to see it in type will be enough for me; to see your name signed to it will be a matter of pride to me. No one will ever be the wiser, for, as I say, no one knows I have written it, and I promise you that no one shall know of it if you decide to do as I not only suggest but ask you to do. No one would believe me after it has appeared as *yours,* even if I should forget my promise and claim it as my own. Take it. It is yours. You are entitled to it as a slight measure of repayment for the debt of gratitude I owe you."

He pressed the manuscript into my hands, and before I could reply had opened the door and disappeared into the darkness of the street. I rushed to the sidewalk and shouted out to him to return, but I might as well have saved my breath and spared the neighborhood, for there was no answer. Holding his story in my hand, I re-entered the house and walked back into my library, where, sitting and reflecting upon the curious interview, I realized for the first time that I was in entire ignorance as to my visitor's name and address.

I opened the envelope hoping to find them, but they were not there. The envelope contained merely a finely written manuscript of thirty-odd pages, unsigned.

And then I read the story. When I began it was with a half-smile upon my lips, and with a feeling that I was wasting my time. The smile soon faded, however; after reading the first paragraph there was no question of wasted time. The story was a masterpiece. It is needless to say to you that I am not a man of enthusiasms. It is difficult to arouse that emotion in my breast, but upon this occasion I yielded to a force too great for me to resist. I have read the tales of Hoffmann and of Poe, the wondrous romances of De La Motte Fouque, the unfortunately little-known tales of the lamented Fitz-James O'Brien, the weird tales of writers of all tongues have been thoroughly sifted by me in the course of my reading, and I say to you now that in the whole of my life I never read one story, one paragraph, one line, that could approach in vivid delineation, in weirdness of conception, in anything, in any quality which goes to make up the tru:y great story, that story which came into my hands as I have told you. I read it once and was amazed. I read it a second time and was—tempted. It was mine. The writer himself had authorized me to treat it as if it were my own; had voluntarily sacrificed his own claim to its authorship that he might relieve me of my very pressing embarrassment. Not only this; he had almost intimated that in putting my name to his work I should be doing him a favor. Why not do so, then, I asked myself; and immediately my better self rejected the idea as impossible. How could I put out as my own another man's work and retain my self-respect? I resolved on another and better course—to send you the story in lieu of my own with a full statement of the circumstances under which it had come into my possession, when that demon rose up out of the floor at my side, this time more evil of aspect than before, more commanding in its manner. With a groan I shrank back into the cushions of my chair, and by passing my hands over my eyes tried to obliterate forever the offending sight; but it was useless. The uncanny thing approached me, and as truly as I write sat upon the edge of my couch, where for the first time it addressed me.

"Fool!" it said, "how can you hesitate? Here is your position: you have made a contract which must be filled; you are already behind, and in a hopeless mental state. Even granting that between this and tomorrow morning you could put together the necessary number of words to fill the space allotted to you, what kind of a thing do you think that story would make? It would be a mere raving like that other precious effort of August. The public, if by some odd chance it ever reached them, would think your mind was utterly gone; your reputation would go with that verdict. On the other hand, if you do not have the story ready by tomorrow, your hold on the *Idler* will be destroyed. They have their announcements printed, and your name and portrait appear among those of the prominent contributors. Do you suppose the editor and publisher will look leniently upon your failure?"

"Considering my past record, yes," I replied. "I have never yet broken a promise to them."

"Which is precisely the reason why they will be severe with you. You, who have been regarded as one of the few men who can do almost any kind of literary work at will—you, of whom it is said that your 'brains are on tap'—will they be lenient with *you?* Bah! Can't you see that the very fact of your invariable readiness heretofore is going to make your present unreadiness a thing incomprehensible?"

"Then what shall I do?" I asked. "If I can't, I can't, that is all."

"You can. There is the story in your hands. Think what it will do for you. It is one of the immortal stories—"

"You have read it, then?" I asked.

"Haven't you?"

"Yes—but—"

"It is the same," it said, with a leer and a contemptuous shrug. "You and I are inseparable. Aren't you glad?" it added, with a laugh that grated on every fibre of my being. I was too overwhelmed to reply, and it resumed: "It is one of the immortal stories. We agree to that. Published over your name, your name will live. The stuff you write yourself will give you present glory; but when you have been dead ten years people won't remember your name even—unless I get control of you, and in that case there is a very pretty though hardly a literary record in store for you."

Again it laughed harshly, and I buried my face in the pillows of my couch, hoping to find relief there from this dreadful vision.

"Curious," it said. "What you call your decent self doesn't dare look me in the eye! What a mistake people make who say that the man who won't look you in the eye is not to be trusted! As if mere brazenness were a sign of honesty; really, the theory of decency is the most amusing thing in the world. But come, time is growing short. Take that story. The writer gave it to you. Begged you to use it as your own. It is yours. It will make your reputation, and save you with your publishers. How can you hesitate?"

"I shall not use it!" I cried, desperately.

"You must—consider your children. Suppose you lose your connection with these publishers of yours?"

"But it would be a crime."

"Not a bit of it. Whom do you rob? A man who voluntarily came to you, and gave you that of which you rob him. Think of it as it is—and act, only act quickly. It is now midnight."

The tempter rose up and walked to the other end of the room, whence, while he pretended to be looking over a few of my books and pictures, I was aware he was eying me closely, and gradually compelling me by sheer force of will to do a thing which I abhorred. And I—I struggled weakly against the temptation, but gradually, little by little, I yielded, and finally succumbed altogether. Springing to my feet, I rushed to the table, seized my pen, and signed my name to the story.

"There!" I said. "It is done. I have saved my position and made my reputation, and am now a thief!"

"As well as a fool," said the other, calmly. "You don't mean to say you are going to send that manuscript in as it is?"

"Good Lord!" I cried. "What under heaven have you been trying to make me do for the last half hour?"

"Act like a sane being," said the demon. "If you send that manuscript to Currier he'll know in a minute it isn't yours. He knows you haven't an amanuensis, and that handwriting isn't yours. Copy it."

"True!" I answered. "I haven't much of a mind for details tonight. I will do as you say."

I did so. I got out my pad and pen and ink, and for three hours diligently applied myself to the task of copying the story. When it was finished I went over it carefully, made a few minor corrections, signed it, put it in an envelope, addressed it to you, stamped it, and went out to the mail-box on the corner, where I dropped it into the slot, and returned home. When I had returned to my library my visitor was still there.

"Well," it said, "I wish you'd hurry and complete this affair. I am tired, and wish to go."

"You can't go too soon to please me," said I, gathering up the original manuscripts of the story and preparing to put them away in my desk.

"Probably not," it sneered. "I'll be glad to go too, but I can't go until that manuscript is destroyed. As long as it exists there is evidence of your having appropriated the work of another. Why, can't you see that? Burn it!"

"I can't see my way clear in crime!" I retorted. "It is not in my line."

Nevertheless, realizing the value of his advice, I thrust the pages one by one into the blazing log fire, and watched them as they flared and flamed and grew to ashes. As the last page disappeared in the embers the demon vanished. I was alone, and throwing myself down for a moment's reflection upon my couch, was soon lost in sleep.

It was noon when I again opened my eyes, and, ten minutes after I awakened, your telegraphic summons reached me.

"Come down at once," was what you said, and I went; and then came the terrible *dénouement,* and yet a *dénouement* which was pleasing to me since it relieved my conscience. You handed me the envelope containing the story.

"Did you send that?" was your question.

"I did—last night, or rather early this morning. I mailed it about three o'clock," I replied.

"I demand an explanation of your conduct," said you.

"Of what?" I asked.

"Look at your so-called story and see. If this is a practical joke, Thurlow, it's a damned poor one."

I opened the envelope and took from it the sheets I had sent you— twenty-four of them.

They were every one of them as blank as when they left the paper-mill!

You know the rest. You know that I tried to speak; that my utterance failed me; and that, finding myself unable at the time to control my emotions, I turned and rushed madly from the office, leaving the mystery unexplained. You know that you wrote demanding a satisfactory explanation of the situation or my resignation from your staff.

This, Currier, is my explanation. It is all I have. It is absolute truth. I beg you to believe it, for if you do not, then is my condition a hopeless one. You will ask me perhaps for a *résumé* of the story which I thought I had sent you.

It is my crowning misfortune that upon that point my mind is an absolute blank. I cannot remember it in form or in substance. I have racked my brains for some recollection of some small portion of it to help to make my explanation more credible, but, alas! it will not come back to me. If I were dishonest I might fake up a story to suit the purpose, but I am not dishonest. I came near to doing an unworthy act; I did do an unworthy thing, but by some mysterious provision of fate my conscience is cleared of that.

Be sympathetic, Currier, or, if you cannot, be lenient with me this time. *Believe, believe, believe,* I implore you. Pray let me hear from you at once.

(Signed)   HENRY THURLOW.

II

(Being a Note from George Currier, Editor of the Idler, *to Henry Thurlow, Author.)*

Your explanation has come to hand. As an explanation it isn't worth the paper it is written on, but we are all agreed here that it is probably the best bit of fiction you ever wrote. It is accepted for the Christmas issue. Enclosed please find check for one hundred dollars.

Dawson suggests that you take another month up in the Adirondacks. You might put in your time writing up some account of that dream-life you are leading while you are there. It seems to me there are possibilities in the idea. The concern will pay all expenses. What do you say?

(Signed)   Yours ever,   G. C.

W. S. GILBERT, *the great English satirist, was born in 1836 and lived to write a huge number of "Bab Ballads," humorous verse from which he drew the plots of several of his comic operettas that he wrote with Arthur Sullivan. The fantastic occurs often in Gilbert (four times in the operettas alone); originally I planned to use the first-night version of the ghost scene of G&S' Ruddigore, but found that it suffers out of context. Here is one of the less familiar "Bab Ballads" written for* Fun *magazine. In it, two supernatural critters vie ferociously for top honors in a scareathon, in which one wonders who is the bigger dummy.*

The Ghost, the Gallant, the Gael, and the Goblin

by W. S. Gilbert

O'er unreclaimed suburban clay
    Some years ago were hobblin',
An elderly ghost of easy ways,
    And an influential goblin.
The ghost was a sombre spectral shape,
    A fine old five-act fogy,
The goblin imp, a lithe young ape,
    A fine low-comedy bogy.

And as they exercised their joints,
    Promoting quick digestion,
They talked on several curious points,
    And raised this pregnant question:
"Which of us two is Number One—
    The ghostie, or the goblin?"
And o'er the point they raised in fun
    They fairly fell a-squabblin'.

They'd barely speak, and each, in fine,
    Grew more and more reflective,
Each thought his own particular line
    By far the more effective.
At length they settled some one should

By each of them be haunted,
And so arranged that either could
Exert his prowess vaunted.

"The Quaint against the Statuesque"—
By competition lawful—
The goblin backed the Quaint Grotesque,
The ghost the Grandly Awful.
"Now," said the goblin, "here's my plan—
In attitude commanding,
I see a stalwart Englishman
By yonder tailor's standing.

"The very fittest man on earth
My influence to try on—
Of gentle, p'raps of noble birth,
And dauntless as a lion!
Now wrap yourself within your shroud—
Remain in easy hearing—
Observe—you'll hear him scream aloud
When I begin appearing!"

The imp with yell unearthly—wild—
Threw off his dark enclosure:
His dauntless victim looked and smiled
With singular composure.
For hours he tried to daunt the youth,
For days, indeed, but vainly—
The stripling smiled!—to tell the truth,
The stripling smiled insanely.

For weeks the goblin weird and wild,
That noble stripling haunted;
For weeks the stripling stood and smiled
Unmoved and all undaunted.
The sombre ghost exclaimed, "Your plan
Has failed you, goblin, plainly:
Now watch yon hardy Hieland man,
So stalwart and ungainly.

"These are the men who chase the roe,
    Whose footsteps never falter,
Who bring with them where'er they go,
    A smack of old SIR WALTER.
Of such as he, the men sublime
    Who lead their troops victorious,
Whose deeds go down to after-time,
    Enshrined in annals glorious!

"Of such as he the bard has said
    'Hech thrawfu' raltie rawkie!
Wi' thecht ta' croonie clapperhead
    And fash' wi' unco pawkie!'
He'll faint away when I appear
    Upon his native heather;
Or p'raps he'll only scream with fear,
    Or p'raps the two together."

The spectre showed himself, alone,
    To do his ghostly battling,
With curdling groan and dismal moan
    And lots of chains a-rattling!
But no—the chiel's stout Gaelic stuff
    Withstood all ghostly harrying.
His fingers closed upon the snuff
    Which upwards he was carrying.

For days that ghost declined to stir,
    A foggy, shapeless giant—
For weeks that splendid officer
    Stared back again defiant!
Just as the Englishman returned
    The goblin's vulgar staring,
Just so the Scotchman boldly spurned
    The ghost's unmannered scaring.

For several years the ghostly twain
    These Britons bold have haunted,
But all their efforts are in vain—
    Their victims stand undaunted.

Unto this day the imp and ghost
(Whose powers the imp derided)
Stand each at his allotted post—
The bet is undecided.

BERNHARDT J. HURWOOD *is a Manhattan novelist, short-story writer and es-
sayist who specializes in many areas, including the supernatural. He has
edited and/or written many collections of short anecdotes about ghosts,
some of them retold from other cultures' folklore. "The Corpse at the Inn"
is one such tale, originating with an oriental tale by Pu Sung Ling. It shows
an interesting variation in the role of the spectre; Western ghosts may have
many guises and purposes, but Chinese phantoms often are really bodies inhabited by demons, a particularly nasty specimen of which appears below.
Hurwood's stories are almost always quite brief, thus I have included three
other terse accounts of unusually unnerving apparitions . . . and these three,
according to the author, are not fictional, but may have "really happened." I
am skeptical of that—but true or not, they are all unusually horrendous.*

A Quartet of Strange Things
by Bernhardt J. Hurwood

I: THE CORPSE AT THE INN
From the Liao Chai of Pu Sung Ling

In a remote village located in the Yang Shin district there was once an
old man who, with the aid of his son, kept a roadside inn. One evening
as the gathering shadows grew long and black, four weary travellers arrived and asked the landlord for a night's lodging. To their dismay the
old man refused their request, explaining that all the rooms were filled.
But as it had become quite dark while they talked, and there was nowhere else for them to go, the men implored the innkeeper to make
room for them anywhere he could. Seeing that the four were genuinely
distressed, the old man offered to put them up in a small outbuilding situated near the women's quarters. The strangers were greatly relieved
and followed their host who led the way carrying a small oil lamp in
one hand.

Now it happened that the innkeeper's daughter-in-law had died that
day, and her corpse was laid out in the very room to which he led his
unsuspecting guests. She was dressed in ceremonial paper robes and
lying on a makeshift wooden bier in deep shadow at the far end of the
chamber. Near the door were four simple cots and a plain wooden table
upon which he placed the flickering, smoky oil lamp. Then taking his
leave, he withdrew as quickly as he could without arousing suspicion

and returned to the inn. The four lodgers were so exhausted that they did not notice the corpse with which they were forced to share quarters. Flinging themselves upon their couches, three of the men soon were sound asleep. The fourth, however, felt a strange premonition and lay staring at the eerie shadows cast by the sputtering lamp.

He had finally begun to doze off when suddenly he heard a creaking noise accompanied by the rustling of paper. Daring not to move anything but his eyes, he glanced sideways in the direction of the ominous sounds. By now he had become accustomed to the murky darkness, and saw at once what was happening. Fingers of ice seemed to grip his heart as he realized there was a corpse in the room. Worse yet, the dead body of the girl was rising stiffly from the bier, the dim light revealing the ghastly pallor of her lifeless face. Paralyzed with terror, the poor man beheld the animated corpse standing upright. In the next moment the dreadful creature began gliding unmistakably toward the three who slept.

As she reached the first man she bent silently over him and exhaled in his face. She rose up and repeated her action over the second and the third sleepers. The fourth man, by now half dead with fright, pulled the cover over his face, held his breath and listened for what seemed a veritable eternity. A chill came over him as she approached his bed and bent down as she had over the others. But then, hearing her footsteps recede, he stealthily peeked out from beneath his coverlet and saw her ascend the bier and stretch out, corpselike, as before.

For a few moments the man lay still. Then, ever so cautiously he stretched out one foot and kicked the nearest of his companions. But he shuddered, for it was like touching a dead man. By now the unhappy fellow had no thought but of flight. Moving as softly as he could, he reached for his clothing so that he could make a dash for the door. But no sooner had he reached under the bed than once more he heard that awful creaking and rustling. Instinctively he buried his head beneath the cover again and held his breath as he had done before. After what seemed to be an eternity the corpse came to him a second time and bent down to breathe its foul breath upon his face. Finally it retreated to the far end of the chamber to resume its place upon the bier.

Now, wasting not an instant, the traveller seized his clothes and dashed to the door as fast as he could. But he was not alone. The dead girl, too, leaped to her feet and followed him into the night. Outdoors, the man plunged wildly into the darkness, shrieking at the top of his lungs. But there was no one to hear him but his ghastly pursuer, who was close upon his heels. Raising his voice as he passed the inn door was to no avail. His screams went unheeded. So he kept running toward the main road which led to the city.

With the corpse keeping up its pace, the fleeing man looked about desperately for a place to hide. Suddenly he noticed a small roadside monastery, and rushing up to the gate, he pounded with all his might. But alas, the priests inside knew not what to make of this unexpected tumult and would not open the door. By now the corpse was only yards away. In desperation, the man ran towards a huge willow tree that stood nearby. And just in time, for the dead girl reached the tree at the precise moment her quarry managed to dodge to one side. It now became a deadly game. The corpse, her eyes glowing fiercely, like live coals, tried to seize her victim with demoniac ferocity. But each time she moved to the left he would rush to the right, and so it went until both were panting hoarsely at the brink of exhaustion. Then both the corpse and her intended victim stood motionless, staring at each other— he in mortal terror, she with the cold rage of an unnatural monster.

Suddenly the corpse lunged forward with outstretched arms to seize its victim once and for all. The man, believing that his end had finally come, fell backward, senseless to the ground. The corpse crashed into the tree with the force of a charging tiger.

By now the priests, who had been hearing the shrieks and moans, rushed out to find the cause of the disturbance. They found the unconscious stranger lying on the ground beside the tree so they carried him into the monastery. By daybreak they succeeded in bringing him to his senses, at which time he told them in detail of his horrible ordeal in the dark. When the sun was shining brightly they went out to investigate the tree and there found the corpse of the girl, hanging limply to the trunk.

The local magistrate was summoned at once, and upon arriving, he ordered that the body be removed. But this was impossible at first, for her long fingernails were imbedded too deeply in the tree. Finally she was detached and word of the night's dreadful events were sent to the inn where, by now, the three other travellers had been found dead. The innkeeper had the body of his daughter-in-law brought back, and the traveller who lived requested that he be given a certificate attesting to the truth of his tale. The magistrate complied with the man's wishes and he was accordingly sent home.

II: THE VAMPIRE OF CROGLIN GRANGE

A number of years ago two brothers and a sister rented a very old house in England called Croglin Grange. The place had no upper floor, so that all the bedrooms were at ground level. They were very fond of it and especially enjoyed the surroundings, which were peaceful and extremely charming. A belt of graceful trees separated the property from an old churchyard, and on moonlit nights the entire area presented a view of unsurpassed beauty.

One summer night, shortly after she had gone to bed, the sister, whose name was Flora, noticed what appeared to be two lights flickering in and out of the trees bordering the churchyard. Watching with mild curiosity, she gradually became aware of something dark coming towards her window. A chill of uncontrollable horror overcame her as the shapeless dark mass came closer. She wanted to get up and run from the room, but by now she was so terrified that she became paralyzed with fear.

Suddenly the hideous thing appeared at the window! Never in her life had she seen anything so ugly, so ghastly. The face was brown and shrivelled like that of a mummy, but it had fierce, blazing eyes that glared like coals from Hell itself. As she cowered in her bed the thing began scratching at the window . . . *scratch, scratch, scratch*. Thank God the window is locked, she thought, but then, to her horror, she realised that it was picking at the leading of the mullioned window. The crash of the glass falling to the floor seemed to break the spell and she leaped from the bed and ran to the door, just as a withered brown hand reached in and turned the lock.

She was so busy fumbling with the doorknob that she wasn't aware of the speed with which the monstrous horror scuttled across the room and threw itself at her. Seizing her long hair with its bony fingers, it dragged her back to the bed, forced her down, then bent over and bit her ferociously in the throat. At that instant her voice came back and she screamed with every ounce of strength that she had, while punching and kicking her hideous assailant with all her might.

Seconds later her brothers rushed into her room, and as one of them ran for a poker, the other gave chase to the creature as it ran like the wind across the lawn, over the low stone wall, and into the churchyard.

As terrible as her experience was, she refused to believe that it was anything supernatural, insisting that it had to be an attack by an escaped mental patient or prisoner. But there was no news of any such thing, and besides, how could she explain the hideous appearance of the thing? After a brief stay in hospital whilst her wound healed, and a short stay abroad, she finally returned to Croglin Grange, assuring her brothers that the chances of any such thing happening again were virtually nil. Nevertheless, thereafter they kept loaded pistols in their rooms, and tried to make her do the same, but she refused on the grounds that she could not stand guns.

After an uneventful winter the woman was awakened from a sound sleep late one March night by the familiar sound of scratching at the window. Seizing the torch she kept by her bed, she switched it on and illuminated the window. There fully bathed by the beam of light was the same ghastly brown shrivelled face with the glaring eyes, and the bony hands. A single bloodcurdling scream brought her brothers on the double, both with pistols in hand. The thing backed off and began retreating across the lawn with the two men hard on its heels. One fired a shot and hit it in the leg, but it kept running and after scrambling back over the churchyard wall, disappeared into a vault showing signs of decay and neglect.

The next day the brothers gathered a number of their neighbours together, and after revealing what had happened the night before, led them to the vault and opened it. The sight that met their eyes was shocking, and unlike anything they had ever seen. Except for one, all the coffins were broken open, and the bones of their occupants scattered on the floor. Upon opening the lid of the single coffin that was intact, they found the brown, shrivelled, hideous figure that had broken into Croglin Grange. In one leg was a fresh bullet hole. After overcoming their initial shock, they removed the dreadful body, drenched it with petrol, and burned it to cinders. Although they never knew its origin, they were never bothered by the vampire again.

III: THE OLD MAN IN YELLOW

There is hardly anything more unnerving than being followed by a hideous stranger on a lonely road at night. When the stranger proves to be *nonhuman* . . . but that is getting ahead of the story. . . .

It happened a few years ago to a young man named Elwyn Thomas, who happened to be visiting friends in a small village in South Wales. It was a warm June night and darkness was just beginning to fall when he left his friends to return to the country inn where he was staying. Judging by past experience, he reckoned on reaching it by about nine o'clock. It was exactly eight-thirty when he said good-night.

He was completely alone in the gathering dusk, and the only sounds were the occasional cries of night birds and the crunch of his own footsteps on the gravel road. Being neither superstitious nor afraid of anything he walked briskly along, glancing now and then towards the banks of an old canal off to one side of the road.

After about ten minutes he began experiencing a peculiar, creepy sensation, as if he were being watched. On an impulse, he stopped, turned around and gasped involuntarily. There, no more than a yard behind him, suspended in mid-air at eye-level, was the most hideous face he had ever seen. The putty-coloured skin was drawn tightly over the features, except for the forehead, which was lined with deep wrinkles. Thin, seemingly bloodless lips formed a crooked grin over a half-open, toothless mouth. The cheeks were hollow and corpse-like, and the eyes were wild, luminous, and piercing. Wrapped around the ghastly object were two pieces of old yellow calico, one under the jaw and tied on top of the head, the other over the forehead and tied behind.

Unable to help himself, Thomas turned and began running as fast as he could. After having covered about a hundred yards, he stopped to catch his breath and turned around again. To his horror the face was still there—as if he hadn't moved an inch. On an impulse he dropped down, grabbed a handful of gravel and hurled it at the face, then turned again and ran.

When he finally reached the inn he stopped at the path leading off the road and looked back again. The head was still behind him. Cautiously he backed up in the direction of the inn and was surprised to observe that this time the head remained above the road, grinning somewhat contemptuously. Taking courage he decided to go back, confront the apparition, and question it. But as he approached, the head began receding, its glowing eyes fixed almost malevolently on his own. Now he felt as though he had to follow. Down the road he went slowly, like a sleepwalker, until the head disappeared over a stone wall surrounding a little graveyard not far from the inn. Suddenly he felt everything begin to spin; then he lost consciousness.

When he came to again, it was late at night. He had lain at the foot of the churchyard wall for more than two hours. Groping through the darkness until he found his way back to the inn, it was with great relief that he finally retired to bed and to a restless night filled with bad dreams.

When he told the innkeeper about his experience the next day he learned that he had not been having hallucinations. An eccentric old recluse fitting the exact description of the apparition had once lived in a cottage whose ruins were quite near to the place where the face had disappeared. No one could remember exactly how long the old man had been dead, but they knew it had been many years since he had been last seen alive.

IV: THE GLOWING MAGGOT OF DOOM

Perhaps the most loathsome and terrifying apparition ever seen was a maggoty creature that was said to have haunted a little Yorkshire churchyard years ago.

The first man to see it was Mr. Mullins, the postman. It was a bright, moonlit night and he was passing the graveyard on his way home. What caught his attention was a large blob of luminous ooze issuing from the fresh grave of a recently dead villager named Peters. Wriggling like a giant, ugly glow-worm it grew bigger as it issued from the ground. Horrified, yet fascinated, Mullins followed the "thing" which now looked exactly like a giant maggot, but he had to summon all his courage, for when he saw its eyes he was forced to avert his own. They seemed to exude pure evil, and somehow appeared strangely human. The ghastly monster slithered along the ground with a caterpillar's wriggle, leaving a gleaming trail of disgusting slime in its wake. To Mullins' amazement, the maggot wriggled in and out between the tombstones, left the graveyard, and disappeared from sight when it reached the threshold of the vicar's house nearby.

The following day Mullins told his wife and his best friend about his chilling experience, and that night the three of them went to the churchyard to see if they could discover what the hideous apparition might be. Just as it had the night before, the dreadful worm oozed from Peters' grave, made its way to the vicar's house, and again disappeared at the threshold. The next day, however, the Mullinses and their friend received a severe shock. The vicar and his entire family had suddenly been taken ill, and were dead by sunset. The doctor who examined them attributed their deaths to ptomaine poisoning.

More determined than ever to get to the bottom of this horrible apparition's origin, Mullins, his wife, and their friend ventured once again to the village churchyard after dark that night. Again the hideous glowing maggot wriggled out of the grave and slithered between the tombstones, leaving the now familiar trail of slime in its path. This time they followed it to the house of the village blacksmith, into which it vanished. There was no need for it to visit him a second time, for he became ill in the morning and died before sunset, like the vicar and his family, of ptomaine poisoning.

Thoroughly alarmed, but more baffled than ever, Mullins and his companions determined to keep watch again that same night. Nothing happened. Somewhat relieved, they nevertheless decided to continue their nightly vigil at the graveyard for at least one more week. Ten nights after it had first appeared, it emerged from its customary place again only to head directly to the Mullins' house! They were horror-stricken, but powerless. That night they spent in sleepless, terrified anticipation. In the morning tragedy struck and their five-year-old son died an hour after being taken ill.

That night their hearts filled with grief and hatred, Mullins and his wife, aided by their friend, went back to the village churchyard. This time they had a plan. Equipped with a hooded lantern and spades, they dug up the grave of the late Mr. Peters.

When they finally struck the coffin, Mullins and his friend pried off the lid while Mrs. Mullins held the lantern. There, on the dead man's face was an expression of such unspeakable malevolence that they slammed the lid down and staggered back involuntarily. But after composing themselves, they put a rope around the corpse and dragged it from the grave. After resting for a few moments, they took the body to a deserted field nearby, saturated it with kerosene, and burned it to cinders. Then, returning to the cemetery, they filled in the grave and covered up all traces of their deed.

For several nights after this they went back, but the monstrous maggot of death was never seen again. Mullins later learned that the dead man had been on bad terms with both the vicar and the blacksmith. But he himself had never had any trouble with Peters. For what reason, then, did the glowing harbinger of evil visit his house? He never learned, but he thanked Providence that he never saw it again.

One of the most unusual themes of ghostly literature is that of the dead soul who receives permission to return to life, usually upon fulfilling certain divinely imposed conditions. Few such tales exist in folk literature, but the plot is quite popular in Hollywood, the most recent major version of it being Heaven Can Wait. Perhaps two decades ago, my friend and collaborator PARKE GODWIN wrote a charming, funny-sad variation on the theme, in which Isolde of Irish legendry finds a way to live again. For some strange reason, Parke stuck the manuscript in a drawer and forgot about it till the 1970s, when he showed it to me while we were collaborating on The Masters of Solitude. He considered "The Lady of Finnigan's Hearth" an embarrassing example of a kind of writing he no longer chose to do, and was all for chucking the story into the wastebasket. But I read it, fell in love with it, and urged Parke to try it out on FANTASTIC STORIES magazine. Editor Ted White also was wildly enthusiastic and bought it immediately. Several months later, this wonderful, lilting love story won one of the top places in the British Fantasy Awards of 1978. The Moral: Never trust an author on the subject of his own writing!

The Lady of Finnigan's Hearth

by Parke Godwin

Isolde, if you remember her story, was the girl queen of Cornwall in the days of King Arthur, and the sweetheart of a bad-luck knight named Tristram.

Though time and legend left their sugary crust, neither these nor any lute-twanging minstrel ever did her justice. She was a joyous, bouncing Irish hellion who died at nineteen, a bundle of brogue and bad manners, all heart and no head; a thoroughly medieval urchin whose first utterance in Glory was that she had been abducted from the world against her will and demanded immediate return. Her claim was not considered.

Isolde was not happy in Heaven. She felt that she just didn't fit in. Some—the women mostly—whispered of her not uneventful past. Others held she was a nice enough little thing if you liked them unpolished. Troubadours protested they would never have put hand to string in her behalf if they had known what she was really like. The immortal Wagner said flatly and to her face she was not worthy of the magnificent opera he had written about her. To most of the romantics she was an artistic embarrassment.

Well, it went this way most of the time. In the beginning, of course, there had been Tristram for company, but that was short-lived. Isolde came to realize that chivalry, while it might beautify a short life (the shorter the better), did not wear well in terms of the eternal. They bored each other until, mutually relieved, they finally went their separate ways.

But Paradise hung heavily upon Isolde, and her harp—an Irish model brought from home—lay discarded and mute. She passed her centuries longing for the good green world below. Such a short life; so little lived, so little known. She wanted to go back. At last when the yearning was too strong to keep silent, she planted herself before the Recording Angel and let him know her mind.

"Hear me, Angel: I said it the day I was brought here—against my will and before my time—and I say it again. I want to go *home!*"

"A very peculiar desire," the Angel acknowledged with some disappointment. "I should think you would have had time to let our place grow on you. Very peculiar." He shook his head. "But not impossible; that is, if you can pass the test. Before you can go back you must tell me what is the secret of life."

"And if I know it, I can go back? I can live again?"

The Angel's eyes were old and kind and sad. "You must know it to live at all, child. Where makes no difference."

Isolde pondered this a moment. "Well now, and where might be a good place to look?"

"I don't want to discourage you, child, but if you didn't find it down there, you probably won't find it here. However—" he had said it so often, "look where the heart is."

Isolde went away and thought for a long time, but it seemed hopeless. In her thoughtless lifetime she had never learned the secret of anything. She was doomed to Paradise, as it were, and it galled her more and more as the centuries passed. The virtuous criticized her for what she had been and the snobbish deplored her for what she was. Isolde walked Heaven alone and found no answer to the question. It was as remote from her as Hell itself.

"Well"—she decided firmly, picking up her harp—"why not?"

The Recording Angel paused in his eternal occupation and gazed up at the familiar figure. "Yes, girl?"

"I've searched my heart, Angel, and I've looked Heaven high and low and across for the secret. 'Tis not in either place."

"You must know it, nevertheless," the Angel said. "Everyone wants to go back at first. We afford the chance, but we afford it only to those grown wise enough to use a life properly. They are very few and most of them would rather leave well enough alone."

"I never lived to learn what well enough was. An end to this." Isolde raised her hand impatiently. "Open the gates and point me out the south stairway."

The Angel read her intention. "I admire your spirit, girl, but not your reasoning. They can't tell you anything constructive down *there*. I doubt if they'd even want to."

Isolde was not to be swayed. "The gates, Sir!"

"Well, if you're determined—" He opened the portals of Paradise, and she skipped through, turning to wave to him. "I'm glad you're taking the harp with you. You do play well and they never get a chance to hear a really good one."

She found the new place better suited to her. The climate was agreeable, the people generally friendly if irresponsible, and there was always something going on. Her coming caused some social stir; she was soon entrenched in the very best circle, a small but powerful clique of Salem women, stoutly traditional and privileged beyond belief.

But Hell, fun as it was, taught her no more than Heaven. Whatever the secret was, she must go *home* to find it, to the world she had left. But how? Her friends were allowed one night on Earth at All Saints' Eve, but she was only a novice. It would be ages before they would trust her with a broom for all of her natural talent. Need sharpened her craft to a fine edge. She evolved her plan and put it to work.

Isolde's closest friend was Prissy O'Gowra, a brilliant Irish witch with most potent broomstick in the trade. Lately, Prissy's carefree spirit was vexed with a bittersweet sadness—her sudden and hopeless love for the American Secretary of State. He was to appear at an international conference in Paris. When the Prince gave her permission to go there, Prissy was ecstatic. Magic and sabbats were not for her. Their charms were flat beside what loomed in Paris. When begged for the broom, she threw it joyously to the grateful Isolde and whirled away on the west wind, trailing a snatch of *chanson*.

And so, on All Saints' Eve, Isolde flew with her friends to Gallows Hill outside Salem. The night was made for revels—raw, cold, and wet with the naked trees bending to the wind against a moonless sky. The Prince himself put in an appearance; there was a quadrille to Isolde's harp accompaniment, and as for spells, their form had never been better. The Washington Senators got another year in the cellar and four gluepots waltzed their way to the Kentucky Derby and a four-way photo finish. It was a glorious night in the finest tradition. When dawn came on dragging a thick fog behind, they sped homeward on the east wind, conscious of a social success.

But Isolde was missing.

It was sorrowfully reported that she had lost control in the fog over the Eastern Seaboard and was presumed to have crashed. Too late they insisted Isolde was too inexperienced for the flight. Now she was marooned on a world grown callous to the ancient art of witchcraft, but she had the awful O'Gowra broom in her hands and was free to roam till All Saints' next.

For days there was no laughter in Hell. Isolde had been the gayest and dearest of all the brilliant society of the Vivacious Fallen. Now she was gone and with her went some of the sparkle of damnation.

Well now, wasn't it a simple thing to let them think her lost? When she was rid of them, Isolde veered her broom a point or two to starboard and swooped down on the unsuspecting Earth, landing in a small wood. It was early morning still, and the fog coiled in erratic patterns over the ground, seeking refuge in the low places before the sun could drive it away. Isolde listened: not a soul about nor the sound of one, but through the trees the windows of a drab white house stared bleakly at her, just visible above the fog.

"Didn't I always have the luck?" she congratulated herself. " 'Tis the castle of some lord, no doubt, and I'm fair in time for breakfast."

It was her first thought to hop the broomstick and *whoosh* up to the house, but it was a grand morning for a walk. She shouldered the broom and in fifteen earthly minutes Isolde found herself in the overgrown front yard of the bald-windowed house.

"What manner of hovel is this?" she wondered. "The paint all peeling and not so much as a candle for light or a fire for warmth. It looked better from afar. An ogre lives here, no doubt—but I'll ask just for surety."

She went up to the mud-splashed door and put her hand on the knob.

"Castle, castle, now will you tell:
Who within your walls doth dwell?"

As one might suppose, there was no answer.

"I'll burn you for kindling, creaking scoundrel!" Isolde hissed, this time in the fairy tongue. "Now open your gawp and tell me who lives here!"

The house groaned, for it had been silent a long time. "Marty Finnigan lives here," it said mournfully. "Alone."

"Sure then, Marty Finnigan keeps a sorry house."

The house sighed deep in its timbers. "No one cares for me," it said with a tremor of self-pity.

"Oh now—and why's that?"

"It's really quite *simple,*" said the house peevishly. "Because no one cares for Marty Finnigan."

"Pile o' knotholes, keep your tongue in your head!"

"Well," the house groaned sulkily, "either knock or go away." It settled once more in a manner designed to signify the interview was ended.

Isolde rapped on the door with her broom handle.

Silence.

Rap! Rap! Rap! "Halloooo! *Marty Finnigan!*"

Isolde heard muffled sounds from the second floor. Someone was up. She knocked again. "Up with your gate, Sir Finnigan, for 'tis a gentlewoman waits on your stoop in the cold and wet—"

A window rumbled up. The next instant, Isolde was drenched from hair to heels with cold water: "All right, you gah-damned kids, Halloween's over. Now *blow!*" A touseled head jutted through the window, and Marty Finnigan stared coldly down at the dampened little queen. "Oh . . . I'm sorry, lady. I thought it was those trick-or-treat punks again."

It was Isolde's hot-tempered impulse to singe him roundly with a fireball, but—*noblesse oblige,* and *noblesse* is all the easier when a man's face is no pain to a woman's eye. She gave him a graceful curtsey and asked, "Did I rouse you from slumber, Sir Finnigan?"

Marty rubbed his weekend growth of beard. "Did she wake me up, she says. No," he growled, "I was just lying there with my eyes closed. What's your problem?"

"Problem?"

"What do you want?"

"Just a morsel of bread and a place by your fire."

"A mors—" The Finnigan features contorted in disbelief. "Get lost."

"—So I can wring out the wet welcome you gave me."

"Well," Marty considered it, "I guess that's fair enough." His head disappeared, and she heard him descending the stairs. The door opened. In flannel pajamas and a ratty blue bathrobe, Marty motioned her into his house.

And Isolde moved in. She stood in the middle of the living room and tried on Marty Finnigan's house for size. It was dirty, dark, and cold—lonely most of all, with no touch of a woman's hand about it. The logs lay in the fireplace unlit and festooned with trash. The dust of the floor swirled up angrily in protest against the fresh air from the open door. In one corner, a battered coffee table displayed a week's run of coffee cups, a wrinkled necktie, two undershirts, and a pile of bills surmounted by a stale cracker, buttered and forgotten some days since.

"Cushnoo!" Isolde clucked. "What a hog-sty!"

"So excuse it." Marty shrugged. "It's the maid's day off."

He had been watching her with growing curiosity. She was small—a hair over five feet, no more—and mercurial in her movements. Her hair, impossibly red, was upswept on her head and held precariously in place with two quaint gold stays. He decided quickly that her face was made for laughter, not for looks. Her figure, if she had any, was well hidden beneath what appeared to be Methuselah's nightshirt, bunched in at the waist with the hem trailing behind like the undecided posterior of a hook-and-ladder engine.

Now Marty was many months a grass widower. Since his wife had left, a motley procession of women had left their perfumed trace about his house, but none of them were in the same league with this one for the new and different. Being essentially religious, he concluded that she had been visited upon him as some kind of penance.

"Make yourself comfortable," he mumbled, turning toward the kitchen. He shuffled sleepily out of the room. Her voice seemed to float musically through the separating wall—

"Shall I light your hearth for you? 'Tis dretful cold."

"No," he grumbled. "The flue's messed up. You couldn't burn gasoline in that thing." He filled the coffee pot with water, chuckling in spite of himself. "Well . . . she *looks* like what I'd get for Halloween, broomstick and all."

The time of year and the thought of the queer old broom summed themselves almost unconsciously in his mind. It *was* Halloween, or the day after. Marty grinned: "Oh, come *on,* Finnigan." But the wry smile softened. *Kind of a nice little thing,* he thought. *I wonder where she's from. . . .*

Isolde strolled to the fireplace, skirts switching behind her, crooning softly—

"Oh Maeldun, son of Ailill
Came from Aran in Thomond . . ."

She knelt beside the logs, stretched out her hand, then withdrew it, beckoning. "Come, fire: so please you, a little of your best for Marty Finnigan."

And the fire blazed up on Finnigan's hearth.

If Marty Finnigan had any true genius, it was in the brewing of coffee. Sitting by the fire, they went through two pots with toast and marmalade. Isolde missed her harp; she would have played gladly for her breakfast, but she had dropped it in her wild plunge to Earth. She stirred the fire, humming to herself, and studied the master of Finnigan's Hall. He was taller by a head and a half than her Trist had been, and leaner. His face was still young but life had happened to it. The eyes were shadowed and the frank mouth lined and drawn too taut for its fullness. The thick brown hair was fading here and there to early gray.

He'd look younger did he smile once a fortnight.

She liked the way his nose wrinkled up when he lit a cigarette. Suddenly she leaned toward him, fixing him with gray eyes: "Marty Finnigan, 'tis a handsome buck you are. Why is it no woman graces your house?"

There was a strange, far-away quality to her voice. It was inside his head, a song remembered from childhood, calling him down the years to where life could still grow green around the heart. *Stay a little,* he wanted to say. . . .

But Marty had been barren soil for the seed of impulse for a long time. He threw his cigarette into the fire. "You *are* an oddball. And you're still soggy from that bath I gave you. Wait, I'll get something you can change into so we can dry out that shroud or whatever it is of yours."

Isolde giggled. "Thank you."

"What's so funny?"

"I just bethought me," she said, "how nice your mouth would be if you let it smile a little now and then."

"You," he said with conviction, "are the *damndest—*"

"Aye," she nodded, taking a piece of toast in three huge bites. As he climbed the stairs, her voice floated after him: "But 'twas not my fault. A tedious long tale it is, and so I'll save it for a winter's night."

Marty returned presently with a faded yellow duster, flapping it vigorously to shake out the wrinkles of long storage. "Here. You're about six sizes smaller than my wife was, but it'll do."

She shrank away from it. "Your . . . wife?"

"What's the matter? She doesn't need it anymore." He dropped it in her lap but she only stared at it.

"You said nought of a wife, Marty."

"Well . . ." Marty made quite an operation out of lighting a cigarette. "She isn't here anymore. We're divorced. Her name is Alice," he concluded irrelevantly.

His glance met hers and was held. "Her name was Alice," Marty heard himself saying, "and all the things I wanted, she didn't. Not even this house. Wants me to move out so we can sell it. Maybe it's a good idea." He looked around the room with new awareness. "God, this place is cruddy."

Fortune brought me here, she thought, and here I'll stay. Plain it is that he needs a woman, and here's as good a place as any to learn what I must learn. If I work my spells right, they won't find me till All Saints' next, and what might I not do for myself *and* this sorry Marty Finnigan before then?

Isolde stood up before the fire, seeming taller than she was. She had once been a queen and the stamp never left her. And as she spoke, the flames leaped in time to the queer movements of her fingers. "Marty, have you never heard that a cricket on the hearth brings marvellous good fortune?"

"In this house," said Marty, "a cricket would die of TB."

"Then I'll be your cricket."

"What—?"

"Let me stay by your hearth and sweep your house with my broom till All Saints' next."

Marty was perplexed. "You know, the dangerous thing about you is you're so believable."

"And, Finnigan," she whispered with mock gravity, "you've grown much too wise to believe in what you see?"

He nodded. "When I found out about Santa Claus." He was vaguely disappointed in her. Only a week before, a dazzling young girl had brightened his threshold for a golden minute till Marty found she had come to sell him a pamphlet on the imminent demise of sinful Mankind.

This one, alas, was compounded of the same unstable elements. He threw the door open and pointed to the Great Beyond. "Good-bye, and take your broom with you." He handed it to her. " 'Sweep my house' . . . You couldn't sweep tennis balls with this thing."

"*Oooooh!*" Isolde was breathless at the sacrilege. "*That* be too much. Soulless imp, know that on just such a broom, Prissy O'Gowra flew the length and breadth of Eire till it carried her *whoosh!* straight into the cottage of the man who became her husband, it did. Not to *mention*, of course, her many and glorious services regarding the heathen English. Well, it's like crystal you don't know a good broom or a bargain when they be thrust in your *snout*, Sir Finnigan!"

He propelled her toward the door. "Yeah. Sure. Good-bye."

"*Unhand me, ogre!*"

He unhanded her out to the front stoop. "Get lost. Break a leg." *Slam!*

Yet her voice through the heavy door was as clear as though she were beside him: "*Just one leg, Marty?*"

"Fine."

He was on his back with a terrible pain in his left leg. The instrument of disaster lay beside him. He had tripped over that damned broom.

"Broken," Isolde crooned over him. "Fair brast below the knee, but it's a clean break and will mend soon."

"How did you—*yikes, quit pawin' at it*—how did you get in here?"

"Oh," she said airily, "I forgot my broom. But how *fortunate* you are I happened back, for here's yourself with your pin broken and like to be days in the mending by the look of it, with no one but me to get your supper—"

He saw the awful defeat of it. "Oh, no. No . . . no . . ."

"—To mend your socks and tend the fire, and take my old broom to the dreadful dust that's on your hearth and heart, Marty Finnigan. Till next All Saints' Eve!"

Isolde stood in the middle of the living room, making little swishing movements with the broom and humming to herself. For the time, at least, she was mistress of Marty's house. Of Heaven, this would suffice her. As for Hell, she had brought fair measure. The sun was well up, and it promised to be a roaring good day.

> "In Laighin fair, I met a lad.
> Who soon came courting me . . ."

She knelt by the hearth. "Prissy!" she whispered. *"Hoo,* Priss, can you hear me?"

The logs crackled furiously for a moment. She listened.

"Oh, I'm grand, Prissy. Thanks for the asking." Isolde took a ball of flame from the fire. Her dexterous fingers kneaded a fiery shamrock as she listened to the small talk of a friend. "Well, if anyone asks, you've not heard one word of me. Promise, now. What? Oh, your old broom's safe with me, and, Priss, it still works soo*peri*orly!"

Marty always said it was just magic the way she took that house and made it shine. She took care of him and so well that he put on five pounds before he was out of bed. Now and then he admitted to himself that there *was* something unworldly about her—but then she would bounce into the room and announce with convincing authority that she had just made the grandest stew this side of Hell, and could he spare a drop of the whiskey his dear uncle had sent him—just to bring out the flavor of the meat, of course?

Unworldly? In all his drab, disenchanted days, Marty had never known anything or anyone whose reality was so completely undeniable. She was as real as the luck that came with her; as real as the twenty-pound turkey which she swore on the soul of St. Bridget just traipsed into the kitchen and dropped stone dead—plucked and dressed—on Thanksgiving Day in the morning; as real as the well-paid job that materialized in a formerly uninterested office; as real as the first paycheck which Isolde set in a place of honor on the kitchen table, toasting it with a royal flourish of her teacup: "Increase, little bag of gold." Then with a wink at Marty: "And good health to the master of Finnigan's Hall."

Marty warmed to the tea, the excellent dinner, the cozy sound of logs crackling lustily on the hearth. "And praise them angels as brung it, my grandmother used to say."

She took his hands across the teacups, and her eyes held something not so heavy as sorrow nor light as laughter. "It's no angel I am, Marty." Then erect and determined: *"As* Mistress Marcianetti will discover, does she not keep her dog from howling and snapping at me when I come near."

"That's Poobah," said Marty. "He's six years older than God. Funny: you're the only one he does that to."

Nevertheless Isolde promised herself that she would inflict the venerable Poobah with fleas enough to make him a Job among canines.

"Mrs. Marcianetti has two interests in life," Marty continued. "Poo-bah and my welfare. I keep hoping she'll run out of home-canned toma-toes, but she never does. She brings them over about once a week, looks around, shakes her head and leaves."

"Aye, and now you have a housekeeper, and the dear old thing's got a fair crick in her neck from spying out her casement at me."

"Spying?"

"Aye, Marty: wondering who I am, and what I be to you."

He read her trailed meaning. "Well, I've been thinking about that," he started shyly. "I know this is foolish, but—" He stopped; the old fear of being hurt melted his purpose. "What I meant to say was, it's been nice having you here."

She rose and came round the table to him. "No, Marty, say what you started to say. Life's far too short to be afraid of it!"

Marty took refuge in the complicated business of lighting a cigarette. "I don't know. You just walked into this house and sort of put it on like a glove. It lives, it really lives because you're in it. When you leave—"

"When I leave—?"

"If you left, I think the life would go out of it. I think it would fall apart."

"Well, now"—her long fingers assured themselves needlessly that her hair was in place—"what a heartwarming concern for your house. And what of yourself?"

Marty blew out a great quantity of smoke. "I guess I go with the house."

Isolde knelt and took his hands. "Listen, Marty. If I knew 'twould all end this night, I'd still say those things you lack the heart to say to me: I love you. You've won me, and your hearth is mine. That's what I'd say, I would."

"Yes." He smiled, and the fear sloughed from him when he looked at her. "And a little more. Marry me and stay here always."

"I will," she whispered, her head in his lap. "I can make you happy, Finnigan."

"I know you can"—he laughed—"and when I'm too old for anything else, you can make me respectable."

"Oh, Marty, what a gallant offer. . . ."

Suddenly, she twisted away from him. Surprised, Marty saw the shadow of a frown cross her face, erasing the happiness and leaving something alien in its place. Her head was inclined sharply as if she had caught some sound beyond his hearing: a footstep lighter than thought, or perhaps a voice on the damp December wind. He started to speak but she stopped him with two fingers across his lips.

"Not a sound, Marty. There now; your supper's gone stone cold whilst you gape at me."

Isolde stood up. Resolutely, she reached for the old broom that was rarely out of her sight. "Eat, Marty. I'll not be gone a minute."

"Well, hurry back. If we're getting married, there's buckets of stuff we have to talk about."

"True," she murmured. Straight-backed and firm, she turned away from him.

Out of Marty's sight, her resolution faltered, and she shrank back from the sliding doors that closed off the living room. Beyond the doors, she heard a faint rustle of movement. Isolde clutched at her broom, quailed and retreated a step, the fear a hod of hot bricks on her heart. She took one hesitant step toward the kitchen. Then her head went up; she turned a scornful eye on the panel doors.

You need not fear the like of him, and you a queen, the proudest Leinster could spawn. Hold tight the broom. Head up. Now, in you go—

At her touch, the doors slid apart. Isolde took one sweeping step, then halted. The fear dissolved in her throat, welled up and poured out in a peal of relieved, irreverent laughter. She fell back against the doors, the helpless victim of her own mirth.

"Oh, God, no!" she gasped, " 'Tis himself . . ."

Tall, tragic, and darkly resplendent in the false ermine and sagging black tights of a stock company Hamlet, her visitor helped himself once more to the Finnigan whiskey, threw back his cape and made a sweeping obeisance before his audience of one. "To Her Majestie, Queen of the Faerie Glen," he declaimed in his best third-balcony register, adding a hint of mockery, "greetings from the Joyous Damned."

"Oh my, oh my." She was still giggling. "Expect the worst and get the best. Give ye good evening, Mr. Booth."

The gaunt young man favored her with a brilliant smile. "The same: John Wilkes Booth, your servant. I am come as herald from our court; *nay*"—Booth put up his hand in protest of her single word—"let not the fear of intrusion mar our meeting. We shall be secret kept, for the time's out of joint, and we are slipped between two broken ticks. That uninspired lout presently absorbing his supper in the scullery will hear no more of us than the wind that brought me."

"Blather, Booth. Spit it out. My supper's cooling while you hold me here."

"The price"—Booth smiled—"of materialization. One reacquires old appetites—as witness that rather artless embrace of a moment ago."

"Oooooh!" Isolde's complexion darkened a shade. "You be no gentleman, John, or the Prince either, and you can tell him that for me."

"Oh, you wrong us, Isolde. For myself, I wanted you home for our annual festival of the Bard. We do Hamlet again, echoing last year's triumph." Booth gathered the ermine to his ebonied breast, pausing for full effect. "The Prince has again chosen me to interpret the Dane. Wanton nymph, he is a lover and a critic of the arts, a gentleman and sportsman. When tidings reached him that you were gone and, through your broom, immune to recall for the nonce, he *smiled* in gracious defeat. Aloud he wished you well and ruled that no unpleasantness attend your holiday."

"Then why are you—?"

"*But*—when he heard that—that *Finnigan* declare his most unpoetic desire, he sent me on the first east wind." Booth smote his temples. "And I in the middle of a rehearsal."

"Sent you to tell me *what,* John? Can you not deliver yourself without suffering so? Tell me what?"

"Say rather to beg, Isolde. Come home now, for come you must, and it will hurt less now than later." Booth moved toward her. "Surrender your broom."

"I'll not!" she snapped, falling back. "Away with you. I'll not return before my time." She swung the broom high, wielding it like a sword. "One step more, John, and I'll sweep eternity clear of you."

Booth halted. "Listen to us, you fool, we know what life is. Madness; blind madness. What was your own time here but misery and heartbreak? What else will you find here now?"

"Life!" She hurled it at him. "Life, you wretched wreck of a soul. Life and its secret, for I left too soon to know what it was. But I'll find it, Booth. You mark me: I'll find it."

"You stole it. You can't steal life, Isolde."

"Then I'll borrow."

"And at what interest?" Booth asked. "You know the Prince never takes a loss. Come home before it is too late."

"Too late?" Isolde lowered the broom. "Tell me, John, why is't I've not been called till now? Why all a-sudden?"

The pale Booth opened his mouth to speak, then stopped. "It is late. I must go. My rehearsal . . ." He swirled the ermine around him with pathetic bravado.

"No!" Isolde demanded. "Tell me why I'm sent for *now*."

"No more . . ." The image of Booth began to blur, each line of the fine, sharp figure dissolving into an amorphous haze until only the magnificent voice remained. "Come home . . . Faerie Queen . . ."

"Back on the wind, Booth," Isolde sobbed, angry and afraid. "Tell it to the Prince, and them Above, if you can: I live! I am! For life's not borrowed, not stolen, but taken free and shaped at will—"

"*Illusion* . . ." came the faint whisper.

"No, 'tis real," she sobbed. "The knowing and the loving of it. Hear me, Booth—"

"*Heartbreak*," said the wind.

The unoiled clock on the mantle roused itself and began to grind away the minutes. Her attention drawn by the sound, Isolde looked at the hands. Even as she watched, they seemed to move faster and faster. But she had found something. *The knowing and the loving of it:* that was something to remember.

To know and to love. That must be the secret.

"Hey, good-lookin'," Marty enticed from the kitchen, "come on! I've poured the wine."

Was that the secret? Was it?

"Hey, come on!"

"*Illusion* . . ." murmured the rain, but she did not hear it.

"Aye, Marty," she answered, "I'm coming."

Well, wasn't she a bride of two days and mistress of her own house, and that house to be put straight this Monday morning?

Marty had gone to work. Isolde stood in the middle of the living room and raised her voice: "Wake, House of Finnigan! A word with you."

The house stirred and came alive. The furniture dented and flexed itself as if supporting a body, the curtains rustled, the furnace groaned. Floors and stairs creaked with the memory of a million footsteps, and out of all these came the voice: "What do you want?"

"Obedience," Isolde snapped, "for I am your mistress now, and you'll bend to my wish and the power of my broom. Hold your roof high and gallant, as if you cost twice the gold he paid, and let no one say that Marty Finnigan's a poor man."

"I hear you," sighed the house, "but it won't work."

"And why not?"

"Because it's not real," said the house. "I need love, not spells. There is no love in you and nothing real."

"He knows I love him."

"Words," said the house. "But the belfry told the wind that the candles broke and the Book burned on the altar where you married him."

"And so I can burn you," she threatened, "if your warped temper runs against my wish. *Mind,* you'll do as I say!"

The furnace rattled violently. "I will do as you say," and the voice began to fade, "but it will only seem . . . not be . . ."

"Enough, then," Isolde commanded. "House—be clean."

There was a rush of a great vacuum that swept every particle of dust from the floor, a flapping and rustling as the curtains and rugs shook out their lint, the swish of a hundred invisible brushes and dust rags rubbing and slapping the dust from woodwork, books, and cranny corners. In the kitchen, last night's dishes washed and dried themselves, sailing gracefully from the sink to the cupboard—and the immaculate house was quiet again.

So the happiness began for Marty Finnigan, and the world was green again. He fell asleep at night with the slight form of her curved like a kitten in his arms and woke in the morning to the joy of her nearness. Drawn by the amazement of his love he would lie on his elbow watching her asleep. Most of the time, she lay still as sleep itself but now and then she was restless and tossed fitfully, whispering aloud in some dream. Sometimes she spoke his name or a word in Irish; sometimes strange words that were like far music at the end of night, like the sound of the day itself breaking in their room.

He loved her and the love made him grow, and if everything about her seemed touched with magic, he reasoned it to this love. She had her moods, though, and when they came over her, she wanted to wander alone in the woods and meadows beyond the house. So it was on a Saturday in March that she rose out of sorts from bed and knew the blackness was on her. Without even bothering to take her broom, she kissed him good-bye almost solemnly and went out with a basket to gather herbs for salads and spells.

With herself gone, it was a slow morning for Marty. He drank coffee and read the papers, and toyed with the idea of beginning his flower bed, but gave it up before it became serious. Sprawled comfortably on the sofa, he became only gradually aware of the sound of a car turning into their lane.

His brow furrowed in a puzzled frown. He wasn't expecting company, and no one just dropped in on a Saturday morning. The frown deepened to irritation: a salesman—blood brother in Marty's eye to the Japanese beetle, the termite, and the housefly. He decided to make short, polite work of it.

The woman on the doorstep was tall and coldly beautiful. "Hello, Martin. I see you still resist shaving on weekends."

"Alice, what—"

They stared at each other for a moment.

"Well," she asked finally, "you do have some manners, don't you? Ask me inside."

Marty followed her into the living room where she stood alertly in the center of the floor, head turned slightly to one side. In this attitude, she reminded Marty of a beagle sniffing out a rabbit.

"Sit down, Alice. How about some coffee?"

She made a little grimace of distaste. "Darling, it's much too early for coffee. Coffee's for evening and regrets, but I will take a martini."

"Sorry, no gin in the house," he said. "We're both whiskey folks here."

Alice laughed drily. "You never did have any taste, Martin. By the way, where's the *new* Mrs. Finnigan? I hear she's quite young."

"Isolde's nineteen," said Marty. "She's out for a while, but she'll be back soon."

"Isolde?" Alice took a cigarette from her purse and put a lighter to it. "Makes you think of a fat soprano. But nineteen! My God, Martin, what do you talk about . . . when you talk?"

"So what's wrong with nineteen? Am I an antique?"

"Too old for *that,* anyway."

It burned Marty that she could still get to him. He thrust himself off the sofa. "All right, knock it off, Alice. What do you want?"

"And what has she *done* to this room?" Alice ignored him. "With my furniture, too." She was ill at ease in the room. It had a new brightness and charm she could never give it despite her driven search for the Room that was Her. "And that's what I came about," she concluded. "Darling, I *am* in a pinch for money, and since the furniture is mine— now that you're doing so well—I want to sell it."

She pronounced it as if the matter was settled and done; it was her way, the way she'd been from the beginning. Marty felt himself beginning to heat. "Why didn't you do this before, when it didn't matter if there was a rug on the floor or even a floor? Why now?"

"Now just a minute, Darling—"

"And dammit, don't call me 'darling.' You're the only woman in the world who could make 'darling' sound like a common noun."

"For that matter, Darling, the house itself is half mine, legally. I let you stay here because I *was* a little sorry for you. I mean, you're so helpless, Martin. It didn't matter then, but the broker says the value's gone up with the new throughway finished, and I do need the cash." Her expression softened. "I know it's been tough for you, Martin, but it's been no bed of roses for me, either. I work hard, too, and no matter how it turned out for us, give a girl credit, hmm?"

"Oh, I give you credit, Alice," Marty said quietly. Suddenly, he wanted Isolde very much. Now, when he needed her.

Go make yourself some coffee, the thought told him, and Marty acted without thinking about it. Somehow it seemed a very good idea at the moment. He left Alice so abruptly, she was startled.

"Where are you going, Martin?"

"To make coffee."

"Oh, for God's sake!" She stubbed out her cigarette with a vicious jab and threw her eyes impatiently around the room. A slight sound made her turn.

The sliding doors that led to the kitchen were drawing slowly together.

"Martin? Why did you close the doors?"

There was no answer, nor could she hear him moving in the kitchen. A deep silence had settled over the entire house, and as if a cloud had slid over the sun, the room was growing darker and somehow chilly.

A storm, she thought. *I'd better finish this up and leave.* She remembered an appointment for the early afternoon and looked at the clock on the mantle: ten thirty-three. . . .

As she looked, the clock stopped ticking.

"What . . . ?" Alice stepped to the mantle to look at it, and her eye fell on a queer old broom, the handle worn black with use and the head no more than a bundle of birch switches. She picked it up. "Shades of Halloween," she snickered, "how quaint can you be?"

"Put it down!"

Alice froze; it was as though the very sound were a pair of hands laid on her will to move. The hands loosened, and she turned. A slight red-haired girl stood behind her with cold gray eyes belying the voice that was softened now to a gentle admonishment.

"Never touch my broom," Isolde took it from her. " 'Tis the luck of Finnigan's Hearth."

Alice felt a tiny chill run like a frightened mouse down her spine. "Oh . . . hello, I didn't hear you come in. You must be Isolde."

"Aye."

"Martin and I have been having a talk." Alice attempted a patronizing grace that fell flat. "I—want to make some arrangement about the furniture and the house. But excuse me, I didn't introduce myself. I'm—"

"I know," said Isolde. "The late Mistress Finnigan."

Alice managed something like a laugh. It was a weak sound.

"Do seat yourself," Isolde invited, "and tell me your pleasure in refreshment."

Alice composed herself and prepared to do battle. She arranged her hands delicately in her lap and crossed her exquisite legs, reassured since Martin's new wife was neither beautiful nor sophisticated. It was true: Martin *must* have gotten her out of some unguarded cradle. "Well, Martin said you didn't have martini makings."

"Oh dear," Isolde laughed. "That be just like a man: not able to find a thing in his own house." She busied herself a moment at the sideboard: "For 'tis here in my hand."

She offered Alice the martini, complete to the olive. Alice blinked. There was nothing on the sideboard but a decanter of whiskey. She tasted the drink and found it superb—but with a something in its tang she couldn't place. "Perfect! Thanks so much. Whatever do you add to get this taste?"

"Herbs," said Isolde.

Those cold eyes on her; gray, but darker than before . . . like smoke. With some irritation, Alice found she was becoming increasingly nervous under that gaze. She attempted to avert it. "I think your clock has stopped."

"Aye," said Isolde, without looking at the clock, "it has."

Alice glanced at her watch. "About—well, that's queer. My watch has stopped, too."

"So it has." Isolde's smile was ice. "Time out of joint, Mistress Alice." She took the decanter from the sideboard and sat down facing Alice. "And Marty be asleep in the kitchen, but just for a bit." Her left hand carved a curious shape in the air and held a glass.

Alice gasped. "What on *earth*—!"

"When the clock rouses," Isolde purred, "so will he. Till then, we'll pass a womanly word or two."

She opened the decanter and poured. The glass was a tall one, but the liquor swelled steadily toward the brim, and Alice's jaw dropped proportionately lower as she watched it rise. "Surely, you're not going to *drink* that."

"Oh, yes." Isolde sipped at the whiskey, nodded her pleased approval, and casually drank it down. " 'Tis not pure, but only 86 proof."

Alice was shaken beyond manners. "You little fool, that's whiskey! You'll kill yourself."

She tried to rise, but her will and legs had turned to water.

"Drink up, Mistress Alice." The voice was music, but the eyes were black. Alice raised her glass; the round brim held her gaze as it spun, developing in concentric circles, drawing her in . . .

"Now," Isolde began calmly, "as to the selling of the house . . ."

. . . There was black Limbo, then Alice felt herself grasped by huge hands, and she was dragged up, up over interminable stone steps by two half-naked brutes. The rays from occasional torches glanced off the crude gold ornaments on their arms and gleamed again in their fierce blue eyes. There was no sound in her ears but the wild beating of her own heart as they passed up over hundreds of steps, ending at the entrance of a great hall. At the far end of the hall, raised on a dais, a familiar figure beckoned them forward. Alice was pushed forward to the foot of the dais.

"Kneel," a voice commanded her. "Kneel to Isolde of the blood of Leinster, daughter of a hundred unblemished kings of Eire."

"Please," Alice croaked, "please, God, this isn't real. It's insane." She raised her head to the slight, erect figure on the throne, but flinched again from the searching eyes. "You . . . what have you done to me?"

"Before I judge you," said Isolde, "one small truth out of a lying life to warm my soul upon. For what reason did you bring the pain of yourself to Marty Finnigan? And taking his heart, unworthy as you are, for what reason did you desert him?"

The truth welled out of the bottom of Alice's being. She had no power to silence it, having never known it, and it passed from her heart to her lips like a stranger.

"I was afraid," said the truth in her voice. "I had nothing to give, but I found that Martin needed giving. There was nothing inside. . . ."

". . . And what a shame it is," Isolde crooned, refilling her glass, "that you come now to talk of selling Finnigan's Hearth that we love so much and our friends, too. But here! I've forgot my graces. Do let me fill your glass like a good hostess." She leaned toward Alice, stretching out her open hand. The long fingers closed in a beckoning motion. Alice's glass was full.

Alice rubbed her eyes, shivering with unaccountable cold. She had been sitting and talking, sipping at a delicious drink and listening to a melodious voice that spoke of furniture and trifles. And yet, she seemed to have wandered out of time in a nightmare, forgotten already but leaving its chill on her mind. "What did you say? I'm afraid I . . . it's very strange. . . ."

"*Drink up, Alice.*"

. . . And Alice groveled on the stone floor while Isolde's long finger lifted and pointed at her. "It was harm enough to take him, even more to leave. Yea, but to come *now* like a cloud in the middle of his brightest day." She leaned back, musing a moment. At a sign of her hand, a giant shadow loomed beside Alice, ready with the sword. With cold pleasure, Isolde commanded: "Give me her head."

"Don't!" Alice shrieked, cowering away from the shadow. "Please, *don't—*"

The sword came down.

". . . So will you wake now, and leave this house," Isolde whispered over the sleeping woman. "You will leave us in peace, and only in dreams will you remember the fear of me, nought but the fear—"

There was a sudden *whirr* of clockwork. The sound jarred Isolde, and she spun around. Unbidden by her, the mantle clock was ticking.

"Name of a black day," she breathed, "who is it?"

Alice woke with a violent start. She stared stupidly at her drink as if looking for a reality she might have misplaced. Between her fingers, the glass and drink dissolved to a fine smoke. Then she saw Isolde—and she remembered. She was too frightened to move, but she could scream. She was still screaming when the panel doors banged open and Marty burst into the room.

"What happened?" he looked dazedly at both women. "I must have passed out. I woke up on the floor and—"

Alice bolted out of the chair and cowered against him, her face white and contorted with fear. "Martin, she tried to kill me . . . it was in a dream . . . a man with a sword . . . there was a glass in my hand and it just disappeared . . ."

Isolde backed toward the fireplace in confusion and fright. Something had broken her spell, and now she was caught with her world falling about her head. The fear became a swelling black anger, hammering harder and faster at her temples.

"I don't know what she is," Alice moaned against Marty's shoulder, "but, Martin, she's not *human!*" She clung to him like a child sobbing out of a nightmare to the safety of a grown-up, and Marty, with the answering instinct, put his arms around her.

The last stroke of the hammer fell. Isolde gasped with a pain that bent her almost double. Only her will remained: "Take your hands from her, Marty, or I'll burn the wench in your arms!"

Marty looked up at her. For a long second, there was only the loud ticking of the clock and Alice's ragged sobbing. Then Marty pushed Alice toward the door. "Get out, Alice," he said. "Don't come back."

"Come away with me, Martin. Please, for your own sake."

But he was already closing the door on her. "No, not with you. This is something between Isolde and me, and you're a stranger, Alice. You always were. Good-bye."

He shut the door and leaned his head against it, eyes shut. From the driveway came the sound of the car started, jerked nervously into gear, and roaring down the lane.

"Marty?"

He didn't answer.

"Marty, will you turn away from me now?"

"Turn away? Turn away from what? You aren't real, are you?"

His voice was quiet and toneless with the knowing. "I know it now. I guess—always—some part of me knew, but I needed someone. Strange—sometimes when I loved you—it was like you weren't there, and I was alone. Not always, no; only a few times when I needed you so much I reached for *something,* I don't know what. Some part of me knew. I guess that's why I never asked how you came."

"From Heaven and Hell," Isolde sighed, "and all the winds between." She was tired, tired as she had not been in fifteen hundred years. "I was searching for life, and 'twas here by your fire I found it. And if I be not your first love, Marty—well you be not mine, either. But that was a long time ago, nor was it half the glory of this."

For the first time, there was something in his expression that escaped her. "Are you afraid, Marty?"

"No," Marty said quietly, "not afraid." He took a step toward the panel doors.

"Then why do you turn away?"

"Don't you know?" He wheeled on her, and Isolde began to understand the thing behind his eyes and in his voice. It was hurt. "Can't you see what you've done? Alice gave nothing, but she promised nothing. She was what she was. You promised everything when you had nothing to give that was *real*."

"And have you lacked since I came?" she asked, with the strange, sick weariness growing in her. "Have I not won your house for you, once and always?"

"Sure, and for what?" The hurt was a hard brightness in the words. "For the years we'll spend in it?"

"The years? No, we haven't got years. . . ."

"For the growing old together—when you'll never grow old, never grow up? For the children we won't have?"

She sank into a chair. "I only had a little time . . . and my broom."

"And you knew that. You knew that, and yet you couldn't know how I'd feel when you—"

"I wanted *life*, Marty!"

"Life!" he screamed at her, lunging at the broom. "With *that!*"

Her hand shut in a fist. *"Don't touch it!"*

She could have cut out her tongue before the wish was half uttered. Marty froze, paralyzed with the sudden agony. It faded slowly, leaving him white and spent.

"Thanks," he said weakly. "That was a quick death."

"God and yourself forgive me, Marty. 'Twas the last hurt I'll ever do you."

"Yes. It's killed. . . ." Marty smiled sadly at her. "Oh, my poor, scared Isolde, I couldn't have hurt you. I couldn't, but you wouldn't take the chance."

He walked out of the living room. Isolde heard his footsteps on the stairs, then in the bedroom above, and the sound of closets and drawers being opened, not in haste but with deliberateness. She rose from the chair and wandered about the living room, unable to think of what might happen. Suddenly she dropped to her knees, a little ball of misery in the middle of the floor.

"Oh, wretched!" she cursed herself, beating futile repentance into the carpet with her fists. "Worthless, white-livered slut! Be you damned twice over for the hurt in his eyes, for the love you took from him, for the life of him you stole, and yourself not fit to kiss his dead, mud-tracking boots."

After a few minutes, Marty came downstairs again, dressed to go out, carrying a small suitcase.

"Where do you go, Marty?"

"Away," he said. "I'll send someone after the rest of my things."

She bowed her head. "And not come back?"

He shook his head. "I don't want to look at this house again. Alice can sell it if she wants, I don't care. But you can work that broom till it wears out; I won't be back."

"No fear, Marty. I said 'twas the last hurt." When she looked at him, the old pride was there but it was gentled. "You've a queen's word for it."

He put his hand on the doorknob, pulled it open. "I guess I just can't take losing again. Good-bye, honey."

"Fare-you-well, Marty. The best of my heart go with you."

The door closed behind him.

Isolde fell forward, burying her face in her arms. "Heaven and Hell, Heaven and Hell, let me die once more."

"How unutterably tragic," said the petulant, cultivated voice behind her. "I really should have brought Booth along. He fairly wallows in this sort of thing."

Isolde raised her head slowly to the well-tailored man in the easy chair, pursing his lips over a tumbler of whiskey. Bitterly and without surprise she said, "Well, now's my day complete."

The Prince sipped at his whiskey, knitting fine brows. "Wonderful stuff! The woman was mad to pass this up for that drowned-olive affair. No—as a matter of fact, I hadn't intended to come myself, only to send again to ask you to come home." He gave her a charming shrug and smile. "But none of your crowd was available. Nero is throwing a party for some American Senator and Booth is still playing Hamlet. Oh! The conceit of that actor! Do you know where he kills the king in the last act? Well, as true as I'm here, whenever the mood strikes him, that unbelievable ham shoots the king with a pistol and gallops off up center bellowing *Sic Semper Tyrannis*. Still, he's in demand. The women, mostly. As for Prissy, her latest passion is Zen, and she doesn't even care about her broom, though *you've* certainly made free with it." He chuckled with reminiscent delight. "That execution effect was superb. That's why I broke your spell. I wanted to see how well you could manage *a capella*, and, my dear—you fizzled."

Isolde stared at her hands. "What's it matter now? Marty's gone. 'Tis over."

"You can't say you weren't warned. You had every chance."

"Aye, I did." She rose heavily, picked up the broom, and held it out to the Prince. " 'Tis over, let's be gone."

He waved it away. "Not for all the world. No, the moment I saw you, I knew the game was changed. There are more interesting considerations now."

Isolde was firm. "Take it. I want no more of this." Another wave of sickness rolled over her. "I said you've won. Must you rack me as well?"

"That's what I meant," said the Prince, "though I must decline the credit. You see, Faerie Queen, you're with child—what a quaint phrase!" He toasted her with his glass. "Congratulations."

"With child . . ." She dropped the broom and sank to her knees, stunned by the wonder of it. "With child! Oh saints, saints, saints, Marty, I have your child!"

"Precisely," the Prince interjected, "and you can hardly blame me for *that*. Nevertheless, you can see why I won't recall you before your time. I will even extend your visit if need be. There'll be the child."

"Marty's child!" she flared. "It belongs to him."

"Of course, Isolde, but you belong to me." An eloquent shrug of his shoulders. "Though it is an unusual case. First of its kind, actually. The possibilities are infinite. For example—how would you like to be mother of a President?" He leaned back, speculating with pleasure. "I'll make him a man of universal insight and intellectual power, a natural leader of men and irresistible to women; yet humble, possessing the common touch. A man of the people. The world will be ready for another Kennedy."

"You'll not have the power of one finger over my son!"

"Oh, stop it!" he snapped. "You're as bad as Booth. He warned you that I never operate at a loss." The Prince picked up her broom. "This is your only hold on the world, and yet its greatest power was only your own lunatic thirst for life. Well, you got everything you wanted. Now, by the same easy method, you want to sweep it all away, and still you don't understand. Not my power but your lack of it will stop you. Yet, with my way, you could have him back."

Isolde was very still for a time, seeming to accept what he said. Finally: "Aye, you do win it all . . . all. You know you can hold me here and that I won't live without Marty. But make me the small promise that Marty and his own will never lack."

The Prince was all graciousness. "They will never lack."

"And my son be happy all the days of his life?"

"Fabulously."

She gave him a cold smile. "Thanks for that."

The Prince nodded benignly. "My pleasure entirely. It's all in the family. So, it's done—now for the last." He held out the broom to her. "Take this and wish your husband back."

She hesitated. "But will he love me?"

"He will want you—not quite the same, but good enough for the time you have left."

"No—not quite the same."

He held out the broom. "But still. . ."

She took the broom. "But still."

"Now, Isolde: wish."

And Isolde wished. "Broom," she commanded, "from the world and the memory of Marty Finnigan, *sweep me out forever.*"

The Prince gasped. "Wait!"

"And that done," she raised the broom with both hands, broke it over her knee, and hurled the pieces into the fireplace, "be quit of me!" the two ends flashed into unearthly flame and disintegrated. Isolde sucked in one last breath of sweet air and held it, waiting—

A low moan ran through the foundations of the house. The curtains tore loose from every window, the paint and wallpaper peeled, the dust of months swirled in a brown cloud and settled over the furniture and the floor. All that the broom had done for her was undone, for the house had said it would only seem, and the seeming was ended.

But Isolde still stood there—corporeal, uneclipsed. She opened her eyes to the fuming anger of the Prince.

"You treacherous slut. You puling, sentimental, self-sacrificing *cow!*"

Dumbly she waited to be consumed, not hearing or caring. Marty was free of her, and what was done was done.

"Fool!" the Prince screamed at her, his voice almost a ludicrous falsetto with rage. "No one since that primal wench in Eden could have been so stupid. To writhe through the agony of this blind hog wallow of a world, not once but *twice.* To feel limbs wither and love die—*twice.* To know the death of every dream and its disillusionment—*twice.* And for what grubby little reason? Why do you think that men have clung through all time to the need for Heaven and Hell? Not for punishment, not for reward. They are refuge, both of them, from trying to find a meaning for life; the pointless end to the grisly joke. And it *is* a joke. The immense cosmic joke that you, you second-rate Guinevere, will never understand in a thousand lifetimes. Because in Heaven are all rewards for virtue except the earthly hunger for reward, and if Hell is empty after all, at least it holds no pain. Why shouldn't they be sought after and prayed for by the brave and cowardly alike, the saints and the greedy, the men who knew they walked alone and the petty bargainers who mortgaged their souls to have them loved for five minutes; why shouldn't they be refuge—these two endings that you've tossed out like an old pair of shoes? Neither gives a meaning, but both make an end to *this!*"

Something was dawning on Isolde, something so immense she dared grasp only the littlest piece of it. "Well, take me if you will. Why do you rage so?" She grinned at him. "You've lost your power over me, haven't you, Prince?"

"I wouldn't say that." But he made no move toward her.

"Yes"—the thing grew in her—"that's it: the meaning. The Secret. That's why you sent Booth when I was about to give of myself to Marty. Afraid you were that I'd learn the secret and be quit of you." She laughed in his face. "Come, try and take me. Here's my hand, Prince. Try!"

The Prince backed away from the contact. "Now, don't be hasty. Keep away from me. Don't touch me, you grimy little *human!*"

She pursued him around the room, hooting with laughter. "I've won! I'm alive, and if I lay hand or foot to you, by the Grail I'll leave a lump for every inch. *There!*"

"*Yi!*"

"And there! And there! Now, out of my house, for 'tis mine at last! Oh, Marty, Marty." She sank down on the sofa, weeping and laughing with her joy. "I'm alive. I don't know how, but I'm alive."

"Well," said the Prince nastily, keeping a safe distance from her, "at least I don't have the bother of you any more. The broom finishes that."

" 'Twas the giving," she said to herself. "The giving."

"Perhaps," the Prince conceded shortly. "I never have understood that sort of thing."

"The giving . . . such a little thing."

The Prince snorted his contempt from the doorway. "Even if I were a man, I'd call you a fool."

"Aye, Prince," she answered, and she was no longer a girl. "But if you were a fool, you'd be a man."

He inclined his head with an old-fashioned courtesy. "Well, Faerie

Queen, your world and welcome to it. Oh, don't get up. I'll let myself out."

The house was drab and dirty as the day she had come to it, unchanged in any way except that Marty was gone. But she was alive, and it was her house, and she knew what to do with it now.

His house in my hands, she thought, and his son beneath my heart. Well now! A new broom and a bucket, a brush and paint, and new curtains to be made and the kitchen to be cleaned and the lawn mowed and his garden started and . . . and what sit you here for, Mistress Finnigan, when there's your toil waiting. Just you wait, Marty, and *then* say I can give you nothing that's real . . . and, oh saints, saints, saints, I'm about to be *sick* again!

She swept and she scrubbed. She chipped and painted. She measured and she sewed. She mowed and raked until, little by little, under blistered hands that now wove no magic but her love, Finnigan's Hearth began to shine once more. She was sick in the mornings with depressing regularity but weathered it with choking curses and went about her work. The spring wind was a bouquet of moselle in her nostrils, and ancient Poobah no longer growled when she passed.

But the days went by and she found what it was to be lonely.

One afternoon, as she was rooting weeds out of the new flower bed, she heard someone call her name. Looking up, she saw a tall, white-haired man standing near the front steps. He seemed familiar but the name escaped her.

"Well, top of the morning, Mrs. Finnigan."

"And the rest of the day for yourself," she responded cordially. "What be you? An insurance peddler?"

"Good heavens, no," he laughed gently. "There's nothing sure in this world. No, I was in the area and I just thought I'd look in. I wondered if you'd found what you were looking for?"

Isolde knew him now. She curtsied in deep respect. "Sure, I forgot the face and the name. Give you good day, Angel. And how be the Blessed?"

"Tolerably well," he nodded. "You too, by your blossoming aspect. Did you find your Secret?"

Isolde wiped the perspiration from her face, leaving it streaked with brown earth. "Not all, but as much as my poor thick skull can hold."

"That's all anyone can do. Tell me, then: what is it?"

"To keep from hurt the heart of Marty Finnigan, to love him with my own, and to give to him all the days of my life."

"Well, now—" The Angel stepped back, regarding her with his kind, sad eyes. "As nicely as I've ever heard it put. Different hearts, different words, but it dresses out about the same."

"Aye, but I learned too late. He's forgot me."

"Yes, I know," said the Angel. "Your finest hour, as that Englishman said. Well, as a woman, you're going to learn that men are very forgetful anyway. It's all a question of what they forget." He indicated the flower bed. "What have you planted?"

"Roses," she said with some enthusiasm. "Marty said when the spring came . . ." the sentence trailed off. "They'll grace the look of the house," she finished, hearing the loneliness in her own voice.

"They will," the Angel said. "I wish you could send me one. But then I never sent you a wedding gift, did I? That just shows you: forgetful, every one of us. Well, let me think. What would be appropriate?" He considered the problem. "How about a new harp?"

And play it to an empty house, she thought.

"Yes," the Angel nodded, pleased with his choice. "A harp. A forgotten art, these days, but you always did have a talent for it." He took her hands in his. "Good-bye for the time, Isolde. We'll meet again, of course."

" 'Twill be my pleasure, Angel."

"Yes—well—next time, *do* plan to stay." He waved to her and disappeared around the corner of the house. Isolde went back to her digging.

A few minutes later a car turned into the lane. It was a police cruiser, manned by two bored officers and bearing a battered passenger in the rear seat. The policemen helped their charge from the car with the care one accords to a cracked Ming vase.

Isolde's heart came up into her throat. She clutched at her trowel as if it were the O'Gowra broom.

The officer gave her a weary, patient nod. "This your husband, Ma'am?"

"Oh, for sure," she swallowed. "Whatever's happened to him?"

Marty's left eye was swollen shut in a small mound of royal purple. The other was bloodshot. He was unshaven, unwashed, and the remains of his suit were only memorials to an epic struggle.

"Who did this?" Isolde snapped. "Who *dast* do this to Martin Finnigan?"

The officer gave Marty a look of professional compassion. "Couldn't tell you all of 'em. Had complaints on him all week. Drunk and disorderly, damage to property, assault, four fights in three days—"

"Oh, dear God! Four?"

"Yes, Ma'am. He must've lost them all. Had him down at the station for two days, drying him out. He wouldn't tell us where he lived." He swung away toward the car. Marty sagged down onto the front stoop, as bleakly silent as Stonehenge. The second policeman regarded him.

"You know, lady," he said, "I think your husband's one of those people who just can't drink."

The first officer returned with something under his arm. He proffered it to Marty, puzzled. "This yours, Mr. Finnigan?"

Marty's one good eye appraised the object, an ancient harp. "Hell, no," he concluded gloomily. "What would I do with it?"

The policeman handed it to Isolde. Her arms and fingers remembered its curve. "Well, it ain't ours, either, so you take it. All right, Ma'am, I guess that's all. Keep him home for a while."

"My thanks, Sir."

The police car rumbled out of the lane, leaving them alone in their world. Isolde took a deep, tired breath. There were so many things to tell him . . . about the house and the missing of himself for days . . . about the lonely expanse of bed at night . . . about the child.

But no: a little at a time. I'll not tell him; I'll show him, a little at a time that what we have is real.

"Well, Marty?"

"Well, what?" he muttered. "Don't think I wanted to come back here. They made me come back."

Isolde fought against the anger, but it rose in her throat. "And—and so you'll be walking off again."

"Yes." Marty's voice was hoarse with fatigue. "But I wouldn't mind an aspirin or two, if we have any."

" 'We,' Finnigan? 'We' have nothing. *I* might have a draught to soothe your head." *There's nothing but to fight him. A little of him must be fought and beaten so all of him can win.* "But when you walk down that road, Finnigan, what pill will you take against the next woman that comes your way and loves you, but, pity her soul, isn't good enough, isn't real enough, isn't perfect enough for you?"

"Don't hand me that, damn it!" Marty lunged up at her. "You know what you are. You're a lie, an illusion," he seethed, "standing there telling me *I* don't have any guts. Telling a real person—"

"*Real!*" She jabbed a finger into his chest. "I am the realest, strongest clout of woman 'twill ever be your good fortune to look on, and, I might add, getting realer by the moment, as time and the sight of your eyes will unfold to your feeble understanding. See!" Isolde spread her hands before his face. "Those be blisters. That be callous. And do you puzzle where I got them? From work. From cleaning and painting the house that's mine now, because I stayed to care for it, whilst you walked away. And this sweat"—she was almost crying now—"is from loving your own dream enough to plant your bloody roses!"

His face cracked in the beginnings of a sardonic grin. "Looks like you used your nose to dig with."

"Does it indeed?" The nose in point was thrust as close as possible to him. "A minute at a glass will tell you you've not exactly the look of a rose yourself, Sir Finnigan. And was I blindfold with only this poor nose to tell me what I was next to, my first thought would not be any kind of flower. God, what a sorry sight you are, and yourself unwashed as a Cornish cowherd. *Crawling* home after days—"

"I did not *crawl* home," Marty bawled. "I am not staying."

"Then crawl away!"

"Don't tell me what to do in my own yard."

"*My* yard!" Isolde dropped the trowel, jabbed her fist into his stomach and kicked him in the shin. Marty doubled for a second in surprise, then grabbed at her, tucked her under one arm and spanked her until they swayed and fell onto the grass. She twisted on her back and looked up at him. Marty was very pale, but laughing. "Ah-h, hell. You're right, where else is there?"

"Marty," she said with the anger gone out of her, "will you go? Or do you come home to stay?"

"To stay." He seemed to consider it. "I think I came home to die. Honey, *please,* do we have any aspirin?"

She couldn't bear it any longer. Her arms were around him and she was sobbing. "Stay . . . stay. Please stay."

"Sure," he soothed her. "I have to. The world isn't ready for you yet, baby."

"Oh, Marty, that be finished and dead, I swear."

"Now listen," he said painfully as if each word weighed a ton, "that part is over. Let's never, never even think about it. Because people—oh, God, my head—because people like Alice . . . and other people . . . well, they're just not very broadminded."

"It's done and done." She drew him up gently. "And nothing left of it but ourselves. Our house stands tall and gallant, Finnigan. Welcome home."

Isolde led him inside and stretched him out with great care on the sofa, his head sandwiched between an icebag and the pillow. She knelt beside him and drew soft chords from the harp.

Marty stirred. "Lovely," he murmured, and then he was asleep. Isolde played softly. Now and then, when he moved, she would replace the icebag gently, as if it were a crown.

The authorship of this terrible little anecdote is uncertain, but has been ascribed to GUY DE MAUPASSANT, *a Frenchman who, born in 1854, became a leading novelist in the same naturalistic school that spawned Émile Zola. He wrote some three hundred tales as well as novels, many of them supernatural and usually tinged with tragedy.*

The Phantom Hag

by Guy de Maupassant (?)

The other evening in an old castle the conversation turned upon apparitions, each one of the party telling a story. As the accounts grew more horrible the young ladies drew closer together.

"Have you ever had an adventure with a ghost?" said they to me. "Do you not know a story to make us shiver? Come, tell us something."

"I am quite willing to do so," I replied. "I will tell you of an incident that happened to myself."

Toward the close of the autumn of 1858 I visited one of my friends, subprefect of a little city in the center of France. Albert was an old companion of my youth, and I had been present at his wedding. His charming wife was full of goodness and grace. My friend wished to show me his happy home, and to introduce me to his two pretty little daughters. I was feted and taken great care of. Three days after my arrival I knew the entire city, curiosities, old castles, ruins, etc. Every day about four o'clock Albert would order the phaeton, and we would take a long ride, returning home in the evening. One evening my friend said to me:

"Tomorrow we will go further than usual. I want to take you to the Black Rocks. They are curious old Druidical stones, on a wild and desolate plain. They will interest you. My wife has not seen them yet, so we will take her."

The following day we drove out at the usual hour. Albert's wife sat by his side. I occupied the back seat alone. The weather was gray and somber that afternoon, and the journey was not very pleasant. When we arrived at the Black Rocks the sun was setting. We got out of the phaeton, and Albert took care of the horses.

We walked some little distance through the fields before reaching the giant remains of the old Druid religion. Albert's wife wished to climb to the summit of the altar, and I assisted her. I can still see her graceful figure as she stood draped in a red shawl, her veil floating around her. "How beautiful it is! But does it not make you feel a little melancholy?" said she, extending her hand toward the dark horizon, which was lighted a little by the last rays of the sun.

The afternoon wind blew violently, and sighed through the stunted trees that grew around the stone cromlechs; not a dwelling nor a human being was in sight. We hastened to get down, and silently retraced our steps to the carriage.

"We must hurry," said Albert; "the sky is threatening, and we shall have scarcely time to reach home before night."

We carefully wrapped the robes around his wife. She tied the veil around her face, and the horses started into a rapid trot. It was growing dark; the scenery around us was bare and desolate; clumps of fir trees here and there and furze bushes formed the only vegetation. We began to feel the cold, for the wind blew with fury; the only sound we heard was the steady trot of the horses and the sharp clear tinkle of their bells.

Suddenly I felt the heavy grasp of a hand upon my shoulder. I turned my head quickly. A horrible apparition presented itself before my eyes. In the empty place at my side sat a hideous woman. I tried to cry out; the phantom placed her fingers upon her lips to impose silence upon me. I could not utter a sound. The woman was clothed in white linen; her head was cowled; her face was overspread with a corpse-like pallor, and in place of eyes were ghastly black cavities.

I sat motionless, overcome by terror.

The ghost suddenly stood up and leaned over the young wife. She encircled her with her arms, and lowered her hideous head as if to kiss her forehead.

"What a wind!" cried Madame Albert, turning precipitately toward me. "My veil is torn."

As she turned I felt the same infernal pressure on my shoulder, and the place occupied by the phantom was empty. I looked out to the right and left—the road was deserted, not an object in sight.

"What a dreadful gale!" said Madame Albert. "Did you feel it? I cannot explain the terror that seized me; my veil was torn by the wind as if by an invisible hand; I am trembling still."

"Never mind," said Albert, smiling; "wrap yourself up, my dear; we will soon be warming ourselves by a good fire at home. I am starving."

A cold perspiration covered my forehead; a shiver ran through me; my tongue clove to the roof of my mouth, and I could not articulate a sound; a sharp pain in my shoulder was the only sensible evidence that

I was not the victim of an hallucination. Putting my hand upon my aching shoulder, I felt a rent in the cloak that was wrapped around me. I looked at it; five perfectly distinct holes—visible traces of the grip of the horrible phantom. I thought for a moment that I should die or that my reason should leave me; it was, I think, the most dreadful moment of my life.

Finally I became more calm; this nameless agony had lasted for some minutes; I do not think it is possible for a human being to suffer more than I did during that time. As soon as I had recovered my senses, I thought at first I would tell my friends all that had passed, but hesitated, and finally did not, fearing that my story would frighten Madame Albert, and feeling sure my friend would not believe me. The lights of the little city revived me, and gradually the oppression of terror that overwhelmed me became lighter.

So soon as we reached home, Madame Albert untied her veil; it was literally in shreds. I hoped to find my clothes whole and prove to myself that it was all imagination. But no, the cloth was torn in five places, just where the fingers had seized my shoulder. There was no mark, however, upon my flesh, only a dull pain.

I returned to Paris the next day, where I endeavored to forget the strange adventure; or at least when I thought of it, I would force myself to think it an hallucination.

The day after my return I received a letter from my friend Albert. It was edged with black. I opened it with a vague fear.

His wife had died the day of my return.

Ghosts often like to associate with religious orders, it seems, and here in the former capital of Sicily, a gruesome though pitiful phantom intrudes itself insidiously into the daily routine of the impressionable narrator when he visits the catacombs of the Capuchins, a branch of the Franciscan order of monks distinguished by the pointed hoods or capuches *they wear.* EUGÈNE MONTFORT, *born in 1877 in Paris, wrote novels and short stories, many of which are set in the sunny Mediterranean clime.*

The Ghost of the Capuchins
by Eugène Montfort

Adapted from the French by
Faith Lancereau
and Marvin Kaye

Toward the end of the last century, I settled for the winter in Palermo, that magnificent city whose rough, majestic architecture is softened by breezes from the Tyrrhenian Sea. My apartment was in an area called Quattro Canti, a place in the very center of town where the houses are richly ornamented and offset by statuary of antique nobility. Four Corners—for that is the meaning of the street's name—is busy morning and night with streams of natives whose features blend the *hauteur* of the proud Castilian and the more voluptuous characteristics of the Arab.

I stayed at the home of a Spanish gentleman named Herrera, whose ancestors came from Sicily. There amid the sculptured marble palaces of the Via Maqueda I dwelled, in a second-floor apartment with windows commanding all the comings and goings of Quattro Canti.

Herrera, my host, was discreet. Though my rooms were part of his home, he never showed himself to me unless I wished him to. Other than the day when he took me up to the apartment, I don't suppose I spoke with him more than twice in as many weeks.

That first day, he unlocked the door, swung it wide and allowed me to discover for myself the merits or shortcomings of the place. No word passed his lips as I investigated the simple quarters. A heavy oak table with sculptured feet distinguished one corner, and a gilded wooden Madonna rested on the bureau. An old painting of a young dark girl in religious habit completed the décor; otherwise the place was unremarkable, but tidy and immaculately clean.

"Who is she?" I asked, indicating the portrait of the pretty girl. She had large, dark, bewildered eyes, and when I stepped closer and examined the canvas and the frame, I guessed it must have been painted at least as far back as the time of Louis XIV. The painting was at the foot of the bed, next to an armchair which I decided would be a fine place to sit and read in. "Who is she?" I asked once more.

Herrera shrugged. "I know no more than you."

I agreed to take the rooms, and settled in that very afternoon. Days passed, and I led a quiet existence in Palermo. My afternoons and evenings were spent in strolls in charming gardens, walks to the market or to the port, and many visits to the Palatine Chapel, so renowned for its beauty. I made few friends, but those I met would usually be at the shipping mall at close of day, and there would I join them.

Thus I became thoroughly familiar with all the sights of that remarkable city . . . all except one.

On the outskirts of Palermo is a Capuchin monastery and burial catacombs famous throughout the town for vaults filled with the skeletons of long times past. Everyone I spoke with recommended the place to me, and my friends asserted more than once that I must not leave Palermo before viewing the great Capuchin city of death.

Yet I stayed away from it for a long time. I do not care for things of a macabre cast; the appurtenances of the grave fill me with loathing and shatter my sleep.

But every week that elapsed made it harder for me to admit to my friends that, as yet, I had not gone to the monastery. I avoided the subject as much as possible, but there came a time when the very word "monk" ensured an unquiet evening abed, and at length I felt compelled to get it over with, so obsessive had the subject become. What matter, I thought, whether I subsequently woke up in a sweat? The mere thought of the place had already rendered some of my nights unbearable.

One morning when the weather was mild and I felt more rested and calm than circumstances lately had permitted, I set off for the monastery. As I neared the boundary of the outer white wall that shut off the Capuchins from the rest of the world, I thought I could detect on the faces of the people of the neighborhood a sort of sardonic satisfaction, as if to say, "Another going in, but he'll look different when he comes out."

By the time I was at the entryway, I felt like turning around and quietly returning to Signor Herrera's. But the distance was far, and I knew if I did not go in today, it would be harder to avoid tomorrow, so I passed the archway and spoke to the clerk.

He exchanged a few polite words, then, without further converse or preparation, opened the gate and ushered me downstairs to the burial vaults.

I was completely taken aback by the vastness of the dreadful vista. A long hallway stacked from floor to ceiling with bodies. Skeletons covered in black, gloved hands crossed at the waist, gaping sockets that once contained flesh stared sightlessly downward. At their feet, rows of glassed-in coffins held more recent human remains, while high up near the ceiling a long ledge held still more skinless piles of bones.

Everywhere, clothed skeletons leaned forward, discussing me, as it were, with silent laughter, but their joke was plain enough, though never uttered.

The monk escorted me through great galleries of the dead. Though I soon felt faint, he merely appeared bored. When I stopped, he stopped; when I stumbled forward, he resumed his pace.

The place stretched out so far I thought there must be no end. After a while—once the first shock grew duller—the hideous spectacle began to assume a ghoulish attraction of its own. I was simultaneously repulsed and fascinated by the rotted faces. The mystery of death possessed me, I sought its secrets in the downcast heads that studied the floor in a stupor, grinning with broken teeth and jaws.

Here a large skeleton rested by a smaller one, the pair posing for some morbid genius of the canvas. Over there, shreds of gray hair and bits of skin still clung to a smooth white skull, its shriveled expression atrocious, as if shrieking out the unfairness of the state of death. Yet its nearest neighbor smiled gently, sadly, while high above its head, an elder statesman reflected deeply, perhaps, on how best to legislate the improved condition of the charnel house. Two bodies away, mere surprise contorted moldering facial bones.

One skeleton stood apart from the others. Instead of leaning toward the ground, its skull pointed forward as if it had raised its head expressly to catch my eye. Its left shoulder brushed familiarly against a smaller adjacent body. I moved closer and read the name of the ghoul whose empty sockets seemed to fix me in their hypnotic command.

PIETRO CATALA
April 8, 1684

So old, then. I could not bear more. I signaled to my guide that I was anxious to return to the world of the living.

But the blue sky brought little relief as I returned to my apartment. Looking out the window, I saw the smiles of the passersby and knew they were, without realizing it, rehearsing for the final death-grin they would share with the skeletons of the vault, the grim wordless jest that ridiculed all projects and prospects we yearn for in life.

That night, I asked my landlord if he had any books on Palermo that I might borrow. He rooted about in his library, gathered up several and passed them to me. I took them to my sitting room, but did not browse in them until the following morning, when, rested by a sound sleep and in good spirits, I began to pick through the pile.

A ray of sunshine lit the apartment. I could hear joyful noises in the street, and, turning my thoughts away from the Capuchin monks and their grisly charges, I anticipated strolling through the city and taking in the good air by portside, perhaps lunching on shellfish.

But as I was about to set aside Herrera's books and quit the room, a parchment-bound old tome at the bottom of the pile arrested my attention. I picked it up, somehow compelled to examine it. Yellowed by time, it bore on the cover the following lengthy title:

Collection of Rare Facts
and Strange Happenings
in Palermo
from 1650 to 1700 A.D.

I sat down in my chair beneath the old picture and turned to the first few entries, but in truth, they were not especially interesting. I closed the book, turned it on its side to study the spine, but my fingers slipped and it fell to the floor. As it did, its leaves opened of their own accord to a place far back in the volume. My eye scanned it for an instant, then, discovering the import, I picked up the tome and read the providential passage word for word.

1684—ON APRIL 8 THERE OCCURRED A DREADFUL THING, AN
EVENT THAT WAS THE SUBJECT OF CONVERSATION FOR A LONG
TIME THEREAFTER. A YOUNG MAN OF TWENTY-THREE YEARS,
ONE PIETRO CATALA, ELDEST SON OF A RENOWNED INHABITANT
OF THE CITY, BECAME ENGAGED TO BIANCA BELFIORE, ALSO OF
AN OLD AND ILLUSTRIOUS CLAN. THEY WERE TO BE PLIGHTED TO
ONE ANOTHER, ACCORDING TO THE FAMILIES' INTENTIONS, ONE
MONTH HENCE, BUT GOD'S WAYS CANNOT BE PERCEIVED BY SIN-
NING MORTALS. AT FOUR IN THE AFTERNOON ON THE EIGHTH DAY
OF APRIL, AS THE COUPLE STROLLED ALONG THE MONREALE
ROAD ADMIRING THE BEAUTY OF THE SPRING SEASON, A VIOLENT
STORM ERUPTED. THE LOVERS TOOK REFUGE BENEATH A TREE,
BUT PROVIDENCE HURLED DOWN A GREAT LIGHTNING BOLT AND
PIETRO WAS STRUCK. HE DIED INSTANTLY, AND BIANCA, OVER-
COME BY GRIEF, FAINTED. THE BEAUTIFUL, SAD YOUNG GIRL
NEVER MARRIED ANOTHER, BUT JOINED A NEARBY CONVENT,
TAKING THE VEIL ON THE VERY DAY SHE WOULD HAVE WED
PIETRO.

As I read, I thought I saw once more the Capuchin skeleton whose
head was erect, whose name was attached to the clothing: Pietro Catala.

The air in my room, so fresh a moment earlier, now seemed to choke
me. I leaped up, grabbed my hat and left the room, slamming the door,
ran downstairs and into the street. Solitude suddenly unsettled me, I
had to be surrounded by the crowd walking along the Quattro Canti.

It was no accident, something whispered to me, that I'd especially
noted the remains of the lad whom lightning struck so long ago. The coincidence held some dreadful significance, I was afraid, though what it
might be I was powerless to discern.

I found my friends at the cafe and eagerly told them the occurrences
of the past day and morning, but they totally missed the point, treated
the affair lightly. They had neither solace nor wisdom to shed or share,
and I quickly quitted the place. Their gaiety, their idle talk was
superficial, vain; it no longer appealed to me. Behind their vacuous
laughter I heard a darker humor.

It was twilight, nearly dark. To get to the center of the city, I took a
small deserted road and walked along it distractedly, sorry I'd chosen
such a lifeless thoroughfare.

In front of me, someone walked slowly, quietly. The absence of any footfall began to worry at my nerves, and when I thought to pass him by, the most mundane of details caught my eye, and I shuddered. His clothing was too large, it looked like the black dress of a Capuchin. I tried to convince myself it was a mistake, that my overexcited brain saw resemblances that were not there. Again I considered walking faster to overtake the creature and look at his face. But I did not. Instead, I stopped in the middle of the roadway, stock-still.

What if I saw nothing there but bone, hollow cavities where eyes once were?

I waited till the silent pedestrian was far ahead of me, still treading along the road in silence, then I ducked down a side path and found another route to the well-lit and busy Maqueda Road.

I could not return yet to the empty rooms of the Quattro Canti. Instead I sought the calculated repartée of the theatre, purchasing a seat where a popular comedy was playing. But I found nothing within to smile about; on the contrary, the so-called playwright's wit seemed stupid and forced and withal so irritating that I left before the final act.

At last, late in the evening, I returned home.

I sensed nothing peculiar upon entering my room. The window was wide open and the usual street sounds wafted up to my ears. It was impossible to sleep when the windows remained open, so I closed the shutters, curtains and blinds in order to muffle the outside noise. I undressed by candlelight and as I did, noted how my room appeared enormous. I had never before heeded how the taper flickered and dimmed and created so many shadowy corners. An urge arose in me to check every cranny, to peer at each nook, even to look under my bed. For a long time, I refrained, thinking how ridiculous I was being, but in the end, I could not help but make a detailed inspection of every corner, the narrowest recesses, places not even large enough for small animals to hide.

At last, finally reassured I was the only person there, I double-checked the lock, then fell into the armchair, wondering why my minute scrutiny failed to calm me down, but rather increased my agitation.

I'd felt ill at ease that morning, but now the sensation was infinitely worse, hardly tolerable. An unknown, invisible presence seemed to stifle the entire room, and even the eyes of the portrait flickered in the candle flame as if lit with awareness that I was also there.

Next to the door stood a great mirror. I tried to avert my gaze from it, lest it reflect something more than the room appeared to hold. Yet time and again, it pulled me back, though I dared not look even as I dared not avoid it. The air was too warm, yet too cold; I sweated and shivered with sudden chill. Something ominous seemed to impend. My heart pounded; my breath rasped unevenly in my chest. I thought I might be growing delirious.

At last, hoping that sleep might banish all terror, I lay down on my bed, hastily throwing the bedclothes aside. I stretched out and breathed deeply, willing myself to become calm. It did not help. I began to toss and turn, but could not sleep. I blamed my insomnia on the unsnuffed candle. I usually slumber in darkness, but that night the idea of no light in the room was too hideous to bear. So I finally pulled the sheet over my face to keep the light out of my eyes.

Rest came after a long, long time.

In the middle of the night, I awoke, suddenly more nervous than I'd ever been. The sheet was still over my head. I saw nothing other than the muted glow of the candle through the cloth.

But I heard a strange sound, a kind of rubbing on the floor as if something was being dragged about the room. Not walking; more of a sliding, scuffing noise.

I didn't dare remove the sheet. I listened, teeth on edge, tight to keep them from chattering. The sliding was too deliberate and too heavy to be a small animal that might have gnawed through the woodwork into the chamber. Yet no human would walk like that, the scraping sound was dreadful to hear.

And then the noise stopped, and a silence even more terrible ensued. It was undoubtedly very late. Nothing could be heard from the street below, and now nothing disturbed the absolute stillness of my room.

I was in a cold sweat, dared not move, but with every second that I heard nothing, I grew more frightened, afraid of what might be hovering just above me in the gloom. My ignorance was an added torment, and at length I resolved I must see what was going on, no matter what it might cost me.

I lifted the sheet and gazed anxiously around the room. There by the armchair where earlier I sat knelt a black-robed figure, its back to me, its body entirely covered in the enveloping rough garb of the Capuchins.

As I gazed in horror and dread, the thing raised its arms in supplication to the old portrait of the woman. As it did, the sleeves fell back to its shoulders, and where arms should have been, I saw nothing but the outstretched bones and splayed fingers of a skeleton.

The picture itself was ringed with pale fire, and the eyes of the long-dead woman depicted in its frame seemed to turn downward to regard the foul creature below with a mixture of pity and fondness.

When I awoke, it was daylight. The room was empty, though still dark. I leaped from bed and pushed back the shutters, letting in the blessed light of morning.

The door was locked from inside, just as I'd left it.

I crossed over to the picture, telling myself such coincidences cannot occur; pictures like this are sold in every gallery or antique shop. The features were not in the least unusual, and the eyes certainly were not cast downward, nor did they seem to smile.

But when I wiped the frame clean with a damp towel, I saw centered in the middle of its bottom edge the name, Bianca Belfiore.

I returned to the Capuchin catacombs that day. The monk who admitted me looked surprised. Visitors rarely return for a second tour.

He followed me as I strode along the avenues of death, this time neither looking right nor left till I came, at last, to the remains of Pietro Catala.

I asked the monk whether he ever moved any of the skeletons. He shook his head, puzzled, and assured me he never, never, never touched them.

Yet the head of Catala now faced the ground. The eyes did not seek mine, nor did he lean any longer against the neighboring skeleton.

I gave the monk a coin and fled.

I left Palermo that morning, telling Signor Herrera I'd received a telegram calling me away immediately. He looked skeptical, knowing very well my mail passed through his hands first.

I did not wish to go to my room, so I asked him to pack my trunk and send all to the address I supplied.

Just before I left, I asked him whether he ever heard anything peculiar at night, but he shook his head.

"It is curious, though," he told me, looking as if he wanted me to say more, but knowing no gentleman pried into another's affairs. "Your room has an excellent view, and I have priced it reasonably enough. Yet I never seem to keep tenants in it for very long. . . ."

EDWARD D. HOCH *is a charming writer, incredibly prolific, yet uncompromisingly excellent. Born in 1930 in Rochester, New York, he still resides there with his wife, Pat, and contributes literally hundreds of detectival and espionage stories to* Ellery Queen's Mystery Magazine. *It is not commonly known that Ed wrote some memorable fantasy tales at the beginning of his career.* "Who Rides with Santa Anna?" *is one of the subtlest; the identity of the mysterious rider is easy to deduce, but unless one is up on dates, it is easy to miss the real riddle that the author proposes.* . . .

Who Rides with Santa Anna?

by Edward D. Hoch

Antonio Lopez de Santa Anna stood pensively on a hardened hill of sand, looking north toward a little cluster of smoldering cottonwoods that had once sheltered the walls of the Alamo Mission. For nearly two weeks, his overwhelming forces had battered at the small band of Texans and Americans. For nearly two weeks every attack had been thrown back—until now the plain between the Mexican camp and the little mission was strewn with the trappings of unsettled battle.

"Once more," Santa Anna breathed to the officer at his side. "Once more we must try it."

"But five hundred of our men have died already, President."

"What is five hundred when seven times that number still ride with us? Prepare for another attack."

And he stood there, alone, searching the horizon with his glass, swinging it from time to time back toward the shell-scarred walls of the Alamo Mission, searching for any sign of movement. Presently the officer, Juan, returned to his side.

"Yes, Juan?"

"I have passed the orders, President."

"Very good."

"But a single rider has come in from the south. . . ."

"A rider?" Santa Anna wheeled around, turning his glass toward camp. "A messenger from Mexico City, perhaps?"

"No, President." Juan shook his head. "He is an old man—though he rides well. He wishes to speak with you."

"Very well. Bring him to me. But be ready to ride."

And presently, a little old man came slowly up the path to the place where Santa Anna stood. A short man, with a face that still seemed to retain some of the shrewdness of youth, combined now with some uncertain wisdom of age.

"Good day, great Santa Anna," the old man spoke. "How does the battle progress?" His words were an odd sort of Spanish, tempered with an accent that might have been French.

"Who are you, old man?" Santa Anna asked. "And whatever brings you to this settlement of San Antonio, before the mission of the Alamo?"

"Word reached me of your difficulties, great general. I only thought to offer my assistance."

Santa Anna smiled, revealing a crooked row of yellow teeth. "Your fighting days are over, old man. The battle today is for the younger."

But the old man stretched out a hand in protest. "I am but sixty-seven years of age, and can still ride a horse with the best of your men."

"What is one more man to me?" Santa Anna asked.

"But I can win you the battle," the little man insisted.

"You are a soldier?"

"I fought in Europe in my younger days. Many great battles!"

Santa Anna nodded. "Some day the history books will remember this as a great battle, also."

The old man took the glass from his hands and peered through it toward the cluster of cottonwoods. "That is the Alamo Mission?"

"Correct," Santa Anna replied. "My objective since February twenty-third. Only now it is more a fort than a mission."

"How many men do they have?"

"Less than two hundred, I'm sure. And with them are men like Travis, Bowie, and Crockett. If I could wipe them off the map at a single stroke, there would be no more trouble with this idea of Texas independence."

The old man dropped the glass from his eye. "I will get it for you. Draw me a map in the sand to show me the layout of the mission. Quickly."

"Well," Santa Anna began, "here are the walls . . ." He sketched quickly with his sword, somehow catching the eagerness of the old man at his side. ". . . and here is an old convent, with a courtyard. And a small hospital, and a chapel. . . ."

"I see. . . . Very well. How many men do you have?"

"Thirty-five hundred. But it's those walls—those confounded walls!"

"You have tried to scale them?"

"We have tried everything. For two weeks . . ."

"But you have cannon."

"A few. More than the defenders, certainly."

"But you have been firing into the mission rather than at the walls! That was your trouble!"

"And what would you suggest?" Santa Anna queried.

"Direct all your cannons at a single point," he said. "Breach the wall and pour your overwhelming forces through the hole."

Santa Anna listened, his eyes glued to the gems as the old man's hands manipulated the snuff. "Will you ride with me?"

"But a moment ago, you thought me too old."

"Never fear. Will you ride with me?"

"How far, Santa Anna?"

"Across all of Texas."

The old man's eyes glistened. "I will ride further. I will ride with you into Washington itself, where ten years from this date you will be emperor of all the continent."

"Then we ride! Jose," he shouted, "prepare the cannon for firing. . . ."

And the air was filled with smoke and fire and screaming, roaring death, and soon the walls of the Alamo Mission trembled and shivered.

"We ride," Santa Anna shouted. "Jose, order a full attack. The horsemen and then the foot soldiers."

"This is the last attack?"

"The last attack, Jose! The wall is breached. . . ."

And at his side, the old man wheeled his white horse high into the air. "Pass the word, Santa Anna. Not a defender must remain alive. We must wipe them out, to bring all of Texas to its knees. . . ."

And Santa Anna passed the word. . . . And then they were thundering across the plain, past the deserted dirt roads, past the crumbling cottonwoods, toward the breach in the Alamo wall. . . .

"I feel victory in my bones," Santa Anna shouted to the man at his side. "This is my day."

The old man produced a dainty jeweled snuffbox, encrusted with a glittering single letter N. Santa Anna wondered where he had gotten it. Then the old man spurred his great horse forward. "Victory, as long as we ride together. This time, I will make no mistake. This time, there will be no Waterloo."

BARBARA GALLOW *is an actress, writer and announcer for a popular New England radio station. Currently at work on a major fantasy novel, she has a gift for quietly incisive character observation that makes* Jane *both sardonic and touching. Original in its setting and loosely based on a true story,* Jane *is one of the gentler tales in this collection, but its muted ironies make it truly haunting. . . .*

Jane

by Barbara Gallow

If you ask me, the only interesting thing about WBZR-FM is our location. The music is formula album rock, but we're housed in a Victorian Gothic nightmare that's right out of a Charles Addams cartoon. It's a twenty-room, chocolate-brown shingle, former Great Estate (or so the local historical society keeps reminding us whenever we suggest knocking down a few hallowed walls to enlarge our studios) with domed turrets, wrought-iron widow's walks, enough black-oak woodwork to fill a dozen funeral parlors and a front-hall fireplace with some copper relief work that looks like the mouth of Hell. There are also a pair of hand-painted and stained-glass windows (depicting Great Ancestors) that are corny, but pretty. When the light is right, they cast rainbows on the paneled hallway.

It's a pretty strange place to locate a radio station, but then our owners are pretty strange themselves—a couple of zonked-out former hippies who went straight, hit it rich in the communications business and decided that a decaying (and consequently low-rent) mansion was a "far out" place for their latest venture, WBZR-FM, Stereo Album Rock. Or, in announcer hype, "Bi-*zarrre* Radio!" I'm told the owners came up with the call letters because they thought this house was so bizarre. Actually, it's our *music* that's bizarre. Not to mention our listeners.

My last gig was evening deejay with a Beautiful Music station in Brookline, Mass. When the beautiful music put me to sleep and I snored through a newscast, a weather report and two commercials, the program director suggested that I might not be ideally suited to their format; so I came to WBZR—weekends, eight-to-four, weekdays, whenever someone is sick, hung over or too stoned to go on. Actually, there isn't much difference between working for a BM station and an album rock station. Both of them play music for most of the hour and all the announcer has to do is come on a few times to give the news and weather, keep the commercials running, and remind the listeners what station they're tuned to. The main difference is that at WBZR I have to sound mellowed-out and into the music.

I like working weekends. Nobody else is around, I get to read a lot, drink a few dozen cups of coffee without anyone telling me how lousy it is for me, and play with Herman, my Labrador and the Eastern States K-9 frisbee champion. Or, rather, I *try* to play with Herman. Mostly he sacks out in front of the studio fireplace (one fireplace in every room, all different, none working) and chews his frisbee. I tried some light practice tosses, but quit that when he nearly went through one of the stained-glass windows on the second-floor landing. I'd hate like Hell to smash the only decent-looking thing in this building.

The one thing I *don't* do is listen to the music. Most of the other announcers sit in the booth with their headphones on, gettin' down; personally, I'd rather listen to a trash-masher than an entire album of New Wave rock. So I usually turn the studio monitors down, put my feet up on the console and stare out the window, watching the neighborhood winos take naps in the street. Sometimes I bring in my portable TV and watch ballgames or old movies. I was suffering through about my fifteenth viewing of *Demetrius and the Gladiators* when I met Jane.

Victor Mature was just being set up for the kill by the evil Messalina when Herman barked and nearly sent me through the ceiling. Normally, Herman's lethargy can only be shaken by the words "food," "frisbee" or "French poodles," but now he was growling in the direction of the outer hall, hackles up.

I couldn't remember if I had locked the front door or not. Technically, we're supposed to leave it open so any of our admiring listeners can stop by and make themselves at home (which they usually do by staring at the giant copper fireplace and the stained glass and breathing, "Oh wow, far out. Hey, you givin' away any tee shirts this week?"), but when I'm alone I prefer it locked. Once I left it open and the PM announcer walked in to find a wino passed out in the entryway.

I flipped off *Demetrius* and gave Herman an encouraging nudge. "Go see who's out there, boy."

Herman, for all his ninety pounds of frisbee-conditioned muscle, is essentially a coward and he seemed a lot more content to stand in the doorway barking than to go into the hall. At last he ventured out and got about as far as the middle of the steps (I figured. Since I'm also essentially a coward I wasn't about to leave the studio to find out) when his barking faded into a sort of whimpering, and then nothing. Next thing, he was walking complacently back into the studio with a giant Milk-Bone in his mouth.

I stopped staring at him when I heard the scratching sound of a diamond stylus across paper and realized that I was now treating my audience to dead air. I snapped off the turntable pot and flipped up the announcer mike, "Now that was the latest chart-buster by (quick check of the label) 'Blondie,' my friends. Randy King here with you all afternoon at *double*-you, *beee, zeee, aarrr!* It is cold outside—just forty-three mean ones—and Uncle Jack in the weather center says keep your eyes peeled for some white stuff! But right now I have a little music to warm you up—Fleetwood Mac." It wasn't at all the right disc to follow "Blondie," but it was the first one I picked up, and I nearly dropped it when I saw the girl.

She was standing in the studio doorway watching me, smiling a little. At first glance, I guessed her to be about twenty; she was bundled up in a long, fur-trimmed coat and most of her hair (blonde and curly-looking) was hidden under a wide-brimmed hat with a feather. Her cheeks were rosy from the cold and she had big, round blue eyes.

And all I could think to say was, "I guess the door wasn't locked, huh?"

She smiled. "I guess it wasn't," she said in a soft, high voice, almost like a little girl's.

And my next question, equally brilliant, was, "Do you carry Milk-Bones around with you?"

She looked a little hurt. "There was a box of them sitting on the desk downstairs. I hope you don't mind. Your dog and I are friends—now."

Considering that most visitors to our station would be more likely to give Herman a swig of Colt 44 than a dog biscuit, I couldn't very well mind. And I like blondes.

I hoped the girl was an announcer (and particularly a Randy King) groupie, even though she looked too classy, but she was looking in mild distaste from me in my Schroeder sweatshirt and old jeans to the studio itself, taking in the albums stacked in the built-in bookcases, the posters of rock stars taped haphazardly on the walls, the empty soda bottles and plastic cupholders lined up along the fireplace mantle, the cigarette ashes ground into the cream shag rug.

"Is it always this . . . untidy?" she asked.

"Uh, it gets kind of messy on weekends," I apologized. "No cleaning crew till Tuesday."

"I love this house," she said abruptly, still in that sweet, little girl's voice. "I hate to see"—she gestured vaguely—"bad things happen to it."

I had the feeling that by "bad things" she meant WBZR in general, not just the bottles and ashes. Then she smiled at me, showing a set of matched dimples on each cheek.

"What must you think of me? Barging in here uninvited, taking dog biscuits and then criticizing your housekeeping? I haven't even said any of the polite things a visitor *ought* to say. You must think I'm very pushy and more than a little rude."

"No, I don't think you're rude at all," I said hastily. "I think you're just being honest. (Where do I dig up these wonderful snippets of repartee?) But, go ahead and say a few polite lies about me and the station anyway."

At this she laughed. "To be, as you say, honest, I don't know very much about the sort of music you play, but it doesn't seem very *tuneful.*"

I couldn't have agreed more.

"But I know who you are. You're Randy King. I think you have a very pleasant voice."

So maybe she was a King groupie after all!

"You know me, but I don't know you," I said, trying to sound pleasant. "What's your name?"

"Jane. Plain Jane."

Jane, maybe, but definitely not plain. When she smiled she showed a perfect set of small white teeth and her blue eyes were sparkly and a little mischievous. Add to that, her nose turned up on the end and her hair *was* curly, although I couldn't tell the length because she still wore her hat. Also, as she neared me I could see she was a little older than I had first thought, despite the little kid voice—but I've nothing against women over twenty-five.

I had the strange feeling that I'd seen her before and then I thought back to her remark about loving this house.

"This isn't your first visit to the station, is it?"

"No, not nearly!" she laughed lightly. "Although I don't appear here as often as I used to. I make the others uncomfortable."

I could see why. They aren't used to seeing straight, sober visitors around here.

"You see, this is my house," she continued, very softly.

"Your house?" I asked stupidly.

"I was born and raised here," Jane said, a little sadly. "And I thought I would never leave."

"Then why *did* you?" The question just sort of slipped out. Jane gave me a strange, brief look, as though deciding how to proceed. "If it had been up to me this would still be my house and not a radio station. But of course it wasn't up to me." She flashed another of her quick smiles. "Not that I didn't try."

I smiled back, trying to picture little Jane (she wasn't very tall) fighting lawyers and corporate hotshots and maybe her parents, for all I knew, to keep from being evicted from her home. Although her family probably had a condominium in the suburbs right now.

I turned up the studio monitor for a second, to check the progress of the record and the sound of Fleetwood filled the room. Jane shook her head.

"To think, here you are sending music over the airwaves for everyone to hear and Mama once yelled at me for whistling out the window."

I laughed at that; I like anyone with a good sense of the ridiculous. Jane continued to check out the studio, as if she still couldn't believe that her old house had come to *this*.

"This was my bedroom."

"*Here?*" No wonder she was bugged about the mess.

"I had a pink room. I would have preferred brown, but Mama said pink was the proper color for girls, so . . ." She spread her hands helplessly. Her mother sounded like a candidate for the Long Live Queen Victoria Society. "My bed was on that wall, facing the fireplace. How I loved a fire on days like these! And I had a bureau and vanity over there and pictures on the walls, too, but not like *those*." Jane wrinkled her nose at the posters.

"What about the other rooms?" I didn't care all that much, but I wanted to keep her talking. When she reminisced about this old place her eyes looked even bluer and her cheeks flushed and this is corny as all Hell but I felt like a twelve-year-old with a crush.

"That big room with all the desks used to be my parents' bedroom, and the little room next to this (she meant the production studio) belonged to my brother Edward, and after . . ." she paused abruptly and made a dismissing gesture with her hand. "Well, what's past is past, I believe the saying goes," she said in a brisk voice. I think she got herself kind of shook up thinking about the good old days, because she suddenly seemed kind of flustered, as if she'd said something she shouldn't.

My experience with women is such that I can spot that "time for an exit" look a mile away, so I flipped over the Fleetwood disc (completely ignoring the fact that I was supposed to do a break; the audience prefers its music uninterrupted anyway) and plunged right in.

"I get off in an hour."

"Excuse me?"

Jane was definitely not a King groupie or she'd have picked up the cue. "I get off work in an hour, if you'd like to go out for a drink or something . . ." and I never saw such a look of total disbelief in my life.

"You want me to *go* somewhere with you?" she asked, just to rub in the absurdity of it, I figured. "But I *can't!*"

That gave me a little hope. Maybe she had a boyfriend who'd kill her (or me) if he caught her fooling around with another man. She's just the sort of woman who brings out the macho protector spirit.

"I'm not making a play or anything," I lied. "I'd just like to see you again."

"You would? Really?" Jane seemed genuinely pleased. "I'd like that. Truly." She had a conspirator's gleam in her eye that was cute as hell. "I could come here again and visit. But not weekdays; it's too . . . crowded then."

Nothing could have suited me better. "Next week then?" I asked, trying not to pant. "Same time, same station—excuse the pun."

She nodded eagerly. "But I have to go now," she half-whispered, sort of drifting back towards the door.

I offered to walk her downstairs, but she laughed and said it wasn't necessary. Then she was gone and Herman and I sat looking at each other glumly. Some of the life had left the room.

Two days later, I got a call at six-thirty in the morning. The mid-morning deejay was "bummed out, you know," and wouldn't be in. So I prepared to face the full-time weekday staffers of WBZR.

After being at work about an hour, the "Have a good day" and "Hey, I hear you man," level of conversation sent me running to the coffee machine in desperate need of a fix. I hoped the pantry would be deserted, but I was out of luck: Karen Sykes, the business manager, was there ahead of me. Since some form of chitchat is obligatory at these brief meetings of the weekday and weekend staffs, I told Karen about my visit from Jane.

She gave me one long look over the top of her oversized executive eyeglasses. "I don't believe it," she said definitively.

"Why would I lie?" I said, resisting the urge to answer with the trendy, "Be-*lieve* it!" "What a sweet lady she is," I couldn't help adding, but I doubt if Karen heard me because she was busy bawling into the reception hall, "Sheila, you'll *never* believe it! *Jane* is back!"

That got a reaction. Four people jammed into the little pantry and stared at me. I felt like I was in a miniature Star Chamber.

"Wow, Jane's really back? That's far out!"

"I thought we'd scared her away for good!"

That got me. "Why the hell would you want to scare away a sweet girl like Jane? After all, this *is* her house!"

"*Was,* man. *Was* her house," said the production chief, known lovingly as Freaky Freddy. "We don't want her around here *now.*"

"You actually saw her and talked to her?" Karen asked.

"That's what I said, isn't it?" I'd about had it with these clowns.

Freaky Freddy was impressed. "Oh wow, that is far out, man. Really saw her in person. Wow. Most people only *hear* her," he tittered a little. "She likes to keep a low profile, you know?"

With these jokers around, who could blame her?

Karen was shaking her head like a doctor on a tough case. "So she's back again," she muttered.

"Yeah, and she's coming to visit me again *next* Sunday," I said with I think justifiable bravado.

This was too much for Freddy. "Oh wow, man, he's got a date with *Jane!*" And he headed for the safety of his production studio.

The others cleared out too, except for Karen. "I really can't believe this," she said.

I was getting pretty tired of that refrain. What was the big deal anyway? I couldn't help comparing Karen mentally with Jane. Or contrasting, I should say. I'm not really a chauvinist, but there was just something so much more—I can't help it—*feminine* about Jane. Almost an old-fashioned gentility. And I couldn't wait for Sunday to come, I can tell you.

For the first time in ages I dressed up to go to work. Oh not a suit and tie, but a real sharp cable-knit sweater and corduroy pants. I even gave Herman a clean frisbee to chew on.

Jane came in wearing the same coat and hat, even though it wasn't nearly as cold out. Her cheeks were just as rosy, her hair just as blonde and her eyes as blue and sparkly as I'd remembered them. She appeared in the studio doorway with a shy little smile on her face that showed all her dimples.

I was all set today, though. I had a double album on the turntable and I'd already promised my listeners that they were gonna be treated, yes indeed, to one solid hour of music, music, music. And I left the TV set at home.

And with all that I still couldn't come up with a decent opening line.

"I was so afraid you weren't gonna come, today," I said.

"Oh, but I promised and I always keep my word," Jane said in that enchanting light, sweet voice. Then she giggled. "Although I must say I never used to be in the habit of making assignations with men."

Mostly we talked about ourselves, our families, schools and all that stuff that sounded so trivial coming from me and so sweet coming from her. I tried to talk politics and films and all that trendy nonsense, but Jane either didn't know or didn't care much about them. So I ended up telling her what I hadn't told anyone in a long time: that I truly intended one day to write the great American novel.

"I do *so* admire writers!" she said. "I know you'll write a good book. You're more sensitive than most." Here she paused. "That's why I'm here, you see." She turned her head away, suddenly uncomfortable.

That shy admission had more effect on me than the sexiest come-on. I think I'd have jumped off the roof at that moment if she had asked me.

"Jane, I haven't been able to get you off my mind all week. Are you sure you couldn't go out with me just once?" I wheedled.

"No!" she flared suddenly. "How can you even think it?" I just about fell off my chair. She amended quickly. "You know so little about me, Randy. Less than you think."

The thought hit me like a bolt and even as I was asking the question she was saying, "I have a husband."

Well. And well again. What did I expect? Beautiful women get snapped up pretty quickly.

"I'm sorry," she said sadly. "I ought to have told you, but I never dreamed . . ." She twisted her hands. "He isn't with me now, you see, but . . . but he wants me to join him. I haven't made up my mind." She seemed to be talking more to herself than to me.

"Stay with me!" I burst out. I've never made a declaration to a woman before.

Jane looked at me with a strange, faraway look in her eyes. "How I would like to stay *here,*" she said. "But the others don't want me."

"Well who cares about the others!" I said, in near exasperation. "*I* want you. And I think you want me."

"What good company you would be!" she said passionately.

"Herman's good company, too," I added; Herman was beginning to sniff the air suspiciously. I think he can smell "involvement" and he hates to be excluded.

"Yes, it's been so long since I had a dog," she whispered quickly. She stood in front of me, smiling down from those blue eyes and very slowly reached out her hand to me.

I felt almost hypnotized, lost in her terrific eyes, and I raised my hand to hers.

My hand had nearly closed on her fingertips, when she drew her hand away quickly, almost angrily.

"What am I thinking of!" she said. "I must go."

The whole scene was moving too fast for my feeble brain to comprehend. I could have sworn she'd just offered herself to me. I hated to think she was just another tease. I guess she knew what I was thinking, because she looked at me beseechingly.

"I like you so very much, Randy. You're the first man since Andrew —my husband—that I have ever wanted to spend my . . . all of my time with. But I cannot. You aren't mine to have."

Before I could think of a rejoinder for this unlikely speech she had practically flown out the door, leaving the studio cold and still. And all I could think of was that I still didn't know her last name.

"Bradford was the family name," Karen told me on Thursday, when I went in to collect my paycheck. "I don't know what her husband's name would have been."

"*Would* have been? You talk like he's dead."

Karen laughed in a particularly superior way as she stamped her signature on my check. "Well, I should certainly think he *is*," she said. "After all, he'd be about a hundred and twenty today!"

A hundred and twenty. "And Jane," I asked tonelessly. "How old is Jane?"

Karen shrugged. "Oh I don't know how old she'd be now, but I heard she was pretty young when she died. Only in her late twenties." She thrust my paycheck at me. "Have a nice day."

I've been doing a lot of walking lately. Around this crummy neighborhood where WBZR, where the old Bradford estate, is located. And around the crummy neighborhood where I live. A hundred years ago my block didn't exist. And this neighborhood was the best in the city; of all the fine houses, the Bradford mansion was the finest. Is still. The hand-carved woodwork is as solid now as it was then. The fireplaces, of copper and rose marble and curly maple, still flame to life when the sun hits them. And the beautiful stained-glass windows send rainbows running along the walls, just like the crystal prisms in my grandmother's chandelier used to do. All of these things have been so carefully preserved by the lady of the house. The lady with whom I could gladly spend all *my* days.

"Jane? Jane, I know you're here. Come in; please come in."

It's only Saturday morning, but there's no reason to wait for Sunday afternoon now. I think I feel the way a groom must the night before a wedding.

Herman barks in greeting, and Jane is standing in the doorway, her feather hat in her hands. Her curly blonde hair falls halfway down her back and I can't wait to run my fingers through it.

"I was afraid you wouldn't come back after last week," I tell her. "But it's okay, now."

"Yes," she says, in her little girl's voice. "Now you know."

"Now I know," I say with a grin.

Jane smiles sadly. "So now you know why I must leave."

I stare at her. "What?"

She nods. "I've been so very foolish."

"What do you mean, leave? This is your *home.*"

"Not any more," she says gazing around wistfully. "My time has passed. This house belongs to the living." She says the last word very pointedly and fixes me with a blue-eyed gaze.

I get out of my chair and go to her. "This house belongs to *you . . .* and to me." I reach out for her.

She steps backward and shakes her head. "You mustn't touch me, don't you see?"

"Yes I *do* see and . . . and I *want* you. I want to be with you forever. That's all I care about." She starts to speak, but I don't let her. "Look, Jane, I've always loved you a little. Even before I really met you; I know that now."

"Yes, I know," she says. "That's why I let you see me. But that was a mistake." Her voice drops to a whisper. "I am very fond of you, Randy."

"Then take my hand."

"I can't do that—not to you and not to me." She adds lightly, "After all, I could not bear to have you tire of me and my house after fifty years or so."

"Jane—"

"I'm going to join Andrew now, as I should have done years ago"— she is drifting away from my outstretched hand—"and you must stay where *you* belong."

She disappears into the hall and I follow, Herman at my heels.

The hall is empty.

But Jane is still there, with the sunlight shining on her curly yellow hair, red cheeks and sparkling blue eyes, gazing at me from the hand-painted, stained-glass window at the top of the second-floor landing.

And I hear, a whisper inside my head, "Take care of my house for me, Randy."

To most readers, WASHINGTON IRVING, born in New York in 1783, is
merely the author of "Rip Van Winkle" and "The Legend of Sleepy Hollow," but though those tales have justly become folk classics, the rest of Irving's work is worthy of a revival of interest, richly endowed as it is with fascinating travel notes of a bygone England that Irving's Sketch Book makes
one long to revisit—as well as several excellent early American examples of
fantasy literature. One such is the following Grand Guignol-esque nightmare, also known as "The Tale of the German Student."

The Tale of the German Student
by Washington Irving

On a stormy night, in the tempestuous times of the French Revolution,
a young German was returning to his lodgings, at a late hour, across the
old part of Paris. The lightning gleamed, and the loud claps of thunder
rattled through the lofty narrow streets—but I should first tell you something about this young German.

Gottfried Wolfgang was a young man of good family. He had studied for some time at Gottingen, but being of a visionary and enthusiastic
character, he had wandered into those wild and speculative doctrines
which have so often bewildered German students. His secluded life, his
intense application, and the singular nature of his studies, had an effect
on both mind and body. His health was impaired; his imagination diseased. He had been indulging in fanciful speculations on spiritual es-
sences, until, like Swedenborg, he had an ideal world of his own around
him. He took up a notion, I do not know from what cause, that there
was an evil influence hanging over him; an evil genius or spirit seeking
to ensnare him and insure his perdition. Such an idea working on his
melancholy temperament produced the most gloomy effects. He became
haggard and desponding. His friends discovered the mental malady
preying upon him, and determined that the best cure was a change of
scene; he was sent, therefore, to finish his studies amidst the splendors
and gayeties of Paris.

Wolfgang arrived in Paris at the breaking out of the Revolution. The
popular delirium at first caught his enthusiastic mind, and he was cap-
tivated by the political and philosophical theories of the day, but the
scenes of blood which followed shocked his sensitive nature, disgusted
him with society and the world, and made him more than ever a recluse.

He shut himself up in a solitary apartment in the Pays Latin, the quarter of students. There, in a gloomy street not far from the monastic walls of the Sorbonne, he pursued his favorite speculations. Sometimes he spent hours in the great libraries of Paris, those catacombs of departed authors, rummaging among their hoards of dusty and obsolete works in quest of food for his unhealthy appetite. He was, in a manner, a literary ghoul, feeding in the charnel-house of decayed literature.

Wolfgang, though solitary and recluse, was of an ardent temperament, but for a time it operated merely upon his imagination. He was too shy and ignorant of the world to make any advances to the fair, but he was a passionate admirer of female beauty, and in his lonely chamber would often lose himself in reveries on forms and faces which he had seen, and his fancy would deck out images of loveliness far surpassing the reality.

While his mind was in this excited and sublimated state, a dream produced an extraordinary effect upon him. It was of a female face of transcendent beauty. So strong was the impression made, that he dreamed of it again and again. It haunted his thoughts by day, his slumbers by night; in fine, he became passionately enamored of his shadow of a dream. This lasted so long that it became one of those fixed ideas which haunt the minds of melancholy men, and are at times mistaken for madness.

Such was Gottfried Wolfgang, and such his situation at the time I mentioned. He was returning home late one stormy night, through some of the old and gloomy streets of the Marais, the ancient part of Paris. The loud claps of thunder rattled among the high houses of the narrow streets. He came to the Place de la Greve, the square where public executions are performed. The lightning quivered about the pinnacles of the ancient Hotel de Ville, and shed flickering gleams over the open space in front. As Wolfgang was crossing the square, he shrank back with horror at finding himself close by the guillotine. It was the height of the Reign of Terror (when this dreadful instrument of death stood ever ready, and its scaffold was continually running with the blood of the virtuous and the brave. It had that very day been actively employed in the work of carnage, and there it stood in grim array, amidst a silent and sleeping city, waiting for fresh victims.

Wolfgang's heart sickened within him, and he was turning shuddering from the horrible engine, when he beheld a shadowy form, cowering as it were at the foot of the steps which led up to the scaffold. A succession of vivid flashes of lightning revealed it more distinctly. It was a female figure, dressed in black. She was seated on one of the lower steps of the scaffold, leaning forward, her face hid in her lap; and her long disheveled tresses hanging to the ground, streaming with the rain which fell in torrents. Wolfgang paused. There was something awful in this solitary monument of woe. The female had the appearance of being above the common order. He knew the times to be full of vicissitude, and that many a fair head, which had been pillowed on down, now wandered houseless. Perhaps this was some poor mourner whom the dreadful ax had rendered desolate, and who sat here heartbroken on the strand of existence, from which all that was dear to her had been launched into eternity.

He approached, and addressed her in the accents of sympathy. She raised her head and gazed wildly at him. What was his astonishment at beholding, by the bright glare of the lightning, the very face which had haunted him in his dreams. It was pale and disconsolate, but ravishingly beautiful.

Trembling with violent and conflicting emotions, Wolfgang again accosted her. He spoke something of her being exposed at such an hour of the night, and to the fury of such a storm, and offered to conduct her to her friends. She pointed to the guillotine with a gesture of dreadful signification.

"I have no friend on earth," said she.

"But you have a home," said Wolfgang.

"Yes—in the grave!"

The heart of the student melted at the words.

"If a stranger dare make an offer," said he, "without danger of being misunderstood, I would offer my humble dwelling as a shelter; myself as a devoted friend. I am friendless myself in Paris, and a stranger in the land; but if my life could be of service, it is at your disposal, and should be sacrificed before harm or indignity should come to you."

There was an honest earnestness in the young man's manner that had its effect. His foreign accent, too, was in his favor; it showed him not to be a hackneyed inhabitant of Paris. Indeed, there is an eloquence in true enthusiasm that is not to be doubted. The homeless stranger confided herself implicitly to the protection of the student.

He supported her faltering steps across the Pont Neuf, and by the place where the statue of Henry the Fourth had been overthrown by the populace. The storm had abated, and the thunder rumbled at a distance. All Paris was quiet; that great volcano of human passion slumbered for a while, to gather fresh strength for the next day's eruption. The student conducted his charge through the ancient streets of the Pays Latin, and by the dusky walls of the Sorbonne, to the great dingy hotel which he inhabited. The old portress who admitted them stared with surprise at the unusual sight of the melancholy Wolfgang with a female companion.

On entering his apartment, the student, for the first time, blushed at the scantiness and indifference of his dwelling. He had but one chamber —an old-fashioned salon—heavily carved, and fantastically furnished with the remains of former magnificence, for it was of those hotels in the quarter of the Luxembourg Palace which had once belonged to nobility. It was lumbered with books and papers, and all the usual apparatus of a student, and his bed stood in a recess at one end.

When lights were brought, and Wolfgang had a better opportunity of contemplating the stranger, he was more than ever intoxicated by her beauty. Her face was pale, but of a dazzling fairness, set off by a profusion of raven hair that hung clustering about it. Her eyes were large and brilliant, with a singular expression approaching almost to wildness. As far as her black dress permitted her shape to be seen, it was of perfect symmetry. Her whole appearance was highly striking, though she was dressed in the simplest style. The only thing approaching to an ornament which she wore, was a broad black band round her neck, clasped by diamonds.

The perplexity now commenced with the student how to dispose of the helpless being thus thrown upon his protection. He thought of abandoning his chamber to her, and seeking she' er for himself elsewhere. Still he was so fascinated by her charms, the , seemed to be such a spell upon his thoughts and senses, that he coula not tear himself from her presence. Her manner, too, was singular and unaccountable. She spoke no more of the guillotine. Her grief had abated. The attentions of the student had first won her confidence, and then, apparently, her heart. She was evidently an enthusiast like himself, and enthusiasts soon understand each other.

In the infatuation of the moment, Wolfgang avowed his passion for her. He told her the story of his mysterious dream, and how she had possessed his heart before he had even seen her. She was strangely affected by his recital, and acknowledged to have felt an impulse toward him equally unaccountable. It was the time for wild theory and wild actions. Old prejudices and superstitions were done away; everything was under the sway of the "Goddess of Reason." Among other rubbish of the old times, the forms and ceremonies of marriage began to be considered superfluous bonds for honorable minds. Social compacts were the vogue. Wolfgang was too much of a theorist not to be tainted by the liberal doctrines of the day.

"Why should we separate?" said he. "Our hearts are united; in the eye of reason and honor we are as one. What need is there of sordid forms to bind high souls together?"

The stranger listened with emotion; she had evidently received illumination at the same school.

"You have no home nor family," continued he; "let me be everything to you, or rather let us be everything to one another. If form is necessary, form shall be observed—there is my hand. I pledge myself to you forever."

"Forever?" said the stranger, solemnly.

"Forever!" repeated Wolfgang.

The stranger clasped the hand extended to her. "Then I am yours," murmured she, and sank upon his bosom.

The next morning the student left his bride sleeping, and sallied forth at an early hour to seek more spacious apartments, suitable to the change in his situation. When he returned, he found the stranger lying with her head hanging over the bed, and one arm thrown over it. He spoke to her, but received no reply. He advanced to awaken her from her uneasy posture. On taking her hand, it was cold—there was no pulsation—her face was pallid and ghastly—in a word, she was a corpse.

Horrified and frantic, he alarmed the house. A scene of confusion ensued. The police were summoned.

As the officer of police entered the room, he started back on beholding the corpse.

"Great heaven!" cried he; "how did this woman come here?"

"Do you know anything about her?" said Wolfgang eagerly.

"Do I?" exclaimed the police officer; "she was guillotined yesterday."

He stepped forward, undid the black collar round the neck of the corpse, and the head rolled on the floor!

The student burst into a frenzy. "The fiend! The fiend has gained possession of me!" shrieked he; "I am lost forever."

They tried to soothe him, but in vain. He was possessed with the frightful belief that an evil spirit had reanimated the dead body to ensnare him. He went distracted, and died in a madhouse.

JOHN MASEFIELD, *born in 1878 in Herefordshire, England, became succes-*
sor to Robert Bridges as poet laureate of Great Britain in 1930. Before his
sixtieth birthday, he had written some seventy-five books of poetry of vary-
ing quality. His earlier lyrical evocations of the sea are generally considered
his finest work. Unjustly obscure is The Hounds of Hell, *a harrowing horror*
story in verse of spectral hounds from the Pit. In spite of the menace of the
title creatures, the aspect of the poem I have always liked the most is the
touching and slyly critical dissection of the monkish hero by an author who
may have believed in miracles, but knew they are often rooted in human de-
termination stemming from meretricious motives.

The Hounds of Hell
by John Masefield

About the crowing of the cock,
    When the shepherds feel the cold,
A horse's hoofs went clip-a-clock
    Along the hangman's wold.

The horse-hoofs trotted on the stone,
    The hoof-sparks glittered by,
And then a hunting horn was blown
    And hounds broke into cry.

There was a strangeness in the horn,
    A wildness in the cry,
A power of devilry forlorn
    Exulting bloodily.

A power of night that ran a prey
    Along the hangman's hill.
The shepherds heard the spent buck bray
    And the horn blow for the kill.

They heard the worrying of the hounds
    About the dead beast's bones;
Then came the horn, and then the sounds
    Of horse-hoofs treading stones.

"What hounds are these that hunt the night?"
  The shepherds asked in fear,
"Look, there are calkins clinking bright;
  They must be coming here."

The calkins clinkered to a spark,
  The hunter called the pack;
The sheep-dogs' fells all bristled stark
  And all their lips went back.

"Lord God!" the shepherds said, "they come;
  And see what hounds he has:
All dripping bluish fire, and dumb,
  And nosing to the grass,

"And trotting scatheless through the gorse,
  And bristling in the fell.
Lord, it is Death upon the horse,
  And they're the hounds of hell!"

They shook to watch them as they sped,
  All black against the sky;
A horseman with a hooded head
  And great hounds padding by.

When daylight drove away the dark
  And larks went up and thrilled,
The shepherds climbed the wold to mark
  What beast the hounds had killed.

They came to where the hounds had fed,
  And in that trampled place
They found a pedlar lying dead,
  With horror in his face.

*   *   *

There was a farmer on the wold
  Where all the brooks begin,
He had a thousand sheep from fold
  Out grazing on the whin.

The next night, as he lay in bed,
    He heard a canterer come
Trampling the wold-top with a tread
    That sounded like a drum.

He thought it was a post that rode,
    So turned him to his sleep;
But the canterer in his dreams abode
    Like horse-hoofs running sheep.

And in his dreams a horn was blown
    And feathering hounds replied,
And all his wethers stood like stone
    In rank on the hillside.

Then, while he struggled still with dreams,
    He saw his wethers run
Before a pack cheered on with screams,
    The thousand sheep as one.

So, leaping from his bed in fear,
    He flung the window back,
And he heard a death-horn blowing clear
    And the crying of a pack,

And the thundering of a thousand sheep,
    All mad and running wild
To the stone-pit seven fathoms deep,
    Whence all the town is tiled.

After them came the hounds of hell,
    With hell's own fury filled;
Into the pit the wethers fell,
    And all but three were killed.

The hunter blew his horn a note
    And laughed against the moon;
The farmer's breath caught in his throat,
    He fell into a swoon.

*   *   *

The next night when the watch was set
    A heavy rain came down,
The leaden gutters dripped with wet
    Into the shuttered town.

So close the shutters were, the chink
    Of lamplight scarcely showed;
The men at fireside heard no clink
    Of horse-hoofs on the road.

They heard the creaking hinge complain,
        And the mouse that gnawed the floor,
And the limping footsteps of the rain
        On the stone outside the door.

And on the wold the rain came down
        Till trickles streakt the grass:
A traveller riding to the town
        Drew rein to let it pass.

The wind sighed in the fir-tree tops,
        The trickles sobb'd in the grass,
The branches ran with showers of drops:
        No other noise there was.

Till up the wold the traveller heard
        A horn blow faint and thin;
He thought it was the curlew bird
        Lamenting to the whin;

And when the far horn blew again,
        He thought an owl hallooed,
Or a rabbit gave a shriek of pain
        As the stoat leapt in the wood.

But when the horn blew next, it blew
        A trump that split the air.
And hounds gave cry to an Halloo!—
        The hunt of hell was there.

"Black" (said the traveller), "black and swift,
   Those running devils came;
Scoring to cry with hackles stifft,
   And grin-jowls dropping flame."

They settled to the sightless scent,
   And up the hill a cry
Told where the frightened quarry went,
   Well knowing it would die.

Then presently a cry rang out,
   And a mort blew for the kill;
A shepherd with his throat torn out
   Lay dead upon the hill.

      *   *   *

When this was known, the shepherds drove
   Their flocks into the town;
No man, for money or for love,
   Would watch them on the down.

But night by night the terror ran,
   The townsmen heard them still;
Nightly the hell-hounds hunted man
   And the hunter whooped the kill.

The men who lived upon the moor
   Would wakèn to the scratch
Of hounds' claws digging at the door
   Or scraping at the latch.

And presently no man would go
   Without doors after dark,
Lest hell's black hunting horn should blow,
   And hell's black bloodhounds mark.

They shivered round the fire at home,
   While out upon the bent
The hounds with black jowls dropping foam
   Went nosing to the scent.

Men let the hay crop run to seed
And the corn crop sprout in ear,
And the root crop choke itself in weed—
That hell-hound hunting year.

Empty to heaven lay the wold,
Village and church grew green;
The courtyard flagstones spread with mould,
And weeds sprang up between.

And sometimes when the cock had crowed,
And the hillside stood out grey,
Men saw them slinking up the road
All sullen from their prey.

A hooded horseman on a black,
With nine black hounds at heel,
After the hell-hunt going back
All bloody from their meal.

And in men's minds a fear began
That hell had over-hurled
The guardians of the soul of man,
And come to rule the world

With bitterness of heart by day,
And terror in the night,
And the blindness of a barren way
And withering of delight.

*   *   *

St. Withiel lived upon the moor,
Where the peat-men live in holes;
He worked among the peat-men poor,
Who only have their souls.

He brought them nothing but his love
And the will to do them good,
But power filled him from above,
His very touch was food.

Men told St. Withiel of the hounds,
    And how they killed their prey.
He thought them far beyond his bounds,
    So many miles away.

Then one whose son the hounds had killed
    Told him the tale at length;
St. Withiel pondered why God willed
    That hell should have such strength.

Then one, a passing traveller, told
    How, since the hounds had come,
The church was empty on the wold
    And all the priests were dumb.

St. Withiel rose at this, and said:
    "This priest will not be dumb;
My spirit will not be afraid
    Though all hell's devils come."

He took his stick and out he went,
    The long way to the wold,
Where the sheep-bells clink upon the bent
    And every wind is cold.

He passed the rivers running red
    And the mountains standing bare;
At last the wold-land lay ahead,
    Un-yellowed by the share.

All in the brown October time
    He clambered to the weald;
The plum lay purpled into slime,
    The harvest lay in field.

Trampled by many-footed rain
    The sunburnt corn lay dead;
The myriad finches in the grain
    Rose bothering at his tread.

The myriad finches took a sheer
And settled back to food:
A man was not a thing to fear
In such a solitude.

The hurrying of their wings died out,
A silence took the hill;
There was no dog, no bell, no shout,
The windmill's sails were still.

The gate swung creaking on its hasp,
The pear splashed from the tree,
In the rotting apple's heart the wasp
Was drunken drowsily.

The grass upon the cart-wheel ruts
Had made the trackways dim;
The rabbits ate and hopped their scuts,
They had no fear of him.

The sunset reddened in the west;
The distant depth of blue
Stretched out and dimmed; to twiggy nest
The rooks in clamour drew.

The oakwood in his mail of brass
Bowed his great crest and stood;
The pine-tree saw St. Withiel pass,
His great bole blushed like blood.

Then tree and wood alike were dim,
Yet still St. Withiel strode;
The only noise to comfort him
Were his footsteps on the road.

The crimson in the west was smoked,
The west wind heaped the wrack,
Each tree seemed like a murderer cloaked
To stab him in the back.

Darkness and desolation came
    To dog his footsteps there;
The dead leaves rustling called his name,
    The death-moth brushed his hair.

The murmurings of the wind fell still;
    He stood and stared around:
He was alone upon the hill,
    On devil-haunted ground.

What was the whitish thing which stood
    In front, with one arm raised,
Like death a-grinning in a hood?
    The saint stood still and gazed.

"What are you?" said St. Withiel. "Speak!"
    Not any answer came
But the night-wind making darkness bleak,
    And the leaves that called his name.

A glow shone on the whitish thing,
    It neither stirred nor spoke:
In spite of faith, a shuddering
    Made the good saint to choke.

He struck the whiteness with his staff—
    It was a withered tree;
An owl flew from it with a laugh,
    The darkness shook with glee.

The darkness came all round him close
    And cackled in his ear;
The midnight, full of life none knows,
    Was very full of fear.

The darkness cackled in his heart
    That things of hell were there,
That the startled rabbit played a part
    And the stoat's leap did prepare—

Prepare the stage of night for blood,
    And the mind of night for death,
For a spirit trembling in the mud
    In an agony for breath.

A terror came upon the saint,
    It stripped his spirit bare;
He was sick body standing faint,
    Cold sweat and stiffened hair.

He took his terror by the throat
    And stamped it underfoot;
Then, far away, the death-horn's note
    Quailed like a screech-owl's hoot.

Still far away that devil's horn
    Its quavering death-note blew,
But the saint could hear the crackling thorn
    That the hounds trod as they drew.

"Lord, it is true," St. Withiel moaned,
    "And the hunt is drawing near!
Devils that Paradise disowned,
    They know that I am here.

"And there, O God, a hound gives tongue,
    And great hounds quarter dim"—
The saint's hands to his body clung,
    He knew they came for him.

Then close at hand the horn was loud,
    Like Peter's cock of old
For joy that Peter's soul was cowed,
    And Jesus' body sold.

Then terribly the hounds in cry
    Gave answer to the horn;
The saint in terror turned to fly
    Before his flesh was torn.

After his body came the hounds,
    After the hounds the horse;
Their running crackled with the sounds
    Of fire that runs in gorse.

The saint's breath failed, but still they came:
    The hunter cheered them on,
Even as a wind that blows a flame
    In the vigil of St. John.

And as St. Withiel's terror grew,
    The crying of the pack
Bayed nearer, as though terror drew
    Those grip teeth to his back.

No hope was in his soul, no stay,
    Nothing but screaming will
To save his terror-stricken clay
    Before the hounds could kill.

The laid corn tripped, the bramble caught,
    He stumbled on the stones—
The thorn that scratched him, to his thought,
    Was hell's teeth at his bones.

His legs seemed bound as in a dream,
    The wet earth held his feet,
He screamed aloud as rabbits scream
    Before the stoat's teeth meet.

A black thing struck him on the brow,
    A blackness loomed and waved;
It was a tree—he caught a bough
    And scrambled up it, saved.

Saved for the moment, as he thought,
    He pressed against the bark:
The hell-hounds missed the thing they sought,
    They quartered in the dark.

They panted underneath the tree,
  They quartered to the call;
The hunter cried: "Yoi doit, go see!"
  His death-horn blew a fall.

Now up, now down, the hell-hounds went
  With soft feet padding wide;
They tried, but could not hit the scent,
  However hard they tried.

Then presently the horn was blown,
  The hounds were called away;
The hoof-beats glittered on the stone
  And trotted on the brae.

          *   *   *

The saint gat strength, but with it came
  A horror of his fear,
Anguish at having failed, and shame,
  And sense of judgment near:

Anguish at having left his charge
  And having failed his trust,
At having flung his sword and targe
  To save his body's dust.

He clambered down the saving tree.
  "I am unclean!" he cried.
"Christ died upon a tree for me,
  I used a tree to hide.

"The hell-hounds bayed about the cross,
  And tore his clothes apart;
But Christ was gold, and I am dross,
  And mud is in my heart."

He stood in anguish in the field;
  A little wind blew by,
The dead leaves dropped, the great stars wheeled
  Their squadrons in the sky.

*   *   *

"Lord, I will try again," he said,
  "Though all hell's devils tear.
This time I will not be afraid,
  And what is sent I'll dare."

He set his face against the slope
  Until he topped the brae;
Courage had healed his fear, and hope
  Had put his shame away.

And then, far-off, a quest-note ran,
  A feathering hound replied:
The hounds still drew the night for man
  Along that countryside.

Then one by one the hell-hounds spoke,
  And still the horn made cheer;
Then the full devil-chorus woke
  To fill the saint with fear.

He knew that they were after him
  To hunt him till he fell;
He turned and fled into the dim,
  And after him came hell.

Over the stony wold he went,
  Through thorns and over quags;
The bloodhounds cried upon the scent,
  They ran like rutting stags.

And when the saint looked round, he saw
  Red eyes intently strained,
The bright teeth in the grinning jaw,
  And running shapes that gained.

Uphill, downhill, with failing breath,
  He ran to save his skin,
Like one who knocked the door of death,
  Yet dared not enter in.

Then water gurgled in the night,
  Dark water lay in front,
The saint saw bubbles running bright;
  The huntsman cheered his hunt.

The saint leaped far into the stream
  And struggled to the shore.
The hunt died like an evil dream,
  A strange land lay before.

He waded to a glittering land,
  With brighter light than ours;
The water ran on silver sand
  By yellow water-flowers.

The fishes nosed the stream to rings
  As petals floated by,
The apples were like orbs of kings
  Against a glow of sky.

On cool and steady stalks of green
  The outland flowers grew.
The ghost-flower, silver like a queen,
  The queen-flower streakt with blue.

The king-flower, crimson on his stalk,
  With frettings in his crown;
The peace-flower, purple, from the chalk,
  The flower that loves the down.

Lilies like thoughts, roses like words,
  In the sweet brain of June;
The bees there, like the stock-dove birds,
  Breathed all the air with croon.

Purple and golden hung the plums;
  Like slaves bowed down with gems
The peach-trees were; sweet-scented gums
  Oozed clammy from their stems.

And birds of every land were there,
  Like flowers that sang and flew;
All beauty that makes singing fair
  That sunny garden knew.

For all together sang with throats
  So tuned, that the intense
Colour and odour pearled the notes
  And passed into the sense.

And as the saint drew near, he heard
  The birds talk, each to each,
The fire-bird to the glory-bird.
  He understood their speech.

One said: "The saint was terrified
  Because the hunters came."
Another said: "The bloodhounds cried,
  And all their eyes were flame."

Another said: "No shame to him,
  For mortal men are blind:
They cannot see beyond the grim
  Into the peace behind."

Another sang: "They cannot know,
  Unless we give the clue,
The power that waits in them below
  The things they are and do."

Another sang: "They never guess
  That deep within them stand
Courage and peace and loveliness,
  Wisdom and skill of hand."

Another sang: "Sing, brothers! come
  Make beauty in the air!
The saint is shamed with martyrdom
  Beyond his strength to bear.

"Sing, brothers! every bird that flies!"
    They stretcht their throats to sing,
With the sweetness known in Paradise
    When the bells of heaven ring.

"Open the doors, good saint!" they cried.
    "Pass deeper to your soul;
There is a spirit in your side
    That hell cannot control.

"Open the doors to let him in,
    That beauty with the sword;
The hounds are silly shapes of sin,
    They shrivel at a word.

"Come, saint!" and as they sang, the air
    Shone with the shapes of flame,
Bird after bright bird glittered there,
    Crying aloud they came.

A rush of brightness and delight,
    White as the snow in drift,
The fire-bird and the glory-bright,
    Most beautiful, most swift.

Sweeping aloft to show the way
    And singing as they flew,
Many and glittering as the spray
    When windy seas are blue.

So cheerily they rushed, so strong
    Their sweep was through the flowers,
The saint was swept into their song
    And gloried in their powers.

He sang, and leaped into the stream,
    And struggled to the shore;
The garden faded like a dream.
    A darkness lay before.

Darkness with glimmery light forlorn
    And quavering hounds in quest,
A huntsman blowing on a horn,
    And lost things not at rest.

He saw the huntsman's hood show black
    Against the greying east;
He heard him hollo to the pack
    And horn them to the feast.

He heard the bloodhounds come to cry
    And settle to the scent;
The black horse made the hoof-casts fly.
    The sparks flashed up the bent.

The saint stood still until they came
    Baying to ring him round:
A horse whose flecking foam was flame,
    And hound on yelling hound.

And jaws that dripped with bitter fire
    Snarled at the saint to tear.
Pilled hell-hounds, balder than the geier,
    Leaped round him everywhere.

St. Withiel let the hell-hounds rave.
    He cried: "Now, in this place,
Climb down, you huntsman of the grave,
    And let me see your face.

"Climb down, you huntsman out of hell
    And show me what you are.
The judge has stricken on the bell,
    Now answer at the bar."

The baying of the hounds fell still,
    Their jaws' salt fire died.
The wind of morning struck in chill
    Along that countryside.

The blackness of the horse was shrunk,
    His sides seemed ribbed and old.
The rider, hooded like a monk,
    Was trembling with the cold.

The rider bowed as though with pain;
    Then clambered down and stood,
The thin thing that the frightened brain
    Had fed with living blood.

"Show me. What are you?" said the saint.
    A hollow murmur spoke.
"This, Lord," it said; a hand moved faint
    And drew aside the cloak.

A Woman Death that palsy shook
    Stood sick and dwindling there;
Her fingers were a bony crook,
    And blood was on her hair.

"Stretch out your hands and sign the Cross,"
    Was all St. Withiel said.
The bloodhounds moaned upon the moss,
    The Woman Death obeyed.

Whimpering with pain, she made the sign.
    "Go, devil-hag," said he,
"Beyond all help of bread and wine,
    Beyond all land and sea,

"Into the ice, into the snow,
    Where Death himself is stark!
Out, with your hounds about you, go,
    And perish in the dark!"

They dwindled as the mist that fades
    At coming of the sun;
Like rags of stuff that fire abrades
    They withered and were done.

The cock, that scares the ghost from earth,
    Crowed as they dwindled down;
The red sun, happy in his girth,
    Strode up above the town.

Sweetly above the sunny wold
    The bells of churches rang;
The sheep-bells clinked within the fold,
    And the larks went up and sang;

Sang for the setting free of men
    From devils that destroyed;
The lark, the robin, and the wren,
    They joyed and over-joyed.

The chats, that harbour in the whin,
    Their little sweet throats swelled,
The blackbird and the thrush joined in,
    The missel-thrush excelled.

Till round the saint the singing made
    A beauty in the air,
An ecstasy that cannot fade
    But is for ever there.

When the great supernatural periodical, Weird Tales, *went out of business, an enormous void opened in American fantasy publishing. But in the 1960s, Robert A. (Doc) Lowndes made a brave effort to recapture the* Weird Tales *spirit with his short-lived* Magazine of Horror. *"Doorslammer" is one of the more evanescent tales to derive from an early issue of MOH, but it has a way of sticking with one when more garish stories have faded from memory.* DONALD A. WOLLHEIM *heads up the science fiction paperback house, DAW Books, and is especially distinguished for having edited what is presumed to be the very first science fiction anthology in U.S. publishing history,* The Pocket Book of Science Fiction *(1943).*

Doorslammer

by Donald A. Wollheim

From somewhere down the darkened hall a door slammed.

I looked up from my papers, looked at Mr. Wilkins questioningly. It was ten-thirty at night and I had supposed we were alone in the office, probably alone in the whole gigantic office building.

"The cleaning woman come back?" I queried. She had been in an hour ago, dusting and mopping and emptying the waste baskets. It was a disturbance and a distraction. We wanted to get the books straightened out and we needed peace and quiet to do it.

Wilkins shook his head. "It was nothing. Let's get on with this."

I frowned, annoyed, went back to my ledgers. I finished four more pages, saw that the work was finished on this book. It wasn't going to be such a long job at that. I'd figured on being at the office until maybe one in the morning. I leaned back, looked up.

Wilkins looked up just then, caught my eye, smiled a bit. I saw he'd probably realized just how close we were to being through.

"I'm done with this one," I said. "Going to stretch my legs a bit." He watched me, said nothing. I got up, walked over to the water cooler at the door, took a drink, looked out into the dark corridor leading towards the editorial offices. I couldn't see what door had slammed. They were all shut, all the little cubbyholes at the far end, the ones with the view of the river from twenty stories up, the best offices reserved for the sensitive souls in Editorial—with the big brains and the lowest salaries.

I walked down the hall towards that end. It was dark and deserted, and there were no lights behind the chilled glass windows of the doors.

It's eerie in an office building after hours, darned eerie. I came back. Wilkins had finished his ledger, was leaning back, lighting a cigarette. "Nobody there," I said. "But somebody slammed a door before. I heard it. And there's no drafts."

He nodded soberly. "I know. I heard it too. Often hear it late at night like this. It's nobody. Only Alice."

"Alice?" I asked. "Thought you said we were alone. Is Alice the cleaning woman's name?"

He shook his head. "No, not Mrs. Flaherty. Just Alice . . . You remember."

I sat down. "Who're you kidding? I don't remember any Alice."

Wilkins looked at me, took his cigarette out of his mouth. "Oh, that's right. You never knew her. You came after her time. Well . . . it's Alice, anyway. Alice Kingsley, I think was her name. Alice C. Kingsley. Mrs."

"So?" I said. "So this Alice is working here tonight. Why doesn't she come in and say hello? One of those stuck-up editors?"

"Alice isn't working here tonight," said Wilkins mildly. "She hasn't been working here for a couple of years. Not here. Not nowhere."

"So who are you talking about?" I asked, beginning to get a little piqued. "First you say Alice, then no—so what Alice is here now?"

"I don't know," he said. "I really don't know for sure. We just think it's Alice. I mean the Kingsley girl. She was a knockout too. A real looker."

For a moment he looked dreamy, as if thinking of some girl he'd maybe had an infatuation for. I could have knocked him on the head. "What are you handing me? Make sense, man. You're a hell of an accountant, sitting there like a goof dreaming of some girl."

He wasn't offended. "Yeah, I guess so. But Alice got us all that way. She was . . . well, you just couldn't look at her without thinking of blue skies and green fields, of Spring mornings and college campuses. She didn't belong in a city office. She was . . . well, she looked like a kid fresh from some rah-rah field."

"Uh huh," I said. "Does your wife know about the way you feel about this chick?"

"Ahh," he shook his head, "you won't believe it, but she wouldn't mind. Alice was that way. She was out of this world—I mean the big-city world. The women didn't seem to object to her. Somehow she just didn't seem to compete. She was in love, you see, and offered no rivalry. She was also nuts."

"Boy, what a picture you're building up. Sweet innocence, a knock-out, lovely, but nuts. Come down to Earth, man." I sat down myself, glanced out at the dark corridor back over my shoulder.

He went on again, this time paying no attention to me, just talking.

"Alice was hired as an assistant editor to the short story department. She was fresh from college, somewhere in the Midwest, and she never lost that look. You don't find it often. She had the blackest hair and the fairest skin, and the brightest, shiniest eyes you ever saw.

"She was like a kid in many ways. Never seemed to have any mind for other folks. She was a door slammer. I remember a big fight she had the first week she was here. Slammed the door going out of Miss Burnside's office and boy, did that queen bee get sore. You know what a touchy old bat the boss' secretary is. You should have heard her give Alice the mouth. And Alice didn't answer back. Just looked at her like a child of twelve would look, sort of wide-eyed and wondering what kind of curious animal this was. Afterwards, Alice only remarked that Miss Burnside must be crazy.

"Fact is, we got to thinking that it wasn't Burnsy that was cracked. Alice just never learned some things. She'd step on people's toes and expect them to pardon her like they'd forgive a pretty brat. It took a while for us to learn. She never stopped slamming doors. Got so we all knew when she was around.

"You should have seen the fellows try to date up Alice. Not one of them got to first base. She just seemed so darned innocent and starry that nothing impressed her. Later, we found out why. She was married, you see. Still loved her husband. He was some fellow she'd met in college, married there.

"We envied him until we found out that one day he'd run off, just skipped out, vanished. That was the day Alice graduated. She came home with her diploma, in that college town to the boarding house they were living in, and he'd gone. Left no notice, just went. Quit.

"Alice went home to her folks—I think they're Des Moines people—threw a wingding, was laid up, left town, came to New York, got a job. Here. She was brilliant, but there was always something . . .

"It's hard to explain to a fellow who never saw her. You'd be amazed at what she could get away with. None of her bosses—the men that is—could get mad at her. She did her work too well for that, yet she never seemed to be present in spirit. I think they were afraid she'd quit if they pressed her too hard to learn some manners. Having her around was a pleasure—just to see that Springlike air. You don't find it around the city, you just don't.

"But there was something else, though. I remember once going down in the elevator with her, and with Joe Simpkins, her boss, the short story editor, you know. She never said goodnight to us, just brushed past and walked off down the street, her brow a little puzzled as if wondering herself what she was doing here away from the green fields. Joe and I walked a block watching her, and then Joe turned to me and said, 'You know, I keep saying to myself that Alice is as nutty as fruit cake. I keep thinking it every once in a while. It sort of bothers me.'

"I knew what he meant, too. Exactly what he meant. Anyway, Alice was with the firm about six months and everybody loved her and everybody knew when you heard a door slam, it was just Alice going somewhere.

"Miss Burnside never forgave her. They had another fight one afternoon and Burnsy gave it to her good. Told her she should wake up and stop acting like a spoiled brat. Burnsy said something else, too. Said she could understand how her husband would walk out on her."

Wilkins stopped, frowned to himself in thought, lit another cigarette. "Alice took it from her without really listening, her usual trick. But the next day it seemed to bother her, because she actually took to closing doors gently. It amazed us all.

"And then one morning, about eleven, the door slammed—violently. Alice was off again, we thought, but we didn't know the whole of it.

"Joe Simpkins told us at lunchtime. He said Alice was very upset. It seems she'd read a manuscript that morning, some short story in the mail unsolicited pile. Something about a guy that fell in love only to find a mirage. Typical college young-love sort of yarn. We saw afterwards who wrote it. Some fellow in California. Last name was Kingsley.

"Alice didn't do much work that afternoon. Just seemed to forget every now and then and sort of visit. She'd drop in on the other readers, sort of stand around vacantly, just sort of dreamy, then breeze out, slamming the door behind her. We were getting real sore after an afternoon of that and Joe swore if she didn't stop it, he'd have to do something. Maybe get rid of her, fire her. Good as she was, he couldn't have people being disrupted.

"He didn't have to fire her though. The door of her own office slammed around four o'clock. When it was half past five and the other girls were leaving, someone looked in and her office was empty and the window open.

"Yeah, it was in the papers. There was quite a funeral, too. She had quite a mob of young fellows there. Nobody ever suspected them, but I think they couldn't help themselves. She was a sort of dream, a dream of sun and fleecy white clouds such as you somehow don't get with city girls. I didn't go myself. They kept the coffin closed.

"Anyway, that was two years ago. Alice made an impression on people that lasted. Nobody that knew her can ever quite get over her. And maybe things feel the same way. We got door trouble in this office, late at night or on quiet afternoons. Nobody pays any attention to it any more."

I looked at him, thinking to myself that he was really going in the deep end. You wouldn't believe he could be such a matter-of-fact, adding and subtracting machine accountant. There was something in his eyes, something perplexed, lit up and yet maybe a little pained.

"Well, enough of this. Let's get this work cleaned up. I want to get home tonight." Wilkins shoved another ledger at me, opened up the other remaining one, and we bent over our tasks again.

Somewhere down the hall a door slammed. I looked up, caught Wilkins' eye. He shrugged.

"It's nothing. Just Alice."

Music is often associated with mystical powers, and there is even a sublitera-
ture of the fantastic that deals with the supposedly demonic characteristics
of the violin. E. T. Hoffmann's The Cremona Violin, *Hugh Conway's* Secret
of the Stradivarius *each may have been influenced by the old anecdote about*
Tartini dreaming that the devil played a solo of such haunting beauty
that when the composer awoke he had to set it down. (The result was
his devilishly difficult violin sonata known as "The Devil's Trill.") "The Ensouled Violin" *is an especially powerful variation on the theme, depending*
partially for its effect on the inclusion of the historic figure, Paganini, as well
as references to the famous Hoffmann tale that preceded it. The author,
HELENA PETROVNA BLAVATSKY, *born in Russia in 1831, was a colorful*
figure in occult circles and a person subject to lifelong nightmares. The ensu-
ing tale reputedly stemmed from one of her bad dreams.

The Ensouled Violin

by Madame Blavatsky

1

In the year 1828, an old German, a music teacher, came to Paris with
his pupil and settled unostentatiously in one of the quiet *faubourgs* of
the metropolis. The first rejoiced in the name of Samuel Klaus; the second answered to the more poetical appellation of Franz Stenio. The
younger man was a violinist, gifted, as rumour went, with extraordinary,
almost miraculous talent. Yet as he was poor and had not hitherto
made a name for himself in Europe, he remained for several years in
the capital of France—the heart and pulse of capricious continental
fashion—unknown and unappreciated. Franz was a Styrian by birth,
and, at the time of the event to be presently described, he was a young
man considerably under thirty. A philosopher and a dreamer by nature,
imbued with all the mystic oddities of true genius, he reminded one of
some of the heroes in Hoffmann's *Contes Fantastiques.* His earlier existence had been a very unusual, in fact, quite an eccentric one, and its
history must be briefly told—for the better understanding of the present
story.

Born of very pious country people, in a quiet burg among the Styrian
Alps; nursed "by the native gnomes who watched over his cradle";
growing up in the weird atmosphere of the ghouls and vampires who

play such a prominent part in the household of every Styrian and Slavonian in Southern Austria; educated later, as a student, in the shadow of the old Rhenish castles of Germany; Franz from his childhood had passed though every emotional stage on the plane of the so-called "supernatural." He had also studied at one time the "occult arts" with an enthusiastic disciple of Paracelsus and Kunrath; alchemy had few theoretical secrets for him; and he had dabbled in "ceremonial magic" and "sorcery" with some Hungarian Tziganes. Yet he loved above all else music, and above music—his violin.

At the age of twenty-two he suddenly gave up his practical studies in the occult, and from that day, though as devoted as ever in thought to the beautiful Grecian Gods, he surrendered himself entirely to his art. Of his classic studies he had retained only that which related to the muses—Euterpe especially, at whose altar he worshipped—and Orpheus whose magic lyre he tried to emulate with his violin. Except his dreamy belief in the nymphs and the sirens, on account probably of the double relationship of the latter to the muses through Calliope and Orpheus, he was interested but little in the matters of this sublunary world. All his aspirations mounted, like incense, with the wave of the heavenly harmony that he drew from his instrument, to a higher and a nobler sphere. He dreamed awake, and lived a real though an enchanted life only during those hours when his magic bow carried him along the wave of sound to the Pagan Olympus, to the feet of Euterpe. A strange child he had ever been in his own home, where tales of magic and witchcraft grow out of every inch of the soil; a still stranger boy he had become, until finally he had blossomed into manhood, without one single characteristic of youth. Never had a fair face attracted his attention; not for one moment had his thoughts turned from his solitary studies to a life beyond that of a mystic Bohemian. Content with his own company, he had thus passed the best years of his youth and manhood with his violin for his chief idol, and with the Gods and Goddesses of old Greece for his audience, in perfect ignorance of practical life. His whole existence had been one long day of dreams, of melody and sunlight, and he had never felt any other aspirations.

How useless, but oh, how glorious those dreams! how vivid! and why should he desire any better fate? Was he not all that he wanted to be, transformed in a second of thought into one or another hero; from Orpheus, who held all nature breathless, to the urchin who piped away under the plane tree to the naiads of Calirrhoë's crystal fountain? Did not the swift-footed nymphs frolic at his beck and call to the sound of the magic flute of the Arcadian shepherd—who was himself? Behold, the Goddess of Love and Beauty herself descending from on high, attracted by the sweet-voiced notes of his violin! . . . Yet there came a time when he preferred Syrinx to Aphrodite—not as the fair nymph pursued by Pan, but after her transformation by the merciful Gods into the reed out of which the frustrated God of the Shepherds had made his magic pipe. For also, with time, ambition grows and is rarely satisfied. When he tried to emulate on his violin the enchanting sounds that resounded in his mind, the whole of Parnassus kept silent under the spell, or joined in heavenly chorus; but the audience he finally craved was composed of more than the Gods sung by Hesiod, verily of the most appreciative *mélomanes* of European capitals. He felt jealous of the magic pipe, and would fain have had it at his command.

"Oh! that I could allure a nymph into my beloved violin!" he often cried, after awakening from one of his daydreams. "Oh, that I could only span in spirit flight the abyss of Time! Oh, that I could find myself for one short day a partaker of the secret arts of the Gods, a God myself, in the sight and hearing of enraptured humanity; and, having learned the mystery of the lyre of Orpheus, or secured within my violin a siren, thereby benefit mortals to my own glory!"

Thus, having for long years dreamed in the company of the Gods of his fancy, he now took to dreaming of the transitory glories of fame upon this earth. But at this time he was suddenly called home by his widowed mother from one of the German universities where he had lived for the last year or two. This was an event which brought his plans to an end, at least so far as the immediate future was concerned, for he had hitherto drawn upon her alone for his meagre pittance, and his means were not sufficient for an independent life outside his native place.

His return had a very unexpected result. His mother, whose only love he was on earth, died soon after she had welcomed her Benjamin back; and the good wives of the burg exercised their swift tongues for many a month after as to the real causes of that death.

Frau Stenio, before Franz's return, was a healthy, buxom, middle-aged body, strong and hearty. She was a pious and a God-fearing soul too, who had never failed in saying her prayers, nor had missed an early mass for years during his absence. On the first Sunday after her son had settled at home—a day that she had been longing for and had antici-pated for months in joyous visions, in which she saw him kneeling by her side in the little church on the hill—she called him from the foot of the stairs. The hour had come when her pious dream was to be realized, and she was waiting for him, carefully wiping the dust from the prayer-book he had used in his boyhood. But instead of Franz, it was his violin that responded to her call, mixing its sonorous voice with the other cracked tones of the peal of the merry Sunday bells. The fond mother was somewhat shocked at hearing the prayer-inspiring sounds drowned by the weird, fantastic notes of the "Dance of the Witches"; they seemed to her so unearthly and mocking. But she almost fainted upon hearing the definite refusal of her well-beloved son to go to church. He never went to church, he coolly remarked. It was a loss of time; besides which, the loud peals of the old church organ jarred on his nerves. Nothing should induce him to submit to the torture of listening to that cracked organ. He was firm, and nothing could move him. To her supplications and remonstrances he put an end by offering to play for her a "Hymn to the Sun" he had just composed.

From that memorable Sunday morning, Frau Stenio lost her usual serenity of mind. She hastened to lay her sorrows and seek for consolation at the foot of the confessional; but that which she heard in response from the stern priest filled her gentle and unsophisticated soul with dismay and almost with despair. A feeling of fear, a sense of profound terror, which soon became a chronic state with her, pursued her from that moment; her nights became disturbed and sleepless, her days passed in prayer and lamentations. In her maternal anxiety for the salvation of her beloved son's soul, and for his *post mortem* welfare, she made a series of rash vows. Finding that neither the Latin petition to the Mother of God written for her by her spiritual adviser, nor yet the humble supplications in German, addressed by herself to every saint she had reason to believe was residing in Paradise, worked the desired effect, she took to pilgrimages to distant shrines. During one of these journeys to a holy chapel situated high up in the mountains, she caught cold, amidst the glaciers of the Tyrol, and redescended only to take to a sick bed, from which she arose no more. Frau Stenio's vow had led her, in one sense, to the desired result. The poor woman was now given an opportunity of seeking out in *propria persona* the saints she had believed in so well, and of pleading face to face for the recreant son, who refused adherence to them and to the Church, scoffed at monk and confessional, and held the organ in such horror.

Franz sincerely lamented his mother's death. Unaware of being the indirect cause of it, he felt no remorse; but selling the modest household goods and chattels, light in purse and heart, he resolved to travel on foot for a year or two, before settling down to any definite profession.

A hazy desire to see the great cities of Europe, and to try his luck in France, lurked at the bottom of this travelling project, but his Bohemian habits of life were too strong to be abruptly abandoned. He placed his small capital with a banker for a rainy day, and started on his pedestrian journey via Germany and Austria. His violin paid for his board and lodging in the inns and farms on his way, and he passed his days in the green fields and in the solemn silent woods, face to face with Nature, dreaming all the time as usual with his eyes open. During the three months of his pleasant travels to and fro, he never descended for one moment from Parnassus; but, as an alchemist transmutes lead into gold, so he transformed everything on his way into a song of Hesiod or Anacreon. Every evening, while fiddling for his supper and bed, whether on a green lawn or in the hall of a rustic inn, his fancy changed the whole scene for him. Village swains and maidens became transfigured into Arcadian shepherds and nymphs. The sand-covered floor was now a green sward; the uncouth couples spinning round in a measured waltz with the wild grace of tamed bears became priests and priestesses of Terpsichore; the bulky, cherry-cheeked and blue-eyed daughters of rural Germany were the Hesperides circling around the trees laden with the golden apples. Nor did the melodious strains of the Arcadian demigods piping on their syrinxes, and audible but to his own enchanted ear, vanish with the dawn. For no sooner was the curtain of sleep raised from his eyes than he would sally forth into a new magic realm of daydreams. On his way to some dark and solemn pine-forest, he played incessantly, to himself and to everything else. He fiddled to the green hill, and forthwith the mountain and the moss-covered rocks moved forward to hear him the better, as they had done at the sound of the Orphean lyre. He fiddled to the merry-voiced brook, to the hurrying river, and both slackened their speed and stopped their waves, and, becoming silent, seemed to listen to him in an entranced rapture. Even the long-legged stork who stood meditatively on one leg on the thatched top of the rustic mill, gravely resolving unto himself the problem of his too-long existence, sent out after him a long and strident cry, screeching, "art thou Orpheus himself, O Stenio?"

It was a period of full bliss, of a daily and almost hourly exaltation. The last words of his dying mother, whispering to him of the horrors of eternal condemnation, had left him unaffected, and the only vision her warning evoked in him was that of Pluto. By a ready association of ideas, he saw the lord of the dark nether kingdom greeting him as he had greeted the husband of Eurydice before him. Charmed with the magic sounds of his violin, the wheel of Ixion was at a standstill once more, thus affording relief to the wretched seducer of Juno, and giving the lie to those who claim eternity for the duration of the punishment of condemned sinners. He perceived Tantalus forgetting his never-ceasing thirst, and smacking his lips as he drank in the heaven-born melody; the stone of Sisyphus becoming motionless, the Furies themselves smiling on him, and the sovereign of the gloomy regions delighted, and awarding preference to his violin over the lyre of Orpheus. Taken *au sérieux,* mythology thus seems a decided antidote to fear, in the face of theological threats, especially when strengthened with an insane and passionate love of music; with Franz, Euterpe proved always victorious in every contest, aye, even with Hell itself!

But there is an end to everything, and very soon Franz had to give up uninterrupted dreaming. He had reached the university town where dwelt his old violin teacher, Samuel Klaus. When this antiquated musician found that his beloved and favourite pupil, Franz, had been left poor in purse and still poorer in earthly affections, he felt his strong attachment to the boy awaken with tenfold force. He took Franz to his heart, and forthwith adopted him as his son.

The old teacher reminded people of one of those grotesque figures which look as if they had just stepped out of some medieval panel. And yet Klaus, with his fantastic *allures* of a night goblin, had the most loving heart, as tender as that of a woman, and the self-sacrificing nature of an old Christian martyr. When Franz had briefly narrated to him the history of his last few years, the professor took him by the hand, and leading him into his study simply said:

"Stop with me, and put an end to your Bohemian life. Make yourself famous. I am old and childless and will be your father. Let us live together and forget all save fame."

And forthwith he offered to proceed with Franz to Paris, *via* several large German cities, where they would stop to give concerts.

In a few days Klaus succeeded in making Franz forget his vagrant life and its artistic independence, and reawakened in his pupil his now dormant ambition and desire for worldly fame. Hitherto, since his mother's death, he had been content to receive applause only from the Gods and Goddesses who inhabited his vivid fancy; now he began to crave once more for the admiration of mortals. Under the clever and careful training of old Klaus his remarkable talent gained in strength and powerful charm with every day, and his reputation grew and expanded with every city and town wherein he made himself heard. His ambition was being rapidly realized; the presiding genii of various musical centres to whose patronage his talent was submitted soon proclaimed him *the one* violinist of the day, and the public declared loudly that he stood unrivalled by any one whom they had ever heard. These laudations very soon made both master and pupil completely lose their heads.

But Paris was less ready with such appreciation. Paris makes reputations for itself, and will take none on faith. They had been living in it for almost three years, and were still climbing with difficulty the artist's Calvary, when an event occurred which put an end even to their most modest expectations. The first arrival of Niccolo Paganini was suddenly heralded, and threw Lutetia into a convulsion of expectation. The unparalleled artist arrived, and—all Paris fell at once at his feet.

2

Now it is a well-known fact that a superstition born in the dark days of medieval superstition, and surviving almost to the middle of the present century, attributed all such abnormal, out-of-the-way talent as that of Paganini to "supernatural" agency. Every great and marvellous artist had been accused in his day of dealings with the devil. A few instances will suffice to refresh the reader's memory.

Tartini, the great composer and violinist of the XVIIth century, was denounced as one who got his best inspirations from the Evil One, with whom he was, it was said, in regular league. This accusation was, of course, due to the almost magical impression he produced upon his audiences. His inspired performance on the violin secured for him in his native country the title of "Master of Nations." The *Sonate du Diable,* also called "Tartini's Dream"—as everyone who has heard it will be ready to testify—is the most weird melody ever heard or invented: hence, the marvellous composition has become the source of endless legends. Nor were they entirely baseless, since it was he, himself, who was shown to have originated them. Tartini confessed to having written it on awakening from a dream, in which he had heard his sonata performed by Satan, for his benefit, and in consequence of a bargain made with his infernal majesty.

Several famous singers, even, whose exceptional voices struck the hearers with superstitious admiration, have not escaped a like accusation. Pasta's splendid voice was attributed in her day to the fact that, three months before her birth, the diva's mother was carried during a trance to heaven, and there treated to a vocal concert of seraphs. Malibran was indebted for her voice to St. Cecelia, while others said she owed it to a demon who watched over her cradle and sung the baby to sleep. Finally, Paganini—the unrivalled performer, the mean Italian, who like Dryden's Jubal striking on the "chorded shell" forced the throngs that followed him to worship the divine sounds produced, and made people say that "less than a God could not dwell within the hollow of his violin"—Paganini left a legend too.

The almost supernatural art of the greatest violin player that the world has ever known was often speculated upon, never understood. The effect produced by him on his audience was literally marvellous, overpowering. The great Rossini is said to have wept like a sentimental German maiden on hearing him play for the first time. The Princess Elisa of Lucca, a sister of the great Napoleon, in whose service Paganini was, as director of her private orchestra, for a long time was unable to hear him play without fainting. In women he produced nervous fits and hysterics at his will; stout-hearted men he drove to frenzy. He changed cowards into heroes and made the bravest soldiers feel like so many nervous schoolgirls. Is it to be wondered at, then, that hundreds of weird tales circulated for long years about and around the mysterious Genoese, that modern Orpheus of Europe. One of these was especially ghastly. It was rumoured, and was believed by more people than would probably like to confess it, that the strings of his violin were made of *human intestines, according to all the rules and requirements of the Black Art.*

Exaggerated as this idea may seem to some, it has nothing impossible in it; and it is more than probable that it was this legend that led to the extraordinary events which we are about to narrate. Human organs are often used by the Eastern Black Magician, so-called, and it is an averred fact that some Bengâlî Tântrikas (reciters of *tantras,* or "invocations to the demon," as a reverend writer has described them) use human corpses, and certain internal and external organs pertaining to them, as powerful magical agents for bad purposes.

However this may be, now that the magnetic and mesmeric potencies of hypnotism are recognized as facts by most physicians, it may be suggested with less danger than heretofore that the extraordinary effects of Paganini's violin-playing were not, perhaps, entirely due to his talent and genius. The wonder and awe he so easily excited were as much caused by his external appearance, "which had something weird and demoniacal in it," according to certain of his biographers, as by the inexpressible charm of his execution and his remarkable mechanical skill. The latter is demonstrated by his perfect imitation of the flageolet, and his performance of long and magnificent melodies on the G string alone. In this performance, which many an artist has tried to copy without success, he remains unrivalled to this day.

It is owing to this remarkable appearance of his—termed by his friends eccentric, and by his too nervous victims, diabolical—that he experienced great difficulties in refuting certain ugly rumours. These were credited far more easily in his day than they would be now. It was whispered throughout Italy, and even in his own native town, that Paganini had murdered his wife and, later on, a mistress, both of whom he had loved passionately, and both of whom he had not hesitated to sacrifice to his fiendish ambition. He had made himself proficient in magic arts, it was asserted, and had succeeded thereby in imprisoning the souls of his two victims in his violin—his famous Cremona.

It is maintained by the immediate friends of Ernst T. W. Hoffmann, the celebrated author of *Die Elixire des Teufels, Meister Martin,* and other charming and mystical tales, that Councillor Crespel, in the *Violin of Cremona,* was taken from the legend about Paganini. It is, as all who have read it know, the history of a celebrated violin, into which the voice and the soul of a famous diva, a woman whom Crespel had loved and killed, had passed, and to which was added the voice of his beloved daughter, Antonia.

Nor was this superstition utterly ungrounded, nor was Hoffmann to be blamed for adopting it, after he had heard Paganini's playing. The extraordinary facility with which the artist drew out of his instrument, not only the most unearthly sounds, but positively human voices, justified the suspicion. Such effects might well have startled an audience and thrown terror into many a nervous heart. Add to this the impenetrable mystery connected with a certain period of Paganini's youth, and the most wild tales about him must be found in a measure justifiable, and even excusable; especially among a nation whose ancestors knew the Borgias and the Medicis of Black Art fame.

3

In those pretelegraphic days, newspapers were limited, and the wings of fame had a heavier flight than they have now.

Franz had hardly heard of Paganini; and when he did, he swore he would rival, if not eclipse, the Genoese magician. Yes, he would either become the most famous of all living violinists, or he would break his instrument an ' ¬ut an end to his life at the same time.

Old Klaus rejoiced at such a determination. He rubbed his hands in glee, and jumping about on his lame leg like a crippled satyr, he flattered and incensed his pupil, believing himself all the while to be performing a sacred duty to the holy and majestic cause of art.

Upon first setting foot in Paris, three years before, Franz had all but failed. Musical critics pronounced him a rising star, but had all agreed that he required a few more years' practice, before he could hope to carry his audiences by storm. Therefore, after a desperate study of over two years and uninterrupted preparations, the Styrian artist had finally made himself ready for his first serious appearance in the great Opera House where a public concert before the most exacting critics of the old world was to be held; at this critical moment Paganini's arrival in the European metropolis placed an obstacle in the way of the realization of his hopes, and the old German professor wisely postponed his pupil's *début*. At first he had simply smiled at the wild enthusiasm, the laudatory hymns sung about the Genoese violinist, and the almost superstitious awe with which his name was pronounced. But very soon Paganini's name became a burning iron in the hearts of both the artists, and a threatening phantom in the mind of Klaus. A few days more, and they shuddered at the very mention of their great rival, whose success became with every night more unprecedented.

The first series of concerts was over, but neither Klaus nor Franz had as yet had an opportunity of hearing him and of judging for themselves. So great and so beyond their means was the charge for admission, and so small the hope of getting a free pass from a brother artist justly regarded as the meanest of men in monetary transactions, that they had to wait for a chance, as did so many others. But the day came when neither master nor pupil could control their impatience any longer; so they pawned their watches, and with the proceeds bought two modest seats.

Who can describe the enthusiasm, the triumphs, of this famous, and at the same time fatal night! The audience was frantic; men wept and women screamed and fainted, while both Klaus and Stenio sat looking paler than two ghosts. At the first touch of Paganini's magic bow, both Franz and Samuel felt as if the icy hand of death had touched them. Carried away by an irresistible enthusiasm, which turned into a violent, unearthly mental torture, they dared neither look into each other's faces, nor exchange one word during the whole performance.

At midnight, while the chosen delegates of the Musical Societies and the Conservatory of Paris unhitched the horses, and dragged the carriage of the grand artist home in triumph, the two Germans returned to their modest lodging, and it was a pitiful sight to see them. Mournful and desperate, they placed themselves in their usual seats at the fire-corner, and neither for a while opened his mouth.

"Samuel!" at last exclaimed Franz, pale as death itself. "Samuel—it remains for us now but to die! . . . Do you hear me? . . . We are worthless! We were two madmen to have ever hoped that anyone in this world would ever rival . . . him!"

The name of Paganini stuck in his throat, as in utter despair he fell into his armchair.

The old professor's wrinkles suddenly became purple. His little greenish eyes gleamed phosphorescently as, bending towards his pupil, he whispered to him in hoarse and broken tones:

"*Nein, nein!* Thou art wrong, my Franz! I have taught thee, and thou hast learned all of the great art that a simple mortal, and a Christian by baptism, can learn from another simple mortal. Am I to blame because these accursed Italians, in order to reign unequalled in the domain of art, have recourse to Satan and the diabolical effects of Black Magic?"

Franz turned his eyes upon his old master. There was a sinister light burning in those glittering orbs; a light telling plainly, that, to secure such a power, he, too, would not scruple to sell himself, body and soul, to the Evil One.

But he said not a word, and, turning his eyes from his old master's face, gazed dreamily at the dying embers.

The same long-forgotten incoherent dreams, which, after seeming such realities to him in his younger days, had been given up entirely, and had gradually faded from his mind, now crowded back into it with the same force and vividness as of old. The grimacing shades of Ixion, Sisyphus and Tantalus resurrected and stood before him, saying:

"What matters hell—in which thou believest not. And even if hell there be, it is the hell described by the old Greeks, not that of the modern bigots—a locality full of conscious shadows, to whom thou canst be a second Orpheus."

Franz felt that he was going mad, and, turning instinctively, he

looked his old master once more right in the face. Then his bloodshot
eye evaded the gaze of Klaus.

Whether Samuel understood the terrible state of mind of his pupil, or
whether he wanted to draw him out, to make him speak, and thus to divert his thoughts, must remain as hypothetical to the reader as it is to
the writer. Whatever may have been in his mind, the German enthusiast
went on, speaking with a feigned calmness:

"Franz, my dear boy, I tell you that the art of the accursed Italian is
not natural; that it is due neither to study nor to genius. It never was
acquired in the usual, natural way. You need not stare at me in that
wild manner, for what I say is in the mouth of millions of people. Listen
to what I now tell you, and try to understand. You have heard the
strange tale whispered about the famous Tartini? He died one fine Sabbath night, strangled by his familiar demon, who had taught him how to
endow his violin with a human voice, by shutting up in it, by means of
incantations, the soul of a young virgin. Paganini did more. In order to
endow his instrument with the faculty of emitting human sounds, such
as sobs, despairing cries, supplications, moans of love and fury—in
short, the most heart-rending notes of the human voice—Paganini became the murderer not only of his wife and his mistress, but also of a
friend, who was more tenderly attached to him than any other being on
this earth. He then made the four chords of his magic violin out of the
intestines of his last victim. This is the secret of his enchanting talent, of
that overpowering melody, that combination of sounds, which you will
never be able to master unless . . ."

The old man could not finish the sentence. He staggered back before
the fiendish look of his pupil, and covered his face with his hands.

Franz was breathing heavily, and his eyes had an expression which
reminded Klaus of those of a hyena. His pallor was cadaverous. For
some time he could not speak, but only gasped for breath. At last he
slowly muttered:

"Are you in earnest?"

"I am, as I hope to help you."

"And . . . and do you really believe that had I only the means of obtaining human intestines for strings, I could rival Paganini?" asked
Franz, after a moment's pause, and casting down his eyes.

The old German unveiled his face, and, with a strange look of determination upon it, softly answered:

"Human intestines alone are not sufficient for our purpose; they must
have belonged to someone who had loved us well, with an unselfish,

holy love. Tartini endowed his violin with the life of a virgin; but that virgin had died of unrequited love for him. The fiendish artist had prepared beforehand a tube, in which he managed to catch her last breath as she expired, pronouncing his beloved name, and he then transferred this breath to his violin. As to Paganini, I have just told you his tale. It was with the consent of his victim, though, that he murdered him to get possession of his intestines.

"Oh, for the power of the human voice!" Samuel went on, after a brief pause. "What can equal the eloquence, the magic spell of the human voice? Do you think, my poor boy, I would not have taught you this great, this final secret, were it not that it throws one right into the clutches of him . . . who must remain unnamed at night?" he added, with a sudden return to the superstitions of his youth.

Franz did not answer; but with a calmness awful to behold, he left his place, took down the violin from the wall where it was hanging, and, with one powerful grasp of the chords, he tore them out and flung them into the fire.

Samuel suppressed a cry of horror. The chords were hissing upon the coals, where, among the blazing logs, they wriggled and curled like so many living snakes.

"By the witches of Thessaly and the dark arts of Circe!" he exclaimed, with foaming mouth and his eyes burning like coals; "by the Furies of Hell and Pluto himself, I now swear, in thy presence, O Samuel, my master, never to touch a violin again until I can string it with four human chords. May I be accursed for ever and ever if I do!" He fell senseless on the floor, with a deep sob, that ended like a funeral wail; old Samuel lifted him up as he would have lifted a child, and carried him to his bed. Then he sallied forth in search of a physician.

4

For several days after this painful scene Franz was very ill, ill almost beyond recovery. The physician declared him to be suffering from brain fever and said that the worst was to be feared. For nine long days the patient remained delirious; and Klaus, who was nursing him night and day with the solicitude of the tenderest mother, was horrified at the work of his own hands. For the first time since their acquaintance began, the old teacher, owing to the wild ravings of his pupil, was able to penetrate into the darkest corners of that weird, superstitious, cold, and, at the same time, passionate nature; and—he trembled at what he discovered. For he saw that which he had failed to perceive before— Franz as he was in reality, and not as he seemed to superficial observers. Music was the life of the young man, and adulation was the air he breathed, without which that life became a burden; from the chords of his violin alone, Stenio drew his life and being, but the applause of men and even of Gods was necessary to its support. He saw unveiled before his eyes a genuine, artistic, *earthly* soul, with its divine counterpart totally absent, a son of the Muses, all fancy and brain poetry, but without a heart. While listening to the ravings of that delirious and unhinged fancy, Klaus felt as if he were for the first time in his long life exploring a marvellous and untravelled region, a human nature not of this world but of some incomplete planet. He saw all this, and shuddered. More than once he asked himself whether it would not be doing a kindness to his "boy" to let him die before he returned to consciousness.

But he loved his pupil too well to dwell for long on such an idea. Franz had bewitched his truly artistic nature, and now old Klaus felt as though their two lives were inseparably linked together. That he could thus feel was a revelation to the old man; so he decided to save Franz, even at the expense of his own old and, as he thought, useless life.

The seventh day of the illness brought on a most terrible crisis. For twenty-four hours the patient never closed his eyes, nor remained for a moment silent; he raved continuously during the whole time. His visions were peculiar, and he minutely described each. Fantastic, ghastly figures kept slowly swimming out of the penumbra of his small, dark room, in regular and uninterrupted procession, and he greeted each by name as he might greet old acquaintances. He referred to himself as Prometheus, bound to the rock by four bands made of human intestines. At the foot of the Caucasian Mount the black waters of the river Styx were running. . . . They had deserted Arcadia, and were now endeavouring to encircle within a sevenfold embrace the rock upon which he was suffering. . . .

"Wouldst thou know the name of the Promethean rock, old man?" he roared into his adopted father's ear. . . . "Listen then . . . its name is . . . called . . . Samuel Klaus. . . ."

"Yes, yes! . . ." the German murmured disconsolately. "It is I who killed him, while seeking to console. The news of Paganini's magic arts struck his fancy too vividly . . . Oh, my poor, poor boy!"

"Ha, ha, ha, ha!" The patient broke into a loud and discordant laugh. "Aye, poor old man, sayest thou? . . . So, so, thou art of poor stuff, anyhow, and wouldst look well only when stretched upon a fine Cremona violin! . . ."

Klaus shuddered, but said nothing. He only bent over the poor maniac, and with a kiss upon his brow, a caress as tender and as gentle as that of a doting mother, he left the sick-room for a few instants, to seek relief in his own garret. When he returned, the ravings were following another channel. Franz was singing, trying to imitate the sounds of a violin.

Towards the evening of that day, the delirium of the sick man became perfectly ghastly. He saw spirits of fire clutching at his violin. Their skeleton hands, from each finger of which grew a flaming claw, beckoned to old Samuel . . . They approached and surrounded the old master, and were preparing to rip him open . . . him, "the only man on this earth who loves me with an unselfish, holy love, and . . . whose intestines can be of any good at all!" he went on whispering, with glaring eyes and demon laugh. . . .

By the next morning, however, the fever had disappeared, and by the end of the ninth day Stenio had left his bed, having no recollection of his illness, and no suspicion that he had allowed Klaus to read his inner thought. Nay; had he himself any knowledge that such a horrible idea as the sacrifice of his old master to his ambition had ever entered his mind? Hardly. The only immediate result of his fatal illness was, that as, by reason of his vow, his artistic passion could find no issue, another passion awoke, which might avail to feed his ambition and his insatiable fancy. He plunged headlong into the study of the Occult Arts, of Alchemy and of Magic. In the practice of Magic the young dreamer sought to stifle the voice of his passionate longing for his, as he thought, forever lost violin. . . .

Weeks and months passed away, and the conversation about Paganini was never resumed between the master and the pupil. But a profound melancholy had taken possession of Franz, the two hardly exchanged a word, the violin hung mute, chordless, full of dust, in its habitual place. It was as the presence of a soulless corpse between them.

The young man had become gloomy and sarcastic, even avoiding the mention of music. Once, as his old professor, after long hesitation, took out his own violin from its dust-covered case and prepared to play, Franz gave a convulsive shudder, but said nothing. At the first notes of the bow, however, he glared like a madman, and rushing out of the house, remained for hours, wandering in the streets. Then old Samuel in his turn threw his instrument down, and locked himself up in his room till the following morning.

One night as Franz sat, looking particularly pale and gloomy, old Samuel suddenly jumped from his seat, and after hopping about the room in a magpie fashion, approached his pupil, imprinted a fond kiss upon the young man's brow, and squeaked at the top of his shrill voice: "Is it not time to put an end to all this? . . ."

Whereupon, starting from his usual lethargy, Franz echoed, as in a dream:

"Yes, it is time to put an end to this."

Upon which the two separated, and went to bed.

On the following morning, when Franz awoke, he was astonished not to see his old teacher in his usual place to greet him. But he had greatly altered during the last few months, and he at first paid no attention to his absence, unusual as it was. He dressed and went into the adjoining room, a little parlour where they had their meals, and which separated their two bedrooms. The fire had not been lighted since the embers had died out on the previous night, and no sign was anywhere visible of the professor's busy hand in his usual housekeeping duties. Greatly puzzled, but in no way dismayed, Franz took his usual place at the corner of the now cold fireplace, and fell into an aimless reverie. As he stretched himself in his old armchair, raising both his hands to clasp them behind his head in a favourite posture of his, his hand came into contact with something on a shelf at his back; he knocked against a case, and brought it violently to the ground.

It was old Klaus's violin-case that came down to the floor with such a sudden crash that the case opened and the violin fell out of it, rolling to the feet of Franz. And then the chords, striking against the brass fender emitted a sound, prolonged, sad and mournful as the sigh of an unrestful soul; it seemed to fill the whole room, and reverberated in the head and the very heart of the young man. The effect of that broken violin-string was magical.

"Samuel!" cried Stenio, with his eyes starting from their sockets, and an unknown terror suddenly taking possession of his whole being. "Samuel! what has happened? . . . My good, my dear old master!" he called out, hastening to the professor's little room, and throwing the door violently open. No one answered, all was silent within.

He staggered back, frightened at the sound of his own voice, so changed and hoarse it seemed to him at this moment. No reply came in response to his call. Naught followed but a dead silence . . . that stillness which, in the domain of sounds, usually denotes death. In the presence of a corpse, as in the lugubrious stillness of a tomb, such silence acquires a mysterious power, which strikes the sensitive soul with a nameless terror. . . . The little room was dark, and Franz hastened to open the shutters.

Samuel was lying on his bed, cold, stiff, and lifeless. . . . At the sight of the corpse of him who had loved him so well, and had been to him more than a father, Franz experienced a dreadful revulsion of feeling, a terrible shock. But the ambition of the fanatical artist got the better of the despair of the man, and smothered the feelings of the latter in a few seconds.

A note bearing his own name was conspicuously placed upon a table near the corpse. With trembling hand, the violinist tore open the envelope, and read the following:

My beloved son, Franz,

When you read this, I shall have made the greatest sacrifice, that your best and only friend and teacher could have accomplished for your fame. He, who loved you most, is now but an inanimate lump of clay. Of your old teacher there now remains but a clod of cold organic matter. I need not prompt you as to what you have to do with it. Fear not stupid prejudices. It is for your future fame that I have made an offering of my body, and you would be guilty of the blackest ingratitude were you now to render useless this sacrifice. When you shall have replaced the chords upon your violin, and these chords a portion of my own self, under your touch it will acquire the power of that accursed sorcerer, all the magic voices of Paganini's instrument. You will find therein my voice, my sighs and groans, my song of welcome, the prayerful sobs of my infinite and sorrowful sympathy, my love for you. And now, my Franz, fear nobody! Take your instrument with you, and dog the steps of him who filled our lives with bitterness and despair! . . . Appear in every arena, where, hitherto, he has reigned without a rival, and bravely throw the gauntlet of defiance in his face. O Franz! then only wilt thou hear with what a magic power the full notes of unselfish love will issue forth from thy violin. Perchance, with a last caressing touch of its chords, thou wilt remember that they once formed a portion of thine old teacher, who now embraces and blesses thee for the last time.
Samuel

Two burning tears sparkled in the eyes of Franz, but they dried up instantly. Under the fiery rush of passionate hope and pride, the two orbs of the future magician-artist, riveted to the ghastly face of the dead man, shone like the eyes of a demon.

Our pen refuses to describe that which took place on that day, after the legal inquiry was over. As another note, written with the view of satisfying the authorities, had been prudently provided by the loving care of the old teacher, the verdict was, "Suicide from causes unknown"; after this the coroner and the police retired, leaving the bereaved heir alone in the deathroom, with the remains of that which had once been a living man.

Scarcely a fortnight had elapsed from that day, ere the violin had been dusted, and four new, stout strings had been stretched upon it. Franz dared not look at them. He tried to play, but the bow trembled in his hand like a dagger in the grasp of a novice-brigand. He then determined not to try again, until the portentous night should arrive, when he should have a chance of rivalling, nay, of surpassing, Paganini.

The famous violinist had meanwhile left Paris, and was giving a series of triumphant concerts at an old Flemish town in Belgium.

5

One night, as Paganini, surrounded by a crowd of admirers, was sitting in the dining-room of the hotel at which he was staying, a visiting card, with a few words written on it in pencil, was handed to him by a young man with wild and staring eyes.

Fixing upon the intruder a look which few persons could bear, but receiving back a glance as calm and determined as his own, Paganini slightly bowed, and then dryly said:

"Sir, it shall be as you desire. Name the night. I am at your service."

On the following morning the whole town was startled by the appearance of bills posted at the corner of every street, and bearing the strange notice:

On the night of . . . at the Grand Theatre of . . . and for the first time, will appear before the public, Franz Stenio, a German violinist, arrived purposely to throw down the gauntlet to the world-famous Paganini and to challenge him to a duel—upon their violins. He purposes to compete with the great "virtuoso" in the execution of the most difficult of his compositions. The famous Paganini has accepted the challenge. Franz Stenio will play, in competition with the unrivalled violinist, the celebrated "Fantaisie Caprice" of the latter, known as "The Witches."

The effect of the notice was magical. Paganini, who, amid his greatest triumphs, never lost sight of a profitable speculation, doubled the usual price of admission, but still the theatre could not hold the crowds that flocked to secure tickets for that memorable performance.

At last the morning of the concert day dawned, and the "duel" was in everyone's mouth. Franz Stenio, who, instead of sleeping, had passed the whole long hours of the preceding midnight in walking up and down his room like an encaged panther, had, towards morning, fallen on his bed from mere physical exhaustion. Gradually he passed into a death-like and dreamless slumber. At the gloomy winter dawn he awoke, but finding it too early to rise he fell asleep again. And then he had a vivid dream—so vivid indeed, so lifelike, that from its terrible realism he felt sure that it was a vision rather than a dream.

He had left his violin on a table by his bedside, locked in its case, the key of which never left him. Since he had strung it with those terrible chords he never let it out of his sight for a moment. In accordance with his resolution he had not touched it since his first trial, and his bow had never but once touched the human strings, for he had since always practised on another instrument. But now in his sleep he saw himself looking at the locked case. Something in it was attracting his attention, and he found himself incapable of detaching his eyes from it. Suddenly he saw the upper part of the case slowly rising, and, within the chink thus produced, he perceived two small, phosphorescent green eyes—eyes but too familiar to him—fixing themselves on his, lovingly, almost beseechingly. Then a thin, shrill voice, as if issuing from these ghastly orbs—the voice and orbs of Samuel Klaus himself—resounded in Stenio's horrified ear, and he heard it say:

"Franz, my beloved boy . . . Franz, I cannot, no, *I cannot* separate myself from . . . *them!*"

And "they" twanged piteously inside the case.

Franz stood speechless, horror-bound. He felt his blood actually freezing, and his hair moving and standing erect on his head. . . .

"It's but a dream, an empty dream!" he attempted to formulate in his mind.

"I have tried my best, Franzchen. . . . I have tried my best to sever myself from these accursed strings, without pulling them to pieces. . . ." pleaded the same shrill, familiar voice. "Wilt thou help me to do so? . . ."

Another twang, still more prolonged and dismal, resounded within the case, now dragged about the table in every direction, by some interior power, like some living, wriggling thing, the twangs becoming sharper and more jerky with every new pull.

It was not for the first time that Stenio heard those sounds. He had often remarked them before—indeed, ever since he had used his master's viscera as a footstool for his own ambition. But on every occasion a feeling of creeping horror had prevented him from investigating their cause, and he had tried to assure himself that the sounds were only a hallucination.

But now he stood face to face with the terrible fact, whether in dream or in reality he knew not, nor did he care, since the hallucination—if hallucination it were—was far more real and vivid than any reality. He tried to speak, to take a step forward; but, as often happens in nightmares, he could neither utter a word nor move a finger . . . He felt hopelessly paralysed.

The pulls and jerks were becoming more desperate with each moment, and at last something inside the case snapped violently. The vision of his Stradivarius, devoid of its magical strings, flashed before his eyes, throwing him into a cold sweat of mute and unspeakable terror.

He made a superhuman effort to rid himself of the incubus that held him spellbound. But as the last supplicating whisper of the invisible Presence repeated:

"Do, oh, do . . . help me to cut myself off—"

Franz sprang to the case with one bound, like an enraged tiger defending its prey, and with one frantic effort breaking the spell.

"Leave the violin alone, you old fiend from hell!" he cried, in hoarse and trembling tones.

He violently shut down the self-raising lid, and while firmly pressing his left hand on it, he seized with the right a piece of rosin from the table and drew on the leather-covered top the sign of the six-pointed star—the seal used by King Solomon to bottle up the rebellious djins inside their prisons.

A wail, like the howl of a she-wolf moaning over her dead little ones, came out of the violin case:

"Thou art ungrateful . . . very ungrateful, my Franz!" sobbed the blubbering "spirit-voice," "But I forgive . . . for I still love thee well. Yet thou canst not shut me in . . . boy. Behold!"

And instantly a greyish mist spread over and covered case and table, and rising upward formed itself first into an indistinct shape. Then it began growing, and as it grew, Franz felt himself gradually enfolded in cold and damp coils, slimy as those of a huge snake. He gave a terrible cry and—awoke; but, strangely enough, not on his bed, but near the table, just as he had dreamed, pressing the violin case desperately with both his hands.

"It was but a dream . . . after all," he muttered, still terrified, but relieved of the load on his heaving breast.

With a tremendous effort he composed himself, and unlocked the case to inspect the violin. He found it covered with dust, but otherwise sound and in order, and he suddenly felt himself as cool and as determined as ever. Having dusted the instrument he carefully rosined the bow, tightened the strings and tuned them. He even went so far as to try upon it the first notes of the "Witches"; first cautiously and timidly, then using his bow boldly and with full force.

The sound of that loud, solitary note—defiant as the war trumpet of a conqueror, sweet and majestic as the touch of a seraph on his golden harp in the fancy of the faithful—thrilled through the very soul of Franz. It revealed to him a hitherto unsuspected potency in his bow, which ran on in strains that filled the room with the richest swell of melody, unheard by the artist until that night. Commencing in uninterrupted *legato* tones, his bow sang to him of sun-bright hope and beauty, of moonlit nights, when the soft and balmy stillness endowed every blade of grass and all things animate and inanimate with a voice and a song of love. For a few brief moments it was a torrent of melody, the harmony of which, "tuned to soft woe," was calculated to make mountains weep, had there been any in the room, and to soothe

> . . . even th' inexorable powers of hell,

the presence of which was undeniably felt in this modest hotel room. Suddenly, the solemn *legato* chant, contrary to all laws of harmony, quivered, became *arpeggios,* and ended in shrill *staccatos,* like the notes of a hyena laugh. The same creeping sensation of terror, as he had before felt, came over him, and Franz threw the bow away. He had recognized the familiar laugh, and would have no more of it. Dressing, he locked the bedevilled violin securely in its case, and, taking it with him to the dining-room, determined to await quietly the hour of trial.

6

The terrible hour of the struggle had come, and Stenio was at his post—calm, resolute, almost smiling.

The theatre was crowded to suffocation, and there was not even standing room to be got for any amount of hard cash or favouritism. The singular challenge had reached every quarter to which the post could carry it, and gold flowed freely into Paganini's unfathomable pockets, to an extent almost satisfying even to his insatiate and venal soul.

It was arranged that Paganini should begin. When he appeared upon the stage, the thick walls of the theatre shook to their foundations with the applause that greeted him. He began and ended his famous composition "The Witches" amid a storm of cheers. The shouts of public enthusiasm lasted so long that Franz began to think his turn would never come. When, at last, Paganini, amid the roaring applause of a frantic public, was allowed to retire behind the scenes, his eye fell upon Stenio, who was tuning his violin, and he felt amazed at the serene calmness, the air of assurance, of the unknown German artist.

When Franz approached the footlights, he was received with icy coldness. But for all that, he did not feel in the least disconcerted. He looked very pale, but his thin white lips wore a scornful smile as response to this dumb unwelcome. He was sure of his triumph.

At the first notes of the prelude of "The Witches" a thrill of astonishment passed over the audience. It was Paganini's touch, and—it was something more. Some—and they were the majority—thought that never, in his best moments of inspiration, had the Italian artist himself, in executing that diabolical composition of his, exhibited such an extraordinary diabolical power. Under the pressure of the long muscular fingers of Franz, the chords shivered like the palpitating intestines of a disembowelled victim under the vivisector's knife. They moaned melodiously, like a dying child. The large blue eye of the artist, fixed with a satanic expression upon the sounding-board, seemed to summon forth Orpheus himself from the infernal regions, rather than the musical notes supposed to be generated in the depths of the violin. Sounds seemed to transform themselves into objective shapes, thickly and precipitately gathering as at the evocation of a mighty magician, and to be whirling around him, like a host of fantastic, infernal figures, dancing the witches' "goat dance." In the empty depths of the shadowy background of the stage, behind the artist, a nameless phantasmagoria, produced by the concussion of unearthly vibrations, seemed to form pictures of shameless orgies, of the voluptuous hymens of a real witches' Sabbat . . . A collective hallucination took hold of the public. Panting for breath, ghastly, and trickling with the icy perspiration of an inexpressible horror, they sat spellbound, and unable to break the spell of the music by the slightest motion. They experienced all the illicit enervating delights of the paradise of Mahommed, that come into the disordered fancy of an opium-eating Mussulman, and felt at the same time the abject terror, the agony of one who struggles against an attack of *delirium tremens* . . . Many ladies shrieked aloud, others fainted, and strong men gnashed their teeth in a state of utter helplessness . . .

Then came the *finale*. Thundering uninterrupted applause delayed its beginning, expanding the momentary pause to a duration of almost a quarter of an hour. The bravos were furious, almost hysterical. At last, when after a profound and last bow, Stenio, whose smile was as sardonic as it was triumphant, lifted his bow to attack the famous *finale*, his eye fell upon Paganini, who, calmly seated in the manager's box, had been behind none in zealous applause. The small and piercing black eyes of the Genoese artist were riveted to the Stradivarius in the hands of Franz, but otherwise he seemed quite cool and unconcerned. His rival's face troubled him for one short instant, but he regained his self-possession and, lifting once more his bow, drew the first note.

Then the public enthusiasm reached its acme, and soon knew no bounds. The listeners heard and saw indeed. The witches' voices resounded in the air, and beyond all the other voices, one voice was heard—

> Discordant, and unlike to human sounds;
> It seem'd of dogs the bark, of wolves the howl;
> The doleful screechings of the midnight owl;
> The hiss of snakes, the hungry lion's roar;
> The sounds of billows beating on the shore;
> The groan of winds among the leafy wood.
> And burst of thunder from the rending cloud;
> 'Twas these, all these in one . . .

The magic bow was drawing forth its last quivering sounds—famous among prodigious musical feats—imitating the precipitate flight of the witches before bright dawn; of the unholy women saturated with the fumes of their nocturnal Saturnalia, when—a strange thing came to pass on the stage. Without the slightest transition, the notes suddenly changed. In their aerial flight of ascension and descent, their melody was unexpectedly altered in character. The sounds became confused, scattered, disconnected . . . and then—it seemed from the sounding-board of the violin—came out squeaking, jarring tones, like those of a street Punch, screaming at the top of a senile voice:

"Art thou satisfied, Franz, my boy? . . . Have not I gloriously kept my promise, eh?"

The spell was broken. Though still unable to realize the whole situation, those who heard the voice and the *Punchinello*-like tones, were freed, as by enchantment, from the terrible charm under which they had been held. Loud roars of laughter, mocking exclamations of half-anger and half-irritation were now heard from every corner of the vast theatre. The musicians in the orchestra, with faces still blanched from weird emotion, were now seen shaking with laughter, and the whole audience rose, like one man, from their seats, unable yet to solve the enigma; they felt, nevertheless, too disgusted, too disposed to laugh to remain one moment longer in the building.

But suddenly the sea of moving heads in the stalls and the pit became once more motionless, and stood petrified as though struck by lightning. What all saw was terrible enough—the handsome though wild face of the young artist suddenly aged, and his graceful, erect figure bent down, as though under the weight of years; but this was nothing to that which some of the most sensitive clearly perceived. Franz Stenio's person was now entirely enveloped in a semi-transparent mist, cloudlike, creeping with serpentine motion, and gradually tightening round the living form, as though ready to engulf him. And there were those also who discerned in this tall and ominous pillar of smoke a clearly-defined figure, a form showing the unmistakable outlines of a grotesque and grinning, but terribly awful-looking old man, whose viscera were protruding and the ends of the intestines stretched on the violin.

Within this hazy, quivering veil, the violinist was then seen, driving his bow furiously across the human chords, with the contortions of a demoniac, as we see them represented on medieval cathedral paintings!

An indescribable panic swept over the audience, and breaking now, for the last time, through the spell which had again bound them motionless, every living creature in the theatre made one mad rush towards the door. It was like the sudden outburst of a dam, a human torrent, roaring amid a shower of discordant notes, idiotic squeakings, prolonged and whining moans, cacophonous cries of frenzy, above which, like the detonations of pistol shots, was heard the consecutive bursting of the four strings stretched upon the sound-board of that bewitched violin.

When the theatre was emptied of the last man of the audience, the terrified manager rushed on the stage in search of the unfortunate performer. He was found dead and already stiff, behind the footlights, twisted up into the most unnatural of postures, with the "catguts" wound curiously around his neck, and his violin shattered into a thousand fragments . . .

When it became publicly known that the unfortunate would-be rival of Niccolo Paganini had not left a cent to pay for his funeral or his hotel-bill, the Genoese, his proverbial meanness notwithstanding, settled the hotel-bill and had poor Stenio buried at his own expense.

He claimed, however, in exchange, the fragments of the Stradivarius —as a memento of the strange event.

*When M. G. Lewis wrote the famous Gothic horror novel, The Monk, the
literary hacks of the day were swift to leap on the bandwagon and grind out
innumerable imitations. Here is one of the better examples, a c. 1798 ghostly
scene in a crypt which, like the Lewis original, dares to suggest the apostles
of Church may be less than holy. The theme may be viewed as part of the
logical process of spiritual redefinition that began long before the Renais-
sance and is raging in today's world.*

The Monk of Horror

or The Conclave of Corpses

Anonymous

Some three hundred years since, when the convent of Kreutzberg was in
its glory, one of the monks who dwelt therein, wishing to ascertain
something of the hereafter of those whose bodies lay all undecayed in
the cemetery, visited it alone in the dead of night for the purpose of
prosecuting his inquiries on that fearful subject. As he opened the trap-
door of the vault a light burst from below; but deeming it to be only the
lamp of the sacristan, the monk drew back and awaited his departure
concealed behind the high altar. The sacristan emerged not, however,
from the opening; and the monk, tired of waiting, approached, and
finally descended the rugged steps which led into the dreary depths. No
sooner had he set foot on the lower-most stair, than the well-known
scene underwent a complete transformation in his eyes. He had long
been accustomed to visit the vault, and whenever the sacristan went
thither, he was almost sure to be with him. He therefore knew every
part of it as well as he did the interior of his own narrow cell, and the
arrangement of its contents was perfectly familiar to his eyes. What,
then, was his horror to perceive that this arrangement, which even but
that morning had come under his observation as usual, was altogether
altered, and a new and wonderful one substituted in its stead.

A dim lurid light pervaded the desolate abode of darkness, and it
just sufficed to give to his view a sight of the most singular description.

On each side of him the dead but imperishable bodies of the long-
buried brothers of the convent sat erect in their lidless coffins, their
cold, starry eyes glaring at him with lifeless rigidity, their withered
fingers locked together on their breasts, their stiffened limbs motionless

and still. It was a sight to petrify the stoutest heart; and the monk's quailed before it, though he was a philosopher, and a sceptic to boot. At the upper end of the vault, at a rude table formed of a decayed coffin, or something which once served the same purpose, sat three monks. They were the oldest corpses in the charnel-house, for the inquisitive brother knew their faces well; and the cadaverous hue of their cheeks seemed still more cadaverous in the dim light shed upon them, while their hollow eyes gave forth what looked to him like flashes of flame. A large book lay open before one of them, and the others bent over the rotten table as if in intense pain, or in deep and fixed attention. No word was said; no sound was heard; the vault was as silent as the grave, its awful tenants still as statues.

Fain would the curious monk have receded from this horrible place; fain would he have retraced his steps and sought again his cell, fain would he have shut his eyes to the fearful scene; but he could not stir from the spot, he felt rooted there; and though he once succeeded in turning his eyes to the entrance of the vault, to his infinite surprise and dismay he could not discover where it lay, nor perceive any possible means of exit. He stood thus for some time. At length the aged monk at the table beckoned him to advance. With slow tottering steps he made his way to the group, and at length stood in front of the table, while the other monks raised their heads and glanced at him with fixed, lifeless looks that froze the current of his blood. He knew not what to do; his senses were fast forsaking him; Heaven seemed to have deserted him for his incredulity. In this moment of doubt and fear he bethought him of a prayer, and as he proceeded he felt himself becoming possessed of a confidence he had before unknown. He looked on the book before him. It was a large volume, bound in black, and clasped with bands of gold, with fastenings of the same metal. It was inscribed at the top of each page.

"Liber Obedientiae."

He could read no further. He then looked, first in the eyes of him before whom it lay open, and then in those of his fellows. He finally glanced around the vault on the corpses who filled every visible coffin in its dark and spacious womb. Speech came to him, and resolution to use it. He addressed himself to the awful beings in whose presence he stood, in the words of one having authority with them.

"Pax vobis," 'twas thus he spake—"Peace be to ye."

"Hic nulla pax," replied an aged monk, in a hollow, tremulous tone, bearing his breast the while—"Here is no peace."

He pointed to his bosom as he spoke, and the monk, casting his eye upon it, beheld his heart within surrounded by living fire, which seemed to feed on it but not consume it. He turned away in affright, but ceased not to prosecute his inquiries.

"*Pax vobis, in nomine Domini,*" he spake again—"Peace be to ye, in the name of the Lord."

"*Hic non pax,*" the hollow and heartrending tones of the ancient monk who sat at the right of the table were heard to answer.

On glancing at the bared bosom of this hapless being also the same sight was exhibited—the heart surrounded by a devouring flame, but still remaining fresh and unconsumed under its operation. Once more the monk turned away and addressed the aged man in the centre.

"*Pax vobis, in nomine Domini,*" he proceeded.

At these words the being to whom they were addressed raised his head, put forward his hand, and closing the book with a loud clap, said—

"Speak on. It is yours to ask, and mine to answer."

The monk felt reassured, and his courage rose with the occasion.

"Who are ye?" he inquired; "who may ye be?"

"We know not!" was the answer, "alas! we know not!"

"We know not, we know not!" echoed in melancholy tones the denizens of the vault.

"What do ye here?" pursued the querist.

"We await the last day, the day of the last judgement! Alas for us! woe! woe!"

"Woe! woe!" resounded on all sides.

The monk was appalled, but still he proceeded.

"What did ye to deserve such doom as this? What may your crime be that deserves such dole and sorrow?"

As he asked the question the earth shook under him, and a crowd of skeletons uprose from a range of graves which yawned suddenly at his feet.

"These are our victims," answered the old monk. "They suffered at our hands. We suffer now, while they are at peace; and we shall suffer."

"For how long?" asked the monk.

"For ever and ever!" was the answer.

"For ever and ever, for ever and ever!" died along the vault.

"May God have mercy on us!" was all the monk could exclaim.

The skeletons vanished, the graves closing over them. The aged men disappeared from his view, the bodies fell back in their coffins, the light fled, and the den of death was once more enveloped in its usual darkness.

On the monk's revival he found himself lying at the foot of the altar. The grey dawn of a spring morning was visible, and he was fain to retire to his cell as secretly as he could, for fear he should be discovered.

From thenceforth he eschewed vain philosophy, says the legend, and, devoting his time to the pursuit of true knowledge, and the extension of the power, greatness, and glory of the Church, died in the odour of sanctity, and was buried in that holy vault, where his body is still visible.

JOSEPH SHERIDAN LE FANU, *grandson of the great comedy-of-manners dramatist Richard Brinsley Sheridan, was born in 1814 in Dublin. He wrote predominantly grim supernatural novels and short stories, including the classic* "Green Tea" *and* "Carmilla," *one of the few important pre-*Dracula *vampire stories (indifferently filmed as* Blood and Roses*).* "Mr. Justice Harbottle" *is a towering tale of spectral revenge that evokes comparison with the tale of the evil judge in Hawthorne's* House of the Seven Gables.

Mr. Justice Harbottle
by Sheridan Le Fanu

CHAPTER I
The Judge's House

Thirty years ago, an elderly man, to whom I paid quarterly a small annuity charged on some property of mine, came on the quarter day to receive it. He was a dry, sad, quiet man, who had known better days, and had always maintained an unexceptionable character. No better authority could be imagined for a ghost story.

He told me one, though with a manifest reluctance; he was drawn into the narration by his choosing to explain what I should not have remarked, that he had called two days earlier than that week after the strict day of payment, which he had usually allowed to elapse. His reason was a sudden determination to change his lodgings, and the consequent necessity of paying his rent a little before it was due.

He lodged in a dark street in Westminster, in a spacious old house, very warm, being wainscoted from top to bottom, and furnished with no undue abundance of windows, and those fitted with thick sashes and small panes.

This house was, as the bills upon the windows testified, offered to be sold or let. But no one seemed to care to look at it.

A thin matron, in rusty black silk, very taciturn, with large, steady, alarmed eyes, that seemed to look in your face, to read what you might have seen in the dark rooms and passages through which you had passed, was in charge of it, with a solitary "maid-of-all-work" under her command. My poor friend had taken lodgings in this house, on account of their extraordinary cheapness. He had occupied them for nearly a year without the slightest disturbance, and was the only tenant, under rent, in the house. He had two rooms; a sitting-room, and a bedroom with a closet opening from it, in which he kept his books and papers locked up. He had gone to his bed, having also locked the outer door. Unable to sleep, he had lighted a candle, and after having read for a time, had laid the book beside him. He heard the old clock at the stair-head strike one; and very shortly after, to his alarm, he saw the closet-door, which he thought he had locked, open stealthily, and a slight dark man, particularly sinister, and somewhere about fifty, dressed in mourning of a very antique fashion, such a suit as we see in Hogarth, entered the room on tiptoe. He was followed by an elder man, stout, and blotched with scurvy, and whose features, fixed as a corpse's, were stamped with dreadful force with a character of sensuality and villainy.

This old man wore a flowered-silk dressing-gown and ruffles, and he remarked a gold ring on his finger, and on his head a cap of velvet, such as, in the days of perukes, gentlemen wore in undress.

This direful old man carried in his ringed and ruffled hand a coil of rope; and these two figures crossed the floor diagonally, passing the foot of his bed, from the closet-door at the farther end of the room, at the left, near the window, to the door opening upon the lobby, close to the bed's head, at his right.

He did not attempt to describe his sensations as these figures passed so near him. He merely said, that so far from sleeping in that room again, no consideration the world could offer would induce him so much as to enter it again alone, even in the daylight. He found both doors, that of the closet, and that of the room opening upon the lobby, in the morning fast locked, as he had left them before going to bed.

In answer to a question of mine, he said that neither appeared the least conscious of his presence. They did not seem to glide, but walked as living men do, but without any sound, and he felt a vibration on the floor as they crossed it. He so obviously suffered from speaking about the apparitions, that I asked him no more questions.

There were in his description, however, certain coincidences so very singular, as to induce me, by that very post, to write to a friend much my senior, then living in a remote part of England, for the information which I knew he could give me. He had himself more than once pointed out that old house to my attention, and told me, though very briefly, the strange story which I now asked him to give me in greater detail.

His answer satisfied me; and the following pages convey its substance.

Your letter (he wrote) tells me you desire some particulars about the closing years of the life of Mr. Justice Harbottle, one of the judges of the Court of Common Pleas. You refer, of course, to the extraordinary occurrences that made that period of his life long after a theme for "winter tales" and metaphysical speculation. I happen to know perhaps more than any other man living of those mysterious particulars.

The old family mansion, when I revisited London, more than thirty years ago, I examined for the last time. During the years that have passed since then, I hear that improvement, with its preliminary demolitions, has been doing wonders for the quarter of Westminster in which it stood. If I were quite certain that the house had been taken down, I should have no difficulty about naming the street in which it stood. As what I have to tell, however, is not likely to improve its letting value, and as I should not care to get into trouble, I prefer being silent on that particular point.

How old the house was, I can't tell. People said it was built by Roger Harbottle, a Turkey merchant, in the reign of King James I. I am not a good opinion upon such questions; but having been in it, though in its forlorn and deserted state, I can tell you in a general way what it was like. It was built of dark-red brick, and the door and windows were faced with stone that had turned yellow by time. It receded some feet from the line of the other houses in the street; and it had a florid and fanciful rail of iron about the broad steps that invited your ascent to the hall-door, in which were fixed, under a file of lamps, among scrolls and twisted leaves, two immense "extinguishers" like the conical caps of fairies, into which, in old times, the footmen used to thrust their flambeaux when their chairs or coaches had set down their great people, in the hall or at the steps, as the case might be. That hall is panelled up to the ceiling, and has a large fire-place. Two or three stately old rooms open from it at each side. The windows of these are tall, with many small panes. Passing through the arch at the back of the hall, you come upon the wide and heavy well-staircase. There is a back staircase also. The mansion is large, and has not as much light, by any means, in proportion to its extent, as modern houses enjoy. When I saw it, it had long been untenanted, and had the gloomy reputation besides of a haunted house. Cobwebs floated from the ceilings or spanned the corners of the cornices, and dust lay thick over everything. The windows were stained with the dust and rain of fifty years, and darkness had thus grown darker.

When I made it my first visit, it was in company with my father, when I was still a boy, in the year 1808. I was about twelve years old, and my imagination impressible, as it always is at that age. I looked about me with great awe. I was here in the very centre and scene of those occurrences which I had heard recounted at the fireside at home, with so delightful a horror.

My father was an old bachelor of nearly sixty when he married. He had, when a child, seen Judge Harbottle on the bench in his robes and wig a dozen times at least before his death, which took place in 1748, and his appearance made a powerful and unpleasant impression, not only on his imagination, but upon his nerves.

The Judge was at that time a man of some sixty-seven years. He had a great mulberry-coloured face, a big, carbuncled nose, fierce eyes, and a grim and brutal mouth. My father, who was young at the time, thought it the most formidable face he had ever seen; for there were evidences of intellectual power in the formation and lines of the forehead. His voice was loud and harsh, and gave effect to the sarcasm which was his habitual weapon on the bench.

This old gentleman had the reputation of being about the wickedest man in England. Even on the bench he now and then showed his scorn of opinion. He had carried cases his own way, it was said, in spite of counsel, authorities, and even of juries, by a sort of cajolery, violence, and bamboozling, that somehow confused and overpowered resistance. He had never actually committed himself; he was too cunning to do that. He had the character of being, however, a dangerous and unscrupulous judge; but his character did not trouble him. The associates he chose for his hours of relaxation cared as little as he did about it.

CHAPTER II

Mr. Peters

One night during the session of 1746 this old Judge went down in his chair to wait in one of the rooms of the House of Lords for the result of a division in which he and his order were interested.

This over, he was about to return to his house close by, in his chair; but the night had become so soft and fine that he changed his mind, sent it home empty, and with two footmen, each with a flambeau, set out on foot in preference. Gout had made him rather a slow pedestrian. It took him some time to get through the two or three streets he had to pass before reaching his house.

In one of those narrow streets of tall houses, perfectly silent at that hour, he overtook, slowly as he was walking, a very singular-looking old gentleman.

He had a bottle-green coat on, with a cape to it, and large stone buttons, a broad-leafed low-crowned hat, from under which a big powdered wig escaped; he stooped very much, and supported his bending knees with the aid of a crutch-handled cane, and so shuffled and tottered along painfully.

"I ask your pardon, sir," said this old man in a very quavering voice, as the burly Judge came up with him, and he extended his hand feebly towards his arm.

Mr. Justice Harbottle saw that the man was by no means poorly dressed, and his manner that of a gentleman.

The Judge stopped short, and said, in his harsh peremptory tones, "Well, sir, how can I serve you?"

"Can you direct me to Judge Harbottle's house? I have some intelligence of the very last importance to communicate to him."

"Can you tell it before witnesses?" asked the Judge.

"By no means; it must reach *his* ear only," quavered the old man earnestly.

"If that be so, sir, you have only to accompany me a few steps farther to reach my house, and obtain a private audience; for I am Judge Harbottle."

With this invitation the infirm gentleman in the white wig complied very readily; and in another minute the stranger stood in what was then termed the front parlour of the Judge's house, *tête-à-tête* with that shrewd and dangerous functionary.

He had to sit down, being very much exhausted, and unable for a little time to speak; and then he had a fit of coughing, and after that a fit of gasping; and thus two or three minutes passed, during which the Judge dropped his roquelaure on an arm-chair, and threw his cocked hat over that.

The venerable pedestrian in the white wig quickly recovered his voice. With closed doors they remained together for some time.

There were guests waiting in the drawing-rooms, and the sound of men's voices laughing, and then of a female voice singing to a harpsichord, were heard distinctly in the hall over the stairs; for old Judge Harbottle had arranged one of his dubious jollifications, such as might well make the hair of godly men's heads stand upright, for that night.

This old gentleman in the powdered white wig, that rested on his stooped shoulders, must have had something to say that interested the Judge very much; for he would not have parted on easy terms with the ten minutes and upwards which that conference filched from the sort of revelry in which he most delighted, and in which he was the roaring king, and in some sort the tyrant also, of his company.

The footman who showed the aged gentleman out observed that the Judge's mulberry-coloured face, pimples and all, were bleached to a dingy yellow, and there was the abstraction of agitated thought in his manner, as he bid the stranger good night. The servant saw that the conversation had been of serious import, and that the Judge was frightened.

Instead of stumping upstairs forthwith to his scandalous hilarities, his profane company, and his great china bowl of punch—the identical bowl from which a bygone Bishop of London, good easy man, had baptised this Judge's grandfather, now clinking round the rim with silver ladles, and hung with scrolls of lemon peel—instead, I say, of stumping and clambering up the great staircase to the cavern of his Circean enchantment, he stood with his big nose flattened against the window-pane, watching the progress of the feeble old man, who clung stiffly to the iron rail as he got down, step by step, to the pavement.

The hall-door had hardly closed, when the old Judge was in the hall bawling hasty orders, with such stimulating expletives as old colonels under excitement sometimes indulge in nowadays, with a stamp or two of his big foot, and a waving of his clenched fist in the air. He commanded the footman to overtake the old gentleman in the white wig, to offer him his protection on his way home, and in no case to show his face again without having ascertained where he lodged, and who he was, and all about him.

"By—, sirrah! if you fail me in this, you doff my livery tonight!"

Forth bounced the stalwart footman, with his heavy cane under his arm, and skipped down the steps, and looked up and down the street after the singular figure, so easy to recognise.

What were his adventures I shall not tell you just now.

The old man, in the conference to which he had been admitted in that stately panelled room, had just told the Judge a very strange story. He might be himself a conspirator; he might possibly be crazed; or possibly his whole story was straight and true.

The aged gentleman in the bottle-green coat, on finding himself alone with Mr. Justice Harbottle, had become agitated. He said,

"There is, perhaps you are not aware, my lord, a prisoner in Shrewsbury jail, charged with having forged a bill of exchange for a hundred and twenty pounds, and his name is Lewis Pyneweck, a grocer of that town."

"Is there?" says the Judge, who knew well that there was.

"Yes, my lord," says the old man.

"Then you had better say nothing to affect this case. If you do, by—I'll commit you; for I'm to try it," says the Judge, with his terrible look and tone.

"I am not going to do anything of the kind, my lord; of him or his case I know nothing, and care nothing. But a fact has come to my knowledge which it behoves you to well consider."

"And what may that fact be?" inquired the Judge; "I'm in haste, sir, and beg you will use dispatch."

"It has come to my knowledge, my lord, that a secret tribunal is in process of formation, the object of which is to take cognisance of the conduct of the judges; and first, of *your* conduct, my lord: it is a wicked conspiracy."

"Who are of it?" demands the Judge.

"I know not a single name as yet. I know but the fact, my lord; it is most certainly true."

"I'll have you before the Privy Council, sir," says the Judge.

"That is what I most desire; but not for a day or two, my lord."

"And why so?"

"I have not as yet a single name, as I told your lordship; but I expect to have a list of the most forward men in it, and some other papers connected with the plot, in two or three days."

"You said one or two just now."

"About that time, my lord."

"Is this a Jacobite plot?"

"In the main I think it is, my lord."

"Why, then, it is political. I have tried no State prisoners, nor am like to try any such. How, then, doth it concern me?"

"From what I can gather, my lord, there are those in it who desire private revenges upon certain judges."

"What do they call their cabal?"

"The High Court of Appeal, my lord."

"Who are you, sir? What is your name?"

"Hugh Peters, my lord."

"That should be a Whig name?"

"It is, my lord."

"Where do you lodge, Mr. Peters?"

"In Thames Street, my lord, over against the sign of the Three Kings."

"Three Kings? Take care one be not too many for you, Mr. Peters! How come you, an honest Whig, as you say, to be privy to a Jacobite plot? Answer me that."

"My lord, a person in whom I take an interest has been seduced to take a part in it; and being frightened at the unexpected wickedness of their plans, he is resolved to become an informer for the Crown."

"He resolves like a wise man, sir. What does he say of the persons? Who are in the plot? Doth he know them?"

"Only two, my lord; but he will be introduced to the club in a few days, and he will then have a list, and more exact information of their plans, and above all of their oaths, and their hours and places of meeting, with which he wishes to be acquainted before they can have any suspicions of his intentions. And being so informed, to whom, think you, my lord, had he best go then?"

"To the king's attorney-general straight. But you say this concerns me, sir, in particular? How about this prisoner, Lewis Pyneweck? Is he one of them?"

"I can't tell, my lord; but for some reason, it is thought your lordship will be well advised if you try him not. For if you do, it is feared 'twill shorten your days."

"So far as I can learn, Mr. Peters, this business smells pretty strong of blood and treason. The king's attorney-general will know how to deal with it. When shall I see you again, sir?"

"If you give me leave, my lord, either before your lordship's court sits, or after it rises, tomorrow. I should like to come and tell your lordship what has passed."

"Do so, Mr. Peters, at nine o'clock tomorrow morning. And see you play me no trick, sir, in this matter; if you do, by ——, sir, I'll lay you by the heels!"

"You need fear no trick from me, my lord; had I not wished to serve you, and acquit my own conscience, I never would have come all this way to talk with your lordship."

"I'm willing to believe you, Mr. Peters; I'm willing to believe you, sir."

And upon this they parted.

"He has either painted his face, or he is consumedly sick," thought the old Judge.

The light had shone more effectually upon his features as he turned to leave the room with a low bow, and they looked, he fancied, unnaturally chalky.

"D— him!" said the Judge ungraciously, as he began to scale the stairs: "he has half-spoiled my supper."

But if he had, no one but the Judge himself perceived it, and the evidence was all, as anyone might perceive, the other way.

CHAPTER III

Lewis Pyneweck

In the meantime, the footman dispatched in pursuit of Mr. Peters speedily overtook that feeble gentleman. The old man stopped when he heard the sound of pursuing steps, but any alarms that may have crossed his mind seemed to disappear on his recognising the livery. He very gratefully accepted the proffered assistance, and placed his tremulous arm within the servant's for support. They had not gone far, however, when the old man stopped suddenly, saying,

"Dear me! as I live, I have dropped it. You heard it fall. My eyes, I fear, won't serve me, and I'm unable to stoop low enough; but if *you* will look, you shall have half the find. It is a guinea; I carried it in my glove."

The street was silent and deserted. The footman had hardly descended to what he termed his "hunkers," and begun to search the pavement about the spot which the old man indicated, when Mr. Peters, who seemed very much exhausted, and breathed with difficulty, struck him a violent blow, from above, over the back of the head with a heavy instrument, and then another; and leaving him bleeding and senseless in the gutter, ran like a lamplighter down a lane to the right, and was gone.

When, an hour later, the watchman brought the man in livery home, still stupid and covered with blood, Judge Harbottle cursed his servant roundly, swore he was drunk, threatened him with an indictment for taking bribes to betray his master, and cheered him with a perspective of the broad street leading from the Old Bailey to Tyburn, the cart's tail, and the hangman's lash.

Notwithstanding this demonstration, the Judge was pleased. It was a disguised "affidavit man," or footpad, no doubt, who had been employed to frighten him. The trick had fallen through.

A "court of appeal," such as the false Hugh Peters had indicated, with assassination for its sanction, would be an uncomfortable institution for a "hanging judge" like the Honourable Justice Harbottle. That sarcastic and ferocious administrator of the criminal code of England, at that time a rather pharisaical, bloody, and heinous system of justice, had reasons of his own for choosing to try that very Lewis Pyneweck, on whose behalf this audacious trick was devised. Try him he would. No man living should take that morsel out of his mouth.

Of Lewis Pyneweck of course, so far as the outer world could see, he knew nothing. He would try him after his fashion, without fear, favour, or affection.

But did he not remember a certain thin man, dressed in mourning, in whose house, in Shrewsbury, the Judge's lodgings used to be, until a scandal of his ill-treating his wife came suddenly to light? A grocer with a demure look, a soft step, and a lean face as dark as mahogany, with a nose sharp and long, standing ever so little awry, and a pair of dark steady brown eyes under thinly traced black brows—a man whose thin lips wore always a faint unpleasant smile.

Had not that scoundrel an account to settle with the Judge? had he not been troublesome lately? and was not his name Lewis Pyneweck, some time grocer in Shrewsbury, and now prisoner in the jail of that town?

The reader may take it, if he pleases, as a sign that Judge Harbottle was a good Christian, that he suffered nothing ever from remorse. That was undoubtedly true. He had nevertheless done this grocer, forger, what you will, some five or six years before, a grievous wrong; but it was not that, but a possible scandal, and possible complications, that troubled the learned Judge now.

Did he not, as a lawyer, know, that to bring a man from his shop to the dock, the chances must be at least ninety-nine out of a hundred that he is guilty?

A weak man like his learned brother Withershins was not a judge to keep the high-roads safe, and make crime tremble. Old Judge Harbottle was the man to make the evil-disposed quiver, and to refresh the world with showers of wicked blood, and thus save the innocent, to the refrain of the ancient saw he loved to quote:

Foolish pity
Ruins a city.

In hanging that fellow he could not be wrong. The eye of a man accustomed to look upon the dock could not fail to read "villain" written sharp and clear in his plotting face. Of course he would try him, and no one else should.

A saucy-looking woman, still handsome, in a mob-cap gay with blue ribbons, in a saque of flowered silk, with lace and rings on, much too fine for the Judge's housekeeper, which nevertheless she was, peeped into his study next morning, and, seeing the Judge alone, stepped in.

"Here's another letter from him, come by the post this morning. Can't you do nothing for him?" she said wheedlingly, with her arm over his neck, and her delicate finger and thumb fiddling with the lobe of his purple ear.

"I'll try," said Judge Harbottle, not raising his eyes from the paper he was reading.

"I knew you'd do what I asked you," she said.

The Judge clapt his gouty claw over his heart, and made her an ironical bow.

"What," she asked, "will you do?"

"Hang him," said the Judge with a chuckle.

"You don't mean to; no, you don't, my little man," said she, surveying herself in a mirror on the wall.

"I'm d—d but I think you're falling in love with your husband at last!" said Judge Harbottle.

"I'm blest but I think you're growing jealous of him," replied the lady with a laugh. "But no; he was always a bad one to me; I've dont with him long ago."

"And he with you, by George! When he took your fortune and your spoons and your earrings, he had all he wanted of you. He drove you from his house; and when he discovered you had made yourself comfortable, and found a good situation, he'd have taken your guineas and your silver and your earrings over again, and then allowed you half a dozen years more to make a new harvest for his mill. You don't wish him good; if you say you do, you lie."

She laughed a wicked saucy laugh, and gave the terrible Rhadamanthus a playful tap on the chops.

"He wants me to send him money to fee a counsellor," she said, while her eyes wandered over the pictures on the wall, and back again to the looking-glass; and certainly she did not look as if his jeopardy troubled her very much.

"Confound his impudence, the *scoundrel!*" thundered the old Judge, throwing himself back in his chair, as he used to do *in furore* on the bench, and the lines of his mouth looked brutal, and his eyes ready to leap from their sockets. "If you answer his letter from my house to please yourself, you'll write your next from somebody else's to please me. You understand, my pretty witch, I'll not be pestered. Come, no pouting; whimpering won't do. You don't care a brass farthing for the villain, body or soul. You came here but to make a row. You are one of Mother Carey's chickens; and where you come, the storm is up. Get you gone, baggage! get you *gone!*" he repeated with a stamp; for a knock at the hall-door made her instantaneous disappearance indispensable.

I need hardly say that the venerable Hugh Peters did not appear again. The Judge never mentioned him. But oddly enough, considering how he laughed to scorn the weak invention which he had blown into dust at the very first puff, his white-wigged visitor and the conference in the dark front parlour was often in his memory.

His shrewd eye told him that allowing for change of tints and such disguises as the playhouse affords every night, the features of this false old man, who had turned out too hard for his tall footman, were identical with those of Lewis Pyneweck.

Judge Harbottle made his registrar call upon the crown solicitor, and tell him that there was a man in town who bore a wonderful resemblance to a prisoner in Shrewsbury jail named Lewis Pyneweck, and to make inquiry through the post forthwith whether anyone was personating Pyneweck in prison, and whether he had thus or otherwise made his escape.

The prisoner was safe, however, and no question as to his identity.

CHAPTER IV

Interruption in Court

In due time Judge Harbottle went circuit; and in due time the judges were in Shrewsbury. News travelled slowly in those days, and newspapers, like the wagons and stage-coaches, took matters easily. Mrs. Pyneweck, in the Judge's house, with a diminished household—the greater part of the Judge's servants having gone with him, for he had given up riding circuit, and travelled in his coach in state—kept house rather solitarily at home.

In spite of quarrels, in spite of mutual injuries—some of them, inflicted by herself, enormous—in spite of a married life of spited bickerings—a life in which there seemed no love or liking or forbearance, for years—now that Pyneweck stood in near danger of death, something like remorse came suddenly upon her. She knew that in Shrewsbury were transacting the scenes which were to determine his fate. She knew she did not love him; but she could not have supposed, even a fortnight before, that the hour of suspense could have affected her so powerfully.

She knew the day on which the trial was expected to take place. She could not get it out of her head for a minute; she felt faint as it drew towards evening.

Two or three days passed; and then she knew that the trial must be over by this time. There were floods between London and Shrewsbury, and news was long delayed. She wished the floods would last for ever. It was dreadful waiting to hear; dreadful to know that the event was over, and that she could not hear till self-willed rivers subsided; dreadful to know that they must subside and the news came at last.

She had some vague trust in the Judge's good nature, and much in the resources of chance and accident. She had contrived to send the money he wanted. He would not be without legal advice and energetic and skilled support.

At last the news did come—a long arrear all in a gush: a letter from a female friend in Shrewsbury; a return of the sentences, sent up for the Judge; and most important, because most easily got at, being told with great aplomb and brevity, the long-deferred intelligence of the Shrewsbury Assizes in the *Morning Advertiser*. Like an impatient reader of a novel, who reads the last page first, she read with dizzy eyes the list of the executions.

Two were respited, seven were hanged; and in that capital catalogue was this line:

"Lewis Pyneweck—forgery."

She had to read it half a dozen times over before she was sure she understood it. Here was the paragraph:

"Sentence, Death—7."

"Executed accordingly, on Friday the 13th instant, to wit:

"Thomas Primer, *alias* Duck—highway robbery.

"Flora Guy—stealing to the value of 11*s*. 6*d*.

"Arthur Pounden—burglary.

"Matilda Mummery—riot.

"Lewis Pyneweck—forgery, bill of exchange."

And when she reached this, she read it over and over, feeling very cold and sick.

This buxom housekeeper was known in the house as Mrs. Carwell—Carwell being her maiden name, which she had resumed.

No one in the house except its master knew her history. Her introduction had been managed craftily. No one suspected that it had been concerted between her and the old reprobate in scarlet and ermine.

Flora Carwell ran up the stairs now, and snatched her little girl, hardly seven years of age, whom she met on the lobby, hurriedly up in her arms, and carried her into her bedroom, without well knowing what she was doing, and sat down, placing the child before her. She was not able to speak. She held the child before her, and looked in the little girl's wondering face, and burst into tears of horror.

She thought the Judge could have saved him. I daresay he could. For a time she was furious with him; and hugged and kissed her bewildered little girl, who returned her gaze with large round eyes.

That little girl had lost her father, and knew nothing of the matter. She had been always told that her father was dead long ago.

A woman, coarse, uneducated, vain, and violent, does not reason, or even feel, very distinctly; but in these tears of consternation were mingling a self-upbraiding. She felt afraid of that little child.

But Mrs. Carwell was a person who lived not upon sentiment, but upon beef and pudding; she consoled herself with punch; she did not trouble herself long even with resentments; she was a gross and material person, and could not mourn over the irrevocable for more than a limited number of hours, even if she would.

Judge Harbottle was soon in London again. Except the gout, this savage old epicurean never knew a day's sickness. He laughed and coaxed and bullied away the young woman's faint upbraidings, and in a little time Lewis Pyneweck troubled her no more; and the Judge secretly chuckled over the perfectly fair removal of a bore, who might have grown little by little into something very like a tyrant.

It was the lot of the Judge whose adventures I am now recounting to try criminal cases at the Old Bailey shortly after his return. He had commenced his charge to the jury in a case of forgery, and was, after his wont, thundering dead against the prisoner, with many a hard aggravation and cynical gibe, when suddenly all died away in silence, and, instead of looking at the jury, the eloquent Judge was gaping at some person in the body of the court.

Among the persons of small importance who stand and listen at the sides was one tall enough to show with a little prominence; a slight mean figure, dressed in seedy black, lean and dark of visage. He had just handed a letter to the crier, before he caught the Judge's eye.

That Judge descried, to his amazement, the features of Lewis Pyneweck. He has the usual faint thin-lipped smile; and with his blue chin raised in air, and as it seemed quite unconscious of the distinguished notice he has attracted, he was stretching his low cravat with his crooked fingers, while he slowly turned his head from side to side—a process which enabled the Judge to see distinctly a stripe of swollen blue round his neck, which indicated, he thought, the grip of the rope.

This man, with a few others, had got a footing on a step, from which he could better see the court. He now stepped down, and the Judge lost sight of him.

His lordship signed energetically with his hand in the direction in which this man had vanished. He turned to the tipstaff. His first effort to speak ended in a gasp. He cleared his throat, and told the astounded official to arrest that man who had interrupted the court.

"He's but this moment gone down *there*. Bring him in custody before me, within ten minutes' time, or I'll strip your gown from your shoulders and fine the sheriff!" he thundered, while his eyes flashed round the court in search of the functionary.

Attorneys, counsellors, idle spectators, gazed in the direction in which Mr. Justice Harbottle had shaken his gnarled old hand. They compared notes. Not one had seen anyone making a disturbance. They asked one another if the Judge was losing his head.

Nothing came of the search. His lordship concluded his charge a great deal more tamely; and when the jury retired, he stared round the court with a wandering mind, and looked as if he would not have given sixpence to see the prisoner hanged.

CHAPTER V

Caleb Searcher

The judge had received the letter; had he known from whom it came, he would no doubt have read it instantaneously. As it was he simply read the direction:

To the Honourable
The Lord Justice
Elijah Harbottle,
One of his Majesty's Justices of
the Honourable Court of Common Pleas.

It remained forgotten in his pocket till he reached home.

When he pulled out that and others from the capacious pocket of his coat, it had its turn, as he sat in his library in his thick silk dressing-gown; and then he found its contents to be a closely written letter, in a clerk's hand, and an enclosure in "secretary hand," as I believe the angular scrivinary of law-writings in those days was termed, engrossed on a bit of parchment about the size of this page. The letter said:

"Mr. Justice Harbottle,—My Lord,

"I am ordered by the High Court of Appeal to acquaint your lordship, in order to your better preparing yourself for your trial, that a true bill hath been sent down, and the indictment lieth against your lordship for the murder of one Lewis Pyneweck of Shrewsbury, citizen, wrongfully executed for the forgery of a bill of exchange, on the —th day of —— last, by reason of the wilful perversion of the evidence, and the undue pressure put upon the jury, together with the illegal admission of evidence by your lordship, well knowing the same to be illegal, by all which the promoter of the prosecution of the said indictment, before the High Court of Appeal, hath lost his life.

"And the trial of the said indictment, I am further ordered to acquaint your lordship is fixed for the 10th day of —— next ensuing, by the right honourable the Lord Chief-Justice Twofold, of the court aforesaid, to wit, the High Court of Appeal, on which day it will most certainly take place. And I am further to acquaint your lordship, to prevent any surprise or miscarriage, that your case stands first for the said day, and that the said High Court of Appeal sits day and night, and never rises; and herewith, by order of the said court, I furnish your lordship with a copy (extract) of the record in this case, except of the indictment, whereof, notwithstanding, the substance and effect is supplied to your lordship in this Notice. And further I am to inform you, that in case the jury then to try your lordship should find you guilty, the right honourable the Lord Chief-Justice will, in passing sentence of death upon you, fix the day of execution for the 10th day of ——, being one calendar month from the day of your trial."

It was signed by   "CALEB SEARCHER,
                                    "Officer of the Crown Solicitor in the
                                    "Kingdom of Life and Death."

The Judge glanced through the parchment.

" 'Sblood! Do they think a man like me is to be bamboozled by their buffoonery?"

The Judge's coarse features were wrung into one of his sneers; but he was pale. Possibly, after all, there was a conspiracy on foot. It was queer. Did they mean to pistol him in his carriage? or did they only aim at frightening him?

Judge Harbottle had more than enough of animal courage. He was not afraid of highwaymen, and he had fought more than his share of duels, being a foul-mouthed advocate while he held briefs at the bar. No one questioned his fighting qualities. But with respect to this particular case of Pyneweck, he lived in a house of glass. Was there not his pretty, dark-eyed, overdressed housekeeper, Mrs. Flora Carwell? Very easy for people who knew Shrewsbury to identify Mrs. Pyneweck, if once put upon the scent; and had he not stormed and worked hard in that case? Had he not made it hard sailing for the prisoner? Did he not know very well what the bar thought of it? It would be the worst scandal that ever blasted judge.

So much there was intimidating in the matter, but nothing more. The Judge was a little bit gloomy for a day or two after, and more testy with every one than usual.

He locked up the papers; and about a week after he asked his housekeeper, one day, in the library:

"Had your husband never a brother?"

Mrs. Carwell squalled on this sudden introduction of the funereal topic, and cried exemplary "piggins full," as the Judge used pleasantly to say. But he was in no mood for trifling now, and he said sternly:

"Come, madam! this wearies me. Do it another time; and give me an answer to my question." So she did.

Pyneweck had no brother living. He once had one; but he died in Jamaica.

"How do you know he is dead?" asked the Judge.

"Because he told me so."

"Not the dead man?"

"Pyneweck told me so."

"Is that all?" sneered the Judge.

He pondered this matter; and time went on. The Judge was growing a little morose, and less enjoying. The subject struck nearer to his thoughts than he fancied it could have done. But so it is with most undivulged vexations, and there was no one to whom he could tell this one.

It was now the ninth; and Mr. Justice Harbottle was glad. He knew nothing would come of it. Still it bothered him; and tomorrow would see it well over.

[What of the paper, I have cited? No one saw it during his life; no one, after his death. He spoke of it to Dr. Hedstone; and what purported to be "a copy," in the old Judge's handwriting, was found. The original was nowhere. Was it a copy of an illusion, incident to brain disease? Such is my belief.]

CHAPTER VI

Arrested

Judge Harbottle went this night to the play at Drury Lane. He was one of those old fellows who care nothing for late hours, and occasionally knocking about in pursuit of pleasure. He had appointed with two cronies of Lincoln's Inn to come home in his coach with him to sup after the play.

They were not in his box, but were to meet him near the entrance, and to get into his carriage there; and Mr. Justice Harbottle, who hated waiting, was looking a little impatiently from the window.

The Judge yawned.

He told the footman to watch for Counsellor Thavies and Counsellor Beller, who were coming; and, with another yawn, he laid his cocked hat on his knees, closed his eyes, leaned back in his corner, wrapped his mantle closer about him, and began to think of pretty Mrs. Abington.

And being a man who could sleep like a sailor, at a moment's notice, he was thinking of taking a nap. Those fellows had no business to keep a judge waiting.

He heard their voices now. Those rake-hell counsellors were laughing, and bantering, and sparring after their wont. The carriage swayed and jerked, as one got in, and then again as the other followed. The door clapped, and the coach was now jogging and rumbling over the pavement. The Judge was a little bit sulky. He did not care to sit up and open his eyes. Let them suppose he was asleep. He heard them laugh with more malice than good-humour, he thought, as they observed it. He would give them a d—d hard knock or two when they got to his door, and till then he would counterfeit his nap.

The clocks were chiming twelve. Beller and Thavies were silent as tombstones. They were generally loquacious and merry rascals.

The Judge suddenly felt himself roughly seized and thrust from his corner into the middle of the seat, and opening his eyes, instantly he found himself between his two companions.

Before he could blurt out the oath that was at his lips, he saw that they were two strangers—evil-looking fellows, each with a pistol in his hand, and dressed like Bow Street officers.

The Judge clutched at the check-string. The coach pulled up. He stared about him. They were not among houses; but through the windows, under a broad moonlight, he saw a black moor stretching lifelessly from right to left, with rotting trees, pointing fantastic branches in the air, standing here and there in groups, as if they held up their arms and twigs like fingers, in horrible glee at the Judge's coming.

A footman came to the window. He knew his long face and sunken eyes. He knew it was Dingly Chuff, fifteen years ago a footman in his service, whom he had turned off at a moment's notice, in a burst of jealousy, and indicted for a missing spoon. The man had died in prison of the jail-fever.

The Judge drew back in utter amazement. His armed companions signed mutely; and they were again gliding over this unknown moor.

The bloated and gouty old man, in his horror, considered the question of resistance. But his athletic days were long over. This moor was a desert. There was no help to be had. He was in the hands of strange servants, even if his recognition turned out to be a delusion, and they were under the command of his captors. There was nothing for it but submission, for the present.

Suddenly the coach was brought nearly to a standstill, so that the prisoner saw an ominous sight from the window.

It was a gigantic gallows beside the road; it stood three-sided, and from each of its three broad beams at top depended in chains some eight or ten bodies, from several of which the cere-clothes had dropped away, leaving the skeletons swinging lightly by their chains. A tall ladder reached to the summit of the structure, and on the peat beneath lay bones.

On top of the dark transverse beam facing the road, from which, as from the other two completing the triangle of death, dangled a row of these unfortunates in chains, a hangman, with a pipe in his mouth, much as we see him in the famous print of the "Idle Apprentice," though here his perch was ever so much higher, was reclining at his ease and listlessly shying bones, from a little heap at his elbow, at the skeletons that hung round, bringing down now a rib or two, now a hand, now half a leg. A long-sighted man could have discerned that he was a dark fellow, lean; and from continually looking down on the earth from the elevation over which, in another sense, he always hung, his nose, his lips, his chin were pendulous and loose, and drawn down into a monstrous grotesque.

This fellow took his pipe from his mouth on seeing the coach, stood up, and cut some solemn capers high on his beam, and shook a new rope in the air, crying with a voice high and distant as the caw of a raven hovering over a gibbet, "A rope for Judge Harbottle!"

The coach was now driving on at its old swift pace.

So high a gallows as that, the Judge had never, even in his most hilarious moments, dreamed of. He thought he must be raving. And the dead footman! He shook his ears and strained his eyelids; but if he was dreaming, he was unable to awake himself.

There was no good in threatening these scoundrels. A *brutum fulmen* might bring a real one on his head.

Any submission to get out of their hands; and then heaven and earth he would move to unearth and hunt them down.

Suddenly they drove round a corner of a vast white building, and under a *porte-cochère*.

CHAPTER VII

Chief-Justice Twofold

The Judge found himself in a corridor lighted with dingy oil-lamps, the walls of bare stone; it looked like a passage in a prison. His guards placed him in the hands of other people. Here and there he saw bony and gigantic soldiers passing to and fro, with muskets over their shoulders. They looked straight before them, grinding their teeth, in bleak fury, with no noise but the clank of their shoes. He saw these by glimpses, round corners, and at the ends of passages, but he did not actually pass them by.

And now, passing under a narrow doorway, he found himself in the dock, confronting a judge in his scarlet robes, in a large courthouse. There was nothing to elevate this temple of Themis above its vulgar kind elsewhere. Dingy enough it looked, in spite of candles lighted in decent abundance. A case had just closed, and the last juror's back was seen escaping through the door in the wall of the jury-box. There were some dozen barristers, some fiddling with pen and ink, others buried in briefs, some beckoning, with the plumes of their pens, to their attorneys, of whom there were no lack; there were clerks to-ing and fro-ing, and the officers of the court, and the registrar, who was handing up a paper to the judge; and the tipstaff, who was presenting a note at the end of his wand to a king's counsel over the heads of the crowd between. If this was the High Court of Appeal, which never rose day or night, it might account for the pale and jaded aspect of everybody in it. An air of indescribable gloom hung upon the pallid features of all the people here; no one ever smiled; all looked more or less secretly suffering.

"The King against Elijah Harbottle!" shouted the officer.

"Is the appellant Lewis Pyneweck in court?" asked Chief-Justice Twofold, in a voice of thunder, that shook the woodwork of the Court, and boomed down the corridors.

Up stood Pyneweck from his place at the table.

"Arraign the prisoner!" roared the Chief; and Judge Harbottle felt the panels of the dock round him, and the floor, and the rails quiver in the vibrations of that tremendous voice.

The prisoner, *in limine,* objected to this pretended court, as being a sham, and nonexistent in point of law; and then, that, even if it were a court constituted by law (the Judge was growing dazed), it had not and could not have any jurisdiction to try him for his conduct on the bench.

Whereupon the chief-justice laughed suddenly, and every one in court, turning round upon the prisoner, laughed also, till the laugh grew and roared all round like a deafening acclamation; he saw nothing but glittering eyes and teeth, a universal stare and grin; but though all the voices laughed, not a single face of all those that concentrated their gaze upon him looked like a laughing face. The mirth subsided as suddenly as it began.

The indictment was read. Judge Harbottle actually pleaded! He pleaded "Not guilty." A jury was sworn. The trial proceeded. Judge Harbottle was bewildered. This could not be real. He must be either mad, or *going* mad, he thought.

One thing could not fail to strike even him. This Chief-Justice Two-fold, who was knocking him about at every turn with sneer and gibe, and roaring him down with his tremendous voice, was a dilated effigy of himself; an image of Mr. Justice Harbottle, at least double his size, and with all his fierce colouring, and his ferocity of eye and visage, enhanced awfully.

Nothing the prisoner could argue, cite, or state was permitted to retard for a moment the march of the case towards its catastrophe.

The chief-justice seemed to feel his power over the jury, and to exult and riot in the display of it. He glared at them, he nodded to them; he seemed to have established an understanding with them. The lights were faint in that part of the court. The jurors were mere shadows, sitting in rows; the prisoner could see a dozen pairs of white eyes shining, coldly, out of the darkness; and whenever the judge in his charge, which was contemptuously brief, nodded and grinned and gibed, the prisoner could see, in the obscurity, by the dip of all these rows of eyes together, that the jury nodded in acquiescence.

And now the charge was over, the huge chief-justice leaned back panting and gloating on the prisoner. Every one in the court turned about, and gazed with steadfast hatred on the man in the dock. From the jury-box where the twelve sworn brethren were whispering together, a sound in the general stillness like a prolonged "hiss-s-s!" was heard; and then, in answer to the challenge of the officer, "How say you, gentlemen of the jury, guilty or not guilty?" came in a melancholy voice the finding, "Guilty."

The place seemed to the eyes of the prisoner to grow gradually darker and darker, till he could discern nothing distinctly but the lumen of the eyes that were turned upon him from every bench and side and corner and gallery of the building. The prisoner doubtless thought that he had quite enough to say, and conclusive, why sentence of death should not be pronounced upon him; but the lord chief-justice puffed it contemptuously away, like so much smoke, and proceeded to pass sentence of death upon the prisoner, having named the 10th of the ensuing month for his execution.

Before he had recovered the stun of this ominous farce, in obedience to the mandate, "Remove the prisoner," he was led from the dock. The lamps seemed all to have gone out, and there were stoves and charcoal fires here and there, that threw a faint crimson light on the walls of the corridors through which he passed. The stones that composed them looked now enormous, cracked and unhewn.

He came into a vaulted smithy, where two men, naked to the waist, with heads like bulls, round shoulders, and the arms of giants, were welding red-hot chains together with hammers that pelted like thunderbolts.

They looked on the prisoner with fierce red eyes, and rested on their hammers for a minute; and said the elder to his companion, "Take out Elijah Harbottle's gyves"; and with a pincers he plucked the end which lay dazzling in the fire from the furnace.

"One end locks," said he, taking the cool end of the iron in one hand, while with the grip of a vice he seized the leg of the Judge, and locked the ring round his ankle. "The other," he said with a grin, "is welded."

The iron band that was to form the ring for the other leg lay still red-hot upon the stone floor, with brilliant sparks sporting up and down its surface.

His companion in his gigantic hands seized the old Judge's other leg, and pressed his foot immovably to the stone floor; while his senior in a twinkling, with a masterly application of pincers and hammer, sped the glowing bar round his ankle so tight that the skin and sinews smoked and bubbled again, and old Judge Harbottle uttered a yell that seemed to chill the very stones, and make the iron chains quiver on the wall.

Chains, vaults, smiths, and smithy all vanished in a moment; but the pain continued. Mr. Justice Harbottle was suffering torture all round the ankle on which the infernal smiths had just been operating.

His friends Thavies and Beller were startled by the Judge's roar in the midst of their elegant trifling about a marriage à la mode case which was going on. The Judge was in panic as well as pain. The street-lamps and the light of his own hall-door restored him.

"I'm very bad," growled he between his set teeth; "my foot's blazing. Who was he that hurt my foot? 'Tis the gout—'tis the gout!" he said, awaking completely. "How many hours have we been coming from the playhouse? 'Sblood, what has happened on the way? I've slept half the night?"

There had been no hitch or delay, and they had driven home at a good pace.

The Judge, however, was in gout; he was feverish too; and the attack, though very short, was sharp; and when, in about a fortnight, it subsided, his ferocious joviality did not return. He could not get this dream, as he chose to call it, out of his head.

CHAPTER VIII

Somebody Has Got into the House

People remarked that the Judge was in the vapours. His doctor said he should go for a fortnight to Buxton.

Whenever the Judge fell into a brown study, he was always conning over the terms of the sentence pronounced upon him in his vision—"in one calendar month from the date of this day"; and then the usual form, "and you shall be hanged by the neck till you are dead," &c. "That will be the 10th—I'm not much in the way of being hanged. I know what stuff dreams are, and I laugh at them; but this is continually in my thoughts, as if it forecast misfortune of some sort. I wish the day my dream gave me were passed and over. I wish I were well purged of my gout. I wish I were as I used to be. 'Tis nothing but vapours, nothing but a maggot." The copy of the parchment and letter which had announced his trial with many a snort and sneer he would read over and over again, and the scenery and people of his dream would rise about him in places the most unlikely, and steal him in a moment from all that surrounded him into a world of shadows.

The Judge had lost his iron energy and banter. He was growing taciturn and morose. The Bar remarked the change, as well they might. His friends thought him ill. The doctor said he was troubled with hypochondria, and that his gout was still lurking in his system, and ordered him to that ancient haunt of crutches and chalk-stones, Buxton.

The Judge's spirits were very low; he was frightened about himself; and he described to his housekeeper, having sent for her to his study to drink a dish of tea, his strange dream in his drive home from Drury Lane playhouse. He was sinking into the state of nervous dejection in which men lose their faith in orthodox advice, and in despair consult quacks, astrologers, and nursery story-tellers. Could such a dream mean that he was to have a fit, and so die on the 10th? She did not think so. On the contrary, it was certain some good luck must happen on that day.

The Judge kindled; and for the first time for many days, he looked for a minute or two like himself, and he tapped her on the cheek with the hand that was not in flannel.

"Odsbud! odsheart! you dear rogue! I had forgot. There is young

Tom—yellow Tom, my nephew, you know, lies sick at Harrogate; why shouldn't he go that day as well as another, and if he does, I get an estate by it? Why, lookee, I asked Doctor Hedstone yesterday if I was like to take a fit any time, and he laughed, and swore I was the last man in town to go off that way."

The Judge sent most of his servants down to Buxton to make his lodgings and all things comfortable for him. He was to follow in a day or two.

It was now the 9th; and the next day well over, he might laugh at his visions and auguries.

On the evening of the 9th, Doctor Hedstone's footman knocked at the Judge's door. The doctor ran up the dusky stairs to the drawing-room. It was a March evening, near the hour of sunset, with an east wind whistling sharply through the chimney-stacks. A wood fire blazed cheerily on the hearth. And Judge Harbottle, in what was then called a brigadier-wig, with his red roquelaure on, helped the glowing effect of the darkened chamber, which looked red all over like a room on fire.

The Judge had his feet on a stool, and his huge grim purple face confronted the fire, and seemed to pant and swell, as the blaze alternately spread upward and collapsed. He had fallen again among his blue devils, and was thinking of retiring from the Bench, and of fifty other gloomy things.

But the doctor, who was an energetic son of Æsculapius, would listen to no croaking, told the Judge he was full of gout, and in his present condition no judge even of his own case, but promised him leave to pronounce on all those melancholy questions, a fortnight later.

In the meantime the Judge must be very careful. He was overcharged with gout, and he must not provoke an attack, till the waters of Buxton should do that office for him, in their own salutary way.

The doctor did not think him perhaps quite so well as he pretended, for he told him he wanted rest, and would be better if he went forthwith to his bed.

Mr. Gerningham, his valet, assisted him, and gave him his drops; and the Judge told him to wait in his bedroom till he should go to sleep.

Three persons that night had specially odd stories to tell.

The housekeeper had got rid of the trouble of amusing her little girl at this anxious time by giving her leave to run about the sitting-rooms and look at the pictures and china, on the usual condition of touching nothing. It was not until the last gleam of sunset had for some time faded, and the twilight had so deepened that she could no longer discern the colours on the china figures on the chimneypiece or in the cabinets, that the child returned to the housekeeper's room to find her mother.

To her she related, after some prattle about the china, and the pictures, and the Judge's two grand wigs in the dressing-room off the library, an adventure of an extraordinary kind.

In the hall was placed, as was customary in those times, the sedan-chair which the master of the house occasionally used, covered with stamped leather, and studded with gilt nails, and with its red silk blinds down. In this case, the doors of this old-fashioned conveyance were locked, the windows up, and, as I said, the blinds down, but not so closely that the curious child could not peep underneath one of them, and see into the interior.

A parting beam from the setting sun, admitted through the window of a back room, shot obliquely through the open door, and lighting on the chair, shone with a dull transparency through the crimson blind.

To her surprise, the child saw in the shadow a thin man dressed in black seated in it; he had sharp dark features; his nose, she fancied, a little awry, and his brown eyes were looking straight before him; his hand was on his thigh, and he stirred no more than the waxen figure she had seen at Southwark fair.

A child is so often lectured for asking questions and on the propriety of silence, and the superior wisdom of its elders, that it accepts most things at last in good faith; and the little girl acquiesced respectfully in the occupation of the chair by this mahogany-faced person as being all right and proper.

It was not until she asked her mother who this man was, and observed her scared face as she questioned her more minutely upon the appearance of the stranger, that she began to understand that she had seen something unaccountable.

Mrs. Carwell took the key of the chair from its nail over the footman's shelf, and led the child by the hand up to the hall, having a lighted candle in her other hand. She stopped at a distance from the chair, and placed the candlestick in the child's hand.

"Peep in, Margery, again, and try if there's anything there," she whispered; "hold the candle near the blind so as to throw its light through the curtain."

The child peeped, this time with a very solemn face, and intimated at once that he was gone.

"Look again, and be sure," urged her mother.

The little girl was quite certain; and Mrs. Carwell, with her mob-cap of lace and cherry-coloured ribbons, and her dark brown hair, not yet powdered, over a very pale face, unlocked the door, looked in, and beheld emptiness.

"All a mistake, child, you see."

"*There,* ma'am! see there! He's gone round the corner," said the child.

"Where?" said Mrs. Carwell, stepping backward a step.

"Into that room."

"Tut, child! 'twas the shadow," cried Mrs. Carwell angrily, because she was frightened. "I moved the candle." But she clutched one of the poles of the chair, which leant against the wall in the corner, and pounded the floor furiously with one end of it, being afraid to pass the open door the child had pointed to.

The cook and two kitchen-maids came running upstairs, not knowing what to make of this unwonted alarm.

They all searched the room; but it was still and empty, and no sign of anyone's having been there.

Some people may suppose that the direction given to her thoughts by this odd little incident will account for a very strange illusion which Mrs. Carwell herself experienced about two hours later.

CHAPTER IX

The Judge Leaves His House

Mrs. Flora Carwell was going up the great staircase with a posset for the Judge in a china bowl, on a little silver tray.

Across the top of the well-staircase there runs a massive oak rail; and, raising her eyes accidentally, she saw an extremely odd-looking stranger, slim and long, leaning carelessly over with a pipe between his finger and thumb. Nose, lips, and chin seemed all to droop downward into extraordinary length, as he leant his odd peering face over the banister. In his other hand he held a coil of rope, one end of which escaped from under his elbow and hung over the rail.

Mrs. Carwell, who had no suspicion at the moment, that he was not a real person, and fancied that he was someone employed in cording the Judge's luggage, called to know what he was doing there.

Instead of answering, he turned about, and walked across the lobby, at about the same leisurely pace at which she was ascending, and entered a room, into which she followed him. It was an uncarpeted and unfurnished chamber. An open trunk lay upon the floor empty, and beside it the coil of rope; but except herself there was no one in the room.

Mrs. Carwell was very much frightened, and now concluded that the child must have seen the same ghost that had just appeared to her. Perhaps, when she was able to think it over, it was a relief to believe so; for the face, figure, and dress described by the child were awfully like Pyneweck; and this certainly was not he.

Very much scared and very hysterical, Mrs. Carwell ran down to her room, afraid to look over her shoulder, and got some companions about her, and wept, and talked, and drank more than one cordial, and talked and wept again, and so on, until, in those early days, it was ten o'clock, and time to go to bed.

A scullery-maid remained up finishing some of her scouring and "scalding" for some time after the other servants—who, as I said, were few in number—that night had got to their beds. This was a low-browed, broad-faced, intrepid wench with black hair, who did not "vally a ghost not a button," and treated the housekeeper's hysterics with measureless scorn.

The old house was quiet, now. It was near twelve o'clock, no sounds were audible except the muffled wailing of the wintry winds, piping high among the roofs and chimneys, or rumbling at intervals, in under gusts, through the narrow channels of the street.

The spacious solitudes of the kitchen level were awfully dark, and this sceptical kitchen-wench was the only person now up and about, in the house. She hummed tunes to herself, for a time; and then stopped and listened; and then resumed her work again. At last, she was destined to be more terrified than even was the housekeeper.

There was a back-kitchen in this house, and from this she heard, as if coming from below its foundations, a sound like heavy strokes that seemed to shake the earth beneath her feet. Sometimes a dozen in sequence, at regular intervals; sometimes fewer. She walked out softly into the passage, and was surprised to see a dusky glow issuing from this room, as if from a charcoal fire.

The room seemed thick with smoke.

Looking in, she very dimly beheld a monstrous figure, over a furnace, beating with a mighty hammer the rings and rivets of a chain.

The strokes, swift and heavy as they looked, sounded hollow and distant. The man stopped, and pointed to something on the floor, that, through the smoky haze, looked, she thought, like a dead body. She remarked no more; but the servants in the room close by, startled from their sleep by a hideous scream, found her in a swoon on the flags, close to the door, where she had just witnessed this ghastly vision.

Startled by the girl's incoherent asseverations that she had seen the Judge's corpse on the floor, two servants having first searched the lower part of the house, went rather frightened upstairs to inquire whether their master was well. They found him, not in his bed, but in his room. He had a table with candles burning at his bedside, and was getting on his clothes again; and he swore and cursed at them roundly in his old style, telling them that he had business, and that he would discharge on the spot any scoundrel who should dare to disturb him again.

So the invalid was left to his quietude.

In the morning it was rumoured here and there in the street that the Judge was dead. A servant was sent from the house three doors away, by Counsellor Traverse, to inquire at Judge Harbottle's hall door.

The servant who opened it was pale and reserved, and would only say that the Judge was ill. He had had a dangerous accident; Doctor Hedstone had been with him at seven o'clock in the morning.

There were averted looks, short answers, pale and frowning faces, and all the usual signs that there was a secret that sat heavily upon their minds, and the time for disclosing which had not yet come. That time would arrive when the coroner had arrived, and the mortal scandal that had befallen the house could be no longer hidden. For that morning Mr. Justice Harbottle had been found hanging by the neck from the banister at the top of the great staircase, and quite dead.

There was not the smallest sign of any struggle or resistance. There had not been heard a cry or any other noise in the slightest degree indicative of violence. There was medical evidence to show that, in his atrabilious state, it was quite on the cards that he might have made away with himself. The jury found accordingly that it was a case of suicide. But to those who were acquainted with the strange story which Judge Harbottle had related to at least two persons, the fact that the catastrophe occurred on the morning to the 10th March seemed a startling coincidence.

A few days after, the pomp of a great funeral attended him to the grave; and so, in the language of scripture, "the rich man died, and was buried."

One of the most famous legends of men who sail the ocean is that of the *Flying Dutchman*. According to tradition, Captain Vanderdecken was a Dutch shipmaster who uttered a fearful curse that he would navigate the formidable Cape of Good Hope and enter Table Bay in Africa "if it takes me forever." Unfortunately, some malevolent deity overheard. Variations of the story abound; Wagner's opera, Die Fliegende Hollender, takes great advantage of the sublegend that Vanderdecken is permitted to put into port with his ghost crew once every seven years, at which time he will be redeemed if he can find the love of one true woman. The folk ballad is truer to the original tradition; the final stanza is my own.

The Flying Dutchman

Traditional

'Twas on a dark and cheerless night
　　To the south'ard of the Cape,
And from a strong nor'wester
　　We had just made our escape.
Like an infant in its cradle,
　　All hands were fast asleep,
And peacefully we sailed along
　　The bosom of the deep,
Peacefully we sailed along the bosom of the deep.

At length our helmsman gave a cry
　　Of terror and of fear,
As if he had just gazed upon
　　Some sudden danger near.
The seas around were clad in foam
　　And just upon our lee
We saw The Flying Dutchman
　　Come bounding o'er the sea,
We saw The Flying Dutchman come bounding o'er the sea.

"Take in our lofty canvas, lads,"
　　Our watchful master cried,
"For me and my ship's company,
　　Some sudden danger bides.

For every seaman who rounds the Cape,
  Although he knows no fear,
Yet knows that there is danger
  When Vanderdecken's near,
He knows that there is danger when Vanderdecken's near.

"Here comes The Flying Dutchman
  Like an eagle o'er the sea!
Pursued along by tempests dire,
  He makes for Table Bay.
Pursued along by tempests dire,
  The lightning'd waves' accursed,
And ere he can cast anchor
  The bay, alas, is past,
And ere he can cast anchor, the bay, alas, is past.

"Let's pity poor Vanderdecken,
  For fearful is his doom:
The seas around this stormy Cape
  Must be his living tomb!
He's doomed to sail the ocean
  Forever and a day,
As he tries in vain his oath to keep
  By entering Table Bay,
He tries in vain his oath to keep by entering Table Bay."

And as we watched that spectral vessel
  Disappear from sight,
Our master glanced to starboard
  And he gave a cry of fright.
A mighty ring of coral loomed
  Beneath the dashing wave,
And many shipmates went that night
  Unto a salt-sea grave,
And many shipmates went that night unto a salt-sea grave.

Here is a lovely, offbeat tale by an unknown author: of a traveling salesman whose experience with trains is not dissimilar to old Vanderdecken's problem with his ship, The Flying Dutchman. Ghost stories can be charming!

The Parlor-Car Ghost

Anonymous

All draped with blue denim—the seaside cottage of my friend, Sara Pyne. She asked me to go there with her when she opened it to have it set in order for the summer. She confessed that she felt a trifle nervous at the idea of entering it alone. And I am always ready for an excursion. So much blue denim rather surprised me, because blue is not complimentary to Sara's complexion—she always wears some shade of red, by preference. She perceived my wonder; she is very nearsighted, and therefore sees everything by some sort of sixth sense.

"You do not like my portieres and curtains and table-covers," said she. "Neither do I. But I did it to accommodate. And now he rests well in his grave, I hope."

"Whose grave, for pity's sake?"

"Mr. J. Billington Price's."

"And who is he? He doesn't sound interesting."

"Then I will tell you about him," said Sara, taking a seat directly in front of one of those curtains. "Last autumn I was leaving this place for New York, traveling on the fast express train known as the Flying Yankee. Of course, I thought of the Flying Dutchman and Wagner's musical setting of the uncanny legend, and how different things are in these days of steam, etc. Then I looked out of the window at the landscape, the horizon that seemed to wheel in a great curve as the train sped on. Every now and then I had an impression at the 'tail of the eye' that a man was sitting in a chair three or four numbers in front of me on the opposite side of the car. Each time that I saw this shape I looked at the chair and ascertained that it was unoccupied. But it was an odd trick of vision. I raised my lorgnette, and the chair showed emptier than before. There was nobody in it, certainly. But the more I knew that it was vacant the more plainly I saw the man. Always with the corner of my eye. It made me nervous. When passengers entered the car I dreaded lest they might take that seat. What would happen if they should? A bag was put in the chair—that made me uncomfortable. The bag was removed at the next station. Then a baby was placed in the seat. It began to laugh as though someone had gently tickled it. There was something odd about that chair—thirteen was its number. When I looked away from it the impression was strong upon me that some person sitting there was watching me.

"Really, it would not do to humor such fancies. So I touched the electric button, asked the porter to bring me a table, and taking from my bag a pack of cards, proceeded to divert myself with a game of patience. I was puzzling where to put a seven of spades. 'Where can it go?' I murmured to myself. A voice behind me prompted: 'Play the four of diamonds on the five, and you can do it.' I started. The only occupants of the car, besides me, were a bridal couple, a mother with three little children, and a typical preacher of one of the straitest sects. Who had spoken? 'Play up the four, madam,' repeated this voice.

"I looked fearfully over my shoulder. At first I saw a bluish cloud, like cigar smoke, but inodorous. Then the vision cleared, and I saw a young man whom I knew by a subtle intuition to be the occupant, seen and not seen, of chair number thirteen. Evidently he was a traveling salesman—and a ghost. Of course, a drummer's ghost sounds ridiculous —they're so extremely alive! Or else you would expect a dead drummer to be particularly dead and not 'walk.' This was a most commonplace-looking ghost, cordial, pushing, businesslike. At the same time, his face had an expression of utter despair and horror which made him still more preposterous. Of course it is not nice to let a stranger speak to one, even on so impersonal a topic as a four of diamonds. But a ghost— there can't be any rule of etiquette about talking with a ghost! My dear, it was dreadful! That forward creature showed me how to play all the cards, and then begged me to lay them out again, in order that he might give me some clever points. I was too much amazed and disturbed to speak. I could only place the cards at his suggestion. This I did so as not to appear to be listening to the empty air, and be supposed to be a crazy woman. Presently the ghost spoke again, and told me his story.

" 'Madam,' he said, 'I have been riding back and forth on this car ever since February 22, 189—. Seven months and eleven days. All this time I have not exchanged a word with anyone. For a drummer, that is pretty hard, you may believe! You know the story of the Flying Dutchman? Well, that is very nearly my case. A curse is upon me and will not be removed until some kind soul——. But I'm getting ahead of my text. That day there were four of us, traveling for different houses. One of the boys was in wool, one in baking powder, one in boots and shoes, and myself in cotton goods. We met on the road, took seats together and fell into talking shop.

" 'Those fellows told big lies about their sales, Washington's Birthday though it was. The baking powder man raised the amount of the bills of goods which he had sold better than a whole can of his stuff could have done. I admitted the straight truth, that I had not yet been able to make a sale. And then I swore—not in a light-minded, chipper style of verbal trimmings, but a great, round, heaven-defying oath—that I would sell a case of blue denims on that trip if it took me forever. We became dry with talk, and when the train stopped at Rivermouth, we went out to have some beer. It is good there, you know—pardon me, I forgot that I was speaking to a lady. Well, we had to run to get aboard. I missed my footing, fell under the wheels, and the next thing that I knew they were holding an inquest over my remains; while I, disemboweled, was sitting on a corner of the undertaker's table, wondering which of the coroner's jury was likely to want a case of blue denims.

" 'Then I remembered my wicked oath, and understood that I was a soul doomed to wander until I could succeed in selling that bill of goods. I spoke once or twice, offering the denims under value, but nobody noticed me. Verdict: accidental death; negligence of deceased; railroad corporation not to blame; deceased got out for beer at his own risk. The other drummers took charge of the remains, and wrote a beautiful letter to my relatives about my social qualities and my impressive conversation. I wish it had been less impressive that time! I might have lied about my sales, or I might have said that I hoped for better luck. But after that oath there was nothing for it. Back and forth, back and forth, on this road, in chair number thirteen, to all eternity. Nobody suspects my presence. They sit on my knees—I'm playing in luck when it is a nice baby as it was this afternoon! They pile wraps, bags, even railway literature on me. They play cards under my nose—and what duffers some of them are! You, madam, are the first person who has perceived me; and therefore I ventured to speak to you, meaning no offense. I can see that you are sorry for me. Now, if you recall the story of the Flying Dutchman, he was saved by the charity of a good woman. In fact, Senta married him. Now I'm not asking anything of that size. I see that you wear a wedding ring, and no doubt you make some man's happiness. I wasn't a marrying man myself, and, naturally, am not a marrying ghost. And that has nothing to do with the matter anyway. But if you could—I don't suppose you would have any use for them—but if you were disposed to do a turn of good, solid, Christian charity—I should be everlastingly grateful, and you may have that case of denims at $72.50. And that quality is quoted today at $80. Does it go, madam?'

"The speech of the poor ghost was not very eloquent, but his eyes had an intense, eager glare, which was terrible. Something—pity, fear, I do not know what—compelled me. I decided to do without that white and gold evening cloak. Instead, I gave $72.50 to the ghost and took from him a receipt for the sum, signed J. Billington Price. Then he smiled contentedly, thanked me with emotion, and returned to chair number thirteen. Several times on the journey, although I did not perceive him again, I felt dazed. When the train arrived at New York, and I, with the other passengers, dismounted, it seemed to me that a strong hand passed under my elbow, steadying me down the steps. As I walked the length of the station my bag—not heavy at any time—appeared to become weightless. I believe that the parlor-car ghost walked beside me, carrying the bag, whose handle still remained in my other hand. Indeed, once or twice I thought I felt the touch of cold fingers against mine. Since then I have no reason to suppose that the poor ghost is not at rest. I hope he is.

"But I never expected nor wished for the blue denims. The next day, however, a dray belonging to a great wholesale house backed up to our door and delivered a case of denims, with a receipted bill for the same. What was I to do? I could not go about selling blue denims; I could not give them away without exciting comment. So I furnished the cottage with them—and you know the effect on my complexion. Pity me, dear! And credit me, frivolous woman as I am, with having saved a soul at the expense of my own vanity. My story is told. What do you think about it?"

"The Red Room" *is a remarkable study of terror created by the power of suggestion, but to say any more would be to tip off the final revelation.* H. G. WELLS *wrote a generous quantity of weird and speculative tales, as well as those justly famous, oft-dramatized and/or filmed classics of science fiction,* The Time Machine, The War of the Worlds, The Invisible Man, The Food of the Gods *and* The Island of Doctor Moreau. *Born in 1866, Wells was the central dramatic figure of the exciting film,* Time After Time . . . *and still seems far ahead of most of his literary successors.*

The Red Room
by H. G. Wells

"I can assure you," said I, "that it will take a very tangible ghost to frighten me." And I stood up before the fire with my glass in my hand.

"It is your own choosing," said the man with the withered arm, and glanced at me askance.

"Eight-and-twenty years," said I, "I have lived, and never a ghost have I seen as yet."

The old woman sat staring hard into the fire, her pale eyes wide open. "Ay," she broke in; "and eight-and-twenty years you have lived and never seen the likes of this house, I reckon. There's a many things to see, when one's still but eight-and-twenty." She swayed her head slowly from side to side. "A many things to see and sorrow for."

I half suspected the old people were trying to enhance the spiritual terrors of their house by their droning insistence. I put down my empty glass on the table and looked about the room, and caught a glimpse of myself, abbreviated and broadened to an impossible sturdiness, in the queer old mirror at the end of the room. "Well," I said, "if I see anything tonight, I shall be so much the wiser. For I come to the business with an open mind."

"It's your own choosing," said the man with the withered arm once more.

I heard the sound of a stick and a shambling step on the flags in the passage outside, and the door creaked on its hinges as a second old man entered, more bent, more wrinkled, more aged even than the first. He supported himself by a single crutch, his eyes were covered by a shade, and his lower lip, half-averted, hung pale and pink from his decaying yellow teeth. He made straight for an arm-chair on the opposite side of the table, sat down clumsily, and began to cough. The man with the withered arm gave this new-comer a short glance of positive dislike; the old woman took no notice of his arrival, but remained with her eyes fixed steadily on the fire.

"I said—it's your own choosing," said the man with the withered arm, when the coughing had ceased for a while.

"It's my own choosing," I answered.

The man with the shade became aware of my presence for the first time, and threw his head back for a moment and sideways, to see me. I caught a momentary glimpse of his eyes, small and bright and inflamed. Then he began to cough and splutter again.

"Why don't you drink?" said the man with the withered arm, pushing the beer towards him. The man with the shade poured out a glassful with a shaky arm that splashed half as much again on the deal table. A monstrous shadow of him crouched upon the wall and mocked his action as he poured and drank. I must confess I had scarce expected these grotesque custodians. There is to my mind something inhuman in senility, something crouching and atavistic; the human qualities seem to drop from old people insensibly day by day. The three of them made me feel uncomfortable, with their gaunt silences, their bent carriage, their evident unfriendliness to me and to one another.

"If," said I, "you will show me to this haunted room of yours, I will make myself comfortable there."

The old man with the cough jerked his head back so suddenly that it startled me, and shot another glance of his red eyes at me from under the shade; but no one answered me. I waited a minute, glancing from one to the other.

"If," I said a little louder, "if you will show me to this haunted room of yours, I will relieve you from the task of entertaining me."

"There's a candle on the slab outside the door," said the man with the withered arm, looking at my feet as he addressed me. "But if you go to the red room to-night—"

("This night of all nights!" said the old woman.)

"You go alone."

"Very well," I answered. "And which way do I go?"

"You go along the passage for a bit," said he, "until you come to a door, and through that is a spiral staircase, and half-way up that is a landing and another door covered with baize. Go through that and down the long corridor to the end, and the red room is on your left up the steps."

"Have I got that right?" I said, and repeated his directions. He corrected me in one particular.

"And are you really going?" said the man with the shade, looking at me again for the third time, with that queer, unnatural tilting of the face.

("This night of all nights!" said the old woman.)

"It is what I came for," I said, and moved towards the door. As I did so, the old man with the shade rose and staggered round the table, so as to be closer to the others and to the fire. At the door I turned and looked at them, and saw they were all close together, dark against the firelight, staring at me over their shoulders, with an intent expression on their ancient faces.

"Good-night," I said, setting the door open.

"It's your own choosing," said the man with the withered arm.

I left the door wide open until the candle was well alight, and then I shut them in and walked down the chilly, echoing passage.

I must confess that the oddness of these three old pensioners in whose charge her ladyship had left the castle, and the deep-toned, old fashioned furniture of the housekeeper's room in which they foregathered, affected me in spite of my efforts to keep myself at a matter-of-fact phase. They seemed to belong to another age, an older age, an age when things spiritual were different from this of ours, less certain; an age when omens and witches were credible, and ghosts beyond denying. Their very existence was spectral; the cut of their clothing, fashions born in dead brains. The ornaments and conveniences of the room about them were ghostly—the thoughts of vanished men, which still haunted rather than participated in the world of to-day. But with an effort I sent such thoughts to the right-about. The long, draughty subterranean passage was chilly and dusty, and my candle flared and made the shadows cower and quiver. The echoes rang up and down the spiral staircase, and a shadow came sweeping up after me, and one fled before me into the darkness overhead. I came to the landing and stopped there for a moment, listening to a rustling that I fancied I heard; then, satisfied of the absolute silence, I pushed open the baize-covered door and stood in the corridor.

The effect was scarcely what I expected, for the moonlight, coming in by the great window on the grand staircase, picked out everything in vivid black shadow or silvery illumination. Everything was in its place: the house might have been deserted on the yesterday instead of eighteen months ago. There were candles in the sockets of the sconces, and whatever dust had gathered on the carpets or upon the polished flooring was distributed so evenly as to be invisible in the moonlight. I was about to advance, and stopped abruptly. A bronze group stood upon the landing, hidden from me by the corner of the wall, but its shadow fell with marvellous distinctness upon the white panelling, and gave me the impression of someone crouching to waylay me. I stood rigid for half a minute perhaps. Then, with my hand in the pocket that held my revolver, I advanced, only to discover a Ganymede and Eagle glistening in the moonlight. That incident for a time restored my nerve, and a porcelain Chinaman on a buhl table, whose head rocked silently as I passed him, scarcely startled me.

The door to the red room and the steps up to it were in a shadowy corner. I moved my candle from side to side, in order to see clearly the nature of the recess in which I stood before opening the door. Here it was, thought I, that my predecessor was found, and the memory of that story gave me a sudden twinge of apprehension. I glanced over my shoulder at the Ganymede in the moonlight, and opened the door of the red room rather hastily, with my face half turned to the pallid silence of the landing.

I entered, closed the door behind me at once, turned the key I found in the lock within, and stood with the candle held aloft, surveying the scene of my vigil, the great red room of Lorraine Castle, in which the young duke had died. Or, rather, in which he had begun his dying, for he had opened the door and fallen headlong down the steps I had just ascended. That had been the end of his vigil, of his gallant attempt to conquer the ghostly tradition of the place; and never, I thought, had apoplexy better served the ends of superstition. And there were other and older stories that clung to the room, back to the half-credible beginning of it all, the tale of a timid wife and the tragic end that came to her husband's jest of frightening her. And looking around that large shadowy room, with its shadowy window bays, its recesses and alcoves, one could well understand the legends that had sprouted in its black corners, its germinating darkness. My candle was a little tongue of flame in its vastness, that failed to pierce the opposite end of the room, and left an ocean of mystery and suggestion beyond its island of light.

I resolved to make a systematic examination of the place at once, and dispel the fanciful suggestions of its obscurity before they obtained a hold upon me. After satisfying myself of the fastening of the door, I began to walk about the room, peering round each article of furniture, tucking up the valances of the bed, and opening its curtains wide. I pulled up the blinds and examined the fastenings of the several windows before closing the shutters, leant forward and looked up the blackness of the wide chimney, and tapped the dark oak panelling for any secret opening. There were two big mirrors in the room, each with a pair of sconces bearing candles, and on the mantelshelf, too, were more candles in china candlesticks. All these I lit one after the other. The fire was laid,—an unexpected consideration from the old housekeeper,—and I lit it, to keep down any disposition to shiver, and when it was burning well, I stood round with my back to it and regarded the room again. I had pulled up a chintz-covered arm-chair and a table, to form a kind of barricade before me, and on this lay my revolver ready to hand. My precise examination had done me good, but I still found the remoter darkness of the place, and its perfect stillness, too stimulating for the imagination. The echoing of the stir and crackling of the fire was no sort of comfort to me. The shadow in the alcove, at the end in particular, had that undefinable quality of a presence, that odd suggestion of a lurking living thing, that comes so easily in silence and solitude. At last, to reassure myself, I walked with a candle into it, and satisfied myself that there was nothing tangible there. I stood that candle upon the floor of the alcove, and left it in that position.

By this time I was in a state of considerable nervous tension, although to my reason there was no adequate cause for the condition. My mind, however, was perfectly clear. I postulated quite unreservedly that nothing supernatural could happen, and to pass the time I began to string some rhymes together, Ingoldsby fashion, of the original legend of the place. A few I spoke aloud, but the echoes were not pleasant. For the same reason I also abandoned, after a time, a conversation with myself upon the impossibility of ghosts and haunting. My mind reverted to the three old and distorted people downstairs, and I tried to keep it upon that topic. The sombre reds and blacks of the room troubled me; even with seven candles the place was merely dim. The one in the alcove flared in a draught, and the fire-flickering kept the shadows and penumbra perpetually shifting and stirring. Casting about for a remedy, I recalled the candles I had seen in the passage, and, with a slight effort, walked out into the moonlight, carrying a candle and leaving the door open, and presently returned with as many as ten. These I put in various knick-knacks of china with which the room was sparsely adorned, lit and placed where the shadows had lain deepest, some on the floor, some in the window recesses, until at last my seventeen candles were so arranged that not an inch of the room but had the direct light of at least one of them. It occurred to me that when the ghost came, I could warn him not to trip over them. The room was now quite brightly illuminated. There was something very cheery and reassuring in these little streaming flames, and snuffing them gave me an occupation, and afforded a reassuring sense of the passage of time.

Even with that, however, the brooding expectation of the vigil weighed heavily upon me. It was after midnight that the candle in the alcove suddenly went out, and the black shadow sprang back to its place. I did not see the candle go out; I simply turned and saw that the darkness was there, as one might start and see the unexpected presence of a stranger. "By Jove!" said I aloud; "that draught's a strong one!" and, taking the matches from the table, I walked across the room in a leisurely manner to relight the corner again. My first match would not strike, and as I succeeded with the second, something seemed to blink on the wall before me. I turned my head involuntarily, and saw that the two candles on the little table by the fireplace were extinguished. I rose at once to my feet.

"Odd!" I said. "Did I do that myself in a flash of absent-mindedness?"

I walked back, relit one, and as I did so, I saw the candle in the right sconce of one of the mirrors wink and go right out, and almost immediately its companion followed it. There was no mistake about it. The flame vanished, as if the wicks had been suddenly nipped between a finger and a thumb, leaving the wick neither glowing nor smoking, but black. While I stood gaping, the candle at the foot of the bed went out, and the shadows seemed to take another step towards me.

"This won't do!" said I, and first one and then another candle on the mantelshelf followed.

"What's up?" I cried, with a queer high note getting into my voice somehow. At that the candle on the wardrobe went out, and the one I had relit in the alcove followed.

"Steady on!" I said. "These candles are wanted," speaking with a half-hysterical facetiousness, and scratching away at a match the while for the mantel candlesticks. My hands trembled so much that twice I missed the rough paper of the matchbox. As the mantel emerged from darkness again, two candles in the remoter end of the window were eclipsed. But with the same match I also relit the larger mirror candles, and those on the floor near the doorway, so that for the moment I seemed to gain on the extinctions. But then in a volley there vanished four lights at once in different corners of the room, and I struck another match in quivering haste, and stood hesitating whither to take it.

As I stood undecided, an invisible hand seemed to sweep out the two candles on the table. With a cry of terror, I dashed at the alcove, then into the corner, and then into the window, relighting three, as two more vanished by the fireplace; then, perceiving a better way, I dropped the matches on the iron-bound deed-box in the corner, and caught up the bedroom candlestick. With this I avoided the delay of striking matches; but for all that the steady process of extinction went on, and the shadows I feared and fought against returned, and crept in upon me, first a step gained on this side of me and then on that. It was like a ragged storm-cloud sweeping out the stars. Now and then one returned for a minute, and was lost again. I was now almost frantic with the horror of coming darkness, and my self-possession deserted me. I leaped panting and dishevelled from candle to candle, in a vain struggle against that remorseless advance.

I bruised myself on the thigh against the table, I sent a chair headlong, I stumbled and fell and whisked the cloth from the table in my fall. My candle rolled away from me, and I snatched another as I rose. Abruptly this was blown out, as I swung it off the table, by the wind of my sudden movement, and immediately the two remaining candles followed. But there was light still in the room, a red light that staved off the shadows from me. The fire! Of course, I could thrust my candle between the bars and relight it!

I turned to where the flames were dancing between the glowing coals, and splashing red reflections upon the furniture, made two steps towards the grate, and incontinently the flames dwindled and vanished, the glow vanished, the reflections rushed together and vanished, and as I thrust the candle between the bars, darkness closed upon me like the shutting of an eye, wrapped about me in a stifling embrace, sealed my vision, and crushed the last vestiges of reason from my brain. The candle fell from my hand. I flung out my arms in a vain effort to thrust that ponderous blackness away from me, and, lifting up my voice, screamed with all my might—once, twice, thrice. Then I think I must have staggered to my feet. I know I thought suddenly of the moonlit corridor, and, with my head bowed and my arms over my face, made a run for the door.

But I had forgotten the exact position of the door, and struck myself heavily against the corner of the bed. I staggered back, turned, and was either struck or struck myself against some other bulky furniture. I have a vague memory of battering myself thus, to and fro in the darkness, of a cramped struggle, and of my own wild crying as I darted to and fro, of a heavy blow at last upon my forehead, a horrible sensation of falling that lasted an age, of my last frantic effort to keep my footing, and then I remember no more.

I opened my eyes in daylight. My head was roughly bandaged, and the man with the withered arm was watching my face. I looked about me, trying to remember what had happened, and for a space I could not recollect. I turned to the corner, and saw the old woman, no longer abstracted, pouring out some drops of medicine from a little blue phial into a glass. "Where am I?" I asked. "I seem to remember you, and yet I cannot remember who you are."

They told me then, and I heard of the haunted Red Room as one who hears a tale. "We found you at dawn," said he, "and there was blood on your forehead and lips."

It was very slowly I recovered my memory of my experience. "You believe now," said the old man, "that the room is haunted?" He spoke no longer as one who greets an intruder, but as one who grieves for a broken friend.

"Yes," said I; "the room is haunted."

"And you have seen it. And we, who have lived here all our lives, have never set eyes upon it. Because we have never dared. . . . Tell us, is it truly the old earl who—"

"No," said I; "it is not."

"I told you so," said the old lady, with the glass in her hand. "It is his poor young countess who was frightened—"

"It is not," I said. "There is neither ghost of earl nor ghost of countess in that room, there is no ghost there at all; but worse, far worse—"

"Well?" they said.

"The worst of all the things that haunt poor mortal man," said I; "and that is, in all its nakedness—*Fear!* Fear that will not have light nor sound, that will not bear with reason, that deafens and darkens and overwhelms. It followed me through the corridor, it fought against me in the room—"

I stopped abruptly. There was an interval of silence. My hand went up to my bandages.

Then the man with the shade sighed and spoke. "That is it," said he. "I knew that was it. A Power of Darkness. To put such a curse upon a woman! It lurks there always. You can feel it even in the daytime, even of a bright summer's day, in the hangings, in the curtains, keeping behind you however you face about. In the dusk it creeps along the corridor and follows you, so that you dare not turn. There is Fear in that room of hers—black Fear, and there will be—so long as this house of sin endures."

CRAIG SHAW GARDNER *is one of the brightest young humorists to enter the ranks of fantasy writers in quite some time. A resident of Cambridge, Massachusetts, he has won a devoted coterie of fans, including me, for his wacky chronicles of Ebenezum, the powerful wizard with a sad occupational affliction: magic makes him sneeze. When Craig heard about this collection of ghost stories, he sat right down and dashed off an appropriate adventure for his sorcerer and Ebenezum's long-suffering apprentice-companion.*

A Gathering of Ghosts

by Craig Shaw Gardner

(1)

"Life is short, death inevitable, and, as the wise men say, it is best to do what one can with your poor, short life. However, should one manage a rich, short life, or even a short life on a moderate income, the 'best' the wise men speak of can be of a better quality altogether."

from *The Teachings of Ebenezum*
Volume 2

It was all luck, I guess you could say. Bad luck. Not that there had been any real catastrophes. Just a string of small misfortunes; beginning, I guess, with that misunderstanding in the tiny kingdom of Melifox, where the ruler had refused to pay us simply because a technicality in a spell had caused most of his wealth to vanish.

I looked to my master, the great wizard Ebenezum, as he descended the hill before me. Even on the steep path we took now, his tread was sure, his dark wizard's robes, tastefully inlaid with silver thread, flowing proud behind him. No matter what hardships we faced on our journey from the Western Kingdoms, no matter how great my master's affliction, Ebenezum would not bow.

It occurred to me, then, that our string of luck really began with my master's sneezing fits. It was the great wizard's battle with a particularly powerful demon from the seventh Netherhell that did it. In the end, of course, my master managed to send the demon back to the foul place from which it came. But my master did not escape the battle unscathed, for he discovered shortly thereafter that, should he even be in the presence of magic, he would begin to sneeze violently.

Now, a malady of this nature might have defeated many a lesser wizard. But not Ebenezum. He still managed to ply his trade, using his wits rather than spells to solve his clients' problems. It became apparent, however, that the mage's malady would not go away of its own accord, and, due to the nature of the affliction, Ebenezum could not cure it through the use of magic. We therefore took to the road, searching for some wizard great enough to cure my master's ills, though we might have to travel to far Vushta, city of a thousand forbidden delights, before we found one as great as that.

And Vushta began to seem more of a possibility with every passing day. What with being chased out of one kingdom and not being particularly welcome in the next two, we hadn't had a chance to meet many wizards at all. Then there'd been the mercenaries King Urfoo of Melifox had sent to kill us, and the seven straight days of rain, and the incident with the giant swamp rats. I didn't even want to think of those.

But still my master walked on, proud and tall, to far, forbidden Vushta. And I would follow him there, and anywhere. Even with his affliction, Ebenezum was the greatest wizard I had ever seen!

I touched my walking stick to my forehead in a silent salute to the man before me. It was then that I lost my footing and slid down the hill, colliding with my master.

Our fall ended in a cluster of bushes at the valley bottom. Not looking at me, the wizard stood with a groan that was like the rumble of an approaching storm. He turned, much too slowly, to face me. I watched the eyes beneath bushy brows and awaited the inevitable.

"Wuntvor," the mage said, his voice like an earthquake splitting a mountainside. "If you can't watch where you put your—"

My master stopped midsentence, and stared over my head. I started to stammer an apology, but the wizard waved me to silence.

"What do you hear, 'prentice?" he asked.

I listened, but heard nothing. I told him so.

"Exactly," he replied. "Nothing at all. 'Tis the midst of summer, deep in the wood, yet I do not see a single bird nor hear an insect. Though I must admit, the absence of the latter does not upset me overmuch." The mage scratched at a pink welt beneath his long, white beard. We had had a great deal of experience, ever since the seven days of rain, with clouds of mosquitoes and biting gnats.

"Methinks, Wunt, something is amiss."

I listened for a moment more. My master was right. The forest was silent, the only sounds the breathing of the wizard and myself. I had never heard quiet like this except perhaps on the coldest days of winter. A chill went up my back, surprising in the summer's heat.

My master dusted off his robes. "We seem to have landed near a clearing." He nodded down what remained of the hill. "Perhaps we shall find some habitation, even someone who can explain the nature of this place. Until then, we will bask in the absence of mosquitoes." He scratched his neck absently as he started down the hill. "Always look at the bright side, Wunt."

I hurriedly gathered up the foodstuffs, books, and magical paraphernalia that had fallen from my pack and followed my master's wizardly strides. He, as usual, carried nothing, preferring, as he often said, to keep his hands free for quick conjuring, his mind free for quick thought. I scrambled after him over the uneven ground, avoiding what underbrush there was. But the brush thinned rapidly as we walked, and we found ourselves facing a large clearing of bare earth, broken only by a ring of seven large boulders in its center.

"Now we've even lost the grasses," Ebenezum rumbled. "Come, Wunt, we'll find the cause of this." He took great strides across the bare ground, clouds of dust rising with every step. I followed close behind, doing my best not to cough.

When we reached the first boulder, something jumped.

"Boo!" the something said. I dropped my pack, but Ebenezum simply stood there and watched the apparition.

"Indeed," he said after a moment.

"Boo! Boo! Boo! Boo!" the creature confronting us shrieked. On closer inspection, I could see that it was definitely human, with long gray hair covering the face and brown rags concealing the body. The person raised frail hands and rushed us on unsteady legs.

Neither of us moved. Our attacker stopped, out of breath. "Not going to work, is it?" she wheezed at last. It was an old woman; her speaking voice was cracked and high.

Ebenezum stroked his moustache. "Is what not going to work?"

"Can't scare you away, huh?" She parted the long hair that covered her face and peered at the sky. "Probably too late for you to get away, anyhow. Might as well sit down and wait." She looked around for a likely rock and sat.

"Indeed," Ebenezum repeated. "Wait for what?"

"You don't know?" The woman's eyes widened in wonder. "Sir, you are in the dreaded Valley of Vrunge!"

"Indeed," Ebenezum said when it became apparent the woman planned to say no more.

"Now don't tell me you've never heard of it. What, do you come from the ignorant Western Kingdoms?" The woman laughed derisively. "Everyone knows of the Valley of Vrunge and the dread curse that falls upon it once every one hundred and thirty-seven years. Not that this place is all that friendly at any time—" She spat on the parched earth. "—but there is one night, every one hundred thirty-seven years, when all hell breaks loose. One night when no one then in the valley will get out alive!"

I didn't like the direction the woman's speech was taking. I swallowed hard and cleared my throat. "Ma'am, would you mind telling us just when that night is?"

"Haven't I made it clear?" The crone laughed again. "This is the cursed night of the Valley of Vrunge. It begins when the sun passes yonder hills." She pointed behind me.

I followed her arm and looked at the sun, already touching the tops of the western hills, then turned to Ebenezum. He stared above me, lost in thought. As I mentioned, our luck seemed to be running true to its course.

"If we are all due to die," Ebenezum said at last, "what are you doing here?"

The old woman looked away from us. "I have my reasons, which I'm sure would be of little interest to anyone but me. Let us just say that once this land was green and fair, and it was ruled over by a princess as lovely as the land itself. But a dark time came upon the earth, and the sky rained toads, and the princess became afraid. But her suitor, the handsome—"

"You're quite right," Ebenezum interrupted. "No one would be interested in that at all. You've decided to die because the sky rained toads?"

The woman sighed and watched the sun disappear behind the hilltop. "Not exactly. I've worn this old body out; I'm due to die. I just thought I'd see old Maggie out in style."

"Maggie?" Ebenezum scratched his insect bite thoughtfully. "That wouldn't be short for Magredel?" He peered into her ancient face.

"Oh, I haven't used that name in years. Not since I got away from those dull Western Kingdoms. Used to practice witchery thereabouts for a time, that's probably where you heard of me. Didn't specialize much, though. More of a general practitioner."

"Maggie?" Ebenezum repeated. "As in Old Aunt Maggie?"

Maggie squinted her eyes in turn. "Say, do I know you from someplace?"

There was an explosion directly behind me. All three of us spun to see a tall, pale apparition atop the tallest of the seven stones.

"Greetings, lady and gentlemen!" the apparition cried with a swirl of its white robe. "And welcome to curse night!"

"Greetings to you, too, Death," Maggie replied. "I hope tonight will be up to your usual standards?"

Death laughed, a high, echoey sound that came near to scaring the life from me. When I mentioned it later to Ebenezum, he said no doubt that was the desired reaction.

The apparition atop the stone disappeared.

"That was our introduction," Maggie remarked. "Soon the fun begins."

I was appalled. "F-fun?" I stammered. "How do you know what happens next?"

"Simple." The crone flashed a toothless smile. "I've been through this night once before."

(2)

"Your average ghost is a much more complex and interesting individual than is generally imagined. Just because someone is dragging chains or has one's head perpetually in flames does not necessarily make them of a lesser class. Some ghosts, especially those with heads still attached and mouths to speak through, are actually quite good conversationalists, with otherworldly stories by the score. In addition, ghosts generally subscribe to the happy custom of disappearing completely at dawn, a habit many living associates and relations might do well to cultivate."

from *The Teachings of Ebenezum*
Volume 6 (Appendix B)

Death had vanished, and the silence was again complete. My master cleared his throat.

"Ebenezum!" the old woman cried. "Of course! I'd recognize that nervous cough anywhere. Poor little Ebby, always coughing or scratching or tugging or doing something. He never could sit still." She winked in my direction. "You know, in the whole first year he studied under me, he didn't get one spell straight? You should have seen the things that showed up in our kitchen!" She laughed.

My master cast a worried glance at the rock where Death had stood. "Please, Aunt Maggie. I don't think this is the proper time to discuss—"

"Oh, keep your cap on!" The woman clapped Ebenezum on the shoulder. "We have a little time. It always takes them a while to get organized. When you only have a performance once every one hundred thirty-seven years, you tend to get a bit rusty."

"But what's going to happen?" I asked. I noticed my hand hurt from my tight grip on the walking stick.

"Ghosts, ghosts and more ghosts." The old woman spat on the ground. "Death is fond of games. He plays a game with every living thing, one in which he's always the victor. Some games he likes more than others, and those great conflicts he brings here, to play over and over again in his arena in the Valley of Vrunge!"

"The spirits just play games?" I asked. That didn't sound so bad.

"All of life is a game, remember. Death brings along the best of all his games, ranging from a nation at war to two people in love."

She jumped and screamed.

"Tickle, tickle, tickle," said a high voice from nowhere.

"Poltergeists! Boo! Boo! Boo! Away from here!" Maggie waved her hands about wildly. "More and more ghosts will appear throughout the night. And Death will try to snare you in his games. Beware, he always wins!" She screamed and jumped again.

"Boo, boo, boo?" the voice from nowhere asked. "That's passé, lady. These days, long, sensitive moans are much more the thing in ghostly circles."

"So it begins. I'm sorry, Ebby, you had to stumble into this!" She ran and screamed as "tickle, tickle, tickle!" chased her around the circle of boulders.

Ebenezum sneezed once and blew his nose on a silver-inlaid sleeve. "Just a minor spirit. Hardly bothers me at all."

I realized then that this was the first time Ebenezum's malady had affected him since we entered the cursed valley. Perhaps the severity of our situation was effecting a cure. Ebenezum had not sneezed once in the presence of Death!

My master shook his head when I explained my theory. "Why should I sneeze? Death is the most natural thing in the world." He pulled at his beard. "And I fear that, should we fail to devise a plan of action, Death will become all too familiar to both of us."

It was then that the beast leapt at me. All I could see was the huge mouth, giant, sharp teeth, slavering tongue. I leapt aside and felt claws of ice graze my shoulder. I rolled over with a groan and looked at my master. He stood at the ready, feet spread, sleeves back, hands in conjuring position. But the clearing was quiet again.

Ebenezum blew his nose. "The apparitions will try to divide us."

A great wind sprang up. My master had to shout to be heard. "Stay close! If we're separated—"

The wizard sneezed as three ghosts on a sled grabbed him and whisked him high in the air. Ghosts, sled and sneezing Ebenezum disappeared around the stones.

Night had fallen completely, and I was alone.

But then there was a crowd around me, sitting on long rows of seats, one atop another, as if they were built on a hillside. The crowd roared, and I saw they were watching a group of uniformed men on a green lawn, a few of whom were running but most of whom were standing still.

A man carrying a big silver box walked up the steps toward me. "Hot dogs!" he cried. "Hot dogs!"

He wasn't real, I told myself. This whole place was beyond my understanding. I stepped aside to let him pass. He stopped next to me anyway.

"Hot dog, mister?"

It was only with a mental effort that I kept from shivering. I looked down at the stout oak staff I used for a walking stick. My grip was firm. If the apparition tried anything, I'd swing at him. And then again, from what I'd heard of ghosts, I might swing through him as well.

With some trepidation, I asked, "What's a hot dog?"

"Like I thought," the spirit nodded sagely, "you're an outsider. So this is your first ball game? Well, you picked a good one, buddy."

I looked out over the field below us. "Ball game," I repeated, struggling to comprehend.

"Yeah," the apparition replied. "*The* ball game. People had counted the Red Sox out, but they came around. Now Torrez will blow the Yankees away! Seventy-eight is going to be our year. It *has* to be."

I looked closely at the spirit, hoping that some gesture or facial mannerism would help me to understand his ravings. All I saw was the haunted look, deep in his eyes.

"Has to be?" I asked.

"Well, yeah." The ghost paused. "I mean, the Sox have to win. Otherwise—" He shuddered. "Do you have any idea what it would be like to have to sell hot dogs throughout eternity?"

He didn't wait for an answer but walked up the stairs beyond me. I turned down to the "ball game" on the field below. I felt a sudden, near overwhelming urge to be drawn into that game and find out just what could move the hot dog spirit to such a frenzy. I'd watch the shifting patterns of men on the bright green lawn, and sooner or later some great secret would be revealed, a joyous revelation that would make my whole existence take on new meaning!

Something in the back of my head told me to turn away. I remembered Aunt Maggie's warning about Death and games.

The ball game disappeared. In its place stood Death.

"There you are," the creature said in his sonorous voice. "I've been looking all over for you. These curse evenings can be so long and boring, sometimes I like to indulge in games to help pass the time. Tell me, do you know how to play 'Red Light, Green Light'?"

Death stood much closer than he had before. I stared at the thin layer of pale skin pulled tight over his skull, and at the shadows where there should have been eyes. Yet his smile was ingratiating; you wanted to believe in what he told you. I decided he would make a good seller of used pack animals on market day.

"Well?" Death prompted.

"No!" I stammered. "I—I don't know the rules!"

"Oh, is that all?" Death reached out to touch my arm. "I'll explain everything. I'm very good with rules."

"No! I have to find my master!" I pulled away from the creature's hand and ran blindly.

Suddenly a pit yawned before me. A pit filled with sharpened spikes, and the roaring creature, all mouth and teeth and claws. I tried to stop, to step backward, but I was over the edge, falling, falling.

Someone barked a command behind me; my master's voice. I found myself on solid ground, standing by Ebenezum. All the ghosts were gone.

Ebenezum sneezed repeatedly, rocking with the force emitted by his nose.

"Temporary exorcism spell," he gasped at last. "Best I can manage."

I did a short jig on the parched earth while my master caught his breath. Ebenezum had freed himself from the sledding spirits! Hope once again rose within my breast.

I asked him how he had accomplished his escape.

The wizard shrugged. "I sneezed my way free. The ghosts were ready for sorcery, a battle of wits, anything but extreme nasal activity. They simply evaporated before the onslaught of my nose."

"That's wonderful!" I cried. "We'll be free of this cursed valley in no time!"

Ebenezum shook his head. "Death does not make the same mistake twice. The next set of apparitions will be ready for my malady."

Aunt Maggie appeared around one of the seven great boulders. She staggered over to Ebenezum's feet and collapsed.

She groaned, then turned and looked at my master. "It's gone! The poltergeist is gone!"

The wizard nodded solemnly. "Exorcism spell."

Maggie sighed in relief. "It kept taunting me, begging me to tickle it back. You can't give in to those things. It would have all been over." She looked at Ebenezum. "Exorcism? That means you followed your calling and graduated into wizardry! I did hesitate to ask you. In the early days, you were very determined, but your aptitude was sometimes less than—"

Ebenezum cleared his throat. " 'Tis only a temporary spell. Death's power is greater than common magic, and the ghosts will push through presently. We must come up with a more permanent solution."

Maggie laughed. "I pulled through this cursed night once, with the aid of magic. Maybe we can do so again. And gain my kingdom back in the bargain!" She slapped my master's shoulder. "So one of my students made good? Let's see you do your stuff. Nothing fancy; a bird out of thin air, water into wine, something to tickle an old woman's fancy."

Ebenezum fixed her with a wizardly stare. "We are in peril for our lives. I need to concentrate." He stalked off and disappeared into the circle of stone.

Maggie shook her head and smiled. "A great wizardly manner. He must be raking in the business." She sighed. "Wish I could work magic the way I used to. After a while, the body wears out. Can toss off a little spell now and again, when I'm feeling spry. But the big ones are beyond my reach."

I hesitated to tell her that, due to my master's affliction, just about all the spells that could save us from our present predicament were beyond his reach as well. Best not to upset her; I was upset enough for both of us.

"But let me tell you my story, and you'll understand why I'm here," she began. "You've already learned of the fair kingdom and the beautiful princess. And then, of course, there were the raining toads. And did I tell you about the princess's handsome suitor, Unwin, killed on their wedding day? No? Well, that's a good place to—"

Maggie jumped and screamed.

"Tickle, tickle, tickle," the disembodied voice chortled. The exorcism spell was over.

A cool breeze blew in my ear. "Hey, big boy," a woman whispered. "What's a fellow like you doing without a date on a night like this?"

I turned to gaze on the most beautiful apparition I had ever seen. I was speechless. She was slender and pale, with long, silver hair. And she wore no clothing at all, ghostly or otherwise. At certain angles, you could see right through her, but at other angles she was more than my eyes could bear.

"Oh, the silent type," she said, and took my hand, her fingers intertwining with mine. Her touch was ice and sent thrills up my arm and across my shoulders. She leaned close, and her breath was the breeze of Autumn. Her lips parted, close to mine. I wanted to kiss those lips more than I wanted life itself.

"I know a little game we can play," the full, cool lips said. "It's called Spin-the-Bottle."

Yes, yes, whatever it was, yes! All those girls I'd known in the Western Kingdoms, women I'd longed for on our travels overland, they were nothing to me now.

But my beloved was pulled away from me and sent spinning through the air, her ectoplasm flying in every direction.

"I can still toss off a spell or two." Maggie smiled. "Got to watch out for Succubi. Not good for your health."

"Crone!" Death was before us. "What would you know of love? Your body has been old and withered for a hundred years. An empty shell which can no longer be filled. Or, can it?"

Death waved his hand and a young man materialized at his side.

"Unwin?" The old woman's voice was little more than a whisper. "Is that you, Unwin?"

"Magredel!" the young man cried. "What's happened to you?"

"It's not me, Unwin. It's you. You've been away. I haven't seen you in so long!"

The old woman was crying.

"Consider, woman," Death said. "Come with me and you will be together always."

But Maggie turned on him, anger replacing sorrow. "No! You've stolen my kingdom for centuries! I'll be with Unwin soon enough! I must free what was tricked from me!"

"Such harsh words." Death examined his skeletal hand. "I have need of this place. My ghosts need their exercise." He looked at me, and I shivered where I stood. "Come, Wuntvor; let's leave these lovers alone while they talk things over. I'll give you the guided tour."

Without thinking, I found myself following him. Death smiled. "Simon says put your hands in the air."

It took all my willpower to keep my hands at my sides.

"We'll find one yet." Death's hands were full of small rectangles, which he fanned out before him. "How about a little 'Go Fish'?"

I found myself staring at the rectangles. I looked the other way.

"My kingdom," Death said.

There were apparitions everywhere. Armies fighting; women laughing, people in costumes familiar and unfamiliar, crawling across the ground, climbing the trees, flying through the air in strange machines.

"Amazing," I said despite myself.

Death nodded. "The paperwork alone is staggering. Yet we pull it off, every one hundred thirty-seven years. It's a shame our audience has to be so small. The Vrunge Curse is my masterpiece. Here are all the great moments of humanity, past, present, future, played out over and over again, from men at war to men at play, games of chance to games of love. A pity. Perhaps I should advertise."

Death coughed gently. "Tell me, Wuntvor. Who is the greatest magician in all the Western Kingdoms?"

Was he trying to trick me? I'd stay firm to my beliefs. "Why, Ebenezum, of course."

"Right!" Death cried as a gong sounded somewhere nearby. "Wuntvor, you've just won an additional five years on your life!"

We were surrounded by bright light. The ghosts all sat in a large amphitheatre now, whistling and cheering. The succubus I had almost kissed stood a little bit to one side, next to a large board that read "5." She was wearing some sort of spangled costume that managed to look more revealing than her nudity had before.

"Okay!" Death smiled broadly. "Now, Wunt, for ten additional years! Tell us, who is the ruler of Melifox?"

The crowd whistled and stamped their feet. Urgent music came from somewhere. The succubus smiled her magnificent smile.

"Uh—King Urfoo the Brave!" I blurted.

"Right, for ten more years!"

The crowd went wild. The spangled beauty flipped a couple of cards over the board to one that read "15."

"All right! All right!" Death raised his hands for silence. "Now it's time for the question we've all been waiting for. Double or nothing!"

The crowd cheered.

"Now, Wuntvor, are you ready to double your life span?"

"Yes! Yes!" the crowd chanted. I nodded my head. Why not? This was easy.

"All right! The big question, Wuntvor, to double your life span or erase it altogether! Who was the famous chamberlain of the Eastern Kingdoms, three centuries ago, who used to mutter to himself, "One of these days, one of these days . . .""

"What?" I asked. How could I know something like that?

"Quick, Wuntvor! The Quiz Lady has set the clock. You have fifteen seconds to answer, or pay the penalty, on 'Forfeit Your Life!'"

What? What could I do? I didn't know anything about the Eastern Kingdoms. The dramatic music was back, louder than ever. The crowd was roaring. I couldn't think. Why hadn't I listened to Maggie and kept away from these games?

"Ten!" the crowd chanted. "Nine! Eight! Seven! Six! Five!"

"Gangway! Gangway! Boo! Boo! Boo!" The entire crowd turned to look at Aunt Maggie, riding atop Ebenezum's shoulders as the wizard rushed into our midst. And Maggie was holding Ebenezum's nose!

"Batwom Ignatius, Wuntvor!" my master cried. "Batwom Ignatius!"

"Batwom Ignatius?" I replied.

"Is right!" Death exclaimed. "You've doubled your life! Barring illness or accident, of course."

The crowd started to go wild, but Maggie chanted a few guttural syllables and Ebenezum waved his hands. The crowd noise receded.

Ebenezum sneezed once, loudly, as Aunt Maggie climbed down from his back. I asked him how he knew about Ignatius.

"Had to learn it for my wizard finals," he replied. "It's amazing the useless knowledge they make you pack into your skull."

"Such a pitiful spell," Death remarked. "Why did you do it? They'll all be back in a moment."

"I wanted to talk to you alone," the wizard replied.

"Your affliction will come back, too, when they return. Is that what you're afraid of? Come with me, Ebenezum, and you need never sneeze again."

"Perhaps I will." Ebenezum tugged at his sleeves. "I have heard, Death, that you are fond of games. Will you play one with me?"

Death sneered. "You toy with me, wizard. No one toys with Death! Quick, what will it be? Parchesi? Contract Bridge? Fifty-two pickup?"

The wizard pulled on his beard for a moment, then intoned, "Arm wrestling."

Death shrugged. "If you insist." He snapped his fingers and a table and chairs materialized between them.

"Now the terms." Ebenezum looked Death in the eye socket. "If I win, the three of us go free, and Maggie regains her kingdom. If I lose, I am yours."

Death smiled. "For someone of your eminence, anything. After you." He indicated a chair.

Ebenezum sat. I thought that the ghostly crowd noises were somewhat closer. Ebenezum would have to hurry, or his nose might betray him.

Death smoothed his snow-white robe and sat opposite my master. His smile, if anything, was broader than before.

"Shall we begin, dear wizard?"

Ebenezum put his elbow to the table. Death did the same. Their hands clasped.

The ghostly crowd was definitely closer. I could see pale flickerings across the clearing.

"Now!" Death said, and Ebenezum tensed his whole body. There was no movement beyond the constant quiver where the two hands met.

And then the ghosts were back upon us, swirling in on top of us, all talking and screaming and laughing at once. "I'm hit!" "You're out!" "Got you!" "Hot dogs!" "Tickle, tickle, tickle!"

"Dishonest Death!" Maggie screamed. "This was to be an even contest, without your ghostly consorts!"

Death laughed. Maggie said something else that I didn't quite catch. And Ebenezum sneezed.

And what a sneeze. Ghosts went flying. Death pulled back in alarm and was caught in the gale, along with his table and chair.

It was silent all around. I saw the first light of dawn in the east.

"Will they be back?" I asked, my voice little more than a whisper.

The sun peeked over the hill, and Ebenezum's chair evaporated beneath him. He sat on the ground rather suddenly.

"Alas, Wuntvor," the wizard said. "I fear they haven't the ghost of a chance." Then he blew his nose.

(3)

"On occasion, a wizard may find himself taking a job that has no monetary rewards. For a good wizard, these jobs will be few and far between, but they happen to us all. They are a wizard's duty, and they do have their benefits, such as letting them be known, loudly and in great detail, anyplace you travel through the kingdom just before the tax collector is due."

from *The Teachings of Ebenezum*
Volume 16

Ebenezum and Maggie sat on one of the great stones so recently toppled by the wizard's sneezing attack, while I surveyed in wonder the devastation a single great sneeze could bring to this already bleak land.

"How?" was my only question.

"Ebby never could keep a secret from me." Maggie cackled. "But his aversion to sorcery presented something of a problem if we were to survive the night."

My master pulled at his beard. "I freed you from Unwin, remember."

"All I had to do was choose to talk to you rather than him. Unwin always was impossibly jealous. Flew off in an ectoplasmic snit. Which made you sneeze about five times."

Ebenezum tried to say something, but Maggie kept right on talking. "That's when I had the idea. If he always sneezed around the supernatural, what if he really sneezed! We couldn't take away his problem, so the two of us worked up a little spell that would increase Ebby's nasal power a hundredfold!"

"Indeed," Ebenezum said, rubbing his nose, which was sore from blowing.

"And now we're safe. And the kingdom is free. Or is it?" Maggie spat on the ground. "Death is such a trickster. I was so afraid of him when Unwin died, I gave in and let him give me five lifetimes for what he termed 'occasional use of my kingdom.' What he didn't tell me was that nothing could live in the kingdom between the times he used it." She looked around her. "Has he kept his word? If only there was a sign."

She slapped Ebenezum's shoulder. "But you still haven't heard my story."

Ebenezum looked out over the hills. "Alas, teacher, we have a long way to travel. Shoulder your pack, Wunt. We'd best move before the sun gets too high."

"You'll sit here and listen!" Maggie commanded. "Ebby never did have any manners. From the beginning. Once there was a beautiful kingdom and a fair princess. But all was not well, for one day came the dreaded rain of—"

"Ow!" I yelled. Something had bitten my arm.

Ebenezum jumped up. "Biting gnats! They're all over us!"

Maggie threw her hands up to the heavens. "My kingdom is saved!"

"Drop us a note when 'tis a little better developed!" the wizard called over his shoulder. "We'll visit then!" And we were once again traveling, somewhat more rapidly than before, with frequent slapping of arms and legs, in the general direction of Vushta.

Born in Kent, England, in 1869, ALGERNON BLACKWOOD is one of the most famous fantasy writers in all English literature. His precise, sometimes journalistic style is coupled with themes of striking originality. "The Woman's Ghost Story" is unusually gentle for him, but its humanistic tone is quietly passionate.

The Woman's Ghost Story
by Algernon Blackwood

"Yes," she said, from her seat in the dark corner, "I'll tell you an experience if you care to listen. And, what's more, I'll tell it briefly, without trimmings—I mean without unessentials. That's a thing story-tellers never do, you know," she laughed. "They drag in all the unessentials and leave their listeners to disentangle; but I'll give you just the essentials, and you can make of it what you please. But on one condition: that at the end you ask no questions, because I can't explain it and have no wish to."

We agreed. We were all serious. After listening to a dozen prolix stories from people who merely wished to "talk" but had nothing to tell, we wanted "essentials."

"In those days," she began, feeling from the quality of our silence that we were with her, "in those days I was interested in psychic things, and had arranged to sit up alone in a haunted house in the middle of London. It was a cheap and dingy lodging-house in a mean street, unfurnished. I had already made a preliminary examination in daylight that afternoon, and the keys from the caretaker, who lived next door, were in my pocket. The story was a good one—satisfied me, at any rate, that it was worth investigating; and I won't weary you with details as to the woman's murder and all the tiresome elaboration as to *why* the place was *alive*. Enough that it was.

"I was a good deal bored, therefore, to see a man, whom I took to be the talkative old caretaker, waiting for me on the steps when I went in at 11 P.M., for I had sufficiently explained that I wished to be there alone for the night.

"'I wished to show you *the* room,' he mumbled, and of course I couldn't exactly refuse, having tipped him for the temporary loan of a chair and table.

"'Come in, then, and let's be quick,' I said.

"We went in, he shuffling after me through the unlighted hall up to the first floor where the murder had taken place, and I prepared myself to hear his inevitable account before turning him out with the half-crown his persistence had earned. After lighting the gas I sat down in the arm-chair he had provided—a faded, brown plush arm-chair—and turned for the first time to face him and get through with the performance as quickly as possible. And it was in that instant I got my first shock. The man was *not* the caretaker. It was not the old fool, Carey, I had interviewed earlier in the day and made my plans with. My heart gave a horrid jump.

" 'Now who are *you*, pray?' I said. 'You're not Carey, the man I arranged with this afternoon. Who are you?'

"I felt uncomfortable, as you may imagine. I was a 'psychical researcher,' and a young woman of new tendencies, and proud of my liberty, but I did not care to find myself in an empty house with a stranger. Something of my confidence left me. Confidence with women, you know, is all humbug after a certain point. Or perhaps you don't know, for most of you are men. But anyhow my pluck ebbed in a quick rush, and I felt afraid.

" 'Who are you?' I repeated quickly and nervously. The fellow was well dressed, youngish and good-looking, but with a face of great sadness. I myself was barely thirty. I am giving you essentials, or I would not mention it. Out of quite ordinary things comes this story. I think that's why it has value.

" 'No,' he said; 'I'm the man who was frightened to death.'

"His voice and his words ran through me like a knife, and I felt ready to drop. In my pocket was the book I had brought to make notes in. I felt the pencil sticking in the socket. I felt, too, the extra warm things I had put on to sit up in, as no bed or sofa was available—a hundred things dashed through my mind, foolishly and without sequence or meaning, as the way is when one is really frightened. Unessentials leaped up and puzzled me, and I thought of what the papers might say if it came out, and what my 'smart' brother-in-law would think, and whether it would be told that I had cigarettes in my pocket, and was a free-thinker.

" 'The man who was frightened to death!' I repeated aghast.

" 'That's me,' he said stupidly.

"I stared at him just as you would have done—any one of you men now listening to me—and felt my life ebbing and flowing like a sort of hot fluid. You needn't laugh! That's how I felt. Small things, you know, touch the mind with great earnestness when terror is there—*real terror*. But I might have been at a middle-class tea party, for all the ideas I had: they were so ordinary!

" 'But I thought you were the caretaker I tipped this afternoon to let me sleep here!' I gasped. 'Did—did Carey send you to meet me?'

" 'No,' he replied in a voice that touched my boots somehow. 'I am the man who was frightened to death. And what is more, I am frightened *now!*'

" 'So am I!' I managed to utter, speaking instinctively. 'I'm simply terrified.'

" 'Yes,' he replied in that same odd voice that seemed to sound within me. 'But you are still in the flesh, and I—*am not!*'

"I felt the need for vigorous self-assertion. I stood up in that empty, unfurnished room, digging the nails into my palms and clenching my teeth. I was determined to assert my individuality and my courage as a new woman and a free soul.

" 'You mean to say you are not in the flesh!' I gasped. 'What in the world are you talking about?'

"The silence of the night swallowed up my voice. For the first time I realised that darkness was over the city; that dust lay upon the stairs; that the floor above was untenanted and the floor below empty. I was alone in an unoccupied and haunted house, unprotected, and a woman. I chilled. I heard the wind round the house, and knew the stars were hidden. My thoughts rushed to policemen and omnibuses, and everything that was useful and comforting. I suddenly realised what a fool I was to come to such a house alone. I was icily afraid. I thought the end of my life had come. I was an utter fool to go in for psychical research when I had not the necessary nerve.

" 'Good God!' I gasped. 'If you're not Carey, the man I arranged with, who are you?'

"I was really stiff with terror. The man moved slowly towards me across the empty room. I held out my arm to stop him, getting up out of my chair at the same moment, and he came to a halt just opposite to me, a smile on his worn, sad face.

" 'I told you who I am,' he repeated quietly with a sigh, looking at me with the saddest eyes I have ever seen, 'and I am frightened *still.'*

"By this time I was convinced that I was entertaining either a rogue or a madman, and I cursed my stupidity in bringing the man in without having seen his face. My mind was quickly made up, and I knew what to do. Ghosts and psychic phenomena flew to the winds. If I angered the creature my life might pay the price. I must humour him till I got to the door, and then race for the street. I stood bolt upright and faced him. We were about of a height, and I was a strong, athletic woman who played hockey in winter and climbed Alps in summer. My hand itched for a stick, but I had none.

" 'Now, of course, I remember,' I said with a sort of stiff smile that was very hard to force. 'Now I remember your case and the wonderful way you behaved. . . .'

"The man stared at me stupidly, turning his head to watch me as I backed more and more quickly to the door. But when his face broke into a smile I could control myself no longer. I reached the door in a run, and shot out on to the landing. Like a fool, I turned the wrong way, and stumbled over the stairs leading to the next storey. But it was too late to change. The man was after me, I was sure, though no sound of footsteps came; I dashed up the next flight, tearing my skirt and banging my ribs in the darkness, and rushed headlong into the first room I came to. Luckily the door stood ajar, and, still more fortunate, there was a key in the lock. In a second I had slammed the door, flung my whole weight against it, and turned the key.

"I was safe, but my heart was beating like a drum. A second later it seemed to stop altogether, for I saw that there was someone else in the room besides myself. A man's figure stood between me and the window, where the street lamps gave just enough light to outline his shape against the glass. I'm a plucky woman, you know, for even then I didn't give up hope, but I may tell you that I have never felt so vilely frightened in all my born days. I had locked myself in with him!

"The man leaned against the window, watching me where I lay in a collapsed heap upon the floor. So there were two men in the house with me, I reflected. Perhaps the other rooms were occupied too! What could it all mean? But, as I stared something changed in the room, or in me— hard to say which—and I realised my mistake, so that my fear, which had so far been physical, at once altered its character and became *psychical*. I became afraid in my soul instead of in my heart, and I knew immediately who this man was.

" 'How in the world did you get up here?' I stammered to him across the empty room, amazement momentarily stemming my fear.

" 'Now, let me tell you,' he began, in that odd far-away voice of his that went down my spine like a knife. 'I'm in different space, for one thing, and you'd find me in any room you went into; for according to your way of measuring, I'm *all over the house*. Space is a bodily condition, but I am out of the body, and am not affected by space. It's my condition that keeps me here. I want something to change my condition for me, for then I could get away. What I want is sympathy. Or, really, more than sympathy; I want affection—I want *love!*'

"While he was speaking I gathered myself slowly upon my feet. I wanted to scream and cry and laugh all at once, but I only succeeded in sighing, for my emotion was exhausted and a numbness was coming over me. I felt for the matches in my pocket and made a movement towards the gas-jet.

" 'I should be much happier if you didn't light the gas,' he said at once, 'for the vibrations of your light hurt me a good deal. You need not be afraid that I shall injure you. I can't touch your body to begin with, for there's a great gulf fixed, you know; and really this half-light suits me best. Now, let me continue what I was trying to say before. You know, so many people have come to this house to see me, and most of them have seen me, and one and all have been terrified. If only, oh! if only someone would be *not* terrified, but kind and loving to me! Then, you see, I might be able to change my condition and get away.'

"His voice was so sad that I felt tears start somewhere at the back of my eyes; but fear kept all else in check, and I stood shaking and cold as I listened to him.

" 'Who are you then? Of course Carey didn't send you, I know now,' I managed to utter. My thoughts scattered dreadfully and I could think of nothing to say. I was afraid of a stroke.

" 'I know nothing about Carey, or who he is,' continued the man quietly, 'and the name my body had I have forgotten, thank God; but I am the man who was frightened to death in this house ten years ago, and I have been frightened ever since, and am frightened still; for the succession of cruel and curious people who come to this house to see the ghost, and thus keep alive its atmosphere of terror, only helps to render my condition worse. If only someone would be kind to me— *laugh,* speak gently and rationally with me, cry if they like, pity, comfort, soothe me—anything but come here in curiosity and tremble as you are now doing in that corner. Now, madam, won't you take pity on me?' His voice rose to a dreadful cry. "Won't you step out into the middle of the room and try to love me a little?'

"A horrible laughter came gurgling up in my throat as I heard him, but the sense of pity was stronger than the laughter, and I found myself actually leaving the support of the wall and approaching the centre of the floor.

" 'By God!' he cried, at once straightening up against the window, 'you have done a kind act. That's the first attempt at sympathy that has been shown me since I died, and I feel better already. In life, you know, I was a misanthrope. Everything went wrong with me, and I came to hate my fellow men so much that I couldn't bear to see them even. Of course, like begets like, and this hate was returned. Finally I suffered from horrible delusions, and my room became haunted with demons that laughed and grimaced, and one night I ran into a whole cluster of them near the bed—and the fright stopped my heart and killed me. It's hate and remorse, as much as terror, that clogs me so thickly and keeps me here. If only someone could feel pity, and sympathy, and perhaps a little love for me, I could get away and be happy. When you came this afternoon to see over the house I watched you, and a little hope came to me for the first time. I saw you had courage, originality, resource— *love*. If only I could touch your heart, without frightening you, I knew I could perhaps tap that love you have stored up in your being there, and thus borrow the wings for my escape!'

"Now I must confess my heart began to ache a little, as fear left me and the man's words sank their sad meaning into me. Still, the whole affair was so incredible, and so touched with unholy quality, and the story of a woman's murder I had come to investigate had so obviously nothing to do with this thing, that I felt myself in a kind of wild dream that seemed likely to stop at any moment and leave me somewhere in bed after a nightmare.

"Moreover, his words possessed me to such an extent that I found it impossible to reflect upon anything else at all, or to consider adequately any ways and means of action or escape.

"I moved a little nearer to him in the gloom, horribly frightened, of course, but with the beginnings of a strange determination in my heart.

" 'You women,' he continued, his voice plainly thrilling at my approach, 'you wonderful women, to whom life often brings no opportunity of spending your great love, oh, if you only could know how many of *us* simply yearn for it! It would save our souls, if you but knew. Few might find the chance that you now have, but if you only spent your love freely, without definite object, just letting it flow openly for all who need, you would reach hundreds and thousands of souls like me, and *release us!* Oh, madam, I ask you again to feel with me, to be kind and gentle—and if you can to love me a little.'

"My heart did leap within me and this time the tears did come, for I could not restrain them. I laughed too, for the way he called me 'madam' sounded so odd, here in this empty room at midnight in a London street, but my laughter stopped dead and merged in a flood of weeping when I saw how my change of feeling had affected him. He had left his place by the window and was kneeling on the floor at my feet, his hands stretched out towards me, and the first signs of a kind of glory about his head.

"'Put your arms round me and kiss me, for the love of God!' he cried. 'Kiss me, oh, kiss me, and I shall be freed! You have done so much already—now do this!'

"I stuck there, hesitating, shaking, my determination on the verge of action, yet not quite able to compass it. But the terror had almost gone.

"'Forget that I'm a man and you're a woman,' he continued in the most beseeching voice I ever heard. 'Forget that I'm a ghost, and come out boldly and press me to you with a great kiss, and let your love flow into me. Forget yourself just for one minute and do a brave thing! Oh, love me, *love me,* LOVE ME! and I shall be free!'

"The words, or the deep force they somehow released in the centre of my being, stirred me profoundly, and an emotion infinitely greater than fear surged up over me and carried me with it across the edge of action. Without hesitation I took two steps forward towards him where he knelt, and held out my arms. Pity and love were in my heart at that moment, genuine pity, I swear, and genuine love. I forgot myself and my little tremblings in a great desire to help another soul.

"'I love you! poor, aching, unhappy thing! I love you,' I cried through hot tears, 'and I am not the least bit afraid in the world.'

"The man uttered a curious sound, like laughter, yet not laughter, and turned his face up to me. The light from the street below fell on it, but there was another light, too, shining all round it that seemed to come from the eyes and skin. He rose to his feet and met me, and in that second I folded him to my breast and kissed him full on the lips again and again."

All our pipes had gone out, and not even a skirt rustled in that dark studio as the story-teller paused a moment to steady her voice, and put a hand softly up to her eyes before going on again.

"Now, what can I say, and how can I describe to you, all you sceptical men sitting there with pipes in your mouths, the amazing sensation I experienced of holding an intangible, impalpable thing so closely to my heart that it touched my body with equal pressure all the way down, and then melted away somewhere into my very being? For it was like seizing a rush of cool wind and feeling a touch of burning fire the moment it had struck its swift blow and passed on. A series of shocks ran all over and all through me; a momentary ecstasy of flaming sweetness and wonder thrilled down into me; my heart gave another great leap— and then I was alone.

"The room was empty. I turned on the gas and struck a match to prove it. All fear had left me, and something was singing round me in the air and in my heart like the joy of a spring morning in youth. Not all the devils or shadows or hauntings in the world could then have caused me a single tremor.

"I unlocked the door and went all over the dark house, even into kitchen and cellar and up among the ghostly attics. But the house was empty. Something had left it. I lingered a short hour, analysing, thinking, wondering—you can guess what and how, perhaps, but I won't detail, for I promised only essentials, remember—and then went out to sleep the remainder of the night in my own flat, locking the door behind me upon a house no longer haunted.

"But my uncle, Sir Henry, the owner of the house, required an account of my adventure, and of course I was in duty bound to give him some kind of a true story. Before I could begin, however, he held up his hand to stop me.

" 'First,' he said, 'I wish to tell you a little deception I ventured to practise on you. So many people have been to that house and seen the ghost that I came to think the story acted on their imaginations, and I wished to make a better test. So I invented for their benefit another story, with the idea that if you did see anything I could be sure it was not due merely to an excited imagination.'

" 'Then what you told me about a woman having been murdered, and all that, was not the true story of the haunting?'

" 'It was not. The true story is that a cousin of mine went mad in that house, and killed himself in a fit of morbid terror following upon years of miserable hypochondriasis. It is his figure that investigators see.'

" 'That explains, then,' I gasped . . .

" 'Explains what?'

"I thought of that poor struggling soul, longing all these years for escape, and determined to keep my story for the present to myself.

" 'Explains, I mean, why I did not see the ghost of the murdered woman,' I concluded.

" 'Precisely,' said Sir Henry, 'and why, if you had seen anything, it would have had value, inasmuch as it could not have been caused by the imagination working upon a story you already knew.' "

WILKIE COLLINS, *born in 1824 in London, is best remembered for* The Moonstone, *usually accepted as the first detective novel in English, and* The Woman in White. *Occasionally one of his short fantasy tales is revived, more often than not the excellent* The Dream Woman. *But most of his writings are little remembered, which is unfortunate because Collins combines a gift for depicting character with an unusually brisk modern style. His pace is easier for the contemporary reader to adapt to than Dickens' earlier novels or some of Poe's overwrought grotesqueries. Out of a choice of several fine little-known tales, I chose "Miss Jéromette and the Clergyman" for its poignancy and the cruel manner in which its moral hero helplessly aids the immoral villain.*

✣Miss Jéromette and the Clergyman

by Wilkie Collins

I

My brother, the clergyman, looked over my shoulder before I was aware of him, and discovered that the volume which completely absorbed my attention was a collection of famous Trials, published in a new edition and in a popular form.

He laid his finger on the Trial which I happened to be reading at the moment. I looked up at him; his face startled me. He had turned pale. His eyes were fixed on the open page of the book with an expression which puzzled and alarmed me.

"My dear fellow," I said, "what in the world is the matter with you?"

He answered in an odd absent manner, still keeping his finger on the open page.

"I had almost forgotten," he said. "And this reminds me."

"Reminds you of what?" I asked. "You don't mean to say you know anything about the Trial?"

"I know this," he said. "The prisoner was guilty."

"Guilty?" I repeated. "Why, the man was acquitted by the jury, with the full approval of the judge! What can you possibly mean?"

"There are circumstances connected with that Trial," my brother answered, "which were never communicated to the judge or the jury—which were never so much as hinted or whispered in court. *I* know them —of my own knowledge, by my own personal experience. They are very sad, very strange, very terrible. I have mentioned them to no mortal creature. I have done my best to forget them. You—quite innocently—have brought them back to my mind. They oppress, they distress me. I wish I had found you reading any book in your library, except *that* book!"

My curiosity was now strongly excited. I spoke out plainly.

"Surely," I suggested, "you might tell your brother what you are unwilling to mention to persons less nearly related to you. We have followed different professions, and have lived in different countries, since we were boys at school. But you know you can trust me."

He considered a little with himself.

"Yes," he said. "I know I can trust you." He waited a moment; and then he surprised me by a strange question.

"Do you believe," he asked, "that the spirits of the dead can return to earth, and show themselves to the living?"

I answered cautiously—adopting as my own the words of a great English writer, touching the subject of ghosts.

"You ask me a question," I said, "which, after five thousand years, is yet undecided. On that account alone, it is a question not to be trifled with."

My reply seemed to satisfy him.

"Promise me," he resumed, "that you will keep what I tell you a secret as long as I live. After my death I care little what happens. Let the story of my strange experience be added to the published experience of those other men who have seen what I have seen, and who believe what I believe. The world will not be the worse, and may be the better, for knowing one day what I am now about to trust to your ear alone."

My brother never again alluded to the narrative which he had confided to me, until the later time when I was sitting by his deathbed. He asked if I still remembered the story of Jéromette. "Tell it to others," he said, "as I have told it to you."

I repeat it, after his death—as nearly as I can in his own words.

II

On a fine summer evening, many years since, I left my chambers in the Temple, to meet a fellow-student, who had proposed to me a night's amusement in the public gardens at Cremorne.

You were then on your way to India; and I had taken my degree at

Oxford. I had sadly disappointed my father by choosing the Law as my profession, in preference to the Church. At that time, to own the truth, I had no serious intention of following any special vocation. I simply wanted an excuse for enjoying the pleasures of a London life. The study of the Law supplied me with that excuse. And I chose the Law as my profession accordingly.

On reaching the place at which we had arranged to meet, I found that my friend had not kept his appointment. After waiting vainly for ten minutes, my patience gave way, and I went into the Gardens by myself.

I took two or three turns round the platform devoted to the dancers, without discovering my fellow-student, and without seeing any other person with whom I happened to be acquainted at that time.

For some reason which I cannot now remember, I was not in my usual good spirits that evening. The noisy music jarred on my nerves, the sight of the gaping crowd round the platform irritated me, the blandishments of the painted ladies of the profession of pleasure saddened and disgusted me. I opened my cigar-case, and turned aside into one of the quiet by-walks of the Gardens.

A man who is habitually careful in choosing his cigar has this advantage over a man who is habitually careless. He can always count on smoking the best cigar in his case, down to the last. I was still absorbed in choosing *my* cigar, when I heard these words behind me—spoken in a foreign accent and in a woman's voice:

"Leave me directly, sir! I wish to have nothing to say to you."

I turned round and discovered a little lady very simply and tastefully dressed, who looked both angry and alarmed as she rapidly passed me on her way to the more frequented part of the Gardens. A man (evidently the worse for the wine he had drunk in the course of the evening) was following her, and was pressing his tipsy attentions on her with the coarsest insolence of speech and manner. She was young and pretty, and she cast one entreating look at me as she went by, which it was not in manhood—perhaps I ought to say, in young-manhood—to resist.

I instantly stepped forward to protect her, careless whether I involved myself in a discreditable quarrel with a blackguard or not. As a matter of course, the fellow resented my interference, and my temper gave way. Fortunately for me, just as I lifted my hand to knock him down, a policeman appeared who had noticed that he was drunk, and who settled the dispute officially by turning him out of the Gardens.

I led her away from the crowd that had collected. She was evidently frightened—I felt her hand trembling on my arm—but she had one great merit: she made no fuss about it.

"If I can sit down for a few minutes," she said in her pretty foreign accent, "I shall soon be myself again, and I shall not trespass any farther on your kindness. I thank you very much, sir, for taking care of me."

We sat down on a bench in a retired part of the Gardens, near a little fountain. A row of lighted lamps ran round the outer rim of the basin. I could see her plainly.

I have said that she was "a little lady." I could not have described her more correctly in three words.

Her figure was slight and small: she was a well-made miniature of a woman from head to foot. Her hair and her eyes were both dark. The hair curled naturally; the expression of the eyes was quiet, and rather sad; the complexion, as I then saw it, very pale; the little mouth perfectly charming. I was especially attracted, I remember, by the carriage of her head; it was strikingly graceful and spirited; it distinguished her, little as she was and quiet as she was, among the thousands of other women in the Gardens, as a creature apart. Even the one marked defect in her—a slight "cast" in the left eye—seemed to add, in some strange way, to the quaint attractiveness of her face. I have already spoken of the tasteful simplicity of her dress. I ought now to add that it was not made of any costly material, and that she wore no jewels or ornaments of any sort. My little lady was not rich: even a man's eye could see that.

She was perfectly unembarrassed and unaffected. We fell as easily into talk as if we had been friends instead of strangers.

I asked how it was that she had no companion to take care of her. "You are too young and too pretty," I said in my blunt English way, "to trust yourself alone in such a place as this."

She took no notice of the compliment. She calmly put it away from her as if it had not reached her ears.

"I have no friend to take care of me," she said simply. "I was sad and sorry this evening, all by myself, and I thought I would go to the Gardens and hear the music, just to amuse me. It is not much to pay at the gate; only a shilling."

"No friend to take care of you?" I repeated. "Surely there must be one happy man who might have been here with you tonight?"

"What man do you mean?" she asked.

"The man," I answered thoughtlessly, "whom we call, in England, a sweetheart."

I would have given worlds to have recalled those foolish words the moment they passed my lips. I felt that I had taken a vulgar liberty with her. Her face saddened; her eyes dropped to the ground. I begged her pardon.

"There is no need to beg my pardon," she said. "If you wish to know, sir—yes, I had once a sweetheart, as you call it in England. He has gone away and left me. No more of him, if you please. I am rested now. I will thank you again, and go home."

She rose to leave me.

I was determined not to part with her in that way. I begged to be allowed to see her safely back to her own door. She hesitated. I took a man's unfair advantage of her, by appealing to her fears. I said, "Suppose the blackguard who annoyed you should be waiting outside the gates?" That decided her. She took my arm. We went away together by the bank of the Thames, in the balmy summer night.

A walk of half an hour brought us to the house in which she lodged— a shabby little house in a by-street, inhabited evidently by very poor people.

She held out her hand at the door, and wished me good-night. I was too much interested in her to consent to leave my little foreign lady without the hope of seeing her again. I asked permission to call on her the next day. We were standing under the light of the street-lamp. She studied my face with a grave and steady attention before she made any reply.

"Yes," she said at last. "I think I do know a gentleman when I see him. You may come, sir, if you please, and call upon me tomorrow."

So we parted. So I entered—doubting nothing, foreboding nothing—on a scene in my life, which I now look back on with unfeigned repentance and regret.

III

I am speaking at this later time in the position of a clergyman, and in the character of a man of mature age. Remember that; and you will understand why I pass as rapidly as possible over the events of the next year of my life—why I say as little as I can of the errors and the delusions of my youth.

I called on her the next day. I repeated my visits during the days and weeks that followed, until the shabby little house in the by-street had become a second and (I say it with shame and self-reproach) a dearer home to me.

All of herself and her story which she thought fit to confide to me under these circumstances may be repeated to you in few words.

The name by which letters were addressed to her was "Mademoiselle Jéromette." Among the ignorant people of the house and the small tradesmen of the neighbourhood—who found her name not easy of pronunciation by the average English tongue—she was known by the friendly nickname of "The French Miss." When I knew her, she was resigned to her lonely life among strangers. Some years had elapsed since she had lost her parents, and had left France. Possessing a small, very small, income of her own, she added to it by colouring miniatures for the photographers. She had relatives still living in France; but she had long since ceased to correspond with them. "Ask me nothing more about my family," she used to say. "I am as good as dead in my own country and among my own people."

This was all—literally all—that she told me of herself. I have never discovered more of her sad story from that day to this.

She never mentioned her family name—never even told me what part of France she came from, or how long she had lived in England. That she was, by birth and breeding, a lady, I could entertain no doubt; her manners, her accomplishments, her ways of thinking and speaking, all proved it. Looking below the surface, her character showed itself in aspects not common among young women in these days. In her quiet way, she was an incurable fatalist, and a firm believer in the ghostly reality of apparitions from the dead. Then again, in the matter of money, she had strange views of her own. Whenever my purse was in my hand, she held me resolutely at a distance from first to last. She refused to move into better apartments; the shabby little house was clean inside, and the poor people who lived in it were kind to her—and that was enough. The most expensive present that she ever permitted me to offer her was a little enamelled ring, the plainest and cheapest thing of the kind in the jeweller's shop. In all her relations with me she was sincerity itself. On all occasions, and under all circumstances, she spoke her mind (as the phrase is) with the same uncompromising plainness.

"I like you," she said to me; "I respect you; I shall always be faithful to you while you are faithful to me. But my love has gone from me. There is another man who has taken it away with him, I know not where."

Who was the other man?

She refused to tell me. She kept his rank and his name strict secrets from me. I never discovered how he had met with her, or why he had left her, or whether the guilt was his of making her an exile from her country and her friends. She despised herself for still loving him; but the passion was too strong for her—she owned it and lamented it with the frankness which was so pre-eminently a part of her character. More than this, she plainly told me, in the early days of our acquaintance, that she believed he would return to her. It might be tomorrow, or it might be years hence. Even if he failed to repent of his own cruel conduct, the man would still miss her, as something lost out of his life; and, sooner or later, he would come back.

"And will you receive him if he does come back?" I asked.

"I shall receive him," she replied, "against my own better judgment—in spite of my own firm persuasion that the day of his return to me will bring with it the darkest days of my life."

I tried to remonstrate with her.

"You have a will of your own," I said. "Exert it, if he attempts to return to you."

"I have no will of my own," she answered quietly, "where *he* is concerned. It is my misfortune to love him." Her eyes rested for a moment on mine, with the utter self-abandonment of despair. "We have said enough about this," she added abruptly. "Let us say no more."

From that time we never spoke again of the unknown man. During the year that followed our first meeting, she heard nothing of him directly or indirectly. He might be living, or he might be dead. There came no word of him, or from him. I was fond enough of her to be satisfied with this—he never disturbed us.

IV

The year passed—and the end came. Not the end as you may have anticipated it, or as I might have foreboded it.

You remember the time when your letters from home informed you of the fatal termination of our mother's illness? It is the time of which I am now speaking. A few hours only before she breathed her last, she called me to her bedside, and desired that we might be left together alone. Reminding me that her death was near, she spoke of my prospects in life; she noticed my want of interest in the studies which were then supposed to be engaging my attention, and she ended by entreating me to reconsider my refusal to enter the Church. "Your father's heart is set upon it," she said. "Do what I ask of you, my dear, and you will help to comfort him when I am gone."

Her strength failed her: she could say no more. Could I refuse the last request she would ever make to me? I knelt at the bedside, and took her wasted hand in mine, and solemnly promised her the respect which a son owes to his mother's last wishes.

Having bound myself by this sacred engagement, I had no choice but to accept the sacrifice which it imperatively exacted from me. The time had come when I must tear myself free from all unworthy associations. No matter what the effort cost me, I must separate myself at once and for ever from the unhappy woman who was not, who never could be, my wife.

At the close of a dull foggy day I set forth with a heavy heart to say the words which were to part us for ever.

Her lodging was not far from the banks of the Thames. As I drew near the place the darkness was gathering, and the broad surface of the river was hidden from me in a chill white mist. I stood for a while, with my eyes fixed on the vaporous shroud that brooded over the flowing water—I stood, and asked myself in despair the one dreary question: "What am I to say to her?"

The mist chilled me to the bones. I turned from the river-bank, and made my way to her lodgings hard by. "It must be done!" I said to myself, as I took out my key and opened the house door.

She was not at her work, as usual, when I entered her little sitting-room. She was standing by the fire, with her head down, and with an open letter in her hand.

The instant she turned to meet me, I saw in her face that something was wrong. Her ordinary manner was the manner of an unusually placid and self-restrained person. Her temperament had little of the liveliness which we associate in England with the French nature. She was not ready with her laugh; and, in all my previous experience, I had never yet known her to cry. Now, for the first time, I saw the quiet face disturbed; I saw tears in the pretty brown eyes. She ran to meet me, and laid her head on my breast, and burst into a passionate fit of weeping that shook her from head to foot.

Could she by any human possibility have heard of the coming change in my life? Was she aware, before I had opened my lips, of the hard necessity which had brought me to the house?

It was simply impossible; the thing could not be.

I waited until her first burst of emotion had worn itself out. Then I asked—with an uneasy conscience, with a sinking heart—what had happened to distress her.

She drew herself away from me, sighing heavily, and gave me the open letter which I had seen in her hand.

"Read that," she said. "And remember I told you what might happen when we first met."

I read the letter.

It was signed in initials only; but the writer plainly revealed himself as the man who had deserted her. He had repented; he had returned to her. In proof of his penitence he was willing to do her the justice which he had hitherto refused—he was willing to marry her; on the condition that she would engage to keep the marriage a secret, so long as his parents lived. Submitting this proposal, he waited to know whether she would consent, on her side, to forgive and forget.

I gave her back the letter in silence. This unknown rival had done me the service of paving the way for our separation. In offering her the atonement of marriage, he had made it, on my part, a matter of duty to *her,* as well as to myself, to say the parting words. I felt this instantly. And yet, I hated him for helping me!

She took my hand, and led me to the sofa. We sat down, side by side. Her face was composed to a sad tranquillity. She was quiet; she was herself again.

"I have refused to see him," she said, "until I had first spoken to you. You have read his letter. What do you say?"

I could make but one answer. It was my duty to tell her what my own position was in the plainest terms. I did my duty—leaving her free to decide on the future for herself. Those sad words said, it was useless to prolong the wretchedness of our separation. I rose, and took her hand for the last time.

I see her again now, at that final moment, as plainly as if it had happened yesterday. She had been suffering from an affection of the throat; and she had a white silk handkerchief tied loosely round her neck. She wore a simple dress of purple merino, with a black-silk apron over it. Her face was deadly pale; her fingers felt icily cold as they closed round my hand.

"Promise me one thing," I said, "before I go. While I live, I am your friend—if I am nothing more. If you are ever in trouble, promise that you will let me know it."

She started, and drew back from me as if I had struck her with a sudden terror.

"Strange!" she said, speaking to herself. "He feels as I feel. *He* is afraid of what may happen to me, in my life to come."

I attempted to reassure her. I tried to tell her what was indeed the truth—that I had only been thinking of the ordinary chances and changes of life, when I spoke.

She paid no heed to me; she came back and put her hands on my shoulders, and thoughtfully and sadly looked up in my face.

"My mind is not your mind in this matter," she said. "I once owned to you that I had my forebodings, when we first spoke of this man's return. I may tell you now, more than I told you then. I believe I shall die young, and die miserably. If I am right, have you interest enough still left in me to wish to hear of it?"

She paused, shuddering—and added these startling words:

"You *shall* hear of it."

The tone of steady conviction in which she spoke alarmed and distressed me. My face showed her how deeply and how painfully I was affected.

"There, there!" she said, returning to her natural manner; "don't take what I say too seriously. A poor girl who has led a lonely life like mine thinks strangely and talks strangely—sometimes. Yes; I give you my promise. If I am ever in trouble, I will let you know it. God bless you—you have been very kind to me—good-bye!"

A tear dropped on my face as she kissed me. The door closed between us. The dark street received me.

It was raining heavily. I looked up at her window, through the drifting shower. The curtains were parted: she was standing in the gap, dimly lit by the lamp on the table behind her, waiting for our last look at each other. Slowly lifting her hand, she waved her farewell at the window, with the unsought native grace which had charmed me on the night when we first met. The curtains fell again—she disappeared—nothing was before me, nothing was round me, but the darkness and the night.

V

In two years from that time, I had redeemed the promise given to my mother on her deathbed. I had entered the Church.

My father's interest made my first step in my new profession an easy one. After serving my preliminary apprenticeship as a curate, I was appointed, before I was thirty years of age, to a living in the West of England.

My new benefice offered me every advantage that I could possibly desire—with the one exception of a sufficient income. Although my wants were few, and although I was still an unmarried man, I found it desirable, on many accounts, to add to my resources. Following the example of other young clergymen in my position, I determined to receive pupils who might stand in need of preparation for a career at the Universities. My relatives exerted themselves; and my good fortune still befriended me. I obtained two pupils to start with. A third would complete the number which I was at present prepared to receive. In course of time, this third pupil made his appearance, under circumstances sufficiently remarkable to merit being mentioned in detail.

It was the summer vacation; and my two pupils had gone home. Thanks to a neighbouring clergyman, who kindly undertook to perform my duties for me, I too obtained a fortnight's holiday, which I spent at my father's house in London.

During my sojourn in the metropolis, I was offered an opportunity of preaching in a church, made famous by the eloquence of one of the popular pulpit-orators of our time. In accepting the proposal, I felt naturally anxious to do my best, before the unusually large and unusually intelligent congregation which would be assembled to hear me.

At the period of which I am now speaking, all England had been startled by the discovery of a terrible crime, perpetrated under circumstances of extreme provocation. I chose this crime as the main subject of my sermon. Admitting that the best among us were frail mortal creatures, subject to evil promptings and provocations like the worst among us, my object was to show how a Christian man may find his certain refuge from temptation in the safeguards of his religion. I dwelt minutely on the hardship of the Christian's first struggle to resist the evil influence—on the help which his Christianity inexhaustibly held out to him in the worst relapses of the weaker and viler part of his nature—on the steady and certain gain which was the ultimate reward of his faith and his firmness—and on the blessed sense of peace and happiness which accompanied the final triumph. Preaching to this effect, with the fervent conviction which I really felt, I may say for myself, at least, that I did no discredit to the choice which had placed me in the pulpit. I held the attention of my congregation, from the first word to the last.

While I was resting in the vestry on the conclusion of the service, a note was brought to me written in pencil. A member of my congregation—a gentleman—wished to see me, on a matter of considerable importance to himself. He would call on me at any place, and at any hour, which I might choose to appoint. If I wished to be satisfied of his respectability, he would beg leave to refer me to his father, with whose name I might possibly be acquainted.

The name given in the reference was undoubtedly familiar to me, as the name of a man of some celebrity and influence in the world of London. I sent back my card, appointing an hour for the visit of my correspondent on the afternoon of the next day.

VI

The stranger made his appearance punctually. I guessed him to be some two or three years younger than myself. He was undeniably handsome; his manners were the manners of a gentleman—and yet, without knowing why, I felt a strong dislike to him the moment he entered the room.

After the first preliminary words of politeness had been exchanged between us, my visitor informed me as follows of the object which he had in view.

"I believe you live in the country, sir?" he began.

"I live in the West of England," I answered.

"Do you make a long stay in London?"

"No. I go back to my rectory tomorrow."

"May I ask if you take pupils?"

"Yes."

"Have you any vacancy?"

"I have one vacancy."

"Would you object to let me go back with you tomorrow, as your pupil?"

The abruptness of the proposal took me by surprise. I hesitated.

In the first place (as I have already said), I disliked him. In the second place, he was too old to be a fit companion for my other two pupils —both lads in their teens. In the third place, he had asked me to receive him at least three weeks before the vacation came to an end. I had my own pursuits and amusements in prospect during that interval, and saw no reason why I should inconvenience myself by setting them aside.

He noticed my hesitation, and did not conceal from me that I had disappointed him.

"I have it very much at heart," he said, "to repair without delay the time that I have lost. My age is against me, I know. The truth is—I have wasted my opportunities since I left school, and I am anxious, honestly anxious, to mend my ways, before it is too late. I wish to prepare myself for one of the Universities—I wish to show, if I can, that I am not quite unworthy to inherit my father's famous name. You are the man to help me, if I can only persuade you to do it. I was struck by your sermon yesterday; and, if I may venture to make the confession in your presence, I took a strong liking to you. Will you see my father, before you decide to say No? He will be able to explain whatever may seem strange in my present application; and he will be happy to see you this afternoon, if you can spare the time. As to the question of terms, I am quite sure it can be settled to your entire satisfaction."

He was evidently in earnest—gravely, vehemently in earnest. I unwillingly consented to see his father.

Our interview was a long one. All my questions were answered fully and frankly.

The young man had led an idle and desultory life. He was weary of it, and ashamed of it. His disposition was a peculiar one. He stood sorely in need of a guide, a teacher, and a friend, in whom he was disposed to confide. If I disappointed the hopes which he had centred in me, he would be discouraged, and he would relapse into the aimless and indolent existence of which he was now ashamed. Any terms for which I might stipulate were at my disposal if I would consent to receive him, for three months to begin with, on trial.

Still hesitating, I consulted my father and my friends.

They were all of opinion (and justly of opinion so far) that the new connection would be an excellent one for me. They all reproached me for taking a purely capricious dislike to a well-born and well-bred young man, and for permitting it to influence me, at the outset of my career, against my own interests. Pressed by these considerations, I allowed myself to be persuaded to give the new pupil a fair trial. He accompanied me, the next day, on my way back to the rectory.

VII

Let me be careful to do justice to a man whom I personally disliked. My senior pupil began well: he produced a decidedly favourable impression on the persons attached to my little household.

The women, especially, admired his beautiful light hair, his crisply-curling beard, his delicate complexion, his clear blue eyes, and his finely shaped hands and feet. Even the inveterate reserve in his manner, and the downcast, almost sullen, look which had prejudiced *me* against him, aroused a common feeling of romantic enthusiasm in my servants' hall. It was decided, on the high authority of the housekeeper herself, that "the new gentleman" was in love—and, more interesting still, that he was the victim of an unhappy attachment which had driven him away from his friends and his home.

For myself, I tried hard, and tried vainly, to get over my first dislike to the senior pupil.

I could find no fault with him. All his habits were quiet and regular; and he devoted himself conscientiously to his reading. But, little by little, I became satisfied that his heart was not in his studies. More than this, I had my reasons for suspecting that he was concealing something from me, and that he felt painfully the reserve on his own part which he could not, or dared not, break through. There were moments when I almost doubted whether he had not chosen my remote country rectory, as a safe place of refuge from some person or persons of whom he stood in dread.

For example, his ordinary course of proceeding, in the matter of his correspondence, was, to say the least of it, strange.

He received no letters at my house. They waited for him at the village post-office. He invariably called for them himself, and invariably forbore to trust any of my servants with his own letters for the post. Again, when we were out walking together, I more than once caught him looking furtively over his shoulder, as if he suspected some person of following him, for some evil purpose. Being constitutionally a hater of mysteries, I determined, at an early stage of our intercourse, on making an effort to clear matters up. There might be just a chance of my winning the senior pupil's confidence, if I spoke to him while the last days of the summer vacation still left us alone together in the house.

"Excuse me for noticing it," I said to him one morning, while we were engaged over our books—"I cannot help observing that you appear to have some trouble on your mind. Is it indiscreet, on my part, to ask if I can be of any use to you?"

He changed colour—looked up at me quickly—looked down again at his book—struggled hard with some secret fear or secret reluctance that was in him—and suddenly burst out with this extraordinary question:

"I suppose you were in earnest when you preached that sermon in London?"

"I am astonished that you should doubt it," I replied.

He paused again; struggled with himself again; and startled me by a second outbreak, even stranger than the first.

"I am one of the people you preached at in your sermon," he said. "That's the true reason why I asked you to take me for your pupil. Don't turn me out! When you talked to your congregation of tortured and tempted people, you talked of Me."

I was so astonished by the confession, that I lost my presence of mind. For the moment, I was unable to answer him.

"Don't turn me out!" he repeated. "Help me against myself. I am telling you the truth. As God is my witness, I am telling you the truth!"

"Tell me the *whole* truth," I said; "and rely on my consoling and helping you—rely on my being your friend."

In the fervour of the moment, I took his hand. It lay cold and still in mine: it mutely warned me that I had a sullen and a secret nature to deal with.

"There must be no concealment between us," I resumed. "You have entered my house, by your own confession, under false pretences. It is your duty to me, and your duty to yourself, to speak out."

The man's inveterate reserve—cast off for the moment only—renewed its hold on him. He considered, carefully considered, his next words before he permitted them to pass his lips.

"A person is in the way of my prospects in life," he began slowly, with his eyes cast down on his book. "A person provokes me horribly. I feel dreadful temptations (like the man you spoke of in your sermon) when I am in the person's company. Teach me to resist temptation! I am afraid of myself, if I see the person again. You are the only man who can help me. Do it while you can."

He stopped, and passed his handkerchief over his forehead.

"Will that do?" he asked—still with his eyes on his book.

"It will *not* do," I answered. "You are so far from really opening your heart to me, that you won't even let me know whether it is a man or a woman who stands in the way of your prospects in life. You use the word 'person,' over and over again—rather than say 'he' or 'she' when you speak of the provocation which is trying you. How can I help a man who has so little confidence in me as that?"

My reply evidently found him at the end of his resources. He tried,

tried desperately, to say more than he had said yet. No! The words seemed to stick in his throat. Not one of them would pass his lips.

"Give me time," he pleaded piteously. "I can't bring myself to it, all at once. I mean well. Upon my soul, I mean well. But I am slow at this sort of thing. Wait till tomorrow."

Tomorrow came—and again he put it off.

"One more day!" he said. "You don't know how hard it is to speak plainly. I am half afraid; I am half ashamed. Give me one more day."

I had hitherto only disliked him. Try as I might (and did) to make merciful allowance for his reserve, I began to despise him now.

VIII

The day of the deferred confession came, and brought an event with it, for which both he and I were alike unprepared. Would he really have confided in me but for that event? He must either have done it, or have abandoned the purpose which had led him into my house.

We met as usual at the breakfast table. My housekeeper brought in my letters of the morning. To my surprise, instead of leaving the room again as usual, she walked round to the other side of the table, and laid a letter before my senior pupil—the first letter, since his residence with me, which had been delivered to him under my roof.

He started, and took up the letter. He looked at the address. A spasm of suppressed fury passed across his face; his breath came quickly; his hand trembled as it held the letter. So far, I said nothing. I waited to see whether he would open the envelope in my presence or not.

He was afraid to open it, in my presence. He got on his feet; he said, in tones so low that I could barely hear him: "Please excuse me for a minute"—and left the room.

I waited for half an hour—for a quarter of an hour, after that—and then I sent to ask if he had forgotten his breakfast.

In a minute more, I heard his footstep in the hall. He opened the breakfast-room door, and stood on the threshold, with a small travelling bag in his hand.

"I beg your pardon," he said, still standing at the door. "I must ask for leave of absence for a day or two. Business in London."

"Can I be of any use?" I asked. "I am afraid your letter has brought you bad news?"

"Yes," he said shortly. "Bad news. I have no time for breakfast."

"Wait a few minutes," I urged. "Wait long enough to treat me like your friend—to tell me what your trouble is before you go."

He made no reply. He stepped into the hall, and closed the door—then opened it again a little way, without showing himself.

"Business in London," he repeated—as if he thought it highly important to inform me of the nature of his errand. The door closed for the second time. He was gone.

I went into my study, and carefully considered what had happened.

The result of my reflections is easily described. I determined on discontinuing my relations with my senior pupil. In writing to his father (which I did, with all due courtesy and respect, by that day's post), I mentioned as my reason for arriving at this decision:—First, that I had found it impossible to win the confidence of his son. Secondly, that his son had that morning suddenly and mysteriously left my house for London, and that I must decline accepting any further responsibility towards him, as the necessary consequence.

I had put my letter in the post-bag, and was beginning to feel a little easier after having written it, when my housekeeper appeared in the study, with a very grave face, and with something hidden apparently in her closed hand.

"Would you please look, sir, at what we have found in the gentleman's bedroom, since he went away this morning?"

I knew the housekeeper to possess a woman's full share of that amiable weakness of the sex which goes by the name of "Curiosity." I had also, in various indirect ways, become aware that my senior pupil's strange departure had largely increased the disposition among the women of my household to regard him as the victim of an unhappy attachment. The time was ripe, as it seemed to me, for checking any further gossip about him, and any renewed attempts at prying into his affairs in his absence.

"Your only business in my pupil's bedroom," I said to the housekeeper, "is to see that it is kept clean, and that it is properly aired. There must be no interference, if you please, with his letters, or his papers, or with anything else that he has left behind him. Put back directly whatever you may have found in his room."

The housekeeper had her full share of a woman's temper as well as of a woman's curiosity. She listened to me with a rising colour, and a just perceptible toss of the head.

"Must I put it back, sir, on the floor, between the bed and the wall?" she inquired, with an ironical assumption of the humblest deference to my wishes. *"That's* where the girl found it when she was sweeping the room. Anybody can see for themselves," pursued the housekeeper indignantly, "that the poor gentleman has gone away broken-hearted. And there, in my opinion, is the hussy who is the cause of it!"

With those words, she made me a low curtsey, and laid a small photographic portrait on the desk at which I was sitting.

I looked at the photograph.

In an instant, my heart was beating wildly—my head turned giddy—the housekeeper, the furniture, the walls of the room, all swayed and whirled round me.

The portrait that had been found in my senior pupil's bedroom was the portrait of Jéromette!

IX

I had sent the housekeeper out of my study. I was alone, with the photograph of the Frenchwoman on my desk.

There could surely be little doubt about the discovery that had burst upon me. The man who had stolen his way into my house, driven by the terror of a temptation that he dared not reveal, and the man who had been my unknown rival in the by-gone time, were one and the same!

Recovering self-possession enough to realize this plain truth, the inferences that followed forced their way into my mind as a matter of course. The unnamed person who was the obstacle to my pupil's prospects in life, the unnamed person in whose company he was assailed by temptations which made him tremble for himself, stood revealed to me now as being, in all human probability, no other than Jéromette. Had she bound him in the fetters of the marriage which he had himself proposed? Had she discovered his place of refuge in my house? And was the letter that had been delivered to him of her writing? Assuming these questions to be answered in the affirmative, what, in that case, was his "business in London"? I remembered how he had spoken to me of his temptations, I recalled the expression that had crossed his face when he recognised the handwriting on the letter—and the conclusion that followed literally shook me to the soul. Ordering my horse to be saddled, I rode instantly to the railway station.

The train by which he had travelled to London had reached the terminus nearly an hour since. The one useful course that I could take, by way of quieting the dreadful misgivings crowding one after another on my mind, was to telegraph to Jéromette at the address at which I had last seen her. I sent the subjoined message—prepaying the reply:

"If you are in any trouble, telegraph to me. I will be with you by the first train. Answer, in any case."

There was nothing in the way of the immediate despatch of my message. And yet the hours passed, and no answer was received. By the advice of the clerk, I sent a second telegram to the London office, requesting an explanation. The reply came back in these terms:

"Improvements in street. Houses pulled down. No trace of person named in telegram."

I mounted my horse, and rode back slowly to the rectory.

"The day of his return to me will bring with it the darkest days of my life." . . . "I shall die young, and die miserably. Have you interest enough still left in me to wish to hear of it?" . . . "You *shall* hear of it." Those words were in my memory while I rode home in the cloudless moonlight night. They were so vividly present to me that I could hear again her pretty foreign accent, her quiet clear tones, as she spoke them. For the rest, the emotions of that memorable day had worn me out. The answer from the telegraph-office had struck me with a strange and stony despair. My mind was a blank. I had no thoughts. I had no tears.

I was about half-way on my road home, and I had just heard the clock of a village church strike ten, when I became conscious, little by little, of a chilly sensation slowly creeping through and through me to the bones. The warm balmy air of a summer night was abroad. It was the month of July. In the month of July, was it possible that any living creature (in good health) could feel cold? It was *not* possible—and yet, the chilly sensation still crept through and through me to the bones.

I looked up. I looked all round me.

My horse was walking along an open high road. Neither trees nor waters were near me. On either side, the flat fields stretched away bright and broad in the moonlight.

I stopped my horse, and looked round me again.

Yes: I saw it. With my own eyes I saw it. A pillar of white mist—between five and six feet high, as well as I could judge—was moving beside me at the edge of the road, on my left hand. When I stopped, the white mist stopped. When I went on, the white mist went on. I pushed my horse to a trot—the pillar of mist was with me. I urged him to a gallop—the pillar of mist was with me. I stopped him again—the pillar of mist stood still.

The white colour of it was the white colour of the fog which I had seen over the river—on the night when I had gone to bid her farewell. And the chill which had then crept through me to the bones was the chill that was creeping through me now.

I went on again slowly. The white mist went on again slowly—with the clear bright night all round it.

I was awed rather than frightened. There was one moment, and one only, when the fear came to me that my reason might be shaken. I caught myself keeping time to the slow tramp of the horse's feet with the slow utterance of these words, repeated over and over again: "Jéromette is dead. Jéromette is dead." But my will was still my own: I was able to control myself, to impose silence on my own muttering lips. And I rode on quietly. And the pillar of mist went quietly with me.

My groom was waiting for my return at the rectory gate. I pointed to the mist, passing through the gate with me.

"Do you see anything there?" I said.

The man looked at me in astonishment.

I entered the rectory. The housekeeper met me in the hall. I pointed to the mist, entering with me.

"Do you see anything at my side?" I asked.

The housekeeper looked at me as the groom had looked at me.

"I am afraid you are not well, sir," she said. "Your colour is all gone —you are shivering. Let me get you a glass of wine."

I went into my study, on the ground floor, and took the chair at my desk. The photograph still lay where I had left it. The pillar of mist floated round the table, and stopped opposite to me, behind the photograph.

The housekeeper brought in the wine. I put the glass to my lips, and set it down again. The chill of the mist was in the wine. There was no taste, no reviving spirit in it. The presence of the housekeeper oppressed me. My dog had followed her into the room. The presence of the animal oppressed me. I said to the woman, "Leave me by myself, and take the dog with you."

They went out, and left me alone in the room.

I sat looking at the pillar of mist, hovering opposite to me.

It lengthened slowly, until it reached to the ceiling. As it lengthened, it grew bright and luminous. A time passed, and a shadowy appearance showed itself in the centre of the light. Little by little, the shadowy appearance took the outline of a human form. Soft brown eyes, tender and melancholy, looked at me through the unearthly light in the mist. The head and the rest of the face broke next slowly on my view. Then the figure gradually revealed itself, moment by moment, downward and downward to the feet. She stood before me as I had last seen her, in her purple-merino dress, with the black-silk apron, with the white handkerchief tied loosely round her neck. She stood before me, in the gentle beauty that I remembered so well; and looked at me as she had looked when she gave me her last kiss—when her tears had dropped on my cheek.

I fell on my knees at the table. I stretched out my hands to her imploringly. I said, "Speak to me—O, once again speak to me, Jéromette."

Her eyes rested on me with a divine compassion in them. She lifted her hand, and pointed to the photograph on my desk, with a gesture which bade me turn the card. I turned it. The name of the man who had left my house that morning was inscribed on it, in her own handwriting.

I looked up at her again, when I had read it. She lifted her hand once more, and pointed to the handkerchief round her neck. As I looked at it, the fair white silk changed horribly in colour—the fair white silk became darkened and drenched in blood.

A moment more—and the vision of her began to grow dim. By slow degrees, the figure, then the face, faded back into the shadowy appearance that I had first seen. The luminous inner light died out in the white mist. The mist itself dropped slowly downwards—floated a moment in airy circles on the floor—vanished. Nothing was before me but the familiar wall of the room, and the photograph lying face downwards on my desk.

X

The next day, the newspapers reported the discovery of a murder in London. A Frenchwoman was the victim. She had been killed by a wound in the throat. The crime had been discovered between ten and eleven o'clock on the previous night.

I leave you to draw your conclusion from what I have related. My own faith in the reality of the apparition is immovable. I say, and believe, that Jéromette kept her word with me. She died young, and died miserably. And I heard of it from herself.

Take up the Trial again, and look at the circumstances that were revealed during the investigation in court. His motive for murdering her is there.

You will see that she did indeed marry him privately; that they lived together contentedly, until the fatal day when she discovered that his fancy had been caught by another woman; that violent quarrels took place between them, from that time to the time when my sermon showed him his own deadly hatred towards her, reflected in the case of another man; that she discovered his place of retreat in my house, and threatened him by letter with the public assertion of her conjugal rights; lastly, that a man, variously described by different witnesses, was seen leaving the door of her lodgings on the night of the murder. The Law—advancing no farther than this—may have discovered circumstances of suspicion, but no certainty. The Law, in default of direct evidence to convict the prisoner, may have rightly decided in letting him go free.

But *I* persist in believing that the man was guilty. *I* declare that he, and he alone, was the murderer of Jéromette. And now, you know why.

One of the most dangerous kinds of ghost is the handsome or beautiful spirit who lures a member of the opposite sex to his or her destruction. One might argue whether such creatures really are incubi and succubi or just ordinary ghosts with a grudge against the opposite sex. Whatever their origin . . . they are especially insidious; but then those who seek comeliness above all other attributes ought to be wary of the results, no matter what plane the object of their affection dwells on. . . .

The Phantom Woman
Anonymous

He took an all-possessing, burning fancy to her from the first. She was neither young nor pretty, so far as he could see—but she was wrapped round with mystery. That was the key of it all; she was noticeable in spite of herself. Her face at the window, sunset after sunset; her eyes, gazing out mournfully through the dusty panes, hypnotized the lawyer. He saw her through the twilight night after night, and he grew at length to wait through the days in a feverish waiting for dusk, and that one look at an unknown woman.

She was always at the same window on the ground floor, sitting doing nothing. She looked beyond, so the infatuated solicitor fancied, at him. Once he even thought that he detected the ghost of a friendly smile on her lips. Their eyes always met with a mute desire to make acquaintance. This romance went on for a couple of months.

Gilbert Dent assured himself that nothing in this life can possibly remain stationary, and he cudgeled his brain for a respectable manner of introducing himself to his idol.

He had hardly arrived at this point when he received a shock. There came an evening when she was not at the window.

Next morning he walked down Wood Lane on his way to the office. He always went by train, but he felt a strong disinclination to go through another day without a sight of her. His heart began to beat like a schoolgirl's as he drew near the house. If she should be at the window. He was almost disposed to take his courage in his hand and call on her, and—yes, even—tell her in a quick burst that she had mysteriously become all the world to him. He could see nothing ridiculous in this course; the possibility of her being married, or having family ties of any sort, had simply never occurred to him.

However, she was not at the window; what was more, there was a sinister silence, a sort of breathlessness about the whole place.

It was a very hot morning in late August. He looked a long time, but no face came, and no movement stirred the house.

He went his way, walking like a man who has been heavily knocked on the brow and sees stars still. That afternoon he left the office early, and in less than an hour stood at the gate again. The window was blank. He pushed the gate back—it hung on one hinge—and walked up the drive to the door. There were five steps—five steps leading up to it. At the foot he wheeled aside sharply to the window; he had a sick dread of looking through the small panes—why he could not have told.

When at last he found courage to look he saw that there was a small round table set just under the window—a work table to all appearance; one of those things with lots of little compartments all round and a lid in the middle which shut over a well-like cavity for holding pieces of needlework. He remembered that his mother had one—thirty years before.

Round the edge of the table was gripped a small, delicate hand. Gilbert Dent's eyes ran from this bloodless hand and slim wrist to a shoulder under a coarse stuff bodice—to a rather wasted throat, which was bare and flung back.

So this was the end—before the beginning. He saw her. She was dead; twisted on the floor with a ghastly face turned up toward the ceiling, and stiff fingers caught in desperation round the work table.

He stumbled away along the path and into the lane.

For a long time he could not realize the horror of this thing. The influence of the decayed house hung over him—nothing seemed real. It was quite dark when he moved away from the gate, and went in the direction of the nearest police station. That she was dead—this woman whose very name he did not know, although she influenced him so powerfully—he was certain; one look at the face would have told anyone that. That she was murdered he more than suspected. He had seen no blood about; there had been no mark on the long, bare throat, and yet the word rushed in his ears, "Murder."

Later on he went back with a police officer.

They broke into the house and entered the room. It was in utter darkness, of course, by now. Dent, his fingers trembling, struck a match. It flared round the walls and lighted them for a moment before he let it fall on the dusty floor.

The policeman began to light his lantern and turned it stolidly on the window. He had no reason for delay; he was eager to get to the bottom of the business. His professional zeal was whetted; this promised to be a mystery with a spice in it.

He turned the light full on the window; he gave a strange, choked cry, half of rage, half of apprehension. Then he went up to Gilbert Dent, who stood in the middle of the room with his hands before his eyes, and took his shoulder and shook it none too gently.

"There ain't nobody," he said.

Dent looked wildly at the window—the recess was empty except for the work table. The woman was gone.

They searched the house; they minutely inspected the garden. Everything was normal; everything told the same mournful tale—of desertion, of death, of long empty years. But they found no woman, nor trace of one.

"This house," said the policeman, looking suspiciously into the lawyer's face, "has been empty for longer than I can remember. Nobody'll live in it. They do say something about foul play a good many years ago. I don't know about that. All I do know is that the landlord can't get it off his hands."

It was doubtful if Gilbert Dent heard one word of what the man was saying. He was too stunned to do anything but creep home—when he was allowed to go—and let himself stealthily into his own house with a latch key; he was afraid even of himself. He did not go to bed that night.

As for the mystery of the woman, the matter was allowed to drop; it ended—officially. There was a shrug and a grin at the police station. The impression there was that the lawyer had been drinking—that the dead woman in the empty room was a gruesome freak of his tipsy brain.

*   *   *

A week or so later Dent called on his brother, Ned—the one near relation he had. Ned was a doctor; perhaps he was a shade more matter-of-fact than Gilbert; at all events, when the latter told his story of the house and the woman, he attributed the affair solely to liver.

"You are overworked"—the elder brother looked at the younger's yellow face. "An experience of this nature is by no means uncommon. Haven't you heard of people having their pet 'spooks'?"

"But this was a real woman," he declared. "I—I, well, I was in love with her. I had made up my mind to marry her—if I could."

Ned gave him a keen, swift glance.

"We'll go to Brighton tomorrow," he said, with quiet decision. "As for your work, everything must be put aside. You've run completely down. You ought to have been taken in hand before."

They went to Brighton, and it really seemed as if Ned was right, and that the woman at the window had been merely a nervous creation. It seemed so, that is, for nearly three weeks, and then the climax came.

It was in the twilight—she had always been part of it—that Gilbert Dent saw her again; the woman that he had found lying dead.

They were walking, the two brothers, along the cliffs.

The wind was blowing in their faces, the sea was booming beneath the cliff. Ned had just said it was about time they turned back to the hotel and had some dinner, when Gilbert with a cry leapt forward to the very edge of the flat grass path on which they were strolling. The movement was so sudden that his brother barely caught him in time. They struggled and swayed on the very edge of the cliff for a second; Gilbert, possessed by some sudden frenzy, seemed resolved to go over, but the other at last dragged him backward, and they rolled together on the close, thick turf.

At this point Gilbert opened his eyes and tried to get on his feet.

"Better?" asked his brother, cheerfully, holding out a helping hand. "Strange! The sea has that effect on some people. Didn't think that you were one of them."

"What effect?"

"Vertigo, my dear fellow."

"Ned," said the other solemnly, "I saw her. It is not worth your while to try to account for anything. I have been inclined to think that you were right—that she, the woman at the window, was a fancy, that I had fallen in love with a creation of my own brain; but I saw her again tonight. You must have seen her yourself—she was within a couple of feet of you. Why did you not try and save her? It was nothing short of murder to let her go over like that. I did my best."

"You certainly did—to kill us both," said Ned, grimly.

Gilbert gave him a wild look.

After luncheon Ned persuaded him to rest—watched him fall asleep, and then went out.

In the porch of the hotel he was met by a waiter on his return who told him that Gilbert had left about a quarter of an hour after he had himself gone out.

Directly he heard this he feared the worst; having, as is usual in such cases, a very hazy idea of what the worst might be. Of course he must follow without a moment's delay; but a reference to the timetable told him that there was not another train for an hour, and that was slow.

It was already getting dusk when he arrived there. He felt certain that Gilbert would go there. He got to the end of the lane and walked up it slowly, examining every house. There would be no difficulty in recognizing the one he wanted; Gilbert had described it in detail more than once.

He stood outside the loosely hanging gate at last, and stared through the darkness at the shabby stucco front and rank garden.

He went down a flight of steps to the back door, and finding it unfastened, stepped into a stone passage. It was one of the problems of the place that he should have avoided the main entrance door with a half-admitted dread, and that, only half admitting still, he was afraid to mount the long flight of stone stairs leading from the servants' quarters. However, he pulled himself together and went up to the room.

It was quite dark inside. He heard something scuttle across the floor; he felt the grit and dust of years under his feet. He struck a match—just as Gilbert had done—and looked first at the recess in which the window was built. The match flared round the room for a moment and gave him a flash picture of his surroundings. He saw the stripes of gaudy paper moving almost imperceptibly, like tentacles of some sea monster, from the wall; he saw a creature—it looked like a rat—scurry across the floor from the window to the great mantelpiece of hard white marble.

If he had seen nothing more than this.

He saw in detail all that the first match had flashed at him. He saw his brother lying on the floor; a ghastly coincidence, his hand was caught round the edge of the work table as hers had been. The other hand was clenched across his breast; there was a look of great agony on his face.

A dead face, of course. This was the end of the affair. He was lying dead by the window where the woman had sat every night at dusk and smiled at him.

The second match went out; the brother of the dead man struck a third. He looked again and closely. Then he staggered to his feet and gave a cry. It rang through the empty rooms and echoed without wearying down the long, stone passages in the basement.

Gilbert's head was thrown back; his chin peaked to the ceiling. On his throat were livid marks. The doctor saw them distinctly; he saw the grip of small fingers; the distinct impression of a woman's little hand.

*   *   *

The curious thing about the whole story—the most curious thing, perhaps—is that no other eye ever saw those murderous marks. So there was no scandal, no chase after the murderer, no undiscovered crime. They faded; when the doctor saw his brother again in the full light and in the presence of others his throat was clear. And the post-mortem proved that death was due to natural causes.

So the matter stands, and will.

But where the house and its overgrown garden stood runs a new road with neat red and white villas.

Whatever secret it knew—if any—it kept discreetly.

Ned Dent is morbid enough to go down the smart new road in the twilight sometimes and wonder.

An anonymous rendition of a folk tale that seems to recur in any country with lots of ice and the need for negotiating the same on skates . . . a good example of the missioned spirit whose duty it is to protect.

The Spectre Bride

Anonymous

The winter nights up at Sault Ste. Marie are as white and luminous as the Milky Way. The silence that rests upon the solitude appears to be white also. Nature has included sound in her arrestment. Save the still white frost, all things are obliterated. The stars are there, but they seem to belong to heaven and not to earth. They are at an immeasurable height, and so black is the night that the opaque ether rolls between them and the observer in great liquid billows.

In such a place it is difficult to believe that the world is peopled to any great extent. One fancies that Cain has just killed Abel, and that there is need for the greatest economy in the matter of human life.

The night Ralph Hagadorn started out for Echo Bay he felt as if he were the only man in the world, so complete was the solitude through which he was passing. He was going over to attend the wedding of his best friend, and was, in fact, to act as the groomsman. Business had delayed him, and he was compelled to make his journey at night. But he hadn't gone far before he began to feel the exhilaration of the skater. His skates were keen, his legs fit for a longer journey than the one he had undertaken, and the tang of the frost was to him what a spur is to a spirited horse.

He cut through the air as a sharp stone cleaves the water. He could feel the tumult of the air as he cleft it. As he went on he began to have fancies. It seemed to him that he was enormously tall—a great Viking of the Northland, hastening over icy fiords to his love. That reminded him that he had a love—though, indeed, that thought was always present with him as a background for other thoughts. To be sure, he had not told her she was his love, because he had only seen her a few times and the opportunity had not presented itself. She lived at Echo Bay, too, and was to be the maid of honor to his friend's bride—which was another reason why he skated on almost as swiftly as the wind, and why, now and then, he let out a shout of exhilaration.

The one drawback in the matter was that Marie Beaujeu's father had money, and that Marie lived in a fine house and wore otter skin about her throat and little satin-lined mink boots on her feet when she went sledding, and that the jacket in which she kept a bit of her dead mother's hair had a black pearl in it as big as a pea. These things made it difficult—nay, impossible—for Ralph Hagadorn to say anything more than "I love you." But that much he meant to have the satisfaction of saying, no matter what came of it.

With this determination growing upon him he swept along the ice which gleamed under the starlight. Indeed, Venus made a glowing path toward the west and seemed to reassure him. He was sorry he could not skim down that avenue of light from the love star, but he was forced to turn his back upon it and face toward the northeast.

It came to him with a shock that he was not alone. His eyelashes were a good deal frosted and his eyeballs blurred with the cold, and at first he thought it an illusion. But he rubbed his eyes hard and at length made sure that not very far in front of him was a long white skater in fluttering garments who sped over the snows fast as ever werewolf went. He called aloud, but there was no answer, and then he gave chase, setting his teeth hard and putting a tension on his firm young muscles. But however fast he might go the white skater went faster. After a time he became convinced, as he chanced to glance for a second at the North Star, that the white skater was leading him out of his direct path. For a moment he hesitated, wondering if he should not keep to his road, but the strange companion seemed to draw him on irresistibly, and so he followed.

Of course it came to him more than once that this might be no earthly guide. Up in those latitudes men see strange things when the hoar frost is on the earth. Hagadorn's father, who lived up there with the Lake Superior Indians and worked in the copper mines, had once welcomed a woman at his hut on a bitter night who was gone by morning, and who left wolf tracks in the snow—yes, it was so, and John Fontanelle, the half-breed, could tell you about it any day—if he were alive. (Alack, the snow where the wolf tracks were is melted now!)

Well, Hagadorn followed the white skater all the night, and when the ice flushed red at dawn and arrows of lovely light shot up into the cold heavens, she was gone, and Hagadorn was at his destination. Then, as he took off his skates while the sun climbed arrogantly up to his place above all other things, Hagadorn chanced to glance lakeward, and he saw there was a great wind-rift in the ice and that the waves showed blue as sapphires beside the gleaming ice. Had he swept along his intended path, watching the stars to guide him, his glance turned upward, all his body at magnificent momentum, he must certainly have gone into that cold grave. The white skater had been his guardian angel!

Much impressed, he went up to his friend's house, expecting to find there the pleasant wedding furore. But someone met him quietly at the door, and his friend came downstairs to greet him with a solemn demeanor.

"Is this your wedding face?" cried Hagadorn. "Why, really, if this is the way you are affected, the sooner I take warning the better."

"There's no wedding today," said his friend.

"No wedding? Why, you're not——"

"Marie Beaujeu died last night——"

"Marie——"

"Died last night. She had been skating in the afternoon, and she came home chilled and wandering in her mind, as if the frost had got in it somehow. She got worse and worse and talked all the time of you."

"Of me?"

"We wondered what it all meant. We didn't know you were lovers."

"I didn't know it myself; more's the pity."

"She said you were on the ice. She said you didn't know about the big breaking up, and she cried to us that the wind was off shore. Then she cried that you could come in by the old French Creek if you only knew——"

"I came in that way," interrupted Hagadorn.

"How did you come to do that? It's out of your way."

So Hagadorn told him how it came to pass.

And that day they watched beside the maiden, who had tapers at her head and feet, and over in the little church the bride who might have been at her wedding said prayers for her friend. Then they buried her in her bridesmaid's white, and Hagadorn was there before the altar with her, as he intended from the first. At midnight the day of the burial her friends were married in the gloom of the cold church, and they walked together through the snow to lay their bridal wreaths on her grave.

Three nights later Hagadorn started back again to his home. They wanted him to go by sunlight, but he had his way and went when Venus made her bright path on the ice. He hoped for the companionship of the white skater. But he did not have it. His only companion was the wind. The only voice he heard was the baying of a wolf on the north shore. The world was as white as if it had just been created and the sun had not yet colored nor man defiled it.

Gothic ghost stories tend to be revoltingly gruesome, but here is a prime example of the period that is comparatively restrained, yet no less awful for the author's judiciousness. M. G. LEWIS, born in 1775, influenced both Germanic and English literature with his collections of fantastic balladry and his novel, The Monk, *considered by most critics to be one of the two pinnacles of Gothic terror fiction (the other is Maturin's* Melmoth the Wanderer). *"The Midnight Embrace" is reminiscent of some of Poe's effects, but on a scale more allied to the wild passions of grand opera.*

The *Midnight* Embrace
by M. G. Lewis

Albert, lord of the ancient castle of Werdendorff, on the borders of the Black Forest, was a nobleman of elegant person, and fascinating manners; but his heart was prone to deceit. He was well versed in all the wily arts of seduction, and he paid slight attention to the fulfilling of either religious or moral duties, when opposed as a bar to his pleasures.

At the distance of half a league from his stately abode, resided the fair Josephine in an humble cottage, happy, virtuous, and respected. Beauty and innocence were the only dower she possessed. Her father had been a subaltern officer in the emperor's service. Her mother was the only child of a very poor, but very respectable pastor. Francisco, her father, had fallen in the field of battle when she had attained her fifth year. His disconsolate widow retired with her trifling pension from Vienna, where she had hitherto resided, to the vicinity of Werdendorff, where she lived with her darling child in a peaceful and retired seclusion now so congenial to their feelings. The education of Josephine she attended to with the most sedulous care, and was amply repaid by the docility of her pupil. At the age of sixteen, Josephine lost her parent, who, previous to her dissolution, gave every advice that a virtuous mind could dictate, with regard to the subsequent conduct of her daughter. Josephine listened to her virtuous counsels with attention, and while the pearly drops chased each other down her pallid cheeks, promised a strict adherence to the wishes of the dying parent. Alas! how little to be depended upon are the promises and resolutions of mortals!

The remains of the mother of Josephine being decently interred, the sorrowing girl soon felt herself obliged to grant less indulgence to heartfelt grief, that she might toil for each day's bread. Her parent's pension expired with her; and our fair maid, to pay the rent of her cottage, and defray her necessary expenditures, was obliged to leave her humble pallet with the first salute of the lark, and ply her needle with assiduous and unremitting industry. Her labour was crowned with success. She lived happy, virtuous, and respected, for the first three years after her mother's decease. She was then predestined to experience a fatal reverse: the veil of innocent simplicity was to be torn from her mind, and the vacancy filled up by the dark cloud of guilt.

Albert of Werdendorff beheld the maid in all her native pride of beauty, softened by angelic modesty, and her unconsciousness of the superlative charms she possessed. Albert longed to call this fair floweret his own; not as a tender admirer, to protect her honourably from all the storms of fate, but as a rude spoiler, that wantonly plucks the rose from its native branch, and then, regardless of its beauties, casts it to wither on the ground.

It is needless to describe minutely the various arts that Lord Albert descended to, in order to seduce the unsuspecting victim of his deceptions. His superior rank, fortune, and connections were so many circumstances to furnish him with favourable pretexts to forward his designs.

Though Albert was lord of the castle of Werdendorff, and had there a splendid establishment, yet he depended on his father for a princely addition to his possessions. He made Josephine to believe that it was impossible for him to espouse her during his father's life; but called on heaven, and every saint, to witness the inviolable faith and constancy he would always maintain towards her: that he should always regard her as his wife; and, as soon as he should be free to offer his hand, their marriage should be legally solemnized. Josephine had many virtuous sentiments; but Albert, by sophistry, overcame those scruples; and the unfortunate maiden added one more to the many that suffer their credulous hearts to be seduced by the wily serpent, like objects of their tender and faithful love.

Josephine's breast was no longer the abode of serenity. In Albert's presence her spirits were elated; she listened with delight to the repetition of his vows, and blinded by delusive passion, esteemed herself one of the happiest of the happy. But in the lone hours of solitude, she was oft times miserable. Regret, remorse, and apprehension, would enter, though obtrusive guests. From the casement of her cottage, Josephine could behold the stately castle of Werdendorff, and discern its portals opened for the reception of guests invited to the noble banquets and festive balls, which often made its lofty roofs resound with their mirth. On these occasions Josephine would sigh, and ponder on the wide difference between herself and Lord Albert in their stations, and wonder if her fond hopes would ever be realized.

At midnight, when all the inhabitants of the castle were wrapt in repose, was the time that Lord Albert paid his visits to Josephine's cottage, which hour was mutually chosen by the lovers for their interviews, that they might elude the observation of those around them. And when the moon gave no ray of light to Lord Albert in his progress over the dark and fenny moor, Josephine would place a lighted taper at her casement, to guide him to her humble abode.

Ah! ill-fated maid! thou didst soon experience the dire truth, that men betray, and that vows can be broken; and that illicit love, though at first ardent, will soon decay, and leave nought but wretchedness behind.

Albert had been Josephine's favoured lover about six months, when, one hapless night, Josephine had placed the taper in her window as usual; and sat wishing the arrival of Albert in anxious expectation. More than once she conjectured she heard his well-known footsteps approach the door. She flew to open it, and her eye fixed on vacancy alone, while she shed bitter tears at the disappointment. Another, and another night elapsed; Albert came not; and Josephine's anguish and suspense became insupportable.

On the fourth morning of Albert's unusual absence, Josephine arose from her pallet after a few hours of restless and perturbed sleep; she approached the window, and her eyes taking their usual direction across the moor to the castle of Werdendorff, she beheld its gay banners streaming on the walls.

Anxious to learn the cause of this rejoicing, Josephine mingled with a group of rustic maidens who were repairing to the castle. She asked them, in tremulous accents, what propitious event they were celebrating at the Chateau; but the villagers were as ignorant as herself. When they came to the outer portal of the edifice, they beheld a gay procession passing from the hall to the chapel.

The sentinel, in reply to Josephine's interrogatories, informed her that Lord Albert was then gone to the chapel to seal his nuptial vows with Lady Guimilda, the proud daughter of a neighbouring baron, whose possessions were immense, and she the sole heiress.

Josephine replied not; her heart was full, even to bursting. She retreated from her companions, and seeking the covert of a friendly wood, gave way to all her frantic ravings of despair, which was still aggravated by every passing gale, bearing along the echoes of the loud shouts of revelry that pervaded the castle, and proclaimed Albert's perjury and her ruin.

As soon as the first violence of her grief was abated, she began to cherish delusive ideas. She thought the sentinel might have deceived her; or, at least, he might have been in an error himself, in supposing Lord Albert the bridegroom of the proud Guimilda; and she thought it more probable that it was some friend of his, who had solemnized his marriage at Werdendorff castle.

Cherishing this weak hope, she returned to her cottage; and partially disguising herself in a long mantle, and a thick white veil, she repaired at twilight to the castle, and, unobserved, mingled in the revelling crowd. But alas! the sentinel's intelligence she soon found to be too true; and the gayest among the gay throng was the false Albert and his bride Guimilda.

Once convinced, Josephine tarried no longer in the castle hall. With torturing sensations, and faltering steps, she left the abode of her haughty rival, and once more sought her lonely dwelling. The night was dark, and the wind shook the rushes, and all around, like her own heart, was drear and forlorn. With folded arms, and her whole person like the statue of despair, sat Josephine by the casement. Fond recollections caused her tears to flow, when she called to mind how oft in that window she had placed the taper to light her then ardent lover over the moor.

While she was thus reflecting, she heard footsteps approach her cottage door; and presently she heard her own name softly pronounced. She instantly recognized Lord Albert's voice; and opening the casement, she cried indignantly, "Away to Guimilda! Away to the pleasures that reign in Werdendorff castle. Why leave you my rival's bed, to add another insult to the woes you have caused me?"

Lord Albert renewed his entreaties for admission; and Josephine, at length, imprudently yielded to his request.

Albert exerted all his eloquence to convince the fair one, that his heart had no share in the nuptial contract with Guimilda; that there Josephine's image reigned triumphant, while her rival could claim nought but his hand. By the stern command of his father, he protested he had joined his fate to Guimilda's, who would only leave him his fortune on that condition: but that his love to Josephine should never be diminished by that circumstance; but that he would transplant her to a more pleasing abode, where she might reside in elegant retirement, and appear in a situation more congenial to his wishes than her present dwelling would allow, or, indeed, her near vicinity to the castle render prudent.

The soft blandishments of her deceiver again lured her to guile; and her anger was completely vanquished by love.

Again was the board spread with the choice delicacies, and delicious wines, that Lord Albert had brought with him from the castle; the flower-footed hours winged away with rapturous delight, and again the soft smile beamed on the lovely countenance of Josephine.

"Adieu, my beloved," said Lord Albert; "the first blush of morn empurples the east, and warns me from thy arms."

Josephine inquired affectionately when she was next to expect her loved lord. He replied, that he would return at the *dark hour of midnight,* and again clasp her in his arms.

Lord Albert's bosom beat high as he sped homewards across the moor. The horrid deed he had committed, did not at that moment appall him. He congratulated himself on being freed from a mistress, whom satiety had for some time past made him detest.

In relating to Josephine the cause of his marriage with the Lady Guimilda, he had been guilty of a great falsehood. The known wealth of the heiress, at first, induced Lord Albert to visit at her father's villa; for avarice was a ruling passion with the youth. But when he beheld the haughty fair one, he instantly became a captive to her beauty, and loathed Josephine.

His nightly visits to Josephine, though conducted with much cautious secrecy, had by some means reached the ears of the proud Guimilda. No pity for the poor maiden filled her breast; she hated her fair rival, for having a prior claim to Lord Albert's heart. Her revengeful temper made her feel that she should never enjoy perfect happiness while Josephine existed. She thought that there was more than a probability, that, for all Albert's declarations to the contrary, when she conversed with him on the subject, that, after a short time would elapse, his heart might grow cold towards the legal partner of his fortune, and return with redoubled ardour to his deserted mistress. She knew the infirmities of her own temper; and the angelic sweetness of disposition which her informants had represented Josephine to possess, contrasted with her own hauteur, caprice, and tyranny, made the confirmation of her fears appear as strong as proofs of holy writ.

To glut her revenge, and leave no room for apprehension, she formed the horrid project of demanding the following sacrifice at the hands of Lord Albert.

This was the removal of Josephine by a poison which should take a quick effect, and cause her to breathe her last ere she should have time to reveal the name of her murderer. The time fixed on by Guimilda for the perpetration of this horrid deed, was their wedding night. Albert was to make some plausible excuse to his guests, to account for his absenting himself at that time, and then to repair to Josephine's cottage; and, as he always, on those occasions, condescended to convey with his own hands, some refreshments, it would be an easy matter for him to infuse into the goblet of wine that he should present to his fair victim, a deadly but tasteless drug that Guimilda prepared for that fatal purpose. The proud Guimilda made a solemn vow, never to admit Lord Albert to her bed, till her horrific demand was complied with.

Alas! her destined husband was too pliantly moulded to her purpose; he made not half the resistance she expected to encounter; but, after a very few scruples, signified his perfect acquiescence with the will of this fiend in female form.

How Lord Albert effected his purpose has been previously described. He had nearly gained the castle on his return, when his own words recurred to his memory: at the dark hour of midnight he would again return, and clasp her in his arms. "Ill-fated Josephine!" exclaimed he, mentally. "Ere that hour arrives, thy fluttering breath will flee amid agonizing pain; and thou, late so beauteous, wilt be a lifeless corpse." The first light of morning cheerfully illumined the dell; but Albert's heart was not gladdened by the scene.

The beams of the sun began to gild the turrets of Werdendorff, yet the bridal ball was not concluded. In vain the blaze of beauty met Lord Albert's eyes; he sighed amid surrounding splendour; for conscience had strongly entwined her chains around his heart. Guimilda was impatient to know if her lord had accomplished the dire deed; and, on his answering in the affirmative, she experienced the most extravagant and unnatural transports. But Albert was clouded with horror; and he kept constantly repeating the words, "At midnight's dark hour thou shalt embrace me again."

On the next evening the guests again assembled in the halls of Werdendorff, again the musicians tuned their instruments to notes of joy; and again the gay knights and their fair partners joined in the mazy dance. Lord Albert alone seemed abstracted; and his woe-expressive countenance gave rise to a variety of conjectures, all very remote from the truth. Guimilda perceived the agony of his mind (which her hardened heart considered as a weakness) with extreme displeasure; nor was she slow in whispering to him the most keen reproaches for the pusillanimity of his conduct, in appearing in this manner before their guests.

But in vain Lord Albert endeavoured to arouse himself, and put on a gay unembarrassed air. His mind, in a few hours, had undergone a total revolution. He now regarded Guimilda as an agent of infernal malice, sent to plunge his soul into an irremediable abyss of guilt. The artless behaviour of his murdered love was the contrast; her gentle unupbraiding manners, the affectionate looks with which she would hang enraptured over him, and listen to the tender oaths he had so basely violated, was in these thoughts; yet they every moment rushed unbidden on his brain.

As midnight's dark hour was proclaimed by the turret bell, Albert's limbs shook with fear. "I hear," said he, aloud, "the fatal summons that calls me hence. Guimilda, farewell forever! this is thy work."

Guimilda was going to make some reply, when a tremendous storm suddenly shook the battlements of the castle: the thunder's loud peals burst on the ancient walls, while the lightning's pointed glare flashed with appalling repetition through the painted casements. Dim burnt the numberless tapers, when Josephine's deathlike form glided from the portal, and, with solemn pace, proceeded along the hall to the spot where Lord Albert stood. Pale was her face, and her features seemed to retain the convulsive marks of the horrid death to which Guimilda had revengefully consigned her. Clad in the habiliments of the grave, her appearance was awe-inspiring. In a hollow, deep-toned voice, she addressed her perjured lover:

"Thou false one! Base assassin of her whom thou lured'st from the flowery paths of virtue; her whom thou had'st sworn to cherish and protect while life was left thee. Thou hast cut short the thread of my existence: but think not to escape the punishment due to thy crimes. 'Tis midnight's dark hour; the hour by thyself appointed: delay not, therefore, thy promised embrace."

With these words Josephine wound her arms around his trembling form. "I am come from the confines of the dead," said she, "to make thee fulfil thy parting promise." She dragged him by a force he could not resist to her breast: she pressed her clammy lips to his; and held him fast in her noisome icy embrace.

At length the horrific spectre released him from her grasp. He started back in breathless agony, and sank senseless on the floor. Thrice he raised his frenzied eye to gaze on his supernatural visitant; thrice he raised his hands, as if to implore the mercy of offended heaven; and then expired with a heavy groan.

Again loud thunder shook the castle to its very foundation. The affrighted guests rushed from the hall, rather choosing to brave the fury of the elements, than remain spectators of the horrid scene within its walls. Even the proud Guimilda fled with terror and dismay. She sought refuge in a convent that stood about a league's distance from the castle; here she remained till death put a period to her mental sufferings, which far exceeded her corporeal ones; though they were many, and severe; for she exhausted her frame by the variety and frequencies of the vigorous penance she imposed on herself, as a chastisement for her heinous, regretted crime.

As soon as Lord Albert's body was interred, the domestics hastily left the horrid castle. The edifice, being greatly damaged by the storm, soon fell to decay. Its dismantled ramparts were skirted with thorns; and the proud turrets of Werdendorff lay scattered on the plain.

Full oft, when the traveller wanders among the time-stricken ruins, a peasant will lead him to his cot, and relate the sad story of Albert and Josephine, and warn the stranger not to rove among the avenues of the castle, lest he should be assailed by the grim spectres, who always punish the temerity of those who intrude with unhallowed steps in the mansion where they keep their mysterious orgies. The hall of the castle still remains entire amid the Gothic ruins. On the anniversary of that fatal night when Josephine's spectre gave the midnight embrace to the false Albert, the same scene is again acted by supernatural beings. Guimilda, her husband, and his murdered love, traverse the haunted hall, which is then illumined with a more than mortal light: and the groans of the spectre lord can be heard afar, while he is clasped in the arms of Josephine's implacable ghost.

Oft will the village maidens, at the sober gloom of evening, review the isolated scene, and relate to those of their juvenile companions, yet unacquainted with the tragic tale, all the particulars of that wondrous legend; while they shuddering pass the mouldering tomb that covers the libertine's remains, to weep over the lowly violet-covered grave of the fair, but frail Josephine.

Can there be ghosts of things to come? Among fantasists, the following story by the author of "The Lady or the Tiger?" is nearly as popular as that remarkable puzzle tale. FRANK R. STOCKTON, born in 1834 in Philadelphia, worked on several magazines and newspapers and produced a large number of novels and short stories, many too sugary for today's taste. But often one finds gems in his collected works, and the story of the semibarbaric princess and her doomed lover who must open one of two doors is recognized as a classic of English letters. (Equally maddening is its less familiar sequel, "The Discourager of Hesitancy," which only compounds the riddle with a second insoluble anecdote.) Here is another fine Stockton tale.

The Philosophy of
Relative Existences
by Frank R. Stockton

In a certain summer, not long gone, my friend Bentley and I found ourselves in a little hamlet which overlooked a placid valley, through which a river gently moved, winding its way through green stretches until it turned the end of a line of low hills and was lost to view. Beyond this river, far away, but visible from the door of the cottage where we dwelt, there lay a city. Through the mists which floated over the valley we could see the outlines of steeples and tall roofs; and buildings of a character which indicated thrift and business stretched themselves down to the opposite edge of the river. The more distant parts of the city, evidently a small one, lost themselves in the hazy summer atmosphere.

Bentley was young, fair-haired, and a poet; I was a philosopher, or trying to be one. We were good friends, and had come down into this peaceful region to work together. Although we had fled from the bustle and distractions of the town, the appearance in this rural region of a city, which, so far as we could observe, exerted no influence on the quiet character of the valley in which it lay, aroused our interest. No craft plied up and down the river; there were no bridges from shore to shore; there were none of those scattered and half-squalid habitations which generally are found on the outskirts of a city; there came to us no distant sound of bells; and not the smallest wreath of smoke rose from any of the buildings.

In answer to our inquiries our landlord told us that the city over the river had been built by one man, who was a visionary, and who had a great deal more money than common sense. "It is not as big a town as you would think, sirs," he said, "because the general mistiness of things in this valley makes them look larger than they are. Those hills, for instance, when you get to them are not as high as they look to be from here. But the town is big enough, and a good deal too big; for it ruined its builder and owner, who when he came to die had not money enough left to put up a decent tombstone at the head of his grave. He had a queer idea that he would like to have his town all finished before anybody lived in it, and so he kept on working and spending money year after year and year after year until the city was done and he had not a cent left. During all the time that the place was building hundreds of people came to him to buy houses or to hire them, but he would not listen to anything of the kind. No one must live in his town until it was all done. Even his workmen were obliged to go away at night to lodge. It is a town, sirs, I am told, in which nobody has slept for even a night. There are streets there, and places of business, and churches, and public halls, and everything that a town full of inhabitants could need; but it is all empty and deserted, and has been so as far back as I can remember, and I came to this region when I was a little boy."

"And is there no one to guard the place?" we asked; "no one to protect it from wandering vagrants who might choose to take possession of the buildings?"

"There are not many vagrants in this part of the country," he said; "and if there were, they would not go over to that city. It is haunted."

"By what?" we asked.

"Well, sirs, I scarcely can tell you; queer beings that are not flesh and blood, and that is all I know about it. A good many people living hereabouts have visited that place once in their lives, but I know of no one who has gone there a second time."

"And travellers," I said; "are they not excited by curiosity to explore that strange uninhabited city?"

"Oh, yes," our host replied; "almost all visitors to the valley go over to that queer city—generally in small parties, for it is not a place in which one wishes to walk about alone. Sometimes they see things, and sometimes they don't. But I never knew any man or woman to show a fancy for living there, although it is a very good town."

This was said at suppertime, and, as it was the period of full moon, Bentley and I decided that we would visit the haunted city that evening. Our host endeavored to dissuade us, saying that no one ever went over there at night; but as we were not to be deterred, he told us where we would find his small boat tied to a stake on the river-bank. We soon crossed the river, and landed at a broad, but low, stone pier, at the land end of which a line of tall grasses waved in the gentle night wind as if they were sentinels warning us from entering the silent city. We pushed through these, and walked up a street fairly wide, and so well paved that we noticed none of the weeds and other growths which generally denote desertion or little use. By the bright light of the moon we could see that the architecture was simple, and of a character highly gratifying to the eye. All the buildings were of stone and of good size. We were greatly excited and interested, and proposed to continue our walks until the moon should set, and to return on the following morning—"to live here, perhaps," said Bentley. "What could be so romantic and yet so real? What could conduce better to the marriage of verse and philosophy?" But as he said this we saw around the corner of a cross-street some forms as of people hurrying away.

"The spectres," said my companion, laying his hand on my arm.

"Vagrants, more likely," I answered, "who have taken advantage of the superstition of the region to appropriate this comfort and beauty to themselves."

"If that be so," said Bentley, "we must have a care for our lives."

We proceeded cautiously, and soon saw other forms fleeing before us and disappearing, as we supposed, around corners and into houses. And now suddenly finding ourselves upon the edge of a wide, open public square, we saw in the dim light—for a tall steeple obscured the moon—the forms of vehicles, horses, and men moving here and there. But before, in our astonishment, we could say a word one to the other, the moon moved past the steeple, and in its bright light we could see none of the signs of life and traffic which had just astonished us.

Timidly, with hearts beating fast, but with not one thought of turning back, nor any fear of vagrants,—for we were now sure that what we had seen was not flesh and blood, and therefore harmless,—we crossed the open space and entered a street down which the moon shone clearly. Here and there we saw dim figures, which quickly disappeared; but, approaching a low stone balcony in front of one of the houses, we were surprised to see, sitting thereon and leaning over a book which lay open upon the top of the carved parapet, the figure of a woman who did not appear to notice us.

"That is a real person," whispered Bentley, "and she does not see us."

"No," I replied; "it is like the others. Let us go near it."

We drew near to the balcony and stood before it. At this the figure raised its head and looked at us. It was beautiful, it was young; but its substance seemed to be of an ethereal quality which we had never seen or known of. With its full, soft eyes fixed upon us, it spoke:—

"Why are you here?" it asked. "I have said to myself that the next time I saw any of you I would ask you why you come to trouble us. Cannot you live content in your own realms and spheres, knowing, as you must know, how timid we are, and how you frighten us and make us unhappy? In all this city there is, I believe, not one of us except myself who does not flee and hide from you whenever you cruelly come here. Even I would do that, had not I declared to myself that I would see you and speak to you, and endeavor to prevail upon you to leave us in peace."

The clear, frank tones of the speaker gave me courage. "We are two men," I answered, "strangers in this region, and living for the time in the beautiful country on the other side of the river. Having heard of this quiet city, we have come to see it for ourselves. We had supposed it to be uninhabited, but now that we find that this is not the case, we would assure you from our hearts that we do not wish to disturb or annoy any one who lives here. We simply came as honest travellers to view the city."

The figure now seated herself again, and as her countenance was nearer to us, we could see that it was filled with pensive thought. For a moment she looked at us without speaking. "Men!" she said. "And so I have been right. For a long time I have believed that the beings who sometimes come here, filling us with dread and awe, are men."

"And you," I exclaimed—"who are you, and who are these forms that we have seen, these strange inhabitants of this city?"

She gently smiled as she answered: "We are the ghosts of the future. We are the people who are to live in this city generations hence. But all of us do not know that, principally because we do not think about it and study about it enough to know it. And it is generally believed that the men and women who sometimes come here are ghosts who haunt the place."

"And that is why you are terrified and flee from us?" I exclaimed. "You think we are ghosts from another world?"

"Yes," she replied; "that is what is thought, and what I used to think."

"And you," I asked, "are spirits of human beings yet to be?"

"Yes," she answered; "but not for a long time. Generations of men, I know not how many, must pass away before we are men and women." "Heavens!" exclaimed Bentley, clasping his hands and raising his eyes to the sky, "I shall be a spirit before you are a woman." "Perhaps," she said again, with a sweet smile upon her face, "you may live to be very, very old."

But Bentley shook his head. This did not console him. For some minutes I stood in contemplation, gazing upon the stone pavement beneath my feet. "And this," I ejaculated, "is a city inhabited by the ghosts of the future, who believe men and women to be phantoms and spectres?"

She bowed her head.

"But how is it," I asked, "that you discovered that you are spirits and we mortal men?"

"There are so few of us who think of such things," she answered, "so few who study, ponder, and reflect. I am fond of study, and I love philosophy; and from the reading of many books I have learned much. From the book which I have here I have learned most; and from its teachings I have gradually come to the belief, which you tell me is the true one, that we are spirits and you men."

"And what book is that?" I asked.

"It is *The Philosophy of Relative Existences,* by Rupert Vance."

"Ye gods!" I exclaimed, springing upon the balcony, "that is my book, and I am Rupert Vance." I stepped toward the volume to seize it, but she raised her hand.

"You cannot touch it," she said. "It is the ghost of a book. And did you write it?"

"Write it? No," I said; "I am writing it. It is not yet finished."

"But here it is," she said, turning over the last pages. "As a spirit book it is finished. It is very successful; it is held in high estimation by intelligent thinkers; it is a standard work."

I stood trembling with emotion. "High estimation!" I said. "A standard work!"

"Oh, yes," she replied with animation; "and it well deserves its great success, especially in its conclusion. I have read it twice."

"But let me see these concluding pages," I exclaimed. "Let me look upon what I am to write."

She smiled, and shook her head, and closed the book. "I would like to do that," she said, "but if you are really a man you must not know what you are going to do."

"Oh, tell me, tell me," cried Bentley from below, "do you know a

book called *Stellar Studies*, by Arthur Bentley? It is a book of poems."
The figure gazed at him. "No," it said presently; "I never heard of it."

I stood trembling. Had the youthful figure before me been flesh and blood, had the book been a real one, I would have torn it from her.

"O wise and lovely being!" I exclaimed, falling on my knees before her, "be also benign and generous. Let me but see the last page of my book. If I have been of benefit to your world; more than all, if I have been of benefit to you, let me see, I implore you—let me see how it is that I have done it."

She rose with the book in her hand. "You have only to wait until you have done it," she said, "and then you will know all that you could see here." I started to my feet, and stood alone upon the balcony.

"I am sorry," said Bentley, as we walked toward the pier where we had left our boat, "that we talked only to that ghost girl, and that the other spirits were all afraid of us. Persons whose souls are choked up with philosophy are not apt to care much for poetry; and even if my book is to be widely known, it is easy to see that she may not have heard of it."

I walked triumphant. The moon, almost touching the horizon, beamed like red gold. "My dear friend," said I, "I have always told you that you should put more philosophy into your poetry. That would make it live."

"And I have always told you," said he, "that you should not put so much poetry into your philosophy. It misleads people."

"It didn't mislead that ghost girl," said I.

"How do you know?" said Bentley. "Perhaps she is wrong, and the other inhabitants of the city are right, and we may be the ghosts after all. Such things, you know, are only relative. Anyway," he continued, after a little pause, "I wish I knew that those ghosts were now reading the poem which I am going to begin tomorrow."

This short ambiguity is intense and upsetting in its implications, and it is by a writer who claims to have seen the black-hooded figures mentioned herein. Z. Z. JEROMM is the pen name of an actor who claims considerable personal concourse with the world of the spectral.

21 Main Street No.
by Z. Z. Jeromm

It is my belief and the belief of my family as well as those who have lived here before me that there are sites—call them châteaus, call them estates, or apartments, or houses, or what you will—that are designated to be forever occupied by ghosts. I do not know why this should be so. I know only that it is. There are some who will dispute this—on both planes, I imagine. They are wrong. Let me cite the facts in my own case.

People have lived here, in this same general locale, maybe even in this very room, where I am now sitting alone at my desk in these dark and lonely hours that pass between dusk and daylight—my wife and children being long asleep in their beds—for some hundreds of years. The portraits that hang, dusty and neglected on the peeling walls in the west wing, are testimony enough to this, and I say dusty and neglected, for that wing is one we rarely visit; it holding such unhappy memories for us.

There is nothing—at least, nothing I know of—that should attract us to this place; rather the reverse, I should say. The weather is rarely pleasant—unenthusiastic rain by day and truculent fog by night; the contour of the land hereabouts is flat and uninteresting; the vegetation on it, boringly ordinary, and of culture—well, the less said, the better. There are no opera houses, no symphony halls, no theatres, no dance companies that visit. There is one tiny museum filled with the most trivial of artifacts and hung with paintings that have been daubed by brushes dipped in the most awful of garish tints and held by hands boasting of the least of small talents. Oh yes, there is one very old movie house with its original seats still intact and which still proudly shows films on its original screen. I have heard—for I have never graced it with my presence—that they distribute to their coarse audiences printed sheets containing the dialogue to these films rather than use and perhaps wear out their sound equipment, but this may be an exaggeration.

I mention all the above merely to illustrate the singular lack of clear motive in most people in even those choices which affect them deeply. What has attracted my ancestors to this place I don't know; any more than I know why I, myself, am here.

It is not a happy place; this house we live in, not a happy home. It has seen more than its share of tears and madness; of murders and suicides; of hauntings and exorcisms; this last a rather futile gesture designed, I should imagine, to satisfy church personnel who must keep up their pride, real estate agents who must keep up the values of those properties they handle, and all those misguided do-gooders who earn their livings toiling in the wastelands of the mass media and who must, needless to say, keep up their circulation.

Certainly, those much publicized exorcisms didn't help us.

Nor any of the others.

For the creatures are here still, now as then; coming and going day and night as they please, in their black hooded capes that fall in heavy folds to the floor, shrouding their evil in shadow; huddling in their damnable semicircles; cackling in high-pitched voices; using for their own ends the energies from the bodies of those poor, still-alive—God help them—souls. There is no defense against them; nothing to stop them in their hysterical glee from reaching into the minds of the inhabitants of this house, twisting and turning them till those minds fill with paranoid fears and suspicions and they turn on each other. I, like you, was taught that good triumphs over evil, that love is stronger than hate. Why then is it that in this house brother has killed brother, that no animal or bird or even rodent is safe, that parents destroy their own issue and each other rather than allow the sickness they feel in their breasts to burst beyond these bounds into outrageous acts against the innocent?

But in here, too, we are—were—innocent.

It was not—is not—our fault that these creatures exist. Where do they come from? I do not know. Where do they hide during those times we do not see them? Again, I do not know.

I know only that I am lonely. I should like to be either alive or dead; not a shadow in this gray world; living in this house of fear with a wife I can no longer touch, and with children whose laughter no longer rings out and who walk sadly through these rooms like the ghosts they are; like the ghosts we are.

All of us; my ancestors and possibly yours; crowding each other, jostling monstrous memories that permit no rest.

And we cannot leave.

Who are they, these creatures that hold us? Bind us to this place? Or, are they themselves bound? Held fast in the grip of an evil even beyond theirs?

Are they controlled by others?

By you, perhaps?

Yes, you, sitting solid and self-satisfied in your armchair reading these lines. Is it your love for us—or that emotion you glorify with the name—so earth-bound, so possessive, so selfish that we must forever stay to satisfy your puny longings?

Think hard.

But for your soul's sake as for ours—be honest, be merciful.

There is a new family moving in here tomorrow.

I am afraid for them.

Shakespearean actors, like most theatre people, are superstitious; a whole subclassification of taboo might be written about the production of plays by The Bard. Much of this lore is wonderfully evoked in the following eerie, amusing and ultimately glorious novella by FRITZ LEIBER, *son of a once-renowned actor of the same name. One of America's finest fantasists, Leiber here portrays the world of the touring "rep" company with rich atmosphere, and it is no surprise, since he spent two seasons himself as a Shakespearean actor in his father's company; his stage name was Francis Lathrop.*

Four Ghosts in Hamlet
by Fritz Leiber

Actors are a superstitious lot, probably because chance plays a big part in the success of a production of a company or merely an actor—and because we're still a little closer than other people to the gypsies in the way we live and think. For instance, it's bad luck to have peacock feathers on stage or say the last line of a play at rehearsals or whistle in the dressing room (the one nearest the door gets fired) or sing "God Save the Sovereign" on a railway train. (A Canadian company got wrecked that way.)

Shakespearean actors are no exceptions. They simply travel a few extra superstitions, such as the one which forbids reciting the lines of the Three Witches, or anything from *Macbeth,* for that matter, except at performances, rehearsals, and on other legitimate occasions. This might be a good rule for outsiders too—then there wouldn't be the endless flood of books with titles taken from the text of *Macbeth*—you know, *Brief Candles, Tomorrow and Tomorrow, The Sound and the Fury, A Poor Player, All Our Yesterdays,* and those are all just from one brief soliloquy.

And our company, the Governor's company, has a rule against the Ghost in *Hamlet* dropping his greenish cheesecloth veil over his helmet-framed face until the very moment he makes each of his entrances. Hamlet's dead father mustn't stand veiled in the darkness of the wings.

This last superstition commemorates something which happened not too long ago, an actual ghost story. Sometimes I think it's the greatest ghost story in the world—though certainly not from my way of telling it, which is gossipy and poor, but from the wonder blazing at its core.

It's not only a true tale of the supernatural, but also very much a story about people, for after all—and before everything else—ghosts are people.

The ghostly part of the story first showed itself in the tritest way imaginable: three of our actresses (meaning practially all the ladies in a Shakespearean company) took to having sessions with a Ouija board in the hour before curtain time and sometimes even during a performance when they had long offstage waits, and they became so wrapped up in it and conceited about it and they squeaked so excitedly at the revelations which the planchette spelled out—and three or four times almost missed entrances because of it—that if the Governor weren't such a tolerant commander-in-chief, he would have forbidden them to bring the board to the theater. I'm sure he was tempted to and might have, except that Props pointed out to him that our three ladies probably wouldn't enjoy Ouija sessions one bit in the privacy of a hotel room, that much of the fun in operating a Ouija board is in having a half-exasperated, half-intrigued floating audience, and that when all's done the basic business of all ladies is glamour, whether of personal charm or of actual witchcraft, since the word means both.

Props—that is, our property man, Billy Simpson—was fascinated by their obsession, as he is by any new thing that comes along, and might very well have broken our Shakespearean taboo by quoting the Three Witches about them, except that Props has no flair for Shakespearean speech at all, no dramatic ability whatsoever, in fact he's the one person in our company who never acts even a bit part or carries a mute spear on stage, though he has other talents which make up for this deficiency —he can throw together a papier-mache bust of Pompey in two hours, or turn out a wooden prop dagger all silvery bladed and hilt-gilded, or fix a zipper, and that's not all.

As for myself, I was very irked at the ridiculous alphabet board, since it seemed to occupy most of Monica Singleton's spare time and satisfy all her hunger for thrills. I'd been trying to promote a romance with her—a long touring season becomes deadly and cold without some sort of heart-tickle—and for a while I'd made progress. But after Ouija came along, I became a ridiculous Guildenstern mooning after an unattainable unseeing Ophelia—which were the parts I and she actually played in *Hamlet*.

I cursed the idiot board with its childish corner-pictures of grinning suns and smirking moons and windblown spirits, and I further alienated Monica by asking her why wasn't it called a Nenein or No-No board (Ninny board!) instead of a Yes-Yes board? Was that, I inquired, because all spiritualists are forever accentuating the positive and behaving like a pack of fawning yes-men?—yes, we're here; yes, we're your uncle Harry; yes, we're happy on this plane; yes, we have a doctor among us who'll diagnose that pain in your chest; and so on.

Monica wouldn't speak to me for a week after that.

I would have been even more depressed except that Props pointed out to me that no flesh-and-blood man can compete with ghosts in a girl's affections, since ghosts being imaginary have all the charms and perfections a girl can dream of, but that all girls eventually tire of ghosts, or if their minds don't, their bodies do. This eventually did happen, thank goodness, in the case of myself and Monica, though not until we'd had a grisly, mind-wrenching experience—a night of terrors before the nights of love.

So Ouija flourished and the Governor and the rest of us put up with it one way or another, until there came that three-night stand in Wolverton, when its dismal uncanny old theater tempted our three Ouija-women to ask the board who was the ghost haunting the spooky place and the swooping planchette spelled out the name S-H-A-K-E-S-P-E-A-R-E. . . .

But I am getting ahead of my story. I haven't introduced our company except for Monica, Props, and the Governor—and I haven't identified the last of those three.

We call Gilbert Usher the Governor out of sheer respect and affection. He's about the last of the old actor-managers. He hasn't the name of Gielgud or Olivier or Evans or Richardson, but he's spent most of a lifetime keeping Shakespeare alive, spreading that magical a-religious gospel in the more remote counties and the Dominions and the United States, like Benson once did. Our other actors aren't names at all—I refuse to tell you mine!—but with the exception of myself they're good troupers, or if they don't become that the first season, they drop out. Gruelingly long seasons, much uncomfortable traveling, and small profits are our destiny.

This particular season had got to that familiar point where the plays are playing smoothly and everyone's a bit tireder than he realizes and the restlessness sets in. Robert Dennis, our juvenile, was writing a novel of theatrical life (he said) mornings at the hotel—up at seven to slave at it, our Robert claimed. Poor old Guthrie Boyd had started to drink again, and drink quite too much, after an abstemious two months which had astonished everyone.

Francis Farley Scott, our leading man, had started to drop hints that he was going to organize a Shakespearean repertory company of his own next year and he began to have conspiratorial conversations with Gertrude Grainger, our leading lady, and to draw us furtively aside one by one to make us hypothetical offers, no exact salary named. F.F. is as old as the Governor—who is our star, of course—and he has no talents at all except for self-infatuation and a somewhat grandiose yet impressive fashion of acting. He's portly like an opera tenor and quite bald and he travels an assortment of thirty toupees, ranging from red to black shot with silver, which he alternates with shameless abandon—they're for wear offstage, not on. It doesn't matter to him that the company knows all about his multicolored artificial toppings, for we're part of his world of illusion, and he's firmly convinced that the stage-struck local ladies he squires about never notice, or at any rate mind the deception. He once gave me a lecture on the subtleties of suiting the color of your hair to the lady you're trying to fascinate—her own age, hair color, and so on.

Every year F.F. plots to start a company of his own—it's a regular midseason routine with him—and every year it comes to nothing, for he's as lazy and impractical as he is vain. Yet F.F. believes he could play any part in Shakespeare or all of them at once in a pinch; perhaps the only F. F. Scott Company which would really satisfy him would be one in which he would be the only actor—a Shakespearean monologue; in fact, the one respect in which F.F. is not lazy is in his eagerness to double as many parts as possible in any single play.

F.F.'s yearly plots never bother the Governor a bit—he keeps waiting wistfully for F.F. to fix him with an hypnotic eye and in a hoarse whisper ask *him* to join the Scott company.

And I of course was hoping that now at last Monica Singleton would stop trying to be the most exquisite ingenue that ever came tripping Shakespeare's way (rehearsing her parts even in her sleep, I guessed, though I was miles from being in a position to know that for certain) and begin to take note and not just advantage of my devoted attentions.

But then old Sybil Jameson bought the Ouija board and Gertrude Grainger dragooned an unwilling Monica into placing her fingertips on the planchette along with theirs "just for a lark." Next day Gertrude announced to several of us in a hushed voice that Monica had the most amazing undeveloped mediumistic talent she'd ever encountered, and from then on the girl was a Ouija-addict. Poor tight-drawn Monica, I suppose she had to explode out of her self-imposed Shakespearean discipline somehow, and it was just too bad it had to be the board instead of me. Though come to think of it, I shouldn't have felt quite so resent-ful of the board, for she might have exploded with Robert Dennis, which would have been infinitely worse, though we were never quite sure of Robert's sex. For that matter I wasn't sure of Gertrude's and suffered agonies of uncertain jealousy when she captured my beloved. I was obsessed with the vision of Gertrude's bold knees pressing Mon-ica's under the Ouija board, though with Sybil's bony ones for chap-erones, fortunately.

Francis Farley Scott, who was jealous too because this new toy had taken Gertrude's mind off their annual plottings, said rather spitefully that Monica must be one of those grabby girls who have to take com-mand of whatever they get their fingers on, whether it's a man or a planchette, but Props told me he'd bet anything that Gertrude and Sybil had "followed" Monica's first random finger movements like the skill-fulest dancers guiding a partner while seeming to yield, in order to coax her into the business and make sure of their third.

Sometimes I thought that F.F. was right and sometimes Props and sometimes I thought that Monica had a genuine supernatural talent, though I don't ordinarily believe in such things, and that last really frightened me, for such a person might give up live men for ghosts for-ever. She was such a sensitive, subtle, wraith-cheeked girl and she could get so keyed up and when she touched the planchette her eyes got such an empty look, as if her mind had traveled down into her fingertips or out to the ends of time and space. And once the three of them gave me a character reading from the board which embarrassed me with its accu-racy. The same thing happened to several other people in the company. Of course, as Props pointed out, actors can be pretty good character an-alysts whenever they stop being egomaniacs.

After reading characters and foretelling the future for several weeks, our Three Weird Sisters got interested in reincarnation and began ask-ing the board and then telling us what famous or infamous people we'd been in past lives. Gertrude Grainger had been Queen Boadicea, I wasn't surprised to hear. Sybil Jameson had been Cassandra. While Monica was once mad Queen Joanna of Castile and more recently a prize hysterical patient of Janet at the Salpetriere—touches which irri-tated and frightened me more than they should have. Billy Simpson—Props—had been an Egyptian silversmith under Queen Hatshepsut and later a servant of Samuel Pepys; he heard this with a delighted chuckle. Guthrie Boyd had been the Emperor Claudius and Robert Dennis had been Caligula. For some reason I had been both John Wilkes Booth and Lambert Simnel, which irritated me considerably, for I saw no romance but only neurosis in assassinating an American president and dying in a burning barn, or impersonating the Earl of Warwick, pretending unsuccessfully to the British throne, being pardoned for it—of all things!—and spending the rest of my life as a scullion in the kitchen of Henry VII and his son. The fact that both Booth and Simnel had been actors of a sort—a poor sort—naturally irritated me the more. Only much later did Monica confess to me that the board had probably made those decisions because I had had such a "tragic, dangerous, defeated look"—a revelation which surprised and flattered me.

Francis Farley Scott was flattered too, to hear he'd once been Henry VIII—he fancied all those wives and he wore his golden-blond toupee after the show that night—until Gertrude and Sybil and Monica announced that the Governor was a reincarnation of no less than William Shakespeare himself. That made F.F. so jealous that he instantly sat down at the prop table, grabbed up a quill pen, and did an impromptu rendering of Shakespeare composing Hamlet's "To be or not to be" soliloquy. It was an effective performance, though with considerably more frowning and eye-rolling and trying of lines for sound than I imagine Willy S. himself used originally, and when F.F. finished, even the Governor, who'd been standing unobserved in the shadows beside Props, applauded with the latter.

Governor kidded the pants off the idea of himself as Shakespeare. He said that if Willy S. were ever reincarnated it ought to be as a world-famous dramatist who was secretly in his spare time the world's greatest scientist and philosopher and left clues to his identity in his mathematical equations—that way he'd get his own back at Bacon, or rather the Baconians.

Yet I suppose if you had to pick someone for a reincarnation of Shakespeare, Gilbert Usher wouldn't be a bad choice. Insofar as a star and director ever can be, the Governor is gentle and self-effacing—as Shakespeare himself must have been, or else there would never have arisen that ridiculous Bacon-Oxford-Marlowe-Elizabeth-take-your-pick-who-wrote-Shakespeare controversy. And the Governor has a sweet melancholy about him, though he's handsomer and, despite his years, more athletic than one imagines Shakespeare being. And he's generous to a fault, especially where old actors who've done brave fine things in the past are concerned.

This season his mistake in that last direction had been in hiring Guthrie Boyd to play some of the more difficult older leading roles, including a couple F.F. usually handles: Brutus, Othello, and, besides those, Duncan in *Macbeth*, Kent in *King Lear*, and the Ghost in *Hamlet*.

Guthrie was a bellowing hard-drinking bear of an actor, who'd been a Shakespearean star in Australia and successfully smuggled some of his reputation west—he learned to moderate his bellowing, while his emotions were always simple and sincere, though explosive—and finally even spent some years in Hollywood. But there his drinking caught up with him, probably because of the stupid film parts he got, and he failed six times over. His wife divorced him. His children cut themselves off. He married a starlet and she divorced him. He dropped out of sight.

Then after several years the Governor ran into him. He'd been rusticating in Canada with a stubborn teetotal admirer. He was only a shadow of his former self, but there was some substance to the shadow —and he wasn't drinking. The Governor decided to take a chance on him—although the company manager Harry Grossman was dead set against it—and during rehearsals and the first month or so of performances it was wonderful to see how old Guthrie Boyd came back, exactly as if Shakespeare were a restorative medicine.

It may be stuffy or sentimental of me to say so, but you know, I think Shakespeare's good for people. I don't know of an actor, except myself, whose character hasn't been strengthened and his vision widened and charity quickened by working in the plays. I've heard that before Gilbert Usher became a Shakespearean, he was a more ruthlessly ambitious and critical man, not without malice, but the plays mellowed him, as they've mellowed Props's philosophy and given him a zest for life.

Because of his contact with Shakespeare, Robert Dennis is a less strident and pettish swish (if he is one), Gertrude Grainger's outbursts of cold rage have an undercurrent of queenly make-believe, and even Francis Farley Scott's grubby little seductions are probably kinder and less insultingly illusionary.

In fact I sometimes think that what civilized serenity the British people possess, and small but real ability to smile at themselves, is chiefly due to their good luck in having had William Shakespeare born one of their company.

But I was telling how Guthrie Boyd performed very capably those first weeks, against the expectations of most of us, so that we almost quit holding our breaths—or sniffing at his. His Brutus was workmanlike, his Kent quite fine—that bluff, rough, honest part suited him well—and he regularly got admiring notices for his Ghost in *Hamlet*. I think his years of living death as a drinking alcoholic had given him an understanding of loneliness and frozen abilities and despair that he put to good use—probably unconsciously—in interpreting that small role.

He was really a most impressive figure in the part, even just visually. The Ghost's basic costume is simple enough—a big all-enveloping cloak that brushes the ground-cloth, a big dull helmet with the tiniest battery light inside its peak to throw a faint green glow on the Ghost's features, and over the helmet a veil of greenish cheesecloth that registers as mist to the audience. He wears a suit of stage armor under the cloak, but that's not important and at a pinch he can do without it, for his cloak can cover his entire body.

The Ghost doesn't switch on his helmet-light until he makes his entrance, for fear of it being glimpsed by an edge of the audience, and nowadays because of that superstition or rule I told you about, he doesn't drop the cheesecloth veil until the last second either, but when Guthrie Boyd was playing the part that rule didn't exist and I have a vivid recollection of him standing in the wings, waiting to go on, a big bearish inscrutable figure about as solid and unsupernatural as a bushy seven-foot evergreen covered by a gray tarpaulin. But then when Guthrie would switch on the tiny light and stride smoothly and silently on stage and his hollow distant tormented voice boomed out, there'd be a terrific shivery thrill, even for us backstage, as if we were listening to words that really had traveled across black windy infinite gulfs from the Afterworld or the Other Side.

At any rate Guthrie was a great Ghost, and adequate or a bit better than that in most of his other parts—for those first nondrinking weeks. He seemed very cheerful on the whole, modestly buoyed up by his comeback, though sometimes something empty and dead would stare for a moment out of his eyes—the old drinking alcoholic wondering what all this fatiguing sober nonsense was about. He was especially looking forward to our three-night stand at Wolverton, although that was still two months in the future then. The reason was that both his children—married and with families now, of course—lived and worked at Wolverton and I'm sure he set great store on proving to them in person his rehabilitation, figuring it would lead to a reconciliation and so on.

But then came his first performance as Othello. (The Governor, although the star, always played Iago—an equal role, though not the title one.) Guthrie was almost too old for Othello, of course, and besides that, his health wasn't good—the drinking years had taken their toll of his stamina and the work of rehearsals and of first nights in eight different plays after years away from the theater had exhausted him. But somehow the old volcano inside him got seething again and he gave a magnificent performance. Next morning the papers raved about him and one review rated him even better than the Governor.

That did it, unfortunately. The glory of his triumph was too much for him. The next night—*Othello* again—he was drunk as a skunk. He remembered most of his lines—though the Governor had to throw him about every sixth one out of the side of his mouth—but he weaved and wobbled, he planked a big hand on the shoulder of every other character he addressed to keep from falling over, and he even forgot to put in his false teeth the first two acts, so that his voice was mushy. To cap that, he started really to strangle Gertrude Grainger in the last scene, until that rather brawny Desdemona, unseen by the audience, gave him a knee in the gut; then, after stabbing himself, he flung the prop dagger high in the flies so that it came down with two lazy twists and piercing the ground-cloth buried its blunt point deep in the soft wood of the stage floor not three feet from Monica, who plays Iago's wife, Emilia, and so was lying dead on the stage at that point in the drama, murdered by her villainous husband—and might have been dead for real if the dagger had followed a slightly different trajectory.

Since a third performance of *Othello* was billed for the following night, the Governor had no choice but to replace Guthrie with Francis Farley Scott, who did a good job (for him) of covering up his satisfaction at getting his old role back. F.F., always a plushy and lascivious-eyed Moor, also did a good job with the part, coming in that way without even a brush-up rehearsal, so that one critic, catching the first and third shows, marveled how we could change big roles at will, thinking we'd done it solely to demonstrate our virtuosity.

Of course the Governor read the riot act to Guthrie and carried him off to a doctor, who without being prompted threw a big scare into him about his drinking and his heart, so that he just might have recovered from his lapse, except that two nights later we did *Julius Caesar* and Guthrie, instead of being satisfied with being workmanlike, decided to recoup himself with a really rousing performance. So he bellowed and groaned and bugged his eyes as I suppose he had done in his palmiest Australian days. His optimistic self-satisfaction between scenes was frightening to behold. Not too terrible a performance, truly, but the critics all panned him and one of them said, "Guthrie Boyd played Brutus —a bunch of vocal cords wrapped up in a toga."

That tied up the package and knotted it tight. Thereafter Guthrie was medium pie-eyed from morning to night—and often more than medium. The Governor had to yank him out of Brutus too (F.F. again replacing), but being the Governor he didn't sack him. He put him into a couple of bit parts—Montano and the Soothsayer—in *Othello* and *Caesar* and let him keep on at the others, and he gave me and Joe Rubens and sometimes Props the job of keeping an eye on the poor old sot and making sure he got to the theater by the half hour and if possible not too plastered. Often he played the Ghost or the Doge of Venice in his street clothes under cloak or scarlet robe, but he played them. And many were the nights Joe and I made the rounds of half the local bars before we corraled him. The Governor sometimes refers to Joe Rubens and me in mild derision as "the American element" in his company, but just the same he depends on us quite a bit; and I certainly don't mind being one of his trouble-shooters—it's a joy to serve him.

All this may seem to contradict my statement about our getting to the point, about this time, where the plays were playing smoothly and the monotony setting in. But it doesn't really. There's always something going wrong in a theatrical company—anything else would be abnormal; just as the Samoans say no party is a success until somebody's dropped a plate or spilled a drink or tickled the wrong woman.

Besides, once Guthrie had got Othello and Brutus off his neck, he didn't do too badly. The little parts and even Kent he could play passably whether drunk or sober. King Duncan, for instance, and the Doge in *The Merchant* are easy to play drunk because the actor always has a couple of attendants to either side of him, who can guide his steps if he weaves and even hold him up if necessary—which can turn out to be an effective dramatic touch, registering as the infirmity of extreme age.

And somehow Guthrie continued to give that same masterful performance as the Ghost and get occasional notices for it. In fact Sybil Jameson insisted he was a shade better in the Ghost now that he was invariably drunk; which could have been true. And he still talked about the three-night stand coming up in Wolverton, though now as often with gloomy apprehension as with proud fatherly anticipation.

Well, the three-night stand eventually came. We arrived at Wolverton on a nonplaying evening. To the surprise of most of us, but especially Guthrie, his son and daughter were there at the station to welcome him with their respective spouses and all their kids and numerous in-laws and a great gaggle of friends. Their cries of greeting when they spotted him were almost an organized cheer and I looked around for a brass band to strike up.

I found out later that Sybil Jameson, who knew them, had been sending them all his favorable notices, so that they were eager as weasels to be reconciled with him and show him off as blatantly as possible.

When he saw his children's and grandchildren's faces and realized the cries were for him, old Guthrie got red in the face and beamed like the sun, and they closed in around him and carried him off in triumph for an evening of celebrations.

Next day I heard from Sybil, whom they'd carried off with him, that everything had gone beautifully. He'd drunk like a fish, but kept marvellous control, so that no one but she noticed, and the warmth of the reconciliation of Guthrie to everyone, complete strangers included, had been wonderful to behold. Guthrie's son-in-law, a pugnacious chap, had got angry when he'd heard Guthrie wasn't to play Brutus the third night, and he declared that Gilbert Usher must be jealous of his magnificent father-in-law. Everything was forgiven twenty times over. They'd even tried to put old Sybil to bed with Guthrie, figuring romantically, as people will about actors, that she must be his mistress. All this was very fine, and of course wonderful for Guthrie, and for Sybil too in a fashion, yet I suppose the unconstrained night-long bash, after two months of uninterrupted semicontrolled drunkenness, was just about the worst thing anybody could have done to the old boy's sodden body and laboring heart.

Meanwhile on that first evening I accompanied Joe Rubens and Props to the theater we were playing at Wolverton to make sure the scenery got stacked right and the costume trunks were all safely arrived and stowed. Joe is our stage manager besides doing rough or Hebraic parts like Caliban and Tubal—he was a professional boxer in his youth and got his nose smashed crooked. Once I started to take boxing lessons from him, figuring an actor should know everything, but during the third lesson I walked into a gentle right cross and, although it didn't exactly stun me, there were bells ringing faintly in my head for six hours afterwards and I lived in a world of faery and that was the end of my fistic career. Joe is actually a most versatile actor—for instance, he understudies the Governor in Macbeth, Lear, Iago, and of course Shylock —though his brutal moon-face is against him, especially when his makeup doesn't include a beard. But he dotes on being genial and in the States he often gets a job by day playing Santa Claus in big department stores during the month before Christmas.

The Monarch was a cavernous old place, very grimy backstage, but with a great warren of dirty little dressing rooms and even a property room shaped like an L stage left. Its empty shelves were thick with dust.

There hadn't been a show in the Monarch for over a year, I saw from the yellowing sheets thumbtacked to the callboard as I tore them off and replaced them with a simple black-crayoned HAMLET: TO-NIGHT AT 8:30.

Then I noticed, by the cold inadequate working lights, a couple of tiny dark shapes dropping down from the flies and gliding around in wide swift circles—out into the house too, since the curtain was up. Bats, I realized with a little start—the Monarch was really halfway through the lich gate. The bats would fit very nicely with *Macbeth,* I told myself, but not so well with *The Merchant of Venice,* while with Hamlet they should neither help nor hinder, provided they didn't descend in nightfighter squadrons; it would be nice if they stuck to the Ghost scenes.

I'm sure the Governor had decided we'd open at Wolverton with *Hamlet* so that Guthrie would have the best chance of being a hit in his children's home city.

Billy Simpson, shoving his properties table into place just in front of the dismal L of the prop room, observed cheerfully, "It's a proper haunted house. The girls'll find some rare ghosts here, I'll wager, if they work their board."

Which turned out to be far truer than he realized at the time—I think.

"Bruce!" Joe Rubens called to me. "We better buy a couple of rat traps and set them out. There's something scuttling back of the drops."

But when I entered the Monarch next night, well before the hour, by the creaky thick metal stage door, the place had been swept and tidied a bit. With the ground-cloth down and the *Hamlet* set up, it didn't look too terrible, even though the curtain was still unlowered, dimly showing the house and its curves of empty seats and the two faint green exit lights with no one but myself to look at them.

There was a little pool of light around the callboard stage right, and another glow the other side of the stage beyond the wings, and lines of light showing around the edges of the door of the second dressing room, next to the star's.

I started across the dark stage, sliding my shoes softly so as not to trip over a cable or stage-screw and brace, and right away I got the magic electric feeling I often do in an empty theater the night of a show. Only this time there was something additional, something that started a shiver crawling down my neck. It wasn't, I think, the thought of the bats which might now be swooping around me unseen, skirling their inaudibly shrill trumpet calls, or even of the rats which *might* be watching sequin-eyed from behind trunks and flats, although not an hour ago Joe had told me that the traps he'd actually procured and set last night had been empty today.

No, it was more as if all of Shakespeare's characters were invisibly there around me—all the infinite possibilities of the theater. I imagined Rosalind and Falstaff and Prospero standing arm-in-arm watching me with different smiles. And Caliban grinning down from where he silently swung in the flies. And side by side, but unsmiling and not arm-in-arm: Macbeth and Iago and Dick the Three Eyes—Richard III. And all the rest of Shakespeare's myriad-minded good-evil crew.

I passed through the wings opposite and there in the second pool of light Billy Simpson sat behind his table with the properties for *Hamlet* set out on it: the skulls, the foils, the lantern, the purses, the parchmenty letters, Ophelia's flowers, and all the rest. It was odd Props having everything ready quite so early and a bit odd too that he should be alone, for Props has the un-actorish habit of making friends with all sorts of locals, such as policemen and porters and flower women and newsboys and shopkeepers and tramps who claim they're indigent actors, and even inviting them backstage with him—a fracture of rules which the Governor allows since Props is such a sensible chap. He has a great liking for people, especially low people, Props has, and for all the humble details of life. He'd make a good writer, I'd think, except for his utter lack of dramatic flair and story-skill—a sort of prosiness that goes with his profession.

And now he was sitting at his table, his stooped shoulders almost inside the doorless entry to the empty-shelfed prop room—no point in using it for a three-night stand—and he was gazing at me quizzically. He has a big forehead—the light was on that—and a tapering chin—that was in shadow—and rather large eyes, which were betwixt the light and the dark. Sitting there like that, he seemed to me for a moment (mostly because of the outspread props, I guess) like the midnight Master of the Show in *The Rubaiyat* round whom all the rest of us move like shadow shapes.

Usually he has a quick greeting for anyone, but tonight he was silent, and that added to the illusion.

"Props," I said, "this theater's got a supernatural smell."

His expression didn't change at that, but he solemnly sniffed the air in several little whiffles adding up to one big inhalation, and as he did so he threw his head back, bringing his weakish chin into the light and shattering the illusion.

"Dust," he said after a moment. "Dust and old plush and scenery water-paint and sweat and drains and gelatin and greasepaint and powder and a breath of whisky. But the supernatural . . . no, I can't smell that. Unless . . ." And he sniffed again, but shook his head.

I chuckled at his materialism—although that touch about whisky did seem fanciful, since I hadn't been drinking and Props never does and Guthrie Boyd was nowhere in evidence. Props has a mind like a notebook for sensory details—and for the minutiae of human habits too. It was Props, for instance, who told me about the actual notebook in which John McCarthy (who would be playing Fortinbras and the Player King in a couple of hours) jots down the exact number of hours he sleeps each night and keeps totting them up, so he knows when he'll have to start sleeping extra hours to average the full nine he thinks he must get each night to keep from dying.

It was also Props who pointed out to me that F.F. is much more careless gumming his offstage toupees to his head than his theater wigs—a studied carelessness, like that in tying a bowtie, he assured me; it indicated, he said, a touch of contempt for the whole offstage world.

Props isn't *only* a detail-worm, but it's perhaps because he is one that he has sympathy for all human hopes and frailties, even the most trivial, like my selfish infatuation with Monica.

Now I said to him, "I didn't mean an actual smell, Billy. But back there just now I got the feeling anything might happen tonight."

He nodded slowly and solemnly. With anyone but Props I'd have wondered if he weren't a little drunk. Then he said, "You were on a stage. You know, the science fiction writers are missing a bet there. We've got time machines right now. Theaters. Theaters are time machines and spaceships too. They take people on trips through the future and the past and the elsewhere and the might-have-been—yes, and if it's done well enough, give them glimpses of Heaven and Hell."

I nodded back at him. Such grotesque fancies are the closest Props ever comes to escaping from prosiness.

I said, "Well, let's hope Guthrie gets aboard the spaceship before the curtain up-jets. Tonight we're depending on his children having the sense to deliver him here intact. Which from what Sybil says about them is not to be taken for granted."

Props stared at me owlishly and slowly shook his head. "Guthrie got here about ten minutes ago," he said, "and looking no drunker than usual."

"That's a relief," I told him, meaning it.

"The girls are having a Ouija session," he went on, as if he were determined to account for all of us from moment to moment. "They smelt the supernatural here, just as you did, and they're asking the board to name the culprit." Then he stooped so that he looked almost hunchbacked and he felt for something under the table.

I nodded. I'd guess the Ouija part from the lines of light showing around the door of Gertrude Grainger's dressing room.

Props straightened up and he had a pint bottle of whisky in his hand. I don't think a loaded revolver would have dumbfounded me as much. He unscrewed the top.

"There's the Governor coming in," he said tranquilly, hearing the stage door creak and evidently some footsteps my own ears missed. "That's seven of us in the theater before the hour."

He took a big slow swallow of whisky and recapped the bottle, as naturally as if it were a nightly action. I goggled at him without comment. What he was doing was simply unheard of—for Billy Simpson.

At that moment there was a sharp scream and a clatter of thin wood and something twangy and metallic falling and a scurry of footsteps. Our previous words must have cocked a trigger in me, for I was at Gertrude Grainger's dressing-room door as fast as I could sprint—no worry this time about tripping over cables or braces in the dark.

I yanked the door open and there by the bright light of the bulbs framing the mirror were Gertrude and Sybil sitting close together with the Ouija board face down on the floor in front of them along with a flimsy wire-backed chair, overturned. While pressing back into Gertrude's costumes hanging on the rack across the little room, almost as if she wanted to hide behind them liked bedclothes, was Monica pale and staring-eyed. She didn't seem to recognize me. The dark-green heavily brocaded costume Gertrude wears as the Queen in *Hamlet,* into which Monica was chiefly pressing herself, accentuated her pallor. All three of them were in their street clothes.

I went to Monica and put an arm around her and gripped her hand. It was cold as ice. She was standing rigidly.

While I was doing that, Gertrude stood up and explained in rather haughty tones what I told you earlier: about them asking the board who the ghost was haunting the Monarch tonight and the planchette spelling out S-H-A-K-E-S-P-E-A-R-E . . .

"I don't know why it startled you so, dear," she ended crossly, speaking to Monica. "It's very natural his spirit should attend performances of his plays."

I felt the slim body I clasped relax a little. That relieved me. I was selfishly pleased at having got an arm around it, even under such public and unamorous circumstances, while at the same time my silly mind was thinking that if Props had been lying to me about Guthrie Boyd having come in no more drunken than usual (this new Props who drank straight whisky in the theater could lie too, I supposed), why then we could certainly use William Shakespeare tonight, since the Ghost in *Hamlet* is the one part in all his plays Shakespeare himself is supposed to have acted on the stage.

"I don't know why myself now," Monica suddenly answered from beside me, shaking her head as if to clear it. She became aware of me at last, started to pull away, then let my arm stay around her.

The next voice that spoke was the Governor's. He was standing in the doorway, smiling faintly, with Props peering around his shoulder. Props would be as tall as the Governor if he ever straightened up, but his stoop takes almost a foot off his height.

The Governor said softly, a comic light in his eyes, "I think we should be content to bring Shakespeare's plays to life, without trying for their author. It's hard enough on the nerves just to *act* Shakespeare."

He stepped forward with one of his swift, naturally graceful movements and kneeling on one knee he picked up the fallen board and planchette. "At all events I'll take these in charge for tonight. Feeling better now, Miss Singleton?" he asked as he straightened and stepped back.

"Yes, quite all right," she answered flusteredly, disengaging my arm and pulling away from me rather too quickly.

He nodded. Gertrude Grainger was staring at him coldly, as if about to say something scathing, but she didn't. Sybil Jameson was looking at the floor. She seemed embarrassed, yet puzzled too.

I followed the Governor out of the dressing room and told him, in case Props hadn't, about Guthrie Boyd coming to the theater early. My momentary doubt of Props's honesty seemed plain silly to me now, although his taking that drink remained an astonishing riddle.

Props confirmed me about Guthrie coming in, though his manner was a touch abstracted.

The Governor nodded his thanks for the news, then twitched a nostril and frowned. I was sure he'd caught a whiff of alcohol and didn't know to which of us two to attribute it—or perhaps even to one of the ladies, or to an earlier passage of Guthrie this way.

He said to me, "Would you come into my dressing room for a bit, Bruce?"

I followed him, thinking he'd picked me for the drinker and wondering how to answer—best perhaps simply silently accept the fatherly lecture—but when he'd turned on the lights and I'd shut the door, his first question was, "You're attracted to Miss Singleton, aren't you, Bruce?"

When I nodded abruptly, swallowing my morsel of surprise, he went on softly but emphatically, "Then why don't you quit hovering and playing Galahad and really go after her? Ordinarily I must appear to frown on affairs in the company, but in this case it would be the best way I know of to break up those Ouija sessions, which are obviously harming the girl."

I managed to grin and tell him I'd be happy to obey his instructions—and do it entirely on my own initiative too.

He grinned back and started to toss the Ouija board on his couch, but instead put it and the planchette carefully down on the end of his long dressing table and put a second question to me.

"What do you think of some of this stuff they're getting over the board, Bruce?"

I said, "Well, that last one gave me a shiver, all right—I suppose because . . ." and I told him about sensing the presence of Shakespeare's characters in the dark. I finished, "But of course the whole idea is nonsense," and I grinned.

He didn't grin back.

I continued impulsively, "There was one idea they had a few weeks back that impressed me, though it didn't seem to impress you. I hope you won't think I'm trying to butter you up, Mr. Usher. I mean the idea of you being a reincarnation of William Shakespeare."

He laughed delightedly and said, "Clearly you don't yet know the difference between a player and a playwright, Bruce. Shakespeare striding about romantically with head thrown back?—and twirling a sword and shaping his body and voice to every feeling handed him? Oh no! I'll grant he might have played the Ghost—it's a part within the scope of an average writer's talents, requiring nothing more than that he stand still and sound off sepulchrally."

He paused and smiled and went on. "No, there's only one person in this company who might be Shakespeare come again, and that's Billy

Simpson. Yes, I mean Props. He's a great listener and he knows how to put himself in touch with everyone and then he's got that rat-trap mind for every hue and scent and sound of life, inside or out the mind. And he's very analytic. Oh, I know he's got no poetic talent, but surely Shakespeare wouldn't have that in *every* reincarnation. I'd think he'd need about a dozen lives in which to gather material for every one in which he gave it dramatic form. Don't you find something very poignant in the idea of a mute inglorious Shakespeare spending whole humble lifetimes collecting the necessary stuff for one great dramatic burst? Think about it some day."

I was doing that already and finding it a fascinating fantasy. It crystalized so perfectly the feeling I'd got seeing Billy Simpson behind his property table. And then Props did have a high-foreheaded poet-school-master's face like that given Shakespeare in the posthumous engravings and woodcuts and portraits. Why, even their initials were the same. It made me feel strange.

Then the Governor put his third question to me.

"He's drinking tonight, isn't he? I mean Props, not Guthrie."

I didn't say anything, but my face must have answered for me—at least to such a student of expressions as the Governor—for he smiled and said, "You needn't worry. I wouldn't be angry with him. In fact, the only other time I know of that Props drank spirits by himself in the theater, I had a great deal to thank him for." His lean face grew thoughtful. "It was long before your time, in fact it was the first season I took out a company of my own. I had barely enough money to pay the printer for the three-sheets and get the first-night curtain up. After that it was touch and go for months. Then in mid-season we had a run of bad luck—a two-night heavy fog in one city, an influenza scare in another, Harvey Wilkins' Shakespearean troupe two weeks ahead of us in a third. And when in the next town we played it turned out the advance sale was very light—because my name was unknown there and the theater an unpopular one—I realized I'd have to pay off the company while there was still money enough to get them home, if not the scenery.

"That night I caught Props swigging, but I hadn't the heart to chide him for it—in fact I don't think I'd have blamed anyone, except perhaps myself, for getting drunk that night. But then during the performance the actors and even the union stagehands we travel began coming to my dressing room by ones and twos and telling me they'd be happy to work without salary for another three weeks, if I thought that might give us a chance of recouping. Well, of course I grabbed at their offers and we got a spell of brisk pleasant weather and we hit a couple of places starved for Shakespeare, and things worked out, even to paying all the back salary owed before the season was ended.

"Later on I discovered it was Props who had put them all up to doing it."

Gilbert Usher looked up at me and one of his eyes was wet and his lips were working just a little. "I couldn't have done it myself," he said, "for I wasn't a popular man with my company that first season—I'd been riding everyone much too hard and with nasty sarcasms—and I hadn't yet learned how to ask anyone for help when I really needed it. But Billy Simpson did what I couldn't, though he had to nerve himself for it with spirits. He's quick enough with his tongue in ordinary circumstances, as you know, particularly when he's being the friendly listener, but apparently when something very special is required of him, he must drink himself to the proper pitch. I'm wondering . . ."

His voice trailed off and then he straightened up before his mirror and started to unknot his tie and he said to me briskly, "Better get dressed now, Bruce. And then look in on Guthrie, will you?"

My mind was churning some rather strange thoughts as I hurried up the iron stairs to the dressing room I shared with Robert Dennis. I got on my Guildenstern make-up and costume, finishing just as Robert arrived; as Laertes, Robert makes a late entrance and so needn't hurry to the theater on *Hamlet* nights. Also, although we don't make a point of it, he and I spend as little time together in the dressing room as we can.

Before going down I looked into Guthrie Boyd's. He wasn't there, but the lights were on and the essentials of the Ghost's costume weren't in sight—impossible to miss that big helmet!—so I assumed he'd gone down ahead of me.

It was almost the half hour. The house lights were on, the curtain down, more stage lights on too, and quite a few of us about. I noticed that Props was back in the chair behind his table and not looking particularly different from any other night—perhaps the drink had been a once-only aberration and not some symptom of a crisis in the company.

I didn't make a point of hunting for Guthrie. When he gets costumed early he generally stands back in a dark corner somewhere, wanting to be alone—perchance to sip, aye, there's the rub!—or visits with Sybil in her dressing room.

I spotted Monica sitting on a trunk by the switchboard, where backstage was brightest lit at the moment. She looked ethereal yet springlike in her blond Ophelia wig and first costume, a pale green one. Recalling my happy promise to the Governor, I bounced up beside her and asked her straight out about the Ouija business, pleased to have something to the point besides the plays to talk with her about—and really not worrying as much about her nerves as I suppose I should have.

She was in a very odd mood, both agitated and abstracted, her gaze going back and forth between distant and near and very distant. My questions didn't disturb her at all, in fact I got the feeling she welcomed them, yet she genuinely didn't seem able to tell me much about why she'd been so frightened at the last name the board had spelled. She told me that she actually did get into a sort of dream state when she worked the board and that she'd screamed before she'd quite comprehended what had shocked her so; then her mind had blacked out for a few seconds, she thought.

"One thing though, Bruce," she said. "I'm not going to work the board any more, at least when the three of us are alone like that."

"That sounds like a wise idea," I agreed, trying not to let the extreme heartiness of my agreement show through.

She stopped peering around as if for some figure to appear that wasn't in the play and didn't belong backstage, and she laid her hand on mine and said, "Thanks for coming so quickly when I went idiot and screamed."

I was about to improve this opportunity by telling her that the reason I'd come so quickly was that she was so much in my mind, but just then Joe Rubens came hurrying up with the Governor behind him in his Hamlet black to tell me that neither Guthrie Boyd nor his Ghost costume was to be found anywhere in the theater.

What's more, Joe had got the phone numbers of Guthrie's son and daughter from Sybil and rung them up. The one phone hadn't answered, while on the other a female voice—presumably a maid's—had informed him that everyone had gone to see Guthrie Boyd in *Hamlet.*

Joe was already wearing his cumbrous chain-mail armor for Marcellus—woven cord silvered—so I knew I was elected. I ran upstairs and in the space of time it took Robert Dennis to guess my mission and advise me to try the dingiest bars first and have a drink or two myself in them, I'd put on my hat, overcoat, and wristwatch and left him.

So garbed and as usual nervous about people looking at my ankles, I sallied forth to comb the nearby bars of Wolverton. I consoled myself with the thought that if I found Hamlet's father's ghost drinking his way through them, no one would ever spare a glance for my own costume.

Almost on the stroke of curtain I returned, no longer giving a damn what anyone thought about my ankles. I hadn't found Guthrie or spoken to a soul who'd seen a large male imbiber—most likely of Irish whisky—in great-cloak and antique armor, with perhaps some ghostly green light cascading down his face.

Beyond the curtain the overture was fading to its sinister close and the backstage lights were all down, but there was an angry hushed-voice dispute going on stage left, where the Ghost makes all his entrances and exits. Skipping across the dim stage in front of the blue-lit battlements of Elsinore—I still in my hat and overcoat—I found the Governor and Joe Rubens and with them John McCarthy all ready to go on as the Ghost in his Fortinbras armor with a dark cloak and some green gauze over it.

But alongside them was Francis Farley Scott in a very similar get-up —no armor, but a big enough cloak to hide his King costume and a rather more impressive helmet than John's.

They were all very dim in the midnight glow leaking back from the dimmed-down blue floods. The five of us were the only people I could see on this side of the stage.

F.F. was arguing vehemently that he must be allowed to double the Ghost with King Claudius because he knew the part better than John and because—this was the important thing—he could imitate Guthrie's voice perfectly enough to deceive his children and perhaps save their illusions about him. Sybil had looked through the curtain hole and seen them and all of their yesterday crowd, with new recruits besides, occupying all of the second, third, and fourth rows center, chattering with excitement and beaming with anticipation. Harry Grossman had confirmed this from the front of the house.

I could tell that the Governor was vastly irked at F.F. and at the same time touched by the last part of his argument. It was exactly the sort of sentimental heroic rationalization with which F.F. cloaked his insatiable yearnings for personal glory. Very likely he believed it himself.

John McCarthy was simply ready to do what the Governor asked him. He's an actor untroubled by inward urgencies—except things like keeping a record of the hours he sleeps and each penny he spends— though with a natural facility for portraying on stage emotions which he doesn't feel one iota.

The Governor shut up F.F. with a gesture and got ready to make his decision, but just then I saw that there was a sixth person on this side of the stage.

Standing in the second wings beyond our group was a dark figure like a tarpaulined Christmas tree topped by a big helmet of unmistakable general shape despite its veiling. I grabbed the Governor's arm and pointed at it silently. He smothered a large curse and strode up to it and rasped, "Guthrie, you old Son of a B! Can you go on?" The figure gave an affirmative grunt.

Joe Rubens grimaced at me as if to say "Show business!" and grabbed a spear from the prop table and hurried back across the stage for his entrance as Marcellus just before the curtain lifted and the first nervous, superbly atmospheric lines of the play rang out, loud at first, but then going low with unspoken apprehension.

"Who's there?"

"Nay, answer me; stand, and unfold yourself."

"Long live the king!"

"Bernardo?"

"He."

"You come most carefully upon your hour."

" 'Tis now struck twelve; get thee to bed, Francisco."

"For this relief much thanks; 'tis bitter cold and I am sick at heart."

"Have you had quiet guard?"

"Not a mouse stirring."

With a resigned shrug, John McCarthy simply sat down. F.F. did the same, though *his* gesture was clench-fisted and exasperated. For a moment it seemed to me very comic that two Ghosts in *Hamlet* should be sitting in the wings, watching a third perform. I unbuttoned my overcoat and slung it over my left arm.

The Ghost's first two appearances are entirely silent ones. He merely goes on stage, shows himself to the soldiers, and comes off again. Nevertheless there was a determined little ripple of hand-clapping from the audience—the second, third, and fourth rows center greeting their patriarchal hero, it seemed likely. Guthrie didn't fall down at any rate and he walked reasonably straight—an achievement perhaps rating applause, if anyone out there knew the degree of intoxication Guthrie was probably burdened with at this moment—a cask-bellied Old Man of the Sea on his back.

The only thing out of normal was that he had forgot to turn on the little green light in the peak of his helmet—an omission which hardly mattered, certainly not on this first appearance. I hurried up to him when he came off and told him about it in a whisper as he moved off toward a dark backstage corner. I got in reply, through the inscrutable green veil, an exhalation of whisky and three affirmative grunts: one, that he knew it; two, that the light was working; three, that he'd remember to turn it on next time.

Then the scene had ended and I darted across the stage as they changed to the room-of-state set. I wanted to get rid of my overcoat. Joe Rubens grabbed me and told me about Guthrie's green light not being on and I told him that was all taken care of.

"Where the hell was he all the time we were hunting for him?" Joe asked me.

"I don't know," I answered.

By that time the second scene was playing, with F.F., his Ghost-coverings shed, playing the King as well as he always does (it's about his best part) and Gertrude Grainger looking very regal beside him as the Queen, her namesake, while there was another flurry of applause, more scattered this time, for the Governor in his black doublet and tights beginning about his seven hundredth performance of Shakespeare's longest and meatiest role.

Monica was still sitting on the trunk by the switchboard, looking paler than ever under her make-up, it seemed to me, and I folded my overcoat and silently persuaded her to use it as a cushion. I sat beside her and she took my hand and we watched the play from the wings.

After a while I whispered to her, giving her hand a little squeeze, "Feeling better now?"

She shook her head. Then leaning toward me, her mouth close to my ear, she whispered rapidly and unevenly, as if she just had to tell someone, "Bruce, I'm frightened. There's something in the theater. I don't think that was Guthrie playing the Ghost."

I whispered back, "Sure it was. I talked with him."

"Did you see his face?" she asked.

"No, but I smelled his breath," I told her and explained to her about him forgetting to turn on the green light. I continued, "Francis and John were both ready to go on as the Ghost, though, until Guthrie turned up. Maybe you glimpsed one of them before the play started and that gave you the idea it wasn't Guthrie."

Sybil Jameson in her Player costume looked around at me warningly. I was letting my whispering get too loud.

Monica put her mouth so close that her lips for an instant brushed my ear and she mouse-whispered, "I don't mean another *person* playing the Ghost—not that exactly. Bruce, there's *something* in the theater."

"You've got to forget that Ouija nonsense," I told her sharply. "And buck up now," I added, for the curtain had just gone down on Scene Two and it was time for her to get on stage for her scene with Laertes and Polonius.

I waited until she was launched into it, speaking her lines brightly enough, and then I carefully crossed the stage behind the backdrop. I was sure there was no more than nerves and imagination to her notions, though they'd raised shivers on me, but just the same I wanted to speak to Guthrie again and see his face.

When I'd completed my slow trip (you have to move rather slowly, so the drop won't ripple or bulge), I was dumbfounded to find myself witnessing the identical backstage scene that had been going on when I'd got back from my tour of the bars. Only now there was a lot more light because the scene being played on stage was a bright one. And Props was there behind his table, watching everything like the spectator he basically is. But beyond him were Francis Farley Scott and John McCarthy in their improvised Ghost costumes again, and the Governor and Joe with them, and all of them carrying on that furious lipreader's argument, now doubly hushed.

I didn't have to wait to get close to them to know that Guthrie must have disappeared again. As I made my way toward them, watching their silent antics, my silly mind became almost hysterical with the thought that Guthrie had at last discovered that invisible hole every genuine alcoholic wishes he had, into which he could decorously disappear and drink during the times between his absolutely necessary appearances in the real world.

As I neared them, Donald Fryer (our Horatio) came from behind me, having made the trip behind the backdrop faster than I had, to tell the Governor in hushed gasps that Guthrie wasn't in any of the dressing rooms or anywhere else stage right.

Just at that moment the bright scene ended, the curtain came down, the drapes before which Ophelia and the others had been playing swung back to reveal again the battlements of Elsinore, and the lighting shifted back to the midnight blue of the first scene, so that for the moment it was hard to see at all. I heard the Governor say decisively, *"You* play the Ghost," his voice receding as he and Joe and Don hurried across the stage to be in place for their proper entrance. Seconds later there came the dull soft hiss of the main curtain opening and I heard the Governor's taut resonant voice saying, "The air bites shrewdly; it is very cold," and Don responding as Horatio with, "It is a nipping and an eager air."

By that time I could see again well enough—see Francis Farley Scott and John McCarthy moving side by side toward the back wing through which the Ghost enters. They were still arguing in whispers. The explanation was clear enough: each thought the Governor had pointed at him in the sudden darkness—or possibly in F.F.'s case was pretending he so thought. For a moment the comic side of my mind, grown a bit hysterical by now, almost collapsed me with the thought of twin Ghosts entering the stage side by side. Then once again, history still repeating itself, I saw beyond them that other bulkier figure with the unmistakable shrouded helmet. They must have seen it too for they stopped dead just before my hands touched a shoulder of each of them. I circled quickly past them and reached out my hands to put them lightly on the third figure's shoulders, intending to whisper, "Guthrie, are you okay?" It was a very stupid thing for one actor to do to another—startling him just before his entrance—but I was made thoughtless by the memory of Monica's fears and by the rather frantic riddle of where Guthrie could possibly have been hiding.

But just then Horatio gasped, "Look, my lord, it comes," and Guthrie moved out of my light grasp onto the stage without so much as turning his head—and leaving me shaking because where I'd touched the rough buckram-braced fabric of the Ghost's cloak I'd felt only a kind of insubstantiality beneath instead of Guthrie's broad shoulders.

I quickly told myself that was because Guthrie's cloak had stood out from his shoulders and his back as he had moved. I had to tell myself something like that. I turned around. John McCarthy and F.F. were standing in front of the dark prop table and by now my nerves were in such a state that their paired forms gave me another start. But I tiptoed after them into the downstage wings and watched the scene from there.

The Governor was still on his knees with his sword held hilt up like a cross doing the long speech that begins, "Angels and ministers of grace defend us!" And of course the Ghost had his cloak drawn around him so you couldn't see what was under it—and the little green light still wasn't lit in his helmet. Tonight the absence of that theatric touch made him a more frightening figure—certainly to me, who wanted so much to see Guthrie's ravaged old face and be reassured by it. Though there was still enough comedy left in the ragged edges of my thoughts that I could imagine Guthrie's pugnacious son-in-law whispering angrily to those around him that Gilbert Usher was so jealous of his great father-in-law that he wouldn't let him show his face on the stage.

Then came the transition to the following scene where the Ghost has led Hamlet off alone with him—just a five-second complete darkening of the stage while a scrim is dropped—and at last the Ghost spoke those first lines of "Mark me" and "My hour is almost come, When I to sulphurous and tormenting flames Must render up myself."

If any of us had any worries about the Ghost blowing up on his lines or slurring them drunkenly, they were taken care of now. Those lines were delivered with the greatest authority and effect. And I was almost certain that it was Guthrie's rightful voice—at least I was at first—but doing an even better job than the good one he had always done of getting the effect of distance and otherworldliness and hopeless alienation from all life on Earth. The theater became silent as death, yet at the same time I could imagine the soft pounding of a thousand hearts, thousands of shivers crawling—and I *knew* that Francis Farley Scott, whose shoulder was pressed against mine, was trembling.

Each word the Ghost spoke was like a ghost itself, mounting the air and hanging poised for an impossible extra instant before it faded towards eternity.

Those great lines came: "I am thy father's spirit; Doomed for a certain term to walk the night . . ." and just at that moment the idea came to me that Guthrie Boyd might be dead, that he might have died and be lying unnoticed somewhere between his children's home and the theater —no matter what Props had said or the rest of us had seen—and that his ghost might have come to give a last performance. And on the heels of that shivery impossibility came the thought that similar and perhaps even eerier ideas must be frightening Monica. I knew I had to go to her.

So while the Ghost's words swooped and soared in the dark—marvellous black-plumed birds—I again made that nervous cross behind the back-drop.

Everyone stage right was standing as frozen and absorbed—motionless loomings—as I'd left John and F.F. I spotted Monica at once. She'd moved forward from the switchboard and was standing, crouched a little, by the big floodlight that throws some dimmed blue on the back-drop and across the back of the stage. I went to her just as the Ghost was beginning his exit stage left, moving backward along the edge of the light from the flood, but not quite in it, and reciting more lonelily and eerily than I'd ever heard them before those memorable last lines:

"Fare thee well at once!
"The glow-worm shows the matin to be near,
"And 'gins to pale his uneffectual fire;
"Adieu, adieu! Hamlet, remember me."

One second passed, then another, and then there came two unexpected bursts of sound at the same identical instant: Monica screamed and a thunderous applause started out front, touched off by Guthrie's people, of course, but this time swiftly spreading to all the rest of the audience.

I imagine it was the biggest hand the Ghost ever got in the history of the theater. In fact, I never heard of him getting a hand before. It certainly was a most inappropriate place to clap, however much the performance deserved it. It broke the atmosphere and the thread of the scene.

Also, it drowned out Monica's scream, so that only I and a few of those behind me heard it.

At first I thought I'd made her scream, by touching her as I had Guthrie, suddenly, like an idiot, from behind. But instead of shrinking or dodging away she turned and clung to me, and kept clinging too even after I'd drawn her back and Gertrude Grainger and Sybil Jameson had closed in to comfort her and hush her gasping sobs and try to draw her away from me.

By this time the applause was through and Governor and Don and Joe were taking up the broken scene and knitting together its finish as best they could, while the floods came up little by little, changing to rosy, to indicate dawn breaking over Elsinore.

Then Monica mastered herself and told us in quick whispers what had made her scream. The Ghost, she said, had moved for a moment into the edge of the blue floodlight, and she had seen for a moment through his veil, and what she had seen had been a face like Shakespeare's. Just that and no more. Except that at the moment when she told us—later she became less certain—she was sure it was Shakespeare himself and no one else.

I discovered then that when you hear something like that you don't exclaim or get outwardly excited. Or even inwardly, exactly. It rather shuts you up. I know I felt at the same time extreme awe and a renewed irritation at the Ouija board. I was deeply moved, yet at the same time pettishly irked, as if some vast adult creature had disordered the toy world of my universe.

It seemed to hit Sybil and even Gertrude the same way. For the moment we were shy about the whole thing, and so, in her way, was Monica, and so were the few others who had overheard in part or all what Monica had said.

I knew we were going to cross the stage in a few more seconds when the curtain came down on that scene, ending the first act, and stagelights came up. At least I knew that I was going across. Yet I wasn't looking forward to it.

When the curtain did come down—with another round of applause from out front—and we started across, Monica beside me with my arm still tight around her, there came a choked-off male cry of horror from ahead to shock and hurry us. I think about a dozen of us got stage left about the same time, including of course the Governor and the others who had been on stage.

F.F. and Props were standing inside the doorway to the empty prop room and looking down into the hidden part of the L. Even from the side, they both looked pretty sick. Then F.F. knelt down and almost went out of view, while Props hunched over him with his natural stoop.

As we craned around Props for a look—myself among the first, just beside the Governor, we saw something that told us right away that this Ghost wasn't ever going to be able to answer that curtain call they were still fitfully clapping for out front, although the house lights must be up by now for the first intermission.

Guthrie Boyd was lying on his back in his street clothes. His face looked gray, the eyes staring straight up. While swirled beside him lay the Ghost's cloak and veil and the helmet and an empty fifth of whisky.

Between the two conflicting shocks of Monica's revelation and the body in the prop room, my mind was in a useless state. And from her helpless incredulous expression I knew Monica felt the same. I tried to put things together and they wouldn't fit anywhere.

F.F. looked up at us over his shoulder. "He's not breathing," he said. "I think he's gone." Just the same he started loosing Boyd's tie and shirt and pillowing his head on the cloak. He handed the whisky bottle back to us through several hands and Joe Rubens got rid of it.

The Governor sent out front for a doctor and within two minutes Harry Grossman was bringing us one from the audience who'd left his seat number and bag at the box office. He was a small man—Guthrie would have made two of him—and a bit awestruck, I could see, though holding himself with greater professional dignity because of that, as we made way for him and then crowded in behind.

He confirmed F.F.'s diagnosis by standing up quickly after kneeling only for a few seconds where F.F. had. Then he said hurriedly to the Governor, as if the words were being surprised out of him against his professional caution, "Mr. Usher, if I hadn't heard this man giving that great performance just now, I'd think he'd been dead for an hour or more."

He spoke low and not all of us heard him, but I did and so did Monica, and there was Shock Three to go along with the other two, raising in my mind for an instant the grisly picture of Guthrie Boyd's spirit, or some other entity, willing his dead body to go through with that last performance. Once again I unsuccessfully tried to fumble together the parts of this night's mystery.

The little doctor looked around at us slowly and puzzledly. He said, "I take it he just wore the cloak over his street clothes?" He paused. Then, "He *did* play the Ghost?" he asked us.

The Governor and several others nodded, but some of us didn't at once and I think F.F. gave him a rather peculiar look, for the doctor cleared his throat and said, "I'll have to examine this man as quickly as possible in a better place and light. Is there—?" The Governor suggested the couch in his dressing room and the doctor designated Joe Rubens and John McCarthy and Francis Farley Scott to carry the body. He passed over the Governor, perhaps out of awe, but Hamlet helped just the same, his black garb most fitting.

It was odd the doctor picked the older men—I think he did it for dignity. And it was odder still that he should have picked two ghosts to help carry a third, though he couldn't have known that.

As the designated ones moved forward, the doctor said, "Please stand back, the rest of you."

It was then that the very little thing happened which made all the pieces of this night's mystery fall into place—for me, that is, and for Monica too, judging from the way her hand trembled in and then tightened around mine. We'd been given the key to what had happened. I won't tell you what it was until I've knit together the ends of this story.

The second act was delayed perhaps a minute, but after that we kept to schedule, giving a better performance than usual—I never knew the Graveyard Scene to carry so much feeling, or the bit with Yorick's skull to be so poignant.

Just before I made my own first entrance, Joe Rubens snatched off my street hat—I'd had it on all this while—and I played all of Guildenstern wearing a wrist-watch, though I don't imagine anyone noticed.

F.F. played the Ghost as an off-stage voice when he makes his final brief appearance in the Closet Scene. He used Guthrie's voice to do it, imitating him very well. It struck me afterwards as ghoulish—but right.

Well before the play ended, the doctor had decided he could say that Guthrie had died of a heart seizure, not mentioning the alcoholism. The minute the curtain came down on the last act, Harry Grossman informed Guthrie's son and daughter and brought them backstage. They were much moved, though hardly deeply smitten, seeing they'd been out of touch with the old boy for a decade. However, they quickly saw it was a Grand and Solemn Occasion and behaved accordingly, especially Guthrie's pugnacious son-in-law.

Next morning the two Wolverton papers had headlines about it and Guthrie got his biggest notices ever in the Ghost. The strangeness of the event carried the item around the world—a six-line filler, capturing the mind for a second or two, about how a once-famous actor had died immediately after giving a performance as the Ghost in *Hamlet,* though in some versions, of course, it became Hamlet's Ghost.

The funeral came on the afternoon of the third day, just before our last performance in Wolverton, and the whole company attended along with Guthrie's children's crowd and many other Wolvertonians. Old Sybil broke down and sobbed.

Yet to be a bit callous, it was a neat thing that Guthrie died where he did, for it saved us the trouble of having to send for relatives and probably take care of the funeral ourselves. And it did give old Guthrie a grand finish, with everyone outside the company thinking him a hero-martyr to the motto The Show Must Go On. And of course we knew too that in a deeper sense he'd really been that.

We shifted around in our parts and doubled some to fill the little gaps Guthrie had left in the plays, so that the Governor didn't have to hire another actor at once. For me, and I think for Monica, the rest of the season was very sweet. Gertrude and Sybil carried on with the Ouija sessions alone.

And now I must tell you about the very little thing which gave myself and Monica a satisfying solution to the mystery of what had happened that night.

You'll have realized that it involved Props. Afterwards I asked him straight out about it and he shyly told me that he really couldn't help me there. He'd had this unaccountable devilish compulsion to get drunk and his mind had blanked out entirely from well before the performance until he found himself standing with F.F. over Guthrie's body at the end of the first act. He didn't remember the Ouija scare or a word of what he'd said to me about theaters and time machines—or so he always insisted.

F.F. told us that after the Ghost's last exit he'd seen him—very vaguely in the dimness—lurch across backstage into the empty prop room and that he and Props had found Guthrie lying there at the end of the scene. I think the queer look F.F.—the old reality-fuddling rogue!— gave the doctor was to hint to him that *he* had played the Ghost, though that wasn't something I could ask him about.

But the very little thing— When they were picking up Guthrie's body and the doctor told the rest of us to stand back, Props turned as he obeyed and straightened his shoulders and looked directly at Monica and myself, or rather a little over our heads. He appeared compassionate yet smilingly serene as always and for a moment transfigured, as if he were the eternal observer of the stage of life and this little tragedy were only part of an infinitely vaster, endlessly interesting pattern.

I realized at that instant that Props could have done it, that he'd very effectively guarded the doorway to the empty prop room during our searches, that the Ghost's costume could be put on or off in seconds (though Props's shoulders wouldn't fill the cloak like Guthrie's), and that I'd never once before or during the play seen him and the Ghost at the same time. Yes, Guthrie had arrived a few minutes before me . . . and died . . . and Props, nerved to it by drink, had covered for him.

While Monica, as she told me later, knew at once that here was the great-browed face she'd glimpsed for a moment through the greenish gauze.

Clearly there had been four ghosts in *Hamlet* that night—John McCarthy, Francis Farley Scott, Guthrie Boyd, and the fourth who had really played the role. Mentally blacked out or not, knowing the lines from the many times he'd listened to *Hamlet* performed in this life, or from buried memories of times he'd taken the role in the days of Queen Elizabeth the First, Billy (or Willy) Simpson, or simply Willy S., had played the Ghost, a good trouper responding automatically to an emergency.

Here is another legend of the sea, of a tar who sails forlornly like the Flying Dutchman (Q.V.), though his itinerant vigil may not be forever—a thought which frightens him, poor ghost. SARALEE TERRY is the pseudonym of an obscure novelist who writes humorous verse on napkins.

The Ghost of Sailboat Fred
by Saralee Terry

From Plymouth to Cape Finistere,
Each sailor, to a man,
Will quake and shake in mortal fear
On spying "the Dutchman."

For Vanderdecken's flying boat
Presages doom at sea;
Don't hail his sail when you're afloat,
Or wrecked ye'll surely be.

But now I sing of Sailboat Fred
Who terrifies no he-man.
Tars laugh and chaff at this poor dead
Befuddled little seaman.

When Freddie breathed, he loved to fish
Upon a placid stream;
Poor lad, he had no other wish
For loafing was his dream.

One day on deck he fell asleep
And snoozed till it was morning.
A bog of fog was sair acreep
And soon, without a warning

A fearful storm began to rage
With furious commotion;
It broke the yoke of his moorage
And swept him to the ocean.

Green Freddie rode the sea so wide
Yet could not find the land;
His sail so frail bobbed on the tide
And never touched the sand.

And now his spectre seeks the beach,
As sailors laugh with glee;
His ghost the coast still tries to reach
Because he's late for tea

And every day that he's not home
Just makes his wife more mad.
Each year, the fear that she will roam
And find him scares him bad.

'Twould mean her patience was no more
And she would have his head . . .
And not a lot of help he'd score
Just from the fact he's dead!

There are several peculiar legends associated with Christmas Eve, one of which is that at midnight, animals briefly enjoy the power of human speech. "The Fisherman's Story" is another Yule legend of peasant superstition concerning fishing for gain on that holiday. ANATOLE LE BRAZ, born in 1859 in Saint-Servais, Brittany, was a professor of philosophy who wrote a small number of books and tales dealing with the legends of his native province, among which is the strange story that follows. Its translator and adapter, FAITH LANCEREAU, has trimmed the original of its conversational prolixity. A native and resident of New York City, she is a psychologist specializing in chronic mental illness; she is devoted to cats and fantasy literature.

The Fisherman's Story

Adapted by Faith Lancereau
from a tale by Anatole Le Braz

We were all gathered at the home of Jean Menguy and his family on the hilly ridge of Crec'h, overlooking the sea. Christmas was near, and we sat about the fire talking of the miracles and events of that holiest of nights.

Everyone had something to say except Cloarec, the pilot. He sat quietly sucking his pipe. Under his thick, bushy brows, his blue eyes turned inward as if he remembered things long past.

"Cloarec," I said, "you are so quiet. Surely you have some story of the season just waiting to be told."

His face, which was always brick-red—having been cooked over and over by the salty sea air—now became fiery red. With embarrassment, he stuttered, "When it comes to tales like the one I have in mind, there is little to wait for. I still do not know what really happened. But it taught me never to go fishing on Christmas Eve. . . ."

Removing the pipe from his mouth, he shook the ash on his thumb, passed the back of his hand under his nose, and sniffed. Then, in the characteristic accents of Brittany, he began his story.

I was about your age, John Junior, when this occurred. Take heed and always listen to the advice of your elders.

One Christmas Eve, I decided I would put out to sea to fish. My father tried to dissuade me from going because it was a Holy Night, but I replied, "Christmas or not, whether you will or won't come, the winds are northwest, and it is a blessed time for turbot, so I'm going."

The previous week had been impossible for putting out the nets. There was a heavy haze like you see sometimes in Ireland, and it darkened the sky for six consecutive days. I was, therefore, doubly eager to go on Christmas Eve, when the sky was lightly overcast and the north wind was well-tempered and not too cold. The ocean was calm and gray with large swells, not choppy; one might wait till mid-March to find such good conditions again for fishing.

"But," my father said, "you would do better to lose the fish than lose your soul. Do not go out tonight, son!"

"And where is there a commandment of God or of the Church forbidding me to earn a living on Christmas Eve?" I demanded. "Isn't it just as necessary to eat tomorrow as any other day?"

"A clever argument to which I have no reply," my father admitted, "yet I was always told that Christmas Eve, beginning at midnight, is a mysterious time and better left alone. However, you are an adult, and if you insist on going, I cannot stop you. But please take one bit of advice with you."

"Yes?"

"If anything strange should happen, hoist your anchor as fast as you can, raise its cross in the air, make your crew kneel and sing 'The Song of Nédélek.'* Do not forget."

I shrugged my shoulders and set out for port. With me were five crew members, all rough tars like myself, all more concerned with keeping the pot boiling in this world, than in assuring themselves a place in the next. Except for the little cabin boy, Dudored (who died twenty years ago of yellow fever in Montevideo), all are still alive. There were the brothers Pierre and René Balanec from Roc'h-vrân, Louis Rudono from Cosquer, and Gonery Mezcam of Kerampoullou.

The five joined me at the landing, their heavy boots on, their oilskin hats tied under their chins. Ten minutes later, with all sails set, we steered toward the Seven Isles.

The breeze was just right, but we were the only anglers out. All other ships were still tied to the pier. Pierre pointed at the fishermen who, with folded arms, lounged on the embankment of the old battery. "Idlers," he spat. "Probably not ten sous in any of their pockets for cel-

* A Christmas carol of Brittany.

ebrating Christmas, yet they loaf around instead of preparing for the holiday."

Rudono agreed with Balanec and worried we all would be expected to treat the shirkers once High Mass ended.

But I knew there was another reason why they did not set out to sea. Uneasily, I mentioned to my crew the discussion I'd had with my father.

"Bah!" Pierre scoffed. "An old woman's idea."

All but Dudored agreed. Working on one of the lines, our cabin boy timidly murmured something about his grandfather being lost forever just after midnight on Christmas Eve, but none of the others paid any attention.

Soon we were in the waters of the Ile aux Moines and let down our lines. But contrary to our expectations, the fish weren't biting. We thought the gentle weather would bring them to the surface, but they seemed in no hurry to leave their dark hiding places in the depths. After an hour or so with nothing to show for the time spent, Pierre suggested we move farther out to sea, and I agreed.

It started out as a good move. As soon as we hit the windward side of the islands, we brought in fish each and every time we put out the net. Our spirits rose with the abundance of our catch; it began to look as if we would empty the sea of fish, and our cabin boy, Dudored, barely had enough time to take the catch out of the nets before the next was hauled into the boat.

The more fish we caught, the more we laughed and chaffed one another. The hours slipped by unnoticed. We didn't even mark the onset of darkness. Our eyes saw nothing but the gray-green waters that lifted the ship with their long regular waves and brought turbot to our lines.

Dudored alone had thoughts of a darker nature, though I did not realize it at the time. But the approach of night bothered him, and finally he spoke to me.

"It's getting late, pilot," he said; "it'll be hard to go in with the ebb tide."

He was right. The tide and the northwest wind would work against us if we didn't hurry to catch the eddy at Seven Isles while the water was still deep enough to get over it. Sea currents are terrible and cannot be approached as if one were jumping a hurdle. So I agreed with Dudored and ordered our departure.

But the other men objected. The more fish they caught, the more they wanted. Pierre's brother, René, when he heard the suggestion originated with Dudored, scowled deeply. "What business is it of his, that unweaned calf?" he growled thickly. "Did we ask him what time it is?"

"No," I said, "but maybe we should listen, anyhow. Look at the horizon. Darkness is falling."

"Let it fall. One last pull on the net, pilot."

He was indeed angry, all of the others were, too—Louis, Pierre, Gonery. To be truthful, I also was annoyed at our cabin boy, so I did not fight them. We stayed.

Cloarec paused to relight his pipe. Bending over the fireplace, he took an ember in his hand and put it to the bowl of the tiny clay pipe. Inhaling, his cheeks become so hollow they seemed to touch the inner walls of his face.

Somewhere outside the house, a cricket began to chirp.

"I regret," he said at last, "that I, too, was so transfigured by the profit motive as to jeopardize the lives of six men, but I spare nothing now, the facts are so few, as it is.

"And now I come to the evil part of my tale."

We finally finished pulling things together on board ship. Our sails were set, and I sat down at the rudder to tack when, shooting a glance at the foresail, I saw it flutter slightly, then grow calm. That was ominous. If the wind disappeared and the waves subsided, we would be in a bad fix. Stranded, at the very least, until half-tide, and even escaping then would mean hard work on the oars. Then we'd still have to wait three or four hours in the dark before being able to set sail for port.

The laughter that claimed us earlier was suddenly gone. My five companions, sitting on the benches at their posts, some facing forward, some backward, distractedly watched the deepening darkness.

Nevertheless, I held on to the hope of reaching the formidable embankment at the right moment. We sailed toward it, and indeed were only a few hundred yards away, when René began to shout obscenities.

"What's wrong with you?" I snapped.

"A horrible mess," he replied, looking west toward the high sea. "There's nothing over there but drizzle."

Louis Rudono looked the same way, then muttered, "No doubt about it. Fog coming."

And they were right. Turning quickly, I saw a confounding fog invading the horizon, a fog weaving a soft weft between sky and water.

"Damn," Pierre muttered, "that's what muzzled the wind."

The sea curled round the sides of the boat. Foam streamed in our wake, and the oak planks shook beneath us. We were in the channel between the islands.

"Hey, cabin boy," I stood up and called, "come steer as best you can. The rest of you, to the oars!" I myself joined them.

Now note carefully how Mezcam and I took the oars on the starboard side, while the brothers Balanec were seated to port. At the prow, Louis Rudono kept a lookout for rocks. He had good eyes, and I thought if anyone could spot trouble ahead, Louis could.

Remember how we were situated: Louis at the prow; little Dudored at the helm; the other four on the oars right and left.

I gave the word and we pulled hard. The vessel responded and we fairly flew over the water. Pierre, an enormous man, groaned loud with the effort.

But no matter how fast we rowed, we could not outrun the fog. Little by little, it overtook us. In the final minutes before it did, we saw the last remnant of daylight gleam eerily on the face of the sea.

Then darkness enveloped the boat, and the fog muffled us in an enormous floating wall of mist. For a little while, we could still make out a light on the Ile aux Moines, suspended like a ghostly star in the distance, but presently, it, too, turned into a blurred halo and vanished.

"That's the last light," Louis said over his shoulder. "Boy, steer to starboard, do you hear?"

"Aye, aye," he answered from his post behind us. His high-pitched voice sounded hoarse.

Now a glacial dampness penetrated our limbs. The fog was around and in us, its strange smoky smell stinging our throats and lungs. We held to the oars, still trying to maneuver across the rapids. Every minute I asked Louis what he saw, if anything.

"Whitecaps." He dipped his hand below the bow. "The water's choppy; we're still in the channel, I think."

The acrid fog stank in our nostrils, the curtain of shadow and night imprisoned us and it became difficult even to see one another seated close by. I reached out and touched Gonery's jersey to assure myself that he hadn't left his seat and that the gigantic silhouette my eyes squinted at was really him. Even the sides of the boat were indistinct against the deeper gloom of the night.

Then from the bow of the boat, as if from far off, our lookout's voice sounded, thin and hard to hear, "We're no longer going forward, friends. We're drifting."

There was nothing we could do. We let go of the oars and sat in near-silence, broken only by the slap-slap of the waves against the sides of our ship. Destiny now was the pilot.

At least, I thought, we would drift into the high sea and be more secure while waiting for the tide to change. If we stayed in the channel waters, we might run upon the reefs. However it turned out, I was sure we would not reach port until dawn.

We glided along, shadows that seemed more like specters than mortals. Wrapped in oilskin, visors pulled down, hands in sleeves, we said nothing, no longer able to talk, to open the mouth was to swallow fog. I thought the dreadful smell must be like the waters of Hell.

Even the noise of the ocean itself eventually faded away. Total silence. We floated alone as if we had ceased to exist, six lost souls on a sea of death.

The silence was suddenly broken by the weak voice of the cabin boy. I could not hear him.

"What, Dudored?"

"I said there is a seventh person on board."

Everyone leaped to their feet.

"What kind of idiocy are you saying?" I snarled at him, furious and frightened at the same time.

Pierre sneered. "The little fool can't count higher than five!"

"Or else he's blind," taunted his brother René.

"Damn you," Dudored swore faintly, "then count yourselves."

I did. Or tried to. But the hazy figures in the fog could not be identified. There, at front, that must be Louis, yes, over there the brothers, but had Mezcam moved? I was not sure, so I counted again. Seven.

"Yes," Pierre whispered, "there is one more on board."

Each had to do it for himself, none took the others' words for it. And every man reached the same tally.

We had started out as six, but there were seven silhouettes etched against the blackness of night.

"Call the roll," Rudono implored me.

I did so, naming each according to age, Pierre first, then Gonery Mezcam. Both answered.

"Louis?"

"Here!"

"René?"

"Here."

"Dudored?"

"Here."

Louis Rudono burst out, "The one who didn't answer is over by me!" He gestured at a figure leaning on the mast, rushed forward to grab him by the collar, but lowered his fist fast when Pierre yelled, "Ass! It's me you're aiming your fist at!"

And then no one said anything further for a long time. My heart beat fast, my skin prickled with terror that longed to cry out and break the heavy silence. Deep breaths on all sides, eyes averted lest the comrade whose face one sought turned out to be the mysterious stranger who came out of the night.

I meditated nervously on the nature of the inexplicable seventh passenger. Was he human or a wraith? A ghost was dreadful to contemplate, but the weight of another body might be too much for our small vessel to bear.

And then the cabin boy spoke again.

"Pilot! The back of the boat is sinking. The inner planks are almost at sea level!"

Pierre let out a cry of pure fear, and the same thought occurred to us all. Our supernatural visitor, whatever his nature, meant to drag us into the midnight depths of the sea.

I shouted that we must throw all we could overboard in order to lighten the load.

All the fish went first.

Total havoc. Everything within reach splashed overboard, but nothing helped, the ship was not lightened.

"Only an inch before we're engulfed," the little cabin boy screamed.

I felt around frantically for anything else that could be tossed into the water, came across the anchor, hefted it high . . . then stopped.

The words of my father rushed into my mind.

"Wait!" I cried out. "Throw nothing else." Then I raised the cross of the anchor above my head and began to sing, "In a town of Galilee—" The hymn of Nédélek.

Later the others told me they thought I'd gone crazy, but Dudored joyfully said that as soon as I started to chant, the boat rose once more. They all joined in on the second verse, Pierre Balanec bellowing like some great church organ.

And then a call from the fog, "Ho, there! Beware of what's alongside, sail nearer to the wind!"

We never found out who spoke. It was not Louis, our lookout. But turning to the indicated side of the ship, we all saw with dread and wonder the great rocks of Triagoz. The sea had almost run us on them.

Had we been under sail with the slightest breeze, we would have been pounded mercilessly, even as we foundered. But Louis saw the lighthouse immediately after the strange warning, and we set to the oars with renewed strength. Soon the watchman greeted us, a lantern in his hand.

"Listen," he said as he tethered our line to the pier, "the midnight mass on the mainland."

And all of us crossed ourselves.

The pilot's pipe had gone out. He stared at it a moment, reflecting on the odd history he'd told us there in Jean Menguy's seaside house.

"Well, that's my tale," he said. "We returned to port by six a.m. without a single fish. My father regarded me with silent knowledge and wonder, but never asked any questions."

"And the seventh?" I asked. "When do you think he disappeared? And who, or what was he?"

Cloarec bowed his curly head and shrugged his shoulders. "I have told you all I know, or wish to know." Blinking his small blue eyes, so full of dreams beneath his bushy brows, he added, "Do not seek for more, but remember always that you must never go fishing on Christmas Eve."

Here is an example of a "historical" haunted house that once existed—so the nameless author says—about ten miles north of Atlantic City. I have the strange feeling that I read some local reference to the very place a few years ago while researching the Miss America Pageant for a series of articles . . . but like ghosts themselves, the reference remains elusive. Still, the site of this sea-haunted hostel ought to be capable of investigation.

The Old Mansion

Anonymous

Down on Long Beach, that narrow strip of sand which stretches along the New Jersey coast from Barnegat Inlet on the north to Little Egg Harbor Inlet on the south, the summer sojourner at some one of the numerous resorts, which of late years have sprung up every few miles, may, in wandering over the sand dunes just across the bay from the village of Manahawkin, stumble over some charred timbers or vestiges of crumbling chimneys, showing that once, years back, a human habitation has stood there. If the find rouses the jaded curiosity of the visitor sufficiently to impel him to question the weather-beaten old bayman who sails him on his fishing trips he will learn that these relics mark the site of one of the first summer hotels erected on the New Jersey coast.

"That's where the Old Mansion stood," he will be informed by Captain Nate or Captain Sam, or whatever particular captain it may chance to be, and if by good fortune it chances to be Captain Jim, he will hear a story that will pleasantly pass away the long wait for a sheepshead bite.

It was my good luck to have secured Captain Jim for a preceptor in the angler's art during my vacation last summer, and his stories and reminiscences of Long Beach were not the least enjoyable features of the two weeks' sojourn.

Captain Jim was not garrulous. Few of the baymen are. They are a sturdy, self-reliant, and self-controlled people, full of strong common sense, but still with that firm belief in the supernatural which seems inherent in dwellers by the sea.

"The Old Mansion," said Captain Jim, "or the Mansion of Health, for that was its full name, was built away back in 1822, so I've heard my father say. There had been a tavern close by years before that was kept by a man named Cranmer, and people used to come from Philadelphia by stage, sixty miles through the pines, to 'Hawkin, and then cross here by boat. Some would stop at Cranmer's and others went on down the beach to Homer's which was clear down at End by the Inlet. Finally some of the wealthy people concluded that they wanted better accommodations than Cranmer gave, so they formed the Great Swamp Long Beach Company, and built the Mansion of Health. I've heard that when it was built it was the biggest hotel on the coast, and was considered a wonder. It was 120 feet long, three stories high, and had a porch running all the way around it, with a balcony on top. It was certainly a big thing for those days. I've heard father tell many a time of the stage loads of gay people that used to come rattling into 'Hawkin, each stage drawn by four horses, and sometimes four or five of them a day in the summer. A good many people, too, used to come in their own carriages, and leave them over on the mainland until they were ready to go home. There were gay times at the Old Mansion then, and it made times good for the people along shore, too."

"How long did the Old Mansion flourish, Captain?" I asked.

"Well, for twenty-five or thirty years people came there summer after summer. Then they built a railroad to Cape May, and that, with the ghosts, settled the Mansion of Health."

"What do you mean by the ghosts?" I demanded.

"Well, you see," said Captain Jim, cutting off a mouthful of navy plug, "the story got around that the old house was haunted. Some people said there were queer things seen there, and strange noises were heard that nobody could account for, and pretty soon the place got a bad name and visitors were so few that it didn't pay to keep it open any more."

"But how did it get the name of being haunted, Captain Jim?" I persisted.

"Why, it was this way," continued the mariner. "Maybe you've heard of the time early in the fifties when the Powhatan was wrecked on the beach here, and every soul on board was lost. She was an emigrant ship, and there were over 400 people aboard—passengers and crew. She came ashore here during the equinoctial storm in September. There wasn't any life-saving stations in them days, and everyone was drowned. You can see the long graves now over in the 'Hawkin churchyard, where the bodies were buried after they came ashore. They put them in three long trenches that were dug from one end of the burying-ground to the other. The only people on the beach that night was the man who took care of the Old Mansion. He lived there with his family, and his son-in-law lived with him. He was the wreckmaster for this part of the coast, too. It wasn't till the second day that the people from 'Hawkin could get over to the beach, and by that time the bodies had all come ashore, and the wreckmaster had them all piled up on the sand. I was a youngster, then, and came over with my father, and, I tell you, it was the awfullest sight I ever saw—them long rows of drowned people, all lying there with their white, still faces turned up to the sky. Some were women, with their dead babies clasped tight in their arms, and some were husbands and wives, whose bodies came ashore locked together in a death embrace. I'll never forget that sight as long as I live. Well, when the coroner came and took charge he began to inquire whether any money or valuables had been found, but the wreckmaster declared that not a solitary coin had been washed ashore. People thought this was rather singular, as the emigrants were, most of them, well-to-do Germans, and were known to have brought a good deal of money with them, but it was concluded that it had gone down with the ship. Well, the poor emigrants were given pauper burial, and the people had begun to forget their suspicions until three or four months later there came another storm, and the sea broke clear over the beach, just below the Old Mansion, and washed away the sand. Next morning early two men from 'Hawkin sailed across the bay and landed on the beach. They walked across on the hard bottom where the sea had washed across, and, when about half way from the bay, one of the men saw something curious close up against the stump of an old cedar tree. He called the other man's attention to it, and they went over to the stump. What they found was a pile of leather money-belts that would have filled a wheelbarrow. Every one was cut open and empty. They had been buried in the sand close by the old stump, and the sea had washed away the covering. The men didn't go any further.

"They carried the belts to their boats and sailed back to 'Hawkin as fast as the wind would take them. Of course, it made a big sensation, and everybody was satisfied that the wreckmaster had robbed the bodies, if he hadn't done anything worse, but there was no way to prove it, and so nothing was done. The wreckmaster didn't stay around here long after that, though. The people made it too hot for him, and he and his family went away South, where it was said he bought a big plantation and a lot of slaves. Years afterward the story came to 'Hawkin somehow that he was killed in a barroom brawl, and that his son-in-law was drowned by his boat upsettin' while he was out fishin'. I don't furnish any affidavits with that part of the story, though.

"However, after that nobody lived in the Old Mansion for long at a time. People would go there, stay a week or two, and leave—and at last it was given up entirely to beach parties in the day time, and ghosts at night."

"But, Captain, you don't really believe the ghost part, do you?" I asked.

Captain Jim looked down the bay, expectorated gravely over the side of the boat, and answered, slowly:

"Well, I don't know as I would have believed in 'em if I hadn't seen the ghost."

"What!" I exclaimed; "you saw it? Tell me about it. I've always wanted to see a ghost, or next best thing, a man who has seen one."

"It was one August, about 1861," said the captain. "I was a young feller then, and with a half dozen more was over on the beach cutting salt hay. We didn't go home at nights, but did our own cooking in the Old Mansion kitchen, and at nights slept on piles of hay upstairs. We were a reckless lot of scamps, and reckoned that no ghosts could scare us. There was a big full moon that night, and it was as light as day. The muskeeters was pretty bad, too, and it was easier to stay awake than go to sleep. Along toward midnight me and two other fellers went out on the old balcony, and began to race around the house. We hollered and yelled, and chased each other for half an hour or so, and then we concluded we had better go to sleep, so we started for the window of the room where the rest were. This window was near one end on the ocean side, and as I came around the corner I stopped as if I had been shot, and my hair raised straight up on top of my head. Right there in front of that window stood a woman looking out over the sea, and in her arms she held a little child. I saw her as plain as I see you now. It seemed to me like an hour she stood there, but I don't suppose it was a second; then she was gone. When I could move I looked around for the other boys, and they were standing there paralyzed. They had seen the woman, too. We didn't say much, and we didn't sleep much that night, and the next night we bunked out on the beach. The rest of the crowd made all manner of fun of us, but we had had all the ghost we wanted, and I never set foot inside the old house after that."

"When did it burn down, Captain?" I asked, as Jim relapsed into silence.

"Somewhere about twenty-five years ago. A beach party had been roasting clams in the old oven, and in some way the fire got to the woodwork. It was as dry as tinder, and I hope the ghosts were all burnt up with it."

Few ghost stories occur in science-fiction; the genres tend to be exclusive by definition. But once in a while, some clever writer manages to concoct a conceit that fits both categories of fantastic literature. Such a tale is "The Haunting of Y-12," a delicious "club" story in the tradition of Lord Dunsany's wonderful "Jorkens" series. AL SARRANTONIO is an editor whose science-fiction appears in major genre periodicals regularly. He is one of a new breed of editor-writers whose taste and energy will do much to shape the best of the future output in American speculative fiction.

The Haunting of Y-12
by Al Sarrantonio

It was business time for the Genial Hauntings Club. Seated after dinner in the well-polished leather chairs of the Club's smoking room, pulled up before a glowing fire which threw dark, warm shadows across the walls and ceiling, with brim-filled brandy glasses and lit cigars or pipes, the Members called on the stranger to tell his story. This, of course, was Tradition at the GHC, for this was the one time during the year, on the Eve of Christmas (or, Dickens' Spirits' Eve, as it was whimsically called at the Club), when a new member might earn admission. Not that admission was so difficult to earn, for the nominee, sponsored by one of the present Members (in this case Porutto, a small, olive-skinned fellow of indistinct nationality with glasses and cool brown eyes, an adventurer by trade who was in the habit of tapping his pipe thoughtfully against his palm), need only tell a story. And the story need only be a true one, a story of ghosts—not a tall order for admission to an establishment known as the Genial Hauntings Club; but perhaps yes, since true stories of ghosts do not jump out of every shadow.

The Members settled themselves in—Thomas, the painter; Maye and Podwin, the writers of somewhat Mutt and Jeff-esque proportions who had cowritten many popular fictions, mostly in the science and fantasy categories; Hewetson, Butler of the Club (an exalted position, akin to Secretary); Petrone, the social scientist; Jenick, the light-bearded editor and wit; Ballestaire, the actor; and the others; even Michelle, the somewhat fiery-tempered World Traveler—and the stranger began his tale.

"Well," he said, drawing himself up in his chair and taking a last leisurely puff on his cigar, "my story begins with a computer." He was a young man of short-medium height, working his way toward stocky, with a florid moustache and tight shiny eyes behind his rimless glasses; there was an air of nervous certainty about him, as if he knew what he was about but hadn't quite discovered how to make others believe it yet.

"A haunted computer," he continued, pausing a moment for effect. And then drawing himself up once again with a sigh, he began in earnest.

These events (he said) occurred some twelve years ago, and the computer, called the Y-12, was lodged in my place of employment, what was then known as a Think Tank. There was a rush-rush project underway, and some very odd things began to happen to a man named Lonnigan.

Robert Lonnigan was in charge of our project, whose task it was to develop one of the first table-top computers; you have to remember that at one time a computer that would now rest on your thumbnail would fill an entire drawing room. Anyway, some strange things began to occur.

Lonnigan was working alone one night when the prototype of the Y-12 suddenly turned itself on and began to type out a message which read, "Robert, are you there?"

Lonnigan was a bit shocked of course, but realizing that there was such a thing as a practical joke and that whatever had happened should not have happened, he turned off the computer and went back to work. But once again Y-12 turned itself on and typed out, "Robert, are you there?" and then added, "This is father."

This shook Lonnigan. There was something eerily familiar about the words, and he had a slight feeling of déjà vu. His own father had died a few years previously, but being of the kind of mind that builds computers he was not about to admit to the possibility that his father's spirit had taken over Y-12. Still, something made his skin crawl about the whole thing.

He quickly checked through all of the input files, which only he had access to, and discovered that no one had programmed Y-12—not officially, anyway—for anything that would include the kind of phrasing the machine had evidenced. And as for practical jokes, he couldn't figure out how it could have been rigged up since he was supposed to see every program that went in and since security was so tight due to government involvement in the project; no research assistant was going to jeopardize his security clearance and career by pulling a scary—and somewhat sick—stunt on the program manager. Lonnigan was resolved, that night if possible, to find out what was going on.

He set up Y-12 for two-way conversation using the IBM keyboard and printout and queried, "Identify program: 'Robert, are you there? This is father.'"

There was no response.

He tried the same command, in as many variations as he could think of, but Y-12 remained silent. There was not even an acknowledgment of the query as a viable one, and according to Y-12 itself, no such statement had ever been made by the computer nor could be, since it did not exist in its memory banks.

Lonnigan was dumbfounded, and shut off the computer, beginning to think that maybe he was going crazy. He was bundling up to leave for the night, and had just turned off the lights in the lab, when Y-12 suddenly turned itself on again and repeated once more, "Robert, are you there? This is father. Please answer me."

A chill went up Lonnigan's spine and that feeling of déjà vu gripped him again, and he stood staring at the machine he had built, the machine he had turned off with his own hands, its amber and green lights now blinking on and off in the darkness and typing out repeatedly on its printer, "Robert, are you there? Please answer. Robert, are you there? Please answer." Lonnigan finally ended it by shutting down the computer completely and pulling the plug from the power outlet. He then left quickly, fearing that Y-12 would somehow turn itself back on despite the fact that its power source had been disconnected.

The following morning the bleary-eyed project manager assembled our entire staff and gave us a small speech, demanding that if anyone had tampered with Y-12 he should make himself known. No one stepped forward. Lonnigan pleaded with us, asking that if anyone knew anything at all about what had happened the night before, he should step forward now because he was endangering the entire project. We remained mute to a man, and I must admit we began to look at him a bit strangely.

There was talk throughout that day that perhaps Lonnigan needed a rest. A decision had actually been made to put him on at least temporary suspension when Y-12 suddenly burst into life with myself and about ten others present and began once more to type out its ghost message.

When the pandemonium died down, Lonnigan set us all to work. It was imperative, he said, that whatever was wrong with Y-12 be corrected before the government, which was funding the project, found out and all hell broke loose. One of my friends, a man named Boylston, asked, "But what if it really is haunted?" and Lonnigan, his face showing things he didn't want to show, answered, "Don't even think about it."

Every nut and bolt on the Y-12 computer was removed, turned over, and, more often than not, replaced. Every circuit was tapped, checked and rechecked, each memory bank drained and carefully reprogrammed. Nearly three days later, when we were through, Y-12 looked exactly as it had before. "Let's hope we've driven it out," Lonnigan said as we ran it through a test program. "Driven what out?" asked Boylston, and the look Lonnigan turned on him made him not ask again.

Y-12 ran through the program perfectly, and then ran through it again perfectly. There was a general sigh of relief. But then, almost as soon as it had been shut down, it blinked back into life and began to type: "Robert, are you there?"

There was complete silence in the room, and Lonnigan's face went white. Heaven knows what thoughts were running through his mind then. Whatever they were he shook his head and refused to dwell on them.

He ordered the lab sealed, ordered Y-12 pulled to pieces again. "Check every component twice, change everything that can be changed. We've got a government man coming tomorrow, dammit, so I want it finished before he gets here."

No one moved, and all eyes were on him, with the same silent statement.

Lonnigan went into a rage. "That's not my father in there, dammit! It's a bug! This is a machine. We built it, we can tear it down, we can smash it to bits and it can't talk back; there's a reason for what happened, and I want to know what it is! It's *not my father!*"

From across the room Y-12 burst into life and typed out, "Robert, please answer me."

"Get to it now!" Lonnigan screamed, and stalked from the room.

An hour before dawn the job was completed, and we all sat huddled across the room from Y-12, drinking coffee. No one spoke; all attention was fastened on the computer, or on Robert Lonnigan who sat huddled over a drafting table, a set of blueprints pinned out beneath his eyes. He was studying those prints minutely, almost obsessively, and muttering to himself under his breath. He looked drawn and haggard.

"There's something here. . . . I know it. Something . . ."

At that moment Y-12 began to clatter and blink into life. Everyone in the room, including Lonnigan, jumped.

"Robert, are you there? This is father. Can you hear me? This is father—"

"Ah!" cried Lonnigan suddenly, grabbing the schematic and waving it aloft. There was a look of triumph on his face, and deep relief. "By God, I know what it is," he said. "I should kick myself for not solving this before. Everyone come and look at this."

He spread the diagram out on the drafting table as we gathered around it. Behind us, Y-12 went on, "Can you hear me? Please answer. This is father—" and some of us glanced back nervously.

"Don't worry about the damn computer," said Lonnigan. "We've got some real work ahead of us before that government man gets here. Look at this section." He indicated a portion of the left upper corner of the sheet. "What happened was this, and it really is fantastic. We took every component out of Y-12, at least two times, right? And some were even replaced."

"A couple of times," I said.

"Right," continued Lonnigan. "But what we forgot about was the fact that some of the components of Y-12 were taken whole from other, earlier units and jerry-rigged into this one."

"So?" said my friend Boylston, who was still casting worried looks over his shoulder at the computer. "We've always done that; it's better than redesigning whole circuits that are basically the same. It just eliminates redundancy."

"Well, that's basically true. But in this case we used a component that was haunted."

Lonnigan savored the looks he got from us for a moment.

"Now before you bolt for the doors, listen to me. Do you remember where we got this component here from?" Again he indicated the upper left corner of the blueprint.

"Sure," I piped in. "From the A-6 model."

"Right. And the A-6 unit we used was one of the first ever manufactured. In fact, I'll wager it was the first off the line. And look at this," he said, pointing to a specific area; "we used almost the whole thing intact."

"No we didn't," I protested. "We went through a lot of circuitry, but we bypassed most of it."

"Ah, but not all of it; this whole section over here was part of the memory banks of the original machine."

"Yes, but we *bypassed* it," I insisted.

"Did we?" This was as an accusation from Lonnigan. "Ever since this business started, I've had the eerie feeling that I had heard some of what Y-12 was saying before. Well, it suddenly came to me.

"When I was fresh out of school I worked briefly with a man named Fleishman Bushyager—a brilliant man, but a little on the dotty side. He was elderly at the time, and pretty close to retirement age; the A-6 project, in any case, was supposed to be his last. You must remember this is a long time ago, and that I haven't thought about any of these things in years, so I may be a little fuzzy on a few points. But this is basically how the story goes.

"Part of the reason Bushyager was being herded out after the A-6 project was the fact that he began to come up with a few strange ideas; his son Robert died in an automobile accident and, like Arthur Conan Doyle, the old man became obsessed with trying to reach his son beyond the grave. He was actually working on some computer circuitry to aid him in this—a sort of computerized medium. Some of the higher-ups found out about it and since Bushyager was a big man they couldn't get rid of him outright; so they ordered him to restrict himself to A-6 work alone while they put through, behind his back, paperwork for his retirement.

"The old man was just about ready to leave by the time I got there, but one day he showed me some of the designs and one of his programs in particular. I stared and stared at this blueprint for hours and then it suddenly all wrapped up in my mind. One of the designs for the final A-6 computer actually contained, embedded in the circuitry, the design for Bushyager's medium. And though it was hidden, it could still do the old man's work for him, though in secret. He'd arranged things in such a way that his input would never show up on a readout, but the way we cannibalized the circuitry freed, as it were, the program for the first time. If you look closely, you can even see how Y-12 turned itself on. A bit eerie, but there's your ghost. The Y-12 really was haunted—in a way. And the Robert our ghost was calling for was Robert Bushyager.

"Well," said Lonnigan, "we haven't much time before that government man arrives. Let's unhook that circuitry and patch it up, and clean this place up. At least we didn't have to see any real ghosts, right?"

"Amen," we all agreed.

"This," said the stranger, sipping at his brandy and relighting his cold cigar, "nearly ends my story. The A-6 circuitry was altered and fixed, and the ghost in Y-12 appeared no more. In fact, my story would end here if not for one thing. You see, a curious thing ensued. During the cleanup before the government inspector arrived that morning, I took the printout sheets from Y-12's ghost messages. I put them into a drawer, intending to show them to my wife when I was able to tell her the story after the security lid on the Y-12 project was lifted, and promptly forgot about them. A few years later, when I was leaving my position for a new one, I came across them while cleaning out my desk; I almost tossed them in the waste basket but then remembered what they were and took a close look. And I found, as I said, a curious thing."

The stranger paused, and, with his eyes, took in his audience who, he was delighted to see, was a captive one; even the somewhat impatient Hewetson was leaning forward in his chair, his attention fixed on the stranger's next words. "And what I found," the stranger continued, "was that between the lines of type, in the blank spaces, a kind of raised lettering had appeared. And, on rubbing at this lettering lightly with a pencil, I discovered a most chilling and interesting message. I tried to get in touch with Robert Lonnigan, who was not to be found; and I tried to get in touch with old Bushyager who, it turned out, was dead—which only deepened my feeling of alarm. For there, printed between all the lines of Fleishman Bushyager's input, was a strange message."

There was a moment of silence and then, with a flourish, the stranger produced the very printout he had been speaking of, spreading it out before their eager eyes.

"I, Robert Bushyager," it read, "am here." And on the very last line, at the end of the printout, "And I, Fleishman Bushyager, with him." And under that, "Tell the other Robert his father forgives him."

"Capital!" cried Porutto, the stranger's sponsor, and there were cries of delight all around.

And, after another filling of glasses and stoking of the red-coaled fire, a vote was made, and a toast proposed and accepted, and another member of the Genial Hauntings Club welcomed.

Professors of American literature sometimes view The Turn of the Screw *as a departure from the mainstream of writing produced by* HENRY JAMES. *But the author of* Daisy Miller, The Ambassadors, The Golden Bowl, The American, *and other revered (though usually unread) milestones in U.S. literary history was preoccupied with the supernatural all his life. Born in New York in 1843, son of a philosopher of the same name, James was an admirer of Le Fanu, Poe, Wilkie Collins, and Hawthorne, and himself contributed quite a few ghost stories to the fiction of the day. The convoluted ambiguities of* The Turn of the Screw *with its ghostly Quint and Jessel, have, to my mind, been somewhat overrated, but I see no flaw at all in the following atmospheric tale that, despite its length, retains its hold on the reader in a way which, I am afraid, the Quint-Jessel haunting does not.*

The Ghostly Rental
by Henry James

I was in my twenty-second year, and I had just left college. I was at liberty to choose my career, and I chose it with much promptness. I afterward renounced it, in truth, with equal ardor, but I have never regretted those two youthful years of perplexed and excited, but also of agreeable and fruitful experiment. I had a taste for theology, and during my college term I had been an admiring reader of Dr. Channing. This was theology of a grateful and succulent savor; it seemed to offer one the rose of faith delightfully stripped of its thorns. And then (for I rather think this had something to do with it), I had taken a fancy to the old Divinity School. I have always had an eye to the back scene in the human drama, and it seemed to me that I might play my part with a fair chance of applause (from myself at least), in that detached and tranquil home of mild casuistry, with its respectable avenue on one side, and its prospect of green fields and contact with acres of woodland on the other. Cambridge, for the lovers of woods and fields, has changed for the worse since those days, and the precinct in question has forfeited much of its mingled pastoral and scholastic quietude. It was then a College-hall in the woods—a charming mixture. What it is now has nothing to do with my story; and I have no doubt that there are still doctrine-haunted young seniors who, as they stroll near it in the summer dusk, promise themselves, later, to taste of its fine leisurely quality. For myself, I was not disappointed. I established myself in a great square, low-browed room, with deep window-benches; I hung prints from Overbeck and Ary Scheffer on the walls; I arranged my books, with great refinement of classification, in the alcoves beside the high chimney-shelf, and I began to read Plotinus and St. Augustine. Among my companions were two or three men of ability and of good fellowship, with whom I occasionally brewed a fireside bowl; and with adventurous reading, deep discourse, potations conscientiously shallow, and long country walks, my initiation into the clerical mystery progressed agreeably enough.

With one of my comrades I formed an especial friendship, and we passed a great deal of time together. Unfortunately he had a chronic weakness of one of his knees, which compelled him to lead a very sedentary life, and as I was a methodical pedestrian, this made some difference in our habits. I used often to stretch away for my daily ramble, with no companion but the stick in my hand or the book in my pocket. But in the use of my legs and the sense of unstinted open air, I have always found company enough. I should, perhaps add that in the enjoyment of a very sharp pair of eyes, I found something of a social pleasure. My eyes and I were on excellent terms; they were indefatigable observers of all wayside incidents, and so long as they were amused I was contented. It is, indeed, owing to their inquisitive habits that I came into possession of this remarkable story.

Much of the country about the old college town is pretty now, but it was prettier thirty years ago. That multitudinous eruption of domiciliary pasteboard which now graces the landscape, in the direction of the low, blue Waltham Hills, had not yet taken place; there were no genteel cottages to put the shabby meadows and scrubby orchards to shame—a juxtaposition by which, in later years, neither element of the contrast has gained. Certain crooked crossroads, then, as I remember them, were more deeply and naturally rural, and the solitary dwellings on the long grassy slopes beside them, under the tall customary elm that curved its foliage in mid-air like the outward dropping ears of a girdled wheatsheaf, sat with their shingled hoods well pulled down on their ears, and no prescience whatever of the fashion of French roofs—weatherwrinkled old peasant women, as you might call them, quietly wearing the native coif, and never dreaming of mounting bonnets, and indecently exposing their venerable brows. That winter was what is called an "open" one; there was much cold, but little snow; the roads were firm and free, and I was rarely compelled by the weather to forego my exercise.

One gray December afternoon I had sought it in the direction of the adjacent town of Medford, and I was retracing my steps at an even pace, and watching the pale, cold tints—the transparent amber and faded rose-color—which curtained, in wintry fashion, the western sky, and reminded me of a sceptical smile on the lips of a beautiful woman. I came, as dusk was falling, to a narrow road which I had never traversed and which I imagined offered me a short cut homeward. I was about three miles away; I was late and would have been thankful to make them two.

I diverged, walked some ten minutes, and then perceived that the road had a very unfrequented air. The wheel-ruts looked old; the stillness seemed peculiarly sensible. And yet down the road stood a house, so it must in some degree have been a thoroughfare. On one side was a high, natural embankment, on the top of which was perched an apple-orchard, whose tangled boughs made a stretch of coarse black lacework, hung across the coldly rosy west. In a short time I came to the house, and I immediately found myself interested in it. I stopped in front of it gazing hard, I hardly knew why, but with a vague mixture of curiosity and timidity. It was a house like more of the houses thereabouts, except that it was decidedly a handsome specimen of its class. It stood on a grassy slope, it had its tall, impartially drooping elm beside it, and its old black-cover at its shoulder. But it was of very large proportions, and it had a striking look of solidity and stoutness of timber. It had lived to a good old age, too, for the woodwork on its doorway and under its eaves, carefully and abundantly carved, referred it to the middle, at the latest, of the last century.

All this had once been painted white, but the broad back of time, leaning against the doorposts for a hundred years, had laid bare the grain of the wood. Behind the house stretched an orchard of apple-trees, more gnarled and fantastic than usual, and wearing, in the deepening dusk, a blighted and exhausted aspect. All the windows of the house had rusty shutters, without slats, and these were closely drawn. There was no sign of life about it; it looked blank, bare and vacant, and yet, as I lingered near it, it seemed to have a familiar meaning—an audible eloquence. I have always thought of the impression made upon me at first sight, by that gray colonial dwelling, as a proof that induction may sometimes be near akin to divination; for after all, there was nothing on the face of the matter to warrant the very serious induction that I made.

I fell back and crossed the road. The last red light of the sunset disengaged itself, as it was about to vanish, and rested faintly for a moment on the time-silvered front of the old house. It touched, with perfect regularity, the series of small panes in the fan-shaped window above the door, and twinkled there fantastically. Then it died away, and left the place more intensely somber. At this moment, I said to myself with the accent of profound conviction—"The house is simply haunted!"

Somehow, immediately, I believed it, and so long as I was not shut up inside, the idea gave me pleasure. It was implied in the aspect of the house, and it explained it. Half an hour before, if I had been asked, I would have said, as befitted a young man who was explicitly cultivating cheerful views of the supernatural, that there were no such things as haunted houses. But the dwelling before me gave a vivid meaning to the empty words; it had been spiritually blighted.

The longer I looked at it, the intenser seemed the secret that it held. I walked all round it, I tried to peep here and there, through a crevice in the shutters, and I took a puerile satisfaction in laying my hand on the doorknob and gently turning it. If the door had yielded, would I have gone in?—would I have penetrated the dusky stillness? My audacity, fortunately, was not put to the test. The portal was admirably solid, and I was unable even to shake it.

At last I turned away, casting many looks behind me. I pursued my way, and, after a longer walk than I had bargained for, reached the high-road. At a certain distance below the point at which the long lane I have mentioned entered it, stood a comfortable, tidy dwelling, which might have offered itself as the model of the house which is in no sense haunted—which has no sinister secrets, and knows nothing but blooming prosperity. Its clean white paint stared placidly through the dusk, and its vine-covered porch had been dressed in straw for the winter. An old, one-horse chaise, freighted with two departing visitors, was leaving the door, and through the undraped windows, I saw the lamplit sitting-room, and the table spread with the early "tea," which had been improvised for the comfort of the guests. The mistress of the house had come to the gate with her friends; she lingered there after the chaise had wheeled creakingly away, half to watch them down the road, and half to give me, as I passed in the twilight, a questioning look. She was a comely, quick young woman, with a sharp, dark eye, and I ventured to stop and speak to her.

"That house down that side-road," I said, "about a mile from here—the only one—can you tell me whom it belongs to?"

She stared at me a moment, and, I thought, colored a little. "Our folks never go down that road," she said, briefly.

"But it's a short way to Medford," I answered.

She gave a little toss of her head. "Perhaps it would turn out a long way. At any rate, we don't use it."

This was interesting. A thrifty Yankee household must have good reasons for this scorn of time-saving processes. "But you know the house, at least?" I said.

"Well, I have seen it."

"And to whom does it belong?"

She gave a little laugh and looked away, as if she were aware that, to a stranger, her words might seem to savor of agricultural superstition. "I guess it belongs to them that are in it."

"But is there any one in it? It is completely closed."

"That makes no difference. They never come out, and no one ever goes in." And she turned away.

But I laid my hand on her arm, respectfully. "You mean," I said, "that the house is haunted?"

She drew herself away, colored, raised her fingers to her lips, and hurried into the house, where, in a moment, the curtains were dropped over the windows.

For several days, I thought repeatedly of this little adventure, but I took some satisfaction in keeping it to myself. If the house was not haunted, it was useless to expose my imaginative whims, and if it was, it was agreeable to drain the cup of horror without assistance. I determined, of course, to pass that way again; and a week later—it was the last day of the year—I retraced my steps. I approached the house from the opposite direction, and found myself before it at about the same hour as before. The light was failing, the sky low and gray; the wind wailed along the hard, bare ground, and made slow eddies of the frost-blackened leaves. The melancholy mansion stood there, seeming to gather the winter twilight around it, and mask itself in it, inscrutably. I hardly knew on what errand I had come, but I had a vague feeling that if this time the doorknob were to turn and the door to open, I should take my heart in my hands, and let them close behind me. Who were the mysterious tenants to whom the good woman at the corner had alluded? What had been seen or heard—what was related? The door was as stubborn as before, and my impertinent fumblings with the latch caused no upper window to be thrown open, nor any strange, pale face to be thrust out. I ventured even to raise the rusty knocker and give it half-a-dozen raps, but they made a flat, dead sound, and aroused no echo.

Familiarity breeds contempt; I don't know what I should have done next, if, in the distance, up the road (the same one I had followed), I had not seen a solitary figure advancing. I was unwilling to be observed hanging about this ill-famed dwelling, and I sought refuge among the dense shadows of a grove of pines near by, where I might peep forth, and yet remain invisible. Presently, the newcomer drew near, and I perceived that he was making straight for the house. He was a little, old man, the most striking feature of whose appearance was a voluminous cloak, of a sort of military cut. He carried a walking-stick, and advanced in a slow, painful, somewhat hobbling fashion, but with an air of extreme resolution. He turned off from the road, and followed the vague wheel-track, and within a few yards of the house he paused. He looked up at it, fixedly and searchingly, as if he were counting the windows, or noting certain familiar marks. Then he took off his hat, and bent over slowly and solemnly, as if he were performing an obeisance.

As he stood uncovered, I had a good look at him. He was, as I have said, a diminutive old man, but it would have been hard to decide whether he belonged to this world or to the other. His head reminded me, vaguely, of the portraits of Andrew Jackson. He had a crop of grizzled hair, as stiff as a brush, a lean, pale, smooth-shaven face, and an eye of intense brilliancy, surmounted with thick brows, which had remained perfectly black. His face, as well as his cloak, seemed to belong to an old soldier; he looked like a retired military man of a modest rank; but he struck me as exceeding the classic privilege of even such a personage to be eccentric and grotesque. When he had finished his salute, he advanced to the door, fumbled in the folds of his cloak, which hung down much further in front than behind, and produced a key. This he slowly and carefully inserted into the lock, and then, apparently, he turned it. But the door did not immediately open; first he bent his head, turned his ear, and stood listening, and then he looked up and down the road. Satisfied or reassured, he applied his aged shoulder to one of the deep-set panels, and pressed a moment. The door yielded—opening into perfect darkness. He stopped again on the threshold, and again removed his hat and made his bow. Then he went in, and carefully closed the door behind him.

Who in the world was he, and what was his errand? He might have been a figure out of one of Hoffmann's tales. Was he vision or a reality —an inmate of the house, or a familiar, friendly visitor? What had been the meaning, in either case, of his mystic genuflexions, and how did he propose to proceed, in that inner darkness? I emerged from my retirement, and observed narrowly, several of the windows. In each of them, at an interval, a ray of light became visible in the chink between the two leaves of the shutters. Evidently, he was lighting up; was he going to give a party—a ghostly revel? My curiosity grew intense, but I was quite at a loss how to satisfy it. For a moment I thought of rapping peremptorily at the door; but I dismissed this idea as unmannerly, and calculated to break the spell, if spell there was. I walked round the house and tried, without violence, to open one of the lower windows. It resisted, but I had better fortune; in a moment, with another. There was a risk, certainly, in the trick I was playing—a risk of being seen from within, or (worse) seeing, myself, something that I should repent of seeing. But curiosity, as I say, had become an inspiration, and the risk was highly agreeable.

Through the parting of the shutters I looked into a lighted room—a room lighted by two candles in old brass flambeaux, placed upon the mantel-shelf. It was apparently a sort of back parlor, and it had retained all its furniture. This was of a homely, old-fashioned pattern, and consisted of hair-cloth chairs and sofas, spare mahogany tables, and framed samplers hung upon the walls. But although the room was furnished, it had a strangely uninhabited look; the tables and chairs were in rigid positions, and no small familiar objects were visible. I could not see everything, and I could only guess at the existence, on my right, of a large folding-door. It was apparently open, and the light of the neighboring room passed through it. I waited for some time, but the room remained empty. At last I became conscious that a large shadow was projected upon the wall opposite the folding-door—the shadow, evidently, of a figure in the adjoining room. It was tall and grotesque, and seemed to represent a person sitting perfectly motionless, in profile. I thought I recognized the perpendicular bristles and far-arching nose of my little old man. There was a strange fixedness in his posture; he appeared to be seated, and looking intently at something. I watched the shadow a long time, but it never stirred.

At last, however, just as my patience began to ebb, it moved slowly, rose to the ceiling, and became indistinct. I don't know what I should have seen next, but by an irresistible impulse, I closed the shutter. Was it delicacy?—was it pusillanimity? I can hardly say. I lingered, nevertheless, near the house, hoping that my friend would reappear. I was not disappointed; for he at last emerged, looking just as when he had gone in, and taking his leave in the same ceremonious fashion. (The lights, I had already observed, had disappeared from the crevice of each of the windows.) He faced about before the door, took off his hat, and made an obsequious bow. As he turned away I had a hundred minds to speak to him, but I let him depart in peace. This, I may say, was pure delicacy—you will answer, perhaps that it came too late. It seemed to me that he had a right to resent my observation; though my own right to exercise it (if ghosts were in the question) struck me as equally positive. I continued to watch him as he hobbled softly down the bank, and along the lonely road. Then I musingly retreated in the opposite direction. I was tempted to follow him, at a distance, to see what became of him; but this, too, seemed indelicate; and I confess, moreover, that I felt the inclination to coquet a little, as it were, with my discovery—to pull apart the petals of the flower one by one.

I continued to smell the flower from time to time, for its oddity of perfume had fascinated me. I passed by the house on the cross-road again, but never encountered the old man in the cloak, or any other wayfarer. It seemed to keep observers at a distance, and I was careful not to gossip about it: one inquirer, I said to myself, may edge his way into the secret, but there is no room for two. At the same time, of course, I would have been thankful for any chance sidelight that might fall across the matter—though I could not well see whence it was to come. I hoped to meet the old man in the cloak elsewhere, but as the days passed by without his reappearing, I ceased to expect it. And yet I reflected that he probably lived in that neighborhood, inasmuch as he had made his pilgrimage to the vacant house on foot. If he had come from a distance, he would have been sure to arrive in some old deep-hooded gig with yellow wheels—a vehicle as venerably grotesque as himself.

One day I took a stroll in Mount Auburn cemetery—an institution at that period in its infancy, and full of a sylvan charm which it has now completely forfeited. It contained more maple and birch than willow and cypress, and the sleepers had ample elbow room. It was not a city of the dead, but at the most a village, and a meditative pedestrian might stroll there without too importunate reminder of the grotesque side of our claims to posthumous consideration. I had come out to enjoy the first foretaste of Spring—one of those mild days of late winter, when the torpid earth seems to draw the first long breath that marks the rupture of the spell of sleep. The sun was veiled in haze, and yet warm, and the frost was oozing from its deepest lurking-places. I had been treading for half an hour the winding ways of the cemetery, when suddenly I perceived a familiar figure seated on a bench against a southward-facing evergreen hedge.

I call the figure familiar, because I had seen it often in memory and in fancy; in fact, I had beheld it but once. Its back was turned to me, but it wore a voluminous cloak, which there was no mistaking. Here, at last, was my fellow-visitor at the haunted house, and here was my chance, if I wished to approach him! I made a circuit, and came toward him from in front. He saw me, at the end of the alley, and sat motionless, with his hands on the head of his stick, watching me from under his black eyebrows as I drew near. At a distance these black eyebrows looked formidable; they were the only thing I saw in his face. But on a closer view I was reassured, simply because I immediately felt that no man could really be as fantastically fierce as this poor old gentleman looked. His face was a kind of caricature of martial truculence. I stopped in front of him, and respectfully asked leave to sit and rest upon his bench. He granted it with a silent gesture, of much dignity, and I placed myself beside him. In this position I was able, covertly, to observe him. He was quite as much an oddity in the morning sunshine, as he had been in the dubious twilight. The lines in his face were as rigid as if they had been hacked out of a block by a clumsy woodcarver. His eyes were flamboyant, his nose terrific, his mouth implacable. And yet, after a while, when he slowly turned and looked at me, fixedly, I perceived that in spite of this portentous mask, he was a very mild old man. I was sure he even would have been glad to smile, but, evidently, his facial muscles were too stiff—they had taken a different fold, once for all. I wondered whether he was demented, but I dismissed the idea; the fixed glitter in his eye was not that of insanity. What his face really expressed was deep and simple sadness; his heart perhaps was broken, but his brain was intact. His dress was shabby but neat, and his old blue cloak had known half a century's brushing.

I hastened to make some observation upon the exceptional softness of the day, and he answered me in a gentle, mellow voice, which it was almost startling to hear proceed from such bellicose lips.

"This is a very comfortable place," he presently added.

"I am fond of walking in graveyards," I rejoined deliberately; flattering myself that I had struck a vein that might lead to something.

I was encouraged; he turned and fixed me with his duskily glowing eyes. Then very gravely—"Walking, yes. Take all your exercise now. Some day you will have to settle down in a graveyard in a fixed position."

"Very true," said I. "But you know there are some people who are said to take exercise even after that day."

He had been looking at me still; at this he looked away.

"You don't understand?" I said, gently.

He continued to gaze straight before him.

"Some people, you know, walk about after death," I went on.

At last he turned, and looked at me more portentously than ever. "You don't believe that," he said simply.

"How do you know I don't?"

"Because you are young and foolish." This was said without acerbity —even kindly; but in the tone of an old man whose consciousness of his own heavy experience made everything else seem light.

"I am certainly young," I answered; "but I don't think that, on the whole, I am foolish. But say I don't believe in ghosts—most people would be on my side."

"Most people are fools!" said the old man.

I let the question rest, and talked of other things. My companion seemed on his guard, he eyed me defiantly, and made brief answers to my remarks; but I nevertheless gathered an impression that our meeting was an agreeable thing to him, and even a social incident of some importance. He was evidently a lonely creature, and his opportunities for gossip were rare. He had had troubles, and they had detached him from the world, and driven him back upon himself; but the social chord in his antiquated soul was not entirely broken, and I was sure he was gratified to find that it could still feebly resound. At last, he began to ask questions himself; he inquired whether I was a student.

"I am a student of divinity," I answered.

"Of divinity?"

"Of theology. I am studying for the ministry."

At this he eyed me with peculiar intensity—after which his gaze wandered away again. "There are certain things you ought to know, then," he said at last.

"I have a great desire for knowledge," I answered. "What things do you mean?"

He looked at me again awhile, but without heeding my question. "I like your appearance," he said. "You seem to me a sober lad."

"Oh, I am perfectly sober!" I exclaimed—yet departing for a moment from my soberness.

"I think you are fair-minded," he went on.

"I don't any longer strike you as foolish, then?" I asked.

"I stick to what I said about people who deny the power of departed spirits to return. They *are* fools!" And he rapped fiercely with his staff on the earth.

I hesitated a moment, and then, abruptly, "You have seen a ghost!" I said.

He appeared not at all startled.

"You are right, sir!" he answered with great dignity. "With me it's not a matter of cold theory—I have not had to pry into old books to learn what to believe. *I know!* With these eyes I have beheld the departed spirit standing before me as near as you are!" And his eyes, as he spoke, certainly looked as if they had rested upon strange things.

I was irresistibly impressed—I was touched with credulity.

"And was it very terrible?" I asked.

"I am an old soldier—I am not afraid!"

"When was it?—where was it?" I asked.

He looked at me mistrustfully, and I saw that I was going too fast.

"Excuse me from going into particulars," he said. "I am not at liberty to speak more fully. I have told you so much, because I cannot bear to hear this subject spoken of lightly. Remember in future, that you have seen a very honest old man who told you—on his honor—that he had seen a ghost!" And he got up, as if he thought he had said enough. Reserve, shyness, pride, the fear of being laughed at, the memory, possibly, of former strokes of sarcasm—all this, on one side, had its weight with him; but I suspected that on the other, his tongue was loosened by the garrulity of old age, the sense of solitude, and the need of sympathy—and perhaps, also, by the friendliness which he had been so good as to express toward myself. Evidently it would be unwise to press him, but I hoped to see him again.

"To give greater weight to my words," he added, "let me mention my name—Captain Diamond, sir. I have seen service."

"I hope I may have the pleasure of meeting you again," I said.

"The same to you, sir!" And brandishing his stick portentously—though with the friendliest intentions—he marched stiffly away.

I asked two or three persons—selected with discretion—whether they knew anything about Captain Diamond, but they were quite unable to enlighten me. At last, suddenly, I smote my forehead, and dubbing myself a dolt, remembered that I was neglecting a source of information to which I had never applied in vain. The excellent person at whose table I had habitually dined, and who dispensed hospitality to students at so much a week, had a sister as good as herself, and of conversational power more varied. The sister, who was known as Miss Deborah, was an old maid in all the force of the term. She was deformed, and she never went out of the house; she sat all day at the window, between a bird-cage and a flower-pot, stitching small linen articles—mysterious bands and frills. She wielded, I was assured, an exquisite needle, and her work was highly prized. In spite of her deformity and her confinement, she had a little, fresh, round face, and an imperturbable serenity of spirit. She had also a very quick little wit of her own, she was extremely observant, and she had a high relish for a friendly chat. Nothing pleased her so much as to have you—especially, I think, if you were a young divinity student—move your chair near her sunny window, and settle yourself for twenty minutes' "talk."

"Well, sir," she used always to say, "what is the latest monstrosity in Biblical criticism?"—for she used to pretend to be horrified at the rationalistic tendency of the age. But she was an inexorable little philosopher, and I am convinced that she was a keener rationalist than any of us, and that, if she had chosen, she could have propounded questions that would have made the boldest of us wince. Her window commanded the whole town—or rather, the whole country. Knowledge came to her as she sat singing, with her little, cracked voice, in her low rocking chair. She was the first to learn everything, and the last to forget it. She had the town gossip at her fingers' ends, and she knew everything about people she had never seen. When I asked her how she had acquired her learning, she said simply—"Oh, I observe!"

"Observe closely enough," she once said, "and it doesn't matter where you are. You may be in a pitch-dark closet. All you want is something to start with; one thing leads to another, and all things are mixed up. Shut me up in a dark closet and I will observe after a while, that some places in it are darker than others. After that (give me time), and I will tell you what the President of the United States is going to have for dinner." Once I paid her a compliment. "Your observation," I said, "is as fine as your needle, and your statements are as true as your stitches."

Of course Miss Deborah had heard of Captain Diamond. He had been much talked about many years before, but he had survived the scandal that attached to his name.

"What was the scandal?" I asked.

"He killed his daughter."

"Killed her?" I cried; "How so?"

"Oh, not with a pistol, or a dagger, or a dose of arsenic! With his tongue. Talk of women's tongues! He cursed her—with some horrible oath—and she died!"

"What had she done?"

"She had received a visit from a young man who loved her, and whom he had forbidden the house."

"The house," I said—"ah yes! The house is out in the country, two or three miles from here, on a lonely cross-road."

Miss Deborah looked sharply at me, as she bit her thread.

"Ah, you know about the house?" she said.

"A little," I answered; "I have seen it. But I want you to tell me more."

But here Miss Deborah betrayed an incommunicativeness which was most unusual.

"You wouldn't call me superstitious, would you?" she asked.

"You?—you are the quintessence of pure reason."

"Well, every thread has its rotten place, and every needle its grain of rust. I would rather not talk about that house."

"You have no idea how you excite my curiosity!" I said.

"I can feel for you. But it would make me very nervous."

"What harm can come to you?" I asked.

"Some harm came to a friend of mine." And Miss Deborah gave a very positive nod.

"What had your friend done?"

"She had told me Captain Diamond's secret, which he had told her with a mighty mystery. She had been an old flame of his, and he took her into his confidence. He bade her tell no one, and assured her that if she did, something dreadful would happen to her."

"And what happened to her?"

"She died."

"Oh, we are all mortal!" I said. "Had she given him a promise?"

"She had not taken it seriously, she had not believed him. She repeated the story to me, and three days afterward, she was taken with inflammation of the lungs. A month afterward, here where I sit now, I was stitching her grave-clothes. Since then, I have never mentioned what she told me."

"Was it very strange?"

"It was strange, but it was ridiculous too. It is a thing to make you shudder and to make you laugh, both. But you can't worry it out of me. I am sure that if I were to tell you, I should immediately break a needle in my finger, and die the next week of lockjaw."

I retired, and urged Miss Deborah no further; but every two or three days, after dinner, I came and sat down by her rocking chair. I made no further allusion to Captain Diamond; I sat silent, clipping tape with her scissors. At last, one day, she told me I was looking poorly. I was pale.

"I am dying of curiosity," I said. "I have lost my appetite. I have eaten no dinner."

"Remember Blue Beard's wife!" said Miss Deborah.

"One may as well perish by the sword as by famine!" I answered.

Still she said nothing, and at last I rose with a melodramatic sigh and departed. As I reached the door she called me and pointed to the chair I had vacated. "I never was hardhearted," she said. "Sit down, and if we are to perish, may we at least perish together."

And then, in very few words, she communicated what she knew of Captain Diamond's secret. "He was a very high-tempered old man, and though he was very fond of his daughter, his will was law. He had picked out a husband for her, and given her due notice. Her mother was dead, and they lived alone together. The house had been Mrs. Diamond's own marriage portion; the Captain, I believe, hadn't a penny.

After his marriage they had come to live there, and he had begun to work the farm. The poor girl's lover was a young man with whiskers from Boston. The Captain came in one evening and found them together; he collared the young man, and hurled a terrible curse at the poor girl. The young man cried that she was his wife, and he asked her if it was true. She said, 'No!' Thereupon Captain Diamond, his fury growing fiercer, repeated his imprecation, ordered her out of the house, and disowned her forever. She swooned away, but her father went raging off and left her. Several hours later, he came back and found the house empty. On the table was a note from the young man telling him that he had killed his daughter, repeating the assurance that she was his own wife, and declaring that he himself claimed the sole right to commit her remains to earth. He had carried the body away in a gig! Captain Diamond wrote him a dreadful note in answer, saying that he didn't believe his daughter was dead, but that, whether or no, she was dead to him.

"A week later, in the middle of the night, he saw her ghost. Then, I suppose, he was convinced. The ghost reappeared several times, and finally began regularly to haunt the house. It made the old man very uncomfortable, for little by little his passion had passed away, and he was given up to grief. He determined at last to leave the place, and tried to sell it or rent it; but meanwhile the story had gone abroad, the ghost had been seen by other persons, the house had a bad name, and it was impossible to dispose of it. With the farm, it was the old man's only property, and his only means of subsistence; if he could neither live in it nor rent it he was beggared. But the ghost had no mercy, as he had had none. He struggled for six months, and at last he broke down. He put on his old blue cloak and took up his staff, and prepared to wander away and beg his bread. Then the ghost relented, and proposed a compromise. 'Leave the house to me!' it said; 'I have marked it for my own. Go off and live elsewhere. But to enable you to live, I will be your tenant, since you can find no other. I will hire the house of you and pay you a certain rent.' And the ghost named a sum. The old man consented, and he goes every quarter to collect his rent!"

I laughed at this recital, but I confess I shuddered too, for my own observation had exactly confirmed it. Had I not been witness of one of the Captain's quarterly visits, had I not all but seen him sit watching his spectral tenant count out the rent money, and when he trudged away in the dark, had he not a little bag of strangely gotten coin hidden in the folds of his old blue cloak? I imparted none of these reflections to Miss Deborah, for I was determined that my observations should have a sequel, and I promised myself the pleasure of treating her to my story in its full maturity. "Captain Diamond," I asked, "has no other known means of subsistence?"

"None whatever. He toils not, neither does he spin—his ghost supports him. A haunted house is valuable property!"

"And in what coin does the ghost pay?"

"In good American gold and silver. It has only this peculiarity—that the pieces are all dated before the young girl's death. It's a strange mixture of matter and spirit!"

"And does the ghost do things handsomely; is the rent large?"

"The old man, I believe, lives decently, and has his pipe and his glass. He took a little house down by the river; the door is sidewise to the street, and there is a little garden before it. There he spends his days, and has an old colored woman to do for him. Some years ago, he used to wander about a good deal, he was a familiar figure in the town, and most people knew his legend. But of late he has drawn back into his shell; he sits over his fire, and curiosity has forgotten him. I suppose he is falling into his dotage. But I am sure, I trust," said Miss Deborah in conclusion, "that he won't outlive his faculties or his powers of locomotion, for, if I remember rightly, it was part of the bargain that he should come in person to collect his rent."

We neither of us seemed likely to suffer any especial penalty for Miss Deborah's indiscretion; I found her, day after day, singing over her work, neither more nor less active than usual. For myself, I boldly pursued my observations. I went again, more than once, to the graveyard, but I was disappointed in my hope of finding Captain Diamond there. I had a prospect, however, which afforded me compensation. I shrewdly inferred that the old man's quarterly pilgrimages were made upon the last day of the old quarter. My first sight of him had been on the 31st of December, and it was probable that he would return to his haunted home on the last day of March. This was near at hand; at last it arrived. I betook myself late in the afternoon to the old house on the cross-road, supposing that the hour of twilight was the appointed season. I was not wrong. I had been hovering about for a short time, feeling very much like a restless ghost myself, when he appeared in the same manner as before, and wearing the same costume. I again concealed myself, and saw him enter the house with the ceremonial which he had used on the former occasion. A light appeared successively in the crevice of each pair of shutters, and I opened the window which had yielded to my importunity before. Again I saw the great shadow on the wall, motionless and solemn. But I saw nothing else. The old man reappeared at last, made his fantastic salaam before the old house, and crept away into the dusk.

One day, more than a month after this, I met him again at Mount Auburn. The air was full of the voice of spring; the birds had come back and were twittering over their winter's travels, and a mild west wind was making a thin murmur in the raw verdure. He was seated on a bench in the sun, still muffled in his enormous mantle, and he recognized me as soon as I approached him. He nodded at me as if he were an old Bashaw giving the signal for my decapitation, but it was apparent that he was pleased to see me.

"I have looked for you here more than once," I said. "You don't come often."

"What did you want of me?" he asked.

"I wanted to enjoy your conversation. I did so greatly when I met you here before."

"You found me amusing?"

"Interesting!" I said.

"You didn't think me cracked?"

"Cracked?—My dear sir—!" I protested.

"I'm the sanest man in the country. I know that is what insane people always say; but generally they can't prove it. I can!"

"I believe it," I said. "But I am curious to know how such a thing can be proved."

He was silent awhile.

"I will tell you. I once committed, unintentionally, a great crime. Now I pay the penalty. I give up my life to it. I don't shirk it; I face it squarely, knowing perfectly what it is. I haven't tried to bluff it off; I haven't begged off from it; I haven't run away from it. The penalty is terrible, but I have accepted it. I have been a philosopher!

"If I were a Catholic, I might have turned monk, and spent the rest of my life in fasting and praying. That is no penalty; that is an evasion. I might have blown my brains out—I might have gone mad. I wouldn't do either. I would simply face the music, take the consequences. As I say, they are awful! I take them on certain days, four times a year. So it has been these twenty years; so it will be as long as I last. It's my business; it's my avocation. That's the way I feel about it. I call that reasonable!"

"Admirably so!" I said. "But you fill me with curiosity and with compassion."

"Especially with curiosity," he said, cunningly.

"Why," I answered, "if I know exactly what you suffer I can pity you more."

"I'm much obliged. I don't want your pity; it won't help me. I'll tell you something, but it's not for myself; it's for your own sake." He paused a long time and looked all round him, as if for chance eavesdroppers. I anxiously awaited his revelation, but he disappointed me. "Are you still studying theology?" he asked.

"Oh, yes," I answered, perhaps with a shade of irritation. "It's a thing one can't learn in six months."

"I should think not, so long as you have nothing but your books. Do you know the proverb, 'A grain of experience is worth a pound of precept'? I'm a great theologian."

"Ah, you have had experience," I murmured sympathetically.

"You have read about the immortality of the soul; you have seen Jonathan Edwards and Dr. Hopkins chopping logic over it, and deciding, by chapter and verse, that it is true. But I have seen it with these eyes; I have touched it with these hands!" And the old man held up his rugged old fists and shook them portentously. "That's better!" he went on; "but I have bought it dearly. You had better take it from the books —evidently you always will. You are a very good young man; you will never have a crime on your conscience."

I answered with some juvenile fatuity, that I certainly hoped I had my share of human passions, good young man and prospective Doctor of Divinity as I was.

"Ah, but you have a nice, quiet little temper," he said. "So have I—now! But once I was very brutal—very brutal. You ought to know that such things are. I killed my own child."

"Your own child?"

"I struck her down to the earth and left her to die. They could not hang me, for it was not with my hand I struck her. It was with foul and damnable words. That makes a difference; it's a grand law we live under! Well, sir, I can answer for it that *her* soul is immortal. We have an appointment to meet four times a year, and then I catch it!"

"She has never forgiven you?"

"She has forgiven me as the angels forgive! That's what I can't stand —the soft, quiet way she looks at me. I'd rather she twisted a knife about in my heart—O Lord, Lord, Lord!" and Captain Diamond bowed his head over his stick, and leaned his forehead on his crossed hands.

I was impressed and moved, and his attitude seemed for the moment a check to further questions. Before I ventured to ask him anything more, he slowly rose and pulled his old cloak around him. He was unused to talking about his troubles, and his memories overwhelmed him. "I must go my way," he said; "I must be creeping along."

"I shall perhaps meet you here again," I said.

"Oh, I'm a stiff-jointed old fellow," he answered, "and this is rather far for me to come. I have to reserve myself. I have sat sometimes a month at a time smoking my pipe in my chair. But I should like to see you again." And he stopped and looked at me, terribly and kindly. "Some day, perhaps, I shall be glad to be able to lay my hand on a young, unperverted soul. If a man can make a friend, it is always something gained. What is your name?"

I had in my pocket a small volume of Pascal's *Thoughts,* on the flyleaf of which were written my name and address. I took it out and offered it to my old friend. "Pray keep this little book," I said. "It is one I am very fond of, and it will tell you something about me."

He took it and turned it over slowly, then looking up at me with a scowl of gratitude, "I'm not much of a reader," he said; "but I won't refuse the first present I shall have received since—my troubles; and the last. Thank you, sir!" And with the little book in his hand he took his departure.

I was left to imagine him for some weeks after that sitting solitary in his armchair with his pipe. I had not another glimpse of him. But I was awaiting my chance, and on the last day of June, another quarter having elapsed, I deemed that it had come. The evening dusk in June falls late, and I was impatient for its coming. At last, toward the end of a lovely summer's day, I revisited Captain Diamond's property. Everything now was green around it save the blighted orchard in its rear, but its own immitigable grayness and sadness were as striking as when I had first beheld it beneath a December sky. As I drew near it, I saw that I was late for my purpose, for my purpose had simply been to step forward on Captain Diamond's arrival, and bravely ask him to let me go in with him. He had preceded me, and there were lights already in the windows. I was unwilling, of course, to disturb him during his ghostly interview, and I waited till he came forth. The lights disappeared in the course of time; then the door opened and Captain Diamond stole out. That evening he made no bow to the haunted house, for the first object he beheld was his fair-minded young friend planted, modestly but firmly, near the doorstep. He stopped short, looking at me, and this time his terrible scowl was in keeping with the situation.

"I knew you were here," I said. "I came on purpose."

He seemed dismayed, and looked round at the house uneasily.

"I beg your pardon if I have ventured too far," I added, "but you know you have encouraged me."

"How did you know I was here?"

"I reasoned it out. You told me half your story, and I guessed the other half. I am a great observer, and I had noticed this house in passing. It seemed to me to have a mystery. When you kindly confided to me that you saw spirits, I was sure that it could only be here that you saw them."

"You are mighty clever," cried the old man. "And what brought you here this evening?"

I was obliged to evade this question.

"Oh, I often come; I like to look at the house—it fascinates me."

He turned and looked up at it himself. "It's nothing to look at outside." He was evidently quite unaware of its peculiar outward appearance, and this odd fact, communicated to me thus in the twilight, and under the very brow of the sinister dwelling, seemed to make his vision of the strange things within more real.

"I have been hoping," I said, "for a chance to see the inside. I thought I might find you here and that you would let me go in with you. I should like to see what you see."

He seemed confounded by my boldness, but not altogether displeased. He laid his hand on my arm. "Do you know what I see?" he asked.

"How can I know, except as you said the other day, by experience? I want to have the experience. Pray, open the door and take me in."

Captain Diamond's brilliant eyes expanded beneath their dusky brows, and after holding his breath a moment, he indulged in the first and last apology for a laugh by which I was to see his solemn visage contorted. It was profoundly grotesque, but it was perfectly noiseless. "Take you in?" he softly growled. "I wouldn't go in again before my time's up for a thousand times that sum." And he thrust out his hand from the folds of his cloak and exhibited a small agglomeration of coins knotted into the corner of an old silk pocket-handkerchief. "I stick to my bargain no less, but no more!"

"But you told me the first time I had the pleasure of talking with you that it was not so terrible."

"I don't say it's terrible—now. But it's damned disagreeable!"

This adjective was uttered with a force that made me hesitate and reflect. While I did so, I thought I heard a slight movement of one of the window-shutters above us. I looked up, but everything seemed motionless. Captain Diamond, too, had been thinking; suddenly he turned toward the house. "If you will go in alone," he said, "you are welcome."

"Will you wait for me here?"

"Yes, you will not stop long."

"But the house is pitch dark. When you go you have lights."

He thrust his hand into the depths of his cloak and produced some matches. "Take these," he said. "You will find two candlesticks with candles on the table in the hall. Light them, take one in each hand and go ahead."

"Where shall I go?"

"Anywhere—everywhere. You can trust the ghost to find you."

I will not pretend to deny that by this time my heart was beating. And yet I imagine I motioned the old man with a sufficiently dignified gesture to open the door. I had made up my mind that there was in fact a ghost. I had conceded the premise. Only I had assured myself that once the mind was prepared, and the thing was not a surprise, it was possible to keep cool. Captain Diamond turned the lock, flung open the door, and bowed low to me as I passed in. I stood in the darkness, and heard the door close behind me. For some moments, I stirred neither finger nor toe; I stared bravely into the impenetrable dusk. But I saw nothing and heard nothing, and at last I struck a match. On the table were two old brass candlesticks rusty from disuse. I lighted the candles and began my tour of exploration.

A wide staircase rose in front of me, guarded by an antique balustrade of that rigidly delicate carving which is found so often in old New England houses. I postponed ascending it, and turned into the room on my right. This was an old-fashioned parlor, meagerly furnished, and musty with the absence of human life. I raised my two lights aloft and saw nothing but its empty chairs and its blank walls. Behind it was the room into which I had peeped from without, and which, in fact, communicated with it, as I had supposed, by folding doors. Here, too, I found myself confronted by no menacing specter. I crossed the hall again, and visited the rooms on the other side; a dining room in front, where I might have written my name with my finger in the deep dust of the great square table; a kitchen behind with its pots and pans eternally cold. All this was hard and grim, but it was not formidable. I came back into the hall, and walked to the foot of the staircase, holding up my candles; to ascend required a fresh effort, and I was scanning the gloom above. Suddenly, with an inexpressible sensation, I became aware that this gloom was animated; it seemed to move and gather itself together.

Slowly—I say slowly, for to my tense expectancy the instants appeared ages—it took the shape of a large, definite figure, and this figure advanced and stood at the top of the stairs. I frankly confess that by this time I was conscious of a feeling to which I am in duty bound to apply the vulgar name of fear. I may poetize it and call it Dread, with a capital letter; it was at any rate the feeling that makes a man yield ground. I measured it as it grew, and it seemed perfectly irresistible; for it did not appear to come from within but from without, and to be embodied in the dark image at the head of the staircase. After a fashion I reasoned—I remember reasoning. I said to myself, "I had always thought ghosts were white and transparent; this is a thing of thick shadows, densely opaque." I reminded myself that the occasion was momentous, and that if fear were to overcome me I should gather all possible impressions while my wits remained. I stepped back, foot behind foot, with my eyes still on the figure and placed my candles on the table. I was perfectly conscious that the proper thing was to ascend the stairs resolutely, face to face with the image, but the soles of my shoes seemed suddenly to have been transformed into leaden weights. I had got what I wanted; I was seeing the ghost. I tried to look at the figure distinctly so that I could remember it, and fairly claim, afterward, not to have lost my self-possession. I even asked myself how long it was expected I should stand looking, and how soon I could honorably retire.

All this, of course, passed through my mind with extreme rapidity, and it was checked by a further movement on the part of the figure. Two white hands appeared in the dark perpendicular mass, and were slowly raised to what seemed to be the level of the head. Here they were pressed together, over the region of the face, and then they were removed, and the face was disclosed. It was dim, white, strange, in every way ghostly. It looked down at me for an instant, after which one of the hands was raised again, slowly, and waved to and fro before it. There was something very singular in this gesture; it seemed to denote resentment and dismissal, and yet it had a sort of trivial, familiar motion. Familiarity on the part of the haunting Presence had not entered into my calculations, and did not strike me pleasantly. I agreed with Captain Diamond that it was "damned disagreeable." I was pervaded by an intense desire to make an orderly, and, if possible, a graceful retreat. I wished to do it gallantly, and it seemed to me that it would be gallant to blow out my candles. I turned and did so, punctiliously, and then I made my way to the door, groped a moment and opened it. The outer light, almost extinct as it was, entered for a moment, played over the dusty depths of the house and showed me the solid shadow.

Standing on the grass, bent over his stick, under the early glimmering stars, I found Captain Diamond. He looked up at me fixedly for a moment, but asked no questions, and then he went and locked the door. This duty performed, he discharged the other—made his obeisance like the priest before the altar—and then without heeding me further, took his departure.

A few days later, I suspended my studies and went off for the summer's vacation. I was absent for several weeks, during which I had plenty of leisure to analyze my impressions of the supernatural. I took some satisfaction in the reflection that I had not been ignobly terrified; I had not bolted nor swooned—I had proceeded with dignity. Nevertheless, I was certainly more comfortable when I had put thirty miles between me and the scene of my exploit, and I continued for many days to prefer the daylight to the dark. My nerves had been powerfully excited; of this I was particularly conscious when, under the influence of the drowsy air of the seaside, my excitement began slowly to ebb. As it disappeared, I attempted to take a sternly rational view of my experience. Certainly I had seen *something*—that was not fancy; but what had I seen? I regretted extremely now that I had not been bolder, that I had not gone nearer and inspected the apparition more minutely. But it was very well to talk; I had done as much as any man in the circumstances would have dared; it was indeed a physical impossibility that I should have advanced. Was not this paralyzation of my powers in itself a supernatural influence? Not necessarily, perhaps, for a sham ghost that one accepted might do as much execution as a real ghost. But why had I so easily accepted the sable phantom that waved its hand? Why had it so impressed itself? Unquestionably, true or false, it was a very clever phantom. I greatly preferred that it should have been true—in the first place because I did not care to have shivered and shaken for nothing, and in the second place because to have seen a well-authenticated goblin is, as things go, a feather in a quiet man's cap. I tried, therefore, to let my vision rest and to stop turning it over. But an impulse stronger than my will recurred at intervals and set a mocking question on my lips. Granted that the apparition was Captain Diamond's daughter; if it was she, it certainly was her spirit. But was it not her spirit and something more?

The middle of September saw me again established among the theologic shades, but I made no haste to revisit the haunted house.

The last of the month approached—the term of another quarter with poor Captain Diamond—and found me indisposed to disturb his pilgrimage on this occasion; though I confess that I thought with a good deal of compassion of the feeble old man trudging away, lonely, in the autumn dusk, on his extraordinary errand. On the thirtieth of September, at noonday, I was drowsing over a heavy octavo, when I heard a feeble rap at my door. I replied with an invitation to enter, but as this produced no effect I repaired to the door and opened it. Before me stood an elderly Negress with her head bound in a scarlet turban, and a white handkerchief folded across her bosom. She looked at me intently and in silence; she had that air of supreme gravity and decency which aged persons of her race so often wear. I stood interrogative, and at last, drawing her hand from her ample pocket, she held up a little book. It was the copy of Pascal's *Thoughts* that I had given to Captain Diamond.

"Please, sir," she said, very mildly, "do you know this book?"

"Perfectly," said I, "my name is on the flyleaf."

"It is your name—no other?"

"I will write my name if you like, and you can compare them," I answered.

She was silent a moment and then, with dignity—"It would be useless, sir," she said, "I can't read. If you will give me your word, that is enough. I come," she went on, "from the gentleman to whom you gave the book. He told me to carry it as a token—a token—that is what he called it. He is right down sick, and he wants to see you."

"Captain Diamond—sick?" I cried. "Is his illness serious?"

"He is very bad—he is all gone."

I expressed my regret and sympathy, and offered to go to him immediately, if his sable messenger would show me the way. She assented deferentially, and in a few moments I was following her along the sunny streets, feeling very much like a personage in the Arabian Nights, led to a postern gate by an Ethiopian slave. My own conductress directed her steps toward the river and stopped at a decent little yellow house in one of the streets that descend to it. She quickly opened the door and let me in, and I very soon found myself in the presence of my old friend. He was in bed, in a darkened room, and evidently in a very feeble state. He lay back on his pillow staring before him, with his bristling hair more erect than ever, and his intensely dark and bright old eyes touched with the glitter of fever. His apartment was humble and scrupulously neat, and I could see that my dusky guide was a faithful servant. Captain Diamond, lying there rigid and pale on his white sheets, resembled some ruggedly carven figure on the lid of a Gothic tomb. He looked at me silently, and my companion withdrew and left us alone.

"Yes, it's you," he said, at last, "it's you, that good young man. There is no mistake, is there?"

"I hope not; I believe I'm a good young man. But I am very sorry you are ill. What can I do for you?"

"I am very bad, very bad; my poor old bones ache so!" and, groaning portentously, he tried to turn toward me.

I questioned him about the nature of his malady and the length of time he had been in bed, but he barely heeded me; he seemed impatient to speak of something else. He grasped my sleeve, pulled me toward him, and whispered quickly: "You know my time's up!"

"Oh, I trust not," I said, mistaking his meaning. "I shall certainly see you on your legs again."

"God knows!" he cried. "But I don't mean I'm dying; not yet a bit. What I mean is, I'm due at the house. This is rent-day."

"Oh, exactly! But you can't go."

"I can't go. It's awful. I shall lose my money. If I am dying, I want it all the same. I want to pay the doctor. I want to be buried like a respectable man."

"It is this evening?" I asked.

"This evening at sunset, sharp."

He lay staring at me, and, as I looked at him in return, I suddenly understood his motive in sending for me. Morally, as it came into my thought, I winced. But, I suppose I looked unperturbed, for he continued in the same tone. "I can't lose my money. Someone else must go. I asked Belinda; but she won't hear of it."

"You believe the money will be paid to another person?"

"We can try, at least. I have never failed before and I don't know. But, if you say I'm as sick as a dog, that my old bones ache, that I'm dying, perhaps she'll trust you. She don't want me to starve!"

"You would like me to go in your place, then?"

"You have been there once; you know what it is. Are you afraid?"

I hesitated.

"Give me three minutes to reflect," I said, "and I will tell you." My glance wandered over the room and rested on the various objects that spoke of the threadbare, decent poverty of its occupant. There seemed to be a mute appeal to my pity and my resolution in their cracked and faded sparseness.

Meanwhile Captain Diamond continued, feebly: "I think she'd trust you, as I have trusted you; she'll like your face; she'll see there is no harm in you. It's a hundred and thirty-three dollars, exactly. Be sure you put them into a safe place."

"Yes," I said at last, "I will go, and, so far as it depends upon me, you shall have the money by nine o'clock tonight."

He seemed greatly relieved; he took my hand and faintly pressed it, and soon afterward I withdrew. I tried for the rest of the day not to think of my evening's work, but, of course, I thought of nothing else. I will not deny that I was nervous; I was, in fact, greatly excited, and I spent my time in alternately hoping that the mystery should prove less deep than it appeared, and yet fearing that it might prove too shallow. The hours passed very slowly, but, as the afternoon began to wane, I started on my mission. On the way, I stopped at Captain Diamond's modest dwelling, to ask how he was doing, and to receive such last instructions as he might desire to lay upon me. The old Negress, gravely and inscrutably placid, admitted me and, in answer to my inquiries said that the Captain was very low; he had sunk since the morning.

"You must be right smart," she said, "if you want to get back before he drops off."

A glance assured me that she knew of my projected expedition, though, in her own opaque black pupil, there was not a gleam of self-betrayal.

"But why should Captain Diamond drop off?" I asked. "He certainly seems very weak; but I cannot make out that he has any definite disease."

"His disease is old age," she said, sententiously.

"But he is not so old as that; sixty-seven or sixty-eight, at most."

She was silent a moment.

"He's worn out; he's used up; he can't stand it any longer."

"Can I see him a moment?" I asked; upon which she led me again to his room.

He was lying in the same way as when I had left him, except that his eyes were closed. But he seemed very "low," as she had said, and he had very little pulse. Nevertheless, I further learned the doctor had been there in the afternoon and professed himself satisfied. "He don't know what's been going on," said Belinda, curtly.

The old man stirred a little, opened his eyes, and after some time recognized me.

"I'm going, you know," I said. "I'm going for your money. Have you anything more to say?" He raised himself slowly, and with a painful effort, against his pillows; but he seemed hardly to understand me. "The house, you know," I said. "Your daughter."

He rubbed his forehead, slowly, awhile, and at last, his comprehension awoke. "Ah, yes," he murmured, "I trust you. A hundred and thirty-three dollars. In old pieces—all in old pieces." Then he added more vigorously, and with a brightening eye: "Be very respectful—be very polite. If not—if not . . ." and his voice failed again.

"Oh, I certainly shall be," I said with a rather forced smile. "But, if not?"

"If not, I shall know it!" he said, very gravely. And with this, his eyes closed and he sunk down again.

I took my departure and pursued my journey with a sufficiently resolute step. When I reached the house, I made a propitiatory bow in front of it, in emulation of Captain Diamond. I had timed my walk so as to be able to enter without delay; night had already fallen. I turned the key, opened the door and shut it behind me. Then I struck a light, and found the two candlesticks I had used before, standing on the tables in the entry. I applied a match to both of them, took them up and went into the parlor. It was empty, and though I waited awhile, it remained empty. I passed them into the other rooms on the same floor, and no dark image rose before me to check my steps. At last, I came out into the hall again, and stood weighing the question of going upstairs. The staircase had been the scene of my discomfiture before, and I approached it with profound mistrust. At the foot, I paused, looking up, with my hand on the balustrade. I was acutely expectant, and my expectation was justified. Slowly, in the darkness above, the black figure that I had seen before took shape. It was not an illusion; it was a figure, and the same. I gave it time to define itself, and watched it stand and look down at me with its hidden face. Then, deliberately, I lifted my voice and spoke.

"I have come in place of Captain Diamond, at his request," I said. "He is very ill; he is unable to leave his bed. He earnestly begs that you will pay the money to me; I will immediately carry it to him." The figure stood motionless, giving no sign. "Captain Diamond would have come if he were able to move," I added, in a moment, appealingly; "but, he is utterly unable."

At this the figure slowly unveiled its face and showed me a dim, white mask; then it began slowly to descend the stairs. Instinctively I fell back before it, retreating to the door of the front sitting room. With my eyes still fixed on it, I moved backward across the threshold; then I stopped in the middle of the room and set down my lights. The figure advanced; it seemed to be that of a tall woman, dressed in various black crepe. As it drew near, I saw that it had a perfectly human face, though it looked extremely pale and sad. We stood gazing at each other; my agitation had completely vanished; I was only deeply interested.

"Is my father dangerously ill?" said the apparition.

At the sound of its voice—gentle, tremulous, and perfectly human—I started forward; I felt a rebound of excitement. I drew a long breath, I gave a sort of cry, for what I saw before me was not a disembodied spirit, but a beautiful woman, an audacious actress. Instinctively, irresistibly, by the force of reaction against my credulity, I stretched out my hand and seized the long veil that muffled her head. I gave it a violent jerk, dragged it nearly off, and stood staring at a large fair person, of about five-and-thirty. I comprehended her at a glance, her long black dress, her pale, sorrow-worn face, painted to look paler, her very fine eyes—the color of her father's—and her sense of outrage at my movement.

"My father, I suppose," she cried, "did not send you here to insult me!" and she turned away rapidly, took up one of the candles and moved toward the door. Here she paused, looked at me again, hesitated, and then drew a purse from her pocket and flung it down on the floor. "There is your money!" she said, majestically.

I stood there, wavering between amazement and shame, and saw her pass out into the hall. Then I picked up the purse. The next moment, I heard a loud shriek and a crash of something dropping, and she came staggering back into the room without her light.

"My father—my father!" she cried; and with parted lips and dilated eyes, she rushed toward me.

"Your father—where?" I demanded.

"In the hall, at the foot of the stairs."

I stepped forward to go out, but she seized my arm.

"He's in white," she cried, "in his shirt. It's not he!"

"Why, your father is in his house, in his bed, extremely ill," I answered.

She looked at me fixedly, with searching eyes.

"Dying?"

"I hope not," I stuttered.

She gave a long moan and covered her face with her hands.

"Oh, heavens, I have seen his ghost!" she cried.

She still held my arm, she seemed too terrified to release it. "His ghost!" I echoed, wondering.

"It's the punishment of my long folly!" she went on.

"Ah," said I, "it's the punishment of my indiscretion—of my violence!"

"Take me away, take me away!" she cried, still clinging to my arm. "Not there"—as I was turning toward the hall and the front door—"not there, for pity's sake! By this door—the back entrance." And snatching the other candles from the table, she led me through the neighboring room into the back part of the house. Here was a door opening from a sort of scullery into the orchard. I turned the rusty lock and we passed out and stood in the cool air, beneath the stars. Here my companion gathered her black drapery about her, and stood for a moment, hesitating. I had been infinitely flurried, but my curiosity touching her was uppermost. Agitated, pale, picturesque, she looked, in the early evening light, very beautiful.

"You have been playing all these years a most extraordinary game," I said.

She looked at me somberly, and seemed disinclined to reply. "I came in perfect good faith," I went on. "The last time—three months ago—you remember?—you greatly frightened me."

"Of course it was an extraordinary game," she answered at last. "But it was the only way."

"Had he not forgiven you?"

"So long as he thought me dead, yes. There have been things in my life he could not forgive."

I hesitated and then—"And where is your husband?" I asked.

"I have no husband—I have never had a husband."

She made a gesture which checked further questions, and moved rapidly away. I walked with her round the house to the road, and she kept murmuring—"It was he—it was he!" When we reached the road she stopped, and asked me which way I was going. I pointed to the road by which I had come, and she said—"I take the other. You are going to my father's?" she added.

"Directly," I said.

"Will you let me know tomorrow what you have found?"

"With pleasure. But how shall I communicate with you?"

She seemed at a loss, and looked about her. "Write a few words," she said, "and put them under that stone?" And she pointed to one of the lava slabs that bordered the old well. I gave her my promise to comply, and she turned away. "I know my road," she said. "Everything is arranged. It's an old story."

She left me with a rapid step, and as she receded into the darkness, resumed, with the dark flowing lines of her drapery, the phantasmal appearance with which she had at first appeared to me. I watched her till she became invisible, and then I took my own leave of the place. I returned to town at a swinging pace, and marched straight to the little yellow house near the river. I took the liberty of entering without a knock, and encountering no interruption, made my way to Captain Diamond's room. Outside the door, on a low bench, with folded arms, sat the sable Belinda.

"How is he?" I asked.

"He's gone to glory."

"Dead?" I cried.

She rose with a sort of tragic chuckle.

"He's as big a ghost as any of them now!"

I passed into the room and found the old man lying there irredeemably rigid and still. I wrote that evening a few lines which I proposed on the morrow to place beneath the stone, near the well; but my promise was not destined to be executed. I slept that night very ill—it was natural—and in my restlessness left my bed to walk about the room. As I did so I caught sight, in passing my window, of a red glow in the northwestern sky. A house was on fire in the country, and evidently burning fast. It lay in the same direction as the scene of my evening's adventures, and as I stood watching the crimson horizon I was startled by a sharp memory. I had blown out the candle which lighted me, with my companion, to the door which we escaped, but I had not accounted for the other light, which she had carried into the hall and dropped— heaven knew where—in her consternation.

The next day I walked out with my folded letter and turned into the familiar crossroad. The haunted house was a mass of charred beams and smoldering ashes; the well-cover had been pulled off, in quest of water, by the few neighbors who had had the audacity to contest what they must have regarded as a demon-kindled blaze, the loose stones were completely displaced, and the earth had been trampled into puddles.

Opera lovers know and love Offenbach's strikingly offbeat Tales of
Hoffmann, *but few are probably aware that the Hoffmann of the title is* E.
T. HOFFMANN, *the German macabre writer who, born in 1776, lived to write
many unforgettable tales of the strange and psychologically unsettling ways
of often-artistic characters. Tschaikovsky based his* Nutcracker *ballet on one
of Hoffmann's stories, and* The Cremona Violin *doubtless inspired Mme. Blavatsky to write* "The Ensouled Violin" (Q.V.). *The following ghost story is
a wholly independent prologue to Hoffmann's short story,* "Automata."

Untitled Ghost Story
by E. T. Hoffmann

A considerable time ago I was invited to a little evening gathering,
where our friend Vincent was, along with some other people. I was de-
tained by business, and did not arrive till very late. I was all the more
surprised not to hear the slightest sound as I came up to the door of the
room. Could it be that nobody had been able to come? I gently opened
the door. There sat Vincent, opposite me, with the others, around a little table; and they were all staring, stiff and motionless like so many
statues, in the profoundest silence up at the ceiling. The lights were on a
table at some distance, and nobody took any notice of me. I went
nearer, full of amazement, and saw a glittering gold ring suspended
from the ceiling, swinging back and forth in the air, and presently beginning to move in circles. One after another they said, "Wonderful!"
"Most wonderful!" "Most inexplicable!" "Curious!" and so on. I could
no longer contain myself, and cried out, "For Heaven's sake, tell me
what you are doing."

At this they all jumped up. But Vincent cried, in that shrill voice of
his: "Creeping Tom! You come slinking in like a sleepwalker, interrupting the most important and interesting experiments. Let me tell you
that a phenomenon which the incredulous have classed without a moment's hesitation as fabulous, has just been verified by this company.
We wished to see whether the pendulum swings of a suspended ring can
be controlled by the concentrated human will. I undertook to fix my
will upon it; and thought as hard as I could of circular oscillations. The
ring, which is fixed to the ceiling by a silk thread, remained motionless
for a very long time, but at last it began to swing, and it was just beginning to go in circles when you came in and interrupted us."

"But what if it were not your will," I said, "so much as the draught of air when I opened the door which set the ring in motion?"

"Materialist!" cried Vincent. Everybody laughed.

"The pendulum oscillations of rings nearly drove me crazy at one time," said Theodore. "This is absolutely certain, and anyone can convince himself of it: the oscillations of a plain gold ring, suspended by a fine thread over the palm of the hand, unquestionably take the direction which the unspoken will directs them to take. I cannot tell you how profoundly and how eerily this phenomenon affected me. I used to sit for hours at a time making the ring go swinging in the most varied directions, as I willed it; and at last I went to the length of making an oracle of it. I would say, mentally, 'If such and such a thing is going to happen, let the ring swing between my thumb and little finger; if it is not going to happen, let it swing at right angles to that direction,' and so on."

"Delightful," said Lothair. "You set up within yourself a higher spiritual principle to speak to you mystically when you conjure it up. Here we have the true 'spiritus familiaris,' the Socratic daemon. From here there is only a very short step to ghosts and supernatural stories, which might easily have their *raison d'être* in the influence of some exterior spiritual principle."

"And I mean to take just this step," said Cyprian, "by telling you, right here and now, the most terrible supernatural story I have ever heard. The peculiarity of this story is that it is vouched for by persons of credibility, and that the manner in which it has been brought to my knowledge, or recollection, has to do with the excited or (if you prefer) disorganized condition which Lothair observed me to be in a short time ago."

Cyprian stood up; and, as was his habit when his mind was occupied, and he needed a little time to arrange his words, he walked several times up and down the room. Presently he sat down, and began: —

"You may remember that some little time ago, just before the last campaign, I was paying a visit to Colonel von P— at his country house. The colonel was a good-tempered, jovial man, and his wife quietness and simpleness personified. At the time I speak of, the son was away with the army, so that the family circle consisted, besides the colonel and his lady, of two daughters and an elderly French lady who was trying to persuade herself that she was fulfilling the duties of a governess—though the young ladies appeared to be beyond the period of being 'governed.' The elder of the two daughters was a most lively and cheerful girl, vivacious even to ungovernability; not without plenty of brains, but so constituted that she could not go five yards without cutting at least three entrechats. She sprang in the same fashion in her conversation and everything that she did, restlessly from one thing to another. I myself have seen her within the space of five minutes work at needlework, read, draw, sing, dance, or cry about her poor cousin who was killed in battle and then while the tears were still in her eyes burst into a splendid infectious burst of laughter when the Frenchwoman spilled the contents of her snuffbox over the pug. The pug began to sneeze frightfully, and the old lady cried, *'Ah, che fatalità! Ah carino! Poverino!"* (She always spoke to the dog in Italian because he was born in Padua.) Moreover, this young lady was the loveliest blonde ever seen, and for all her odd caprices, full of the utmost charm, goodness, kindliness, and attractiveness, so that whether she wanted to or not she exerted the most irresistible charm over everyone.

"Her younger sister was the greatest possible contrast to her (her name was Adelgunda). I try in vain to find words in which to express to you the extraordinary impression which this girl produced upon me when I first saw her. Picture to yourselves the most exquisite figure, and the most marvellously beautiful face; but her cheeks and lips wear a deathly pallor, and she moves gently, softly, slowly, with measured steps; and then, when you hear a low-toned word from her scarcely opened lips you feel a sort of shudder of spectral awe. Of course I soon got over this eerie feeling, and, when I managed to get her to emerge from her deep self-absorbed condition and converse, I was obliged to admit that the strangeness, the eeriness, was only external; and by no means came from within. In the little she said she displayed a delicate womanliness, a clear head, and a kindly disposition. She had not a trace of overexcitability, though her melancholy smile, and her glance, heavy as if with tears, seemed to speak of some morbid bodily condition producing a hostile influence on her mental state. It struck me as very strange that the whole family, not excepting the French lady, seemed to get into a state of anxiety as soon as anyone began to talk to this girl, and tried to interrupt the conversation, often breaking into it in a very forced manner. But the most extraordinary thing of all was that, as soon as it was eight o'clock in the evening, the young lady was reminded, first by the French lady and then by her mother, sister, and father, that it was time to go to her room, just as little children are sent to bed so that they will not overtire themselves. The French lady went with her, so that neither of them ever appeared at supper, which was at nine o'clock.

The lady of the house, probably noticing my surprise at those proceedings, threw out (by way of preventing indiscreet inquiries) a sort of sketchy statement to the effect that Adelgunda was in very poor health, that, particularly about nine in the evening, she was liable to feverish attacks, and that the doctors had ordered her to have complete rest at that time. I saw there must be more in the affair than this, though I could not imagine what it might be; and it was only today that I ascertained the terrible truth, and discovered what the events were which have wrecked the peace of that happy circle in the most frightful manner.

"Adelgunda was at one time the most blooming, vigorous, cheerful creature to be seen. Her fourteenth birthday came, and a number of her friends and companions had been invited to spend it with her. They were all sitting in a circle in the shrubbery, laughing and amusing themselves, taking little heed that the evening was getting darker and darker, for the soft July breeze was blowing refreshingly, and they were just beginning thoroughly to enjoy themselves. In the magic twilight they set about all sorts of dances, pretending to be elves and woodland sprites. Adelgunda cried, 'Listen, children! I shall go and appear to you as the White Lady whom our gardener used to tell us about so often while he was alive. But you must come to the bottom of the garden, where the old ruins are.' She wrapped her white shawl round her, and went lightly dancing down the leafy path, the girls following her, in full tide of laughter and fun. But Adelgunda had scarcely reached the old crumbling arches, when she suddenly stopped, and stood as if paralyzed in every limb. The castle clock struck nine.

" 'Look, look!' cried she, in a hollow voice of the deepest terror. 'Don't you see it? the figure—close before me—stretching her hand out at me. Don't you see her?'

"The children saw nothing whatever; but terror came upon them, and they all ran away, except one, more courageous than the rest, who hastened up to Adelgunda, and was going to take her in her arms. But Adelgunda, turning pale as death, fell to the ground. At the screams of the other girl everybody came hastening from the castle, and Adelgunda was carried in. At last she recovered from her faint, and, trembling all over, told them that as soon as she reached the ruins she saw an airy form, as if shrouded in mist, stretching its hand out towards her. Of course everyone ascribed this vision to some deceptiveness of the twilight; and Adelgunda recovered from her alarm so completely that night that no further evil consequences were anticipated, and the whole affair was supposed to be at an end. However, it turned out altogether otherwise. The next evening, when the clock struck nine, Adelgunda sprang up, in the midst of the people about her, and cried, 'There she is! there she is. Don't you see her—just before me?'

"Since that unlucky evening, Adelgunda declared that as soon as the clock struck nine, the figure stood before her, remaining visible for several seconds, although no one but herself could see anything of it, or trace by any psychic sensation the proximity of an unknown spiritual principle. So that poor Adelgunda was thought to be out of her mind; and, in a strange perversion of feeling, the family were ashamed of this condition of hers. I have told you already how she was dealt with in consequence. There was, of course, no lack of doctors, or of plans of treatment for ridding the poor soul of the *idée fixe,* as people were pleased to term the apparition which she said she saw. But nothing had any effect; and she implored, with tears, to be left in peace, inasmuch as the form which in its vague, uncertain traits had nothing terrible or alarming about it no longer caused her any fear; although for a time after seeing it she felt as if her inner being and all her thoughts and ideas were turned out from her, and were hovering, bodiless, outside of her. At last the colonel made the acquaintance of a celebrated doctor who had the reputation of being specially clever in the treatment of the mentally afflicted. When this doctor heard Adelgunda's story he laughed aloud, and said nothing could be easier than to cure a condition of the kind, which resulted solely from an overexcited imagination. The idea of the appearing of the spectre was so intimately associated with the striking of nine o'clock that the mind could not dissociate them. So that all that was necessary was to effect this separation by external means. About this there would be no difficulty, as it was only necessary to deceive the patient as to the time, and let nine o'clock pass without her being aware of it. If the apparition did not then appear, she would be convinced herself that it was an illusion; and measures to give tone to the general system would be all that would then be necessary to complete the cure.

"This unfortunate advice was taken. One night all the clocks at the castle were put back an hour—the hollow, booming tower clock included—so that, when Adelgunda awoke in the morning, although she did not know it, she was really an hour wrong in her time. When evening came, the family were assembled, as usual, in a cheerful corner room; no stranger was present, and the mother constrained herself to talk about all sorts of cheerful subjects. The colonel began (as was his habit, when in specially good humour) to carry on an encounter of wit with the old French lady, in which Augusta, the older of the daughters, aided and abetted him. Everybody was laughing, and more full of enjoyment than ever. The clock on the wall struck eight (although it was really nine o'clock) and Adelgunda fell back in her chair, pale as death. Her work dropped from her hands; she rose, with a face of horror, stared before her into the empty part of the room, and murmured, in a hollow voice, 'What! an hour early! Don't you see it? Don't you see it? Right before me!'

"Everyone rose up in alarm. But as none of them saw the smallest vestige of anything, the colonel cried, 'Calm yourself, Adelgunda, there is nothing there! It is a vision of your brain, only your imagination. We see nothing, nothing whatever; and if there really were a figure close to you we should see it as well as you! Calm yourself.'

" 'Oh God!' cried Adelgunda, 'they think I am out of my mind. See! it is stretching out its long arm, it is making signs to me!'

"And, as though she were acting under the influence of another, without exercise of her own will, with eyes fixed and staring, she put her hand back behind her, took up a plate which chanced to be on the table, held it out before her into vacancy, and let it go.

"The plate did not drop, but floated about among the persons present, and then settled gently on the table. Augusta and her mother fainted; and these fainting fits were succeeded by violent nervous fever. The colonel forced himself to retain his self-control, but the profound impression which this extraordinary occurrence made on him was evident in his agitated and disturbed condition.

"The French lady had fallen on her knees and prayed in silence with her face turned to the floor, and both she and Adelgunda remained free from evil consequences. The mother very soon died. Augusta survived the fever; but it would have been better had she died. She who, when I first saw her, was an embodiment of vigorous, magnificent youthful happiness, is now hopelessly insane, and that in a form which seems to me the most terrible and gruesome of all the forms of idée fixe ever heard of. For she thinks she is the invisible phantom which haunts Adelgunda; and therefore she avoids everyone, or, at all events, refrains from speaking, or moving if anybody is present. She scarce dares to breathe, because she firmly believes that if she betrays her presence in any way everyone will die. Doors are opened for her, and her food is set down, she slinks in and out, eats in secret, and so forth. Can a more painful condition be imagined?

"The colonel, in his pain and despair, followed the colours to the next campaign, and fell in the victorious engagement at W——. It is remarkable, most remarkable that since then Adelgunda has never seen the phantom. She nurses her sister with the utmost care, and the French lady helps her. Only this very day Sylvester told me that the uncle of these poor girls is here, taking the advice of our celebrated R——, as to the means of cure to be tried in Augusta's case. God grant that the cure may succeed, improbable as it seems."

When Cyprian finished, the friends all kept silence, looking meditatively before them. At last Lothair said, "It is certainly a very terrible ghost story. I must admit it makes me shudder, although the incident of the hovering plate is rather trifling and childish."

"Not so fast, my dear Lothair," Ottmar interrupted. "You know my views about ghost stories, and the manner in which I swagger towards visionaries; maintaining, as I do, that often as I have thrown down my glove to the spirit world challenging it to enter the lists with me, it has never taken the trouble to punish me for my presumption and irreverence. But Cyprian's story suggests another consideration. Ghost stories may often be mere chimeras; but, whatever may have been at the bottom of Adelgunda's phantom, and the hovering plate, this much is certain: that on that evening, in the family of Colonel von P—— something happened which produced in three of the persons present such a shock to the system that the result was the death of one and the insanity of another; if we do not ascribe at least indirectly the colonel's death to it, too. For I happen to remember that I heard from officers who were on the spot, that he suddenly dashed into the thick of the enemy's fire as if impelled by the furies. Then the incident of the plate differs so completely from anything in the ordinary *mise en scène* of supernatural stories. The hour when it happened is so remote from ordinary supernatural use and wont, and the event so simple that its improbability acquires probability, and thereby becomes gruesome to me. But if one were to assume that Adelgunda's imagination carried along those of her father, mother and sister—that it was only within her brain that the plate moved about—would not this vision of the imagination striking three people dead in a moment, like a shock of electricity, be the most terrible supernatural event imaginable?"

"Certainly," said Theodore, "and I share with you, Ottmar, your opinion that the very horror of the incident lies in its utter simplicity. I can imagine myself enduring fairly well the sudden alarm produced by some fearful apparition; but the weird actions of some invisible thing would infallibly drive me mad. The sense of the most utter, most helpless powerlessness must grind the spirit to dust. I remember that I could hardly resist the profound terror which made me afraid to sleep in my room alone, like a silly child, when I once read of an old musician who was haunted in a terrible manner for a long time (almost driving him out of his mind) by an invisible being which used to play on his piano in the night, compositions of the most extraordinary kind, with the power and the technique of the most accomplished master. He heard every note, saw the keys going up and down, but never any form of a player."

"Really," Lothair said, "the way in which this class of subject is flourishing among us is becoming unendurable, I have admitted that the incident of that accursed plate produced the profoundest impression on me. Ottmar is right; if events are to be judged by their results, this is the most terrible supernatural story conceivable. Therefore I pardon the disturbed condition which Cyprian displayed earlier in the evening, and which has passed away considerably now. But not another word on the subject of supernatural horrors."

Tender ghost stories do exist in the literature of the supernatural, but many come dangerously close to being cloying. "The Doll's Ghost" is an exception; though touching enough, it is rooted in sufficient darkness to make it quietly tragic. F. MARION CRAWFORD, author of several highly regarded weird fictions, was born in 1854 in Italy, son of American parents.

The Doll's Ghost

by F. Marion Crawford

It was a terrible accident, and for one moment the splendid machinery of Cranston House got out of gear and stood still. The butler emerged from the retirement in which he spent his elegant leisure, two grooms appeared simultaneously, there were actually housemaids on the grand staircase, and Mrs. Pringle herself stood upon the landing. Mrs. Pringle was the housekeeper. As for the head nurse, the under nurse, and the nursery maid, their feelings cannot be described.

The Lady Gwendolen Lancaster-Douglas-Scroop, youngest daughter of the ninth Duke of Cranston, and aged six years and three months, picked herself up quite alone, and sat down on the third step from the foot of the grand staircase in Cranston House.

"Oh!" ejaculated the butler, and he disappeared again.

"Ah!" responded the grooms as they also went away.

"It's only that doll," Mrs. Pringle was distinctly heard to say, in a tone of contempt. Then the three nurses gathered round Lady Gwendolen and hurried her out of Cranston House as fast as they could, lest it should be found out upstairs that they had allowed the Lady Gwendolen to tumble down the grand staircase with her doll in her arms. And as the doll was badly broken, the nursery maid carried it, with the pieces, wrapped up in Lady Gwendolen's little cloak. It was not far to Hyde Park, and when they had reached a quiet place they took means to find out that Lady Gwendolen had no bruises.

Lady Gwendolen Douglas-Scroop sometimes yelled, but she never cried. It was because she had yelled that the nurse had allowed her to go downstairs alone with Nina, the doll, under one arm, while she steadied herself with her other hand on the balustrade, and trod upon the polished marble steps beyond the edge of the carpet. So she had fallen, and Nina had come to grief.

When the nurses were quite sure that she was not hurt, they

unwrapped the doll and looked at her in her turn. She had been a very beautiful doll, very large, and fair, and healthy, with real yellow hair, and eyelids that would open and shut over very grown-up dark eyes. Moreover, when you moved her right arm up and down she said, "Pa-pa," and when you moved the left she said, "Ma-ma," very distinctly.

"I heard her say 'Pa' when she fell," said the under nurse, who heard everything. "But she ought to have said 'Pa-pa.' "

"That's because her arm went up when she hit the step," said the head nurse. "She'll say the other 'Pa' when I put it down again."

"Pa," said Nina, as her right arm was pushed down, and speaking through her broken face. It was cracked right across, from the upper corner of the forehead, with a hideous gash, through the nose and down to the little frilled collar of the pale green silk Mother Hubbard frock, and two little three-cornered pieces of porcelain had fallen out.

"It's a wonder she can speak at all, being all smashed," said the under nurse.

"You'll have to take her to Mr. Puckler," said her superior. "It's not far, and you'd better go at once." The under nurse wrapped Nina up again and departed.

Mr. Bernard Puckler and his little daughter lived in a little house in a little alley, which led out off a quiet little street not very far from Belgrave Square. He was the great doll doctor, and his extensive practice lay in the most aristocratic quarter. He mended dolls of all sizes and ages, boy dolls and girl dolls, baby dolls in long clothes, and grown-up dolls in fashionable gowns, talking dolls and dumb dolls, those that shut their eyes when they lay down, and those whose eyes had to be shut for them by means of a mysterious wire. His daughter Else was only just over twelve years old, but she was already very clever at mending dolls' clothes, and at doing their hair, which is harder than you might think, though the dolls sit quite still while it is being done.

Mr. Puckler had originally been a German, but he had dissolved his nationality in the ocean of London many years ago, like a great many foreigners. He still had one or two German friends, however, who came on Saturday evenings, and smoked with him and played picquet or "skat" with him for farthing points, and called him "Herr Doctor," which seemed to please Mr. Puckler very much.

He looked older than he was, for his beard was rather long and ragged, his hair was grizzled and thin, and he wore horn-rimmed spectacles. As for Else, she was a thin, pale child, very quiet and neat, with dark eyes and brown hair that was plaited down her back and tied with a bit of black ribbon. She mended the dolls' clothes and took the dolls back to their homes when they were quite strong again.

The house was a little one, but too big for the two people who lived in it. There was a small sitting-room on the street, and the workshop was at the back, and there were three rooms upstairs. But the father and daughter lived most of their time in the workshop, because they were generally at work, even in the evenings.

Mr. Puckler laid Nina on the table and looked at her a long time, till the tears began to fill his eyes behind the horn-rimmed spectacles. He was a very susceptible man, and he often fell in love with the dolls he mended, and found it hard to part with them when they had smiled at him for a few days. They were real little people to him, with characters and thoughts and feelings of their own, and he was very tender with them all. But some attracted him especially from the first, and when they were brought to him maimed and injured, their state seemed so pitiful to him that the tears came easily. You must remember that he had lived among dolls during a great part of his life, and understood them.

"How do you know that they feel nothing?" he went on to say to Else. "You must be gentle with them. It costs nothing to be kind to the little beings, and perhaps it makes a difference to them."

And Else understood him, because she was a child, and she knew that she was more to him than all the dolls.

He fell in love with Nina at first sight, perhaps because her beautiful brown glass eyes were something like Else's own, and he loved Else first and best, with all his heart. And, besides, it was a very sorrowful case. Nina had evidently not been long in the world, for her complexion was perfect, her hair was smooth where it should be smooth, and curly where it should be curly, and her silk clothes were perfectly new. But across her face was that frightful gash, like a saber cut, deep and shadowy within, but clean and sharp at the edges. When he tenderly pressed her head to close the gaping wound, the edges made a fine grating sound, that was painful to hear, and the lids of the dark eyes quivered as though Nina were suffering dreadfully.

"Poor Nina!" he exclaimed sorrowfully. "But I shall not hurt you much, though you will take a long time to get strong."

He always asked the names of the broken dolls when they were brought to him, and sometimes the people knew what the children called them, and told him. He liked "Nina" for a name. Altogether and in every way she pleased him more than any doll he had seen for many years, and he felt drawn to her, and made up his mind to make her perfectly strong and sound, no matter how much labor it cost him.

Mr. Puckler worked patiently and Else watched him. She could do nothing for poor Nina, whose clothes needed no mending. The longer the doll doctor worked, the more fond he became of the yellow hair and the beautiful brown glass eyes. He sometimes forgot all the other dolls that were waiting to be mended, lying side by side on a shelf, and sat for an hour gazing at Nina's face, while he racked his ingenuity for some new invention by which to hide even the smallest trace of the terrible accident.

She was wonderfully mended. Even he was obliged to admit that; but the scar was still visible to his keen eyes, a very fine line right across the face, downwards from right to left. Yet all the conditions had been most favorable for a cure, since the cement had set quite hard at the first attempt and the weather had been fine and dry, which makes a great difference in a dolls' hospital.

At last he knew that he could do no more, and the under nurse had already come twice to see whether the job was finished.

"Nina is not quite strong yet," Mr. Puckler had answered each time, for he could not make up his mind to face the parting.

And now he sat before the square deal table at which he worked, and Nina lay before him for the last time with a big brown paper box beside her. It stood there like her coffin, waiting for her, he thought. He must put her into it, and lay tissue paper over her dear face, and then put on the lid, and at the thought of tying the string his sight was dim with tears again. He was never to look into the glassy depths of the beautiful brown eyes any more, nor to hear the little wooden voice say "Pa-pa" and "Ma-ma." It was a very painful moment.

In the vain hope of gaining time before the separation, he took up the little sticky bottles of cement and glue and gum and color, looking at each one in turn, and then at Nina's face. And all his small tools lay there, neatly arranged in a row, but he knew that he could not use them again for Nina. She was quite strong at last, and in a country where there should be no cruel children to hurt her she might live a hundred years, with only that almost imperceptible line across her face to tell of the fearful thing that had befallen her on the marble steps of Cranston House.

Suddenly Mr. Puckler's heart was quite full, and he rose abruptly from his seat and turned away.

"Else," he said unsteadily, "you must do it for me. I cannot bear to see her go into the box."

So he went and stood at the window with his back turned, while Else did what he had not the heart to do.

"Is it done?" he asked, not turning round. "Then take her away, my dear. Put on your hat, and take her to Cranston House quickly, and when you are gone I will turn round."

Else was used to her father's queer ways with the dolls, and though she had never seen him so much moved by a parting, she was not much surprised.

"Come back quickly," he said, when he heard her hand on the latch. "It is growing late, and I should not send you at this hour. But I cannot bear to look forward to it any more."

When Else was gone, he left the window and sat down in his place before the table again, to wait for the child to come back. He touched the place where Nina had lain, very gently, and he recalled the softly tinted pink face, and the glass eyes, and the ringlets of yellow hair, till he could almost see them.

The evenings were long, for it was late in the spring. But it began to grow dark soon, and Mr. Puckler wondered why Else did not come back. She had been gone an hour and a half, and that was much longer than he had expected, for it was barely half a mile from Belgrave Square to Cranston House. He reflected that the child might have been kept waiting, but as the twilight deepened he grew anxious, and walked up and down in the grim workshop, no longer thinking of Nina, but of Else, his own living child, whom he loved.

An undefinable, disquieting sensation came upon him by fine degrees, a chilliness and a faint stirring of his thin hair, joined with a wish to be in any company rather than to be alone much longer. It was the beginning of fear.

He told himself in strong German-English that he was a foolish old man, and he began to feel about for the matches in the dusk. He knew just where they should be, for he always kept them in the same place, close to the little tin box that held bits of sealing-wax of various colors, for some kinds of mending. But somehow he could not find the matches in the gloom.

Something had happened to Else, he was sure, and as his fear increased, he felt as though it might be allayed if he could get a light and see what time it was. Then he called himself a foolish old man again, and the sound of his own voice startled him in the dark. He still could not find the matches.

The window was gray; he might see what time it was if he went close to it, and he could go and get matches out of the cupboard afterwards. He stood back from the table, to get out of the way of the chair, and began to cross the board floor.

Something was following him in the dark. There was a small pattering, as of tiny feet upon the boards. He stopped and listened, and the roots of his hair tingled. It was nothing, and he was a foolish old man. He made two steps more, and he was sure that he heard the little pattering again. He turned his back to the window, leaning against the sash so that the panes began to crack, and he faced the dark. Everything was quite still, and it smelt of paste and cement and wood-filings as usual.

"Is that you, Else?" he asked, and he was surprised by the fear in his voice.

There was no answer in the room, and he held up his watch and tried to make out what time it was by the gray dusk that was just not darkness. So far as he could see, it was within two or three minutes of ten o'clock. He had been a long time alone. He was shocked, and frightened for Else, out in London, so late, and he almost ran across the room to the door. As he fumbled for the latch, he distinctly heard the running of the little feet after him.

"Mice!" he exclaimed feebly, just as he got the door open.

He shut it quickly behind him, and felt as though some cold thing had settled on his back and were writhing upon him. The passage was quite dark, but he found his hat and was out in the alley in a moment, breathing more freely, and surprised to find how much light there still was in the open air. He could see the pavement clearly under his feet, and far off in the street to which the alley led he could hear the laughter and calls of children, playing some game out of doors. He wondered how he could have been so nervous, and for an instant he thought of going back into the house to wait quietly for Else. But instantly he felt that nervous fright of something stealing over him again. In any case it was better to walk up to Cranston House and ask the servants about the child. One of the women had perhaps taken a fancy to her, and was even now giving her tea and cake.

He walked quickly to Belgrave Square, and then up the broad streets, listening as he went, whenever there was no other sound, for the tiny footsteps. But he heard nothing, and was laughing at himself when he rang the servants' bell at the big house. Of course, the child must be there.

The person who opened the door was quite an inferior person, for it was a back door, but affected the manners of the front, and stared at Mr. Puckler superciliously under the strong light.

No little girl had been seen, and he knew "nothing about no dolls."

"She is my little girl," said Mr. Puckler tremulously, for all his anxiety was returning tenfold, "and I am afraid something has happened."

The inferior person said rudely that "nothing could have happened to her in that house, because she had not been there, which was a jolly good reason why;" and Mr. Puckler was obliged to admit that the man ought to know, as it was his business to keep the door and let people in. He wished to be allowed to speak to the under nurse, who knew him; but the man was ruder than ever, and finally shut the door in his face.

When the doll doctor was alone in the street, he steadied himself by the railing, for he felt as though he were breaking in two, just as some dolls break, in the middle of the backbone.

Presently he knew that he must be doing something to find Else, and that gave him strength. He began to walk as quickly as he could through the streets, following every highway and byway which his little girl might have taken on her errand. He also asked several policemen in vain if they had seen her, and most of them answered him kindly, for they saw that he was a sober man and in his right senses, and some of them had little girls of their own.

It was one o'clock in the morning when he went up to his own door again, worn out and hopeless and broken-hearted. As he turned the key in the lock, his heart stood still, for he knew that he was awake and not dreaming, and that he really heard those tiny footsteps pattering to meet him inside the house.

But he was too unhappy to be much frightened any more, and his heart went on again with a dull regular pain, that found its way all through him with every pulse. So he went in, and hung up his hat in the dark, and found the matches in the cupboard and the candlestick in its place in the corner.

Mr. Puckler was so much overcome and so completely worn out that he sat down in his chair before the work-table and almost fainted, as his face dropped forward upon his folded hands. Beside him the solitary candle burned steadily with a low flame in the still warm air.

"Else! Else!" he moaned against his yellow knuckles. And that was all he could say, and it was no relief to him. On the contrary, the very sound of the name was a new and sharp pain that pierced his ears and his head and his very soul. For every time he repeated the name it meant that little Else was dead, somewhere out in the streets of London in the dark.

He was so terribly hurt that he did not even feel something pulling gently at the skirt of his old coat, so gently that it was like the nibbling of a tiny mouse. He might have thought that it was really a mouse if he had noticed it.

"Else! Else!" he groaned right against his hands.

Then a cool breath stirred his thin hair, and the low flame of the one candle dopped down almost to a mere spark, not flickering as though a draught were going to blow it out, but just dropping down as if it were tired out. Mr. Puckler felt his hands stiffening with fright under his face; and there was a faint rustling sound, like some small silk thing blown in a gentle breeze. He sat up straight, stark and scared, and a small wooden voice spoke in the stillness.

"Pa-pa," it said, with a break between the syllables.

Mr. Puckler stood up in a single jump, and his chair fell over backwards with a smashing noise upon the wooden floor. The candle had almost gone out.

It was Nina's doll voice, and he should have known it among the voices of a hundred other dolls. And yet there was something more in it, a little human ring, with a pitiful cry and a call for help, and the wail of a hurt child. Mr. Puckler stood up, stark and stiff, and tried to look round, but at first he could not, for he seemed to be frozen from head to foot.

Then he made a great effort, and he raised one hand to each of his temples, and pressed his own head round as he would have turned a doll's. The candle was burning so low that it might as well have been out altogether, for any light it gave, and the room seemed quite dark at first. Then he saw something. He would not have believed that he could be more frightened than he had been just before that. But he was, and his knees shook, for he saw the doll standing in the middle of the floor, shining with a faint and ghostly radiance, her beautiful glassy brown eyes fixed on his. And across her face the very thin line of the break he had mended with such care shone as though it were drawn in light with a fine point of white flame.

Yet there was something human in her face, like Else's own, as if only the doll saw him through them, and not Else. And there was enough of Else to bring back all his pain and to make him forget his fear.

"Else, my little Else!" he cried aloud.

The small ghost moved, and its doll-arm slowly rose and fell with a stiff, mechanical motion.

"Pa-pa," it said.

It seemed this time that there was even more of Else's tone echoing somewhere between the wooden notes that reached his ears so distinctly, and yet so far away. Else was calling him, he was sure.

His face was perfectly white in the gloom, but his knees did not shake any more, and he felt that he was less frightened.

"Yes, child! But where? Where?" he asked. "Where are you, Else?"

"Pa-pa!"

The syllables died away in the quiet room. There was a low rustling of silk, the glassy brown eyes turned slowly away, and Mr. Puckler heard the pitter-patter of the small feet in the bronze kid slippers as the figure ran straight to the door. Then the candle burned high again, the room was full of light, and he was alone.

Mr. Puckler passed his hand over his eyes and looked about him. He could see everything quite clearly, and he felt that he must have been dreaming, though he was standing instead of sitting down, as he should have been if he had just waked up. The candle burned brightly now. There were the dolls to be mended, lying in a row with their toes up. The third one had lost her right shoe, and Else was making one. He knew that, and he was certainly not dreaming now. He had not been dreaming when he had come in from his fruitless search and had heard the doll's footsteps running to the door. He had not fallen asleep in his chair. How could he possibly have fallen asleep when his heart was breaking? He had been awake all the time.

He steadied himself, set the fallen chair upon its legs, and said to himself again very emphatically that he was a foolish old man. He ought to be out in the streets looking for his child, asking questions, and inquiring at the police stations, where all accidents were reported as soon as they were known, or at the hospitals.

"Pa-pa!"

The longing, wailing, pitiful little wooden cry rang from the passage, outside the door, and Mr. Puckler stood for an instant with white face, transfixed and rooted to the spot. A moment later his hand was on the latch. Then he was in the passage, with the light streaming from the open door behind him.

Quite at the other end he saw the little phantom shining clearly in the shadow, and the right hand seemed to beckon to him as the arm rose and fell once more. He knew all at once that it had not come to frighten him but to lead him, and when it disappeared, and he walked boldly towards the door, he knew that it was in the street outside, waiting for him. He forgot that he was tired and had eaten no supper, and had walked many miles, for a sudden hope ran through and through him, like a golden stream of life.

And sure enough, at the corner of the alley, and at the corner of the street, and out in Belgrave Square, he saw the small ghost flitting before him. Sometimes it was only a shadow, where there was other light, but then the glare of the lamps made a pale green sheen on its little Mother Hubbard frock of silk; and sometimes, where the streets were dark and silent, the whole figure shone out brightly, with its yellow curls and rosy neck. It seemed to trot along like a tiny child, and Mr. Puckler could almost hear the pattering of the bronze kid slippers on the pavement as it ran. But it went very fast, and he could only just keep up with it, tearing along with his hat on the back of his head and his thin hair blown by the night breeze, and his horn-rimmed spectacles firmly set upon his broad nose.

On and on he went, and he had no idea where he was. He did not even care, for he knew certainly that he was going the right way.

Then at last, in a wide, quiet street, he was standing before a big, sober-looking door that had two lamps on each side of it, and a polished brass bellhandle, which he pulled.

And just inside, when the door was opened, in the bright light, there was the little shadow, and the pale green sheen of the little silk dress, and once more the small cry came to his ears, less pitiful, more longing.

"Pa-pa!"

The shadow turned suddenly bright, and out of the brightness the beautiful brown glass eyes were turned up happily to his, while the rosy mouth smiled so divinely that the phantom doll looked almost like a little angel.

"A little girl was brought in soon after ten o'clock," said the quiet voice of the hospital doorkeeper. "I think they thought she was only stunned. She was holding a big brown-paper box against her, and they could not get it out of her arms. She had a long plait of brown hair that hung down as they carried her."

"She is my little girl," said Mr. Puckler, but he hardly heard his own voice.

He leaned over Else's face in the gentle light of the children's ward, and when he had stood there a minute the beautiful brown eyes opened. "Pa-pa!" cried Else. "I knew you would come!"

Then Mr. Puckler did not know what he did or said for a moment, and what he felt was worth all the fear and terror and despair that had almost killed him that night. But by and by Else was telling her story, and the nurse let her speak, for there were only two other children in the room, who were getting well and were sound asleep.

"They were big boys with bad faces!" said Else, "and they tried to get Nina away from me, but I held on and fought as well as I could till one of them hit me with something, and I don't remember any more, for I tumbled down, and I suppose the boys ran away, and somebody found me there. But I'm afraid Nina is all smashed."

"Here is the box," said the nurse. "We could not take it out of her arms till she came to herself. Would you like to see if the doll is broken?"

And she undid the string cleverly, but Nina was all smashed to pieces. Only the gentle light of the children's ward made a pale green sheen in the folds of the little Mother Hubbard frock.

Spectral hounds occur more than once in genre fiction: the original version of Faulkner's "The Hound" concerned a departed canine who sought revenge for its own, and its master's murders; Masefield's vicious pack harrows mortals elsewhere in this volume, and you don't have to be a Doyle buff to be acquainted with the Hound of the Baskervilles. Here is another nasty mutt, courtesy of AMBROSE BIERCE, who grew from a poverty-stricken Connecticut childhood to become one of America's best-known essayists and prosodists. The essence of Bierce is savagely withering satire; he was so disenchanted with his fellows that it is little wonder he disappeared in Mexico and was never again heard from. He was born in 1842, but it is unlikely that anyone will ever know when he left this plane—probably with a disgusted sneer on his lip.

Staley Fleming's Hallucination

by Ambrose Bierce

Of two men who were talking one was a physician.

"I sent for you, Doctor," said the other, "but I don't think you can do me any good. Maybe you can recommend a specialist in psychopathy. I fancy I'm a bit loony."

"You look all right," the physician said.

"You shall judge—I have hallucinations. I wake every night and see in my room, intently watching me, a big black Newfoundland dog with a white forefoot."

"You say you wake; are you sure about that? 'Hallucinations' are sometimes only dreams."

"Oh, I wake, all right. Sometimes I lie still a long time, looking at the dog as earnestly as the dog looks at me—I always leave the light going. When I can't endure it any longer I sit up in bed—and nothing is there!"

" 'M, 'm—what is the beast's expression?"

"It seems to me sinister. Of course I know that, except in art, an animal's face in repose has always the same expression. But this is not a real animal. Newfoundland dogs are pretty mild-looking, you know; what's the matter with this one?"

"Really, my diagnosis would have no value: I am not going to treat the dog."

The physician laughed at his own pleasantry, but narrowly watched his patient from the corner of his eye. Presently he said: "Fleming, your description of the beast fits the dog of the late Atwell Barton."

Fleming half rose from his chair, sat again and made a visible attempt at indifference. "I remember Barton," he said, "I believe he was—it was reported that—wasn't there something suspicious in his death?"

Looking squarely now into the eyes of his patient, the physician said: "Three years ago the body of your old enemy, Atwell Barton, was found in the woods near his home and yours. He had been stabbed to death. There have been no arrests; there was no clue. Some of us had 'theories.' I had one. Have you?"

"I? Why, bless your soul, what could I know about it? You remember that I left for Europe almost immediately afterward—a considerable time afterward. In the few weeks since my return you could not expect me to construct a 'theory.' In fact, I have not given the matter a thought. What about his dog?"

"It was first to find the body. It died of starvation on his grave."

We do not know the inexorable law underlying coincidences. Staley Fleming did not, or he would perhaps not have sprung to his feet as the night wind brought in through the open window the long wailing howl of a distant dog. He strode several times across the room in the steadfast gaze of the physician; then, abruptly confronting him, almost shouted: "What has all this to do with my trouble, Dr. Halderman? You forget why you were sent for."

Rising, the physician laid his hand upon his patient's arm and said, gently: "Pardon me. I cannot diagnose your disorder off-hand—tomorrow, perhaps. Please go to bed, leaving your door unlocked; I will pass the night here with your books. Can you call me without rising?"

"Yes, there is an electric bell."

"Good. If anything disturbs you push the button without sitting up. Good night."

Comfortably installed in an armchair, the man of medicine stared into the glowing coals and thought deeply and long, but apparently to little purpose, for he frequently rose and opening a door leading to the staircase, listened intently; then resumed his seat. Presently, however, he fell asleep, and when he woke it was past midnight. He stirred the failing fire, lifted a book from the table at his side and looked at the title. It was Denneker's *Meditations*. He opened it at random and began to read:

"Forasmuch as it is ordained of God that all flesh hath spirit and thereby taketh on spiritual powers, so, also, the spirit hath powers of the flesh, even when it is gone out of the flesh and liveth as a thing apart, as many a violence performed by wraith and lemure sheweth. And there be those who say that man is not single in this, but the beasts have the like evil inducement, and—"

The reading was interrupted by a shaking of the house, as by the fall of a heavy object. The reader flung down the book, rushed from the room, and mounted the stairs to Fleming's bedchamber. He tried the door, but contrary to his instructions it was locked. He set his shoulder against it with such force that it gave way. On the floor near the disordered bed, in his night clothes, lay Fleming gasping away his life.

The physician raised the dying man's head from the floor and observed a wound in the throat. "I should have thought of this," he said, believing it suicide.

When the man was dead an examination disclosed the unmistakable marks of an animal's fangs deeply sunken into the jugular vein.

But there was no animal.

Mirrors and cameras traditionally have been objects of distrust in folk tradition, probably because they are believed to have the power to entrap an essential part of the human soul. Here is an anonymous rendition of that theme; the plot is often encountered in oral ghost tales.

The Dead Woman's Photograph

Anonymous

Virgil Hoyt is a photographer's assistant up at St. Paul, and a man of a good deal of taste. He has been in search of the picturesque all over the West, and hundreds of miles to the north in Canada, and can speak three or four Indian dialects, and put a canoe through the rapids. That is to say, he is a man of an adventurous sort and no dreamer. He can fight well and shoot well and swim well enough to put up a winning race with the Indian boys, and he can sit all day in the saddle and not dream about it at night.

Wherever he goes he uses his camera.

"The world," Hoyt is in the habit of saying to those who sit with him when he smokes his pipe, "was created in six days to be photographed. Man—and especially woman—was made for the same purpose. Clouds are not made to give moisture, nor trees to cast shade. They were created for the photographer."

In short, Virgil Hoyt's view of the world is whimsical, and he doesn't like to be bothered with anything disagreeable. That is the reason that he loathes and detests going to a house of mourning to photograph a corpse. The horribly bad taste of it offends him partly, and partly he is annoyed at having to shoulder, even for a few moments, a part of someone's burden of sorrow. He doesn't like sorrow, and would willingly canoe 500 miles up the cold Canadian rivers to get rid of it. Nevertheless, as assistant photographer, it is often his duty to do this very kind of thing.

Not long ago he was sent for by a rich Jewish family at St. Paul to photograph the mother, who had just died. He was very much put out, but he went. He was taken to the front parlor, where the dead woman lay in her coffin. It was evident that there was some excitement in the household and that a discussion was going on, but Hoyt wasn't concerned, and so he paid no attention to the matter.

The daughter wanted the coffin turned on end, in order that the corpse might face the camera properly, but Hoyt said he could overcome the recumbent attitude and make it appear that the face was taken in the position it would naturally hold in life, and so they went out and left him alone with the dead.

The face was a strong and positive one, such as may often be seen among Jewish matrons. Hoyt regarded it with some admiration, thinking to himself that she was a woman who had been used to having her own way. There was a strand of hair out of place, and he pushed it back from her brow. A bud lifted its head too high from among the roses on her breast and spoiled the contour of the chin, so he broke it off. He remembered these things later very distinctly and that his hand touched her bare face two or three times.

Then he took the photographs and left the house.

He was very busy at the time and several days elapsed before he was able to develop the plates. He took them from the bath, in which they had lain with a number of others, and went to work upon them. There were three plates, he having taken that number merely as a precaution against any accident. They came up well, but as they developed he became aware of the existence of something in the photograph which had not been apparent to his eye. The mysterious always came under the head of the disagreeable with him, and was therefore to be banished, so he made only a few prints and put the things away out of sight. He hoped that something would intervene to save him from attempting an explanation.

But it is a part of the general perplexity of life that things do not intervene as they ought and when they ought, so one day his employer asked him what had become of those photographs. He tried to evade him, but it was futile, and he got out the finished photographs and showed them to him. The older man sat staring at them a long time.

"Hoyt," said he, at length, "you're a young man, and I suppose you have never seen anything like this before. But I have. Not exactly the same thing, but similar phenomena have come my way a number of times since I went into the business, and I want to tell you there are things in heaven and earth not dreamt of——"

"Oh, I know all that tommy-rot," cried Hoyt, angrily, "but when anything happens I want to know the reason why, and how it is done."

"All right," said his employer, "then you might explain why and how the sun rises."

But he humored the younger man sufficiently to examine with him the bath in which the plates were submerged and the plates themselves.

All was as it should be. But the mystery was there and could not be done away with.

Hoyt hoped against hope that the friends of the dead woman would somehow forget about the photographs, but of course the wish was unreasonable, and one day the daughter appeared and asked to see the photographs of her mother.

"Well, to tell the truth," stammered Hoyt, "those didn't come out as well as we could wish."

"But let me see them," persisted the lady. "I'd like to look at them, anyway."

"Well, now," said Hoyt, trying to be soothing, as he believed it was always best to be with women—to tell the truth, he was an ignoramus where women were concerned—"I think it would be better if you didn't see them. There are reasons why——" he ambled on like this, stupid man that he was, and of course the Jewess said she would see those pictures without any further delay.

So poor Hoyt brought them out and placed them in her hand, and then ran for the water pitcher, and had to be at the bother of bathing her forehead to keep her from fainting.

For what the lady saw was this: Over face and flowers and the head of the coffin fell a thick veil, the edges of which touched the floor in some places. It covered the features so well that not a hint of them was visible.

"There was nothing over mother's face," cried the lady at length.

"Not a thing," acquiesced Hoyt. "I know, because I had occasion to touch her face just before I took the picture. I put some of her hair back from her brow."

"What does it mean, then?" asked the lady.

"You know better than I. There is no explanation in science. Perhaps there is some in psychology."

"Well," said the lady, stammering a little and coloring, "mother was a good woman, but she always wanted her own way, and she always had it, too."

"Yes?"

"And she never would have her picture taken. She didn't admire herself. She said no one should ever see a picture of hers."

"So?" said Hoyt, meditatively. "Well, she's kept her word, hasn't she?"

The two stood looking at the pictures for a time. Then Hoyt pointed to the open blaze in the grate.

"Throw them in," he commanded. "Don't let your father see them—don't keep them yourself. They wouldn't be good things to keep."

"That's true enough," said the lady, slowly. And she threw them in the fire. Then Virgil Hoyt brought out the plates and broke them before her eyes.

And that was the end of it—except that Hoyt sometimes tells the story to those who sit beside him when his pipe is lighted.

BRAM STOKER *is the justly famous author of* Dracula, *the book which both defined and effectively ended the vampire horror novel—since no fantasist has ever written anything to surpass it on its own terms. Born in Dublin in 1847, Stoker lived a vigorous life as actor Henry Irving's personal manager and wrote a small number of mostly weird novels and tales in his spare time. His first and perhaps rarest work of fiction was* Under the Sunset, *consisting of a series of darkly poetic episodes about the land of Death where the pale ghosts of the living may be sought.* "The Castle of the King" *is a self-contained chapter from that work, a bleak odyssey to the shores of night. It is astounding that the haunted Irishman thought he was writing the following tone poem for children!*

The Castle of the King
by Bram Stoker

When they told the poor Poet that the One he loved best was lying sick in the shadow of danger, he was nigh distraught.

For weeks past he had been alone; she, his Wife, having gone afar to her old home to see an aged grandsire ere he died.

The Poet's heart had for some days been oppressed with a strange sorrow. He did not know the cause of it; he only knew with the deep sympathy which is the poet's gift, that the One he loved was sick. Anxiously had he awaited tidings. When the news came, the shock, although he expected a sad message, was too much for him, and he became nigh distraught.

In his sadness and anxiety he went out into the garden which long years he had cultured for Her. There, amongst the bright flowers, where the old statues stood softly white against the hedges of yew, he lay down in the long uncut summer grass, and wept with his head buried low.

He thought of all the past—of how he had won his Wife and how they loved each other; and to him it seemed a sad and cruel thing that she was afar and in danger, and he not near to comfort her or even to share her pain.

Many many thoughts came back to him, telling the story of the weary years whose gloom and solitude he had forgotten in the brightness of his lovely home.—

How in youth they twain had met and in a moment loved. How his poverty and her greatness had kept them apart. How he had struggled and toiled in the steep and rugged road to fame and fortune.

How all through the weary years he had striven with the single idea of winning such a place in the history of his time, that he should be able to come and to her say, "I love you," and to her proud relations, "I am worthy, for I too have become great."

How amid all this dreaming of a happy time which might come, he had kept silent as to his love. How he had never seen her or heard her voice, or even known her habitation, lest, knowing, he should fail in the purpose of his life.

How time—as it ever does to those who work with honesty and singleness of purpose—crowned the labours and the patience of his life.

How the world had come to know his name and reverence and love it as of one who had helped the weak and weary by his example; who had purified the thoughts of all who listened to his words; and who had swept away baseness before the grandeur and simpleness of his noble thoughts.

How success had followed in the wake of fame.

How at length even to his heart, timorous with the doubt of love, had been borne the thought that he had at last achieved the greatness which justified him in seeking the hand of her he loved.

How he had come back to his native place, and there found her still free.

How when he had dared to tell her of his love she had whispered to him that she, too, had waited all the years, for that she knew that he would come to claim her at the end.

How she had come with him as his bride into the home which he had been making for her all these years. How, there, they had lived happily; and had dared to look into the long years to come for joy and content without a bar.

How he thought that even then, when though somewhat enfeebled in strength by the ceaseless toil of years and the care of hoping, he might look to the happy time to come.

But, alas! for hope; for who knoweth what a day may bring forth? Only a little while ago his Dear One had left him hale, departing in the cause of duty; and now she lay sick and he not nigh to help her.

All the sunshine of his life seemed passing away. All the long years of waiting and the patient continuance in well-doing which had crowned their years with love, seemed as but a passing dream, and was all in vain—all, all in vain.

Now with the shadow hovering over his Beloved One, the cloud seemed to be above and around them, and to hold in its dim recesses the doom of them both.

"Why, oh why," asked the poor Poet to the viewless air, "did love come to us? Why came peace and joy and happiness, if the darkening wings of peril shadow the air around her, and leave me to weep alone?"

Thus he moaned, and raved, and wept; and the bitter hours went by him in his solitude.

As he lay in the garden with his face buried in the long grass, they came to him and told him with weeping, that tidings—sad, indeed—had come.

As they spoke he lifted his poor head and gazed at them; and they saw in the great, dark, tender eyes that now he was quite distraught. He smiled at them sadly, as though not quite understanding the import of their words. As tenderly as they could they tried to tell him that the One he loved best was dead.

They said:—

"She has walked in the Valley of the Shadow;" but he seemed to understand them not.

They whispered,

"She has heard the Music of the Spheres," but still he comprehended not.

Then they spoke to him sorrowfully and said:

"She now abides in the Castle of the King."

He looked at them eagerly, as if to ask:

"What castle? What king?"

They bowed their heads; and as they turned away weeping they murmured to him softly—

"The Castle of the King of Death."

He spake no word; so they turned their weeping faces to him again. They found that he had risen and stood with a set purpose on his face. Then he said sweetly:

"I go to find her, that where she abideth, I too may there abide."

They said to him:

"You cannot go. Beyond the Portal she is, and in the Land of Death."

Set purpose shone in the Poet's earnest, loving eyes as he answered them for the last time:

"Where she has gone, there go I too. Through the Valley of the Shadow shall I wend my way. In these ears also shall ring the Music of the Spheres. I shall seek, and I shall find my Beloved in the Halls of the Castle of the King. I shall clasp her close—even before the dread face of the King of Death."

As they heard these words they bowed their heads again and wept, and said:

"Alas! alas!"

The poet turned and left them; and passed away. They fain would have followed; but he motioned them that they should not stir. So, alone, in his grief he went.

As he passed on he turned and waved his hand to them in farewell. Then for a while with uplifted hand he stood, and turned him slowly all around.

Suddenly his outstretched hand stopped and pointed. His friends looking with him saw, where, away beyond the Portal, the idle wilderness spread. There in the midst of desolation the mist from the marshes hung like a pall of gloom on the far off horizon.

As the Poet pointed there was a gleam of happiness—very very faint it was—in his poor sad eyes, distraught with loss, as if afar he beheld some sign or hope of the Lost One.

Swiftly and sadly the Poet fared on through the burning day.

The Rest Time came; but on he journeyed. He paused not for shade or rest. Never, even for an instant did he stop to cool his parched lips with an icy draught from the crystal springs.

The weary wayfarers resting in the cool shadows beside the fountains raised their tired heads and looked at him with sleepy eyes as he hurried. He heeded them not; but went ever onward with set purpose in his eyes, as though some gleam of hope bursting through the mists of the distant marshes urged him on.

So he fared on through all the burning day, and all the silent night. In the earliest dawn, when the promise of the still unrisen sun quickened the eastern sky into a pale light, he drew anigh the Portal. The horizon stood out blackly in the cold morning light.

There, as ever, stood the Angels who kept watch and ward, and oh, wondrous! although invisible to human eyes, they were seen of him.

As he drew nigh they gazed at him pityingly and swept their great wings out wide, as if to shelter him. He spake; and from his troubled heart the sad words came sweetly through the pale lips:

"Say, Ye who guard the Land, has my Beloved One passed hither on the journey to the Valley of the Shadow, to hear the Music of the Spheres, and to abide in the Castle of the King?"

The Angels at the Portal bowed their heads in token of assent; and they turned and looked outward from the Land to where, far off in the idle wilderness, the dank mists crept from the lifeless bosom of the marsh.

They knew well that the poor lonely Poet was in quest of his Beloved One; so they hindered him not, neither urged they him to stay. They pitied him much for that much he loved.

They parted wide, that through the Portal he might pass without let.

So, the Poet went onwards into the idle desert to look for his Beloved One in the Castle of the King.

For a time he went through gardens whose beauty was riper than the gardens of the Land. The sweetness of all things stole on the senses like the odours from the Isles of the Blest.

The subtlety of the King of Death, who rules in the Realms of Evil, is great. He has ordered that the way beyond the Portal be made full of charm. Thus those straying from the paths ordained for good see around them such beauty that in its joy the gloom and cruelty and guilt of the desert are forgotten.

But as the Poet passed onwards the beauty began to fade away.

The fair gardens looked as gardens do when the hand of care is taken off, and when the weeds in their hideous luxuriance choke, as they spring up, the choicer life of the flowers.

From cool alleys under spreading branches, and from crisp sward which touched as soft as velvet the Wanderer's aching feet, the way became a rugged stony path, full open to the burning glare. The flowers began to lose their odour, and to dwarf to stunted growth. Tall hemlocks rose on every side, infecting the air with their noisome odour.

Great fungi grew in the dark hollows where the pools of dank water lay. Tall trees, with branches like skeletons, rose—trees which had no leaves, and under whose shadow to pause were to die.

Then huge rocks barred the way. These were only passed by narrow, winding passages, overhung by the ponderous cliffs above, which ever threatened to fall and engulph the Sojourner.

Here the night began to fall; and the dim mist rising from the far-off marshes, took weird shapes of gloom. In the distant fastnesses of the mountains the wild beasts began to roar in their cavern lairs. The air became hideous with the fell sounds of the night season.

But the poor Poet heeded not ill sights or sounds of dread. Onward he went ever—unthinking of the terrors of the night. To him there was no dread of darkness—no fear of death—no consciousness of horror. He sought his Beloved One in the Castle of the King; and in that eager quest all natural terrors were forgot.

So fared he onward through the livelong night. Up the steep defiles he trod. Through the shadows of the huge rocks he passed unscathed. The wild animals came around him roaring fiercely—their great eyes flaming like fiery stars through the blackness of the night.

From the high rocks great pythons crawled and hung to seize their prey. From the crevices of the mountain steeps, and from cavernous rifts in the rocky way poisonous serpents glided and rose to strike.

But close though the noxious things came, they all refrained to attack; for they knew that the lonely Sojourner was bound for the Castle of their King.

Onward still, onward he went—unceasing—pausing not in his course—but pressing ever forward in his quest.

When daylight broke at last, the sun rose on a sorry sight. There toiling on the rocky way, the poor lonely Poet went ever onwards, unheeding of cold or hunger or pain.

His feet were bare, and his footsteps on the rock-strewn way were marked by blood. Around and behind him, and afar off keeping equal pace on the summits of the rocky ridges, came the wild beasts that looked on him as their prey, but that refrained from touching him because he sought the Castle of their King.

In the air wheeled the obscene birds who follow ever on the track of the dying and the lost. Hovered the bare-necked vultures with eager eyes, and hungry beaks. Their great wings flapped lazily in the idle air as they followed in the Wanderer's track. The vultures are a patient folk, and they await the falling of the prey.

From the cavernous recesses in the black mountain gorges crept, with silent speed, the serpents that there lurk. Came the python, with his colossal folds and endless coils, whence looked forth cunningly the small flat head. Came the boa and all his tribe, which seize their prey by force and crush it with the dread strictness of their embrace. Came the hooded snakes and all those which with their venom destroy their prey. Here, too, came those serpents most terrible of all to their quarry—

which fascinate with eyes of weird magic and by the slow gracefulness of their approach.

Here came or lay in wait, subtle snakes, which take the colour of herb, or leaf, or dead branch, or slimy pool, amongst which they lurk, and so strike their prey unsuspecting.

Great serpents there were, nimble of body, which hang from rock or branch. These griping tight to their distant hold, strike downward with the rapidity of light as they hurl their whip-like bodies from afar upon their prey.

Thus came forth all these noxious things to meet the Questing Man, and to assail him. But when they knew he was bound for the dread Castle of their King, and saw how he went onward without fear, they abstained from attack.

The deadly python and the boa towering aloft, with colossal folds, were passive, and for the nonce, became as stone. The hooded serpents drew in again their venomous fangs. The mild, deep earnest eyes of the fascinating snake became lurid with baffled spleen, as he felt his power to charm was without avail. In its deadly descent the hanging snake arrested its course, and hung a limp line from rock or branch.

Many followed the Wanderer onwards into the desert wilds, waiting and hoping for a chance to destroy.

Many other perils also were there for the poor Wanderer in the desert idleness. As he went onward the rocky way got steeper and darker. Lurid fogs and deadly chill mists arose.

Then in this path along the trackless wilderness were strange and terrible things.

Mandrakes—half plant, half man—shrieked at him with despairing cry, as, helpless for evil, they stretched out their ghastly arms in vain.

Giant thorns arose in the path; they pierced his suffering feet and tore his flesh as onward he trod. He felt the pain, but he heeded it not.

In all the long, terrible journey he had but one idea other than his eager search for his Beloved One. He thought that the children of men might learn much from the journey towards the Castle of the King, which began so fair, amidst the odorous gardens and under the cool shadow of the spreading trees. In his heart the Poet spake to the multitude of the children of men; and from his lips the words flowed like music, for he sang of the Golden Gate which the Angels call TRUTH.

"Pass not the Portal of the Sunset Land!
Pause where the Angels at their vigil stand.

Be warned! and press not though the gates lie wide,
But rest securely on the hither side.
Though odorous gardens and cool ways invite,
Beyond are darkest valleys of the night.
Rest! Rest contented.— Pause whilst undefiled,
Nor seek the horrors of the desert wild."

Thus treading down all obstacles with his bleeding feet, passed ever onwards, the poor distraught Poet, to seek his Beloved One in the Castle of the King.

Even as onward he went the life that is of the animals seemed to die away behind him. The jackals and the more cowardly savage animals slunk away. The lions and tigers, and bears, and wolves, and all the braver of the fierce beasts of prey which followed on his track even after the others had stopped, now began to halt in their career.

They growled low and then roared loudly with uplifted heads; the bristles of their mouths quivered with passion, and the great white teeth champed angrily together in baffled rage. They went on a little further; and stopped again roaring and growling as before. Then one by one they ceased, and the poor Poet went on alone.

In the air the vultures wheeled and screamed, pausing and halting in their flight, as did the savage beasts. These too ceased at length to follow in air the Wanderer in his onward course.

Longest of all kept up the snakes. With many a writhe and stealthy onward glide, they followed hard upon the footsteps of the Questing Man. In the blood marks of his feet upon the flinty rocks they found a joy and hope, and they followed ever.

But time came when the awful aspect of the places where the Poet passed checked even the serpents in their track—the gloomy defiles whence issue the poisonous winds that sweep with desolation even the dens of the beasts of prey—the sterile fastnesses which march upon the valleys of desolation. Here even the stealthy serpents paused in their course; and they too fell away. They glided back, smiling with deadliest rancour, to their obscene clefts.

Then came places where plants and verdure began to cease. The very weeds became more and more stunted and inane. Farther on they declined into the sterility of lifeless rock. Then the most noxious herbs that grew in ghastly shapes of gloom and terror lost even the power to harm, which outlives their living growth. Dwarfed and stunted even of evil, they were compact of the dead rock. Here even the deadly Upas tree could strike no root into the pestiferous earth.

Then came places where, in the entrance to the Valley of the Shadow, even solid things lost their substance, and melted in the dank and cold mists which swept along.

As he passed, the distraught Poet could feel not solid earth under his bleeding feet. On shadows he walked, and amid them, onward through the Valley of the Shadow to seek his Beloved One in the Castle of the King.

The Valley of the Shadow seemed of endless expanse. Circled by the teeming mist, no eye could pierce to where rose the great mountains between which the Valley lay.

Yet they stood there—Mount Despair on the one hand, and the Hill of Fear upon the other.

Hitherto the poor bewildered brain of the Poet had taken no note of all the dangers, and horrors, and pains which surrounded him—save only for the lesson which they taught. But now, lost as he was in the shrouding vapour of the Valley of the Shadow, he could not but think of the terrors of the way. He was surrounded by grisly phantoms that ever and anon arose silent in the mist, and were lost again before he could catch to the full their dread import.

Then there flashed across his soul a terrible thought—

Could it be possible that hither his Beloved One had travelled? Had there come to her the pains which shook his own form with agony? Was it indeed necessary that she should have been appalled by all these surrounding horrors?

At the thought of her, his Beloved One, suffering such pain and dread, he gave forth one bitter cry that rang through the solitude—that cleft the vapour of the Valley, and echoed in the caverns of the mountains of Despair and Fear.

The wild cry prolonged with the agony of the Poet's soul rang through the Valley, till the shadows that peopled it woke for the moment into life-in-death. They flitted dimly along, now melting away and anon springing again into life—till all the Valley of the Shadow was for once peopled with quickened ghosts.

Oh, in that hour there was agony to the poor distraught Poet's soul.

But presently there came a calm. When the rush of his first agony passed, the Poet knew that to the Dead came not the horrors of the journey that he undertook. To the Quick alone is the horror of the passage to the Castle of the King. With the thought came to him such peace that even there—in the dark Valley of the Shadow—stole soft music that sounded in the desert gloom like the Music of the Spheres.

Then the poor Poet remembered what they had told him; that his Beloved One had walked through the Valley of the Shadow, that she had known the Music of the Spheres, and that she abode in the Castle of the King. So he thought that as he was now in the Valley of the Shadow, and as he heard the Music of the Spheres, that soon he should see the Castle of the King where his Beloved One abode. Thus he went on in hope.

But alas! that very hope was a new pain that ere this he wot not of.

Hitherto he had gone on blindly, recking not of where he went or what came a-nigh him, so long as he pressed onward on his quest; but now the darkness and the peril of the way had new terrors, for he thought of how they might arrest his course. Such thoughts made the way long indeed, for the moments seemed an age with hoping. Eagerly he sought for the end to come, when, beyond the Valley of the Shadow through which he fared, he should see rising the turrets of the Castle of the King.

Despair seemed to grow upon him; and as it grew there rang out, ever louder, the Music of the Spheres.

Onward, ever onward, hurried in mad haste the poor distraught Poet. The dim shadows that peopled the mist shrank back as he passed, extending towards him warning hands with long gloomy fingers of deadly cold. In the bitter silence of the moment, they seemed to say:

"Go back! Go back!"

Louder and louder rang now the Music of the Spheres. Faster and faster in mad, feverish haste rushed the Poet, amid the shrinking Shadows of the gloomy valley. The peopling shadows as they faded away before him, seemed to wail in sorrowful warning:

"Go back! Go back!"

Still in his ears rang ever the swelling tumult of the music.

Faster and faster he rushed onward; till, at last, wearied nature gave way and he fell prone to earth, senseless, bleeding, and alone.

After a time—how long he could not even guess—he awoke from his swoon.

For awhile he could not think where he was; and his scattered senses could not help him.

All was gloom and cold and sadness. A solitude reigned around him, more deadly than aught he had ever dreamt of. No breeze was in the air; no movement of a passing cloud. No voice or stir of living thing in earth, or water, or air. No rustle of leaf or sway of branch—all was silent, dead, and deserted. Amid the eternal hills of gloom around, lay the valley devoid of aught that lived or grew.

The sweeping mists with their multitude of peopling shadows had gone by. The fearsome terrors of the desert even were not there. The Poet, as he gazed around him, in his utter loneliness, longed for the sweep of the storm or the roar of the avalanche to break the dread horror of the silent gloom.

Then the Poet knew that through the Valley of the Shadow had he come; that scared and maddened though he had been, he had heard the Music of the Spheres. He thought that now hard by the desolate Kingdom of Death he trod.

He gazed all around him, fearing lest he should see anywhere the dread Castle of the King, where his Beloved One abode; and he groaned as the fear of his heart found voice:

"Not here! oh not here, amid this awful solitude."

Then amid the silence around, upon distant hills his words echoed:

"Not here! oh not here," till with the echoing and reechoing rock, the idle wilderness was peopled with voices.

Suddenly the echo voices ceased.

From the lurid sky broke the terrible sound of the thunder peal. Along the distant skies it rolled. Far away over the endless ring of the grey horizon it swept—going and returning—pealing—swelling—dying away. It traversed the æther, muttering now in ominous sound as of threats, and anon crashing with the voice of dread command.

In its roar came a sound as of a word:

"Onward."

To his knees the Poet sank and welcomed with tears of joy the sound of the thunder. It swept away as a Power from Above the silent desolation of the wilderness. It told him that in and above the Valley of the Shadow rolled the mighty tones of Heaven's command.

Then the Poet rose to his feet, and with new heart went onwards into the wilderness.

As he went the roll of the thunder died away, and again the silence of desolation reigned alone.

So time wore on; but never came rest to the weary feet. Onwards, still onwards he went, with but one memory to cheer him—the echo of the thunder roll in his ears, as it pealed out in the Valley of Desolation:

"Onward! Onward!"

Now the road became less and less rocky, as on his way he passed. The great cliffs sank and dwindled away, and the ooze of the fens crept upward to the mountain's feet.

At length the hills and hollows of the mountain fastnesses disappeared. The Wanderer took his way amid mere trackless wastes, where was nothing but quaking marsh and slime.

On, on he wandered; stumbling blindly with weary feet on the endless road.

Over his soul crept ever closer the blackness of despair. Whilst amid the mountain gorges he had been wandering, some small cheer came from the hope that at any moment some turn in the path might show him his journey's end. Some entry from a dark defile might expose to him, looming great in the distance—or even anigh him—the dread Castle of the King. But now with the flat desolation of the silent marsh around him, he knew that the Castle could not exist without his seeing it.

He stood for a while erect, and turned him slowly round, so that the complete circuit of the horizon was swept by his eager eyes. Alas! never a sight did he see. Nought was there but the black line of the horizon, where the sad earth lay against the level sky. All, all was compact of a silent gloom.

Still on he tottered. His breath came fast and laboured. His weary limbs quivered as they bore him feebly up. His strength—his life—was ebbing fast.

On, on, he hurried, ever on, with one idea desperately fixed in his poor distraught mind—that in the Castle of the King he should find his Beloved One.

He stumbled and fell. There was no obstacle to arrest his feet; only from his own weakness he declined.

Quickly he arose and went onward with flying feet. He dreaded that should he fall he might not be able to arise again.

Again he fell. Again he rose and went on his way desperately, with blind purpose.

So for a while went he onwards, stumbling and falling; but arising ever and pausing not on his way. His quest he followed, of his Beloved One abiding in the Castle of the King.

At last so weak he grew that when he sank he was unable to rise again.

Feebler and feebler he grew as he lay prone; and over his eager eyes came the film of death.

But even then came comfort; for he knew that his race was run, and that soon he would meet his Beloved One in the Halls of the Castle of the King.

To the wilderness his thoughts he spoke. His voice came forth with a feeble sound, like the moaning before a storm of the wind as it passes through reeds in the grey autumn:

"A little longer. Soon I shall meet her in the Halls of the King; and we shall part no more. For this it is worth to pass through the Valley of the Shadow and to listen to the Music of the Spheres with their painful hope. What boots it though the Castle be afar? Quickly speed the feet of the dead. To the fleeting spirit all distance is but a span. I fear not now to see the Castle of the King; for there, within its chiefest Hall, soon shall I meet my Beloved—to part no more.

Even as he spoke he felt that the end was nigh.

Forth from the marsh before him crept a still, spreading mist. It rose silently, higher—higher—enveloping the wilderness for far around. It took deeper and darker shades as it arose. It was as though the Spirit of Gloom were hid within, and grew mightier with the spreading vapour.

To the eyes of the dying Poet the creeping mist was as a shadowy castle. Arose the tall turrets and the frowning keep. The gateway with its cavernous recesses and its beetling towers took shape as a skull. The distant battlements towered aloft into the silent air. From the very ground whereon the stricken Poet lay, grew, dim and dark, a vast causeway leading into the gloom of the Castle gate.

The dying Poet raised his head and looked. His fast failing eyes, quickened by the love and hope of his spirit, pierced through the dark walls of the keep and the gloomy terrors of the gateway.

There, within the great Hall where the grim King of Terrors himself holds his court, he saw her whom he sought. She was standing in the ranks of those who wait in patience for their Beloved to follow them into the Land of Death.

The Poet knew that he had but a little while to wait, and he was patient—stricken though he lay, amongst the Eternal Solitudes.

Afar off, beyond the distant horizon, came a faint light as of the dawn of a coming day.

As it grew brighter the Castle stood out more and more clearly; till in the quickening dawn it stood revealed in all its cold expanse.

The dying Poet knew that the end was at hand. With a last effort he raised himself to his feet, that standing erect and bold, as is the right of manhood, he might so meet face to face the grim King of Death before the eyes of his Beloved One.

The distant sun of the coming day rose over the horizon's edge.

A ray of light shot upward.

As it struck the summit of the Castle keep the Poet's Spirit in an instant of time swept along the causeway. Through the ghostly portal of the Castle it swept, and met with joy the kindred Spirit that it loved before the very face of the King of Death.

Quicker then than the lightning's flash the whole Castle melted into nothingness; and the sun of the coming day shone calmly down upon the Eternal Solitudes.

In the Land within the Portal rose the sun of the coming day. It shone calmly and brightly on a fair garden, where, among the long summer grass lay the Poet, colder than the marble statues around him.

OSCAR WILDE *was born in Dublin in 1856, went to Trinity College and Oxford, then spent his life creating some of the most urbane, scintillant prose and drama in the English tongue. The fame of his novel,* The Picture of Dorian Gray, *and his enduring comedic plays,* Lady Windermere's Fan *and* The Importance of Being Earnest, *has somewhat obscured his poetic fiction, much of which falls within the category of fable.* "The Canterville Ghost" *is better known than most of his tales, partly because of the film starring the great Charles Laughton in the title role, partly because it is one of the best ghost stories ever written.*

The Canterville Ghost
by Oscar Wilde

I

When Mr. Hiram B. Otis, the American Minister, bought Canterville Chase, everyone told him he was doing a very foolish thing, as there was no doubt at all that the place was haunted. Indeed, Lord Canterville himself, who was a man of the most punctilious honour, had felt it his duty to mention the fact to Mr. Otis when they came to discuss terms.

"We have not cared to live in the place ourselves," said Lord Canterville, "since my grand-aunt, the Dowager Duchess of Bolton, was frightened into a fit, from which she never really recovered, by two skeleton hands being placed on her shoulders as she was dressing for dinner, and I feel bound to tell you, Mr. Otis, that the ghost has been seen by several living members of my family, as well as by the rector of the parish, the Rev. Augustus Dampier, who is a Fellow of King's College, Cambridge. After the unfortunate accident to the Duchess, none of our younger servants would stay with us, and Lady Canterville often got very little sleep at night, in consequence of the mysterious noises that came from the corridor and the library."

"My Lord," answered the Minister, "I will take the furniture and the ghost at a valuation. I come from a modern country, where we have everything that money can buy; and with all our spry young fellows painting the Old World red, and carrying off your best actresses and primadonnas, I reckon that if there were such a thing as a ghost in Europe, we'd have it at home in a very short time in one of our public museums, or on the road as a show."

"I fear that the ghost exists," said Lord Canterville, smiling, "though it may have resisted the overtures of your enterprising impresarios. It has been well known for three centuries, since 1584 in fact, and always makes its appearance before the death of any member of our family."

"Well, so does the family doctor for that matter, Lord Canterville. But there is no such thing, sir, as a ghost, and I guess the laws of Nature are not going to be suspended for the British aristocracy."

"You are certainly very natural in America," answered Lord Canterville, who did not quite understand Mr. Otis's last observation, "and if you don't mind a ghost in the house, it is all right. Only you must remember I warned you."

A few weeks after this, the purchase was completed, and at the close of the season the Minister and his family went down to Canterville Chase. Mrs. Otis, who, as Miss Lucretia R. Tappan, of West 53rd Street, had been a celebrated New York belle, was now a very handsome, middle-aged woman, with fine eyes, and a superb profile. Many American ladies on leaving their native land adopt an appearance of chronic ill-health, under the impression that it is a form of European refinement, but Mrs. Otis had never fallen into this error. She had a magnificent constitution, and a really wonderful amount of animal spirits. Indeed, in many respects, she was quite English, and was an excellent example of the fact that we have really everything in common with America nowadays, except, of course, language. Her eldest son, christened Washington by his parents in a moment of patriotism, which he never ceased to regret, was a fair-haired, rather good-looking young man, who had qualified himself for American diplomacy by leading the German at the Newport Casino for three successive seasons, and even in London was well known as an excellent dancer. Gardenias and the peerage were his only weaknesses. Otherwise he was extremely sensible. Miss Virginia E. Otis was a little girl of fifteen, lithe and lovely as a fawn, and with a fine freedom in her large blue eyes. She was a wonderful amazon, and had once raced old Lord Bilton on her pony twice round the park, winning by a length and a half, just in front of the Achilles statue, to the huge delight of the young Duke of Cheshire, who proposed for her on the spot, and was sent back to Eton that very night by his guardians, in floods of tears. After Virginia came the twins, who were usually called "The Stars and Stripes," as they were always getting swished. They were delightful boys, and with the exception of the worthy Minister the only true republicans of the family.

As Canterville Chase is seven miles from Ascot, the nearest railway station, Mr. Otis had telegraphed for a waggonette to meet them, and they started on their drive in high spirits. It was a lovely July evening, and the air was delicate with the scent of the pinewoods. Now and then they heard a wood pigeon brooding over its own sweet voice, or saw, deep in the rustling fern, the burnished breast of the pheasant. Little squirrels peered at them from the beech-trees as they went by, and the rabbits scudded away through the brushwood and over the mossy knolls, with their white tails in the air. As they entered the avenue of Canterville Chase, however, the sky became suddenly overcast with clouds, a curious stillness seemed to hold the atmosphere, a great flight of rooks passed silently over their heads, and, before they reached the house, some big drops of rain had fallen.

Standing on the steps to receive them was an old woman, neatly dressed in black silk, with a white cap and apron. This was Mrs. Umney, the housekeeper, whom Mrs. Otis, at Lady Canterville's earnest request, had consented to keep on in her former position. She made them each a low curtsey as they alighted, and said in a quaint, old-fashioned manner, "I bid you welcome to Canterville Chase." Following her, they passed through the fine Tudor hall into the library, a long, low room, panelled in black oak, at the end of which was a large stained-glass window. Here they found tea laid out for them, and, after taking off their wraps, they sat down and began to look round, while Mrs. Umney waited on them.

Suddenly Mrs. Otis caught sight of a dull red stain on the floor just by the fireplace and, quite unconscious of what it really signified, said to Mrs. Umney, "I am afraid something has been spilt there."

"Yes, madam," replied the old housekeeper in a low voice, "blood has been spilt on that spot."

"How horrid," cried Mrs. Otis; "I don't at all care for blood-stains in a sitting-room. It must be removed at once."

The old woman smiled, and answered in the same low, mysterious voice, "It is the blood of Lady Eleanore de Canterville, who was murdered on that very spot by her own husband, Sir Simon de Canterville, in 1575. Sir Simon survived her nine years, and disappeared suddenly under very mysterious circumstances. His body has never been discovered, but his guilty spirit still haunts the Chase. The blood-stain has been much admired by tourists and others, and cannot be removed."

"That is all nonsense," cried Washington Otis; "Pinkerton's Champion Stain Remover and Paragon Detergent will clean it up in no time," and before the terrified housekeeper could interfere he had fallen upon his knees, and was rapidly scouring the floor with a small stick of what looked like a black cosmetic. In a few moments no trace of the bloodstain could be seen.

"I knew Pinkerton would do it," he exclaimed triumphantly, as he looked round at his admiring family; but no sooner had he said these words than a terrible flash of lightning lit up the sombre room, a fearful peal of thunder made them all start to their feet, and Mrs. Umney fainted.

"What a monstrous climate!" said the American Minister calmly, as he lit a long cheroot. "I guess the old country is so over-populated that they have not enough decent weather for everybody. I have always been of opinion that emigration is the only thing for England."

"My dear Hiram," cried Mrs. Otis, "what can we do with a woman who faints?"

"Charge it to her like breakages," answered the Minister; "she won't faint after that;" and in a few moments Mrs. Umney certainly came to. There was no doubt, however, that she was extremely upset, and she sternly warned Mr. Otis to beware of some trouble coming to the house.

"I have seen things with my own eyes, sir," she said, "that would make any Christian's hair stand on end, and many and many a night I have not closed my eyes in sleep for the awful things that are done here." Mr. Otis, however, and his wife warmly assured the honest soul that they were not afraid of ghosts, and, after invoking the blessings of Providence on her new master and mistress, and making arrangements for an increase of salary, the old housekeeper tottered off to her own room.

II

The storm raged fiercely all that night, but nothing of particular note occurred. The next morning, however, when they came down to breakfast, they found the terrible stain of blood once again on the floor. "I don't think it can be the fault of the Paragon Detergent," said Washington, "for I have tried it with everything. It must be the ghost." He accordingly rubbed out the stain a second time, but the second morning it appeared again. The third morning also it was there, though the library had been locked up at night by Mr. Otis himself, and the key carried upstairs. The whole family were now quite interested; Mr. Otis began to suspect that he had been too dogmatic in his denial of the existence of ghosts, Mrs. Otis expressed her intention of joining the Psychical Society, and Washington prepared a long letter to Messrs. Myers and Podmore on the subject of the Permanence of Sanguineous Stains when connected with Crime. That night all doubts about the objective existence of phantasmata were removed for ever.

The day had been warm and sunny; and, in the cool of the evening, the whole family went out for a drive. They did not return home till nine o'clock, when they had a light supper. The conversation in no way turned upon ghosts, so there were not even those primary conditions of receptive expectation which so often precede the presentation of psychical phenomena. The subjects discussed, as I have since learned from Mr. Otis, were merely such as form the ordinary conversation of cultured Americans of the better class, such as the immense superiority of Miss Fanny Davenport over Sarah Bernhardt as an actress; the difficulty of obtaining green corn, buckwheat cakes, and hominy, even in the best English houses; the importance of Boston in the development of the world-soul; the advantages of the baggage check system in railway travelling; and the sweetness of the New York accent as compared to the London drawl. No mention at all was made of the supernatural, nor was Sir Simon de Canterville alluded to in any way. At eleven o'clock the family retired, and by half-past all the lights were out. Some time after, Mr. Otis was awakened by a curious noise in the corridor, outside his room. It sounded like the clank of metal, and seemed to be coming nearer every moment. He got up at once, struck a match, and looked at the time. It was exactly one o'clock. He was quite calm, and felt his pulse, which was not at all feverish. The strange noise still continued, and with it he heard distinctly the sound of footsteps. He put on his slippers, took a small oblong phial out of his dressing-case, and opened the door. Right in front of him he saw, in the wan moonlight, an old man of terrible aspect. His eyes were as red burning coals; long grey hair fell over his shoulders in matted coils; his garments, which were of antique cut, were soiled and ragged, and from his wrists and ankles hung heavy manacles and rusty gyves.

"My dear sir," said Mr. Otis, "I really must insist on your oiling those chains, and have brought you for that purpose a small bottle of the Tammany Rising Sun Lubricator. It is said to be completely efficacious upon one application, and there are several testimonials to that effect on the wrapper from some of our most eminent native divines. I shall leave it here for you by the bedroom candles, and will be happy to supply you with more should you require it." With these words the

United States Minister laid the bottle down on a marble table, and, closing his door, retired to rest.

For a moment the Canterville ghost stood quite motionless in natural indignation; then, dashing the bottle violently upon the polished floor, he fled down the corridor, uttering hollow groans, and emitting a ghastly green light. Just, however, as he reached the top of the great oak staircase, a door was flung open, two little white-robed figures appeared, and a large pillow whizzed past his head! There was evidently no time to be lost, so, hastily adopting the Fourth Dimension of Space as a means of escape, he vanished through the wainscoting, and the house became quite quiet.

On reaching a small secret chamber in the left wing, he leaned up against a moonbeam to recover his breath, and began to try and realise his position. Never, in a brilliant and uninterrupted career of three hundred years, had he been so grossly insulted. He thought of the Dowager Duchess, whom he had frightened into a fit as she stood before the glass in her lace and diamonds; of the four housemaids, who had gone off into hysterics when he merely grinned at them through the curtains of one of the spare bedrooms; of the rector of the parish, whose candle he had blown out as he was coming late one night from the library, and who had been under the care of Sir William Gull ever since, a perfect martyr to nervous disorders; and of old Madame de Tremouillac, who, having wakened up one morning early and seen a skeleton seated in an armchair by the fire reading her diary, had been confined to her bed for six weeks with an attack of brain fever, and, on her recovery, had become reconciled to the Church, and broken off her connection with that notorious sceptic Monsieur de Voltaire. He remembered the terrible night when the wicked Lord Canterville was found choking in his dressing-room, with the knave of diamonds halfway down his throat, and confessed, just before he died, that he had cheated Charles James Fox out of £50,000 at Crockford's by means of that very card, and swore that the ghost had made him swallow it. All his great achievements came back to him again, from the butler who had shot himself in the pantry because he had seen a green hand tapping at the window pane, to the beautiful Lady Stutfield, who was always obliged to wear a black velvet band round her throat to hide the mark of five fingers burnt upon her white skin, and who drowned herself at last in the carp-pond at the end of the King's Walk. With the enthusiastic egotism of the true artist he went over his most celebrated performances, and smiled bitterly to himself as he recalled to mind his last appearance as "Red Ruben, or the Strangled Babe," his *début* as "Gaunt Gibeon, the Blood-sucker of Bexley Moor," and the *furore* he had excited one lovely June evening by merely playing ninepins with his own bones upon the lawn-tennis ground. And after all this, some wretched modern Americans were to come and offer him the Rising Sun Lubricator, and throw pillows at his head! It was quite unbearable. Besides, no ghost in history had ever been treated in this manner. Accordingly, he determined to have vengeance, and remained till daylight in an attitude of deep thought.

III

The next morning when the Otis family met at breakfast, they discussed the ghost at some length. The United States Minister was naturally a little annoyed to find that his present had not been accepted. "I have no wish," he said, "to do the ghost any personal injury, and I must say that, considering the length of time he has been in the house, I don't think it is at all polite to throw pillows at him"—a very just remark, at which, I am sorry to say, the twins burst into shouts of laughter. "Upon the other hand," he continued, "if he really declines to use the Rising Sun Lubricator, we shall have to take his chains from him. It would be quite impossible to sleep, with such a noise going on outside the bedrooms."

For the rest of the week, however, they were undisturbed, the only thing that excited any attention being the continual renewal of the blood-stain on the library floor. This certainly was very strange, as the door was always locked at night by Mr. Otis, and the windows kept closely barred. The chameleon-like colour, also, of the stain excited a good deal of comment. Some mornings it was a dull (almost Indian) red, then it would be vermilion, then a rich purple, and once when they came down for family prayers, according to the simple rites of the Free American Reformed Episcopalian Church, they found it a bright emerald-green. These kaleidoscopic changes naturally amused the party very much, and bets on the subject were freely made every evening. The only person who did not enter into the joke was little Virginia, who for some unexplained reason, was always a good deal distressed at the sight of the blood-stain, and very nearly cried the morning it was emerald-green.

The second appearance of the ghost was on Sunday night. Shortly after they had gone to bed they were suddenly alarmed by a fearful crash in the hall. Rushing downstairs, they found that a large suit of old armour had become detached from its stand, and had fallen on the stone floor, while, seated in a high-backed chair, was the Canterville ghost, rubbing his knees with an expression of acute agony on his face. The twins, having brought their pea-shooters with them, at once discharged two pellets on him, with that accuracy of aim which can only be attained by long and careful practice on a writing-master, while the United States Minister covered him with his revolver, and called upon him, in accordance with Californian etiquette, to hold up his hands! The ghost started up with a wild shriek of rage, and swept through them like a mist, extinguishing Washington Otis's candle as he passed, and so leaving them all in total darkness. On reaching the top of the staircase he recovered himself, and determined to give his celebrated peal of demoniac laughter. This he had on more than one occasion found extremely useful. It was said to have turned Lord Raker's wig grey in a single night, and had certainly made three of Lady Canterville's French governesses give notice before their month was up. He accordingly laughed his most horrible laugh, till the old vaulted roof rang and rang again, but hardly had the fearful echo died away when a door opened, and Mrs. Otis came out in a light blue dressing-gown. "I am afraid you are far from well," she said, "and have brought you a bottle of Dr. Dobell's tincture. If it is indigestion, you will find it a most excellent remedy." The ghost glared at her in fury, and began at once to make preparations for turning himself into a large black dog, an accomplishment for which he was justly renowned, and to which the family doctor always attributed the permanent idiocy of Lord Canterville's uncle, the Hon. Thomas Horton. The sound of approaching footsteps, however, made him hesitate in his fell purpose, so he contented himself with becoming faintly phosphorescent, and vanished with a deep church-yard groan, just as the twins had come up to him.

On reaching his room he entirely broke down, and became a prey to the most violent agitation. The vulgarity of the twins, and the gross materialism of Mrs. Otis, were naturally extremely annoying, but what really distressed him most was, that he had been unable to wear the suit of mail. He had hoped that even modern Americans would be thrilled by the sight of a Spectre In Armour, if for no more sensible reason, at least out of respect for their national poet Longfellow, over whose graceful and attractive poetry he himself had whiled away many a weary hour when the Cantervilles were up in town. Besides, it was his own suit. He had worn it with great success at the Kenilworth tournament, and had been highly complimented on it by no less a person than the Virgin Queen herself. Yet when he had put it on, he had been completely overpowered by the weight of the huge breastplate and steel casque, and had fallen heavily on the stone pavement, barking both his knees severely, and bruising the knuckles of his right hand.

For some days after this he was extremely ill, and hardly stirred out of his room at all, except to keep the blood-stain in proper repair. However, by taking great care of himself, he recovered, and resolved to make a third attempt to frighten the United States Minister and his family. He selected Friday, the 17th of August, for his appearance, and spent most of that day in looking over his wardrobe, ultimately deciding in favour of a large slouched hat with a red feather, a winding-sheet frilled at the wrists and neck, and a rusty dagger. Towards evening a violent storm of rain came on, and the wind was so high that all the windows and doors in the old house shook and rattled. In fact, it was just such weather as he loved. His plan of action was this. He was to make his way quietly to Washington Otis's room, gibber at him from the foot of the bed, and stab himself three times in the throat to the sound of slow music. He bore Washington a special grudge, being quite aware that it was he who was in the habit of removing the famous Canterville blood-stain, by means of Pinkerton's Paragon Detergent. Having reduced the reckless and foolhardy youth to a condition of abject terror, he was then to proceed to the room occupied by the United States Minister and his wife, and there to place a clammy hand on Mrs. Otis's forehead, while he hissed into her trembling husband's ear the awful secrets of the charnel-house. With regard to little Virginia, he had not quite made up his mind. She had never insulted him in any way, and was pretty and gentle. A few hollow groans from the wardrobe, he thought, would be more than sufficient, or, if that failed to wake her, he might grabble at the counterpane with palsy-twitching fingers. As for the twins, he was quite determined to teach them a lesson. The first thing to be done, was of course, to sit upon their chests, so as to produce the stifling sensation of nightmare. Then, as their beds were quite close to each other, to stand between them in the form of a green, icy-cold corpse, till they became paralysed with fear, and finally, to throw off the winding-sheet, and crawl round the room, with white bleached bones and one rolling eye-ball, in the character of "Dumb Daniel, or the Suicide's Skeleton," a rôle in which he had on more than one occasion produced a great effect, and which he considered quite equal to his famous part of "Martin the Maniac, or the Masked Mystery."

At half-past ten he heard the family going to bed. For some time he was disturbed by wild shrieks of laughter from the twins, who, with the light-hearted gaiety of schoolboys, were evidently amusing themselves before they retired to rest, but at a quarter past eleven all was still, and, as midnight sounded, he sallied forth. The owl beat against the window panes, the raven croaked from the old yew-tree, and the wind wandered moaning round the house like a lost soul; but the Otis family slept unconscious of their doom, and high above the rain and storm he could hear the steady snoring of the Minister for the United States. He stepped stealthily out of the wainscoting, with an evil smile on his cruel, wrinkled mouth, and the moon hid her face in a cloud as he stole past the great oriel window, where his own arms and those of his murdered wife were blazoned in azure and gold. On and on he glided, like an evil shadow, the very darkness seeming to loathe him as he passed. Once he thought he heard something call, and stopped; but it was only the baying of a dog from the Red Farm, and he went on, muttering strange sixteenth-century curses, and ever and anon brandishing the rusty dagger in the midnight air. Finally he reached the corner of the passage that led to luckless Washington's room. For a moment he paused there, the wind blowing his long grey locks about his head, and twisting into grotesque and fantastic folds the nameless horror of the dead man's shroud. Then the clock struck the quarter, and he felt the time was come. He chuckled to himself, and turned the corner; but no sooner had he done so, than, with a piteous wail of terror, he fell back, and hid his blanched face in his long, bony hands. Right in front of him was standing a horrible spectre, motionless as a carved image, and monstrous as a madman's dream! Its head was bald and burnished; its face round, and fat, and white; and hideous laughter seemed to have writhed its features into an eternal grin. From the eyes streamed rays of scarlet light, the mouth was a wide well of fire, and a hideous garment, like to his own, swathed with its silent snows the Titan form. On its breast was a placard with strange writing in antique characters, some scroll of shame it seemed, some record of wild sins, some awful calendar of crime, and, with its right hand, it bore aloft a falchion of gleaming steel.

Never having seen a ghost before, he naturally was terribly frightened, and, after a second hasty glance at the awful phantom, he fled back to his room, tripping up in his long winding-sheet as he sped down the corridor, and finally dropping the rusty dagger into the Minister's jack-boots, where it was found in the morning by the butler. Once in the privacy of his own apartment, he flung himself down on a small pallet-bed, and hid his face under the clothes. After a time, however, the brave old Canterville spirit asserted itself, and he determined to go and speak to the other ghost as soon as it was daylight. Accordingly, just as the dawn was touching the hills with silver, he returned towards the spot where he had first laid eyes on the grisly phantom, feeling that, after all, two ghosts were better than one, and that, by the aid of his new friend, he might safely grapple with the twins. On reaching the spot, however, a terrible sight met his gaze. Something had evidently happened to the spectre, for the light had entirely faded from its hollow eyes, the gleaming falchion had fallen from its hand, and it was leaning up against the wall in a strained and uncomfortable attitude. He rushed forward and seized it in his arms, when, to his horror, the head slipped off and rolled on the floor, the body assumed a recumbent posture, and he found himself clasping a white dimity bed-curtain, with a sweeping-brush, a kitchen cleaver, and a hollow turnip lying at his feet! Unable to understand this curious transformation, he clutched the placard with feverish haste, and there, in the grey morning light, he read these fearful words:

> ## YE OTIS GHOSTE.
> Ye Onlie True and Originale Spook.
> Beware of Ye Imitationes.
> All others are Counterfeite.

The whole thing flashed across him. He had been tricked, foiled, and outwitted! The old Canterville look came into his eyes; he ground his toothless gums together; and, raising his withered hands high above his head, swore, according to the picturesque phraseology of the antique school, that when Chanticleer had sounded twice his merry horn, deeds of blood would be wrought, and Murder walk abroad with silent feet.

Hardly had he finished this awful oath when, from the red-tiled roof of a distant homestead, a cock crew. He laughed a long, low, bitter laugh, and waited. Hour after hour he waited, but the cock, for some strange reason, did not crow again. Finally, at half-past seven, the arrival of the housemaids made him give up his fearful vigil, and he stalked back to his room, thinking of his vain hope and baffled purpose.

There he consulted several books of ancient chivalry, of which he was exceedingly fond, and found that, on every occasion on which his oath had been used, Chanticleer had always crowed a second time. "Perdition seize the naughty fowl," he muttered, "I have seen the day when, with my stout spear, I would have run him through the gorge, and made him crow for me as 'twere in death!" He then retired to a comfortable lead coffin, and stayed there till evening.

IV

The next day the ghost was very weak and tired. The terrible excitement of the last four weeks was beginning to have its effect. His nerves were completely shattered, and he started at the slightest noise. For five days he kept to his room and at last made up his mind to give up the point of the stain on the library floor. If the Otis family did not want it, they clearly did not deserve it. They were evidently people on a low, material plane of existence, and quite incapable of appreciating the symbolic value of sensuous phenomena. The question of phantasmic apparitions, and the development of astral bodies, was of course quite a different matter, and really not under his control. It was his solemn duty to appear in the corridor once a week, and to gibber from the large oriel window on the first and third Wednesday in every month, and he did not see how he could honourably escape from his obligations. It is quite true that his life had been very evil, but, upon the other hand, he was most conscientious in all things connected with the supernatural. For the next three Saturdays, accordingly, he traversed the corridor as usual between midnight and three o'clock, taking every possible precaution against being either heard or seen. He removed his boots, trod as lightly as possible on the old worm-eaten boards, wore a large black velvet cloak, and was careful to use the Rising Sun Lubricator for oiling his chains. I am bound to acknowledge that it was with a good deal of difficulty that he brought himself to adopt this last mode of protection. However, one night, while the family were at dinner, he slipped into Mr. Otis's bedroom and carried off the bottle. He felt a little humiliated at first, but afterwards was sensible enough to see that there was a great deal to be said for the invention, and, to a certain degree, it served his purpose. Still, in spite of everything, he was not left unmolested. Strings were continually being stretched across the corridor, over which he tripped in the dark, and on one occasion, while dressed for the part of

"Black Isaac, or the Huntsman of Hogley Woods," he met with a severe fall, through treading on a butter-slide, which the twins had constructed from the entrance of the Tapestry Chamber to the top of the oak staircase. This last insult so enraged him, that he resolved to make one final effort to assert his dignity and social position, and determined to visit the insolent young Etonians the next night in his celebrated character of "Reckless Rupert, or the Headless Earl."

He had not appeared in this disguise for more than seventy years; in fact, not since he had so frightened pretty Lady Barbara Modish by means of it, that she suddenly broke off her engagement with the present Lord Canterville's grandfather, and ran away to Gretna Green with handsome Jack Castleton, declaring that nothing in the world would induce her to marry into a family that allowed such a horrible phantom to walk up and down the terrace at twilight. Poor Jack was afterwards shot in a duel by Lord Canterville on Wandsworth Common, and Lady Barbara died of a broken heart at Tunbridge Wells before the year was out, so, in every way, it had been a great success. It was, however, an extremely difficult "make-up," if I may use such a theatrical expression in connection with one of the greatest mysteries of the supernatural, or, to employ a more scientific term, the higher-natural world, and it took him fully three hours to make his preparations. At last everything was ready, and he was very pleased with his appearance. The big leather riding-boots that went with the dress were just a little too large for him, and he could only find one of the two horse-pistols, but, on the whole, he was quite satisfied, and at a quarter past one he glided out of the wainscoting and crept down the corridor. On reaching the room occupied by the twins, which I should mention was called the Blue Bed Chamber, on account of the colour of its hangings, he found the door just ajar. Wishing to make an effective entrance, he flung it wide open, when a heavy jug of water fell right down on him, wetting him to the skin, and just missing his left shoulder by a couple of inches. At the same moment he heard stifled shrieks of laughter proceeding from the four-post bed. The shock to his nervous system was so great that he fled back to his room as hard as he could go, and the next day he was laid up with a severe cold. The only thing that at all consoled him in the whole affair was the fact that he had not brought his head with him, for had he done so, the consequences might have been very serious.

He now gave up all hope of ever frightening this rude American family, and contented himself, as a rule, with creeping about the passages in list slippers, with a thick red muffler round his throat for fear of draughts, and a small arquebuse, in case he should be attacked by the twins. The final blow he received occurred on the 19th of September. He had gone downstairs to the great entrance-hall, feeling sure that there, at any rate, he would be quite unmolested, and was amusing himself by making satirical remarks on the large Saroni photographs of the United States Minister and his wife, which had now taken the place of the Canterville family pictures. He was simply but neatly clad in a long shroud, spotted with churchyard mould, had tied up his jaw with a strip of yellow linen, and carried a small lantern and a sexton's spade. In fact, he was dressed for the character of "Jonas the Graveless, or the Corpse-Snatcher of Chertsey Barn," one of his most remarkable impersonations, and one which the Cantervilles had every reason to remember, as it was the real origin of their quarrel with their neighbour, Lord Rufford. It was about a quarter past two o'clock in the morning, and, as far as he could ascertain, no one was stirring. As he was strolling towards the library, however, to see if there were any traces left of the blood-stain, suddenly there leaped out on him from a dark corner two figures, who waved their arms wildly above their heads, and shrieked out "BOO!" in his ear.

Seized with a panic, which, under the circumstances, was only natural, he rushed for the staircase, but found Washington Otis waiting for him there with the big garden-syringe; and being thus hemmed in by his enemies on every side, and driven almost to bay, he vanished into the great iron stove, which, fortunately for him, was not lit, and had to make his way home through the flues and chimneys, arriving at his own room in a terrible state of dirt, disorder, and despair.

After this he was not seen again on any nocturnal expedition. The twins lay in wait for him on several occasions, and strewed the passages with nutshells every night to the great annoyance of their parents and the servants, but it was of no avail. It was quite evident that his feelings were so wounded that he would not appear. Mr. Otis consequently resumed his great work on the history of the Democratic Party, on which he had been engaged for some years; Mrs. Otis organised a wonderful clam-bake, which amazed the whole county; the boys took to lacrosse, euchre, poker, and other American national games; and Virginia rode about the lanes on her pony, accompanied by the young Duke of Cheshire, who had come to spend the last week of his holidays at Canterville Chase. It was generally assumed that the ghost had gone away, and, in fact, Mr. Otis wrote a letter to that effect to Lord Canterville, who, in reply, expressed his great pleasure at the news, and sent his best congratulations to the Minister's worthy wife.

The Otises, however, were deceived, for the ghost was still in the house, and though now almost an invalid, was by no means ready to let matters rest, particularly as he heard that among the guests was the young Duke of Cheshire, whose grand-uncle, Lord Francis Stilton, had once bet a hundred guineas with Colonel Carbury that he would play dice with the Canterville ghost, and was found the next morning lying on the floor of the card-room in such a helpless paralytic state, that though he lived on to a great age, he was never able to say anything again but "Double Sixes." The story was well known at the time, though, of course, out of respect to the feelings of the two noble families, every attempt was made to hush it up; and a full account of all the circumstances connected with it will be found in the third volume of Lord Tattle's *Recollections of the Prince Regent and his Friends*. The ghost, then, was naturally very anxious to show that he had not lost his influence over the Stiltons, with whom, indeed, he was distantly connected, his own first cousin having been married *en secondes noces* to the Sieur de Bulkeley, from whom, as every one knows, the Dukes of Cheshire are lineally descended. Accordingly, he made arrangements for appearing to Virginia's little lover in his celebrated impersonation of "The Vampire Monk, or, the Bloodless Benedictine," a performance so horrible that when old Lady Startup saw it, which she did on one fatal New Year's Eve, in the year 1764, she went off into the most piercing shrieks, which culminated in violent apoplexy, and died in three days, after disinheriting the Cantervilles, who were her nearest relations, and leaving all her money to her London apothecary. At the last moment, however, his terror of the twins prevented his leaving his room, and the little Duke slept in peace under the great feathered canopy in the Royal Bedchamber, and dreamed of Virginia.

V

A few days after this, Virginia and her curly-haired cavalier went out riding on Brockley meadows, where she tore her habit so badly in getting through a hedge, that, on her return home, she made up her mind to go up by the back staircase so as not to be seen. As she was running past the Tapestry Chamber, the door of which happened to be open, she fancied she saw someone inside, and thinking it was her mother's maid, who sometimes used to bring her work there, looked in to ask her to mend her habit. To her immense surprise, however, it was the Canterville Ghost himself! He was sitting by the window, watching the ruined gold of the yellowing trees fly through the air, and the red leaves dancing madly down the long avenue. His head was leaning on his hand, and his whole attitude was one of extreme depression. Indeed, so forlorn, and so much out of repair did he look, that little Virginia, whose first idea had been to run away and lock herself in her room, was filled with pity, and determined to try and comfort him. So light was her footfall, and so deep his melancholy, that he was not aware of her presence till she spoke to him.

"I am so sorry for you," she said, "but my brothers are going back to Eton tomorrow, and then, if you behave yourself, no one will annoy you."

"It is absurd asking me to behave myself," he answered, looking round in astonishment at the pretty little girl who had ventured to address him, "quite absurd. I must rattle my chains, and groan through keyholes, and walk about at night, if that is what you mean. It is my only reason for existing."

"It is no reason at all for existing, and you know you have been very wicked. Mrs. Umney told us, the first day we arrived here, that you killed your wife."

"Well, I quite admit it," said the Ghost petulantly, "but it was a purely family matter, and concerned no one else."

"It is very wrong to kill anyone," said Virginia, who at times had a sweet Puritan gravity, caught from some old New England ancestor.

"Oh, I hate the cheap severity of abstract ethics! My wife was very plain, never had my ruffs properly starched, and knew nothing about cookery. Why, there was a buck I had shot in Hogley Woods, a magnificent pricket, and do you know how she had it sent up to table? However, it is no matter now, for it is all over, and I don't think it was very nice of her brothers to starve me to death, though I did kill her."

"Starve you to death? Oh, Mr. Ghost, I mean Sir Simon, are you hungry? I have a sandwich in my case. Would you like it?"

"No, thank you, I never eat anything now; but it is very kind of you, all the same, and you are much nicer than the rest of your horrid, rude, vulgar, dishonest family."

"Stop!" cried Virginia, stamping her foot, "it is you who are rude, and horrid, and vulgar, and as for dishonesty, you know you stole the paints out of my box to try and furbish up that ridiculous blood-stain in the library. First you took all my reds, including the vermilion, and I couldn't do any more sunsets, then you took the emerald-green and the chrome-yellow, and finally I had nothing left but indigo and Chinese white, and could only do moonlight scenes, which are always depressing to look at, and not at all easy to paint. I never told on you, though I was very much annoyed, and it was most ridiculous, the whole thing; for who ever heard of emerald-green blood?"

"Well, really," said the Ghost, rather meekly, "what was I to do? It is a very difficult thing to get real blood nowadays, and, as your brother began it all with his Paragon Detergent, I certainly saw no reason why I should not have your paints. As for colour, that is always a matter of taste: the Cantervilles have blue blood, for instance, the very bluest in England; but I know you Americans don't care for things of this kind."

"You know nothing about it, and the best thing you can do is to emigrate and improve your mind. My father will be only too happy to give you a free passage, and though there is a heavy duty on spirits of every kind, there will be no difficulty about the Custom House, as the officers are all Democrats. Once in New York, you are sure to be a great success. I know lots of people there who would give a hundred thousand dollars to have a grandfather, and much more than that to have a family Ghost."

"I don't think I should like America."

"I suppose because we have no ruins and no curiosities," said Virginia satirically.

"No ruins! no curiosities!" answered the Ghost; "you have your navy and your manners."

"Good evening; I will go and ask papa to get the twins an extra week's holiday."

"Please don't go, Miss Virginia," he cried; "I am so lonely and so unhappy, and I really don't know what to do. I want to go to sleep and I cannot."

"That's quite absurd! You have merely to go to bed and blow out the candle. It is very difficult sometimes to keep awake, especially at church, but there is no difficulty at all about sleeping. Why, even babies know how to do that, and they are not very clever."

"I have not slept for three hundred years," he said sadly, and Virginia's beautiful blue eyes opened in wonder; "for three hundred years I have not slept, and I am so tired."

Virginia grew grave, and her little lips trembled like rose-leaves. She came towards him, and kneeling down at his side, looked up into his old withered face.

"Poor, poor Ghost," she murmured; "have you no place where you can sleep?"

"Far away beyond the pine-woods," he answered, in a low dreamy voice, "there is a little garden. There the grass grows long and deep, there are the great white stars of the hemlock flower, there the nightingale sings all night long. All night long he sings, and the cold, crystal moon looks down, and the yew-tree spreads out its giant arms over the sleeper."

Virginia's eyes grew dim with tears, and she hid her face in her hands.

"You mean the Garden of Death," she whispered.

"Yes, Death. Death must be so beautiful. To lie in the soft brown earth, with the grasses waving above one's head, and listen to silence. To have no yesterday, and no tomorrow. To forget time, to forgive life, to be at peace. You can help me. You can open for me the portals of Death's house, for Love is always with you, and Love is stronger than Death is."

Virginia trembled, a cold shudder ran through her, and for a few moments there was silence. She felt as if she was in a terrible dream.

Then the Ghost spoke again, and his voice sounded like the sighing of the wind.

"Have you ever read the old prophecy on the library window?"

"Oh, often," cried the little girl, looking up; "I know it quite well. It is painted in curious black letters, and it is difficult to read. There are only six lines:

> When a golden girl can win
> Prayer from out the lips of sin,
> When the barren almond bears,
> And a little child gives away its tears,
> Then shall all the house be still
> And peace come to Canterville.

But I don't know what they mean."

"They mean," he said sadly, "that you must weep for me for my sins, because I have no tears, and pray with me for my soul, because I have no faith, and then, if you have always been sweet, and good, and gentle, the Angel of Death will have mercy on me. You will see fearful shapes in darkness, and wicked voices will whisper in your ear, but they will not harm you, for against the purity of a little child the powers of Hell cannot prevail."

Virginia made no answer, and the Ghost wrung his hands in wild despair as he looked down at her bowed golden head. Suddenly she stood up, very pale, with a strange light in her eyes. "I am not afraid," she said firmly, "and I will ask the Angel to have mercy on you."

He rose from his seat with a faint cry of joy, and taking her hand bent over it with old-fashioned grace and kissed it. His fingers were as cold as ice, and his lips burned like fire, but Virginia did not falter, as he led her across the dusky room. On the faded green tapestry were embroidered little huntsmen. They blew their tasselled horns and with their tiny hands waved to her to go back. "Go back! little Virginia," they cried, "go back!" but the Ghost clutched her hand more tightly, and she shut her eyes against them. Horrible animals with lizard tails, and goggle eyes, blinked at her from the carved chimney-piece, and murmured "Beware! little Virginia, beware! we may never see you again," but the Ghost glided on more swiftly, and Virginia did not listen. When they reached the end of the room he stopped, and muttered some words she could not understand. She opened her eyes, and saw the wall slowly fading away like a mist, and a great black cavern in front of her. A bitter cold wind swept round them, and she felt something pulling at her dress. "Quick, quick," cried the Ghost, "or it will be too late," and, in a moment, the wainscoting had closed behind them, and the Tapestry Chamber was empty.

VI

About ten minutes later, the bell rang for tea, and, as Virginia did not come down, Mrs. Otis sent up one of the footmen to tell her. After a little time he returned and said that he could not find Miss Virginia anywhere. As she was in the habit of going out to the garden every evening to get flowers for the dinner-table, Mrs. Otis was not at all alarmed at first, but when six o'clock struck, and Virginia did not appear, she became really agitated, and sent the boys out to look for her, while she herself and Mr. Otis searched every room in the house. At half-past six the boys came back and said that they could find no trace of their sister anywhere. They were all now in the greatest state of excitement, and did not know what to do, when Mr. Otis suddenly remembered that, some few days before, he had given a band of gypsies permission to camp in the park. He accordingly at once set off for Blackfell Hollow, where he knew they were, accompanied by his eldest son and two of the farm-servants. The little Duke of Cheshire, who was perfectly frantic with anxiety, begged hard to be allowed to go too, but Mr. Otis would not allow him, as he was afraid there might be a scuffle. On arriving at the spot, however, he found that the gypsies had gone, and it was evident that their departure had been rather sudden, as the fire was still burning, and some plates were lying on the grass. Having sent off Washington and the two men to scour the district, he ran home, and despatched telegrams to all the police inspectors in the county, telling them to look out for a little girl who had been kidnapped by tramps or gypsies. He then ordered his horse to be brought round, and, after insisting on his wife and the three boys sitting down to dinner, rode off down the Ascot Road with a groom. He had hardly, however, gone a couple of miles when he heard somebody galloping after him, and, looking round, saw the little Duke coming up on his pony, with his face very flushed and no hat. "I'm awfully sorry, Mr. Otis," gasped out the boy, "but I can't eat any dinner as long as Virginia is lost. Please, don't be angry with me; if you had let us be engaged last year, there would never have been all this trouble. You won't send me back, will you? I can't go! I won't go!"

The Minister could not help smiling at the handsome young scapegrace, and was a good deal touched at his devotion to Virginia, so leaning down from his horse, he patted him kindly on the shoulders, and said, "Well, Cecil, if you won't go back I suppose you must come with me, but I must get you a hat at Ascot."

"Oh, bother my hat! I want Virginia!" cried the little Duke, laughing, and they galloped on to the railway station. There Mr. Otis inquired of the station-master if anyone answering the description of Virginia had been seen on the platform, but could get no news of her. The station-master, however, wired up and down the line, and assured him that a strict watch would be kept for her, and, after having bought a hat for the little Duke from a linen-draper, who was just putting up his shutters, Mr. Otis rode off to Bexley, a village about four miles away, which he was told was a well-known haunt of the gypsies, as there was a large common next to it. Here they roused up the rural policeman, but could get no information from him, and, after riding all over the common, they turned their horses' heads homewards, and reached the Chase about eleven o'clock, dead-tired and almost heart-broken. They found

Washington and the twins waiting for them at the gatehouse with lanterns, as the avenue was very dark. Not the slightest trace of Virginia had been discovered. The gypsies had been caught on Brockley meadows, but she was not with them, and they had explained their sudden departure by saying that they had mistaken the date of Chorton Fair, and had gone off in a hurry for fear they might be late. Indeed, they had been quite distressed at hearing of Virginia's disappearance, as they were very grateful to Mr. Otis for having allowed them to camp in his park, and four of their number had stayed behind to help in the search. The carp-pond had been dragged, and the whole Chase thoroughly gone over, but without any result. It was evident that, for that night at any rate, Virginia was lost to them; and it was in a state of the deepest depression that Mr. Otis and the boys walked up to the house, the groom following behind with the two horses and the pony. In the hall they found a group of frightened servants, and lying on a sofa in the library was poor Mrs. Otis, almost out of her mind with terror and anxiety, and having her forehead bathed with eau-de-cologne by the old housekeeper. Mr. Otis at once insisted on her having something to eat, and ordered up supper for the whole party. It was a melancholy meal, as hardly anyone spoke, and even the twins were awestruck and subdued, as they were very fond of their sister. When they had finished, Mr. Otis, in spite of the entreaties of the little Duke, ordered them all to bed, saying that nothing more could be done that night, and that he would telegraph in the morning to Scotland Yard for some detectives to be sent down immediately. Just as they were passing out of the dining-room, midnight began to boom from the clock tower, and when the last stroke sounded they heard a crash and a sudden shrill cry; a dreadful peal of thunder shook the house, a strain of unearthly music floated through the air, a panel at the top of the staircase flew back with a loud noise, and out on the landing, looking very pale and white, with a little casket in her hand, stepped Virginia. In a moment they had all rushed up to her. Mrs. Otis clasped her passionately in her arms, the Duke smothered her with violent kisses, and the twins executed a wild war-dance round the group.

"Good heavens! child, where have you been?" said Mr. Otis, rather angrily, thinking that she had been playing some foolish trick on them. "Cecil and I have been riding all over the country looking for you, and your mother has been frightened to death. You must never play these practical jokes any more."

"Except on the Ghost! except on the Ghost!" shrieked the twins, as they capered about.

"My own darling, thank God you are found; you must never leave my side again," murmured Mrs. Otis, as she kissed the trembling child, and smoothed the tangled gold of her hair.

"Papa," said Virginia quietly, "I have been with the Ghost. He is dead, and you must come and see him. He had been very wicked, but he was really sorry for all that he had done, and he gave me this box of beautiful jewels before he died."

The whole family gazed at her in mute amazement, but she was quite grave and serious; and, turning round, she led them through the opening in the wainscoting down a narrow secret corridor, Washington following with a lighted candle, which he had caught up from the table. Finally, they came to a great oak door, studded with rusty nails. When Virginia touched it, it swung back on its heavy hinges, and they found themselves in a little low room, with a vaulted ceiling, and one tiny grated window. Imbedded in the wall was a huge iron ring, and chained to it was a gaunt skeleton, that was stretched out at full length on the stone floor, and seemed to be trying to grasp with its long fleshless fingers an old-fashioned trencher and ewer, that were placed just out of its reach. The jug had evidently been once filled with water, as it was covered inside with green mould. There was nothing on the trencher but a pile of dust. Virginia knelt down beside the skeleton, and, folding her little hands together, began to pray silently, while the rest of the party looked on in wonder at the terrible tragedy whose secret was now disclosed to them.

"Hallo!" suddenly exclaimed one of the twins, who had been looking out of the window to try and discover in what wing of the house the room was situated. "Hallo! the old withered almond tree has blossomed. I can see the flowers quite plainly in the moonlight."

"God has forgiven him," said Virginia gravely, as she rose to her feet, and a beautiful light seemed to illumine her face.

"What an angel you are!" cried the young Duke, and he put his arm round her neck and kissed her.

VII

Four days after these curious incidents a funeral started from Canterville Chase at about eleven o'clock at night. The hearse was drawn by eight black horses, each of which carried on its head a great tuft of nodding ostrich-plumes, and the leaden coffin was covered by a rich purple pall, on which was embroidered in gold the Canterville coat-of-arms. By the side of the hearse and the coaches walked the servants with lighted torches, and the whole procession was wonderfully impressive. Lord Canterville was the chief mourner, having come up specially from Wales to attend the funeral, and sat in the first carriage along with little Virginia. Then came the United States Minister and his wife, then Washington and the three boys, and in the last carriage was Mrs. Umney. It was generally felt that, as she had been frightened by the ghost for more than fifty years of her life, she had a right to see the last of him. A deep grave had been dug in the corner of the churchyard, just under the old yew-tree, and the service was read in the most impressive manner by the Rev. Augustus Dampier. When the ceremony was over, the servants, according to an old custom observed in the Canterville family, extinguished their torches, and, as the coffin was being lowered into the grave, Virginia stepped forward and laid on it a large cross made of white and pink almond-blossoms. As she did so, the moon came out from behind a cloud, and flooded with its silent silver the little churchyard, and from a distant copse a nightingale began to sing. She thought of the ghost's description of the Garden of Death, her eyes became dim with tears, and she hardly spoke a word during the drive home.

The next morning, before Lord Canterville went up to town, Mr. Otis had an interview with him on the subject of the jewels the ghost had given to Virginia. They were perfectly magnificent, especially a certain ruby necklace with old Venetian setting, which was really a superb specimen of sixteenth-century work, and their value was so great that Mr. Otis felt considerable scruples about allowing his daughter to accept them.

"My lord," he said, "I know that in this country mortmain is held to apply to trinkets as well as to land, and it is quite clear to me that these jewels are, or should be, heirlooms in your family. I must beg you, accordingly, to take them to London with you, and to regard them simply as a portion of your property which has been restored to you under certain strange conditions. As for my daughter, she is merely a child, and has as yet, I am glad to say, but little interest in such appurtenances of idle luxury. I am also informed by Mrs. Otis, who, I may say, is no mean authority upon Art—having had the privilege of spending several winters in Boston when she was a girl—that these gems are of great monetary worth, and if offered for sale would fetch a tall price. Under these circumstances, Lord Canterville, I feel sure that you will recognise how impossible it would be for me to allow them to remain in the possession of any member of my family; and, indeed, all such vain gauds and toys, however suitable or necessary to the dignity of the British aristocracy, would be completely out of place among those who have been brought up on the severe, and I believe immortal, principles of republican simplicity. Perhaps I should mention that Virginia is very anxious that you should allow her to retain the box as a memento of your unfortunate but misguided ancestor. As it is extremely old, and consequently a good deal out of repair, you may perhaps think fit to comply with her request. For my own part, I confess I am a good deal surprised to find a child of mine expressing sympathy with mediaevalism in any form, and can only account for it by the fact that Virginia was born in one of your London suburbs shortly after Mrs. Otis had returned from a trip to Athens."

Lord Canterville listened very gravely to the worthy Minister's speech, pulling his grey moustache now and then to hide an involuntary smile, and when Mr. Otis had ended, he shook him cordially by the hand, and said, "My dear sir, your charming little daughter rendered my unlucky ancestor, Sir Simon, a very important service, and I and my family are much indebted to her for her marvellous courage and pluck. The jewels are clearly hers, and, egad, I believe that if I were heartless enough to take them from her, the wicked old fellow would be out of his grave in a fortnight, leading me the devil of a life. As for their being heirlooms, nothing is an heirloom that is not so mentioned in a will or legal document, and the existence of these jewels has been quite unknown. I assure you I have no more claim on them than your butler, and when Miss Virginia grows up I daresay she will be pleased to have pretty things to wear. Besides, you forget, Mr. Otis, that you took the furniture and the ghost at a valuation, and anything that belonged to the ghost passed at once into your possession, as, whatever activity Sir Simon may have shown in the corridor at night, in point of law he was really dead, and you acquired his property by purchase."

Mr. Otis was a good deal distressed at Lord Canterville's refusal, and begged him to reconsider his decision, but the good-natured peer was quite firm, and finally induced the Minister to allow his daughter to retain the present the ghost had given her, and when, in the spring of 1890, the young Duchess of Cheshire was presented at the Queen's first drawing-room on the occasion of her marriage, her jewels were the universal theme of admiration. For Virginia received the coronet, which is the reward of all good little American girls, and was married to her boy-lover as soon as he came of age. They were both so charming, and they loved each other so much, everyone was delighted at the match, except the old Marchioness of Dumbleton, who had tried to catch the Duke for one of her seven unmarried daughters, and had given no less than three expensive dinner-parties for that purpose, and, strange to say, Mr. Otis himself. Mr. Otis was extremely fond of the young Duke personally, but, theoretically, he objected to titles, and, to use his own words, "was not without apprehension lest, amid the enervating influences of a pleasure-loving aristocracy, the true principles of republican simplicity should be forgotten." His objections, however, were completely overruled, and I believe that when he walked up the aisle of St. George's, Hanover Square, with his daughter leaning on his arm, there was not a prouder man in the whole length and breadth of England.

The Duke and Duchess, after the honeymoon was over, went down to Canterville Chase, and on the day after their arrival they walked over in the afternoon to the lonely churchyard by the pine-woods. There had been a great deal of difficulty at first about the inscription on Sir Simon's tombstone, but finally it had been decided to engrave on it simply the initials of the old gentleman's name, and the verse from the library window. The Duchess had brought with her some lovely roses, which she strewed upon the grave, and after they had stood by it for some time they strolled into the ruined chancel of the old abbey. There the Duchess sat down on a fallen pillar, while her husband lay at her feet smoking a cigarette and looking up at her beautiful eyes. Suddenly he threw his cigarette away, took hold of her hand, and said to her, "Virginia, a wife should have no secrets from her husband."

"Dear Cecil! I have no secrets from you."

"Yes, you have," he answered, smiling, "you have never told me what happened to you when you were locked up with the ghost."

"I have never told anyone, Cecil," said Virginia gravely.

"I know that, but you might tell me."

"Please don't ask me, Cecil, I cannot tell you. Poor Sir Simon! I owe him a great deal. Yes, don't laugh, Cecil, I really do. He made me see what Life is, and what Death signifies, and why Love is stronger than both."

The Duke rose and kissed his wife lovingly.

"You can have your secret as long as I have your heart," he murmured.

"You have always had that, Cecil."

"And you will tell our children some day, won't you?"

Virginia blushed.

Atmosphere and the evidence of the senses are powerful tools when crafting a ghost myth, and "Blind Man's Buff" takes great advantage of both— though through most of its short length, the author ignores the sense of vision entirely . . . an astonishing tour de force *from a modern master of weird tales, H. R.* WAKEFIELD, *a Briton who wrote most of his supernatural tales between 1928 and 1935.*

Blind Man's Buff

by H. R. Wakefield

"Well, thank heavens that yokel seemed to know the place," said Mr. Cort to himself. " 'First to the right, second to the left, black gates.' I hope the oaf in Wendover who sent me six miles out of my way will freeze to death. It's not often like this in England—cold as the penny in a dead man's eye." He'd barely reach the place before dusk. He let the car out over the rasping, frozen roads. " 'First to the right' "—must be this—second to the left, must be this—and there were the black gates. He got out, swung them open, and drove cautiously up a narrow, twisting drive, his headlights peering suspiciously round the bends. Those hedges wanted clipping, he thought, and this lane would have to be remetaled— full of holes. Nasty drive up on a bad night; would cost some money, though.

The car began to climb steeply and swing to the right, and presently the high hedges ended abruptly, and Mr. Cort pulled up in front of Lorn Manor. He got out of the car, rubbed his hands, stamped his feet, and looked about him.

Lorn Manor was embedded halfway up a Chiltern spur and, as the agent had observed, "commanded extensive vistas." The place looked its age, Mr. Cort decided, or rather ages, for the double Georgian brick chimneys warred with the Queen Anne left front. He could just make out the date, 1703, at the base of the nearest chimney. All that wing must have been added later. "Big place, marvellous bargain at seven thousand, can't understand it. How those windows with their little curved eyebrows seem to frown down on one!" And then he turned and examined the "vistas." The trees were tinted exquisitely to an uncertain glory as the great red sinking sun flashed its rays on their crystal mantle. The vale of Aylesbury was drowsing beneath a slowly deepening shroud of mist. Above it the hills, their crests rounded and shaded by silver and rose coppices, seemed to have set in them great smoky eyes of flame where the last rays burned in them.

"It is like some dream world," thought Mr. Cort. "It is curious how, wherever the sun strikes, it seems to make an eye, and each one fixed on me; those hills, even those windows. But, judging from that mist, I shall have a slow journey home; I'd better have a quick look inside, though I have already taken a prejudice against the place—I hardly know why. Too lonely and isolated, perhaps." And then the eyes blinked and closed, and it was dark. He took a key from his pocket and went up three steps and thrust it into the key-hole of the massive oak door. The next moment he looked forward into absolute blackness, and the door swung to and closed behind him. This, of course, must be the "palatial panelled hall" which the agent described. He must strike a match and find the light-switch. He fumbled in his pockets without success, and then he went through them again. He thought for a moment, "I must have left them on the seat in the car," he decided; "I'll go and fetch them. The door must be just behind me here."

He turned and groped his way back, and then drew himself up sharply, for it had seemed that something had slipped past him, and then he put out his hands—to touch the back of a chair, brocaded, he judged. He moved to the left of it and walked into a wall, changed his direction, went back past the chair, and found the wall again. He went back to the chair, sat down, and went through his pockets again, more thoroughly and carefully this time. Well, there was nothing to get fussed about; he was bound to find the door sooner or later. Now let him think. When he came in he had gone straight back, because he'd stumbled into this chair. The door must be a little to the left or the right of it. He'd try each in turn. He turned to the left first, and found himself going down a little narrow passage; he could feel its sides when he stretched out his hands. Well, then, he'd try his right. He did so, and walked into a wall. He groped his way along it, and again it seemed as if something slipped past him. "I wonder if there's a bat in here?" he asked himself, and then found himself back at the chair.

How Rachel would laugh if she could see him now. Surely he had a stray match somewhere. He took off his overcoat and ran his hands round the seam of every pocket, and then he did the same to the coat of his suit. And then he put them on again. Well, he'd try again. He'd follow the wall along. He did so, and found himself in a little narrow passage. Suddenly he shot out his right hand, for he had the impression that something had brushed his face very lightly. "I'm beginning to get a little bored with that bat, and with this blasted room generally," he said to himself. "I could imagine a more nervous person than myself getting a little fussed and panicky; but that's the one thing not to do." Ah, here was that chair again. "Now, I'll try the wall the other side." Well, that seemed to go on forever, so he retraced his steps till he found the chair, and sat down again. He whistled a little snatch resignedly. What an echo! The little tune had been flung back at him so fiercely, almost menacingly. Menacingly: that was just the feeble, panicky word a nervous person would use. Well, he'd go to the left again this time.

As he got up, a quick spurt of cold air fanned his face. "Is anyone there?" he said. He had purposely not raised his voice—there was no need to shout. Of course, no one answered. Who could there have been to answer since the caretaker was away? Now let him think it out. When he came in he must have gone straight forward and then swerved slightly on the way back; therefore—no, he was getting confused. At that moment he heard the whistle of a train, and felt reassured. The line from Wendover to Aylesbury ran half-left from the front door, so it should be about there—he pointed with his finger, got up, groped his way forward, and found himself in a little narrow passage. Well, he must turn back and go to the right this time. He did so, and something seemed to slip just past him, and then he scratched his finger slightly on the brocade of the chair. "Talk about a maze," he thought to himself; "it's nothing to this." And then he said to himself, under his breath: "Curse this vile, godforsaken place!" A silly, panicky thing to do he realised—almost as bad as shouting aloud. Well, it was obviously no use trying to find the door, he *couldn't* find it—*couldn't*. He'd sit in the chair till the light came. He sat down.

How very silent it was; his hands began searching in his pockets once more. Except for that sort of whispering sound over on the left somewhere—except for that, it was absolutely silent—except for that. What could it be? The caretaker was away. He turned his head slightly and listened intently. It was almost as if there were several people whispering together. One got curious sounds in old houses. How absurd it was! The chair couldn't be more than three or four yards from the door. There was no doubt about that. It must be slightly to one side or the other. He'd try the left once more. He got up, and something lightly brushed his face. "Is anyone there?" he said, and this time he knew he had shouted. "Who touched me? Who's whispering? Where's the door?" What a nervous fool he was to shout like that; yet someone outside might have heard him. He went groping forward again, and touched a wall. He followed along it, touching it with his fingertips, and there was an opening.

The door, the door, it must be! And he found himself going down a little narrow passage. He turned and ran back. And then he remembered! He had put a match-booklet in his note-case! What a fool to have forgotten it, and make such an exhibition of himself. Yes, there it was; but his hands were trembling, and the booklet slipped through his fingers. He fell to his knees, and began searching about on the floor. "It must be just here, it can't be far"—and then something icy-cold and damp was pressed against his forehead. He flung himself forward to seize it, but there was nothing there. And then he leapt to his feet, and with tears streaming down his face cried: "Who is there? Save me! Save me!" And then he began to run round and round, his arms outstretched. At last he stumbled against something, the chair—and something touched him as it slipped past. And then he ran screaming round the room; and suddenly his screams slashed back at him, for he was in a little narrow passage.

* * *

"Now, Mr. Runt," said the coroner, "you say you heard screaming coming from the direction of the Manor. Why didn't you go to find out what was the matter?"

"None of us chaps goes to Manor after sundown," said Mr. Runt.

"Oh, I know there's some absurd superstition about the house; but you haven't answered the question. There were screams, obviously coming from someone who wanted help. Why didn't you go to see what was the matter, instead of running away?"

"None of us chaps goes to Manor after sundown," said Mr. Runt.

"Don't fence with the question. Let me remind you that the doctor said Mr. Cort must have had a seizure of some kind, but that had help been quickly forthcoming, his life might have been saved. Do you mean to tell me that, even if you had known this, you would still have acted in so cowardly a way?"

Mr. Runt fixed his eyes on the ground and fingered his cap.

"None of us chaps goes to Manor after sundown," he repeated.

"A Suffolk Miracle" *is one of the more harrowing ghostly ballads from* **Francis James Child's** English and Scottish Popular Ballads (#27). *This tale of parental interference with the course of true love depends for its power on two details of supernatural lore: that a* revenant *such as is described in the poem is not an insubstantial wraith, but the actual mouldering body reanimated for a time; that the kiss of a* revenant *will prove swiftly fatal to the mortal enduring it. The version of the tale below is my own reshuffling of the original crude Child stanzas and some U.S. variations.*

A Suffolk Miracle
Traditional

A tale I'll tell and vow it will
Enfold thee in its icy chill;
A father's folly it doth tell;
I prithee, mark its moral well:
    There was an old and wealthy man,
    A farmer rich who had much land.
    In Suffolk he did lately dwell,
    His wife and he were known full well.

They had a daughter fair and bright,
She was her parents' chief delight;
She was handsome, neat and tall,
And answered to no lover's call.
    Many a squire came that way
    The handsome lady for to see,
    But at length it was a widow's son
    Who turned out to be her chosen one.

He had no riches, had no land,
But still she offered him her hand,
But when her father came to hear,
He parted her and her poor dear.
    He sent her forty miles away
    Unto her uncle's, and did say,
    "So far from home you shall remain
    Until you change your mind again."

It broke the young man's tender heart
When he and his true love did part;
He sighed and sobbed and sadly grieved
That his true love was from him reaved.
　　　She by no means could to him send
　　　Who was her heart's espoused friend;
　　　She beat her breast, but all in vain,
　　　For she confined must still remain.

He mourned so much, that doctor's art
Could give no ease unto his heart.
He paled and pined and then did say,
"Upon my deathbed I do lay."
　　　His day had come, his hour had passed;
　　　Into his grave he fell at last,
　　　But when he had been twelve months dead—
　　　Up from the grave he raised his head!

The dead man rose, put on his clothes,
And after her he chose to go.
It was a wild and dark and stormy night
When he rode away for his heart's delight.
　　　The girl who had been sent away
　　　Knew nothing of his dying day,
　　　And in the middle of the night,
　　　She joyed to see her heart's delight.

Her father's horse, which well she knew,
Her mother's hood she saw there, too.
The corpse brought them to testify
Her parents' order he came by.
　　　And when he saw his love so true,
　　　He said, "My dear, I've come for you
　　　At your mother's wish, and your father's heed.
　　　I come for you all in great speed."

Her uncle thought he understood,
And said it would be for her good.
He gave consent that straightaway
That with him she should ride away.

So she dressed herself in rich attire
And sped away with her heart's desire.
They rode as swiftly as the wind
He rode in front, and she behind.

And in two hours, scarcely more,
He brought her to her father's door,
But as they reached her parents' gate,
He complained and he cried how his head did ache.
    Her handkerchief she then took out,
    And with it, tied his head about.
    She kissed his lips, and then did say,
    "My dear, you're colder than the clay."

"Get down, get down, get down," said he,
"While I go put this steed away."
And as she knocked at her father's door,
The sight of her lover she saw no more.
    When her father saw her, he did say,
    "Who came with you this very long way?"
    "With the one I love, I love so well,
    I love him more than tongue can tell."

Well, the hair did rise on the old man's head,
For he knew her love had long been dead.
"Where is he now?" he to her said.
"He's in the stable," quoth the maid.
    "Pray, sir, did you not send for me
    By such a messenger?" asked she.
    "O hush, my child, and go to bed,
    I'll see the horse well littered."

He shook as in the stable, he
No shape of any man did see,
But found his horse all in a sweat,
Which made him wring his hands and fret.
    His daughter he told nothing to,
    Nor none else, though all rightly knew
    Her loved one died a year before,
    And all were wrought with fear full sore.

Her father to the mother went
Of the deceased, with full intent
To tell her what his daughter said.
He did, and both went to this maid.
    They asked her, and she still did say
    'Twas he that brought her that long way.
    They gaped at her, and were amazed,
    As on the maid they strangely gazed.

A handkerchief she said she tied
About his head, and that they tried:
The sexton they did speak unto
To ask if he'd the grave undo.
    Well, he sent for clerks, and clergy, too,
    To open up the grave, the corpse to view,
    And though he had been twelve months dead,
    The handkerchief was round his head.

Affrighted then, she did behold
His body turning into mould.
She was thereat so terrified
And grieved at heart, she quickly died.
    So do not part true lovers twain,
    For broken hearts ne'er mend again.
    O let your children go their way
    For force oft breeds their lives' decay.

Little data is available on ROBERT HUGH BENSON, *other than the fact that he is an older brother of the better-known E. F. Benson (Q.V.). Robert rose to the position of Monsignor in the Catholic archdiocese of Westminster and wrote a small number of rare books on the supernatural from a Catholic viewpoint.* "Father Stein's Tale" *is taken from one of those,* A Mirror of Shalott.

Father Stein's Tale

by Robert Hugh Benson

Old Father Stein was a figure that greatly fascinated me during my first weeks in Rome, after I had got over the slight impatience that his personality roused in me. He was slow of speech and thought and movement, and had that distressing grip of the obvious that is characteristic of the German mind. I soon rejoiced to look at his heavy face, generally unshaven, his deep twinkling eyes, and the ponderous body that had such an air of eternal immovability, and to watch his mind, as through a glass case, laboring like an engine over a fact that he had begun to assimilate. He took a kind of paternal interest in me, too, and would thrust his thick hand under my arm as he stood by me, or clap me heavily on the shoulder as we met. But he was excellently educated, had seen much of the world, although always through a haze of the Fatherland that accompanied him everywhere, and had acquired an exceptional knowledge of English during his labors in a London mission. He used his large vocabulary with a good deal of skill.

I was pleased then when Monsignor announced on the following evening that Father Stein was prepared to contribute a story. But the German, knowing that he was master of the situation, would utter nothing at first but hoarse ejaculations at the thought of his reminiscences, and it was not until we had been seated for nearly half an hour before the fire that he consented to begin.

* * *

"It is of a dream," he said; "no more than that; and yet dreams, too, are under the hand of the good God, so I hold. Some, I know, are just folly, and tell us nothing but the confusion of our own nature when the controlling will is withdrawn; but some, I hold, are the whispers of God, and tell us of what we are too dull to hear in our waking life. You do not believe me? Very well; then listen.

"I knew a man in Germany, thirty years ago, who had lived many years away from God. He had been a Catholic, and was well educated in religion till he grew to be a lad. Then he fell into sin, and dared not confess it; and he lied, and made bad confessions, and approached the altar so. He once went to a strange priest to tell his sin, and dared not when the time came; and so added sin to sin, and lost his faith. It is ever so. We know it well. The soul dare not go on in that state, believing in God, and so by an inner act of the will renounces Him. It is not true, it is not true, she cries; and at last the voice of faith is silent and her eyes blind."

The priest stopped and looked round him, and the old Rector nodded once or twice and murmured assent.

"For twenty years he had lived so, without God, and he was not unhappy; for the powers of his soul died one by one, and he could no longer feel. Once or twice they struggled, in their death agony, and he stamped on them again. Once, when his mother died, he nearly lived again; and his soul cried once more within him, and stirred herself; but he would not hear her; it is useless, he said to her; there is no hope for you; lie still; there is nothing for you; you are dreaming; there is no life such as you think; and he trampled her again, and she lay still."

We were all very quiet now. I certainly had not suspected such passion in this old priest; he had seemed to me slow and dull and not capable of any sort of delicate thought or phrase, far less of tragedy; but somehow now his great face was lighted up, his eyebrows twitched as he talked, and it seemed as if we were hearing of a murder that this man had seen for himself. Monsignor sat perfectly motionless, staring intently into the fire, and Father Brent was watching the German sideways; Father Stein took a deliberate pinch of snuff, snapped his box, and put it away, and went on.

"This man had lived on the sea coast as a child, but was now in business in a town on the Rhine, and had never visited his old home since he left it with his mother on his father's death. He was now about thirty-five years of age, when God was gracious to him. He was living in a cousin's house, with whom he was partner.

"One night he dreamed he was a child, and walking with one whom he knew was his sister who had died before he was born, but he could not see her face. They were on a white, dusty road, and it was the noon of a hot summer day. There was nothing to be seen round him but great slopes of a dusty country with dry grass, and the burning sky overhead, and the sun. He was tired, and his feet ached, and he was crying as he walked, but he dared not cry loud for fear that his sister would turn and look at him, and he knew she was a—a *revenant,* and did not wish to see her eyes. There was no wind and no birds and no clouds; only the grasshoppers sawed in the dry grass, and the blood drummed in his ears until he thought he would go mad with the noise. And so they walked, the boy behind his sister, up a long hill. It seemed to him that they had been walking so for hours, for a lifetime, and that there would be no end to it. His feet sank to the ankles in dust, the sun beat on to his brain from above, the white road glared from below, and the tears ran down his cheeks.

"Then there was a breath of salt wind in his face, and his sister began to go faster, noiselessly; and he tried, too, to go faster, but could not; his heart beat like a hammer in his throat, and his feet lagged more and more, and little by little his sister was far in front, and he dared not cry out to her not to leave him for fear she should turn and look at him; and at last he was walking alone, and he dared not lie down or rest.

"The road passed up a slope, and when he reached the top of it at last he saw her again, far away, a little figure that turned to him and waved its hand, and behind her was the blue sea, very faint and in a mist of heat, and then he knew that the end of the bitter journey was very near.

"As he passed up the last slope the sea-line rose higher against the sky, but the line was only as the fine mark of a pencil where sea and sky met, and a dazzling white bird or two passed across it and then dropped below the cliff. By the time he came near his sister the dusty road had died away into the grass, and he was walking over the fresh turf that felt cool to his hot feet. He threw himself down on the edge of it by his sister, where she was lying with her head on her hands looking out at the sea where it spread itself out, a thousand feet below; and still he had not seen her face.

"At the foot of the cliff was a little white beach, and the rocks ran down into deep water on every side of it, and threw a purple shadow across the sand; there were birds here, too, floating out from the cliff and turning and returning; and the sea beneath them was a clear blue, like a Cardinal's ring that I saw once, and the breeze blew up from the water and made him happy again."

Father Stein stopped again, with something of a sob in his old heavy voice, and then he turned to us.

"You know such dreams," he said; "I cannot tell it as—as he told me;

but he said it was like the bliss of the redeemed to look down on the sea and feel the breeze in his hair, and taste its saltness.

"He did not wish his sister to speak, though he was afraid of her no more; and yet he knew that there was some secret to be told that would explain all—why they were here, and why she had come back to him, and why the sea was here, and the little beach below them, and the wind and the birds. But he was content to wait until it was time for her to tell him, as he knew she would. It was enough to lie here, after the dusty journey, beside her, and to wait for the word that should be spoken.

"Now, at first he was so out of breath and his heart beat so in his ears that he could hear nothing but that and his own panting; but it grew quieter soon, and he began to hear something else—the noises of the sea beneath him. It was a still day, but there was movement down below, and the surge heaved itself softly against the cliff and murmured in deep caves below, like the pedal note of the Frankfort organ, solemn and splendid; and the waves leaned over and crashed gently on the sand. It was all so far beneath that he saw the breaking wave before the sound came up to him, and he lay there and watched and listened; and that great sound made him happier even than the light on the water and the coolness and rest; for it was the sea itself that was speaking now.

"Then he saw suddenly that his sister had turned on her elbow and was looking at him; and he looked into her eyes, and knew her, though she had died before he was born. And she, too, was listening, with her lips parted, to the sound of the surge. And now he knew that the secret was to be told; and he watched her eyes, smiling. And she lifted her hand, as if to hold him silent, and waited, and again the sweet murmur and crash rose up from the sea, and she spoke softly.

" 'It is the Precious Blood,' she said."

Father Stein was silent, and we all were silent for a while. As far as I was concerned, at least, the story had somehow held me with an extraordinary fascination, I scarcely knew why.

There was a movement among the others, and presently the Frenchman spoke.

"*Et puis?*" he said.

"The man awoke," said Father Stein, "and found tears on his face."

*   *   *

It was such a short story that there were still a few minutes before the time for night-prayers, and we sat there without speaking again until the clock sounded in the campanile overhead, and the Rector rose and led the way into the west gallery of the church. I saw Father Stein waiting at the door for me to come up, and I knew why he was waiting.

He took my arm in his thick hand and held it a moment as the others passed down the two steps.

"I was that man," he said.

Christmas and ghosts go hand in hand. It is a custom which dates back long before the English tradition of sitting about the wintry fireside to listen to a spectral family history; it probably has its roots in the pagan analogues of the death of Balder and the mourning of sun-death. Dickens is rich in ghosts, Richard Matheson's Hell House *(see Appendix D) takes place during the final week of December, and elsewhere in this volume, Yule phantoms flit through the Burrage, Bangs, and Lancereau-Le Braz tales.* ELIZABETH GASKELL, *born in 1810, was a close friend of Charlotte Brontë, and little wonder: both dwell on the unspoken terror of the wind-swept British countryside. The following story is steeped in the snowy atmosphere of rural England, and has a child-ghost more unpleasant than half-a-dozen full-grown sheet-wavers.*

The Old Nurse's Story
by Elizabeth Gaskell

You know, my dears, that your mother was an orphan, and an only child; and I dare say you have heard that your grandfather was a clergyman up in Westmorland, where I come from. I was just a girl in the village school, when, one day, your grandmother came in to ask the mistress if there was any scholar there who would do for a nurse-maid; and mighty proud I was, I can tell ye, when the mistress called me up, and spoke to my being a good girl at my needle, and a steady honest girl, and one whose parents were very respectable, though they might be poor. I thought I should like nothing better than to serve the pretty young lady, who was blushing as deep as I was, as she spoke of the coming baby, and what I should have to do with it. However, I see you don't care so much for this part of my story, as for what you think is to come, so I'll tell you at once. I was engaged and settled at the parsonage before Miss Rosamond (that was the baby, who is now your mother) was born. To be sure, I had little enough to do with her when she came, for she was never out of her mother's arms, and slept by her all night long; and proud enough was I sometimes when missis trusted her to me. There never was such a baby before or since, though you've all of you been fine enough in your turns; but for sweet, winning ways, you've none of you come up to your mother. She took after her mother, who was a real lady born; a Miss Furnivall, a grand-daughter of Lord Furnivall's, in Northumberland. I believe she had neither brother nor sister, and had been brought up in my lord's family till she had married your grandfather, who was just a curate, son to a shopkeeper in Carlisle —but a clever, fine gentleman as ever was—and one who was a right-down hard worker in his parish, which was very wide, and scattered all abroad over the Westmorland Fells. When your mother, little Miss Rosamond, was about four or five years old, both her parents died in a fortnight—one after the other. Ah! that was a sad time. My pretty young mistress and me was looking for another baby, when my master came home from one of his long rides, wet, and tired, and took the fever he died of; and then she never held up her head again, but just lived to see her dead baby, and have it laid on her breast before she sighed away her life. My mistress had asked me, on her death-bed, never to leave Miss Rosamond; but if she had never spoken a word, I would have gone with the little child to the end of the world.

The next thing, and before we had well stilled our sobs, the executors and guardians came to settle the affairs. They were my poor young mistress's own cousin, Lord Furnivall, and Mr. Esthwaite, my master's brother, a shopkeeper in Manchester; not so well to do then, as he was afterwards, and with a large family rising about him. Well! I don't know if it were their settling, or because of a letter my mistress wrote on her death-bed to her cousin, my lord; but somehow it was settled that Miss Rosamond and me were to go to Furnivall Manor House, in Northumberland, and my lord spoke as if it had been her mother's wish that she should live with his family, and as if he had no objections, for that one or two more or less could make no difference in so grand a household. So, though that was not the way in which I should have wished the coming of my bright and pretty pet to have been looked at—who was like a sunbeam in any family, be it never so grand—I was well pleased that all the folks in the Dale should stare and admire, when they heard I was going to be young lady's maid at my Lord Furnivall's at Furnivall Manor.

But I made a mistake in thinking we were to go and live where my lord did. It turned out that the family had left Furnivall Manor House fifty years or more. I could not hear that my poor young mistress had ever been there, though she had been brought up in the family; and I was sorry for that, for I should have liked Miss Rosamond's youth to have passed where her mother's had been.

My lord's gentleman, from whom I asked as many questions as I durst, said that the Manor House was at the foot of the Cumberland Fells, and a very grand place; that an old Miss Furnivall, a great-aunt of my lord's, lived there, with only a few servants; but that it was a very healthy place, and my lord had thought that it would suit Miss Rosamond very well for a few years, and that her being there might perhaps amuse his old aunt.

I was bidden by my lord to have Miss Rosamond's things ready by a certain day. He was a stern proud man, as they say all the Lords Furnivall were; and he never spoke a word more than was necessary. Folk did say he had loved my young mistress; but that, because she knew that his father would object, she would never listen to him, and married Mr. Esthwaite; but I don't know. He never married at any rate. But he never took much notice of Miss Rosamond; which I thought he might have done if he had cared for her dead mother. He sent his gentleman with us to the Manor House, telling him to join him at Newcastle that same evening; so there was no great length of time for him to make us known to all the strangers before he, too, shook us off; and we were left, two lonely young things (I was not eighteen), in the great old Manor House. It seems like yesterday that we drove there. We had left our own dear parsonage very early, and we had both cried as if our hearts would break, though we were travelling in my lord's carriage, which I thought so much of once. And now it was long past noon on a September day, and we stopped to change horses for the last time at a little smoky town, all full of colliers and miners. Miss Rosamond had fallen asleep, but Mr. Henry told me to waken her, that she might see the park and the Manor House as we drove up. I thought it rather a pity; but I did what he bade me, for fear he should complain of me to my lord. We had left all signs of a town, or even a village, and were then inside the gates of a large wild park—not like the parks here in the south, but with rocks, and the noise of running water, and gnarled thorn-trees, and old oaks, all white and peeled with age.

The road went up about two miles, and then we saw a great and stately house, with many trees close around it, so close that in some places their branches dragged against the walls when the wind blew; and some hung broken down; for no one seemed to take much charge of the place;—to lop the wood, or to keep the moss-covered carriage-way in order. Only in front of the house all was clear. The great oval drive was without a weed; and neither tree nor creeper was allowed to grow over the long, many-windowed front; at both sides of which a wing projected, which were each the ends of other side fronts; for the house, although it was so desolate, was even grander than I expected. Behind it rose the Fells, which seemed unenclosed and bare enough; and on the left hand of the house, as you stood facing it, was a little, old-fashioned flower-garden, as I found out afterwards. A door opened out upon it from the west front; it had been scooped out of the thick dark wood for some old Lady Furnivall; but the branches of the great forest trees had grown and overshadowed it again, and there were very few flowers that would live there at that time.

When we drove up to the great front entrance, and went into the hall I thought we should be lost—it was so large, and vast, and grand. There was a chandelier all of bronze, hung down from the middle of the ceiling; and I had never seen one before, and looked at it all in amaze. Then, at one end of the hall, was a great fire-place, as large as the sides of the houses in my country, with massy andirons and dogs to hold the wood; and by it were heavy old-fashioned sofas. At the opposite end of the hall, to the left as you went in—on the western side—was an organ built into the wall, and so large that it filled up the best part of that end. Beyond it, on the same side, was a door; and opposite, on each side of the fire-place, were also doors leading to the east front; but those I never went through as long as I stayed in the house, so I can't tell you what lay beyond.

The afternoon was closing in and the hall, which had no fire lighted in it, looked dark and gloomy, but we did not stay there a moment. The old servant, who had opened the door for us bowed to Mr. Henry, and took us in through the door at the further side of the great organ, and led us through several smaller halls and passages into the west drawing-room, where he said that Miss Furnivall was sitting. Poor little Miss Rosamond held very tight to me, as if she were scared and lost in that great place, and as for myself, I was not much better. The west drawing-room was very cheerful-looking, with a warm fire in it, and plenty of good, comfortable furniture about. Miss Furnivall was an old lady not far from eighty, I should think, but I do not know. She was thin and tall, and had a face as full of fine wrinkles as if they had been drawn all over it with a needle's point. Her eyes were very watchful to make up, I suppose, for her being so deaf as to be obliged to use a trumpet. Sitting with her, working at the same great piece of tapestry, was Mrs. Stark, her maid and companion, and almost as old as she was. She had lived with Miss Furnivall ever since they both were young, and now she seemed more like a friend than a servant; she looked so cold and grey, and stony, as if she had never loved or cared for any one; and I don't suppose she did care for any one, except her mistress; and, owing to the great deafness of the latter, Mrs. Stark treated her very much as if she were a child. Mr. Henry gave some message from my lord, and then he bowed good-bye to us all—taking no notice of my sweet little Miss Rosamond's out-stretched hand—and left us standing there, being looked at by the two old ladies through their spectacles.

I was right glad when they rung for the old footman who had shown us in at first, and told him to take us to our rooms. So we went out of that great drawing-room, and into another sitting-room, and out of that, and then up a great flight of stairs, and along a broad gallery—which was something like a library, having books all down one side, and windows and writing-tables all down the other—till we came to our rooms, which I was not sorry to hear were just over the kitchens; for I began to think I should be lost in that wilderness of a house. There was an old nursery, that had been used for all the little lords and ladies long ago, with a pleasant fire burning in the grate, and the kettle boiling on the hob, and tea things spread out on the table; and out of that room was the night-nursery, with a little crib for Miss Rosamond close to my bed. And old James called up Dorothy, his wife, to bid us welcome; and both he and she were so hospitable and kind, that by and by Miss Rosamond and me felt quite at home; and by the time tea was over, she was sitting on Dorothy's knee, and chattering away as fast as her little tongue could go. I soon found out that Dorothy was from Westmorland, and that bound her and me together, as it were; and I would never wish to meet with kinder people than were old James and his wife. James had lived pretty nearly all his life in my lord's family, and thought there was no one so grand as they. He even looked down a little on his wife; because, till he had married her, she had never lived in any but a farmer's household. But he was very fond of her, as well he might be. They had one servant under them, to do all the rough work. Agnes they called her; and she and me, and James and Dorothy, with Miss Furnivall and Mrs. Stark, made up the family; always remembering my sweet little Miss Rosamond. I used to wonder what they had done before she came, they thought so much of her now. Kitchen and drawing-room, it was all the same. The hard, sad Miss Furnivall, and the cold Mrs. Stark, looked pleased when she came fluttering in like a bird, playing and pranking hither and thither, with a continual murmur, and pretty prattle of gladness. I am sure, they were sorry many a time when she flitted away into the kitchen, though they were too proud to ask her to stay with them, and were a little surprised at her taste; though to be sure, as Mrs. Stark said, it was not to be wondered at, remembering what stock her father had come of. The great, old rambling house, was a famous place for little Miss Rosamond. She made expeditions all over it, with me at her heels; all, except the east wing, which was never opened, and whither we never thought of going. But in the western and northern part was many a pleasant room; full of things that were curiosities to us, though they might not have been to people who had seen more. The windows were darkened by the sweeping boughs of the trees, and the ivy which had overgrown them: but, in the green gloom, we could manage to see old China jars and carved ivory boxes, and great heavy books, and, above all, the old pictures!

Once, I remember, my darling would have Dorothy go with us to tell us who they all were; for they were all portraits of some of my lord's family, though Dorothy could not tell us the names of every one. We had gone through most of the rooms, when we came to the old state drawing-room over the hall, and there was a picture of Miss Furnivall; or, as she was called in those days, Miss Grace, for she was the younger sister. Such a beauty she must have been! but with such a set, proud look, and such scorn looking out of her handsome eyes, with her eyebrows just a little raised, as if she wondered how any one could have the impertinence to look at her; and her lip curled at us, as we stood there gazing. She had a dress on, the like of which I had never seen before, but it was all the fashion when she was young: a hat of some soft white stuff like beaver, pulled a little over her brows, and a beautiful plume of feathers sweeping round it on one side; and her gown of blue satin was open in front to a quilted white stomacher.

"Well, to be sure!" said I, when I had gazed my fill. "Flesh is grass, they do say; but who would have thought that Miss Furnivall had been such an out-and-out beauty, to see her now?"

"Yes," said Dorothy. "Folks change sadly. But if what my master's father used to say was true, Miss Furnivall, the elder sister, was handsomer than Miss Grace. Her picture is here somewhere; but, if I show it you, you must never let on, even to James, that you have seen it. Can the little lady hold her tongue, think you?" asked she.

I was not so sure, for she was such a little sweet, bold, open-spoken child, so I set her to hide herself; and then I helped Dorothy to turn a great picture, that leaned with its face towards the wall, and was not hung up as the others were. To be sure, it beat Miss Grace for beauty; and, I think, for scornful pride, too, though in that matter it might be hard to choose. I could have looked at it an hour, but Dorothy seemed half frightened at having shown it to me, and hurried it back again, and bade me run and find Miss Rosamond, for that there were some ugly places about the house, where she should like ill for the child to go. I was a brave, high-spirited girl, and thought little of what the old woman said, for I liked hide-and-seek as well as any child in the parish; so off I ran to find my little one.

As winter drew on, and the days grew shorter, I was sometimes almost certain that I heard a noise as if some one was playing on the great organ in the hall. I did not hear it every evening; but, certainly, I did very often; usually when I was sitting with Miss Rosamond, after I had put her to bed, and keeping quite still and silent in the bedroom. Then I used to hear it booming and swelling away in the distance. The first night, when I went down to my supper, I asked Dorothy who had been playing music, and James said very shortly that I was a gowk to take the wind soughing among the trees for music; but I saw Dorothy look at him very fearfully, and Bessy, the kitchen-maid, said something beneath her breath, and went quite white. I saw they did not like my question, so I held my peace till I was with Dorothy alone, when I knew I could get a good deal out of her. So, the next day, I watched my time, and I coaxed and asked her who it was that played the organ; for I knew that it was the organ and not the wind well enough, for all I had kept silence before James. But Dorothy had had her lesson I'll warrant, and never a word could I get from her. So then I tried Bessy, though I had always held my head rather above her, as I was evened to James and Dorothy, and she was little better than their servant. So she said I must never, never tell; and if I ever told, I was never to say *she* had told me; but it was a very strange noise, and she had heard it many a time, but most of all on winter nights, and before storms; and folks did say, it was the old lord playing on the great organ in the hall, just as he used to do when he was alive; but who the old lord was, or why he played, and why he played on stormy winter evenings in particular, she either could not or would not tell me. Well! I told you I had a brave heart; and I thought it was rather pleasant to have that grand music rolling about the house, let who would be the player; for now it rose above the great gusts of wind, and wailed and triumphed just like a living creature, and then it fell to a softness most complete; only it was always music, and tunes, so it was nonsense to call it the wind. I thought at first, that it might be Miss Furnivall who played, unknown to Bessy; but, one day when I was in the hall by myself, I opened the organ and peeped all about it and around it, as I had done to the organ in Crosthwaite Church once before, and I saw it was all broken and destroyed inside, though it looked so brave and fine; and then, though it was noon-day, my flesh began to creep a little, and I shut it up, and run away pretty quickly to my own bright nursery; and I did not like hearing the music for some time after that, any more than James and Dorothy did. All this time Miss Rosamond was making herself more, and more beloved. The old ladies liked her to dine with them at their early dinner; James stood behind Miss Furnivall's chair, and I behind Miss Rosamond's all in state; and, after dinner, she would play about in a corner of the great drawing-room, as still as any mouse, while Miss Furnivall slept, and I had my dinner in the kitchen. But she was glad enough to come to me in the nursery afterwards; for, as she said, Miss Furnivall was so sad, and Mrs. Stark so dull; but she and I were merry enough; and, by-and-by, I got not to care for that weird rolling music, which did one no harm, if we did not know where it came from.

That winter was very cold. In the middle of October the frosts began, and lasted many, many weeks. I remember, one day at dinner, Miss Furnivall lifted up her sad, heavy eyes, and said to Mrs. Stark, "I am afraid we shall have a terrible winter," in a strange kind of meaning way. But Mrs. Stark pretended not to hear, and talked very loud of something else. My little lady and I did not care for the frost; not we! As long as it was dry we climbed up the steep brows, behind the house, and went up on the Fells, which were bleak, and bare enough, and there we ran races in the fresh, sharp air; and once we came down by a new path that took us past the two old gnarled holly trees, which grew about half-way down by the east side of the house. But the days grew shorter, and shorter; and the old lord, if it was he, played away more, and more stormily and sadly on the great organ. One Sunday afternoon—it must have been towards the end of November—I asked Dorothy to take charge of little Missey when she came out of the drawing-room, after Miss Furnivall had had her nap; for it was too cold to take her with me to church, and yet I wanted to go. And Dorothy was glad enough to promise, and was so fond of the child that all seemed well; and Bessy and I set off very briskly, though the sky hung heavy and black over the white earth, as if the night had never fully gone away; and the air, though still, was very biting and keen.

"We shall have a fall of snow," said Bessy to me. And sure enough, even while we were in church, it came down thick, in great large flakes, so thick it almost darkened the windows. It had stopped snowing before we came out, but it lay soft, thick and deep beneath our feet, as we tramped home. Before we got to the hall the moon rose, and I think it was lighter then—what with the moon, and what with the white dazzling snow—than it had been when we went to church, between two and three o'clock. I have not told you that Miss Furnivall and Mrs. Stark never went to church: they used to read the prayers together, in their quiet gloomy way; they seemed to feel the Sunday very long without their tapestry-work to be busy at. So when I went to Dorothy in the kitchen, to fetch Miss Rosamond and take her upstairs with me, I did not much wonder when the old woman told me that the ladies had kept the child with them, and that she had never come to the kitchen, as I had bidden her, when she was tired of behaving pretty in the drawing-room. So I took off my things and went to find her, and bring her to her supper in the nursery. But when I went into the best drawing-room, there sat the two old ladies, very still and quiet, dropping out a word now and then, but looking as if nothing so bright and merry as Miss Rosamond had ever been near them. Still I thought she might be hiding from me; it was one of her pretty ways; and that she had persuaded them to look as if they knew nothing about her; so I went softly peeping under this sofa, and behind that chair, making believe I was sadly frightened at not finding her.

"What's the matter, Hester?" said Mrs. Stark sharply. I don't know if Miss Furnivall had seen me, for, as I told you, she was very deaf, and she sat quite still, idly staring into the fire, with her hopeless face. "I'm only looking for my little Rosy-Posy," replied I, still thinking that the child was there, and near me, though I could not see her.

"Miss Rosamond is not here," said Mrs. Stark. "She went away more than an hour ago to find Dorothy." And she too turned and went on looking into the fire.

My heart sank at this, and I began to wish I had never left my darling. I went back to Dorothy and told her. James was gone out for the day, but she and me and Bessy took lights and went up into the nursery first, and then we roamed over the great large house, calling and entreating Miss Rosamond to come out of her hiding place, and not frighten us to death in that way. But there was no answer; no sound.

"Oh!" said I at last, "can she have got into the east wing and hidden there?"

But Dorothy said it was not possible, for that she herself had never been in there; that the doors were always locked, and my lord's steward had the keys, she believed; at any rate, neither she, nor James had ever seen them: so, I said I would go back, and see if, after all, she was not hidden in the drawing-room, unknown to the old ladies; and if I found her there, I said, I would whip her well for the fright she had given me;

but I never meant to do it. Well, I went back to the west drawing-room, and I told Mrs. Stark we could not find her anywhere, and asked for leave to look all about the furniture there, for I thought now, that she might have fallen asleep in some warm hidden corner; but no! we looked, Miss Furnivall got up and looked, trembling all over, and she was nowhere there; then we set off again, every one in the house, and looked in all the places we had searched before, but we could not find her. Miss Furnivall shivered and shook so much, that Mrs. Stark took her back into the warm drawing-room; but not before they had made me promise to bring her to them when she was found. Well-a-day! I began to think she never would be found, when I bethought me to look out into the great front court, all covered with snow. I was upstairs when I looked out; but, it was such clear moonlight, I could see quite plain two little footprints, which might be traced from the hall door, and round the corner of the east wing. I don't know how I got down, but I tugged open the great, stiff hall door; and, throwing the skirt of my gown over my head for a cloak, I ran out. I turned the east corner, and there a black shadow fell on the snow; but when I came again into the moonlight, there were the little footmarks going up—up to the Fells. It was bitter cold; so cold that the air almost took the skin off my face as I ran, but I ran on, crying to think how my poor little darling must be perished, and frightened. I was within sight of the holly trees, when I saw a shepherd coming down the hill, bearing something in his arms wrapped in his maud. He shouted to me, and asked me if I had lost a bairn; and, when I could not speak for crying, he bore towards me, and I saw my wee bairnie lying still, and white, and stiff, in his arms, as if she had been dead. He told me he had been up the Fells to gather in his sheep, before the deep cold of night came on, and that under the holly trees (black marks on the hill-side, where no other bush was for miles around) he had found my little lady—my lamb—my queen—my darling— stiff, and cold, in the terrible sleep which is frost-begotten. Oh! the joy, and the tears of having her in my arms once again! for I would not let him carry her; but took her, maud and all, into my own arms, and held her near my own warm neck, and heart, and felt the life stealing slowly back again into her little gentle limbs. But she was still insensible when we reached the hall, and I had no breath for speech. We went in by the kitchen door.

"Bring the warming-pan," said I; and I carried her upstairs and began undressing her by the nursery fire, which Bessy had kept up. I called my little lammie all the sweet and playful names I could think of

—even while my eyes were blinded by my tears; and at last, oh! at length she opened her large blue eyes. Then I put her into her warm bed, and sent Dorothy down to tell Miss Furnivall that all was well; and I made up my mind to sit by my darling's bedside the livelong night. She fell away into a soft sleep as soon as her pretty head had touched the pillow, and I watched by her till morning light; when she wakened up bright and clear—or so I thought at first—and, my dears, so I think now.

She said, that she had fancied that she should like to go to Dorothy, for that both the old ladies were asleep, and it was very dull in the drawing-room; and that, as she was going through the west lobby, she saw the snow through the high window falling—falling—soft and steady; but she wanted to see it lying pretty and white on the ground; so she made her way into the great hall; and then, going to the window, she saw it bright and soft upon the drive; but while she stood there, she saw a little girl, not so old as she was, "but so pretty," said my darling, "and this little girl beckoned to me to come out; and oh, she was so pretty and so sweet I could not choose but go." And then this other little girl had taken her by the hand, and side by side the two had gone round the east corner.

"Now you are a naughty little girl, and telling stories," said I. "What would your good mamma, that is in heaven, and never told a story in her life, say to her little Rosamond, if she heard her—and I dare say she does—telling stories!"

"Indeed, Hester," sobbed out my child, "I'm telling you true. Indeed I am."

"Don't tell me!" said I, very stern. "I tracked you by your foot-marks through the snow; there were only yours to be seen: and if you had had a little girl to go hand-in-hand with you up the hill, don't you think the foot-prints would have gone along with yours?"

"I can't help it, dear, dear Hester," said she, crying, "if they did not; I never looked at her feet, but she held my hand fast and tight in her lit-tle one, and it was very, very cold. She took me up the Fell path, up to the holly trees; and there I saw a lady weeping and crying; but when she saw me, she hushed her weeping, and smiled very proud and grand, and took me on her knee, and began to lull me to sleep; and that's all, Hester—but that is true; and my dear mamma knows it is," said she, crying. So I thought the child was in a fever, and pretended to believe her, as she went over her story—over and over again, and always the same. At last Dorothy knocked at the door with Miss Rosamond's breakfast; and she told me the old ladies were down in the eating parlour, and that they wanted to speak to me. They had both been into the night-nursery the evening before, but it was after Miss Rosamond was asleep; so they had only looked at her—not asked me any questions.

"I shall catch it," thought I to myself, as I went along the north gallery. "And yet," I thought, taking courage, "it was in their charge I left her; and it's they that's to blame for letting her steal away unknown and unwatched." So I went in boldly, and told my story. I told it all to Miss Furnivall, shouting it close to her ear; but when I came to the mention of the other little girl out in the snow, coaxing and tempting her out, and willing her up to the grand and beautiful lady by the holly tree, she threw her arms up—her old and withered arms—and cried aloud, "Oh! Heaven, forgive! Have mercy!"

Mrs. Stark took hold of her; roughly enough, I thought; but she was past Mrs. Stark's management, and spoke to me, in a kind of wild warning and authority.

"Hester! keep her from that child! It will lure her to her death! That evil child! Tell her it is a wicked, naughty child." Then, Mrs. Stark hurried me out of the room; where, indeed, I was glad enough to go; but Miss Furnivall kept shrieking out, "Oh! have mercy! Wilt Thou never forgive! It is many a long year ago—"

I was very uneasy in my mind after that. I durst never leave Miss Rosamond, night or day, for fear lest she might slip off again, after some fancy or other; and all the more, because I thought I could make out that Miss Furnivall was crazy, from their odd ways about her; and I was afraid lest something of the same kind (which might be in the family, you know) hung over my darling. And the great frost never ceased all this time; and, whenever it was a more stormy night than usual, between the gusts, and through the wind, we heard the old lord playing on the great organ. But, old lord, or not, wherever Miss Rosamond went, there I followed; for my love for her, pretty helpless orphan, was stronger than my fear for the grand and terrible sound. Besides, it rested with me to keep her cheerful and merry, as beseemed her age. So we played together, and wandered together, here and there, and everywhere; for I never dared to lose sight of her again in that large and rambling house. And so it happened, that one afternoon, not long before Christmas day, we were playing together on the billiard-table in the great hall (not that we knew the right way of playing, but she liked to roll the smooth ivory balls with her pretty hands, and I liked to do whatever she did); and, by-and-by, without our noticing it, it grew dusk indoors, though it was still light in the open air, and I was thinking of taking her back into the nursery, when, all of a sudden, she cried out: "Look, Hester! look! there is my poor little girl out in the snow!"

I turned towards the long narrow windows, and there, sure enough, I saw a little girl, less than my Miss Rosamond—dressed all unfit to be out-of-doors such a bitter night—crying, and beating against the window-panes, as if she wanted to be let in. She seemed to sob and wail, till Miss Rosamond could bear it no longer, and was flying to the door to open it, when, all of a sudden, and close upon us, the great organ pealed out so loud and thundering, it fairly made me tremble; and all the more, when I remembered me that, even in the stillness of that dead-cold weather, I had heard no sound of little battering hands upon the window-glass, although the Phantom Child had seemed to put forth all its force; and, although I had seen it wail and cry, no faintest touch of sound had fallen upon my ears. Whether I remembered all this at the very moment, I do not know; the great organ sound had so stunned me into terror; but this I know, I caught up Miss Rosamond before she got the hall-door opened, and clutched her, and carried her away, kicking and screaming, into the large bright kitchen, where Dorothy and Agnes were busy with their mince-pies.

"What is the matter with my sweet one?" cried Dorothy, as I bore in Miss Rosamond, who was sobbing as if her heart would break.

"She won't let me open the door for my little girl to come in; and she'll die if she is out on the Fells all night. Cruel, naughty Hester," she said, slapping me; but she might have struck harder, for I had seen a look of ghastly terror on Dorothy's face, which made my very blood run cold.

"Shut the back kitchen door fast, and bolt it well," said she to Agnes. She said no more; she gave me raisins and almonds to quiet Miss Rosamond: but she sobbed about the little girl in the snow, and would not touch any of the good things. I was thankful when she cried herself to sleep in bed. Then I stole down to the kitchen, and told Dorothy I had made up my mind. I would carry my darling back to my father's house in Applethwaite; where, if we lived humbly, we lived at peace. I said I had been frightened enough with the old lord's organ-playing; but now, that I had seen for myself this little moaning child, all decked out as no child in the neighbourhood could be, beating and battering to get in, yet always without any sound or noise—with the dark wound on its right shoulder; and that Miss Rosamond had known it again for the phantom that had nearly lured her to her death (which Dorothy knew was true); I would stand it no longer.

I saw Dorothy change colour once or twice. When I had done, she told me she did not think I could take Miss Rosamond with me, for that she was my lord's ward, and I had no right over her; and she asked me, would I leave the child that I was so fond of, just for sounds and sights that could do me no harm; and that they had all had to get used to in their turns? I was all in a hot, trembling passion; and I said it was very well for her to talk, that knew what these sights and noises betokened, and that had, perhaps, had something to do with the Spectre-Child while it was alive. And I taunted her so, that she told me all she knew, at last; and then I wished I had never been told, for it only made me more afraid than ever.

She said she had heard the tale from old neighbours, that were alive when she was first married; when folks used to come to the hall sometimes, before it had got such a bad name on the country side: it might not be true, or it might, what she had been told.

The old lord was Miss Furnivall's father—Miss Grace, as Dorothy called her, for Miss Maude was the elder, and Miss Furnivall by rights. The old lord was eaten up with pride. Such a proud man was never seen or heard of; and his daughters were like him. No one was good enough to wed them, although they had choice enough; for they were the great beauties of their day, as I had seen by their portraits, where they hung in the state drawing-room. But, as the old saying is, "Pride will have a fall"; and these two haughty beauties fell in love with the same man, and he no better than a foreign musician, whom their father had down from London to play music with him at the Manor House. For, above all things, next to his pride, the old lord loved music. He could play on nearly every instrument that ever was heard of: and it was a strange thing it did not soften him; but he was a fierce dour old man, and had broken his poor wife's heart with his cruelty, they said. He was mad after music, and would pay any money for it. So he got this foreigner to come; who made such beautiful music, that they said the very birds on the trees stopped their singing to listen. And, by degrees, this foreign gentleman got such a hold over the old lord, that nothing would serve him but that he must come every year; and it was he that had the great organ brought from Holland, and built up in the hall, where it stood now. He taught the old lord to play on it; but many and many a time, when Lord Furnivall was thinking of nothing but his fine organ, and his finer music, the dark foreigner was walking abroad in the woods with one of the young ladies; now Miss Maude, and then Miss Grace.

Miss Maude won the day and carried off the prize, such as it was; and he and she were married, all unknown to any one; and before he made his next yearly visit, she had been confined of a little girl at a farm-house on the Moors, while her father and Miss Grace thought she was away at Doncaster Races. But though she was a wife and a mother, she was not a bit softened, but was haughty and as passionate as ever; and perhaps more so, for she was jealous of Miss Grace, to whom her foreign husband paid a deal of court—by way of blinding her—as he told his wife. But Miss Grace triumphed over Miss Maude, and Miss Maude grew fiercer and fiercer, both with her husband and with her sister; and the former—who could easily shake off what was disagreeable, and hide himself in foreign countries—went away a month before his usual time that summer, and half-threatened that he would never come back again. Meanwhile, the little girl was left at the farm-house, and her mother used to have her horse saddled and gallop wildly over the hills to see her once every week, at the very least—for where she loved, she loved; and where she hated, she hated. And the old lord went on play-ing—playing on his organ; and the servants thought the sweet music he made had soothed down his awful temper, of which (Dorothy said) some terrible tales could be told. He grew infirm too, and had to walk with a crutch; and his son—that was the present Lord Furnivall's father—was with the army in America, and the other son at sea; so Miss Maude had it pretty much her own way, and she and Miss Grace grew colder and bitterer to each other every day; till at last they hardly ever spoke, except when the old lord was by. The foreign musician came again the next summer, but it was for the last time; for they led him such a life with their jealousy and their passions, that he grew weary, and went away, and never was heard of again. And Miss Maude, who had always meant to have her marriage acknowledged when her father should be dead, was left now a deserted wife—whom nobody knew to have been married—with a child that she dared not own, although she loved it to distraction; living with a father whom she feared, and a sister whom she hated. When the next summer passed over and the dark foreigner never came, both Miss Maude and Miss Grace grew gloomy and sad; they had a haggard look about them, though they looked handsome as ever. But by-and-by Miss Maude brightened; for her father grew more and more infirm, and more than ever carried away by his music; and she and Miss Grace lived almost entirely apart, having separate rooms, the one on the west side, Miss Maude on the east—those very rooms which were now shut up. So she thought she might have her little girl with her, and no one need ever know except those who dared not speak about it, and were bound to believe that it was, as she said, a cottager's child she had taken a fancy to. All this, Dorothy said, was pretty well known; but what came afterwards no one knew, except Miss Grace, and Mrs. Stark, who was even then her maid, and much more of a friend to her than ever her sister had been. But the servants supposed, from words that were dropped, that Miss Maude had triumphed over Miss Grace, and told her that all the time the dark foreigner had been mocking her with pretended love—he was her own husband; the colour left Miss Grace's cheek and lips that very day for ever, and she was heard to say many a time that sooner or later she would have her revenge; and Mrs. Stark was for ever spying about the east rooms.

One fearful night, just after the New Year had come in, when the snow was lying thick and deep, and the flakes were still falling—fast enough to blind any one who might be out and abroad—there was a great and violent noise heard, and the old lord's voice above all, cursing and swearing awfully—and the cries of a little child—and the proud defiance of a fierce woman—and the sound of a blow—and a dead stillness—and moans and wailings dying away on the hill-side! Then the old lord summoned all his servants, and told them, with terrible oaths, and words more terrible, that his daughter had disgraced herself, and that he had turned her out of doors—her and her child—and that if ever they gave her help—or food—or shelter—he prayed that they might never enter Heaven. And, all the while, Miss Grace stood by him, white and still as any stone; and when he had ended she heaved a great sigh, as much as to say her work was done, and her end was accomplished. But the old lord never touched his organ again, and died within the year; and no wonder! for, on the morrow of that wild and fearful night, the shepherds, coming down the Fell side, found Miss Maude sitting, all crazy and smiling, under the holly trees, nursing a dead child—with a terrible mark on its right shoulder. "But that was not what killed it," said Dorothy; "it was the frost and the cold;—every wild creature was in its hole, and every beast in its fold—while the child and its mother were turned out to wander on the Fells! And now you know all! and I wonder if you are less frightened now?"

I was more frightened than ever; but I said I was not. I wished Miss Rosamond and myself well out of that dreadful house for ever; but I would not leave her, and I dared not take her away. But oh! how I watched her, and guarded her! We bolted the doors, and shut the window-shutters fast, an hour or more before dark, rather than leave them open five minutes too late. But my little lady still heard the weird child crying and mourning; and not all we could do or say, could keep her from wanting to go to her, and let her in from the cruel wind and the snow. All this time, I kept away from Miss Furnivall and Mrs. Stark, as much as ever I could; for I feared them—I knew no good could be about them, with their grey hard faces, and their dreamy eyes, looking back into the ghastly years that were gone. But, even in my fear, I had a kind of pity—for Miss Furnivall, at least. Those gone down to the pit can hardly have a more hopeless look than that which was ever on her face. At last I even got so sorry for her—who never said a word but what was quite forced from her—that I prayed for her; and I taught Miss Rosamond to pray for one who had done a deadly sin; but often when she came to those words, she would listen, and start up from her knees, and say, "I hear my little girl plaining and crying very sad— Oh! let her in, or she will die!"

One night—just after New Year's Day had come at last, and the long winter had taken a turn, as I hoped—I heard the west drawing-room bell ring three times, which was the signal for me. I would not leave Miss Rosamond alone, for all she was asleep—for the old lord had been playing wilder than ever—and I feared lest my darling should waken to hear the spectre child; see her I knew she could not. I had fastened the windows too well for that. So, I took her out of her bed and wrapped her up in such outer clothes as were most handy, and carried her down to the drawing-room, where the old ladies sat at their tapestry work as usual. They looked up when I came in, and Mrs. Stark asked, quite astounded, "Why did I bring Miss Rosamond there, out of her warm bed?" I had begun to whisper, "Because I was afraid of her being tempted out while I was away, by the wild child in the snow," when she stopped me short (with a glance at Miss Furnivall), and said Miss Furnivall wanted me to undo some work she had done wrong, and which neither of them could see to unpick. So, I laid my pretty dear on the sofa, and sat down on a stool by them, and hardened my heart against them, as I heard the wind rising and howling.

Miss Rosamond slept on sound, for all the wind blew so; and Miss Furnivall said never a word, nor looked round when the gusts shook the windows. All at once she started up to her full height, and put up one hand, as if to bid us listen.

"I hear voices!" said she. "I hear terrible screams—I hear my father's voice!"

Just at that moment, my darling wakened with a sudden start: "My little girl is crying, oh, how she is crying!" and she tried to get up and go to her, but she got her feet entangled in the blanket, and I caught her up; for my flesh had begun to creep at these noises, which they heard while we could catch no sound. In a minute or two the noises came, and gathered fast, and filled our ears; we, too, heard voices and screams, and no longer heard the winter's wind that raged abroad. Mrs. Stark looked at me, and I at her, but we dared not speak. Suddenly Miss Furnivall went towards the door, out into the ante-room, through the west lobby, and opened the door into the great hall. Mrs. Stark followed, and I durst not be left, though my heart almost stopped beating for fear. I wrapped my darling tight in my arms, and went out with them. In the hall the screams were louder than ever; they sounded to come from the east wing—nearer and nearer—close on the other side of the locked-up doors—close behind them. Then I noticed that the great bronze chandelier seemed all alight, though the hall was dim, and that a fire was blazing in the vast hearth-place, though it gave no heat; and I shuddered up with terror, and folded my darling closer to me. But as I did so, the east door shook, and she, suddenly struggling to get free from me, cried, "Hester! I must go! My little girl is there; I hear her; she is coming! Hester, I must go!"

I held her tight with all my strength; with a set will, I held her. If I had died, my hands would have grasped her still, I was so resolved in my mind. Miss Furnivall stood listening, and paid no regard to my darling, who had got down to the ground, and whom I, upon my knees now, was holding with both my arms clasped round her neck; she still striving and crying to get free.

All at once, the east door gave way with a thundering crash, as if torn open in a violent passion, and there came into that broad and mysterious light, the figure of a tall old man, with grey hair and gleaming eyes. He drove before him, with many a relentless gesture of abhorrence, a stern and beautiful woman, with a little child clinging to her dress.

"Oh Hester! Hester!" cried Miss Rosamond. "It's the lady! the lady below the holly trees; and my little girl is with her. Hester! Hester! let me go to her; they are drawing me to them. I feel them—I feel them. I must go!"

Again she was almost convulsed by her efforts to get away; but I held her tighter and tighter, till I feared I should do her a hurt; but rather that than let her go towards those terrible phantoms. They passed along towards the great hall-door, where the winds howled and ravened for their prey; but before they reached that, the lady turned; and I could see that she defied the old man with a fierce and proud defiance; but then she quailed—and then she threw up her arms wildly and piteously to save her child—her little child—from a blow from his uplifted crutch.

And Miss Rosamond was torn as by a power stronger than mine, and writhed in my arms, and sobbed (for by this time the poor darling was growing faint).

"They want me to go with them on to the Fells—they are drawing me to them. Oh, my little girl! I would come, but cruel, wicked Hester holds me very tight." But when she saw the uplifted crutch she swooned away, and I thanked God for it. Just at this moment—when the tall old man, his hair streaming as in the blast of a furnace, was going to strike the little shrinking child—Miss Furnivall, the old woman by my side, cried out, "Oh, father! father! spare the little innocent child!" But just then I saw—we all saw—another phantom shape itself, and grow clear out of the blue and misty light that filled the hall; we had not seen her till now, for it was another lady who stood by the old man, with a look of relentless hate and triumphant scorn. That figure was very beautiful to look upon, with a soft white hat drawn down over the proud brows, and a red and curling lip. It was dressed in an open robe of blue satin. I had seen that figure before. It was the likeness of Miss Furnivall in her youth; and the terrible phantoms moved on, regardless of old Miss Furnivall's wild entreaty—and the uplifted crutch fell on the right shoulder of the little child, and the younger sister looked on, stony and deadly serene. But at that moment, the dim lights, and the fire that gave no heat, went out of themselves, and Miss Furnivall lay at our feet stricken down by the palsy—death-stricken.

Yes! she was carried to her bed that night never to rise again. She lay with her face to the wall, muttering low but muttering alway: "Alas! alas! what is done in youth can never be undone in age! What is done in youth can never be undone in age!"

DICK BALDWIN *is a transplanted Long Islander living and working in Mount Vernon, New York. Both vocationally and avocationally involved in the film business, he is an expert on cinematic horror—yet here he delivers, with deadpan slyness, a low blow (that is still absolutely logical) to the vampire tradition. And be it remembered that the undead are technically considered to be reanimated corpses, manipulated by spectres dispatched from Hell. The vampire in "Money Talks" is one of the most enterprising of that breed, and may indeed have been taking lessons over in 'Salem's Lot, but if he did, he hasn't quite got all the bugs out yet.*

Money Talks

by Dick Baldwin

On Wednesday evening, August the fourth, a vampire will visit. Welcome him into your home. It is advisable to remove reflective items (such as mirrors) and all religious icons from your person and the immediate area of reception.

There were no flyers.

Not even a prepaid reply envelope.

Just the single sheet of cream-colored stationery without a letterhead, the message typed dead center of the page, folded neatly in thirds, and tucked squarely into the number-ten envelope.

Boyer reread it, regarding the fact that in this enlightened era, rich with tangible wonders like wafer-thin calculators, kids' toys with electronic brains, and vast computer reliance systems, belief in bogeymen was as antiquated as believing in God. But he reread it anyway, sitting in his sunken living room, leaning back on the comfortable Saporiti Italia sofa. The room was furnished in gold Missoni fabrics, and the late afternoon sunlight coming through the expansive picture window played wonderfully off the material, giving it all a rich, warm glow. Boyer himself was still dressed from work: gray Oscar de la Renta suit, pale blue Yves Saint Laurent shirt with pencil-stripe Pierre Cardin tie. He was a man in his thirties who carried himself well—even at home, reading over the mail.

This particular letter had been at the bottom of a stack of charity-club newsletters and parchment-like store-sale circulars left on the sofa's end table for him. He had examined the locally postmarked envelope and found it to be poor bulk-bought quality, but what piqued

Boyer's curiosity, causing him to open this letter first, was that the familiar addressograph label was in red. Usually the labels were printed in a standard black ink spread so thin that impressions were little more than faint specks. The red ink was a neat angle, he thought, and knew, even before he sliced the flap, that this was an unusual piece of junk mail. The stationery inside had an enjoyable coarse texture: definitely some of the better stuff.

As he finished the second reading, he pictured how Wednesday evening might be: a well-scrubbed young man dressed in a barely afforded three-piece suit, sample case at his side like a trained puppy, pointing out an obscure bit of jargon linking the word *salesman* to the word *vampire*. A thumbmarked page from a volume of some encyclopedia or out-of-print reference tome would pop open in the salesman-cum-vampire's hand, and there would be the exact quotation to back his claim. Handy. The sales pitch would come next.

Boyer grinned, like a child discovering the hidden cookie jar. He knew the sales game; you can't sell a salesman . . . still, the approach was different. Unique, in fact. He admired the technique, the style, because money talks when used on eye-catching devices for tenuous selling ventures.

Wednesday evening would be interesting.

Wednesday afternoon was hot. When Boyer came home from the office at four, he noticed first his refreshing central air conditioning, and then the blank space on the landing wall where, up to that afternoon, the gilt-edged mirror had been firmly hooked. Both contingencies were quite agreeable to him. Still standing inside the front door, he accepted his wife's melodious hello and cursory kiss. She was thirty-four, had glossy good looks, a designer's figure, and there was a fluidity of movement when she walked that was nothing short of elegant.

They dined, as usual, at seven. At eight they freshened the living room to receive a visitor. By nine o'clock they doubted a salesman would call and settled for the evening in the stillness of the house.

Mrs. Boyer sat reading a best seller, her long legs curled up on the sofa under her, and Boyer pored over the final draft of a contract, perched in his easy chair. At ten-thirty there was a knock at their door. Mrs. Boyer was so startled by its suddenness she nearly bit her tongue.

Boyer stepped authoritatively up the riser onto the landing, straightening his tie automatically in the spot where the mirror should be. Mrs. Boyer slipped into her shoes and stayed behind primping her hair as Boyer opened the door.

Outside, in the pale moonlight, stood a tall figure. Boyer could see the streetlamp across the way outlined through the long and loose coat the caller wore. A balaclava covered both head and lower portion of face so that only red eyes, flecked with silver, shone out of sockets set deep in cold, white skin. There wasn't a doubt in Boyer's mind that this was not a salesman. He stepped back into the protection of the house. The caller did not move, but silently stood in the doorway.

"Hello!" Mrs. Boyer called brightly from the living room. She started up the landing. "Do come in and—" There was a catch in her smooth voice as the visitor entered.

Still without a word, the newcomer took his hand from his pocket. It was a pasty-looking, clawlike thing with which he effortlessly pushed closed the door behind him, effecting a force that made the picture window rattle. He unfastened his coat, which then slid down to the floor. Underneath, his clothes were stale and of a style indescribably old. The headgear followed, to rest on top of the coat. There were no eyebrows or hair on his mounded head, although there were remnants of what might have been hair hanging down over ears that were lupine. His nose was beaked; his mouth, canine. He was extraordinarily thin and looked cold and hungry.

"Good evening," he said, finally, his voice deep and vapory. He gestured toward the living room with a cordial wave of hand. The Boyers edged in, pressed together, their hands lightly touching. The guest followed. They backed to the sofa and stood, unsure of what to do.

"You are the Boyers," he said, rather than asked, drawing a notepad from inside his decrepit jacket.

Their attention was riveted on the gaunt figure at the foot of their coffee table. Boyer nodded.

"Sit down," he invited them.

They sat.

To Boyer, this was inconceivable: it could not be true that a vampire was in his house—*checking his name off a list!* Yet . . . He tried to speak, but seemed as if he were talking inside a vacuum. He asked about the mailing list.

The guest smiled. "Oh, yes. Mass communication. It benefits everyone. Don't you agree? Progress is very important to survival, and is especially helpful to me when coupled with your mortal's desire to believe only what your puny intellects dictate as truth. A simple letter of introduction opens wide the door of your skepticism and drops what remains of your protective shield of belief. You ask yourself why *I* would bother with exchange of remuneration for paper and postage: I have lackeys to handle that. My hands are never soiled. What concerns me are the host of names at my disposal." He replaced the well-used notepad inside his pocket.

"But . . . why?" Boyer managed to ask.

"A reasonable question. For countless years—centuries—I have done little more than beg and use devious methods of mind control to gain entrance into hovels such as this for the purpose of fulfilling my hunger. I have been at the mercy of the dawn and those of your kind knowledgeable enough to destroy me. I have survived, at times poorly, finding sustenance only on crude animal life—inferior by anyone's standard.

"Thirty years ago the last descendant of the last vampire hunter left your plane and with him took the remaining link of belief in my race. This loss of belief has become chief bastion of my power and the sole reason I have flourished. But I weary of the demeaning devices I must employ for fresh pap. I wish to retire to an easy existence. And what could be easier, more trouble-free, and more fulfilling than the method I have chosen? Once invited, I am free to return as often as I need, and offsetting my calls with other hosts assures time between visits for replenishing supplies. I would not want my visits to be too draining."

Eyes downcast to the coffee table, Boyer saw a grim future reflected back in fear-filled eyes. He sensed once the vampire took possession they would be lost. There must be a way to rid his house of this unwanted guest . . . or at least buy time until dawn . . .

. . . and tomorrow. Cash bonds. Empty bank accounts. Sell the house and leave no forwarding address. Perhaps settle in Mexico.

There were three things he knew about the vampire: one was the warning to remove reflective objects before the visit. This connoted a fear or weakness. Then there was the caution about religious items. Another fear? The third was the vampire's stated dread of dawn—which brought Boyer back to the problem of delaying the monster. The landing mirror was, of course, taken down to humor the expected salesman, and the only religious artifact in the house was a cross his wife hadn't worn for years. It was probably lost now in a drawer upstairs, useless as the oak-leaf mirror in the hall closet.

It suddenly occurred to him that he might be looking the solution in the eye: the highly polished coffee table.

He stood quickly, fighting a strange lethargy. The vampire eyed him with suspicion. Using strength from some untapped source, Boyer upended the heavy mahogany table to face the adversary. Magazines, cut-glass bowls and ashtrays, as well as an oversize art book slid down the slick wood to lay at the vampire's feet.

Mrs. Boyer reacted with horror when she saw that the finish reflected no trace of the gaunt figure. She shuddered back against the sofa, then pushed further, curling protectively as a flash of white, clawing flesh sliced through the air. The table was now nothing more than a pile of rubble.

"That was exceptionally rude, Boyer." Fury glazed the marmoreal face. "You annoy me."

Boyer, stunned, turned to his wife and noticed the pendant which had tumbled outside her blouse. It was the tiny cross, hanging on a thin gold chain. He knew instantly she must have worn it in the same attitude that prompted him to have the mirror removed. He felt a surge of hope. Boyer snatched the chain from around her neck, breaking the delicate clasp, and, holding the ridiculously small crucifix outstretched, rushed toward the vampire.

Air thickened and lights hazed. Time stood stock-still and there was a pure soundlessness not even the beat of two human hearts could penetrate. Blazing cold radiated from the figure in the Boyers' living room.

The vampire reached out his hand and the cross seemed to twist from Boyer's grasp into it.

"Besides loss of belief in my race, another stronghold I possess is the complete disintegration of mortal's religious faith." He closed his hand, then released a lump of jagged metal to the floor. "It was never crosses or stars of David or sacred cows, you see. It was the faith behind them which held power over me. And because you have faith in *nothing*, they are nothing more than detested objects, irritating baubles which disgust me.

"Now I hunger for rich, male blood."

Boyer searched his brain for a ploy or weapon. A way out. The vampire advanced, grinning: an eternity of hell with glazed fangs. Boyer backed recklessly into his stereo unit.

"Look," he said wildly. "Leave me alone. I can make it worth your while—I have money!" Insanely, he tore bills from his wallet. The vampire halted.

"Lots of money!" Boyer cried, thrusting twenties and tens and fives forward, pushing them into a clammy hand.

There arose a shriek so laden with pain and rage that Boyer felt his hair hackle. The living room was swept with an explosion of mouldy frigid wind, sucking books from pine shelves and house plants from quaint wooden buckets. The picture window shattered outward.

It happened so suddenly, Mr. and Mrs. Boyer did not immediately realize they were alone.

Spirits walk the earth for a relatively small number of reasons (see Appendix B). In this anonymous first-person narrative, one of the classic reasons for a haunting is set forth.

The Ghost of the Count
Anonymous

Not far from the Alameda, in the City of Mexico, there is a great old stone building, in which once lived a very wealthy and wicked Spanish count. The house has about four floors, and ninety rooms, more or less. The entire fourth floor is rented and occupied by a big American firm, and their bookkeeper, an American girl, has given us the following true account of the ghost that for years haunted the building. The second floor is unoccupied, as no one cares to live there for obvious reasons. And the bottom floor is also unoccupied, save for lumber rooms, empty boxes and crates and barrels. And last of all is the great patio with its tiled floor, where secretly in the night a duel was fought to the death by the wicked count and a famous Austrian prince, who was one of Maximilian's men. The count was killed.

No one knows why the duel was fought; some say it was because of a beautiful Spanish woman; some say that it was because of treasure that the two jointly "conveyed," and which the count refused to divide with his princely *"socio,"* and more people—Mexicans—shrug their shoulders if you ask about it, and say, *"Quien sabe?"*

"I saw a ghost here last night, Miss James," announces our cashier with much eclat and evident pride.

So great is the shock that I gasp, and my pen drops, spattering red ink on my nice fresh cuffs, and (worse luck!) on the ledger page that I had just totted up. It is ruined, and I will have to erase it, or—something! Wretched man!

"I wish to goodness it had taken you off," I cry, wrathfully, as I look at the bespattered work. "Now will you just look here and see what you have done? I wish you and your ghosts were in——"

"Gehenna?" he inquires, sweetly; "I'll fix that—it won't take half a minute. And don't look so stern, else I won't tell you about the *espanto*. And you will be sorry if you don't hear about it—it would make such a good story." (Insinuatingly.)

"Then go ahead with it." (Ungraciously.)

"Well, last night I was waiting for West. He was to meet me here, after which it was our intention to hit the—that is, I mean we were going out together. (I nod scornfully.) And it seems that while I was patiently waiting here, in my usual sweet-tempered way, the blank idiot had his supper and then lay down to rest himself for a while. You know how delicate he is? (Another contemptuous nod.) Unfortunately he forgot the engagement, and slept on. He says he never awoke until three o'clock, and so didn't come, thinking I wouldn't be there. Meantime I also went to sleep, and might have snoozed on until three, likewise, but for the fact that the ghost woke me——"

"Well? Do go on," I urge.

"The ghost woke me, as I said," proceeds the simpleton, slowly. "It was passing its cold fingers over my face and groaning. Really, it was most extraordinary. At first I didn't know what it was; then, as I felt the icy fingers stroking my face and heard blood-curdling groans issuing from the darkness, I knew what it was. And I remembered the story of the prince and his little duel down in the patio, and knew it was the ghost of the prince's victim. By the way, you don't know what a funny sensation it is to have a ghost pat your face, Miss James——"

"Pat nothing," I retort, indignantly. "I wonder you are not ashamed to tell me such fibs. Such a ta-ra-diddle! And as for the man that the prince killed downstairs, you know as well as I do that he was taken home to Spain and buried there. Why, then, should he come back here into our offices, and pat your face?"

"Ah, that I can't say," with a supercilious drawl. "I can only account for it by thinking that the ghost has good taste—better than that of some people I know," meaningly. "But honestly, I swear that I am telling you the truth—cross my heart and hope to die if I am not! And you don't know how brave I was—I never screamed; in fact, I never made a sound; oh, I was brave!"

"Then what did you do?" sternly.

"I ran. *Por Dios,* how I ran! You remember with what alacrity we got down the stairs during the November earthquake? (I remember only too distinctly.) Well, last night's run wasn't a run, in comparison—it was a disappearance, a flight, a sprint! I went down the four flights of stairs like a streak of blue lightning, and the ghost flew with me. I heard the pattering of its steps and its groans clean down to the patio door, and I assure you I quite thought I had made such an impression that it was actually going on home with me. And the thought made me feel so weak that I felt perforce obliged to take a—have a—that is, strengthen myself with a cocktail. After which I felt stronger and went home quite peacefully. But it was an uncanny experience, wasn't it?"

"Was it before or after taking that cocktail?" I ask, incredulously. "And did you take one only or eleven?"

I am hard on the man, but he really deserves it. Ghosts! Spirits, perhaps, but not ghosts. Whereat his feelings are quite "hurted"—so much so that he vows he will never tell me anything again; I had better read about Doubting Thomas; he never has seen such an unbelieving woman in all his life, and if I were only a man he would be tempted to pray that I might see the ghost; it would serve me right. Then, wrathfully departs, to notice me no more that day.

Not believing the least bit in ghosts I gave the matter no more thought. In fact, when you fall heir to a set of books that haven't been posted for nineteen days, and you have to do it all, and get up your trial balance, too, or else give up your Christmas holidays, you haven't much time to think about ghosts, or anything else, except entries. And though I had been working fourteen hours per day, the 24th of December, noon hour, found me with a difference of $13.89. The which I, of course, must locate and straighten out before departing next morning on my week's holiday. *Por supuesto,* it meant night work. Nothing else would do; and besides, our plans had all been made to leave on the eight o'clock train next morning. So I would just sit up all night, if need be, and find the wretched balance and be done with it.

Behold me settled for work that night at seven o'clock in my own office, with three lamps burning to keep it from looking dismal and lonely, and books and ledgers and journals piled up two feet high around me. If hard work would locate that nasty, hateful $13.89 it would surely be found. I had told the *portero* downstairs on the ground floor to try and keep awake for a time, but if I didn't soon finish the work I would come down and call him when I was ready to go home.

He lived in a little room, all shut off from the rest of the building, so that it was rather difficult to get at him. Besides, he was the very laziest and sleepiest peon possible, and though he was supposed to take care of the big building at night, patrolling it so as to keep off *ladrones,* he in reality slept so soundly that the last trumpet, much less Mexican robbers, would not have roused him.

And for this very reason, before settling to my work I was careful to go around and look to locks and bolts myself; everything was secure, and the doors safely fastened. So that if *ladrones* did break through they would have to be in shape to pass through keyholes or possess false keys.

With never a thought of spirits or *porteros,* or anything else, beyond the thirteen dollars and eighty-nine cents, I worked and added and re-added and footed up. And at eleven o'clock, *grazia a Dios,* I had the thirteen dollars all safe, and would have whooped for joy, had I the time. However, I wasn't out of the woods yet, the sum of eighty-nine dollars being often more easy of location than eighty-nine cents. The latter must be found, also, before I could have the pleasure of shouting in celebration thereof.

At it I went again. After brain cudgeling and more adding and prayerful thought I at last had under my thumb that abominable eighty cents. Eureka! Only nine cents out. I could get it all straight and have some sleep, after all! Inspired by which thought I smothered my yawns and again began to add. I looked at my watch—ten minutes to twelve. Perhaps I could get it fixed before one.

I suppose I had worked at the nine cents for about twenty minutes. One of the cash entries looked to me to be in error. I compared it with the voucher—yes, that was just where the trouble lay! Eleven cents—ten —nine——

S-t-t! Out went the lights in the twinkling of an eye—as I sat, gaping in my astonishment, from out of the pitchy darkness of the room came the most dreary, horrible, blood-curdling groan imaginable. As I sat paralyzed, not daring to breathe, doubting my senses for a moment, and then thinking indignantly that it was some trick of that wretched cashier, I felt long, thin, icy fingers passing gently over my face. *Malgame Dios!* what a sensation! At first I was afraid to move. Then I nervously tried to brush the icy, bony things away. As fast as I brushed, with my heart beating like a steam-hammer, and gasping with deadly fear, the fingers would come back again; a cold wind was blowing over me. Again came that dreadful groan, and too frightened to move or scream, I tumbled in a heap on the floor, among the books and ledgers. Then I suppose I fainted.

When I regained my senses I was still in a heap with the ledgers; still it was dark and still I felt the cold fingers caressing my face. At which I became thoroughly desperate. No ghost should own me! I had laughed at the poor cashier and hinted darkly at cocktails. Pray, what better was I?

I scrambled to my feet, the fingers still stroking my face. I must address them—what language—did they understand English or Spanish, I wondered? Spanish would doubtless be most suitable, if indeed, it was the ghost of the murdered count——.

"Will you do me the favor, Señor Ghost," I started out bravely, in my best Spanish, but with a very trembling voice, "to inform me what it is that you desire? Is there anything I can do for you? Because, if not, I would like very much to be allowed to finish my work, which I cannot do (if you will pardon my abruptness) if I am not alone."

(Being the ghost of a gentleman and a diplomat, surely he would take the hint and vanish. *Ojala!*)

Perhaps the ghost did not understand my Spanish; at any rate there was no articulate reply; there was another groan—again the fingers touched me, and then there was such a mournful sigh that I felt sorry for the poor thing—what could be the matter with it? With my pity, all fear was lost for a moment, and I said to the darkness all about me:

"What is it that you wish, *pobre señor?* Can I not aid you? I am not afraid—let me help you!"

The fingers moved uncertainly for a moment; then the ledgers all fell down, with a loud bang; a cold hand caught mine, very gently—I tried not to feel frightened, but it was difficult—and I was led off blindly, through the offices. I could not see a thing—not a glimmer of light showed; not a sound was heard except my own footsteps, and the faint sound of the invisible something that was leading me along—there were no more groans, thank goodness, else I should have shrieked and fainted, without a doubt. Only the pattering footsteps and the cold hand that led me on and on.

We—the fingers and I—were somehow in the great hall, then on the second floor, and at last on the stairs, going on down, flight after flight. Then I knew that I was being led about by the fingers on the tiled floor of the patio, and close to the *portero's* lodge. Simpleton that he was! Sleeping like a log, no doubt, while I was being led about in the black darkness by an invisible hand, and no one to save me! I would have yelled, of course, but for one fact—I founc it utterly impossible to speak or move my tongue, being a rare and uncomfortable sensation.

But where were we going? Back into the unused lumber rooms, joining onto the patio? Nothing there, except barrels and slabs and empty boxes. What could the ghost mean? He must be utterly demented, surely.

In the middle of the first room we paused. I had an idea of rushing out and screaming for the *portero,* but abandoned it when I found that my feet wouldn't go. I heard steps passing to and fro about the floor, and waited, cold and trembling. They approached me; again my hand was taken, and I was led over near the corner of the room. Obedient to the unseen will, I bent down and groped about the floor, guided by the cold fingers holding mine, until I felt something like a tiny ring, set firmly in the floor. I pulled at it faintly, but it did not move, at which the ghost gave a faint sigh. For a second the cold fingers pressed mine, quite affectionately, then released me, and I heard steps passing slowly into the patio, then dying away. Where was it going, and what on earth did it all mean?

But I was so tired and wrought up I tried to find the door, but couldn't (the cashier would have been revenged could he have seen me stupidly fumbling at a barrel, thinking it was the door), and at last, too fatigued and sleepy to stand, I dropped down on the cold stone floor and went to sleep.

I must have slept for some hours, for when I awoke the light of dawn was coming in at the window, and I sat up and wondered if I had taken leave of my senses during the night. What on earth could I be doing here in the lumber room? Then, like a flash, I remembered, and, half unconsciously, crept about on the floor seeking the small ring. There it was! I caught it and jerked at it hard. Hey, presto, change! For it seemed to me that the entire floor was giving way. There was a sliding, crashing sound, and I found myself hanging on for dear life to a barrel that, fortunately, retained its equilibrium, and with my feet dangling into space. Down below me was a small, stone-floored room, with big boxes and small ones ranged about the walls. Treasure! Like a flash the thought struck me, and with one leap I was down in the secret room gazing about at the boxes.

But, alas! upon investigation, the biggest chests proved empty. The bad, wicked count! No wonder he couldn't rest in his Spanish grave, but must come back to the scene of his wickedness and deceit to make reparation! But the smaller chests were literally crammed with all sorts of things—big heavy Spanish coins, in gold and silver—gold and silver dinner services, with the crest of the unfortunate emperor; magnificent pieces of jeweled armor and weapons, beautiful jewelry and loose precious stones. I deliberately selected handfuls of the latter, giving my preference to the diamonds and pearls—I had always had a taste for them, which I had never before been able to gratify!—and packed them in a wooden box that I found in the lumber room. The gold and dinner services and armor, etc., I left as they were, being rather cumbersome, and carried off, rejoicing, my big box of diamonds and pearls and other jewelry.

Needless to say we didn't go away for the holidays on the eight-o'clock train. But I did come down to the office and proceeded to locate my missing nine cents. After which I unfolded the tale of the ghost and the treasure—only keeping quiet the matter of my private loot. Of which I was heartily glad afterwards. For when the government learned of the find, what do you suppose they offered me for going about with the ghost and discovering the secret room and treasure? Ten thousand dollars! When I refused, stating that I would take merely, as my reward, one of the gold dinner services, the greedy things objected at first, but I finally had my way. And to this very day they have no idea that I—even I—have all the beautiful jewels. Wouldn't they be furious if they knew it? But they aren't apt to, unless they learn English and read this story. Which isn't likely.

"Tusitala," the teller of tales, was what the natives affectionately called ROB-
ERT LOUIS STEVENSON *when he retired to Samoa late in his short, disease-
racked life. Born in Edinburgh in 1850, son of a lighthouse engineer,
Stevenson wanted to take up his father's occupation but proved too sickly
for it. Instead, he penned some of our best-beloved adventure stories, including* Kidnapped, The Master of Ballantrae *and, of course,* Treasure Island.
He wrote many tales of suspense and horror, the most famous of which are
The Strange Case of Dr. Jekyll and Mr. Hyde, The Suicide Club, A Lodging
for the Night *and* "The Body Snatcher," *one of the literary byproducts of
the murderous cadaver-dealing of the ghoulish team, Burke and Hare.* "The
Body Snatcher" *was turned into one of the two or three greatest ghost-terror
films in the history of cinema.*

The Body Snatcher

by Robert Louis Stevenson

Every night in the year, four of us sat in the small parlour of the *George*
at Debenham—the undertaker, and the landlord, and Fettes, and myself.
Sometimes there would be more; but blow high, blow low, come rain or
snow or frost, we four would be each planted in his own particular arm-
chair. Fettes was an old drunken Scotsman, a man of education obviously, and a man of some property, since he lived in idleness. He had
come to Debenham years ago, while still young, and by a mere continuance of living had grown to be an adopted townsman. His blue
camlet cloak was a local antiquity, like the church-spire. His place in
the parlour at the *George,* his absence from church, his old, crapulous,
disreputable vices, were all things of course in Debenham. He had some
vague Radical opinions and some fleeting infidelities, which he would
now and again set forth and emphasize with tottering slaps upon the
table. He drank rum—five glasses regularly every evening; and for the
greater portion of his nightly visit to the *George* sat, with his glass in
his right hand, in a state of melancholy alcoholic saturation. We called
him the Doctor, for he was supposed to have some special knowledge
of medicine and had been known, upon a pinch, to set a fracture or re-
duce a dislocation; but beyond these slight particulars, we had no
knowledge of his character and antecedents.

One dark winter night—it had struck nine some time before the landlord joined us—there was a sick man in the *George,* a great neighbour-

ing proprietor suddenly struck down with apoplexy on his way to Parliament; and the great man's still greater London doctor had been telegraphed to his bedside. It was the first time that such a thing had happened in Debenham, for the railway was but newly open, and we were all proportionately moved by the occurrence.

"He's come," said the landlord, after he had filled and lighted his pipe.

"He?" said I. "Who?—not the doctor?"

"Himself," replied our host.

"What is his name?"

"Dr. Macfarlane," said the landlord.

Fettes was far through his third tumbler, stupidly fuddled, now nodding over, now staring mazily around him; but at the last word he seemed to awaken and repeated the name "Macfarlane" twice, quietly enough the first time, but with sudden emotion at the second.

"Yes," said the landlord, "that's his name, Doctor Wolfe Macfarlane."

Fettes became instantly sober; his eyes awoke, his voice became clear, loud and steady, his language forcible and earnest. We were all startled by the transformation, as if a man had risen from the dead.

"I beg your pardon," he said, "I am afraid I have not been paying much attention to your talk. Who is this Wolfe Macfarlane?" And then, when he had heard the landlord out, "It cannot be, it cannot be," he added; "and yet I would like well to see him face to face."

"Do you know him, Doctor?" asked the undertaker, with a gasp.

"God forbid!" was the reply. "And yet the name is a strange one; it were too much to fancy two. Tell me, landlord, is he old?"

"Well," said the host, "he's not a young man, to be sure, and his hair is white; but he looks younger than you."

"He is older, though; years older. But," with a slap upon the table, "it's the rum you see in my face—rum and sin. This man, perhaps, may have an easy conscience and a good digestion. Conscience! Hear me speak. You would think I was some good, old, decent Christian, would you not? But no, not I; I never canted. Voltaire might have canted if he'd stood in my shoes; but the brains"—with a rattling fillip on his bald head—"the brains were clear and active and I saw and made no deductions."

"If you know this doctor," I ventured to remark, after a somewhat awful pause, "I should gather that you do not share the landlord's good opinion."

Fettes paid no regard to me.

"Yes," he said, with sudden decision, "I must see him face to face."

There was another pause and then a door was closed rather sharply on the first floor and a step was heard upon the stair.

"That's the doctor," cried the landlord. "Look sharp and you can catch him."

It was but two steps from the small parlour to the door of the old *George* inn; the wide oak staircase landed almost in the street; there was room for a Turkey rug and nothing more between the threshold and the last round of the descent; but this little space was every evening brilliantly lit up, not only by the light upon the stair and the great signal-lamp below the sign, but by the warm radiance of the bar-room window. The *George* thus brightly advertised itself to passers-by in the cold street. Fettes walked steadily to the spot and we, who were hanging behind, beheld the two men meet, as one of them had phrased it, face to face. Dr. Macfarlane was alert and vigorous. His white hair set off his pale and placid, although energetic, countenance. He was richly dressed in the finest of broadcloth and the whitest of linen, with a great gold watchchain, and studs and spectacles of the same precious material. He wore a broad-folded tie, white and speckled with lilac, and he carried on his arm a comfortable driving-coat of fur. There was no doubt but he became his years, breathing, as he did, of wealth and consideration; and it was a surprising contrast to see our parlour sot—bald, dirty, pimpled and robed in his old camlet cloak—confront him at the bottom of the stairs.

"Macfarlane!" he said somewhat loudly, more like a herald than a friend.

The great doctor pulled up short on the fourth step, as though the familiarity of the address surprised and somewhat shocked his dignity.

"Toddy Macfarlane!" repeated Fettes.

The London man almost staggered. He stared for the swiftest of seconds at the man before him, glanced behind him with a sort of scare, and then in a startled whisper, "Fettes!" he said, "you!"

"Ay," said the other, "me! Did you think I was dead too? We are not so easy shut of our acquaintance."

"Hush, hush!" exclaimed the doctor. "Hush, hush! this meeting is so unexpected—I can see you are unmanned. I hardly knew you, I confess, at first, but I am overjoyed—overjoyed to have this opportunity. For the present it must be how-d'ye-do and goodbye in one, for my fly is waiting and I must not fail the train; but you shall—let me see—yes—you shall give me your address and you can count on early news of me. We must do something for you, Fettes. I fear you are out at elbows; but we must see to that for auld lang syne, as once we sang at suppers."

"Money!" cried Fettes; "money from you! The money that I had from you is lying where I cast it in the rain."

Dr. Macfarlane had talked himself into some measure of superiority and confidence, but the uncommon energy of this refusal cast him back into his first confusion.

A horrible, ugly look came and went across his almost venerable countenance. "My dear fellow," he said, "be it as you please; my last thought is to offend you. I would intrude on none. I will leave you my address, however—"

"I do not wish it—I do not wish to know the roof that shelters you," interrupted the other. "I heard your name; I feared it might be you; I wished to know if, after all, there were a God; I know now that there is none. Begone!"

He still stood in the middle of the rug, between the stair and the doorway; and the great London physician, in order to escape, would be forced to step to one side. It was plain that he hesitated before the thought of this humiliation. White as he was, there was a dangerous glitter in his spectacles; but while he still paused uncertain, he became aware that the driver of his fly was peering in from the street at this unusual scene and caught a glimpse at the same time of our little body from the parlour, huddled by the corner of the bar. The presence of so many witnesses decided him at once to flee. He crouched together, brushing on the wainscot, and made a dart like a serpent, striking for the door. But his tribulation was not yet entirely at an end, for even as he was passing Fettes clutched him by the arm and these words came in a whisper, and yet painfully distinct, "Have you seen it again?"

The great rich London doctor cried out aloud with a sharp, throttling cry; he dashed his questioner across the open space, and, with his hands over his head, fled out of the door like a detected thief. Before it had occurred to one of us to make a movement, the fly was already rattling towards the station. The scene was over like a dream, but the dream had left proofs and traces of its passage. Next day the servant found the fine gold spectacles broken on the threshold, and that very night we were all standing breathless by the bar-room window, and Fettes at our side, sober, pale, and resolute in look.

"God protect us, Mr. Fettes!" said the landlord, coming first into possession of his customary senses. "What in the universe is all this? These are strange things you have been saying."

Fettes turned towards us; he looked us each in succession in the face. "See if you can hold your tongues," said he. "That man Macfarlane is not safe to cross; those that have done so already have repented it too late."

And then, without so much as finishing his third glass, far less waiting for the other two, he bade us goodbye and went forth, under the lamp of the hotel, into the black night.

We three turned to our places in the parlour, with the big red fire and four clear candles; and as we recapitulated what had passed, the first chill of our surprise soon changed into a glow of curiosity. We sat late; it was the latest session I have known in the old *George*. Each man, before we parted, had his theory that he was bound to prove; and none of us had any nearer business in this world than to track out the past of our condemned companion, and surprise the secret that he shared with the great London doctor. It was no great boast, but I believe I was a better hand at worming out a story than either of my fellows at the *George;* and perhaps there is now no other man alive who could narrate to you the following foul and unnatural events.

In his young days Fettes studied medicine in the schools of Edinburgh. He had talent of a kind, the talent that picks up swiftly what it hears and readily retails it for its own. He worked little at home; but he was civil, attentive, and intelligent in the presence of his masters. They soon picked him out as a lad who listened closely and remembered well; nay, strange as it seemed to me when I first heard it, he was in those days well favoured, and pleased by his exterior. There was, at that period, a certain extramural teacher of anatomy, whom I shall here designate by the letter K. His name was subsequently too well known. The man who bore it skulked through the streets of Edinburgh in disguise, while the mob that applauded at the execution of Burke called loudly for the blood of his employer. But Mr. K—— was then at the top of his vogue; he enjoyed a popularity due partly to his own talent and address, partly to the incapacity of his rival, the university professor. The students, at least, swore by his name, and Fettes believed himself, and was believed by others, to have laid the foundations of success when he had acquired the favour of this meteorically famous man. Mr. K—— was a *bon vivant* as well as an accomplished teacher; he liked a sly allusion no less than a careful preparation. In both capacities Fettes enjoyed and deserved his notice, and by the second year of his attendance he held the half-regular position of second demonstrator or sub-assistant in his class.

In this capacity, the charge of the theatre and lecture-room devolved in particular upon his shoulders. He had to answer for the cleanliness of the premises and the conduct of the other students, and it was a part of his duty to supply, receive, and divide the various subjects. It was with a view to this last—at that time very delicate—affair that he was lodged by Mr. K—— in the same wynd, and at last in the same building, with the dissecting-rooms. Here, after a night of turbulent pleasures, his hand still tottering, his sight still misty and confused, he would be called out of bed in the black hours before the winter dawn by the unclean and desperate interlopers who supplied the table. He would open the door to these men, since infamous throughout the land. He would help them with their tragic burthen, pay them their sordid price, and remain alone, when they were gone, with the unfriendly relics of humanity. From such a scene he would return to snatch another hour or two of slumber, to repair the abuses of the night, and refresh himself for the labours of the day.

Few lads could have been more insensible to the impressions of a life thus passed among the ensigns of mortality. His mind was closed against all general considerations. He was incapable of interest in the fate and fortunes of another, the slave of his own desires and low ambitions. Cold, light, and selfish in the last resort, he had that modicum of prudence, miscalled morality, which keeps a man from inconvenient drunkenness or punishable theft. He coveted, besides, a measure of consideration from his masters and his fellow-pupils, and he had no desire to fail conspicuously in the external parts of life. Thus he made it his pleasure to gain some distinction in his studies, and day after day rendered unimpeachable eye-service to his employer, Mr. K——. For his day of work he indemnified himself by nights of roaring, blackguardly enjoyment; and when that balance had been struck, the organ that he called his conscience declared itself content.

The supply of subjects was a continual trouble to him as well as to his master. In that large and busy class, the raw material of the anatomists kept perpetually running out; and the business thus rendered necessary was not only unpleasant in itself, but threatened dangerous consequences to all who were concerned. It was the policy of Mr. K—— to ask no questions in his dealings with the trade. "They bring the body, and we pay the price," he used to say, dwelling on the alliteration—"*quid pro quo.*" And again, and somewhat profanely, "Ask no questions," he would tell his assistants, "for conscience' sake." There was no understanding that the subjects were provided by the crime of murder. Had that idea been broached to him in words, he would have recoiled in horror; but the lightness of his speech upon so grave a matter was, in itself, an offence against good manners, and a temptation to the men with whom he dealt. Fettes, for instance, had often remarked to himself upon the singular freshness of the bodies. He had been struck again and again by the hang-dog, abominable looks of the ruffians who came to him before the dawn; and, putting things together clearly in his private thoughts, he perhaps attributed a meaning too immoral and too categorical to the unguarded counsels of his master. He understood his duty, in short, to have three branches: to take what was brought, to pay the price, and to avert the eye from any evidence of crime.

One November morning this policy of silence was put sharply to the test. He had been awake all night with a racking toothache—pacing his room like a caged beast or throwing himself in fury on his bed—and had fallen at last into that profound, uneasy slumber that so often follows on a night of pain, when he was awakened by the third or fourth angry repetition of the concerted signal. There was a thin, bright moonshine: it was bitter cold, windy, and frosty; the town had not yet awakened, but an indefinable stir already preluded the noise and business of the day. The ghouls had come later than usual, and they seemed more than usually eager to be gone. Fettes, sick with sleep, lighted them upstairs. He heard their grumbling Irish voices through a dream; and as they stripped the sack from their sad merchandise he leaned dozing with his shoulder propped against the wall; he had to shake himself to find the men their money. As he did so his eyes lighted on the dead face. He started; he took two steps nearer, with the candle raised.

"God Almighty!" he cried. "That is Jane Galbraith!"

The men answered nothing, but they shuffled nearer the door.

"I know her, I tell you," he continued. "She was alive and hearty yesterday. It's impossible she can be dead; it's impossible you should have got this body fairly."

"Sure, sir, you're mistaken entirely," asserted one of the men.

But the other looked Fettes darkly in the eyes, and demanded the money on the spot.

It was impossible to misconceive the threat or to exaggerate the danger. The lad's heart failed him. He stammered some excuses, counted out the sum, and saw his hateful visitors depart. No sooner were they gone than he hastened to confirm his doubts. By a dozen unquestionable marks he identified the girl he had jested with the day before. He saw, with horror, marks upon her body that might well betoken violence. A panic seized him, and he took refuge in his room. There he reflected at length over the discovery that he had made; considered soberly the bearing of Mr. K——'s instructions and the danger to himself of interference in so serious a business, and at last, in sore perplexity, determined to wait for the advice of his immediate superior, the class assistant.

This was a young doctor, Wolfe Macfarlane, a high favourite among all the restless students, clever, dissipated, and unscrupulous to the last degree. He had travelled and studied abroad. His manners were agreeable and a little forward. He was an authority on the stage, skilful on the ice or the links with skate or golf-club; he dressed with nice audacity, and, to put the finishing touch upon his glory, he kept a gig and a strong trotting-horse. With Fettes he was on terms of intimacy; indeed their relative positions called for some community of life; and when subjects were scarce the pair would drive far into the country in Macfarlane's gig, visit and desecrate some lonely graveyard, and return before dawn with their booty to the door of the dissecting-room.

On that particular morning Macfarlane arrived somewhat earlier than his wont. Fettes heard him, and met him on the stairs, told him his story, and showed him the cause of his alarm. Macfarlane examined the marks on her body.

"Yes," he said with a nod, "it looks fishy."

"Well, what should I do?" asked Fettes.

"Do?" repeated the other. "Do you want to do anything? Least said soonest mended, I should say."

"Someone else might recognize her," objected Fettes. "She was as well known as the Castle Rock."

"We'll hope not," said Macfarlane, "and if anybody does—well you didn't, don't you see, and there's an end. The fact is, this has been going on too long. Stir up the mud, and you'll get K—— into the most unholy trouble; you'll be in a shocking box yourself. So will I, if you come to that. I should like to know how any one of us would look, or what the devil we should have to say for ourselves, in any Christian witness-box. For me, you know there's one thing certain—that, practically speaking, all our subjects have been murdered."

"Macfarlane!" cried Fettes.

"Come now!" sneered the other. "As if you hadn't suspected it yourself!"

"Suspecting is one thing—"

"And proof another. Yes, I know; and I'm as sorry as you are this should have come here," tapping the body with his cane. "The next best thing for me is not to recognize it; and," he added coolly, "I don't. You may, if you please. I don't dictate, but I think a man of the world would do as I do; and I may add, I fancy that is what K—— would look for at our hands. The question is, why did he choose us two for his assistants? And I answer, because he didn't want old wives."

This was the tone of all others to affect the mind of a lad like Fettes. He agreed to imitate Macfarlane. The body of the unfortunate girl was duly dissected, and no one remarked or appeared to recognize her.

One afternoon, when his day's work was over, Fettes dropped into a popular tavern and found Macfarlane sitting with a stranger. This was a small man, very pale and dark, with coal-black eyes. The cut of his features gave a promise of intellect and refinement which was but feebly realized in his manners, for he proved, upon a nearer acquaintance, coarse, vulgar, and stupid. He exercised, however, a very remarkable control over Macfarlane; issued orders like the Great Bashaw; became inflamed at the least discussion or delay, and commented rudely on the servility with which he was obeyed. This most offensive person took a fancy to Fettes on the spot, plied him with drinks, and honoured him with unusual confidences on his past career. If a tenth part of what he confessed were true, he was a very loathsome rogue; and the lad's vanity was tickled by the attention of so experienced a man.

"I'm a pretty bad fellow myself," the stranger remarked, "but Macfarlane is the boy—Toddy Macfarlane I call him. Toddy, order your friend another glass." Or it might be, "Toddy, you jump up and shut the door." "Toddy hates me," he said again. "Oh, yes, Toddy, you do!"

"Don't call me that confounded name," growled Macfarlane.

"Hear him! Did you ever see the lads play knife? He would like to do that all over my body," remarked the stranger.

"We medicals have a better way than that," said Fettes. "When we dislike a dead friend of ours, we dissect him."

Macfarlane looked up sharply, as though this jest was scarcely to his mind.

The afternoon passed. Gray, for that was the stranger's name, invited Fettes to join them at dinner, ordered a feast so sumptuous that the tavern was thrown in commotion, and when all was done commanded Macfarlane to settle the bill. It was late before they separated; the man Gray was incapably drunk. Macfarlane, sobered by his fury, chewed the cud of the money he had been forced to squander and the slights he had been obliged to swallow. Fettes, with various liquors singing in his head, returned home with devious footsteps and a mind entirely in abeyance. Next day Macfarlane was absent from the class, and Fettes smiled to himself as he imagined him still squiring the intolerable Gray from tavern to tavern. As soon as the hour of liberty had struck he posted from place to place in quest of his last night's companions. He could find them, however, nowhere; so returned early to his rooms, went early to bed, and slept the sleep of the just.

At four in the morning he was awakened by the well-known signal. Descending to the door, he was filled with astonishment to find Macfarlane with his gig, and in the gig one of those long and ghastly packages with which he was so well acquainted.

"What?" he cried. "Have you been out alone? How did you manage?"

But Macfarlane silenced him roughly, bidding him turn to business. When they had got the body upstairs and laid it on the table, Macfarlane made at first as if he were going away. Then he paused and seemed to hesitate; and then, "You had better look at the face," said he, in tones of some constraint. "You had better," he repeated, as Fettes only stared at him in wonder.

"But where, and how, and when did you come by it?" cried the other.

"Look at the face," was the only answer.

Fettes was staggered; strange doubts assailed him. He looked from the young doctor to the body, and then back again. At last, with a start, he did as he was bidden. He had almost expected the sight that met his eyes, and yet the shock was cruel. To see, fixed in the rigidity of death and naked on that coarse layer of sackcloth, the man whom he had left well-clad and full of meat and sin upon the threshold of a tavern, awoke, even in the thoughtless Fettes, some of the terrors of the conscience. It was a *cras tibi* which re-echoed in his soul, that two whom he had known should have come to lie upon these icy tables. Yet these were only secondary thoughts. His first concern regarded Wolfe. Unprepared for a challenge so momentous, he knew not how to look his comrade in the face. He durst not meet his eye, and he had neither words nor voice at his command.

It was Macfarlane himself who made the first advance. He came up quietly behind and laid his hand gently but firmly on the other's shoulder.

"Richardson," said he, "may have the head."

Now Richardson was a student who had long been anxious for that portion of the human subject to dissect. There was no answer, and the murderer resumed: "Talking of business, you must pay me; your accounts, you see, must tally."

Fettes found a voice, the ghost of his own: "Pay you!" he cried. "Pay you for that?"

"Why, yes, of course you must. By all means and on every possible account, you must," returned the other. "I dare not give it for nothing, you dare not take it for nothing; it would compromise us both. This is another case like Jane Galbraith's. The more things are wrong the more we must act as if all were right. Where does old K—— keep his money—"

"There," answered Fettes hoarsely, pointing to a cupboard in the corner.

"Give me the key, then," said the other, calmly, holding out his hand.

There was an instant's hesitation, and the die was cast. Macfarlane could not suppress a nervous twitch, the infinitesimal mark of an immense relief, as he felt the key turn between his fingers. He opened the cupboard, brought out pen and ink and a paper-book that stood in one compartment, and separated from the funds in a drawer a sum suitable to the occasion.

"Now, look here," he said, "there is the payment made—first proof of your good faith: first step to your security. You have now to clinch it by a second. Enter the payment in your book, and then you for your part may defy the devil."

The next few seconds were for Fettes an agony of thought; but in balancing his terrors it was the most immediate that triumphed. Any future difficulty seemed almost welcome if he could avoid a present quarrel with Macfarlane. He sat down the candle which he had been carrying all the time, and with a steady hand entered the date, the nature, and the amount of the transaction.

"And now," said Macfarlane, "it's only fair that you should pocket the lucre. I've had my share already. By-the-by, when a man of the world falls into a bit of luck, has a few shillings extra in his pocket—I'm ashamed to speak of it, but there's a rule of conduct in the case. No treating, no purchase of expensive class-books, no squaring of old debts; borrow, don't lend."

"Macfarlane," began Fettes, still somewhat hoarsely. "I have put my neck in a halter to oblige you."

"To oblige me?" cried Wolfe. "Oh, come! You did, as near as I can see the matter, what you downright had to do in self defence. Suppose I got into trouble, where would you be? This second little matter flows clearly from the first. Mr. Gray is the continuation of Miss Galbraith. You can't begin and then stop. If you begin, you must keep on beginning; that's the truth. No rest for the wicked."

A horrible sense of blackness and the treachery of fate seized hold upon the soul of the unhappy student.

"My God!" he cried, "but what have I done? and when did I begin? To be made a class assistant—in the name of reason, where's the harm in that? Service wanted the position; Service might have got it. Would *he* have been where *I* am now?"

"My dear fellow," said Macfarlane, "what a boy you are! What harm *has* come to you? What harm *can* come to you if you hold your tongue? Why, man, do you know what this life is? There are two squads of us— the lions and the lambs. If you're a lamb, you'll come to lie upon these tables like Gray or Jane Galbraith; if you're a lion, you'll live and drive a horse like me, like K——, like all the world with any wit or courage. You're staggered at the first. But look at K——! My dear fellow, you're clever, you have pluck. I like you, and K—— likes you. You were born to lead the hunt: and I tell you, on my honour and my experience of life, three days from now you'll laugh at all these scarecrows like a high-school boy at a farce."

And with that Macfarlane took his departure and drove off up the wynd in his gig to get under cover before daylight. Fettes was thus left alone with his regrets. He saw the miserable peril in which he stood involved. He saw, with inexpressible dismay, that there was no limit to his weakness, and that, from concession to concession, he had fallen from the arbiter of Macfarlane's destiny to his paid and helpless accomplice. He would have given the world to have been a little braver at the time, but it did not occur to him that he might still be brave. The secret of Jane Galbraith and the cursed entry in the daybook closed his mouth.

Hours passed; the class began to arrive; the members of the unhappy Gray were dealt out to one and to another, and received without remark. Richardson was made happy with the head; and before the hour of freedom rang Fettes trembled with exultation to perceive how far they had already gone towards safety.

For two days he continued to watch, with increasing joy, the dreadful process of disguise.

On the third day Macfarlane made his appearance. He had been ill, he said; but he made up for lost time by the energy with which he directed the students. To Richardson in particular he extended the most valuable assistance and advice, and that student, encouraged by the praise of the demonstrator, burned high with ambitious hopes, and saw the medal already in his grasp.

Before the week was out Macfarlane's prophecy had been fulfilled. Fettes had outlived his terrors and had forgotten his baseness. He began to plume himself upon his courage, and had so arranged the story in his mind that he could look back on these events with an unhealthy pride. Of his accomplice he saw but little. They met, of course, in the business of the class; they received their orders together from Mr. K——. At times they had a word or two in private, and Macfarlane was from first to last particularly kind and jovial. But it was plain that he avoided any reference to their common secret; and even when Fettes whispered to him that he had cast in his lot with the lions and forsworn the lambs, he only signed to him smilingly to hold his peace.

At length an occasion arose which threw the pair once more into a closer union. Mr. K—— was again short of subjects; pupils were eager, and it was a part of this teacher's pretensions to be always well supplied. At the same time there came the news of a burial in the rustic graveyard of Glencorse. Time has little changed the place in question. It stood then, as now, upon the crossroad, out of call of human habitations, and buried fathom deep in the foliage of six cedar trees. The cries of the sheep upon the neighbouring hills, the streamlets upon either hand, one loudly singing among pebbles, the other dripping furtively from pond to pond, the stir of the wind in mountainous old flowering chestnuts, and once in seven days the voice of the bell and the old tunes of the precentor, were the only sounds that disturbed the silence around the rural church. The Resurrection Man—to use a by-name of the period—was not to be deterred by any of the sanctities of customary piety. It was part of his trade to despise and desecrate the scrolls and trumpets of old tombs, the paths worn by the feet of worshippers and mourners, and the offerings and the inscriptions of bereaved affection. To rustic neighbourhoods, where love is more than commonly tenacious, and where some bonds of blood or fellowship unite the entire society of a parish, the body-snatcher, far from being repelled by natural respect, was attracted by the ease and safety of the task. To bodies that had been laid in earth, in joyful expectation of a far different awakening, there came that hasty, lamp-lit, terror-haunted resurrection of the spade and mattock. The coffin was forced, the cerements torn, and the melancholy relics, clad in sackcloth, after being rattled for hours on moonless by-ways, were at length exposed to uttermost indignities before a class of gaping boys.

Somewhat as two vultures may swoop upon a dying lamb, Fettes and Macfarlane were to be let loose upon a grave in that green and quiet resting-place. The wife of a farmer, a woman who had lived for sixty years, and been known for nothing but good butter and a godly conversation, was to be rooted from her grave at midnight and carried, dead and naked, to that far-away city that she had always honoured with her Sunday best; the place beside her family was to be empty till the crack of doom; her innocent and almost venerable members to be exposed to that last curiosity of the anatomist.

Late one afternoon the pair set forth, well wrapped in cloaks and furnished with a formidable bottle. It rained without remission—a cold, dense, lashing rain. Now and again there blew a puff of wind, but these sheets of falling water kept it down. Bottle and all, it was a sad and silent drive as far as Penicuik, where they were to spend the evening. They stopped once, to hide their implements in a thick bush not far from the churchyard, and once again at the Fisher's Tryst, to have a toast before the kitchen fire and vary their nips of whisky with a glass of ale. When they reached their journey's end the gig was housed, the horse was fed and comforted, and the two young doctors in a private room sat down to the best dinner and the best wine the house afforded. The lights, the fire, the beating rain upon the window, the cold, incongruous work that lay before them, added zest to their enjoyment of the meal. With every glass their cordiality increased. Soon Macfarlane handed a little pile of gold to his companion.

"A compliment," he said. "Between friends these little damned accommodations ought to fly like pipe-lights."

Fettes pocketed the money, and applauded the sentiment to the echo. "You are a philosopher," he cried. "I was an ass till I knew you. You and K—— between you, by the Lord Harry! but you'll make a man of me."

"Of course we shall," applauded Macfarlane. "A man? I tell you, it required a man to back me up the other morning. There are some big, brawling, forty-year-old cowards who would have turned sick at the look of the damned thing; but not you—you kept your head. I watched you."

"Well, and why not?" Fettes thus vaunted himself. "It was no affair of mine. There was nothing to gain on the one side but disturbance, and on the other I could count on your gratitude, don't you see?" And he slapped his pocket till the gold pieces rang.

Macfarlane somehow felt a certain touch of alarm at these unpleasant words. He may have regretted that he had taught his young companion so successfully, but he had no time to interfere, for the other noisily continued in this boastful strain:

"The great thing is not to be afraid. Now, between you and me, I don't want to hang—that's practical; but for all cant, Macfarlane, I was born with a contempt. Hell, God, Devil, right, wrong, sin, crime, and all the old gallery of curiosities—they may frighten boys, but men of the world, like you and me, despise them. Here's to the memory of Gray!"

It was by this time growing somewhat late. The gig, according to order, was brought round to the door with both lamps brightly shining, and the young men had to pay their bill and take the road. They announced that they were bound for Peebles, and drove in that direction till they were clear of the last houses of the town; then, extinguishing the lamps, returned upon their course, and followed a by-road towards Glencorse. There was no sound but that of their own passage, and the incessant, strident pouring of the rain. It was pitch dark; here and there a white gate or a white stone in the wall guided them for a short space across the night; but for the most part it was at a foot pace, and almost groping, that they picked their way through that resonant blackness to their solemn and isolated destination. In the sunken woods that traverse the neighbourhood of the burying-ground the last glimmer failed them, and it became necessary to kindle a match and re-illumine one of the lanterns of the gig. Thus, under the dripping trees, and environed by huge and moving shadows, they reached the scene of their unhallowed labours.

They were both experienced in such affairs, and powerful with the spade; and they had scarce been twenty minutes at their task before they were rewarded by a dull rattle on the coffin lid. At the same moment Macfarlane, having hurt his hand upon a stone, flung it carelessly above his head. The grave, in which they now stood almost to the shoulders, was close to the edge of the plateau of the graveyard; and the gig lamp had been propped, the better to illuminate their labours, against a tree, and on the immediate verge of the steep bank descending to the stream. Chance had taken a sure aim with the stone. Then came a clang of broken glass; night fell upon them; sounds alternately dull and ringing announced the bounding of the lantern down the bank, and its occasional collision with the trees. A stone or two, which it had dislodged in its descent rattled behind it into the profundities of the glen; and then silence, like night, resumed its sway; and they might bend their hearing to its utmost pitch, but naught was to be heard except the rain, now marching to the wind, now steadily falling over miles of open country.

They were so nearly at an end of their abhorred task that they judged it wisest to complete it in the dark. The coffin was exhumed and broken open; the body inserted in the dripping sack and carried between them to the gig; one mounted to keep it in its place, and the other, taking the horse by the mouth, groped along by the wall and bush until they reached the wider road by the Fisher's Tryst. Here was a faint disused radiancy, which they hailed like daylight; by that they pushed the horse to a good pace and began to rattle along merrily in the direction of the town.

They had both been wetted to the skin during their operations, and now, as the gig jumped among the deep ruts, the thing that stood propped between them fell now upon one and now upon the other. At every repetition of the horrid contact each instinctively repelled it with greater haste; and the process, natural although it was, began to tell upon the nerves of the companions. Macfarlane made some ill-favoured jest about the farmer's wife, but it came hollowly from his lips, and was allowed to drop in silence. Still their unnatural burthen bumped from side to side; and now the head would be laid, as if in confidence, upon their shoulders, and now the drenching sackcloth would flap icily about their faces. A creeping chill began to possess the soul of Fettes. He peered at the bundle, and it seemed somehow larger than at first. All over the countryside, and from every degree of distance, the farm dogs accompanied their passage with tragic ululations; and it grew and grew upon his mind that some unnatural miracle had been achieved, that some nameless change had befallen the dead body, and that it was in fear of their unholy burthen that the dogs were howling.

"For God's sake," said he, making a great effort to arrive at speech, "for God's sake, let's have a light!"

Seemingly Macfarlane was affected in the same direction; for though he made no reply, he stopped the horse, passed the reins to his companion, got down, and proceeded to kindle the remaining lamp. They had by that time got no farther than the crossroad down to Auchendinny. The rain still poured as though the deluge were returning, and it was no easy matter to make a light in such a world of wet and darkness. When at last the flickering blue flame had been transferred to the wick and began to expand and clarify, and shed a wide circle of misty brightness round the gig, it became possible for the two young men to see each other and the thing they had along with them. The rain had moulded the rough sacking to the outlines of the body underneath; the head was distinct from the trunk, the shoulders plainly modelled; something at once spectral and human riveted their eyes upon the ghastly comrade of their drive.

For some time Macfarlane stood motionless, holding up the lamp. A nameless dread was swathed, like a wet sheet, about the body, and tightened the white skin upon the face of Fettes; a fear that was meaningless, a horror of what could not be, kept mounting to his brain. Another beat of the watch, and he had spoken. But his comrade forestalled him.

"That is not a woman," said Macfarlane, in a hushed voice.

"It was a woman when we put her in," whispered Fettes.

"Hold that lamp," said the other. "I must see her face."

And as Fettes took the lamp his companion untied the fastenings of the sack and drew down the cover from the head. The light fell very clear upon the dark, well-moulded features and smooth-shaven cheeks of a too familiar countenance, often beheld in dreams of both of these young men. A wild yell rang up into the night; each leaped from his own side into the roadway; the lamp fell, broke, and was extinguished; and the horse, terrified by this unusual commotion, bounded and went off towards Edinburgh at a gallop, bearing along with it, sole occupant of the gig, the body of the dead and long-dissected Gray.

"The Penhale Broadcast" *is surely the most remarkable idea for a ghost story I have ever encountered. It is eerie, beautiful and unforgettable.* JACK SNOW *was a native of Piqua, Ohio, where he was born in 1907. His career in radio eventually led him to New York and a position with NBC. In his spare time, he wrote a handful of fantastic stories, collected in a scarce edition,* Dark Music. *But he is probably best known for his lifelong love of the wonderful Oz tales created by L. Frank Baum. Snow wrote two Oz novels himself:* Magical Mimics in Oz *and* The Shaggy Man of Oz . . . *as well as the indispensable guide to that fairyland,* Who's Who in Oz.

"The Penhale Broadcast"

by Jack Snow

All arrangements were completed for the strangest and most unusual radio broadcast ever conceived.

WXAT, New York key station of a coast-to-coast chain of ninety some radio stations, was ready to broadcast the voice of a woman, dead for fifteen years.

Sonya Parrish had died at the height of an operatic career without parallel in musical annals. Her path of glory had led her to the thrones of European monarchs. It had brought her the laudations of the severest music critics. And, most important of all, it had showered her with the adulation of the general public. When she died in 1919, she was an international favorite. Every civilized nation in the world had mourned her passing with a sincerity that was in itself a remarkable tribute to her art and personal charm. Dignified, lovely and gifted, Sonya Parrish was one of the few to whom the word, genius, was correctly applied.

And now, after fifteen years of silence—a silence that was sealed by the grave—it was said that Sonya Parrish would sing again; that her lovely voice would rise sweet and clear in Gounod's inspired "Ave Maria," and mourn plaintively through the haunting beauty of Wagner's "Traume."

WXAT and its affiliated stations publicized the broadcast months previous to the memorable night when it was scheduled to go on the air. It was an experiment, the network officials admitted. There was a possibility that it might not be a success. But they believed it would be. Sonya Parrish—living or dead—was not the sort of artist to disappoint an audience. And this would be an audience of entire nations—uncounted millions—waiting to hear the long-stilled voice of the great soprano. Short wave broadcast would carry the program to South America and European stations for re-broadcast. The whole world would be a world of ears, a world of hushed voices, waiting for that one voice from the beyond. And Sonya Parrish, station officials believed, would not fail to sing for those hushed, awed listeners.

A brief newspaper clipping from Penhale, an obscure Connecticut town, was the first in the series of incidents which led to the plans for the incredible broadcast. By the merest chance, the clipping had come to the attention of a high official of WXAT. The item told, half-humorously in a self-consciously reportorial style, of the strange singing which had been heard recently in the graveyard at Penhale. The clipping proceeded to link the ghostly singing with the grave of Sonya Parrish, whose body had been interred in the humble cemetery fifteen years ago. Penhale had been Sonya's early home and now she lay buried there, beside her father and mother. It was her voice that had been heard.

The WXAT official put the notice aside with mild curiosity. Several weeks passed. Then this same official's attention had been caught by an article in a New York tabloid. It was the Penhale reporter's story retold more ambitiously and lavishly illustrated with photographs of the late Sonya Parrish. The article was further embellished with the work of an imaginative artist who pictured Sonya, radiantly lovely and sad, singing triumphantly against the gruesome background of the Penhale graveyard. It was this vivid picture, stirring his imagination, which sent the WXAT official off on an investigation which was eventually to lead to plans for the broadcast.

Slipping quietly away from New York, the official motored to Penhale and spent some time questioning the villagers. He found it to be an established and accepted belief that Sonya Parrish sang almost nightly in the graveyard. He had been invited to hear her. And he had gone, half-amused at his own credulity, to the graveyard. At midnight, the hour when Sonya was said to sing, he had heard it himself. He had started violently at the first note. It was Sonya Parrish's voice! There was no denying it! There was no other voice in the world—or out of it—like that one. He had listened, enraptured, the first tremor of fear quickly displaced by the magical beauty of the voice that held him spellbound. It was Sonya Parrish! No one could deny it! The radio official hadn't slept the rest of the night. Early in the morning he motored back

to New York in record time. In a few weeks plans for the amazing
broadcast were announced.

At first the public laughed at the announcements. It was some publicity stunt to introduce a new singer. It was merely a scheme to gain the
public's attention and columns of priceless publicity for WXAT and its
stations. Of course they could broadcast the voice of Sonya Parrish—
hadn't she made scores of phonograph records? But the network
officials vigorously denied these charges. No records would be used.
This was no stunt. In an effort to convince the public of the sincerity of
the venture, the radio officials invited the co-operation of several celebrated psychologists and investigators of psychical phenomena. With
the names of these well known men of science back of it, the venture
assumed solemnity and dignity in the layman's mind, and much of the
public jeering and ridiculing of the proposed broadcast subsided. Thus,
the almost magical power of the mere mention of the name of Science
to render logical in the public mind the most extravagant project.

The broadcast was set for the night of August 30th. At five minutes
before midnight, the remote control line from Penhale would be
plugged into the key station WXAT in New York, and the announcer
would open the broadcast. Five minutes later—at midnight—it was
hoped that the voice of Sonya Parrish would bridge the gap of fifteen
years of death and sing again.

Adrian Ramsey, gifted young announcer of WXAT and winner of the
coveted gold medal diction award from the Academy of Arts and Letters for two successive years, was assigned to handle the broadcast. It
was arranged that Ramsey would be alone in the graveyard beside the
great monolith which marked the hallowed ground in which the body
of Sonya Parrish lay resting.

A slender cable, extending from Ramsey's microphone to a point just
outside the graveyard gate, connected the microphone with an amplify-
ing system, operated by WXAT engineers. Telephone wires would then
carry the broadcast to the local telephone exchange in Penhale, from
which point it would be dispatched by long distance telephone lines to
WXAT in New York, and thence by radio to the listening world.

It was decided that no one was to be in the graveyard but Ramsey, as
it had been found that the singing was always clearest when the cemetery
was nearly deserted. On several evenings, following the wide-spread
publicizing of the phenomena, curious crowds had collected in the
graveyard, and as a result there had been no singing. Upon formulating
its plans for the broadcast, WXAT had secured permission from the

Penhale authorities to station a strict guard about the cemetery after nightfall. On the night of the broadcast, it was planned to double the guard.

At last the great night arrived. Long before midnight, practically every radio receiver in the United States was tuned to WXAT and its network of stations. Foreign listeners awaited the short wave rebroadcast, which would reach them through their local stations. Heretofore neglected radios suddenly loomed as instruments of the utmost importance, and became the center of interest of excited groups of listeners.

Adrian Ramsey stood just outside the gate of the gloomy little Penhale graveyard. It was 11:30. In just twenty-five minutes he would walk into the shadows of those trees—alone—and take his solitary position before the microphone, which had been set up hours previous beside the grave of Sonya Parrish, the greatest singer the world had ever known.

In spite of his training in the commercial world of radio, Adrian was an artist with an artist's temperament. While he was possessed of a naturally keen and vivid imagination, he wasn't the nervous type, nor likely to become easily excited—radio announcers can't afford to—yet he was conscious of a mounting tenseness and an eerie sense of the unreal. Certainly no man had ever been assigned to a stranger duty—to announce to an audience of uncounted millions the singing of a woman, fifteen years dead!

Adrian glanced at the slender gold watch on his wrist. Ten minutes till twelve. It was time he took his place at the microphone. A small group of WXAT officials and technicians stood about, talking in lowered tones.

"Everything's ready, Ramsey," said a tall dark man. He was Turner, program director of WXAT. "We have men stationed every few feet about the place. You won't be disturbed." The program director paused. Then, placing his hand on Adrian's shoulder, he added quietly, "It's got to work." In those four words he expressed the fear that haunted every member of the WXAT staff.

"It's got to work!" If it didn't, there would be no choice but to return the control to New York and proceed with the blaring of a night club orchestra. WXAT and its great nation-wide network of stations would be the laughing stock of the world. It didn't matter that every item of publicity had carried a clause stating that the broadcast was an experiment—a great experiment—and there was a possibility, through no default of the network, that the experiment would fail. All that and the fact that the chain officials were courageous enough to attempt so unusual a broadcast would quickly be lost sight of in the torrent of jeering and ridicule which would follow the unsuccessful venture. The rival network would see to that!

And so, there is small wonder that misgivings and last minute doubts crowded into Adrian Ramsey's mind, as he walked silently through the Penhale graveyard to the tomb of Sonya Parrish.

There was the microphone. He could see it gleaming in the moonlight. Cold, polished steel—an electric ear—insensible to the drama of the moment, waiting only to pick up and record with mechanical precision whatever sounds chanced to strike and agitate its sensitive diaphragm.

Arriving at the microphone, Adrian looked about him. He might be the only human being within miles—so silent, so lonely was the spot. He felt as if he were the only person on earth—save Sonya Parrish. There was her grave, a rounded mound of sod, silver-black in the moonlight, and at its head—the monolith, whitely gleaming and drenched with the rays of the moon that filtered through the leaves of a great elm tree. On either side of the imposing monument were the humble stones marking the resting places of Sonya Parrish's New England forebears.

Adrian Ramsey consulted his watch again. One minute more. Then he would be on the air. During the first few minutes, he would picture the eerie scene about him, and tell something of the greatness that had been Sonya Parish's. Then at midnight—

Now that the actual moment for action had arrived, Adrian was cool and collected. He forgot his doubts. He thought only of his part of the broadcast. Intently his eyes followed his stop watch. Slowly it neared the sixty mark—fifteen seconds—ten seconds—five seconds—11:55. A tiny amber signal light on the microphone stand glowed dully.

"Good evening, Ladies and Gentlemen of the radio audience." It was the cultured and flawlessly correct voice of Adrian Ramsey. He might have been speaking from the luxurious studios in New York, announcing a routine program, surrounded by every refinement of modern civilization. His diction was perfect. His carefully modulated voice was calm and controlled.

For five minutes Adrian talked. He pictured in vivid simple phrases the humble little village graveyard, where this first broadcast of its kind ever attempted was taking place. He read the inscription from the monolith that surmounted Sonya Parrish's resting place. He spoke of the hardy New England forebears of this great woman, all of whom lay buried here. He recalled Sonya's early life, her singing as a child in the village choir, and later her great gift of artistry which had carried her across the ocean to study under the tutelage of European masters. He pictured her triumphs in Continental capitals, the multitudes of Berlin, Paris, Vienna, London, worshipping at her feet. His voice rose as he graphically portrayed her triumphal return to her native shores and her sensational debut with the Metropolitan Opera Company. Then followed her long and full years of glorious singing, her concert tours in which she had swept over the land like a great wave of melody and song —this had been before the days of radio.

Then in lowered tones, Adrian spoke compassionately of the lingering illness which had stricken the singer, when she was at the heights of her powers and fame. He told of her death and of how every nation of the world had paid sorrowful homage to the memory of the great woman whose voice was stilled. Adrian paused. Then in a few words he told of the singing in the graveyard and of the plans of WXAT which had culminated in this memorable experiment. In closing, he expressed the hope that the radio audience would be considerate of the spirit in which the experiment had been attempted, and, if it failed, would think rather of the noble motives which had inspired the venture, than of its failure.

It was intensely moving. Millions heard Adrian's voice. Millions were thrilled by it. The glowing tones—the dramatic phrasing—the supreme significance of the moment.

Again Adrian paused. He himself had been carried away. He trembled slightly. Even as he paused, a sound rose above the night silence and the monotonous chirruping of the crickets. It was the bell of the village church of Penhale tolling the hour of midnight. The vibrations carried clear and pure through the summer night. The microphone was hearing it, even as he was, Adrian knew. What better introduction to what was to follow than the eerie tolling of that distant bell?

Adrian listened, himself spellbound. Eight—nine—ten—eleven—twelve. Breathlessly Adrian counted them off. Then he moved closer to the microphone.

"It is midnight, Ladies and Gentlemen," he spoke in a subdued voice, little more than a whisper. "If Sonya Parrish can hear my voice, she will come now, and sing for the millions who are listening throughout the world." Adrian stepped back from the microphone and waited. Tiny beads of perspiration appeared on his forehead. There was nothing more he could do. His part was finished.

In New York excited groups of apartment dwellers clustered about loudspeakers. The ticking of millions of Gotham's clocks was suddenly, and perhaps for the first time, audible. In restaurants and places of entertainment, all music and talking stopped. No one stirred. New York was an ear.

Across the Middle West there were lights in the living rooms of farm homes at an hour when the occupants were customarily long abed. Hard-working farmers and their wives and families grouped tensely about loudspeakers—waiting. The bass of frogs sounded from nearby pools and streams, and the faint night wind set home-fashioned draperies fluttering in windows that looked out onto spreading fields and well-tended farm lands.

In the South, the moon shone down on wide acres of cotton, white and rolling, like the foam-crested waves of the sea. In humble cabins, far back from the deserted highways, cheap radio receivers inspired a reverent silence. A silence, breathless with the mingled emotions born in the superstitious hearts of the colored folk to whom all this was as a miracle that had passed so many long centuries ago in ancient Jerusalem, pervaded the tiny dwellings. In the mansions of the South, the fine old aristocratic families—last of the Barons of the soil—gathered in the ancestral halls to listen and wait.

On the plains of the West, cattle herders and ranchers sat on their rude bunks, their eyes mesmerized by illuminated dials. Occasionally the stillness was broken by the lonely cry of a coyote.

And in the Far West, up and down the great Pacific coast line with its string of thriving cities, millions more listened and waited, silently enduring the emptiness of those few moments that was like the emptiness that stretches into eternity.

In foreign lands, encircling the globe, the picture was the same. The world was an ear—a vast, multitudinous ear, an ear that listened tensely, hoping for a merest shred of the assurance that had been sought since the birth of the race—the assurance that death holds something more than the grave.

And then, into that ear, softly at first, softly and with incredible sweetness, flowed the unforgettable voice of Sonya Parrish. The world's heart stopped beating for a moment, as it listened. The voice sounded on. It was "Solvejg's Song" from the "Peer Gynt Suite." Delicately lovely, rising at one moment to rich crescendoes of warm beauty, and descending the next to notes of minor plaintiveness that pierced the heart with wistful beauty, the melody wavered and waned across the night air.

This was no hoax. This was Parrish—Sonya Parrish, the incomparable! Many older listeners, recalling the occasions when they had been thrilled by this sublime voice in concert halls and opera houses, listened awe-struck. Tears welled to their eyes.

A warm note of thanks swept through hearts separated by thousands of miles, linking them in a common tide of thanksgiving. There was no more distance—no more space—no more loneliness—even no more death —the impossible had happened—Sonya Parrish was singing again!

The last note of the incredible singing wavered into silence. Then came the voice of Adrian Ramsey. But it was a different Adrian Ramsey who spoke. He, too, had been touched and exalted by the magic that had happened. His voice was vibrant and rich with the strange heady excitement of the moment. He was speaking:

"Sonya Parrish has sung," a slight tremble in his voice betrayed his emotion. "Sonya Parrish has sung for the greatest audience ever assembled. As I look about me, I bow my head in humility. Never was mortal man favored with such a sight. I see the world's immortals gathered in this little graveyard to pay homage to the divine artistry of Sonya Parrish. There—not twenty paces from me—stands great Cæsar with his Roman court. And there—resplendent in the many-colored robes of the Orient—Marco Polo, the dreamer and adventurer. And there—kindly-visaged Shakespeare, mightiest of all the men of letters. His keen eyes gleam with heart-felt appreciation of the artistry he has just witnessed. And there is another divine woman, whose memory the world cherishes—the great Bernhardt, more magnetic and lovely than words can tell. Her eyes are moist with tears, a beautiful tribute to Sonya Parrish's art."

In New York, the WXAT official, who had conceived the broadcast, started. This was carrying the thing a little too far! Even he had been moved by the almost unbelievable success of the weird venture, but Ramsey was going too far. What did he mean? There was no way to stop him now. The official listened again. Ah, Sonya Parrish was singing once more! He listened, enchanted. God! Never had there been such singing as this! The beauty was heart-wringing. It was almost a relief when it wavered into silence.

Ramsey was speaking again. The official listened. "Sonya Parrish has sung again," came the voice from the loudspeaker. "She will sing no more tonight. For those who have assembled here she has displayed the magic of her great art. I bow my head in the glory of the moment in which I am permitted to speak. Such glory has never before come to man. I am humble before the multitude that is Sonya Parrish's audience." Ramsey paused, then continued in a voice that was curiously subdued. "And reverently, worshipfully I speak of One who has lately joined the multitude. For Him the great ones made way as for a King. He is garbed simply in a white robe that falls from His shoulders. A circlet of thorns crowns His head. His eyes are kind and gentle and more wise than—"

There was silence. Quickly the announcer in the New York studios stepped to the microphone and made the customary station identification and the concluding announcement for the program.

The broadcast had been a superb success! It was perfect—save for Ramsey's odd behavior. The man had obviously broken down, a prey to a bad attack of nerves. But even the official of WXAT couldn't find it in his heart to censure him. He was much too elated with the amazing success of the broadcast. And Ramsey's position had undoubtedly been a difficult one. An iron man might have faltered.

At the Penhale graveyard, the little group of station officials and technicians, who had listened breathlessly, just outside the cemetery, with ear-phones clasped to their heads, turned from their equipment and gazed at one another. They breathed a sigh of relief. It was over. It had been a success—more of a success than they had dared hope for. And Ramsey—what an ordeal it must have been for him! Alone there in the graveyard with that singing!

They started along the white-pebbled path of the graveyard to meet Ramsey and congratulate him on the splendid broadcast. But Ramsey wasn't in sight. They could distinguish the gleaming white marble that marked the grave of Sonya Parrish. Still, Ramsey was nowhere to be seen. Then one of the engineers, who was in the lead, shouted and broke into a run. In a few moments they were all standing before the grave of Sonya Parrish. There was the microphone with the familiar call letters, WXAT, across its top. At the base of the instrument, lay the body of Adrian Ramsey. He was dead.

In his eyes shone the light of a greater glory than any living man had ever before looked upon.

"The Last Traveler" *is a most frightening short story, largely because of the author's meticulous attention to setting and atmosphere. Whether the menacing entity is a ghost or not is difficult to say, but the chilling little coda suggests it has something to do with the spirits of the dead.* JEAN RAY *is represented in this country by one obscure book,* Ghouls in My Grave. *Ray's Gallic cruelties are redolent of that country's most famous institution of terror, the Grand Guignol, which, though defunct as a "live" theatre, still has a vast untapped literature waiting to be mined by scholars of the macabre.*

The Last Traveler
by Jean Ray

In his checkered cap and his old overcoat, John was no longer the imposing waiter of the Ocean Queen Hotel; for the next seven months, until the end of the off-season at the seaside, he was going to become once again an ironmonger on Humber Street in Hull.

Mr. Buttercup, the owner of the hotel, gave him a friendly handshake.

"I'll see you next year, John. I intend to open on the fifteenth of May."

"If it's God's will, yes," said John, solemnly drinking the farewell whisky that his employer had poured for him.

The dissatisfied rumble of a strong tide filled the mist-dulled air.

"The season is really over," said John.

"We're the last ones, the very last ones," added Mr. Buttercup.

Distant figures, bent beneath shapeless burdens, were walking along the coast, toward the little railroad station.

"The Stalkers are leaving," observed John. "The watchman on the pier told them there would be snow today."

"Snow!" Mr. Buttercup said indignantly. "Why, we're scarcely into October!"

John looked up at the sky rusted by sea mists. Cranes were passing in melancholy parades.

"They're going past the marshes," he said. "It's a bad sign when they do that."

A pure white bird flew by, crying, "Snow. . . . Snow. . . . Snow. . . ."

"You hear?" said John, trying to laugh.

"Snow? That's outrageous!" said Mr. Buttercup. Then he added philosophically, "Anyway, what difference does it make to me? Tomorrow the men will come to get the furniture that isn't going to hibernate here, and day after tomorrow I'll be in London."

"Yes, what difference does it make?" John said approvingly.

In the distance, a hammer was tapping feverishly on wood.

"Good heavens!" exclaimed Mr. Buttercup. "Windgery is going too! Listen: he's nailing the shutters of his house."

"But then you'll be alone, completely alone," remarked John. "When the last train has gone, the stationmaster goes to the village."

Mr. Buttercup started: alone!

"That's what I get for buying a hotel in this Godforsaken hole," he grumbled, "instead of in Margate or Folkestone."

"But business wasn't too bad," John protested gently, patting the pocket in which his wallet was sleeping.

"No, I suppose not," conceded Mr. Buttercup.

A locomotive whistled from behind the horizon in a long, threadlike wail.

"Here comes the train," said John. "Well, good-by, Mr. Buttercup."

"Oh, you still have a little time. Have another drink."

"Just one more drop, Mr. Buttercup; at my age, I can't run after trains any more!"

Mr. Buttercup remained alone in the dark, empty lobby. The hammer was no longer pounding beyond the road.

"Finiiished. . . . Finiiished . . . ," creaked a snipe, flying up from a nearby pond.

"The season's finished but I'm not," said Mr. Buttercup, trying to show the twelve rattan armchairs in the lobby that he was still light-hearted. But neither the snipe nor the chairs cared about his undaunted spirit.

Then he saw a man running desperately beside the railroad track. A whistle from the locomotive goaded the latecomer; he ran still faster, gesticulating like an unhappy puppet.

Mr. Buttercup grunted with pleasure.

"Mr. Windgery has missed the train," he said to himself. "Ah, that's amusing!"

The ringing of the telephone interrupted his joy. It was the electricity works calling to tell him that the current was going to be cut off, since the season was over.

"But *I'm* still here!" protested Mr. Buttercup.

"We can't keep a dynamo going just for you."

Mr. Buttercup lit one of the two green candles that adorned the piano, used a bottle as a candlestick, and gloomily poured himself another drink.

Twilight was dying in the west. The flame of the candle flickered, pointing its tip at the formidable shadows that had stealthily crept into the lobby.

Someone opened the door and sank into one of the rattan armchairs with a sigh.

Mr. Buttercup looked at him incredulously. At first he had taken him for one of the shadows that were now moving boldly in the lobby, but another sigh, more painful this time, convinced him that it was a man who had sat down in the chair.

The candle did not enable him to recognize him until he was only a few feet away.

"Mr. Windgery!" he exclaimed, relieved. "Well, this *is* a surprise! I saw you going to the station."

"Missed the train," panted Mr. Windgery.

"You ran as fast as you could, though, I saw that. Good heavens, but you're out of breath!"

"Lungs . . . very bad. . . . Wanted to leave . . . snow. . . ."

"Again! But it's not going to snow!"

Mr. Windgery's only answer was to extend a translucent hand toward the darkened windows, and the hotelkeeper saw delicate white flakes fluttering through the evening shadows.

"Well, well . . . ," he murmured. "After all, what of it?"

"Not good for me," complained Mr. Windgery.

"I'll accompany you to your house."

Mr. Windgery shook his head.

"Never mind: everything in my house is either empty or locked up. I'll stay here, if you have a room and a little hot tea."

"Why, of course!" Mr. Buttercup said eagerly, quickly resuming his role as a paid host. "Would you like some supper? I can give you cold beef, pâté, tinned fish, and cheese."

"No, thank you. I only want some hot tea and a little rum, if you don't mind."

"Of course not. You'll keep me company," Mr. Buttercup said good-humoredly. "I was all alone here; everyone else had left—you were the last to go. I can't think of a worse punishment for a decent man than not having anyone to talk to on an October night, a hundred yards from the bellowing sea, with no living voices around him except those of wild geese."

But his companion was as gloomy as the night itself. Mr. Buttercup was alarmed to see him redden his handkerchief with large gobs of sputum. They looked black in the dim light of the candle, and that made them all the uglier.

After a plaintive "Good night," Mr. Windgery went up to his room, taking the last green candle.

Sitting before the pointed flame and drinking from the bottle, Mr. Buttercup felt more alone than ever. He found the whisky bitter and drank it in big swallows, without savoring it.

When he awoke, shivers of horror were running over his skin, but he did not know why, especially since the snow-padded night was perfectly quiet. As he was falling asleep, he had cursed Mr. Windgery's rough cough; he no longer heard it now.

"He's asleep," he thought, but he could not explain the instinct that urged him to huddle down into the warm cave of his covers.

Although twilight, with its gliding shadows, should have seemed more hostile than this silent and splendidly clear night, he had not feared it; but he now said aloud in a quavering voice, "Come, come, what's going on here?"

Nothing was going on. The moonlight was accentuating the silence, that was all.

"What can it be?" he said in the same thin voice.

And suddenly, from the depths of the motionless night, the answer came.

It came in the form of dull, heavy footsteps.

"Mr. Windgery! Mr. Windgery!" called Mr. Buttercup.

Only the imperturbable footsteps answered his cry; they seemed to leave Mr. Windgery's room and calmly go down the stairs.

Mr. Buttercup threw on some unmatched clothes. He wanted to react against a nameless terror that was flowing toward him like shadowy water. He joked foolishly: "I can't complain of not having any company. First I was alone, then Windgery came, and now here's another traveler."

He leaned over the railing but saw nothing, even though the staircase was reflecting a silvery light. The footsteps were at the bottom now.

"Hello there!" said Mr. Buttercup. "Mr. Traveler. . . . Mr. Last Traveler. . . . Let's have a look at you!"

But his voice was more tenuous than a child's hair, and it scarcely reached his trembling lips.

He fell silent without even thinking of calling Mr. Windgery again, but he started down the stairs.

The footsteps were coming from the lobby. A short time later, without any sound of locks or doors, they faded away in the basement.

It later seemed strange to Mr. Buttercup that he did not think of getting a gun.

When the footsteps had ceased, the silence gave him the courage to go prudently down the stairs. He took such minute precautions that he seemed to have become a burglar in his own hotel. Despite the triply-posted notice—Bolt Your Door at Night—the door of Mr. Windgery's room was not locked, and the hotelkeeper was able to open it noiselessly.

The moonlight showed him instantly that there was something tragic and baleful in that room.

Mr. Windgery was lying on the bed with his head sunk deeply into the pillow and his mouth black, opened for a cry that seemed to be still audible; his open eyes reflected the blue light from the window.

"Dead!" gasped Mr. Buttercup. "Good Lord, what a predicament!"

Two seconds later, he was fleeing wildly toward the upper stories: the footsteps had just abruptly crossed the lobby and begun going up the stairs.

If a man of science had later told Mr. Buttercup that at that moment a sixth sense, related to the animal instinct of self-preservation, had taken possession of his whole being, he would no doubt have been answered by a skeptical shrug. One thing is certain, however: Mr. Buttercup was in the grip of absolute terror.

The shrill little voice of human reason had almost immediately stopped advising him to prepare an armed ambush in some dark corner. An imperious instinct resounded in his soul: "I must get away! Against *that* I'm powerless!"

He had just reached the top floor, reserved for the hotel staff and the guests' servants. He stumbled against an artful disorder left by his dissatisfied employees. The footsteps were now going from room to room, as though making a methodical inspection.

"It's in number twelve," murmured the hotelkeeper. "Now it's in number eighteen . . . twenty-two . . . twenty-nine. . . . Dear God, it's in *my* room!"

It chilled his heart to know that the Unknown that walked in the night was moving among the familiar and personal objects he had just left, as though a little of his being still clung to the things in that room.

In the last of the servants' rooms he saw a holy-water basin. He had a strange idea. Without making any noise, he blocked the hall with furniture and placed the holy-water basin on top of this frail barricade.

"It has to come this way," he thought, "and then . . ."

He would have been at a loss if he had been asked to explain what he meant by "it," but he had no time to reflect or reason: the footsteps were falling heavily on the bare steps that led to his refuge. They sounded more ominous and ferocious than ever; they seemed to make the whole building cry out in terror.

"I must go higher!" he groaned.

He reached the empty, dusty attic with its creaking floor. He looked around, wild-eyed. Was this going to be the wretched setting of his death? Suddenly his hand touched a thin metal ladder. The observation platform! He ran up the ladder. The trap door in the ceiling, welded shut by rust and dirt, would not open. The footsteps reached the floor below, then passed the childish barricade.

"Even that doesn't stop it!" thought Mr. Buttercup, weeping. He desperately thrust his head and shoulders against the trap door. It opened onto the vast blue night, blurred by snow but still sparkling with bright stars.

The observation platform overlooked the whole surrounding countryside. He had never ventured onto it before. He felt waves of dizziness rising inside him.

"I'd rather jump off than have *that* get me!" he cried.

Walking on a thick mattress of snow, he went to the edge of the platform. A feeling of immense desolation seized his heart. Far away, on the black surface of the sea, one light was following another. The yellow eye of the pier was insolently staring up at him from the depths of the darkness.

"Yes, yes, I'd rather jump . . . ," he sobbed.

A grating sound made him start; it came from the rusty rungs of the metal ladder. . . . It came closer and closer until it reached the trap door.

Then Mr. Buttercup saw the long stem of the lightning rod gleaming softly in the moonlight. He took hold of it with a gasp of horror, stepped over the railing of the platform, and, with the wail of a soul in hell, let himself slide down into emptiness.

Something jumped onto the platform.

A pale tongue of light licked the horizon. At the bottom of the ashy trench of the railroad, a green lamp went on; the window panes of the little station were whitened by the icy glow of a gaslight, and the first train whistled lazily in the invisible distance. Mr. Buttercup left the pile of creosoted crossties that had served as his shelter all night and, with stiff bones, bleeding hands, and a crazed brain, he ran to the lighted and inhabited little station, which seemed to him the most desirable oasis in the world.

It was not until eleven o'clock, when he had heard the opinion of the doctor who had come from a nearby village on his bicycle and declared that Mr. Windgery had died a natural death from consumption, that Mr. Buttercup resolved to look over the hotel.

He had found nothing suspicious in it, and was already accusing solitude, fear, and whisky, when he reached the observation platform. There, beside his own footprints faithfully retained by the snow, he saw other footprints, hideous, terrifying, and incredibly large. They, too, went to the edge of the platform, but they did not return; it was as though the thing that walked in the night had made a monstrous leap. . . .

When he went back down to the lobby, he uttered an exclamation of joy on seeing the black vehicle that had come for the remains of poor Mr. Windgery. He held its driver with whisky and amusing stories until the arrival of the moving van, and he promised such a large tip to the moving men if everything was gone an hour before the departure of the last train that they hurried so much they nearly broke everything, including their own limbs.

An hour before the last train whistled its farewell, Mr. Buttercup was on the station platform.

He had brought two bottles of whisky for the stationmaster, who helped him up the steps with brotherly affection and waved to him until the train was a tiny black lizard on the horizon.

At a long table of the Silver Dragon, a friendly tavern on Richmond Road where Mr. Buttercup went to tell his story, his companions asked for cards, dice, and a checkerboard.

"It's what's known as suggestion, autosuggestion," said Mr. Chickenbread, who sold musical instruments in the spacious shop next door.

"A hallucination," said Mr. Bitterstone, who was in the oil business.

Mr. Buttercup scratched his cheek.

"No one in the Buttercup family has hallucinations," he retorted, somewhat offended.

Dice rattled, decreeing wins and losses. The white disks melted before the dark advance of the blacks on the neutral checkerboard. Only old Dr. Hellermond remained thoughtful.

"I know," he murmured, speaking more to himself than to the placid Mr. Buttercup, "I know those footsteps. When I was an intern, I often heard them during quiet nights in the hospital, when nothing was awake except formaldehyde fumes and tearful grief. They moved without echoes down the long halls studded with dim night-lights; they preceded nocturnal stretchers being carried to the cold mortuary by silent-footed attendants.

"All of us—doctors, nurses, and attendants—used to hear them, but we had a tacit agreement never to mention them. Sometimes, though, a novice would pray aloud. Each time we heard them we knew that a void had just been made in the painful life of the white-walled wards.

"When the somber sergeants of Newgate Prison prepare the black flag bearing a capital *N* for the approaching dawn, they hear those footsteps moving along a stone corridor toward a cell more sinister than all the others."

Dr. Hellermond fell silent and began watching a game of checkers with interest.

No ghost story has ever approached the mundane horrors of one's daily newspaper, particularly in times of war. JAMES GRANT, born in 1822 of the family of Sir Walter Scott, was the son of a military captain—a fact which surely must have influenced the following grisly narrative.

The Phantom Regiment
by James Grant

Though the continued march of intellect and education have nearly obliterated from the mind of the Scots a belief in the marvellous, still a love of the supernatural lingers among the more mountainous districts of the northern kingdom; for "the Schoolmaster" finds it no easy task, even when aided by all the light of science, to uproot the prejudices of more than two thousand years.

I was born in Strathnairn, about the year 1802, and, on the death of my mother, was given, when an infant, to the wife of a cotter to nurse. With these good people I remained for some years, and thus became cognizant of the facts I am about to relate.

There was a little romance connected with my old nurse Meinie and her gudeman.

In their younger days they had been lovers—lovers as a boy and girl— but were separated by poverty, and then Ewen Mac Ewen enlisted as a soldier, in the 26th or Cameronian Regiment, with which he saw some sharp service in the West Indies and America. The light-hearted young highlander became, in time, a grave, stern, and morose soldier, with the most rigid ideas of religious deportment and propriety: for this distinguished Scottish regiment was of Puritan origin, being one of those raised among the Westland Covenanters, after the deposition of King James VII by the Estates of Scotland. England surrendered to William of Orange without striking a blow; but the defence of Dunkeld, and the victorious battle of Killycrankie, ended the northern campaign, in which the noble Dundee was slain, and the army of the cavaliers dispersed. The Cameronian Regiment introduced their sectarian forms, their rigorous discipline, and plain mode of public worship into their own ranks, and so strict was their code of morals, that even the Non-jurors and Jacobins admitted the excellence and stern propriety of their bearing. They left the Scottish Service for the British, at the Union, in 1707, but still wear on their appointments the five-pointed star, which was the armorial bearing of the colonel who embodied them; and, moreover, retain the privilege of supplying their own regimental Bibles.

After many years of hard fighting in the old 26th, and after carrying a halbert in the kilted regiment of the Isles, Ewen Mac Ewen returned home to his native place, the great plain of Moray, a graver, and, in bearing, a sadder man than when he left it.

His first inquiry was for Meinie.

She had married a rival of his, twenty years ago.

"God's will be done," sighed Ewen, as he lifted his bonnet, and looked upwards.

He built himself a little cottage, in the old highland fashion, in his native strath, at a sunny spot, where the Uise Nairn—the Water of Alders —flowed in front, and a wooded hill arose behind. He hung his knapsack above the fireplace; deposited his old and sorely thumbed regimental Bible (with the Cameronian star on its boards), and the tin case containing his colonel's letter recommending him to the minister, and the discharge, which gave sixpence per diem as the reward of sixteen battles—all on the shelf of the little window, which contained three panes of glass, with a yoke in the centre of each, and there he settled himself down in peace, to plant his own kail, knit his own hose, and to make his own kilts, a grave and thoughtful but contented old fellow, awaiting the time, as he said, "when the Lord would call him away."

Now it chanced that a poor widow, with several children, built herself a little thatched house on the opposite side of the drove road—an old Fingalian path—which ascended the pastoral glen; and the ready-handed veteran lent his aid to thatch it, and to sling her kail-pot on the cruicks, and was wont thereafter to drop in of an evening to smoke his pipe, to tell old stories of the storming of Ticonderoga, and to ask her little ones the catechism and biblical questions. Within a week or so, he discovered that the widow was Meinie—the ripe, blooming Meinie of other years—an old, a faded, and a sad-eyed woman now; and poor Ewen's lonely heart swelled within him, as he thought of all that had passed since last they met, and as he spake of what they were, and what they might have been, had fate been kind, or fortune proved more true.

We have heard much about the hidden and mysterious principle of affinity, and more about the sympathy and sacredness that belong to a first and early love; well, the heart of the tough old Cameronian felt these gentle impulses, and Meinie was no stranger to them. They were married, and for fifteen years, there was no happier couple on the banks of the Nairn. Strange to say, they died on the same day, and were interred in the ancient burying-ground of Dalcross, where now they lie, near the ruined walls of the old vicarage kirk of the Catholic times. God rest them in their humble highland graves! My father, who was the minister of Croy, acted as chief mourner, and gave the customary funeral prayer. But I am somewhat anticipating, and losing the thread of my own story in telling theirs.

In process of time the influx of French and English tourists who came to visit the country of the clans, and to view the plain of Culloden, after the publication of "Waverley" gave to all Britain that which we name in Scotland "the tartan fever," and caused the old path which passed the cot of Ewen to become a turnpike road; a tollbar—that most obnoxious of all impositions to a Celt—was placed across the mouth of the little glen, barring the way directly to the battlefield; and of this gate the old pensioner Ewen naturally became keeper; and during the summer season, when, perhaps, a hundred carriages per day rolled through, it became a source of revenue alike to him, and to the Lord of Cawdor and the Laird of Kilravock, the road trustees. And the chief pleasure of Ewen's existence was to sit on a thatched seat by the gate, for then he felt conscious of being in office—on duty—a species of sentinel; and it smacked of the old time when the Generale was beaten in the morning, and the drums rolled tattoo at night; when he had belts to pipe-clay, and boots to blackball; when there were wigs to frizzle and queues to tie, and to be all trim and in order to meet Monseigneur le Marquis de Montcalm, or General Washington "right early in the morning"; and there by the new barrier of the glen Ewen sat the live-long day, with spectacles on nose, and the Cameronian Bible on his knee, as he spelled his way through Deuteronomy and the tribes of Judah.

Slates in due time replaced the green thatch of his little cottage; then a diminutive additional story, with two small dormer windows, was added thereto, and the thrifty Meinie placed a paper in her window informing shepherds, the chance wayfarers, and the wandering deerstalkers that she had a room to let; but summer passed away, the sportsman forsook the brown scorched mountains, the gay tourist ceased to come north, and the advertisement turned from white to yellow, and from yellow to flyblown green in her window; the winter snows descended on the hills, the pines stood in long and solemn ranks by the white frozen Nairn, but "the room upstairs" still remained without a tenant.

Anon the snow passed away; the river again flowed free, the flowers began to bloom; the young grass to sprout by the hedgerows, and the mavis to sing on the fauld-dykes, for spring was come again, and joyous summer soon would follow; and one night—it was the 26th of April—Ewen was exhibiting his penmanship in large text-hand by preparing the new announcement of "a room to let," when he paused, and looked up as a peal of thunder rumbled across the sky; a red gleam of lightning flashed in the darkness without, and then they heard the roar of the deep broad Nairn, as its waters, usually so sombre and so slow, swept down from the wilds of Badenoch, flooded with the melting snows of the past winter.

A dreadful storm of thunder, rain, and wind came on, and the little cottage rocked on its foundations; frequently the turf-fire upon the hearth was almost blown about the clay-floor, by the downward gusts that bellowed in the chimney. The lightning gleamed incessantly, and seemed to play about the hill of Urchany and the ruins of Caistel Fionlah; the woods groaned and creaked, and the trees seemed to shriek as their strong limbs were torn asunder by the gusts which in some places laid side by side the green sapling of last summer, and the old oak that had stood for a thousand years—that had seen Macbeth and Duncan ride from Nairn, and had outlived the wars of the Comyns and the Clanehattan.

The swollen Nairn tore down its banks, and swept trees, rocks, and stones in wild confusion to the sea, mingling the pines of Aberarder with the old oaks of Cawdor; while the salt spray from the Moray Firth was swept seven miles inland, where it encrusted with salt the trees, the houses, and windows, and whatever it fell on as it mingled with the ceaseless rain, while deep, hoarse, and loud the incessant thunder rattled across the sky, "as if all the cannon on earth," according to Ewen, "were exchanging salvoes between Urchany and the Hill of Geddes."

Meinie grew pale, and sat with a finger on her mouth, and a startled expression in her eyes, listening to the uproar without; four children, two of whom were Ewen's, and her last addition to the clan, clung to her skirts.

Ewen had just completed the invariable prayer and chapter for the night, and was solemnly depositing his old regimental companion, with "Baxter's Saints' Rest," in a place of security, when a tremendous knock—a knock that rang above the storm—shook the door of the cottage.

"Who can this be, and in such a night?" said Meinie.

"The Lord knoweth," responded Ewen, gravely; "but he knocks both loud and late."

"Inquire before you open," urged Meinie, seizing her husband's arm, as the impatient knock was renewed with treble violence.

"Who comes there?" demanded Ewen, in a soldierly tone.

"A friend," replied a strange voice without, and in the same manner.

"What do you want?"

"Fire and smoke!" cried the other, giving the door a tremendous kick; "do you ask that in such a devil of a night as this? You have a room to let, have you not?"

"Yes."

"Well; open the door, or blood and 'oons I'll bite your nose off!"

Ewen hastened to undo the door; and then, all wet and dripping as if he had just been fished up from the Moray Firth, there entered a strange-looking old fellow in a red coat; he stumped vigorously on a wooden leg, and carried on his shoulders a box, which he flung down with a crash that shook the dwelling, saying,—

"There—damn you—I have made good my billet at last."

"So it seems," said Ewen, reclosing the door in haste to exclude the tempest, lest his house should be unroofed and torn asunder.

"Harkee, comrade, what garrison or fortress is this," asked the visitor, "that peaceable folks are to be challenged in this fashion, and forced to give parole and countersign before they march in—eh?"

"It is my house, comrade; and so you had better keep a civil tongue in your head."

"Civil tongue? Fire and smoke, you mangy cur! I can be as civil as my neighbours; but get me a glass of grog, for I am as wet as we were the night before Minden."

"Where have you come from in such a storm as this?"

"Where you'd not like to go—so never mind; but, grog, I tell you—get me some grog, and a bit of tobacco; it is long since I tasted either."

Ewen hastened to get a large quaighful of stiff Glenlivat, which the veteran drained to his health, and that of Meinie; but first he gave them a most diabolical grin, and threw into the liquor some black stuff, say-ing,—

"I always mix my grog with gunpowder—it's a good tonic; I learned that of a comrade who fell at Minden on the glorious 1st of August, '59."

"You have been a soldier, then?"

"Right! I was one of the 25th, or old Edinburgh Regiment; they enlisted me, though an Englishman, I believe; for my good old dam was a follower of the camp."

"Our number was the 26th—the old Cameronian Regiment—so we were near each other, you see, comrade."

"Nearer than you would quite like, mayhap," said Wooden-leg, with another grin and a dreadful oath.

"And you have served in Germany?" asked Ewen.

"Germany—aye, and marched over every foot of it, from Hanover to Hell, and back again. I have fought in Flanders, too."

"I wish you had come a wee while sooner," said Ewen gravely, for this discourse startled his sense of propriety.

"Sooner," snarled this shocking old fellow, who must have belonged to that army "which swore so terribly in Flanders," as good Uncle Toby says; "sooner—for what?"

"To have heard me read a chapter, and to have joined us in prayer."

"Prayers be d——ned!" cried the other, with a shout of laughter, and a face expressive of fiendish mockery, as he gave his wooden leg a thundering blow on the floor; "fire and smoke—another glass of grog—and then we'll settle about my billet upstairs."

While getting another dram, which hospitality prevented him from refusing, Ewen scrutinised this strange visitor, whose aspect and attire were very remarkable; but wholly careless of what any one thought, he sat by the hearth, wringing his wet wig, and drying it at the fire.

He was a little man, of a spare, but strong and active figure, which indicated great age; his face resembled that of a rat; behind it hung a long queue that waved about like a pendulum when he moved his head, which was quite bald, and smooth as a cricket-ball, save where a long and livid scar—evidently a sword cut—traversed it. This was visible while he sat drying his wig; but as that process was somewhat protracted, he uttered an oath, and thrust his cocked hat on one side of his head, and very much over his left eye, which was covered by a patch. This head-dress was the old military triple-cocked hat, bound with yellow braid, and having on one side the hideous black leather cockade of the House of Hanover, now happily disused in the British army, and retained as a badge of service by liverymen alone. His attire was an old threadbare red coat, faced with yellow, having square tails and deep cuffs, with braided holes; he wore knee-breeches on his spindle shanks, one of which terminated, as I have said, in a wooden pin; he carried a large knotted stick; and, in outline and aspect, very much resembled, as Ewen thought, Frederick the Great of Prussia, or an old Chelsea pensioner, or the soldiers he had seen delineated in antique prints of the Flemish wars. His solitary orb possessed a most diabolical leer, and, whichever way you turned, it seemed to regard you with the fixed glare of a basilisk.

"You are a stranger hereabout, I presume?" said Ewen drily.

"A stranger now, certainly; but I was pretty well known in this locality once. There are some bones buried hereabout that may remember me," he replied, with a grin that showed his fangless jaws.

"Bones!" reiterated Ewen, aghast.

"Yes, bones—Culloden Muir lies close by here, does it not?"

"It does—then you have travelled this road before?"

"Death and the Devil! I should think so, comrade; on this very night sixty years ago I marched along this road, from Nairn to Culloden, with the army of His Royal Highness, the Great Duke of Cumberland, Captain-General of the British troops, in pursuit of the rebels under the Popish Pretender—"

"Under His Royal Highness Prince Charles, you mean, comrade," said Ewen, in whose breast—Cameronian though he was—a tempest of Highland wrath and loyalty swelled up at these words.

"Prince—ha! ha! ha!" laughed the other; "had you said as much then, the gallows had been your doom. Many a man I have shot, and many a boy I have brained with the butt end of my musket, for no other crime than wearing the tartan, even as you this night wear it."

Ewen made a forward stride as if he would have taken the wicked boaster by the throat; his anger was kindled to find himself in presence of a veritable soldier of the infamous "German Butcher," whose merciless massacre of the wounded clansmen and their defenceless families will never be forgotten in Scotland while oral tradition and written record exist; but Ewen paused, and said in his quiet way,—

"Blessed be the Lord! these times and things have passed away from the land, to return to it no more. We are both old men now; by your own reckoning, you must at least have numbered four-score years, and in that, you are by twenty my better man. You are my guest tonight, moreover, so we must not quarrel, comrade. My father was killed at Culloden."

"On which side?"

"The right one—for he fell by the side of old Keppoch, and his last words were, 'Righ Hamish gu Bragh!' "

"Fire and smoke!" laughed the old fellow, "I remember these things as if they only happened yesterday—mix me some more grog and put it in the bill—I was the company's butcher in those days—it suited my taste —so when I was not stabbing and slashing the sheep and cattle of the rascally commissary, I was cutting the throats of the Scots and French, for there were plenty of them, and Irish too, who fought against the king's troops in Flanders. We had hot work, that day at Culloden—hotter than at Minden, where we fought in heavy marching order, with our blankets, kettles, and provisions, on a broiling noon, when the battlefield was cracking under a blazing sun, and the whole country was sweltering like the oven of the Great Baker."

"Who is he?"

"What! you don't know him? Ha! ha! ha! Ho! ho! ho! come, that is good."

Ewen expostulated with the boisterous old fellow on this style of conversation, which, as you may easily conceive, was very revolting to the prejudices of a well-regulated Cameronian soldier.

"Come, come, you old devilskin," cried the other, stirring up the fire with his wooden leg, till the sparks flashed and gleamed like his solitary eye; "you may as well sing psalms to a dead horse, as preach to me. Hark how the thunder roars, like the great guns at Carthagena! More grog—put it in the bill—or, halt, d——me! pay yourself," and he dashed on the table a handful of silver of the reigns of George II, and the Glencoe assassin, William of Orange.

He obtained more whiskey, and drank it raw, seasoning it from time to time with gunpowder, just as an Arab does his cold water with ginger.

"Where did you lose your eye, comrade?"

"At Culloden; but I found the fellow who pinked me, next day, as he lay bleeding on the field; he was a Cameron, in a green velvet jacket, all covered with silver; so I stripped off his lace, as I had seen my mother do, and then I brained him with the butt-end of brown-bess—and before his wife's eyes, too! What the deuce do you growl at, comrade? Such things will happen in war, and you know that orders must be obeyed. My eye was gone—but it was the left one, and I was saved the trouble of closing it when taking aim. This slash on the sconce I got at the battle of Preston Pans, from the Celt who slew Colonel Gardiner."

"That Celt was my father—the Miller of Invernahyle," said Meinie, proudly.

"Your father! fire and smoke! do you say so? His hand was a heavy one!" cried Wooden-leg, while his eye glowed like the orb of a hyaena.

"And your leg?"

"I lost at Minden, in Kingsley's Brigade, comrade; aye, my leg—d——n!—that was indeed a loss."

"A warning to repentance, I would say."

"Then you would say wrong. Ugh! I remember when the shot—a twelve-pounder—took me just as we were rushing with charged bayonets on the French cannoniers. Smash! my leg was gone, and I lay sprawling and bleeding in a ploughed field near the Weser, while my comrades swept over me with a wild hurrah! the colours waving, and drums beating a charge."

"And what did you do?"

"I lay there and swore, believe me."

"That would not restore your limb again."

"No; but a few hearty oaths relieve the mind; and the mind relieves the body; you understand me, comrade; so there I lay all night under a storm of rain like this, bleeding and sinking; afraid of the knives of the plundering death-hunters, for my mother had been one, and I remembered well how she looked after the wounded, and cured them of their agony."

"Was your mother one of those infer——" began Mac Ewen.

"Don't call her hard names now, comrade; she died on the day after the defeat at Val; with the Provost Marshal's cord round her neck—a cordon less ornamental than that of St. Louis."

"And your father?"

"Was one of Howard's Regiment; but which the devil only knows, for it was a point on which the old lady, honest woman, had serious doubts herself."

"After the loss of your leg, of course you left the service?"

"No, I became the company's butcher; but, fire and smoke, get me another glass of grog; take a share yourself, and don't sit staring at me like a Dutch Souterkin conceived of a winter night over a 'pot de feu,' as all the world knows King William was. Dam! let us be merry together—ha, ha, ha! ho, ho, ho! and I'll sing you a song of the old whig times."

> " 'O, brother Sandie, hear ye the news,
>   Lillibulero, bullen a la!
> An army is coming sans breeches and shoes,
>   Lillibulero, bullen a la!
>
> " 'To arms! to arms! brave boys to arms!
>   A true British cause for your courage doth ca';
> Country and city against a kilted banditti,
>   Lillibulero, bullen a la!' "

And while he continued to rant and sing the song (once so obnoxious to the Scottish Cavaliers), he beat time with his wooden leg, and endeavoured to outroar the stormy wind and the hiss of the drenching rain. Even Mac Ewen, though he was an old soldier, felt some uneasiness, and Meinie trembled in her heart, while the children clung to her skirts and hid their little faces, as if this singing, riot, and jollity were impious at such a time, when the awful thunder was ringing its solemn peals across the midnight sky.

Although this strange old man baffled or parried every inquiry of Ewen as to whence he had come, and how and why he wore that antiquated uniform, on his making a lucrative offer to take the upper room of the little toll-house for a year—exactly a year—when Ewen thought of his poor pension of sixpence per diem, of their numerous family, and Meinie now becoming old and requiring many little comforts, all scruples were overcome by the pressure of necessity, and the mysterious old soldier was duly installed in the attic, with his corded chest, scratch-wig, and wooden leg; moreover, he paid the first six months' rent in advance, dashing the money—which was all coin of the first and second Georges, on the table with a bang and an oath, swearing that he disliked being indebted to any man.

The next morning was calm and serene; the green hills lifted their heads into the blue and placid sky. There was no mist on the mountains, nor rain in the valley. The flood in the Nairn had subsided, though its waters were still muddy and perturbed; but save this, and the broken branches that strewed the wayside—with an uprooted tree, or a paling laid flat on the ground, there was no trace of yesterday's hurricane, and Ewen heard Wooden-leg (he had no other name for his new lodger) stumping about overhead, as the old fellow left his bed betimes, and after trimming his queue and wig, pipeclaying his yellow facings, and beating them well with the brush, in a soldier-like way, he descended to breakfast, but, disdaining porridge and milk, broiled salmon and bannocks of barley-meal, he called for a can of stiff grog, mixed it with powder from his wide waistcoat pocket, and drank it off at a draught. Then he imperiously desired Ewen to take his bonnet and staff, and accompany him so far as Culloden, "because," said he, "I have come a long, long way to see the old place again."

Wooden-leg seemed to gather—what was quite unnecessary to him—new life, vigour, and energy—as they traversed the road that led to the battlefield, and felt the pure breeze of the spring morning blowing on their old and wrinkled faces.

The atmosphere was charmingly clear and serene. In the distance lay the spires of Inverness, and the shining waters of the Moray Firth, studded with sails, and the ramparts of Fort George were seen jutting out at the termination of a long and green peninsula. In the foreground stood the castle of Dalcross, raising its square outline above a wood, which terminates the eastern side of the landscape. The pine-clad summit of Dun Daviot incloses the west, while on every hand between, stretched the dreary moor of Drummossie—the Plain of Culloden—whilom drenched in the blood of Scotland's bravest hearts.

Amid the purple heath lie two or three grass-covered mounds.

These are the graves of the dead—the graves of the loyal Highlanders, who fell on that disastrous field, and of the wounded, who were so mercilessly murdered next day by an order of Cumberland, which he pencilled on the back of a card (the Nine of Diamonds); thus they were dispatched by platoons, stabbed by bayonets, slashed by swords and spontoons, or brained by the butt-end of musket and carbine; officers and men were to be seen emulating each other in this scene of cowardice and cold-blooded atrocity, which filled every camp and barrack in Continental Europe with scorn at the name of an English soldier.

Ewen was a Highlander, and his heart filled with such thoughts as these, when he stood by the grassy tombs where the fallen brave are buried with the hopes of the house they died for; he took off his bonnet and stood bare-headed, full of sad and silent contemplation; while his garrulous companion viewed the field with his single eye, that glowed like a hot coal, and pirouetted on his wooden pin in a very remarkable manner, as he surveyed on every side the scene of that terrible encounter, where, after enduring a long cannonade of round shot and grape, the Highland swordsmen, chief and gillie, the noble and the nameless, flung themselves with reckless valour on the ranks of those whom they had already routed in two pitched battles.

"It was an awful day," said Ewen, in a low voice, but with a gleam in his grey Celtic eye; "yonder my father fell wounded; the bullet went through his shield and pierced him here, just above the belt; he was living next day, when my mother—a poor wailing woman with a babe at her breast—found him; but an officer of Barrel's Regiment ran a sword twice through his body and killed him; for the orders of the German Duke were, 'that no quarter should be given.' This spring is named MacGillivray's Well, because here they butchered the dying chieftain who led the MacIntoshes—aye bayonetted him, next day at noon, in the arms of his bonnie young wife and his puir auld mother! The inhuman monsters! I have been a soldier," continued Ewen, "and I have fought for my country; but had I stood, that day on this Moor of Culloden, I would have shot the German Butcher, the coward who fled from Flanders—I would, by the God who hears me, though that moment had been my last!"

"Ha, ha, ha! Ho, ho, ho!" rejoined his queer companion. "It seems like yesterday since I was here; I don't see many changes, except that the dead are all buried, wheras we left them to the crows, and a carriage-road has been cut across the field, just where we seized some women, who were looking among the dead for their husbands, and who—"

"Well?"

Wooden-leg whistled, and gave Ewen a diabolical leer with his snaky eye, as he resumed,—

"I see the ridge where the clans formed line—every tribe with its chief in front, and his colours in the centre, when we, hopeless of victory, and thinking only of defeat, approached them; and I can yet see standing the old stone wall which covered their right flank. Fire and smoke! It was against that wall we placed the wounded, when we fired at them by platoons next day. I finished some twenty rebels there myself."

Ewen's hand almost caught the haft of his skene-dhu, as he said, hoarsely—

"Old man, do not call them rebels in my hearing, and least of all by the graves where they lie; they were good men and true; if they were in error, they have long since answered to God for it, even as we one day must answer; therefore let us treat their memory with respect, as soldiers should ever treat their brothers in arms who fall in war."

But Wooden-leg laughed with his strange eldritch yell, and then they returned together to the toll-house in the glen; but Ewen felt strongly dissatisfied with his lodger, whose conversation was so calculated to shock alike his Jacobitical and his religious prejudices. Every day this sentiment grew stronger, and he soon learned to deplore in his inmost heart having ever accepted the rent, and longed for the time when he should be rid of him; but, at the end of the six months, Wooden-leg produced the rent for the remainder of the year, still in old silver of the two first Georges, with a few Spanish dollars, and swore he would set the house on fire, if Ewen made any more apologies about their inability to make him sufficiently comfortable and so forth; for his host and hostess had resorted to every pretence and expedient to rid themselves of him handsomely.

But Wooden-leg was inexorable.

He had bargained for his billet for a year; he had paid for it; and a year he would stay, though the Lord Justice General of Scotland himself should say nay!

Boisterous and authoritative, he awed every one by his terrible gimlet eye and the volleys of oaths with which he overwhelmed them on suffering the smallest contradiction; thus he became the terror of all; and shepherds crossed the hills by the most unfrequented routes rather than pass the toll-bar, where they vowed that his eye bewitched their sheep and cattle. To every whispered and stealthy inquiry as to where his lodger had come from, and how or why he had thrust himself upon this lonely toll-house, Ewen could only groan and shrug his shoulders, or reply,—

"He came on the night of the hurricane, like a bird of evil omen; but on the twenty-sixth of April we will be rid of him, please Heaven! It is close at hand, and he shall march then, sure as my name is Ewen Mac Ewen!"

He seemed to be troubled in his conscience, too, or to have strange visitors; for often in stormy nights he was heard swearing or threatening, and expostulating; and once or twice, when listening at the foot of the stair, Ewen heard him shouting and conversing from his window with persons on the road, although the bar was shut, locked, and there was no one visible there.

On another windy night, Ewen and his wife were scared by hearing Wooden-leg engaged in a furious altercation with some one overhead.

"Dog, I'll blow out your brains!" yelled a strange voice.

"Fire and smoke! blow out the candle first—ha, ha, ha! ho, ho, ho!" cried Wooden-leg; then there ensued the explosion of a pistol, a dreadful stamping of feet, with the sound of several men swearing and fighting. To all this Ewen and his wife hearkened in fear and perplexity; at last something fell heavily on the floor, and then all became still, and not a sound was heard but the night wind sighing down the glen.

Betimes in the morning Ewen, weary and unslept, left his bed and ascended to the door of this terrible lodger and tapped gently.

"Come in; why the devil this fuss and ceremony, eh, comrade?" cried a hoarse voice, and there was old Wooden-leg, not lying dead on the floor as Ewen expected, or perhaps hoped; but stumping about in his shirt sleeves, pipeclaying his facings, and whistling the "Point of War."

On being questioned about the most unearthly "row" of last night, he only bade Ewen mind his own affairs, or uttered a volley of oaths, some of which were Spanish, and mixing a can of gunpowder grog drained it at a draught.

He was very quarrelsome, dictatorial, and scandalously irreligious; thus his military reminiscences were of so ferocious and blood-thirsty a nature, that they were sufficient to scare any quiet man out of his seven senses. But it was more particularly in relating the butcheries, murders, and ravages of Cumberland in the highlands, that he exulted, and there was always a terrible air of probability in all he said. On Ewen once asking of him if he had ever been punished for the many irregularities and cruelties he so freely acknowledged having committed,—

"Punished? Fire and smoke, comrade, I should think so; I have been flogged till the bones of my back stood through the quivering flesh; I have been picquetted, tied neck and heels, or sent to ride the wooden horse, and to endure other punishments which are now abolished in the king's service. An officer once tied me neck and heels for eight and forty hours—ay, damme, till I lost my senses; but he lost his life soon after, a shot from the rear killed him; you understand me, comrade: ha, ha, ha! ho, ho, ho! a shot from the rear."

"You murdered him?" said Ewen, in a tone of horror.

"I did not say so," cried Wooden-leg with an oath, as he dealt his landlord a thwack across the shins with his stump; "but I'll tell you how it happened. I was on the Carthagena expedition in '41, and served amid all the horrors of that bombardment, which was rendered unsuccessful by the quarrels of the general and admiral; then the yellow fever broke out among the troops, who were crammed on board the ships of war like figs in a cask, or like the cargo of a slaver, so they died in scores—and in scores their putrid corpses lay round the hawsers of the shipping, which raked them up every day as they swung round with the tide; and from all the open gunports, where their hammocks were hung, our sick men saw the ground sharks gorging themselves on the dead, while they daily expected to follow. The air was black with flies, and the scorching sun seemed to have leagued with the infernal Spaniards against us. But, fire and smoke, mix me some more grog, I am forgetting my story!

"Our Grenadiers, with those of other regiments, under Colonel James Grant of Carron, were landed on the Island of Tierrabomba, which lies at the entrance of the harbour of Carthagena, where we stormed two small forts which our ships had cannonaded on the previous day.

" 'Grenadiers—open your pouches—handle grenades—blow your fuses!' cried Grant, 'forward.'

"And then we bayonetted the dons, or with the clubbed musket smashed their heads like ripe pumpkins, while our fleet, anchored with broadsides to the shore, threw shot and shell, grape, cannister, carcasses, and hand-grenades in showers among the batteries, booms, cables, chains, ships of war, gunboats, and the devil only knows what more.

"It was evening when we landed, and as the ramparts of San Luiz de Bocca Chica were within musket shot of our left flank, the lieutenant of our company was left with twelve grenadiers (of whom I was one) as a species of out-picquet to watch the Spaniards there, and to acquaint the officer in the captured forts if anything was essayed by way of sortie.

"About midnight I was posted as an advanced sentinel, and ordered to face La Bocca Chica with all my ears and eyes open. The night was close and sultry; there was not a breath of wind stirring on the land or waveless sea; and all was still save the cries of the wild animals that preyed upon the unburied dead, or the sullen splash caused by some half-shrouded corpse, as it was launched from a gun-port, for our ships were moored within pistol-shot of the place where I stood.

"Towards the west the sky was a deep and lurid red, as if the midnight sea was in flames at the horizon; and between me and this fiery glow, I could see the black and opaque outline of the masts, the yards, and the gigantic hulls of those floating charnel-houses our line-of-battle ships, and the dark solid ramparts of San Luiz de Bocca Chica.

"Suddenly I saw before me the head of a Spanish column!

"I cocked my musket, they seemed to be halted in close order, for I could see the white coats and black hats of a single company only. So I fired at them point blank, and fell back on the picquet, which stood to arms.

"The lieutenant of our grenadiers came hurrying towards me.

" 'Where are the dons?' said he.

" 'In our front, sir,' said I, pointing to the white line which seemed to waver before us in the gloom under the walls of San Luiz, and then it disappeared.

" 'They are advancing,' said I.

" 'They have vanished, fellow,' said the lieutenant, angrily.

" 'Because they have marched down into a hollow.'

"In a moment after they reappeared, upon which the lieutenant brought up the picquet, and after firing three volleys retired towards the principal fort where Colonel Grant had all the troops under arms; but not a Spaniard approached us, and what, think you, deceived me and caused this alarm? Only a grove of trees, fire and smoke! yes, it was a grove of manchineel trees, which the Spaniards had cut down or burned to within five feet of the ground; and as their bark is white it resembled the Spanish uniform, while the black burned tops easily passed for their grenadier caps to the overstrained eyes of a poor anxious lad, who found himself under the heavy responsibility of an advanced sentinel for the first time in his life."

"And was this the end of it?" asked Ewen.

"Hell and Tommy?" roared Wooden-leg, "no—but you shall hear. I was batooned by the lieutenant; then I was tried at the drumhead for causing a false alarm, and sentenced to be tied neck and heels, and lest you may not know the fashion of this punishment I shall tell you of it. I was placed on the ground; my firelock was put under my hams, and another was placed over my neck; then the two were drawn close together by two cartouch-box straps; and in this situation, doubled up as round as a ball, I remained with my chin wedged between my knees until the blood spouted out of my mouth, nose, and ears, and I became insensible. When I recovered my senses the troops were forming in column, preparatory to assaulting Fort San Lazare; and though almost blind, and both weak and trembling, I was forced to take my place in the ranks; and I ground my teeth as I handled my musket and saw the lieutenant of our company, in lace-ruffles and powdered wig, prepare to join the forlorn hope, which was composed of six hundred chosen grenadiers, under Colonel Grant, a brave Scottish officer. I loaded my piece with a charmed bullet, cast in a mould given to me by an Indian warrior, and marched on with my section. The assault failed. Of the forlorn hope I alone escaped, for Grant and his Grenadiers perished to a man in the breach. There, too, lay our lieutenant. A shot had pierced his head behind, just at the queue. Queer, was it not? when I was his covering file?"

As he said this, Wooden-leg gave Ewen another of those diabolical leers, which always made his blood run cold, and continued,—

"I passed him as he lay dead, with his sword in his hand, his fine ruffled shirt and silk waistcoat drenched with blood—by the bye, there was a pretty girl's miniature, with powdered hair peeping out of it too. 'Ho, ho!' thought I, as I gave him a hearty kick; 'you will never again have me tied neck-and-heels for not wearing spectacles on sentry, or get me a hundred lashes, for not having my queue dressed straight to the seam of my coat.'"

"Horrible!" said Ewen.

"I will wager my wooden leg against your two of flesh and bone, that your officer would have been served in the same way, if he had given you the same provocation."

"Heaven forbid!" said Ewen.

"Ha, ha, ha! Ho, ho, ho!" cried Wooden-leg.

"You spoke of an Indian warrior," said Ewen, uneasily, as the atrocious anecdotes of this hideous old man excited his anger and repugnance; "then you have served, like myself, in the New World?"

"Fire and smoke! I should think so; but long before your day."

"Then you fought against the Cherokees?"

"Yes."

"At Warwomans Creek?"

"Yes; I was killed there."

"You were—what?" stammered Ewen.

"Killed there."

"Killed?"

"Yes, scalped by the Cherokees; dam! don't I speak plain enough?"

"He is mad," thought Ewen.

"I am not mad," said Wooden-leg gruffly.

"I never said so," urged Ewen.

"Thunder and blazes! but you thought it, which is all the same."

Ewen was petrified by this remark, and then Wooden-leg, while fixing his hyaena-like eye upon him, and mixing a fresh can of his peculiar grog, continued thus,—

"Yes, I served in the Warwomans Creek expedition in '60. In the preceding year I had been taken prisoner at Fort Ninety-six, and was carried off by the Indians. They took me into the heart of their own country, where an old Sachem protected me, and adopted me in place of a son he had lost in battle. Now this old devil of a Sachem had a daughter—a graceful, pretty and gentle Indian girl, whom her tribe named the Queen of the Beaver dams. She was kind to me, and loved to call me her pale-faced brother. Ha, ha, ha! Ho, ho, ho! Fire and smoke! Do I now look like a man that could once attract a pretty girl's eye— now, with my wooden-leg, patched face and riddled carcase? Well, she loved me, and I pretended to be in love too, though I did not care for her the value of an old snapper. She was graceful and round in every limb, as a beautiful statue. Her features were almost regular—her eyes black and soft; her hair hung nearly to her knees, while her smooth glossy skin, was no darker than a Spanish brunette's. Her words were like notes of music, for the language of the Cherokees, like that of the Iroquois, is full of the softest vowels. This Indian girl treated me with love and kindness, and I promised to become a Cherokee warrior, a thundering turtle and scalp-hunter for her sake—just as I would have promised anything to any other woman, and had done so a score of times before. I studied her gentle character in all its weak and delicate points, as a general views a fortress he is about to besiege, and I soon knew every avenue to the heart of the place. I made my approaches with modesty, for the mind of the Indian virgin was timid, and as pure as the new fallen snow. I drew my parallels and pushed on the trenches whenever the old Sachem was absent, smoking his pipe and drinking firewater at the council of the tribe; I soon reached the base of the glacis and stormed the breast-works—dam! I did, comrade.

"I promised her everything, if she would continue to love me, and swore by the Great Spirit to lay at her feet the scalp-lock of the white chief, General the Lord Amherst, K.C.B., and all that, with every other protestation that occurred to me at the time; and so she soon loved me— and me alone—as we wandered on the green slopes of Tennessee, when the flowering forest-trees, and the magnolias, the crimson strawberries, and the flaming azalea made the scenery beautiful; and where the shrill cry of the hawk, and the carol of the merry mocking-bird, filled the air with sounds of life and happiness.

"We were married in the fantastic fashion of the tribe, and the Indian girl was the happiest squaw in the Beaver dams. I hoed cotton and planted rice; I cut rushes that she might plait mats and baskets; I helped her to weave wampum, and built her a wig-wam, but I longed to be gone, for in six months I was wearied of her and the Cherokees too. In short, one night, I knocked the old Sachem on the head, and without perceiving that he still breathed, pocketed his valuables, such as they were, two necklaces of amber beads and two of Spanish dollars, and without informing my squaw of what I had done, I prevailed upon her to guide me far into the forest, on the skirts of which lay a British out-post, near the lower end of the vale, through which flows the Tennessee River. She was unable to accompany me more than a few miles, for she was weak, weary, and soon to become a mother; so I gave her the slip in the forest, and, leaving her to shift for herself, reached headquarters, just as the celebrated expedition from South Carolina was preparing to march against the Cherokees.

"Knowing well the localities, I offered myself as a guide, and was at once accepted—"

"Cruel and infamous!" exclaimed honest Ewen, whose chivalric Highland spirit fired with indignation at these heartless avowals; "and the poor girl you deceived—"

"Bah! I thought the wild beasts would soon dispose of her."

"But then the infamy of being a guide, even for your comrades, against those who had fed and fostered, loved and protected you! By my soul, this atrocity were worthy of King William and his Glencoe assassins!"

"Ho, ho, ho! fire and smoke! you shall hear.

"Well, we marched from New York in the early part of 1760. There were our regiment, with four hundred of the Scots Royals, and Montgomery's Highlanders. We landed at Charleston, and marched up the country to Fort Ninety-six on the frontier of the Cherokees. Our route was long and arduous, for the ways were wild and rough, so it was the first of June before we reached Twelve-mile River. I had been so long unaccustomed to carry my knapsack, that its weight rendered me savage and ferocious, and I cursed the service and my own existence; for in addition to our muskets and accoutrements, our sixty rounds of ball cartridge per man, we carried our own tents, poles, pegs, and cooking utensils. Thunder and blazes! when we halted, which we did in a pleasant valley, where the great shady chestnuts and the flowering hickory made our camp alike cool and beautiful, my back and shoulders were nearly skinned; for as you must know well, comrade, the knapsack straps are passed so tightly under the armpits, that they stop the circulation of the blood, and press upon the lungs almost to suffocation. Scores of our men left the ranks on the march, threw themselves down in despair, and were soon tomahawked and scalped by the Indians.

"We marched forward next day, but without perceiving the smallest vestige of an Indian trail; thus we began to surmise that the Cherokees knew not that we were among them; but just as the sun was sinking behind the blue hills, we came upon a cluster of wig-wams, which I knew well; they were the Beaver dams, situated on a river, among wild woods that never before had echoed to the drum or bugle.

"Bad and wicked as I was, some strange emotions rose within me at this moment. I thought of the Sachem's daughter—her beauty—her love for me, and the child that was under her bosom when I abandoned her in the vast forest through which we had just penetrated; but I stifled all regret, and heard with pleasure the order to 'examine flints and priming.'

"Then the Cherokee warwhoop pierced the echoing sky; a scattered fire was poured upon us from behind the rocks and trees; the sharp steel tomahawks came flashing and whirling through the air; bullets and arrows whistled, and rifles rung, and in a moment we found ourselves surrounded by a living sea of dark-skinned and yelling Cherokees, with plumes on their scalp locks, their fierce visages streaked with war paint, and all their moccasins rattling.

"Fire and fury, such a time it was!

"We all fought like devils, but our men fell fast on every side; the Royals lost two lieutenants, and several soldiers whose scalps were torn from their bleeding skulls in a moment. Our regiment, though steady under fire as a battalion of stone statues, now fell into disorder, and the brown warriors, like fiends in aspect and activity, pressed on with musket and war-club brandished, and with such yells as never rang in mortal ears elsewhere. The day was lost, until the Highlanders came up, and then the savages were routed in an instant, and cut to pieces. 'Shoot and slash' was the order; and there ensued such a scene of carnage as I had not witnessed since Culloden, where His Royal Highness, the fat Duke of Cumberland, galloped about the field, overseeing the wholesale butchery of the wounded.

"We destroyed their magazines of powder and provisions; we laid the wig-wams in ashes, and shot or bayonetted every living thing, from the babe on its mother's breast, to the hen that sat on the roost; for as I had made our commander aware of all the avenues, there was no escape for the poor devils of Cherokees. Had the pious, glorious, and immortal King William been there, he would have thought we had modelled the whole affair after his own exploit at Glencoe.

"All was nearly over, and among the ashes of the smoking wig-wams and the gashed corpses of king's soldiers and Indian warriors, I sat down beneath a great chestnut to wipe my musket, for butt, barrel, and bayonet were clotted with blood and human hair—ouf, man, why do you shudder? it was only Cherokee wool;—all was nearly over, I have said, when a low fierce cry, like the hoarse hiss of a serpent, rang in my ear; a brown and bony hand clutched my throat as the fangs of a wolf would have done, and hurled me to the earth! A tomahawk flashed above me, and an aged Indian's face, whose expression, was like that of a fiend, came close to mine, and I felt his breath upon my cheek. It was the visage of the sachem, but hollow with suffering and almost green with fury, and he laughed like a hyaena, as he poised the uplifted axe.

"Another form intervened for a moment; it was that of the poor Indian girl I had so heartlessly deceived; she sought to stay the avenging hand of the frantic sachem; but he thrust her furiously aside, and in the next moment the glittering tomahawk was quivering in my brain—a knife swept round my head—my scalp was torn off, and I remember no more."

"A fortunate thing for you," said Ewen, drily; "memory such as yours were worse than a knapsack to carry; and so you were killed there?"

"Don't sneer, comrade," said Wooden-leg, with a diabolical gleam in his eye; "prithee, don't sneer; I was killed there, and, moreover, buried too, by the Scots Royals, when they interred the dead next day."

"Then how came you to be here?" said Ewen, not very much at ease, to find himself in company with one he deemed a lunatic.

"Here? that is my business—not yours," was the surly rejoinder.

Ewen was silent, but reckoned over that now there were but thirty days to run until the 26th of April, when the stipulated year would expire.

"Yes, comrade, just thirty days," said Wooden-leg, with an affirmative nod, divining the thoughts of Ewen; "and then I shall be off, bag and baggage, if my friends come."

"If not?"

"Then I shall remain where I am."

"The Lord forbid!" thought Ewen; "but I can apply to the sheriff."

"Death and fury! Thunder and blazes! I should like to see the rascal of a sheriff who would dare to meddle with me!" growled the old fellow, as his one eye shot fire, and, limping away, he ascended the stairs grumbling and swearing, leaving poor Ewen terrified even to think, on finding that his thoughts, although only half conceived, were at once divined and responded to by this strange inmate of his house.

"His friends," thought Ewen, "who may they be?"

Three heavy knocks rang on the floor overhead, as a reply.

It was the wooden leg of the Cherokee invader.

This queer old fellow (continued the quarter-master) was always in a state of great excitement, and used an extra number of oaths, and mixed his grog more thickly with gunpowder, when a stray red coat appeared far down the long green glen, which was crossed by Ewen's lonely toll-bar. Then he would get into a prodigious fuss and bustle, and was wont to pack and cord his trunk, to brush up his well-worn and antique regimentals, and to adjust his queue and the black cockade of his triple-cornered hat, as if preparing to depart.

As the time of that person's wished-for departure drew nigh, Ewen took courage, and shaking off the timidity with which the swearing and boisterous fury of Wooden-leg had impressed him, he ventured to expostulate a little on the folly and sin of his unmeaning oaths, and the atrocity of the crimes he boasted of having committed.

But the wicked old Wooden-leg laughed and swore more than ever, saying that a "true soldier was never a religious one."

"You are wrong, comrade," retorted the old Cameronian, taking fire at such an assertion; "religion is the lightest burden a poor soldier can carry; and, moreover, it hath upheld me on many a long day's march, when almost sinking under hunger and fatigue, with my pack, kettle, and sixty rounds of ball ammunition on my back. The duties of a good and brave soldier are no way incompatible with those of a Christian man; and I never lay down to rest on the wet bivouac or bloody field, with my knapsack, or it might be a dead comrade, for a pillow, without thanking God—"

"Ha, ha, ha!"

"—The God of Scotland's covenanted Kirk for the mercies he vouchsafed to Ewen Mac Ewen, a poor grenadier of the 26th Regiment."

"Ho, ho, ho!"

The old Cameronian took off his bonnet and lifted up his eyes, as he spoke fervently, and with the simple reverence of the olden time; but Wooden-leg grinned and chuckled and gnashed his teeth as Ewen resumed.

"A brave soldier may rush to the cannon's mouth, though it be loaded with grape and cannister; or at a line of levelled bayonets—and rush fearlessly too—and yet he may tremble without shame, at the thought of hell, or of offended Heaven. Is it not so, comrade? I shall never forget the words of our chaplain before we stormed the Isles of Saba and St. Martin from the Dutch, with Admiral Rodney, in '81."

"Bah—that was after I was killed by the Cherokees. Well?"

"The Cameronians were formed in line, mid leg in the salt water, with bayonets fixed, the colours flying, the pipes playing and drums beating 'Britons strike home,' and our chaplain, a reverend minister of God's word, stood beside the colonel with the shot and shell from the Dutch batteries flying about his old white head, but he was cool and calm, for he was the grandson of Richard Cameron, the glorious martyr of Airdsmoss.

" 'Fear not, my bairns,' cried he (he aye called us his bairns, having ministered unto us for fifty years and more)— 'fear not; but remember that the eyes of the Lord are on every righteous soldier, and that His hand will shield him in the day of battle!'

" 'Forward, my lads,' cried the colonel, waving his broad sword, while the musket shot shaved the curls of his old brigadier wig; 'forward, and at them with your bayonets'; and bravely we fell on—eight hundred Scotsmen, shoulder to shoulder—and in half an hour the British flag was waving over the Dutchman's Jack on the ramparts of St. Martin."

But to all Ewen's exordiums, the Wooden-leg replied by oaths, or mockery, or his incessant laugh,—

"Ha, ha, ha! Ho, ho, ho!"

At last came the long-wished for twenty-sixth of April!

The day was dark and louring. The pine woods looked black, and the slopes of the distant hills seemed close and near, and yet gloomy withal. The sky was veiled by masses of hurrying clouds, which seemed to chase each other across the Moray Firth. That estuary was flecked with foam, and the ships were riding close under the lee of the Highland shore, with topmasts struck, their boats secured, and both anchors out, for everything betokened a coming storm.

And with night it came in all its fury;—a storm similar to that of the preceding year.

The fierce and howling wind swept through the mountain gorges, and levelled the lonely shielings, whirling their fragile roofs into the air, and uprooting strong pines and sturdy beeches; the water was swept up from the Loch of the Clans, and mingled with the rain which drenched the woods around it. The green and yellow lightning played in ghastly gleams about the black summit of Dun Daviot, and again the rolling thunder bellowed over the graves of the dead on the bleak, dark moor of Culloden. Attracted by the light in the windows of the toll-house, the red deer came down from the hills in herds and cowered near the little dwelling; while the cries of the affrighted partridges, blackcocks, and even those of the gannets from the Moray Firth were heard at times, as they were swept past, with branches, leaves, and stones, on the skirts of the hurrying blast.

"It is just such a storm as we had this night twelvemonths ago," said Meinie, whose cheek grew pale at the elemental uproar.

"There will be no one coming up the glen tonight," replied Ewen; "so I may as well secure the toll-bar, lest a gust should dash it to pieces."

It required no little skill or strength to achieve this in such a tempest; the gate was strong and heavy, but it was fastened at last, and Ewen retreated to his own fireside. Meanwhile, during all this frightful storm without, Wooden-leg was heard singing and carolling upstairs, stumping about in the lulls of the tempest, and rolling, pushing, and tumbling his chest from side to side; then he descended to get a fresh can of grog—for "grog, grog, grog," was ever his cry. His old withered face was flushed, and his excited eye shone like a baleful star. He was conscious that a great event would ensue.

Ewen felt happy in his soul that his humble home should no longer be the resting-place of this evil bird whom the last tempest had blown hither.

"So you leave us tomorrow, comrade?" said he.

"I'll march before daybreak," growled the other; "'twas our old fashion in the days of Minden. Huske and Hawley always marched off in the dark."

"Before daybreak?"

"Fire and smoke, I have said so, and you shall see; for my friends are on the march already; but good night, for I shall have to parade betimes. They come; though far, far off as yet."

He retired with one of his diabolical leers, and Ewen and his wife ensconced themselves in the recesses of their warm box-bed; Meinie soon fell into a sound sleep, though the wind continued to howl, the rain to lash against the trembling walls of the little mansion, and the thunder to hurl peal after peal across the sky of that dark and tempestuous night.

The din of the elements and his own thoughts kept Ewen long awake; but though the gleams of electric light came frequent as ever through the little window, the glow of the "gathering peat" sank lower on the hearth of hard-beaten clay, and the dull measured tick-tack of the drowsy clock as it fell on the drum of his ear, about midnight, was sending him to sleep, by the weariness of its intense monotony, when from a dream that the fierce hawk eye of his malevolent lodger was fixed upon him, he started suddenly to full consciousness. An uproar of tongue now rose and fell upon the gusts of wind without; and he heard an authoritative voice requiring the toll-bar to be opened.

Overhead rang the stumping of the Wooden-leg, whose hoarse voice was heard bellowing in reply from the upper window.

"The Lord have a care of us!" muttered Mac Ewen, as he threw his kilt and plaid round him, thrust on his bonnet and brogues, and hastened to the door, which was almost blown in by the tempest as he opened it.

The night was as dark, and the hurricane as furious as ever; but how great was Ewen's surprise to see the advanced guard of a corps of Grenadiers, halted at the toll-bar gate, which he hastened to unlock, and the moment he did so, it was torn off its iron hooks and swept up the glen like a leaf from a book, or a lady's handkerchief; as with an unearthly howling the wind came tearing along in fitful and tremendous gusts, which made the strongest forests stoop, and dashed the struggling coasters on the rocks of the Firth—the Æstuarium Vararis of the olden time.

As the levin brands burst in lurid fury overhead, they seemed to strike fire from the drenched rocks, the dripping trees, and the long line of flooded roadway, that wound through the pastoral glen towards Culloden.

The advanced guard marched on in silence with arms slung; and Ewen, to prevent himself from being swept away by the wind, clung with both hands to a stone pillar of the bar gate, that he might behold the passage of this midnight regiment, which approached in firm and silent order in sections of twelve files abreast, all with muskets slung. The pioneers were in front, with their leather aprons, axes, saws, bill-hooks, and hammers; the band was at the head of the column; the drums, fifes, and colours were in the centre; the captains were at the head of their companies; the subalterns on the reverse flank, and the field-officers were all mounted on black chargers, that curvetted and pranced like shadows, without a sound.

Slowly they marched, but erect and upright, not a man of them seeming to stoop against the wind or rain, while overhead the flashes of the broad and blinding lightning were blazing like a ghastly torch, and making every musket-barrel, every belt-plate, sword-blade, and buckle, gleam as this mysterious corps filed through the barrier, with who? Wooden-leg among them!

By the incessant gleams Ewen could perceive that they were Grenadiers, and wore the quaint old uniform of George II's time; the sugarloaf-shaped cap of red cloth embroidered with worsted; the great square-tailed red coat with its heavy cuffs and close-cut collar; the stockings rolled above the knee, and enormous shoe-buckles. They carried grenado-pouches; the officers had espontoons; the sergeants shouldered heavy halberds, and the coats of the little drum-boys were covered with fantastic lace.

It was not the quaint and antique aspect of this solemn battalion that terrified Ewen, or chilled his heart; but the ghastly expression of their faces, which were pale and hollow-eyed, being, to all appearance, the visages of spectres; and they marched past like a long and wavering panorama, without a sound; for though the wind was loud, and the rain was drenching, neither could have concealed the measured tread of so many mortal feet; but there was no footfall heard on the roadway, nor the tramp of a charger's hoof; the regiment defiled past, noiseless as a wreath of smoke.

The pallor of their faces, and the stillness which accompanied their march, were out of the course of nature; and the soul of Mac Ewen died away within him; but his eyes were riveted upon the marching phantoms —if phantoms, indeed, they were—as if by fascination; and, like one in a terrible dream, he continued to gaze until the last files were past; and with them rode a fat and full-faced officer, wearing a three-cocked hat, and having a star and blue ribbon on his breast. His face was ghastly like the rest, and dreadfully distorted, as if by mental agony and remorse. Two aides-de-camps accompanied him, and he rode a wild-looking black horse, whose eyes shot fire. At the neck of the fat spectre—for a spectre he really seemed—hung a card.

It was the Nine of Diamonds!

The whole of this silent and mysterious battalion passed in line of march up the glen, with the gleams of lightning flashing about them. One bolt more brilliant than the rest brought back the sudden flash of steel.

They had fixed bayonets, and shouldered arms!

And on, and on they marched, diminishing in the darkness and the distance, those ghastly Grenadiers, towards the flat bleak moor of Culloden, with the green lightning playing about them, and gleaming on the storm-swept waste.

The Wooden-leg—Ewen's unco' guest—disappeared with them, and was never heard of more in Strathnairn.

He had come with a tempest, and gone with one. Neither was any trace ever seen or heard of those strange and silent soldiers. No regiment had left Nairn that night, and no regiment reached Inverness in the morning; so unto this day the whole affair remains a mystery, and a subject for ridicule with some, although Ewen, whose story of the midnight march of a corps in time of war—caused his examination by the authorities in the Castle of Inverness—stuck manfully to his assertions, which were further corroborated by the evidence of his wife and children. He made a solemn affidavit of the circumstances I have related before the sheriff, whose court books will be found to confirm them in every particular; if not, it is the aforesaid sheriff's fault, and not mine.

There were not a few (but these were generally old Jacobite ladies of decayed Highland families, who form the gossiping tabbies and wallflowers of the Northern Meeting) who asserted that in their young days they had heard of such a regiment marching by night, once a year to the field of Culloden; for it is currently believed by the most learned on such subjects in the vicinity of the "Clach na Cudden," that on the anniversary of the sorrowful battle, a *certain place,* which shall be nameless, opens, and that the restless souls of the murderers of the wounded clansmen march in military array to the green graves upon the purple heath, in yearly penance; and this story was thought to receive full corroboration by the apparition of a fat lubberly spectre with the nine of diamonds chained to his neck; as it was on that card—since named the Curse of Scotland—the Duke of Cumberland hastily pencilled the savage order to "show no quarter to the wounded, but to slaughter all."

The year 1812 was famous for yet another bloody war, but it also saw the birth of CHARLES DICKENS, *who, in spite of critical backlash, may well endure as England's greatest novelist. His deprived childhood and difficult mature years found echoes in his darker pages, many of which were devoted to the ghostly. But* "The Tale of the Bagman's Uncle" *is a thoroughly high-spirited romp, a dashing tale of swashbuckling ghosts that ends in a devastating punchline.*

The Tale of the Bagman's Uncle
by Charles Dickens

"My uncle, gentlemen," said the bagman, "was one of the merriest, pleasantest, cleverest fellows that ever lived. I wish you had known him, gentlemen. On second thoughts, gentlemen, I *don't* wish you had known him, for if you had, you would have been all, by this time, in the ordinary course of nature, if not dead, at all events so near it, as to have taken to stopping at home and giving up company: which would have deprived me of the inestimable pleasure of addressing you at this moment. Gentlemen, I wish your fathers and mothers had known my uncle. They would have been amazingly fond of him, especially your respectable mothers; I know they would. If any two of his numerous virtues predominated over the many that adorned his character, I should say they were his mixed punch and his after supper song. Excuse my dwelling on these melancholy recollections of departed worth; you won't see a man like my uncle every day in the week.

"I have always considered it a great point in my uncle's character, gentlemen, that he was the intimate friend and companion of Tom Smart, of the great house of Bilson and Slum, Cateaton Street, City. My uncle collected for Tiggin and Welps, but for a long time he went pretty near the same journey as Tom; and the very first night they met, my uncle took a fancy for Tom, and Tom took a fancy for my uncle. They made a bet of a new hat before they had known each other half an hour, who should brew the best quart of punch and drink it the quickest. My uncle was judged to have won the making, but Tom Smart beat him in the drinking by about half a salt-spoonfull. They took another quart a-piece to drink each other's health in, and were staunch friends ever afterwards. There's a destiny in these things, gentlemen; we can't help it.

"In personal appearance, my uncle was a trifle shorter than the middle size; he was a thought stouter too, than the ordinary run of people, and perhaps his face might be a shade redder. He had the jolliest face you ever saw, gentlemen: something like Punch, with a handsomer nose and chin; his eyes were always twinkling and sparkling with good humour; and a smile—not one of your unmeaning wooden grins, but a real, merry, hearty, good-tempered smile—was perpetually on his countenance. He was pitched out of his gig once, and knocked, head first, against a mile-stone. There he lay, stunned, and so cut about the face with some gravel which had been heaped up alongside it, that, to use my uncle's own strong expression, if his mother could have revisited the earth, she wouldn't have known him. Indeed, when I come to think of the matter, gentlemen, I feel pretty sure she wouldn't, for she died when my uncle was two years and seven months old, and I think it's very likely that, even without the gravel, his top-boots would have puzzled the good lady not a little: to say nothing of his jolly red face. However, there he lay, and I have heard my uncle say, many a time, that the man said who picked him up that he was smiling as merrily as if he had tumbled out for a treat, and that after they had bled him, the first faint glimmerings of returning animation, were, his jumping up in bed, bursting out into a loud laugh, kissing the young woman who held the basin, and demanding a mutton chop and a pickled walnut. He was very fond of pickled walnuts, gentlemen. He said he always found that, taken without vinegar, they relished the beer.

"My uncle's great journey was in the fall of the leaf, at which time he collected debts, and took orders, in the north: going from London to Edinburgh, from Edinburgh to Glasgow, from Glasgow back to Edinburgh, and thence to London by the smack. You are to understand that his second visit to Edinburgh was for his own pleasure. He used to go back for a week, just to look up his old friends; and what with breakfasting with this one, lunching with that, dining with a third, and supping with another, a pretty tight week he used to make of it. I don't know whether any of you, gentlemen, ever partook of a real substantial hospitable Scotch breakfast, and then went out to a slight lunch of a bushel of oysters, a dozen or so of bottled ale, and a noggin or two of whiskey to close up with. If you ever did, you will agree with me that it requires a pretty strong head to go out to dinner and supper afterwards.

"But, bless your hearts and eye-brows, all this sort of thing was nothing to my uncle! He was so well seasoned, that it was mere child's play. I have heard him say that he could see the Dundee people out, any day, and walk home afterwards without staggering; and yet the Dundee people have as strong heads and as strong punch, gentlemen, as you are likely to meet with, between the poles. I have heard of a Glasgow man and a Dundee man drinking against each other for fifteen hours at a sitting. They were both suffocated, as nearly as could be ascertained, at the same moment, but with this trifling exception, gentlemen, they were not a bit the worse for it.

"One night, within four-and-twenty hours of the time when he had settled to take shipping for London, my uncle supped at the house of a very old friend of his, a Baillie Mac something and four syllables after it, who lived in the old town of Edinburgh. There were the baillie's wife, and the baillie's three daughters, and the baillie's grown-up son, and three or four stout, bushy eye-browed, canny old Scotch fellows, that the baillie had got together to do honour to my uncle, and help to make merry. It was a glorious supper. There were kippered Salmon, and Finnan haddocks, and a lamb's head, and a haggis—a celebrated Scotch dish, gentlemen, which my uncle used to say always looked to him, when it came to table, very much like a cupid's stomach—and a great many other things besides, that I forget the names of, but very good things notwithstanding. The lassies were pretty and agreeable; the baillie's wife was one of the best creatures that ever lived; and my uncle was in thoroughly good cue. The consequence of which was, that the young ladies tittered and giggled, and the old lady laughed out loud, and the baillie and the other old fellows roared till they were red in the face, the whole mortal time. I don't quite recollect how many tumblers of whiskey toddy each man drank after supper; but this I know, that about one o'clock in the morning, the baillie's grown-up son became insensible while attempting the first verse of 'Willie brewed a peck o' maut'; and he having been, for half an hour before, the only other man visible above the mahogany, it occurred to my uncle that it was almost time to think about going: especially as drinking had set in at seven o'clock, in order that he might get home at a decent hour. But, thinking it might not be quite polite to go just then, my uncle voted himself into the chair, mixed another glass, rose to propose his own health, addressed himself in a neat and complimentary speech, and drank the toast with great enthusiasm. Still nobody woke; so my uncle took a little drop more—neat this time, to prevent the toddy from disagreeing with him—and, laying violent hands on his hat, sallied forth into the street.

"It was a wild gusty night when my uncle closed the baillie's door, and settling his hat firmly on his head, to prevent the wind from taking it, thrust his hands into his pockets, and looking upward, took a short survey of the state of the weather. The clouds were drifting over the moon at their giddiest speed: at one time wholly obscuring her: at another, suffering her to burst forth in full splendour and shed her light on all the objects around; anon, driving over her again, with increased velocity, and shrouding everything in darkness. 'Really, this won't do,' said my uncle, addressing himself to the weather, as if he felt himself personally offended. 'This is not at all the kind of thing for my voyage. It will not do, at any price,' said my uncle very impressively. Having repeated this, several times, he recovered his balance with some difficulty —for he was rather giddy with looking up into the sky so long—and walked merrily on.

"The baillie's house was in the Canongate, and my uncle was going to the other end of Leith Walk, rather better than a mile's journey. On either side of him, there shot up against the dark sky, tall gaunt straggling houses, with time-stained fronts, and windows that seemed to have shared the lot of eyes in mortals, and to have grown dim and sunken with age. Six, seven, eight stories high, were the houses; story piled above story, as children build with cards—throwing their dark shadows over the roughly paved road, and making the dark night darker. A few oil lamps were scattered at long distances, but they only served to mark the dirty entrance to some narrow close, or to show where a common stair communicated, by steep and intricate windings, with the various flats above. Glancing at all these things with the air of a man who had seen them too often before, to think them worthy of much notice now, my uncle walked up the middle of the street, with a thumb in each waistcoat pocket, indulging from time to time in various snatches of song, chaunted forth with such good will and spirit, that the quiet honest folk started from their first sleep and lay trembling in bed till the sound died away in the distance; when, satisfying themselves that it was only some drunken ne'er-do-weel finding his way home, they covered themselves up warm and fell asleep again.

"I am particular in describing how my uncle walked up the middle of the street, with his thumbs in his waistcoat pockets, gentlemen, because, as he often used to say (and with great reason too) there is nothing at all extraordinary in this story, unless you distinctly understand at the beginning that he was not by any means of a marvellous or romantic turn.

"Gentlemen, my uncle walked on with his thumbs in his waistcoat pockets, taking the middle of the street to himself, and singing, now a verse of a love song, and then a verse of a drinking one, and when he was tired of both, whistling melodiously, until he reached the North Bridge, which, at this point, connects the old and new towns of Edinburgh. Here he stopped for a minute, to look at the strange irregular clusters of lights piled one above the other, and twinkling afar off so high, that they looked like stars, gleaming from the castle walls on the one side and the Calton Hill on the other, as if they illuminated veritable castles in the air; while the old picturesque town slept heavily on, in gloom and darkness below: its palace and chapel of Holyrood, guarded day and night, as a friend of my uncle's used to say, by old Arthur's Seat, towering, surly and dark, like some gruff genius over the ancient city he has watched so long. I say, gentlemen, my uncle stopped here, for a minute, to look about him; and then, paying a compliment to the weather which had a little cleared up, though the moon was sinking, walked on again, as royally as before; keeping the middle of the road with great dignity, and looking as if he would very much like to meet with somebody who would dispute possession of it with him. There was nobody at all disposed to contest the point, as it happened; and so, on he went, with his thumbs in his waistcoat pockets, like a lamb.

"When my uncle reached the end of Leith Walk, he had to cross a pretty large piece of waste ground which separated him from a short street which he had to turn down, to go direct to his lodging. Now, in this piece of waste ground, there was, at that time, an enclosure belonging to some wheelwright who contracted with the Post-office for the purchase of old worn-out mail coaches; and my uncle, being very fond of coaches, old, young, or middle-aged, all at once took it into his head to step out of his road for no other purpose than to peep between the palings at these mails—about a dozen of which, he remembered to have seen, crowded together in a very forlorn and dismantled state, inside. My uncle was a very enthusiastic, emphatic sort of person, gentlemen; so, finding that he could not obtain a good peep between the palings, he got over them, and sitting himself quietly down on an old axletree, began to contemplate the mail coaches with a deal of gravity.

"There might be a dozen of them, or there might be more—my uncle was never quite certain on this point, and being a man of very scrupulous veracity about numbers, didn't like to say—but there they stood, all huddled together in the most desolate condition imaginable. The doors had been torn from their hinges and removed; the linings had been stripped off: only a shred hanging here and there by a rusty nail; the lamps were gone, the poles had long since vanished, the iron-work was rusty, the paint was worn away; the wind whistled through the chinks in the bare wood work; and the rain, which had collected on the roofs, fell, drop by drop, into the insides with a hollow and melancholy sound. They were the decaying skeletons of departed mails, and in that lonely place, at that time of night, they looked chill and dismal.

"My uncle rested his head upon his hands, and thought of the busy bustling people who had rattled about, years before, in the old coaches, and were now as silent and changed; he thought of the numbers of people to whom one of those crazy mouldering vehicles had borne, night after night, for many years, and through all weathers, the anxiously expected intelligence, the eagerly looked-for remittance, the promised assurance of health and safety, the sudden announcement of sickness and death. The merchant, the lover, the wife, the widow, the mother, the schoolboy, the very child who tottered to the door at the postman's knock—how had they all looked forward to the arrival of the old coach. And where were they all now!

"Gentlemen, my uncle used to *say* that he thought all this at the time, but I rather suspect he learnt it out of some book afterwards, for he distinctly stated that he fell into a kind of doze, as he sat on the old axletree looking at the decayed mail coaches, and that he was suddenly awakened by some deep church bell striking two. Now, my uncle was never a fast thinker, and if he had thought all these things, I am quite certain it would have taken him till full half-past two o'clock, at the very least. I am, therefore, decidedly of opinion, gentlemen, that my uncle fell into the kind of doze, without having thought about anything at all.

"Be this as it may, a church bell struck two. My uncle woke, rubbed his eyes, and jumped up in astonishment.

"In one instant after the clock struck two, the whole of this deserted and quiet spot had become a scene of most extraordinary life and animation. The mail-coach doors were on their hinges, the lining was replaced, the iron-work was as good as new, the paint was restored, the lamps were alight, cushions and great coats were on every coach box, porters were thrusting parcels into every boot, guards were stowing away letter bags, hostlers were dashing pails of water against the renovated wheels; numbers of men were rushing about, fixing poles into every coach; passengers arrived, portmanteaus were handed up, horses were put to; in short, it was perfectly clear that every mail there was to be off directly. Gentlemen, my uncle opened his eyes so wide at all this, that, to the very last moment of his life, he used to wonder how it fell out that he had ever been able to shut 'em again.

" 'Now then!' said a voice, as my uncle felt a hand on his shoulder, 'You're booked for one inside. You'd better get in.'

" '*I* booked!' said my uncle, turning round.

" 'Yes, certainly.'

"My uncle, gentlemen, could say nothing; he was so very much astonished. The queerest thing of all, was, that although there was such a crowd of persons, and although fresh faces were pouring in, every moment, there was no telling where they came from. They seemed to start up, in some strange manner, from the ground, or the air, and disappear in the same way. When a porter had put his luggage in the coach, and received his fare, he turned round and was gone; and before my uncle had well begun to wonder what had become of him, half-a-dozen fresh ones started up, and staggered along under the weight of parcels which seemed big enough to crush them. The passengers were all dressed so oddly too! Large, broad-skirted laced coats with great cuffs and no collars; and wigs, gentlemen—great formal wigs with a tie behind. My uncle could make nothing of it.

" 'Now, *are* you going to get in?' said the person who had addressed my uncle before. He was dressed as a mail guard, with a wig on his head and most enormous cuffs to his coat, and had a lantern in one hand, and a huge blunderbuss in the other, which he was going to stow away in his little arm-chest. '*Are* you going to get in, Jack Martin?' said the guard, holding the lantern to my uncle's face.

" 'Hallo!' said my uncle, falling back a step or two. 'That's familiar!'

" 'It's so on the way-bill,' replied the guard.

" 'Isn't there a "Mister" before it?' said my uncle. For he felt, gentlemen, that for a guard he didn't know, to call him Jack Martin, was a liberty which the Post-office wouldn't have sanctioned if they had known it.

" 'No, there is not,' rejoined the guard coolly.

" 'Is the fare paid?' inquired my uncle.

" 'Of course it is,' rejoined the guard.

" 'It is, is it?' said my uncle. 'Then here goes! Which coach?'

" 'This,' said the guard, pointing to an old-fashioned Edinburgh and London Mail, which had the steps down, and the door open. 'Stop! Here are the other passengers. Let them get in first.'

"As the guard spoke, there all at once appeared, right in front of my uncle, a young gentleman in a powdered wig, and a sky-blue coat trimmed with silver, made very full and broad in the skirts, which were lined with buckram. Tiggin and Welps were in the printed calico and waistcoat piece line, gentlemen, so my uncle knew all the materials at once. He wore knee breeches, and a kind of leggings rolled up over his silk stockings, and shoes with buckles; he had ruffles at his wrists, a three-cornered hat on his head, and a long taper sword by his side. The flaps of his waistcoat came half way down his thighs, and the end of his cravat reached to his waist. He stalked gravely to the coach-door, pulled off his hat, and held it above his head at arm's length: cocking his little finger in the air at the same time, as some affected people do, when they take a cup of tea. Then he drew his feet together, and made a low grave bow, and then put out his left hand. My uncle was just going to step forward, and shake it heartily, when he perceived that these attentions were directed, not towards him, but to a young lady who just then appeared at the foot of the steps, attired in an old-fashioned green velvet dress with a long waist and stomacher. She had no bonnet on her head, gentlemen, which was muffled in a black silk hood, but she looked round for an instant as she prepared to get into the coach, and such a beautiful face as she disclosed, my uncle had never seen—not even in a picture. She got into the coach, holding up her dress with one hand; and, as my uncle always said with a round oath, when he told the story, he wouldn't have believed it possible that legs and feet could have been brought to such a state of perfection unless he had seen them with his own eyes.

"But, in this one glimpse of the beautiful face, my uncle saw that the young lady cast an imploring look upon him, and that she appeared terrified and distressed. He noticed, too, that the young fellow in the powdered wig, notwithstanding his show of gallantry, which was all very fine and grand, clasped her tight by the wrist when she got in, and followed himself immediately afterwards. An uncommonly ill-looking fellow, in a close brown wig and a plum-coloured suit, wearing a very large sword, and boots up to his hips, belonged to the party; and when he sat himself down next to the young lady, who shrunk into a corner at his approach, my uncle was confirmed in his original impression that something dark and mysterious was going forward, or, as he always said himself, that 'there was a screw loose somewhere.' It's quite surprising how quickly he made up his mind to help the lady at any peril, if she needed help.

"'Death and lightning!' exclaimed the young gentleman, laying his hand upon his sword as my uncle entered the coach.

" 'Blood and thunder!' roared the other gentleman. With this, he whipped his sword out, and made a lunge at my uncle without further ceremony. My uncle had no weapon about him, but with great dexterity he snatched the ill-looking gentleman's three-cornered hat from his head, and, receiving the point of his sword right through the crown, squeezed the sides together, and held it tight.

" 'Pink him behind!' cried the ill-looking gentleman to his companion, as he struggled to regain his sword.

" 'He had better not,' cried my uncle, displaying the heel of one of his shoes, in a threatening manner. 'I'll kick his brains out, if he has any, or fracture his skull if he hasn't.' Exerting all his strength, at this moment, my uncle wrenched the ill-looking man's sword from his grasp, and flung it clean out of the coach-window: upon which the younger gentleman vociferated 'Death and lightning!' again, and laid his hand upon the hilt of his sword, in a very fierce manner, but didn't draw it. Perhaps, gentlemen, as my uncle used to say with a smile, perhaps he was afraid of alarming the lady.

" 'Now, gentlemen,' said my uncle, taking his seat deliberately, 'I don't want to have any death, with or without lightning, in a lady's presence, and we have had quite blood and thundering enough for one journey; so, if you please, we'll sit in our places like quiet insides. Here, guard, pick up that gentleman's carving-knife.'

"As quickly as my uncle said the words, the guard appeared at the coach-window, with the gentleman's sword in his hand. He held up his lantern, and looked earnestly in my uncle's face, as he handed it in: when, by its light, my uncle saw, to his great surprise, that an immense crowd of mail-coach guards swarmed round the window, every one of whom had his eyes earnestly fixed upon him too. He had never seen such a sea of white faces, red bodies, and earnest eyes, in all his born days.

" 'This is the strangest sort of thing I ever had anything to do with,' thought my uncle; 'allow me to return you your hat, sir.'

"The ill-looking gentleman received his three-cornered hat in silence, looked at the hole in the middle with an inquiring air, and finally stuck it on the top of his wig with a solemnity the effect of which was a trifle impaired by his sneezing violently at the moment, and jerking it off again.

" 'All right!' cried the guard with the lantern, mounting into his little seat behind. Away they went. My uncle peeped out of the coach-window as they emerged from the yard, and observed that the other mails, with coachmen, guards, horses, and passengers, complete, were driving round and round in circles, at a slow trot of about five miles an hour. My uncle burnt with indignation, gentlemen. As a commercial man, he felt that the mail bags were not to be trifled with, and he resolved to memorialise the Post-office on the subject, the very instant he reached London.

"At present, however, his thoughts were occupied with the young lady who sat in the farthest corner of the coach, with her face muffled closely in her hood; the gentleman with the sky-blue coat sitting opposite to her; the other man in the plum-coloured suit, by her side, and both watching her intently. If she so much as rustled the folds of her hood, he could hear the ill-looking man clap his hand upon his sword, and could tell by the other's breathing (it was so dark he couldn't see his face) that he was looking as big as if he were going to devour her at a mouthful. This roused my uncle more and more, and he resolved, come what might, to see the end of it. He had a great admiration for bright eyes, and sweet faces, and pretty legs and feet; in short, he was fond of the whole sex. It runs in our family, gentlemen—so am I.

"Many were the devices which my uncle practised, to attract the lady's attention, or at all events, to engage the mysterious gentlemen in conversation. They were all in vain; the gentlemen wouldn't talk, and the lady didn't dare. He thrust his head out of the coach-window at intervals, and bawled out to know why they didn't go faster? But he called till he was hoarse; nobody paid the least attention to him. He leant back in the coach, and thought of the beautiful face, and the feet and legs. This answered better; it whiled away the time, and kept him from wondering where he was going, and how it was that he found himself in such an odd situation. Not that this would have worried him much, any way—he was a mighty free and easy, roving, devil-may-care sort of person, was my uncle, gentlemen.

"All of a sudden the coach stopped. 'Hallo!' said my uncle, 'what's in the wind now?'

" 'Alight here,' said the guard, letting down the steps.

" 'Here!' cried my uncle.

" 'Here,' rejoined the guard.

" 'I'll do nothing of the sort,' said my uncle.

" 'Very well, then stop where you are,' said the guard.

" 'I will,' said my uncle.

" 'Do,' said the guard.

"The other passengers had regarded this colloquy with great attention, and, finding that my uncle was determined not to alight, the younger man squeezed past him, to hand the lady out. At this moment, the ill-looking man was inspecting the hole in the crown of his three-cornered hat. As the young lady brushed past, she dropped one of her gloves into my uncle's hand, and softly whispered, with her lips so close to his face that he felt her warm breath on his nose, the single word 'Help!' Gentlemen, my uncle leaped out of the coach at once, with such violence that it rocked on the springs again.

" 'Oh! You've thought better of it, have you?' said the guard when he saw my uncle standing on the ground.

"My uncle looked at the guard for a few seconds, in some doubt whether it wouldn't be better to wrench his blunderbuss from him, fire it in the face of the man with the big sword, knock the rest of the company over the head with the stock, snatch up the young lady, and go off in the smoke. On second thoughts, however, he abandoned this plan, as being a shade too melodramatic in the execution, and followed the two mysterious men, who, keeping the lady between them, were now entering an old house in front of which the coach had stopped. They turned into the passage, and my uncle followed.

"Of all the ruinous and desolate places my uncle had ever beheld, this was the most so. It looked as if it had once been a large house of entertainment; but the roof had fallen in, in many places, and the stairs were steep, rugged, and broken. There was a huge fire-place in the room into which they walked, and the chimney was blackened with smoke; but no warm blaze lighted it up now. The white feathery dust of burnt wood was still strewed over the hearth, but the stove was cold, and all was dark and gloomy.

" 'Well,' said my uncle, as he looked about him, 'a mail travelling at the rate of six miles and a half an hour, and stopping for an indefinite time at such a hole as this, is rather an irregular sort of proceeding, I fancy. This shall be made known. I'll write to the papers.'

"My uncle said this in a pretty loud voice, and in an open unreserved sort of manner, with the view of engaging the two strangers in conversation if he could. But, neither of them took any more notice of him than whispering to each other, and scowling at him as they did so. The lady was at the farther end of the room, and once she ventured to wave her hand, as if beseeching my uncle's assistance.

"At length the two strangers advanced a little, and the conversation began in earnest.

"'You don't know this is a private room, I suppose, fellow?' said the gentleman in sky-blue.

"'No, I do not, fellow,' rejoined my uncle. 'Only if this is a private room specially ordered for the occasion, I should think the public room must be a *very* comfortable one'; with this my uncle sat himself down in a high-backed chair, and took such an accurate measure of the gentleman, with his eyes, that Tiggin and Welps could have supplied him with printed calico for a suit, and not an inch too much or too little, from that estimate alone.

"'Quit this room,' said both the men together, grasping their swords.

"'Eh?' said my uncle, not at all appearing to comprehend their meaning.

"'Quit the room, or you are a dead man,' said the ill-looking fellow with the large sword, drawing it at the same time and flourishing it in the air.

"'Down with him!' cried the gentleman in sky-blue, drawing his sword also, and falling back two or three yards. 'Down with him!' The lady gave a loud scream.

"Now, my uncle was always remarkable for great boldness, and great presence of mind. All the time that he had appeared so indifferent to what was going on, he had been looking slyly about, for some missile or weapon of defence, and at the very instant when the swords were drawn, he espied, standing in the chimney corner, an old basket-hilted rapier in a rusty scabbard. At one bound, my uncle caught it in his hand, drew it, flourished it gallantly above his head, called aloud to the lady to keep out of the way, hurled the chair at the man in sky-blue, and the scabbard at the man in plum-colour, and taking advantage of the confusion, fell upon them both, pell-mell.

"Gentleman, there is an old story—none the worse for being true—regarding a fine young Irish gentleman, who being asked if he could play the fiddle, replied he had no doubt he could, but he couldn't exactly say, for certain, because he had never tried. This is not inapplicable to my uncle and his fencing. He had never had a sword in his hand before, except once when he played Richard the Third at a private theatre: upon which occasion it was arranged with Richmond that he was to be run through, from behind, without showing fight at all. But here he was, cutting and slashing with two experienced swordsmen: thrusting and guarding and poking and slicing, and acquitting himself in the most manful and dexterous manner possible, although up to that time he had never been aware that he had the least notion of the science. It only shows how true the old saying is, that a man never knows what he can do till he tries, gentlemen.

"The noise of the combat was terrific; each of the three combatants swearing like troopers, and their swords clashing with as much noise as if all the knives and steels in Newport market were rattling together, at the same time. When it was at its very height, the lady (to encourage my uncle most probably) withdrew her hood entirely from her face, and disclosed a countenance of such dazzling beauty, that he would have fought against fifty men, to win one smile from it, and die. He had done wonders before, but now he began to powder away like a raving mad giant.

"At this very moment, the gentleman in sky-blue turning round, and seeing the young lady with her face uncovered, vented an exclamation of rage and jealousy, and, turning his weapon against her beautiful bosom, pointed a thrust at her heart, which caused my uncle to utter a cry of apprehension that made the building ring. The lady stepped lightly aside, and snatching the young man's sword from his hand, before he had recovered his balance, drove him to the wall, and running it through him, and the panelling, up to the very hilt, pinned him there, hard and fast. It was a splendid example. My uncle, with a loud shout of triumph, and a strength that was irresistible, made his adversary retreat in the same direction, and plunging the old rapier into the very centre of a large red flower in the pattern of his waistcoat, nailed him beside his friend; there they both stood, gentlemen, jerking their arms and legs about, in agony, like the toy-shop figures that are moved by a piece of packthread. My uncle always said, afterwards, that this was one of the surest means he knew of, for disposing of an enemy; but it was liable to one objection on the ground of expense, inasmuch as it involved the loss of a sword for every man disabled.

" 'The mail, the mail!' cried the lady, running up to my uncle and throwing her beautiful arms round his neck; 'we may yet escape.'

" '*May!*' cried my uncle; 'why, my dear, there's nobody else to kill, is there?' My uncle was rather disappointed, gentlemen, for he thought a little quiet bit of love-making would be agreeable after the slaughtering, if it were only to change the subject.

" 'We have not an instant to lose here,' said the young lady. 'He (pointing to the young gentleman in sky-blue) is the only son of the powerful Marquess of Filletoville.'

" 'Well, then, my dear, I'm afraid he'll never come to the title,' said my uncle, looking coolly at the young gentleman as he stood fixed up against the wall, in the cockchafer fashion I have described. You have cut off the entail, my love.'

" 'I have been torn from my home and friends by these villains,' said the young lady, her features glowing with indignation. 'That wretch would have married me by violence in another hour.'

" 'Confound his impudence!' said my uncle, bestowing a very contemptuous look on the dying heir of Filletoville.

" 'As you may guess from what you have seen,' said the young lady, 'the party were prepared to murder me if I appealed to any one for assistance. If their accomplices find us here, we are lost. Two minutes hence may be too late. The mail!' With these words, overpowered by her feelings, and the exertion of sticking the young Marquess of Filletoville, she sunk into my uncle's arms. My uncle caught her up, and bore her to the house-door. There stood the mail, with four long-tailed, flowing-maned, black horses, ready harnessed; but no coachman, no guard, no hostler even, at the horses' heads.

"Gentlemen, I hope I do no injustice to my uncle's memory, when I express my opinion, that although he was a bachelor, he *had* held some ladies in his arms, before this time; I believe indeed, that he had rather a habit of kissing barmaids; and I know, that in one or two instances, he had been seen by credible witnesses, to hug a landlady in a very perceptible manner. I mention the circumstance, to show what a very uncommon sort of person this beautiful young lady must have been, to have affected my uncle in the way she did; he used to say, that as her long dark hair trailed over his arm, and her beautiful dark eyes fixed themselves upon his face when she recovered, he felt so strange and nervous that his legs trembled beneath him. But, who can look in a sweet soft pair of dark eyes, without feeling queer? *I* can't, gentlemen. I am afraid to look at some eyes I know, and that's the truth of it.

" 'You will never leave me,' murmured the young lady.

" 'Never,' said my uncle. And he meant it too.

" 'My dear preserver!' exclaimed the young lady. 'My dear, kind, brave preserver!'

" 'Don't,' said my uncle, interrupting her.

" 'Why?' inquired the young lady.

" 'Because your mouth looks so beautiful when you speak,' rejoined my uncle, 'that I'm afraid I shall be rude enough to kiss it.'

"The young lady put up her hand as if to caution my uncle not to do so, and said—no, she didn't say anything—she smiled. When you are looking at a pair of the most delicious lips in the world, and see them

gently break into a roguish smile—if you are very near them, and nobody else by—you cannot better testify your admiration of their beautiful form and colour than by kissing them at once. My uncle did so, and
I honour him for it.

" 'Hark!' cried the young lady, starting. 'The noise of wheels and
horses!'

" 'So it is,' said my uncle, listening. He had a good ear for wheels,
and the trampling of hoofs; but there appeared to be so many horses
and carriages rattling towards them, from a distance, that it was impossible to form a guess at their number. The sound was like that of fifty
breaks, with six blood cattle in each.

" 'We are pursued!' cried the young lady, clasping her hands. 'We are
pursued. I have no hope but in you!'

"There was such an expression of terror in her beautiful face, that
my uncle made up his mind at once. He lifted her into the coach, told
her not to be frightened, pressed his lips to hers once more, and then
advising her to draw up the window to keep the cold air out, mounted
to the box.

" 'Stay, love,' cried the young lady.

" 'What's the matter?' said my uncle, from the coach-box.

" 'I want to speak to you,' said the young lady: 'only a word. Only
one word, dearest.'

" 'Must I get down?' inquired my uncle. The lady made no answer,
but she smiled again. Such a smile, gentlemen! It beat the other one, all
to nothing. My uncle descended from his perch in a twinkling.

" 'What is it, my dear?' said my uncle, looking in at the coach-window. The lady happened to bend forward at the same time, and my
uncle thought she looked more beautiful than she had done yet. He was
very close to her just then, gentlemen, so he really ought to know.

" 'What is it, my dear?' said my uncle.

" 'Will you never love any one but me; never marry any one beside?'
said the young lady.

"My uncle swore a great oath that he never would marry anybody
else, and the young lady drew in her head, and pulled up the window. He
jumped upon the box, squared his elbows, adjusted the ribands, seized
the whip which lay on the roof, gave one flick to the off leader, and
away went the four long-tailed flowing-maned black horses, at fifteen
good English miles an hour, with the old mail coach behind them.
Whew! How they tore along!

"The noise behind grew louder. The faster the old mail went, the faster came the pursuers—men, horses, dogs, were leagued in the pursuit. The noise was frightful, but, above all, rose the voice of the young lady, urging my uncle on, and shrieking, 'Faster! Faster!'

"They whirled past the dark trees, as feathers would be swept before a hurricane. Houses, gates, churches, haystacks, objects of every kind they shot by, with a velocity and noise like roaring waters suddenly let loose. Still the noise of pursuit grew louder, and still my uncle could hear the young lady wildly screaming, 'Faster! Faster!'

"My uncle plied whip and rein, and the horses flew onward till they were white with foam; and yet the noise behind increased; and yet the young lady cried 'Faster! Faster!' My uncle gave a loud stamp on the boot in the energy of the moment, and—found that it was grey morning, and he was sitting in the wheelwright's yard, on the box of an old Edinburgh mail, shivering with the cold and wet and stamping his feet to warm them! He got down, and looked eagerly inside for the beautiful young lady. Alas! There was neither door nor seat to the coach. It was a mere shell.

"Of course my uncle knew very well that there was some mystery in the matter, and that everything had passed exactly as he used to relate it. He remained staunch to the great oath he had sworn to the beautiful young lady: refusing several eligible landladies on her account, and dying a bachelor at last. He always said, what a curious thing it was that he should have found out, by such a mere accident as his clambering over the palings, that the ghosts of mail coaches and horses, guards, coachmen, and passengers, were in the habit of making journeys regularly every night. He used to add, that he believed he was the only living person who had ever been taken as a passenger on one of these excursions. And I think he was right, gentlemen—at least I never heard of any other."

"I wonder what these ghosts of mail coaches carry in their bags," said the landlord, who had listened to the whole story with profound attention.

"The dead letters, of course," said the bagman.

"Oh, ah! to be sure," rejoined the landlord. "I never thought of that."

In the preceding story, CHARLES DICKENS showed us what high adventure might be found in the company of ghostly passengers of antique coaches. But there is another side to the question, as the following dreadful tale shows. AMELIA B. EDWARDS was born in 1831 and showed literary tendencies as early as age seven.

The North Mail

by Amelia B. Edwards

The circumstances I am about to relate to you have truth to recommend them. They happened to myself, and my recollection of them is as vivid as if they had taken place only yesterday. Twenty years, however, have gone by since that night. During those twenty years I have told the story to but one other person. I tell it now with a reluctance which I find it difficult to overcome. All I entreat, meanwhile, is that you will abstain from forcing your own conclusions upon me. I want nothing explained away. I desire no arguments. My mind on this subject is quite made up; and, having the testimony of my own senses to rely upon, I prefer to abide by it.

Well! It was just twenty years ago, and within a day or two of the end of the grouse season. I had been out all day with my gun, and had had no sport to speak of. The wind was due east; the month, December; the place, a bleak wide moor in the far north of England. And I had lost my way. It was not a pleasant place in which to lose one's way, with the first feathery flakes of a coming snow-storm just fluttering down upon the heather, and the leaden evening closing in all around. I shaded my eyes with my hand, and stared anxiously into the gathering darkness, where the purple moorland melted into a range of low hills, some ten or twelve miles distant. Not the faintest smoke-wreath, not the tiniest cultivated patch, or fence, or sheep-track, met my eyes in any direction. There was nothing for it but to walk on, and take my chance of finding what shelter I could, by the way. So I shouldered my gun again, and pushed wearily forward; for I had been on foot since an hour after daybreak, and had eaten nothing since breakfast.

Meanwhile, the snow began to come down with ominous steadiness, and the wind fell. After this, the cold grew more intense, and the night came rapidly up. As for me, my prospects darkened with the darkening sky, and my heart grew heavy as I thought how my young wife was already watching for me through the window of our little inn parlour, and imagined all the suffering in store for her throughout this weary night. We had been married four months, and, having spent our autumn in the Highlands, were now lodging in a remote little village situated just on the verge of the great English moorlands. We were very much in love, and, of course, very happy. This morning, when we parted, she had implored me to return before dusk, and I had promised her that I would. What would I not have given to keep my word!

Even now, weary as I was, I felt that with a supper, an hour's rest, and a guide, I might still get back to her before midnight, if only guide and shelter could be found.

And all this time the snow fell, and the night thickened. I stopped and shouted every now and then, but my shouts seemed only to make the silence deeper. Then a vague sense of uneasiness came upon me, and I began to remember stories of travellers who had walked on and on in the falling snow until, wearied out, they were fain to lie down and sleep their lives away. Would it be possible, I asked myself, to keep on thus through all the long dark night? Would there not come a time when my limbs must fail, and my resolution give way? When I, too, must sleep the sleep of death. Death! I shuddered. How hard to die just now, when life lay all so bright before me! How hard for my darling, whose whole loving heart . . . but that thought was not to be borne! To banish it, I shouted again, louder and longer, and then listened eagerly. Was my shout answered, or did I only fancy that I heard a far-off cry? I halloed again, and again the echo followed. Then a wavering speck of light came suddenly out of the dark, shifting, disappearing, growing momentarily nearer and brighter. Running towards it at full speed, I found myself, to my great joy, face to face with an old man and a lantern.

"Thank God!" was the exclamation that burst involuntarily from my lips.

Blinking and frowning, he lifted the lantern and peered into my face. "What for?" growled he, sulkily.

"Well—for you. I began to fear I should be lost in the snow."

"Eh, then, folks do get cast away hereabouts fra' time to time, an' what's to hinder you from bein' cast away likewise, if the Lord's so minded?"

"If the Lord is so minded that you and I shall be lost together, friend, we must submit," I replied; "but I don't mean to be lost without you. How far am I now from Dwolding?"

"A gude twenty mile, more or less."

"And the nearest village?"

"The nearest village is Wyke, an' that's twelve mile t'other side."

"Where do you live, then?"

"Out yonder," said he, with a vague jerk of the lantern.

"You're going home, I presume?"

"Maybe I am."

"Then I'm going with you."

The old man shook his head, and rubbed his nose reflectively with the handle of the lantern.

"It ain't o' no use," growled he. "He 'ont let you in—not he."

"We'll see about that," I replied, briskly. "Who is He?"

"The master."

"Who is the master?"

"That's now't to you," was the unceremonious reply.

"Well, well; you lead the way, and I'll engage that the master shall give me shelter and a supper tonight."

"Eh, you can try him!" muttered my reluctant guide; and, still shaking his head, he hobbled, gnome-like, away through the falling snow.

A large mass loomed up presently out of the darkness, and a huge dog rushed out barking furiously.

"Is this the house?" I asked.

"Ay, it's the house. Down, Bey!" And he fumbled in his pocket for the key.

I drew up close behind him, prepared to lose no chance of entrance, and saw in the little circle of light shed by the lantern that the door was heavily studded with iron nails, like the door of a prison. In another minute he had turned the key, and I had pushed past him into the house.

Once inside, I looked round with curiosity, and found myself in a great raftered hall, which served, apparently, a variety of uses. One end was piled to the roof with corn, like a barn. The other was stored with flour-sacks, agricultural implements, casks, and all kinds of miscellaneous lumber; while from the beams overhead hung rows of hams, flitches, and bunches of dried herbs for winter use. In the centre of the floor stood some huge object gauntly dressed in a dingy wrapping-cloth, and reaching halfway to the rafters. Lifting a corner of this cloth, I saw, to my surprise, a telescope of very considerable size, mounted on a rude moveable platform with four small wheels. The tube was made of painted wood, bound round with bands of metal rudely fashioned; the speculum, so far as I could estimate its size by the dim light, measured at least fifteen inches in diameter. While I was yet examining the instrument, and asking myself whether it was not the work of some self-taught optician, a bell rang sharply.

"That's for you," said my guide, with a malicious grin. "Yonder's his room."

He pointed to a low black door at the opposite side of the hall. I crossed over, rapped somewhat loudly, and went in, without waiting for an invitation. A huge, white-haired old man rose from a table covered with books and papers, and confronted me sternly.

"Who are you?" said he. "How came you here? What do you want?"

"James Murray, barrister-at-law. On foot across the moor. Meat, drink, and sleep."

He bent his bushy brows in a portentous frown.

"Mine is not a house of entertainment," he said, haughtily. "Jacob, how dared you admit this stranger?"

"I didn't admit him," grumbled the old man. "He followed me over the muir, and shouldered his way in before me. I'm no match for six foot two."

"And pray, sir, by what right have you forced an entrance into my house?"

"The same by which I should have clung to your boat, if I were drowning. The right of self-preservation."

"Self-preservation?"

"There's an inch of snow on the ground already," I replied briefly; "and it will be deep enough to cover my body before daybreak."

He strode to the window, pulled aside a heavy black curtain, and looked out.

"It is true," he said. "You can stay, if you choose, till morning. Jacob, serve the supper."

With this he waved me to a seat, resumed his own, and became at once absorbed in the studies at which I had disturbed him.

I placed my gun in a corner, drew a chair to the hearth, and examined my quarters at leisure. Smaller and less incongruous in its arrangements than the hall, this room contained, nevertheless, much to awaken my curiosity. The floor was carpetless. The whitewashed walls were in parts scrawled over with strange diagrams, and in others covered with shelves crowded with philosophical instruments, the uses of many of which were unknown to me. On one side of the fireplace stood a bookcase filled with dingy folios; on the other, a small organ, fantastically decorated with painted carvings of mediaeval saints and devils.

Through the half-opened door of a cupboard at the further end of the room, I saw a long array of geological specimens, surgical preparations, crucibles, retorts, and jars of chemicals; while on the mantelshelf beside me, amid a number of small objects, stood a model of the solar system, a small galvanic battery, and a microscope. Every chair had its burden. Every corner was heaped high with books. The very floor was littered over with maps, casts, papers, tracings, and learned lumber of all conceivable kinds.

I stared about me with an amazement increased by every fresh object upon which my eyes chanced to rest. So strange a room I had never seen; yet seemed it stranger still to find such a room in a lone farmhouse, amid these wild and solitary moors! Over and over again, I looked from my host to his surroundings, and from his surroundings back to my host, asking myself who and what he could be? His head was singularly fine; but it was more the head of a poet than a philosopher. Broad in the temples, prominent over the eyes, and clothed with a rough profusion of perfectly white hair, it had all the ideality and much of the ruggedness that characterises the head of Louis von Beethoven. There were the same deep lines about the mouth, and the same stern furrows in the brow. There was the same concentration of expression. While I was yet observing him, the door opened, and Jacob brought in the supper. His master then closed his book, rose, and with more courtesy of manner than he had yet shown, invited me to the table.

A dish of ham and eggs, a loaf of brown bread, and a bottle of admirable sherry, were placed before me.

"I have but the homeliest farmhouse fare to offer you, sir," said my entertainer. "Your appetite, I trust, will make up for the deficiencies of our larder."

I had already fallen upon the viands, and now protested, with the enthusiasm of a starving sportsman, that I had never eaten anything so delicious.

He bowed stiffly, and sat down to his own supper, which consisted, primitively, of a jug of milk and a basin of porridge. We ate in silence, and, when we had done, Jacob removed the tray. I then drew my chair back to the fireside. My host, somewhat to my surprise, did the same, and turning abruptly towards me said:—

"Sir, I have lived here in strict retirement for three-and-twenty years. During that time, I have not seen as many strange faces, and I have not read a single newspaper. You are the first stranger who has crossed my threshold for more than four years. Will you favour me with a few words of information respecting that outer world from which I have parted company so long?"

"Pray interrogate me," I replied. "I am heartily at your service."

He bent his head in acknowledgement; leaned forward, with his elbows resting on his knees, and his chin supported in the palms of his hands; stared fixedly into the fire, and proceeded to question me.

His inquiries related chiefly to scientific matters, with the later progress of which, as applied to the practical purposes of life, he was almost wholly unacquainted. No student of science myself, I replied as well as my slight information permitted; but the task was far from easy, and I was much relieved when, passing from interrogation to discussion, he began pouring forth his own conclusions upon the facts which I had been attempting to place before him. He talked, and I listened spellbound. He talked till I believe he almost forgot my presence, and only thought aloud. I had never heard anything like it then; I have never heard anything like it since. Familiar with all systems of all philosophies, subtle in analysis, bold in generalisation, he poured forth his thoughts in an uninterrupted stream, and, still leaning forward in the same moody attitude with his eyes fixed upon the fire, wandered from topic to topic, from speculation to speculation, like an inspired dreamer. From practical science to mental philosophy; from electricity in the wire to electricity in the nerve; from Watts to Mesmer, from Mesmer to Reichenbach, from Reichenbach to Swedenborg, Spinoza, Condillac, Descartes, Berkeley, Aristotle, Plato, and the Magi and Mystics of the East, were transitions which, however bewildering in their variety and scope, seemed easy and harmonious upon his lips as sequences in music. By-and-by—I forget now by what link of conjecture or illustration—he passed on to that field which lies beyond the boundary line of even conjectural philosophy, and reaches no man knows whither. He spoke of the soul and its aspirations; of the spirit and its powers; of second sight; of prophecy; of those phenomena which, under the names of ghosts, spectres, and supernatural appearances, have been denied by the sceptics and attested by the credulous, of all ages.

"The world," he said, "grows hourly more and more sceptical of all that lies beyond its own narrow radius; and our men of science foster the fatal tendency. They condemn as fable all that resists experiment. They reject as false all that cannot be brought to the test of the laboratory or the dissecting-room. Against what superstition have they waged so long and obstinate a war, as against the belief in apparitions? And yet what superstition has maintained its hold upon the minds of men so long and so firmly? Show me any fact in physics, in history, in archaeology, which is supported by testimony so wide and so various. Attested by all races of men, in all ages, and in all climates, by the soberest sages of antiquity, by the rudest savages of today, by the Christian, the Pagan, the Pantheist, the Materialist, this phenomenon is treated as a nursery tale by the philosophers of our century. Circumstantial evidence weighs with them as a feather in the balance. The comparison of causes with effects, however valuable in physical science, is put aside as worthless and unreliable. The evidence of competent witnesses, however conclusive in a court of justice, counts for nothing. He who pauses before he pronounces, is condemned as a trifler. He who believes, is a dreamer or a fool."

He spoke with bitterness, and, having said thus, relapsed for some minutes into silence. Presently he raised his head from his hands, and added, with an altered voice and manner—

"I, sir, paused, investigated, believed, and was not ashamed to state my convictions to the world. I, too, was branded as a visionary, held up to ridicule by my contemporaries, and hooted from that field of science in which I had laboured with honour during all the best years of my life. These things happened just three-and-twenty years ago. Since then, I have lived as you see me living now, and the world has forgotten me, as I have forgotten the world. You have my history."

"It is a very sad one," I murmured, scarcely knowing what to answer.

"It is a very common one," he replied. "I have only suffered for the truth, as many a better and wiser man has suffered before me."

He rose, as if desirous of ending the conversation, and went over to the window.

"It has ceased snowing," he observed, as he dropped the curtain, and came back to the fireside.

"Ceased!" I exclaimed, starting eagerly to my feet. "Oh, if it were only possible—but no! it is hopeless. Even if I could find my way across the moor, I could not walk twenty miles tonight."

"Walk twenty miles tonight!" repeated my host. "What are you thinking of?"

"Of my wife," I replied, impatiently. "Of my young wife, who does not know that I have lost my way, and who is at this moment breaking her heart with suspense and terror."

"Where is she?"

"At Dwolding, twenty miles away."

"At Dwolding," he echoed, thoughtfully. "Yes, the distance, it is true, is twenty miles; but—are you so anxious to save the next six or eight hours?"

"So anxious, that I would give ten guineas at this moment for a guide and a horse."

"Your wish can be gratified at a less costly rate," said he, smiling. "The night mail from the north, which changes horses at Dwolding, passes within five miles of this spot, and will be due at a certain crossroad in about an hour and a quarter. If Jacob were to go with you across the moor, and put you into the old coach road, you could find your way, I suppose, to where it joins the new one?"

"Easily—gladly."

He smiled again, rang the bell, gave the old servant his directions, and, taking a bottle of whiskey and a wine-glass from the cupboard in which he kept his chemicals, said—

"The snow lies deep, and it will be difficult walking tonight on the moor. A glass of usquebaugh before you start."

I would have declined the spirit, but he pressed it on me, and I drank it. It went down my throat like liquid flame, and almost took my breath away.

"It is strong," he said; "but it will help to keep out the cold. And now you have no moments to spare. Good night!"

I thanked him for his hospitality, and would have shaken hands, but that he had turned away before I could finish my sentence. In another minute I had traversed the hall, Jacob had locked the outer door behind me, and we were out on the wide white moor.

Although the wind had fallen, it was still bitterly cold. Not a star glimmered in the black vault overhead. Not a sound, save the rapid crunching of the snow beneath our feet, disturbed the heavy stillness of the night. Jacob, not too well pleased with his mission, shambled on before in sullen silence, his lantern in his hand, and his shadow at his feet. I followed, with my gun over my shoulder, as little inclined for conversation as himself. My thoughts were full of my late host. His voice yet rang in my ears. His eloquence yet held my imagination captive. I remember to this day, with surprise, how my over-excited brain retained whole sentences and parts of sentences, troops of brilliant images, and fragments of splendid reasoning, in the very words in which he had uttered them. Musing thus over what I had heard, and striving to recall a lost link here and there, I strode on at the heels of my guide, absorbed and unobservant. Presently—at the end, as it seemed to me, of only a few minutes—he came to a sudden halt, and said:

"Yon's your road. Keep the stone fence to your right hand, and you can't fail of the way."

"This, then, is the old coach-road?"

"Ay, 'tis the old coach-road."

"And how far do I go, before I reach the cross-roads?"

"Nigh upon three miles."

I pulled out my purse, and he became more communicative.

"The road's a fair road enough," said he, "for foot passengers; but 'twas over steep and narrow for the northern traffic. You'll mind where the parapet's broken away, close again the sign-post. It's never been mended since the accident."

"What accident?"

"Eh, the night mail pitched right over into the valley below—a gude sixty feet an' more—just at the worst bit o' road in the whole county."

"Horrible! Were many lives lost?"

"All. Four were found dead, and t'other two died next morning."

"How long is it since this happened?"

"Just nine year."

"Near the sign-post, you say? I will bear it in mind. Good night."

"Gude night, sir, and thankee."

Jacob pocketed his half-crown, made a faint pretence of touching his hat, and trudged back by the way he had come.

I watched the light of his lantern till it quite disappeared, and then turned to pursue my way alone. This was no longer a matter of the slightest difficulty, for, despite the dead darkness overhead, the line of stone fence showed distinctly enough against the pale gleam of the snow. How silent it seemed now, with only my own footsteps to listen to; how silent and how solitary! A strange disagreeable sense of loneliness stole over me. I walked faster. I hummed a fragment of a tune. I cast up enormous sums in my head, and accumulated them at compound interest. I did my best, in short, to forget the startling speculations to which I had but just been listening and to some extent, I succeeded.

Meanwhile the night air seemed to become colder and colder, and though I walked fast, I found it impossible to keep myself warm. My feet were like ice. I lost sensation in my hands, and grasped my gun mechanically. I even breathed with difficulty, as though, instead of traversing a quiet north country highway, I were sealing the uppermost heights of some gigantic Alp. This last symptom became presently so distressing, that I was forced to stop for a few minutes, and lean against the stone fence. As I did so, I chanced to look back up the road, and there, to my infinite relief, I saw a distant point of light, like the gleam of an approaching lantern. I at first concluded that Jacob had retraced his steps and followed me; but even as the conjecture presented itself, a second light flashed into sight—a light evidently parallel with the first, and approaching at the same rate of motion. It needed no second thought to show me that these must be the carriage-lamps of some private vehicle; though it seemed strange that any private vehicle should take a road professedly disused and dangerous.

There could be no doubt, however, of the fact, for the lamps grew larger and brighter every moment, and I even fancied I could already see the dark outline of the carriage between them. It was coming up very fast, and quite noiselessly; the snow being nearly a foot deep under the wheels.

And now the body of the vehicle became distinctly visible behind the lamps. It looked strangely lofty. A sudden suspicion flashed upon me. Was it possible that I had passed the cross-roads in the dark without observing the sign-post, and could this be the very coach which I had come to meet?

No need to ask myself that question a second time, for here it came round the bend of the road, guard and driver, one outside passenger, and four steaming greys, all wrapped in a soft haze of light, through which the lamps blazed out like a pair of fiery meteors.

I jumped forward, waved my hat, and shouted. The mail came down at full speed, and passed me. For a moment I feared that I had not been seen or heard, but it was only for a moment. The coachman pulled up; the guard, muffled to the eyes in capes and comforters, and apparently sound asleep in the rumble, neither answered my hail nor made the slightest effort to dismount; the outside passenger did not even turn his head. I opened the door for myself, and looked in. There were but three travellers inside, so I stepped in, shut the door, slipped into the vacant corner, and congratulated myself on my good fortune.

The atmosphere of the coach seemed, if possible, colder than that of the outer air, and was pervaded by a singularly damp and disagreeable smell. I looked round at my fellow passengers. They were all three men; and all silent. They did not seem to be asleep, but each leaned back in his corner of the vehicle, as if absorbed in his own reflections. I attempted to open a conversation.

"How intensely cold it is tonight," I said, addressing my opposite neighbour.

He lifted his head, looked at me, but made no reply.

"The winter," I added, "seems to have begun in earnest."

Although the corner in which he sat was so dim that I could distinguish none of his features very clearly, I saw that his eyes were still turned full upon me. And yet he answered never a word.

At any other time I should have felt, and perhaps expressed, some annoyance; but at that moment I felt too ill to do either. The icy coldness of the night air had struck a chill to my very marrow, and the strange smell inside the coach was affecting me with an intolerable nausea. I shivered from head to foot, and, turning to my left-hand neighbour, asked if he had any objection to an open window.

He neither spoke nor stirred.

I repeated the question somewhat more loudly, but with the same result. Then I lost patience, and let the sash down. As I did so, the leather strap broke in my hand, and I observed that the glass was covered with a thick coat of mildew, the accumulation, apparently, of years. My attention being thus drawn to the condition of the coach, I examined it more narrowly, and saw by the uncertain light of the outer lamps that it was in the last state of dilapidation. Every part of it was not only out of repair, but in a state of actual decay. The sashes splintered at a touch. The leather fittings were crusted over with mould, and literally rotting from the woodwork. The floor was almost breaking away beneath my feet. The whole machine, in short, was foul with damp, and had evidently been dragged from some outhouse in which it had been mouldering away for years, to do another day of two of duty on the road.

I turned to the third passenger, whom I had not yet addressed, and hazarded one more remark.

"This coach," I said, "is in a deplorable condition. The regular mail, I suppose, is under repair?"

He moved his head slowly, and looked me in the face, without speaking a word. I shall never forget that look while I live. I turned cold at heart under it. I turn cold at heart even now when I recall it. His eyes glowed with a fiery unnatural lustre. His face was livid as the face of a corpse. His bloodless lips were drawn back as if in the agony of death, and showed the gleaming teeth between.

The words that I was about to utter died upon my lips, and a strange horror came upon me. My sight had by this time become used to the gloom of the coach, and I could see with tolerable distinctness. I turned to my opposite neighbour. He, too, was looking at me, with the same startling pallor in his face, and the same stony glitter in his eyes. I passed my hand across my brow. I turned to the passenger on the seat beside my own, and saw—oh Heaven! how shall I describe what I saw? I saw that he was no living man—that none of them were living men, like myself! A pale phosphorescent light—the light of putrefaction—played upon their awful faces; upon their hair, dank with the dews of the grave; upon their clothes, earth-stained and dropping to pieces; upon their hands, which were as the hands of corpses long buried. Only their eyes, their terrible eyes, were living; and those eyes were all turned menacingly upon me!

A shriek of terror, a wild unintelligible cry for help and mercy, burst from my lips as I flung myself against the door, and strove in vain to open it.

In that single instant, brief and vivid as a landscape beheld in the flash of summer lightning, I saw the moon shining down through a rift of stormy cloud—the ghastly sign-post rearing its warning finger by the wayside—the broken parapet—the plunging horses—the black gulf below. Then the coach reeled like a ship at sea. Then came a mighty crash—a sense of crushing pain—and then, darkness.

It seemed as if years had gone by, when I awoke one morning from a deep sleep, and found my wife watching by my bedside. I will pass over the scene that ensued, and give you, in half a dozen words, the tale she told me with tears of thanksgiving. I had fallen over a precipice, close against the junction of the old coach-road and the new, and had only been saved from certain death by lighting upon a deep snowdrift that had accumulated at the foot of the rock beneath. In this snowdrift I was discovered at daybreak by a couple of shepherds, who carried me to the nearest shelter, and brought a surgeon to my aid. The surgeon found me in a state of raving delirium, with a broken arm and a compound fracture of the skull. The letters in my pocket-book showed my name and address; my wife was summoned to nurse me; and, thanks to youth and a fine constitution, I came out of danger at last. The place of my fall, I need scarcely say, was precisely that at which a frightful accident had happened to the north mail nine years before.

I never told my wife the fearful events which I have just related to you. I told the surgeon who attended me; but he treated the whole adventure as a mere dream born of the fever in my brain. We discussed the question over and over again, until we found that we could discuss it with temper no longer, and then we dropped it. Others may form what conclusions they please—I *know* that twenty years ago I was the fourth inside passenger in that Phantom Coach.

The supernatural stories of EDWARD FREDERICK BENSON *are some of the most effective and frightening in all supernatural literature.* "The Room in the Tower" *is my personal nominee for the most chilling tale I've ever read. Less familiar is the wonderful story that follows. Benson, born in 1867, was the youngest of three sons of a former archbishop of Canterbury. He wrote many recently revived comedic novels of manners, and a very few ghostly tales.* "How Fear Departed from the Long Gallery" *creates a surprising variety of moods: beginning with drollness, it passes through several pages of disquieting prologue leading to the final episode, which is dreadful and terrifying, yet unexpectedly . . . but that would spoil the ending. I have given this tale the last position because I do not believe it can be bettered.*

How Fear Departed
from the Long Gallery

by E. F. Benson

Church-Peveril is a house so beset and frequented by spectres, both visible and audible, that none of the family which it shelters under its acre and a half of green copper roofs takes psychical phenomena with any seriousness. For to the Peverils the appearance of a ghost is a matter of hardly greater significance than the appearance of the post to those who live in more ordinary houses. It arrives, that is to say, practically every day, it knocks (or makes other noises), it is observed coming up the drive (or in other places). I myself, when staying there have seen the present Mrs. Peveril, who is rather short-sighted, peer into the dusk, while we were taking our coffee on the terrace after dinner, and say to her daughter:

"My dear, was not that the Blue Lady who has just gone into the shrubbery? I hope she won't frighten Flo. Whistle for Flo, dear."

(Flo, it may be remarked, is the youngest and most precious of many dachshunds.)

Blanche Peveril gave a cursory whistle, and crunched the sugar left unmelted at the bottom of her coffee-cup between her very white teeth.

"Oh, darling, Flo isn't so silly as to mind," she said. "Poor blue Aunt Barbara is such a bore! Whenever I meet her she always looks as if she wanted to speak to me, but when I say, 'What is it, Aunt Barbara?' she never speaks, but only points somewhere toward the house, which is so vague. I believe there was something she wanted to confess about two hundred years ago, but she has forgotten what it is."

Here Flo gave two or three short pleased barks, and came out of the shrubbery wagging her tail, and capering round what appeared to me to be a perfectly empty space on the lawn.

"There! Flo has made friends with her," said Mrs. Peveril. "I wonder why she dresses in that very stupid shade of blue."

From this it may be gathered that even with regard to psychic phenomena there is some truth in the proverb that speaks of familiarity. But the Peverils do not exactly treat their ghosts with contempt, since most of that delightful family never despised anybody except such people as avowedly did not care for hunting or shooting, or golf or skating. And as all of their ghosts are of their family, it seems reasonable to suppose that they all, even the poor Blue Lady, excelled at one time in field-sports. So far then they harbor no such unkindness or contempt, but only pity. Of one Peveril, indeed, who broke his neck in vainly attempting to ride up the main staircase on a thoroughbred mare after some monstrous and violent deed in the back-garden, they are very fond, and Blanche comes downstairs in the morning with an eye unusually bright when she can announce that Master Anthony was "very loud" last night. He (apart from the fact of his having been so foul a ruffian) was a tremendous fellow across country, and they like these indications of the continuance of his superb vitality. In fact, it is supposed to be a compliment, when you go to stay at Church-Peveril, to be assigned a bedroom which is frequented by defunct members of the family. It means that you are worthy to look on the august and villainous dead, and you will find yourself shown into some vaulted or tapestried chamber, without benefit of electric light, and are told that great-great-grandmamma Bridget occasionally has vague business by the fire-place, but it is better not to talk to her, and that you will hear Master Anthony "awfully well" if he attempts the front staircase any time before morning. There you are left for your night's repose, and, having quakingly undressed, begin reluctantly to put out your candles. It is draughty in these great chambers, and the solemn tapestry swings and bellows and subsides, and the firelight dances on the forms of huntsmen and warriors and stern pursuits. Then you climb into your bed, a bed so huge that you feel as if the desert of Sahara was spread for you, and pray, like the mariners who sailed with St. Paul, for day. And, all the time, you are aware that Freddy and Harry and Blanche and possibly even

Mrs. Peveril are quite capable of dressing up and making disquieting tappings outside your door, so that when you open it some inconjecturable horror fronts you. For myself, I stick steadily to the assertion that I have an obscure valvular disease of the heart, and so sleep undisturbed in the new wing of the house, where Aunt Barbara and great-great-grandmamma Bridget and Master Anthony never penetrate. I forget the details of great-great-grandmamma Bridget, but she certainly cut the throat of some distant relation before she disembowelled herself with the axe that had been used at Agincourt. Before that she had led a very sultry life, crammed with amazing incidents.

But there is one ghost at Church-Peveril at which the family never laugh, in which they feel no friendly and amused interest, and of which they only speak just as much as is necessary for the safety of their guests. More properly it should be described as two ghosts, for the "haunt" in question is that of two very young children, who were twins. These, not without reason, the family take very seriously indeed. The story of them, as told me by Mrs. Peveril, is as follows:

In the year 1602, the same being the last of Queen Elizabeth's reign, a certain Dick Peveril was greatly in favor at Court. He was brother to Master Joseph Peveril, then owner of the family house and lands, who two years previously, at the respectable age of seventy-four, became father of twin-boys, first-born of his progeny. It is known that the royal and ancient virgin had said to handsome Dick, who was nearly forty years his brother's junior, " 'Tis pity that you are not master of Church-Peveril," and these words probably suggested to him a sinister design. Be that as it may, handsome Dick, who very adequately sustained the family reputation for wickedness, set off to ride down to Yorkshire, and found that, very conveniently, his brother Joseph had just been seized with an apoplexy, which appeared to be the result of a continued spell of hot weather combined with the necessity of quenching his thirst with an augmented amount of sack, and had actually died while handsome Dick, with God knows what thoughts in his mind, was journeying northwards. Thus it came about that he arrived at Church-Peveril just in time for his brother's funeral. It was with great propriety that he attended the obsequies, and returned to spend a sympathetic day or two of mourning with his widowed sister-in-law, who was but a faint-hearted dame, little fit to be mated with such hawks as these. On the second night of his stay, he did that which the Peverils regret to this day. He entered the room where the twins slept with their nurse and quietly strangled the latter as she slept. Then he took the twins and put them into the fire which warms the long gallery. The weather, which up to the day of Joseph's death had been so hot, had changed suddenly to bitter cold, and the fire was heaped high with burning logs and was exultant with flame. In the core of this conflagration he struck out a cremation-chamber, and into that he threw the two children, stamping them down with his riding-boots. They could just walk, but they could not walk out of that ardent place. It is said that he laughed as he added more logs. Thus he became master of Church-Peveril.

The crime was never brought home to him, but he lived no longer than a year in the enjoyment of his blood-stained inheritance. When he lay adying he made his confession to the priest who attended him, but his spirit struggled forth from its fleshly coil before Absolution could be given him. On that very night there began in Church-Peveril the haunting which to this day is but seldom spoken of by the family, and then only in low tones with serious mien. For, only an hour or two after handsome Dick's death, one of the servants passing the door of the long gallery heard from within peals of the loud laughter so jovial and yet so sinister, which he had thought would never be heard in the house again. In a moment of that cold courage which is so nearly akin to mortal terror, he opened the door and entered, expecting to see he knew not what manifestation of him who lay dead in the room below. Instead he saw two little white-robed figures toddling towards him hand in hand across the moonlit floor.

The watchers in the room below ran upstairs startled by the crash of his fallen body, and found him lying in the grip of some dread convulsion. Just before morning he regained consciousness and told his tale. Then pointing with trembling and ash-grey finger towards the door, he screamed aloud, and so fell back dead.

During the next fifty years this strange and terrible legend of the twin-babies became fixed and consolidated. Their appearance, luckily for those who inhabited the house, was exceedingly rare, and during these years they seem to have been seen four or five times only. On each occasion they appeared at night, between sunset and sunrise, always in the same long gallery, and always as two toddling children scarcely able to walk. And on each occasion the luckless individual who saw them died either speedily or terribly, or with both speed and terror, after the accursed vision had appeared to him. Sometimes he might live for a few months: he was lucky if he died, as did the servant who first saw them, in a few hours. Vastly more awful was the fate of a certain

Mrs. Canning, who had the ill-luck to see them in the middle of the next century, or to be quite accurate, in the year 1760. By this time the hours and the place of their appearance were well-known, and, as up till a year ago, visitors were warned not to go between sunset and sunrise into the long gallery.

But Mrs. Canning, a brilliantly clever and beautiful woman, admirer also and friend of the notorious sceptic M. Voltaire, wilfully went and sat night after night in spite of all protestations, in the haunted place. For four evenings she saw nothing, but on the fifth she had her will, for the door in the middle of the gallery opened, and there came toddling towards her the ill-omened, innocent little pair. It seemed that even then she was not frightened, but she thought good, poor wretch, to mock at them, telling them it was time for them to get back into the fire. They gave no word in answer, but turned away from her, crying and sobbing. Immediately after they disappeared from her vision, she rustled downstairs to where the family and guests in the house were waiting for her, with the triumphant announcement that she had seen them both, and must needs write to M. Voltaire, saying that she had spoken to spirits made manifest. It would make him laugh. But when some months later the whole news reached him he did not laugh at all.

Mrs. Canning was one of the great beauties of her day, and in the year 1760 she was at the height and zenith of her blossoming. The chief beauty, if it is possible to single out one point where all was so exquisite, lay in the dazzling color and incomparable brilliance of her complexion. She was now just thirty years of age, but in spite of the excesses of her life, retained the snow and roses of girlhood, and she courted the bright light of day which other women shunned, for it but showed to greater advantage the splendor of her skin. In consequence she was very considerably dismayed one morning, about a fortnight after her strange experience in the long gallery, to observe on her left cheek an inch or two below her turquoise-colored eyes, a little greyish patch of skin, about as big as a threepenny piece. It was in vain that she applied her accustomed washes and unguents; vain, too, were the arts of her *fardeuse* and of her medical adviser. For a week she kept herself secluded, martyring herself with solitude and unaccustomed physics, and for result at the end of the week she had no amelioration to comfort herself with: instead, this woeful grey patch had doubled itself in size. Thereafter the nameless disease, whatever it was, developed in new and terrible ways. From the center of the discolored place there sprouted forth little lichen-like tendrils of greenish-grey, and another patch appeared on her lower lip. This, too, soon vegetated, and one morning on opening her eyes to the horror of the new day, she found that her vision was strangely blurred. She sprang to her looking-glass, and what she saw caused her to shriek aloud with horror. From under her upper eyelid a fresh growth had sprung up, mushroom-like, in the night, and its filaments extended downwards, screening the pupil of her eye. Soon after her tongue and throat were attacked: the air passages became obstructed, and death by suffocation was merciful after such suffering.

More terrible yet was the case of a certain Colonel Blantyre who fired at the children with his revolver. What he went through is not to be recorded here.

It is this haunting, then, that the Peverils take quite seriously, and every guest on his arrival in the house is told that the long gallery must not be entered after nightfall on any pretext whatever. By day, however, it is a delightful room and intrinsically merits description, apart from the fact that the due understanding of its geography is necessary for the account that here follows. It is full eighty feet in length, and is lit by a row of six tall windows looking over the gardens at the back of the house. A door communicates with the landing at the top of the main staircase, and about halfway down the gallery in the wall facing the windows is another door communicating with the back staircase and servants' quarters, and thus the gallery forms a constant place of passage for them in going to the rooms on the first landing. It was through this door that the baby-figures came when they appeared to Mrs. Canning, and on several other occasions they have been known to make their entry here, for the room out of which handsome Dick took them lies just beyond at the top of the back stairs. Further on again in the gallery is the fireplace into which he thrust them, and at the far end a large box-window looks straight down the avenue. Above this fireplace, there hangs with grim significance a portrait of handsome Dick, in the insolent beauty of early manhood, attributed to Holbein, and a dozen other portraits of great merit face the windows. During the day this is the most frequented sitting-room in the house, for its other visitors never appear there then, nor does it then ever resound with the harsh jovial laugh of handsome Dick, which sometimes, after dark has fallen, is heard by passers-by on the landing outside. But Blanche does not grow bright-eyed when she hears it: she shuts her ears and hastens to put a greater distance between her and the sound of that atrocious mirth.

But during the day the long gallery is frequented by many occupants, and much laughter in no wise sinister or saturnine resounds there. When summer lies hot over the land, those occupants lounge in the deep window-seats, and when winter spreads his icy fingers and blows shrilly between his frozen palms, congregate around the fireplace at the far end, and perch, in companies of cheerful chatterers, upon sofa and chair, and chair-back and floor. Often have I sat there on long August evenings up till dressing-time, but never have I been there when anyone has seemed disposed to linger over-late without hearing the warning: "It is close on sunset: shall we go?" Later on in the shorter autumn days they often have tea laid there, and sometimes it has happened that, even while merriment was most uproarious, Mrs. Peveril has suddenly looked out of the window and said, "My dears, it is getting so late: let us finish our nonsense downstairs in the hall." And then for a moment a curious hush always falls on loquacious family and guests alike, and as if some bad news had just been known, we all make our silent way out of the place. But the spirits of the Peverils (of the living ones, that is to say) are the most mercurial imaginable, and the blight which the thought of handsome Dick and his doings casts over them passes away again with amazing rapidity.

A typical party, large, young, and peculiarly cheerful, was staying at Church-Peveril shortly after Christmas last year, and as usual on December 31, Mrs. Peveril was giving her annual New Year's Eve ball. The house was quite full, and she had commandeered as well the greater part of the Peveril Arms to provide sleeping-quarters for the overflow from the house. For some days past a black and windless frost had stopped all hunting, but it is an ill windlessness that blows no good (if so mixed a metaphor may be forgiven), and the lake below the house had for the last day or two been covered with an adequate and admirable sheet of ice. Everyone in the house had been occupied all the morning of that day in performing swift and violent manoeuvres on the elusive surface, and as soon as lunch was over we all, with one exception, hurried out again. This one exception was Madge Dalrymple, who had had the misfortune to fall rather badly earlier in the day, but hoped, by resting her injured knee, instead of joining the skaters again, to be able to dance that evening. The hope, it is true, was of the most sanguine sort, for she could but hobble ignobly back to the house, but with the breezy optimism which characterizes the Peverils (she is Blanche's first cousin), she remarked that it would be but tepid enjoyment that she could, in her present state, derive from further skating, and thus she sacrificed little, but might gain much.

Accordingly after a rapid cup of coffee which was served in the long gallery, we left Madge comfortably reclined on the big sofa at right-angles to the fireplace, with an attractive book to beguile the tedium till tea. Being of the family, she knew all about handsome Dick and the babies, and the fate of Mrs. Canning and Colonel Blantyre, but as we went out I heard Blanche say to her, "Don't run it too fine, dear," and Madge had replied, "No, I'll go away well before sunset." And so we left her alone in the long gallery.

Madge read her attractive book for some minutes, but failing to get absorbed in it, put it down and limped across to the window. Though it was still but little after two, it was but a dim and uncertain light that entered, for the crystalline brightness of the morning had given place to a veiled obscurity produced by flocks of thick clouds which were coming sluggishly up from the northeast. Already the whole sky was overcast with them, and occasionally a few snowflakes fluttered waveringly down past the long windows. From the darkness and bitter cold of the afternoon, it seemed to her that there was like to be a heavy snowfall before long, and these outward signs were echoed inwardly in her by that muffled drowsiness of the brain, which to those who are sensitive to the pressures and lightness of weather portends storm. Madge was peculiarly the prey of such external influences: to her a brisk morning gave an ineffable brightness and briskness of spirit, and correspondingly the approach of heavy weather produced a somnolence in sensation that both drowsed and depressed her.

It was in such mood as this that she limped back again to the sofa beside the log-fire. The whole house was comfortably heated by waterpipes, and though the fire of logs and peat, an adorable mixture, had been allowed to burn low, the room was very warm. Idly she watched the dwindling flames, not opening her book again, but lying on the sofa with face towards the fireplace, intending drowsily and not immediately to go to her own room and spend the hours, until the return of the skaters made gaiety in the house again, in writing one or two neglected letters. Still drowsily she began thinking over what she had to communicate: one letter several days overdue should go to her mother, who was immensely interested in the psychical affairs of the family. She would tell her how Master Anthony had been prodigiously active on the staircase a night or two ago, and how the Blue Lady, regardless of the severity of the weather, had been seen by Mrs. Peveril that morning, strolling about. It was rather interesting: the Blue Lady had gone down the laurel walk and had been seen by her to enter the stables, where, at the moment, Freddy Peveril was inspecting the frost-bound hunters. Identically then, a sudden panic had spread through the stables, and the horses had whinnied and kicked, and shied, and sweated. Of the fatal twins nothing had been seen for many years past, but, as her mother knew, the Peverils never used the long gallery after dark.

Then for a moment she sat up, remembering that she was in the long gallery now. But it was still but a little after half-past two, and if she went to her room in half an hour, she would have ample time to write this and another letter before tea. Till then she would read her book. But she found she had left it on the window-sill, and it seemed scarcely worth while to get it. She felt exceedingly drowsy.

The sofa where she lay had been lately re-covered, in a greyish green shade of velvet, somewhat the color of lichen. It was of very thick, soft texture, and she luxuriously stretched her arms out, one on each side of her body, and pressed her fingers into the nap. How horrible that story of Mrs. Canning was: the growth on her face was of the color of lichen. And then without further transition or blurring of thought Madge fell asleep.

She dreamed. She dreamed that she awoke and found herself exactly where she had gone to sleep, and in exactly the same attitude. The flames from the logs had burned up again, and leaped on the walls, fitfully illuminating the picture of handsome Dick above the fireplace. In her dream she knew exactly what she had done today, and for what reason she was lying here now instead of being out with the rest of the skaters. She remembered also (still dreaming), that she was going to write a letter or two before tea, and prepared to get up in order to go to her room. As she half-rose she caught sight of her own arms lying out on each side of her on the grey velvet sofa. But she could not see where her hands ended, and where the grey velvet began: her fingers seemed to have melted into the stuff. She could see her wrists quite clearly, and a blue vein on the backs of her hands, and here and there a knuckle. Then, in her dream she remembered the last thought which had been in her mind before she fell asleep, namely the growth of the lichen-colored vegetation on the face and the eyes and the throat of Mrs. Canning. At that thought the strangling terror of real nightmare began: she knew that she was being transformed into this grey stuff, and she was absolutely unable to move. Soon the grey would spread up her arms, and over her feet; when they came in from skating they would find here nothing but a huge misshapen cushion of lichen-colored velvet, and that would be she. The horror grew more acute, and then by a violent effort she shook herself free of the clutches of this very evil dream, and she awoke.

For a minute or two she lay there, conscious only of the tremendous relief at finding herself awake. She felt again with her fingers the pleasant touch of the velvet, and drew them backwards and forwards, assuring herself that she was not, as her dream had suggested, melting into greyness and softness. But she was still, in spite of the violence of her awakening, very sleepy, and lay there till, looking down, she was aware that she could not see her hands at all. It was very nearly dark.

At that moment a sudden flicker of flame came from the dying fire, and a flare of burning gas from the peat flooded the room. The portrait of handsome Dick looked evilly down on her, and her hands were visible again. And then a panic worse than the panic of her dreams seized her. Daylight had altogether faded, and she knew that she was alone in the dark and terrible gallery. The panic was of the nature of nightmare, for she felt unable to move for terror. But it was worse than nightmare because she knew she was awake. And then the full cause of this frozen fear dawned on her; she knew with the certainty of absolute conviction that she was about to see the twin-babies.

She felt a sudden moisture break out on her face, and within her mouth her tongue and throat went suddenly dry, and she felt her tongue grate along the inner surface of her teeth. All power of movement had slipped from her limbs, leaving them dead and inert, and she stared with wide eyes into the blackness. The spurt of flame from the peat had burned itself out again, and darkness encompassed her.

Then on the wall opposite her, facing the windows, there grew a faint light of dusky crimson. For a moment she thought it but heralded the approach of the awful vision, then hope revived in her heart, and she remembered that thick clouds had overcast the sky before she went to sleep, and guessed that this light came from the sun not yet quite sunk and set. This sudden revival of hope gave her the necessary stimulus, and she sprang off the sofa where she lay. She looked out of the window and saw the dull glow on the horizon. But before she could take a step forward it was obscured again. A tiny sparkle of light came from the hearth which did not more than illuminate the tiles of the fireplace, and snow falling heavily tapped at the window panes. There was neither light nor sound except these.

But the courage that had come to her, giving her the power of movement, had not quite deserted her, and she began feeling her way down the gallery. And then she found that she was lost. She stumbled against a chair, and, recovering herself, stumbled against another. Then a table barred her way, and, turning swiftly aside, she found herself up against the back of the sofa. Once more she turned and saw the dim gleam of the firelight on the side opposite to that on which she expected it. In her blind gropings she must have reversed her direction. But which way was she to go now? She seemed blocked in by furniture. And all the time insistent and imminent was the fact that the two innocent terrible ghosts were about to appear to her.

Then she began to pray, "Lighten our darkness, O Lord," she said to herself. But she could not remember how the prayer continued, and she had sore need of it. There was something about the perils of the night. All this time she felt about her with groping, fluttering hands. The fireglimmer which should have been on her left was on her right again; therefore she must turn herself round again. "Lighten our darkness," she whispered, and then aloud she repeated, "Lighten our darkness."

She stumbled up against a screen, and could not remember the existence of any such screen. Hastily she felt beside it with blind hands, and touched something soft and velvety. Was it the sofa on which she had lain? If so, where was the head of it? It had a head and a back and feet —it was like a person, all covered with grey lichen. Then she lost her head completely. All that remained to her was to pray; she was lost, lost in this awful place, where no one came in the dark except the babies that cried. And she heard her voice rising from whisper to speech, and speech to scream. She shrieked out the holy words, she yelled them as if blaspheming as she groped among tables and chairs and the pleasant things of ordinary life which had become so terrible.

Then came a sudden and awful answer to her screamed prayer. Once more a pocket of inflammable gas in the peat on the hearth was reached by the smouldering embers, and the room started into light. She saw the evil eyes of handsome Dick, she saw the little ghostly snowflakes falling thickly outside. And she saw where she was, just opposite the door through which the terrible twins made their entrance. Then the flame went out again, and left her in blackness once more. But she had gained something, for she had her geography now. The center of the room was bare of furniture, and one swift dart would take her to the door of the landing above the main staircase and into safety. In that gleam she had been able to see the handle of the door, bright-brassed, luminous like a star. She would go straight for it; it was but a matter of a few seconds now.

She took a long breath, partly of relief, partly to satisfy the demands of her galloping heart. But the breath was only half-taken when she was stricken once more into the immobility of nightmare.

There came a little whisper, it was no more than that, from the door opposite which she stood, and through which the twin-babies entered. It was not quite dark outside, for she could see that the door was opening. And there stood in the opening two little white figures, side by side. They came towards her slowly, shufflingly. She could not see face or form at all distinctly, but the two little white figures were advancing. She knew them to be the ghosts of terror, innocent of the awful doom they were bound to bring, even as she was innocent. With the inconceivable rapidity of thought, she made up her mind what to do. She had not hurt them or laughed at them, and they, they were but babies when the wicked and bloody deed had sent them to their burning death. Surely the spirits of these children would not be inaccessible to the cry of one who was of the same blood as they, who had committed no fault that merited the doom they brought. If she entreated them they might have mercy, they might forbear to bring the curse upon her, they might allow her to pass out of the place without blight, without the sentence of death, or the shadow of things worse than death upon her.

It was but for the space of a moment that she hesitated, then she sank down on to her knees, and stretched out her hands towards them.

"Oh, my dears," she said, "I only fell asleep. I have done no more wrong than that——"

She paused a moment, and her tender girl's heart thought no more of herself, but only of them, those little innocent spirits on whom so awful a doom was laid, that they should bring death where other children bring laughter, and doom for delight. But all those who had seen them before had dreaded and feared them, or had mocked at them.

Then, as the enlightenment of pity dawned on her, her fear fell from her like the wrinkled sheath that holds the sweet folded buds of spring.

"Dears, I am so sorry for you," she said. "It is not your fault that you must bring me what you must bring, but I am not afraid any longer. I am only sorry for you. God bless you, you poor darlings."

She raised her head and looked at them. Though it was so dark, she could now see their faces, though all was dim and wavering, like the light of pale flames shaken by a draught. But the faces were not miserable or fierce—they smiled at her with shy little baby smiles. And as she looked they grew faint, fading slowly away like wreaths of vapor in frosty air.

Madge did not at once move when they had vanished, for instead of fear there was wrapped round her a wonderful sense of peace, so happy and serene that she would not willingly stir, and so perhaps disturb it. But before long she got up, and feeling her way, but without any sense of nightmare pressing her on, or frenzy of fear to spur her, she went out of the long gallery, to find Blanche just coming upstairs whistling and swinging her skates.

"How's the leg, dear?" she asked. "You're not limping any more."

Till that moment Madge had not thought of it.

"I think it must be all right," she said. "I had forgotten it anyhow. Blanche, dear, you won't be frightened for me, will you, but—I have seen the twins."

For a moment Blanche's face whitened with terror.

"What?" she said in a whisper.

"Yes, I saw them just now. But they were kind, they smiled at me, and I was so sorry for them. And somehow I am sure I have nothing to fear."

It seems that Madge was right, for nothing untoward has come to her. Something, her attitude to them, we must suppose, her pity, her sympathy, touched and dissolved and annihilated the curse. Indeed, I was at Church-Peveril only last week, arriving there after dark. Just as I passed the gallery door, Blanche came out.

"Ah, there you are," she said. "I've just been seeing the twins. They looked too sweet and stopped nearly ten minutes. Let us have tea at once."

Appendices

APPENDIX A:

"RALPH"

I have always believed that when an editor's own tale appears in an anthology, an explanation is due the reader. While proper pride is a necessary emotion, it is unduly frowned on in these United States. Thus, one must justify the decision to choose one's own work in any selection which purports to be a representation of excellence.

The following narrative is not fiction, though my imperfect memory has doubtless simplified and compacted and chronologically shifted some of the events. But the basic points made and occurrences all are true.

"Ralph" is both trivial and significant, as I suspect all putative paranormal events are. In a way it is as enigmatic as Stockton's famous lady-tiger riddle, but the lack of resolution is not besides the point—it *is* the point. I am neither convinced in nor dissuaded from the hypothesis that ghosts exist. The phenomena recounted in this personal history urge me toward acceptance, but the rational mind—the one tool modern man most needs to survive the millennium—proposes other possibilities. Thus, somewhat like Claudius, I stand in pause what I shall most believe, and both distrust.

I have elected to include "Ralph" as an appendix because its theme is rare in ghostly literature: that the need to believe is an almost inescapable trap of the ego.

Ralph
by Marvin Kaye

His name is Ralph Baroski. He was my uncle. How long ago he died is
not as important as the fact that once he lived.

He has haunted me most of my life.

At what level may the word "haunted" be defined? I am not sure,
and that is the point of what follows. I cannot be objective about it. My
perceptions of my uncle are tangled, and reality itself is arbitrary, for I
have sometimes dreamed so vividly that I thought myself awake . . .
until I woke to learn I still dreamed. Then can I state, dogmatically,
that now I do not slumber, perhaps a whim of someone else's subconscious? Possibly Ralph's?

I was born in the late 1930s in Philadelphia, the youngest of four
children, separated by nine years from the next eldest. It was a small,
artificially comfortable world for me, marred only by a too-early
awareness of death and the vague terrors of all-encompassing night. To
bolster my courage, I met the Gorgon head-on, investing my imagination with a fascination for supernatural fiction in whatever form it was
available: literature, comics, films, radio.

I had few friends. My play-life came chiefly from listening to radio,
reading sensationalistic comics, worshiping at the Holy Cinema across
the street, where, every Saturday, at least one of a double bill would be
a film of the supernatural. In that theatre, I first dreamed of being an
actor, of mingling with those *belles gens* whose worries and delights had
so little in common with my family's, and of course, seemed somehow
infinitely preferable . . .

Yet though I craved the theatre, hindsight reveals that circumstances
were actually preparing me for the creative discipline of writing. Of
shaping words, of juggling concept and timbre. Words, of words, of all

the words I heard: an auditory kaleidoscope of tonal tang and texture, from the Philadelphianisms—down-inflected questions and localisms like "gaz" or "gaw 'head"—through a lush ethnic legato, capped by that compote of accents and unfamiliar rhythms heard in cinema or on radio. A burdensome multitude of words sharpening eye and adjusting the ear to the bulk and line of our language.

Later, creation would appeal to me more than interpretation, but as the edge of familial security gradually frayed, it became positively determined that I must adopt some work that would lead to that uppercase Achievement which, essentially, is an unsuccessful substitute for the charmed circle of early love, unearned.

I learned about Ralph a few months before I was thirteen. My mother's parents hailed from Poland, land of dybbuks, golems and a peculiarly Christian strain of mysticism dividing Chasidic folklore from its southern Judaistic counterparts.

My maternal grandparents came from Warsaw, and if I remember correctly, lived for a time in Salem, N.J., where my late mother was born. Besides a sister, she had four brothers, and the eldest (I think) was Ralph.

When she spoke of him, it was with wistful affection, tinged by something darker. Later I learned what it was.

Once she showed me his picture. He was a good-looking boy with a most solemn expression, a mien I do not think reflected his true character. The characteristic attitude in family portraiture of bygone days seems to have been to regard children as diminutive adults, beset with the cares and responsibilities of that state. Youngsters were dressed in rigid "company's-coming" garb and arranged in unbending attitudes. Examine portraits of children in museums and marvel at the machined joylessness of their expressions. Is it possible they did not long to grimace into the lens or stick their tongues out at the painter? I wonder, too, whether it was the artist's choice to so freeze youth in time, or whether it was a style principally dictated by a sterner philosophy of parentage than today is rife.

Well, Ralph may have been mischievous. His photo does not reveal it. Yet I assume him to have been bright, good-humored, slightly raucous at times, a spirit of fun and adventure, a brother that my mother might have delighted in.

There are three facts about him that are not conjecture.

1. I looked like him. My mother said so. I doubt whether my introverted, reclusive nature was much like his, but even I noted the remarkable physical resemblance of the photograph.
2. He died a few weeks before his thirteenth birthday, victim to that influenza epidemic which, shortly after the turn of the century, decimated the populations of Europe and America.
3. Because he did not attain the initiatory age of thirteen, Ralph was not Bar Mitzvah, that is, he never was inducted into the adult Jewish community. Thirteen is that religion's customary milestone for spiritual coming of age. Thus the interpreted tradition of the time held that Ralph never was born and had no right to a Jewish funeral and burial. Non-persons have no rites.

I heard this repulsive detail directly from my mother who, decades later, when she told it to me, still was understandably upset about it. Of course, Judaism is not centrally organized like Roman Catholicism; its tenets are variously interpreted by local rabbinical authority, as anyone who reads Potok or Kemelman knows. So Ralph may have been denied ritual by the stunted sway of some unfeeling icicle. Yet such uncompassionate insistence on Form is common enough in orthodoxy's stubborn circles. Read Bertrand Russell's *Portraits from Memory* and note the similar coldness in the pious lifestyle of his Christian grandparents. Rigid sectarianism too often puts a low priority on revering the living, and therefore is universally capable of withholding that spiritual comfort which is the *raison d'être* of all religion.

So it would not have discredited the ethics of denominational bookkeeping to rubber-stamp Ralph's existence at another time or place. But dogmatic authority was invested with ill-deserved awe three-score and ten years ago. It is ironic that it should take more than five times as long as Ralph lived for one of his apostate relatives to rage, like Laertes: *"What ceremony else?"*

Our contemporary literature is preoccupied with the terror of nonbeing. Faulkner, Beckett, Joyce, Camus and Pinter tilt at it to greater or lesser degree, and even such a "pop" entertainment as, say, *Jesus Christ, Superstar,* is darkened by the horror that fervent embracement of Oriental solipsism cannot overcome. Ibsen raises the issue to cosmic tragi-comedy in *Peer Gynt,* while even Dickens' Scrooge strikes a respondent chord as the archetype of eleventh-hour redemption and apotheosis of Self.

Personally, I am probably stylistically cursed by immortal longings, and even when I read for pleasure, I find it hard to put aside a tedious tome, for such an action smacks too much of divine denial of another creator's "personhood."

Like Ibsen's wastrel-hero, Peer, my uncle Ralph's memory stayed green in the memory of a woman, my mother. When she told me about him and his *de facto* excommunication, I was about twelve years old. I spent much of that year in mute fear that I, too, would die before my thirteenth birthday and therefore cease to exist in my parents' world. I had, even then, some self-derisive strain within me, but it was insufficient to dispel the terror.

Yet I reached and passed the ominous birthday. In so doing, I reaped a crop of guilt which hindsight suggests has haunted me all my life. For my mother loved her brother, but he died; she cared for me, and I lived. These arbitrarily-bestowed gifts must be justified, and so I have forced myself to Achieve, for the circumstances of my survival compel me to recreate myself over and yet over again.

2

Fantasy writers have long postulated mechanistic afterlifes. But an event suggesting a plane beyond death not only does not automatically authenticate sectarian claims, it cannot be lightly credited by speculating parapsychologists, either. Our tools for measuring the supposed paranormal are imprecise. Yet too many rush to judgment.

It is perhaps understandable in an age of deep psychological disorientation, especially since we have been deluged of late with shoddy *psi* testament: cynically reported myths about PK, ESP, ghosts and OBEs. Unscrupulous psychic "wonder-workers" exploit ignorant, longing humanity and headline-hungry rags provide the platforms on which charlatans stand.

Other psychic researchers, sincere enough, suffer from a blinding need to *believe:* virtually an inescapable trap of our spiritually-unanchored century.

I have had several so-called out-of-body experiences but am not convinced they were anything but unusual mental states akin to the ecstatic hallucinations of antique witch-worship reported by such cultural historians as Pennethorne Hughes or Margaret Murray. It is an area whose very nature makes it impossible for the person undergoing the phenomenon to report it accurately. The most objective fact-finder is highly suspect when attempting to catalog the deceptive events of a trance.

Occasionally, one reads about an OBE seen by an independent eyewitness, but nothing may be surmised from these narratives except that something odd may have occurred. The objectification of the "travel" is undermined by the real possibility that a mere telepathic exchange accounted for it.

Telepathy is widely conceded to be a mundane mechanistic function. Whether one subscribes to the hypotheses of similar frequencies or sympathetic fields, one hardly can avoid viewing "lep" as an electrical curiosity. For those who crave cosmic meaning, thought interchange must appear as important as the latest news broadcast to an all-music-FM-station radio announcer.

Ghosts, however, are quite another matter.

I am rather sensitive to atmospheres. I trained as an actor, a discipline which stresses mental monitoring of muscular function through concentration and isolation of parts of the body. To do this, one must consciously channel thoughts, breathing, physical sensation, selecting and editing all at one or another time in the training stages. This means that advanced acting technique, as in other meditative exercises, often brings about gradations of mental process not normally noticeable in less contemplative life-modes.

Once, I visited the Joseph Priestley home in Northumberland, Pennsylvania. Priestley, discoverer of oxygen and inventor of the air rifle, was a churchman who eventually modified his beliefs and became something of a freethinker. In order to hold his own spiritual views without communal disapproval, he left England and settled at the confluence of the north and west branches of the Susquehanna River.

In that historic shrine, filled with period furniture, much of it repurchased articles once belonging to Priestley, I became strongly aware of a friendly, inquisitive presence, or an atmosphere, if one prefers: looking into an oval mirror, I almost fancied someone stood behind, watching with detached amusement.

I was a reporter sent to write a space-filler. When I sheepishly told my impressions to my assignments editor, I was surprised that, instead of ridiculing the conceit, he said, "Priestley is supposed to haunt the house. One of his descendants once told me, 'Joseph potters about in his laboratory still, especially at night. I've often seen lights inside, though we always lock it up carefully.' "

The Priestley atmosphere was pleasant, but I cannot say the same thing for that which I experienced in 1973 in a Manhattan theatre.

At that time, I was engaged on the staff of a repertory company. Late one night, I sat alone in the business office behind the auditorium working on one of my non-fiction books.

Outside, a worklight burned above the bare stage. All doors were locked from inside.

At one a.m., or a few minutes after, I heard a loud clump from what seemed to be dead-center stage. I rose, walked to the door of the office and peered out over the empty seats but saw nothing within the arch of the proscenium.

As I stared, a dreadful coldness came over me. I sensed an enormous malevolence. I can put it no other way than to state that hatred seemed to surge from the empty stage, washing over the darkened auditorium like a polar tide, lapping at the furthest shingle.

A thought entered my mind that I had a time limit for gathering my things and going. I did so swiftly, leaving on lights and appliances, hurrying till I stood safely outside on the sidewalk. There, feeling ashamed of myself, I attempted to mock my own irrational behavior. But I lacked the courage to go back inside.

The next morning, the company House Manager berated me for forgetting to turn off the electricity, especially the air conditioner, which brought the landlord down on his head. Feeling foolish, I explained why I'd failed to do so. To my surprise, the House Manager was instantly mollified, and later, reported that the landlord, too, was completely sympathetic to my explanation.

The next day, the same official, looking extremely pale, took me aside and said the preceding evening he'd let himself into the business office to get a tape recorder he'd accidentally left behind.

"All of a sudden," said he, "I heard a crash backstage. I investigated —and felt the same awful cold you described. I was also positive I had a time limit—a short one—to quit the theatre. I almost didn't make it! I've got a weak heart, and it was pounding dreadfully!"

The above paragraphs were written with calculated intent. It is so easy to accept ephemera when it is profoundly to our interest to do so: yet neither case proves anything conclusively. Priestley's home, fitted out with his original furniture, could not help but feel "lived in," while the theatre was often spoken of, in my presence, as being haunted by two spectres. The House Manager, poor in health, rich in imagination, heard all the particulars of my experience and underwent them the very next night.

Emotionally, I feel there *was* something more than an overexcitated fancy in each case, but just as in the case of the out-of-body experience, the testimony of he to whom paranormal phenomenon occurs is gravely suspect because it is almost never objective in nature.

The price of mind is doubt, and it is a fair assessment; I would rather be unsure than too easily deluded. Tradition has immortalized ancient error with ages of rote repetition, but logic, too, is a two-edged sword. One avoids one blade only to be sliced by the other.

And so, with this apt metaphor, we end our long prologue and examine the homely incidents of the missing knives.

3

1979: Eight or nine months precedent to the moment these words are written. Dinnertime. My wife serves a roast.

I reach into a drawer to fetch the twin blades of our electric knife. One is missing. The gadget cannot operate without both, so my wife and I clatter about the kitchen, opening one drawer after another, turning dishes, forks, skewers, saucers out, upside-down, but all to no avail.

There was a cleaning-person in the day before. Maybe she accidentally misplaced the blade.

Saralee, my wife, wonders whether she didn't lose it herself. "I might have absent-mindedly dumped it into the trash."

What about the drain? I investigate, but see it could not possibly fit.

We agree to carve the roast manually, and buy another electric knife blade soon. (We never got around to it.)

A few weeks later: I prepare to slice vegetables for a soup. I open the same drawer to get a large dark-handled carving knife.

It is not there. In its place is a light-handled knife I have never seen before.

Later, my wife says the light-handled one is a relative's recent gift.

Two weeks later: the dark-handled knife is back in the drawer. The light-handled one is gone.

We own a set of four sharp steak knives, which are kept in a different drawer. Because they are tarnishable, they are stored in protective cardboard holders. After being used, they are immediately washed, dried and returned to their containers. So their inflexible "life cycle" is: sleeves-in-drawer to table to sink to drawer-and-sleeves.

Yet, a few weeks after the bread knife business, a steak knife vanishes. At this writing, it is still missing.

By then, Saralee and I joke that our precocious nine-year-old, Terry Ellen, is ahead of schedule, as usual, taking up poltergeisting well before attaining her teens.

But we really regard the knife problem as an ongoing case of human carelessness.

And then one afternoon, while I am in the bedroom reading, Saralee enters and, behind me, begins to make the bed. She takes a set of distinctively-patterned sheets and smooths them onto the bed. While she performs that activity, the matching pillowcases rest on a chair that neither one of us is watching.

She reaches for the pillowcases, but cannot find them. She ransacks chair and linen closet, even pulls apart the bed, in case she accidentally tucked them in while making it. Still nothing.

While she searches, I ponder this latest in an irksome series of episodes. Though I still want to attribute them to a prosaic cause, their regularity of occurrence, every two or three weeks, is remarkable.

I decide to do a rather silly thing at that moment. It is so preposterous to me that I do not bother to mention it to my wife.

Before I tell about it, I must first introduce a friend.

She is an actress and a writer *manquée*. We met several years ago at The Bedside Network of the Veterans Hospital Radio-TV Guild. She claims a high level of psychic sensitivity and has told me many personal experiences which I audit with a polite skepticism, not as to her veracity, but rather, her interpretation of the events. (I ought to explain that this habit of doubting is not some easy, offhanded quirk of temperament, but rather the result of long research and practice of the subtle dodges of the professional psychic. I reported my findings in considerable detail in *The Handbook of Mental Magic,* Stein & Day, 1975.)

One day, without revealing why, I invited our friend to visit our apartment. After she chatted with me for a while, I asked whether she noticed any psychic presences in the room.

"Yes," she said, "there's a young boy sitting on the edge of your sofa. He has wide eyes and is looking straight at me, wondering who I am. He seems whimsical, prankish. Does that remind you of anyone, perhaps a relative who might need to visit you?"

I shrugged, but accepted her scenario. "Can't think of anyone."

"He's dressed quaintly. He may have died quite a while ago."

A long-buried memory surfaced. "How old would you guess he is?"

"Perhaps eleven or twelve years."

"I had an uncle Ralph who died at twelve, long before I was born."

"Oh," my friend remarked, "there's an older person with him, a woman."

Hearing that, I found a family wedding album and showed it to her, in case she could pick out my mother's photo as the mystery woman she claimed she saw.

Instead, she stopped at a different picture. "Who's this young man? He looks like the boy on the sofa."

I stared at my own wedding photo, taken when I was much younger and heavier.

Then something else came to my mind. I started.

"What is it?" my friend asked.

"A while ago," I explained, "a pair of pillowcases disappeared in a peculiar manner while Saralee was making the bed. While she looked for them, I tried an experiment in automatic writing . . ."

Automatic writing has always struck me as particularly idiotic. Ouija boards operate similarly to the old Chevreul pendulum, which sways when its holder thinks of a circle or a straight line, and minute muscular information runs from the brain to the fingertips, setting the pendulum in motion in the appropriate pattern.

Automatic writing, I have always suspected, is just another innocent way to delude oneself, drawing on the subconscious for answers fervently desired by occult acolytes.

Yet I picked up a pencil that afternoon and positioned it above a sheet of typing paper, shut my eyes and waited.

The pencil moved. My mind naturally edited the response, thereby stopping it. I opened my eyes, expecting to see a meaningless scrawl.

But on the paper was a short mark that looked like a word; it was perhaps five letters long.

Partially illegible, it clearly began with an "R" and the second letter was either "O" or "A."

"It would be as hard for a ghost to move your arm," said my friend, "as for you to haul a load of bricks."

I was still very skeptical, though. The whole thing was an intellectual game, playing with random evidence in hopes of discovering a significant schematic.

"What could your uncle possibly want from you? It's seventy-some years since he died."

"I have no idea. Granting your premise, why would he come back and play pranks?"

"To get your attention."

I laughed. "All right. He's got it. Now what?"

That night I discussed it with my wife.

"If it *were* true, what could *I* do for him?"

She said, simply enough, "You can write. . . ."

I can write. I can tell that my uncle lived. That, despite the judgment of an unfeeling orthodoxy, he spent twelve years upon this earth. He existed.

Has he waited for me and my craft to grow so I could tell of him? If so, have I failed, lacking all but the baldest facts about my uncle?

It is ironic that a recurrent theme in my work is psychological manipulation. Have I myself been handled and shaped?

The afternoon before my wife and I held that final discussion about Ralph, I'd been working in the kitchen, making a one-pot meal for dinner. I had reason, therefore, to go into the pot compartment directly below the drawer where the bread knife and electric knife blade are kept.

Because Ralph was so much on my mind, I remembered that three knives still were missing. So once more I took out all the drawers and examined them, inside and out. I looked in the pot section of the cabinet, thinking that a knife might fall into it if it got improperly lodged in the drawer above.

My efforts bore no results, and I replaced everything as I'd found it.

Hours later, after dinner, once our daughter went to bed, Saralee and I engaged in our talk. I said that whether Ralph existed in some other form in our apartment or not, it *was* a good idea for me to write something about him. Except I had no idea where I could sell such an amorphous essay.

My wife reminded me I had a contract to provide Doubleday with a collection of my shorter fiction.* "Why not include it there?"

"Begging the definition a bit, isn't it?" I mused. "But I suppose that *is* the place to have it appear in print, since it will be a fantasy collection."

Once I made up my mind to do it, the same thought occurred to both of us, and we exchanged a smile.

"All right," Saralee said, raising her voice, "is *that* what you wanted him to do? If it is, how about returning our knives?"

Laughing, I walked into the kitchen, flicked on the light and opened the bread-knife drawer. Naturally, nothing was out of place. I shut it again.

Two seconds later, I heard a muted but unmistakably metallic *clash*.

Suddenly tense, I pulled the drawer open a second time, but still saw nothing. Then, on impulse, I totally removed it and looked into the cavity where the drawer had been.

Below, clearly framed in the rectangle of space, teetering precariously on the domed lid of the pot I'd used that afternoon, was the long-missing gleaming second blade of our electric knife.

The steak knife is still missing. My spiritualistic friend claims the returned blade was a down payment for drafting this piece. One Doubleday editor thinks the missing knives constitute the second half of a royalty advance upon completion of a satisfactory final manuscript.

But what do *I* think, knowing that every psychic event is capable of mechanistic interpretation? Do I imagine I painstakingly examined that pot compartment because I actually did so, or have I come to accept it as fact because my ego is impelled to fashion circumstances it yearns to believe in? (I have dreamed and thought myself awake.)

* *The Possession of Immanuel Wolf and Other Improbable Tales* (Doubleday, 1981).

Though my uncle's existence is at least confirmed in the twin rhythms of my life and this work, yet what if he actually is here at this moment, standing over me, reading? Will he return the steak knife as a sign? (I checked the drawer a day or two ago. The fourth cardboard sleeve still was empty.)

If it is there now, will that prove that Ralph returned it? (When *did* I look in that drawer? *When?*)

If the knife is not there, will that mean this chain of events has no significance, the haunting illusory?

Will it merely mean Ralph cannot summon sufficient psychic energy tonight to accomplish the feat?

Or might it be because he is enjoined not to perform any action that cannot be ambiguously interpreted?

Or, if it is still missing, might it suggest, instead, that my uncle is displeased with an essay which tells too much of me . . . and not enough about Ralph?

I will go now to the drawer and look.

APPENDIX B:

SO YOU WANT TO MEET A GHOST?

There are two traditional ways to encounter phantoms: go where they are supposed to lurk, or else wait for one to come to you. The latter method generally ensures that the ghost you meet will be someone (or thing) known to you, whereas itinerant spook-seeking might bring you into contact with the kind of spectral riffraff that you would have avoided, had they been alive.

However, if you are determined to pry into funereal matters, consult the two ensuing appendices. They will get you started on your way. How it all ends, though, is up to you . . . and your quarry.

For those who prefer to stay at home and hobnob solely with departed family and friends, several suggestions may prove helpful:

1. Always allow for the relativistic nature of experience (see Appendix A). If you ever expect to persuade others, let alone yourself, of the objectivity of your psychic adventures, you must study the methods of scientific parapsychological research and apply them. The well-known (though controversial) psychic investigator and author, Harry Price, once issued a list of rules for observing occult phenomena. Some of the highlights include:

   a. Always have notebooks, pencils and a reliable watch handy, so time and character of the "event" may be swiftly and accurately recorded. A flashlight and/or candle and matches are also advisable.

   b. Always presearch the reputedly haunted site. Be sure windows and doors are locked, or even sealed, to help rule out chicanery.

   c. Visit all suspicious rooms on a regular schedule throughout the night. From time to time, sit in darkness, if you dare. Some ghosts are shy.

   d. If possible, keep vigil with another observer so impressions may be compared.

   e. If you see what seems to be a ghost, do not approach or it may vanish. Or worse, it may become offended, like Hamlet's father, and who wants to outrage an apparition?

  f. Keep in mind that most reports of "factual" wraiths begin with a sudden drop in room temperature. A clammy, chilly sensation along the spine could merely be nerves. Or it might be a signal to pay attention.

2. If you believe you are seeing and/or speaking with the spectre of a relative or friend, be polite and find out if anything is wanted. According to Dr. Louis C. Jones in his fascinating work, *Things That Go Bump in the Night,* spooks in the oral folk tradition in America tend to appear for one of five reasons:

  a. To replay their own death, especially if it is of a violent nature;
  b. To perform again normal and/or favored activities of their previous lifetimes;
  c. To tend to business that should have been finished before they died;
  d. To object to the actions of a descendant (and possibly to punish the same for ditto);
  e. To warn or protect or comfort or reward the living.

3. Once the reason for the activity has been ascertained, do not delay in carrying it out, or, according to folklore, the haunting will worsen. Of course, there isn't much one can do about reasons *a* or *b* above, but *c* and *e* are worth becoming involved in, if we believe those tales of hidden treasures yielded up to mortals by benevolent spirits.

4. If you suspect that it is reason *d* which motivates the hypothetical haunt, it might be well to avoid its favorite appearing places. Unless, of course, you wish to embark upon a one-way field trip into the sphere of the supernatural.

Good luck and pleasant dreams!

APPENDIX C:

A BAEDEKER OF FAVORITE U.S. HAUNTS

Once upon a time, the threat of legal reprisal forced journalists to keep the location of reputedly haunted houses a secret, and the custom was often utilized by fabulists to make their fictions appear more authentic. Thus we read about the ghastly Villa d'_____ situated on the B_____ River not far from the bustling northern town of L_____, and wonder if perhaps we didn't pass within two miles of it on our last vacation.

But today, though some rental agents still are shy about branding a property as ghost-ridden, others find the presence of a putative phantom actually enhances the value of the estate. (See "Ghost Stories for Daring Househunters," the New York *Times,* October 26, 1975.)

Still, avocational ghost-hunters can't always rely on the suspicious appearance of a brooding mansion; looks can be deceptive. Local gossip may focus around an occasional questionable site, but serious spook-seekers would do well to get in touch with parapsychological societies, or simply scan the headlines of back-dated newspapers in any given area.

Chasing ghosts may be like trying to outrun a will-o'-the-wisp, but for those diehards (!) who intend to persevere despite frequent disappointment, the following list of allegedly haunted sites should prove useful. Many come from a list provided by the U. S. Department of Commerce—all open to the public (and so designated by an asterisk). Some come from older and/or less reliable sources and may not still exist or be viewable. Those without an asterisk before the listing ought to be checked into with local chambers of commerce lest fruitless travel end in disappointment.

STATE	LOCATION	NATURE OF HAUNTING
California	* THE WHALEY HOUSE, Old Town, 2482 San Diego Avenue, San Diego 92110.	Built in 1865, Whaley House was San Diego's first brick mansion, and served as the seat of local government through the 1870s. Built by Judge Thomas Whaley, it is said to be haunted by the ghost of a hanged man.
	* THE WINCHESTER MYSTERY HOUSE, 525 S. Winchester Boulevard, San Jose 95128.	Surely the most bizarre mansion ever built, this sprawling nightmare has more than 160 rooms, secret chambers, stairs that lead nowhere, a ballroom with mysterious mottos worked into the glass of the windows, and other eerie features that must be seen with the aid of a guide lest one lose one's way. Stories conflict on why the late Sarah Winchester built the house that way [it took more than thirty years]; the most popular legend is that she was afraid she would be haunted by the ghosts of people killed by the Winchester firearms that were manufactured by her husband's firm. By building a confusing network of rooms and passages, it is said she hoped to confuse pursuing spectres and also provide a home for gentler victims of Winchester ballistics. She kept workmen busy every day of the year— no holidays—for decades. Before an earthquake leveled part of the house in 1906, the house was even bigger!

STATE	LOCATION	NATURE OF HAUNTING
Connecticut	Stony Creek; Frisbie Island.	According to a hearsay report in the New York *Sun*, September 1, 1885, an old summer hotel even then decaying was often seen to have mysterious lights in its windows late at night. Local sailors spoke of investigating, but never did, says the paper.
Delaware	* Woodburn (Governor's Mansion), Dover; c/o Travel Development Bureau, Dept. of Economic Development, 630 State College Road, Dover 19901.	The home of Delaware's chief executive is open to the public a limited time each week. Look for the bibulous phantom who is supposed to empty wine decanters in the dining room.
District of Columbia	* Decatur House, c/o National Trust for Historic Preservation, 748 Jackson Place, N.W., Washington 20006.	Stephen Decatur, early American naval hero, died in a duel and is said to still walk in the home he lived in. His house is right across Lafayette Park from The White House (see below).
	* The Capitol, Washington 20515.	It is not generally known that America's governmental seat is reportedly haunted by at least fifteen ghosts (according to the Philadelphia *Press*, October 2, 1898). The worst of the group is a phantom cat which, when seen by members of the security staff on a certain stairway at night, grows to *elephant* size. Statuary Hall at night is an eerie place because footsteps supposedly have been heard following timid mortals intruding there. In the House

STATE	LOCATION	NATURE OF HAUNTING
		wing, the ghost of John Quincy Adams has reportedly appeared near his own desk, while Woodrow Wilson occasionally is said to turn up in the Senate portion.
	* The Octagon, 1799 New York Avenue, N.W., Washington 20006.	Built during the 1700s, Octagon House is a frequently discussed treasure-trove of ghostly phenomena. Many tales of ghosts may be uncovered by visiting any Tuesday through Sunday.
	* The White House, 1600 Pennsylvania Avenue, Washington 20500.	One of the responsibilities of our Chief Executive is to tolerate the ghostly inhabitants of the presidential residence—among them, according to legend, the spirits of Abraham Lincoln and James Garfield.
Illinois	Diamond Island, two miles from Hardin, Ill.	According to the St. Louis *Globe-Democrat* of September 18, 1888, the fiery spectre of a murdered man once appeared to foolhardy, young investigators whose boat was commandeered by the apparition. Their screams brought rescue from the residents living on the far shore.
Louisiana	* Beauregard House (also known as LeCarpentier House), 1113 Chartres Street, New Orleans 70116.	Civil War General P. G. T. Beauregard rented this columned mansion and liked it so much he is still said to walk its halls.

STATE	LOCATION	NATURE OF HAUNTING
	* Oaklawn Manor, Franklin 70538.	A white-pillared mansion with marble floors and a fine collection of imported antiques, Oaklawn Manor was frequently visited by statesman Henry Clay, who is still thought to visit, though a shade.
	* Parlange Plantation, Route 1, Box M73A, New Roads 70760.	A beautiful young girl is said to haunt this early Louisiana estate.
	* Pharmacie Française, c/o The Historical Pharmacy Museum, 514 Chartres Street, New Orleans 70130.	Voodoo artifacts are on display in this museum, and where there is black magic, can spirits be far away?
	* St. Louis Cemetery #1, c/o Greater New Orleans Tourist & Convention Commission, 334 Royal Street, New Orleans 70130.	Because of the damp character of the local soil, tombs are constructed above-ground. One of them houses the late Marie Levaux, said to be a voodoo queen. Some residents still mark hex signs thereon and consult her advice.
	* St. Maurice Plantation, St. Maurice 71471.	This huge estate supposedly is troubled by poltergeists and a child-ghost.
	* The Cottage Plantation, Route 5, Box 425, St. Francisville (near Baton Rouge) 70775.	A picturesque plantation, now in ruins, was a showplace visited by American politicos and the Marquis de Lafayette. It is uncertain which of them still lingers.

STATE	LOCATION	NATURE OF HAUNTING
	* The Myrtles Plantation, P.O. Box 757, St. Francisville 70775.	Sleepers used to complain that the ghost of a French governess would enter the bedroom and wake them by staring into their faces. The Myrtles is Louisiana's oldest and biggest plantation.
	* The Voodoo Museum, 739 Bourbon Street, New Orleans 70116.	The rise and progress of New Orleans voodoo is traced in this tourist attraction. Whether or not it is visited by ghosts, too, remains to be reported.
	* Valcour Aime Plantation Gardens, c/o Louisiana State Tourist Division, P.O. Box 44291, Baton Rouge 70804.	These ruins in Vacherie, Louisiana, were once known as the "Versailles of Louisiana." A nameless spectre supposedly haunts the grounds.
Maine	* Marine Antique Shop, c/o Wiscasset Chamber of Commerce, P.O. Box 274, Wiscasset 04578.	This store formerly was a restaurant where the employees claimed to see chairs and tables move unnaturally.
	* Musical Wonder House, c/o Wiscasset Chamber of Commerce, P.O. Box 274, Wiscasset 04578.	This museum contains hundreds of mechanical music machines and spirits of the dead, so folks say.
Maryland	Peg Alley's Point, a peninsula near Baltimore.	According to the Baltimore *American,* May 1866, a woman named Peg Alley was murdered by her husband on a two-mile-long wooded strip between the Miles River and one of its tributaries. Her ghost was seen by rail workers laboring in the vicinity.

STATE	LOCATION	NATURE OF HAUNTING
	* U. S. F. *Constellation,* Pier 1, Constellation Dock, Baltimore 21202.	A haunted ship? Tradition has it that a sailor who died in 1799 still lurks on this floating museum, possibly till his name is cleared of charges of cowardice.
Massachusetts	Cape Cod.	In the November 1934 issue of *Harper's Monthly Magazine,* a "Harlan Jacobs" told of a series of frightening occurrences while he and his family spent "Four Months in a Haunted House." Though he only stated that it was an isolated spot near a summer resort community—a characterization that fits almost any site on the Cape—the story attains veracity by being included in Louis C. Jones's eminently respectable study, *Things That Go Bump in the Night.* Jones, who knew "Jacobs," wrote that he was a Columbia University professor who told him his experience before it appeared in print. Obviously, it would take investigation to pinpoint the site of this cottage, but determined ghost lovers *might* manage it.
Missouri	Spooks' Hollow, on an old turnpike road four miles from Cape Girardeau, going toward Jackson.	Reported in the October 6, 1887, St. Louis *Globe-Democrat:* salesmen traveling on this road saw a white, diaphanous object rise into the air at a point where the road rounds a high bluff.

STATE	LOCATION	NATURE OF HAUNTING
New Jersey	522 North 5th Street, Camden.	A woman who fell to her death on the stairs of this railroad-flat home, and also a child-ghost, were reported by Hans Holzer in his book, *Houses of Horror.*
	"The Old Mansion," (see story of that title in this collection), on the sand dunes of Long Beach, ten miles north of Atlantic City.	Ghosts of a shipwreck reportedly haunted a long-gone hotel near Manahawkin, New Jersey. The site might still be worth investigating, provided it is not now private property.
New York	Cherry Hill, South Pearl Street, Albany.	Alleged scene of a murder, this colonial mansion has a terrace where a ghost is said to stroll.
	* Morris-Jumel Mansion, 160th Street at Edgecombe, Manhattan 10030.	This museum was once the home of Colonel Roger Morris and served as Washington's headquarters during the Revolutionary Battle of Long Island. Hans Holzer, in *Some of My Best Friends are Ghosts,* says that more than one group of visiting schoolchildren have seen mysterious figures, especially a woman in blue; also a Colonial soldier was seen by a teacher, and yet a third spectre is said to occupy the historical premises.
	Montauk Point, Long Island.	A horrible feline phantom is described in one of Bernhardt J. Hurwood's books: in one of the smaller tourist houses in this resort on the tip of Long Island, a visitor was reportedly annoyed

STATE	LOCATION	NATURE OF HAUNTING
		by a cat that kept snuggling up to him. One night he woke to find the cat crouching over him drinking his blood. When he hurled it away, it vanished. The story may be fiction, but if I ever vacation in Montauk, I do not plan to roll in catnip beforehand.
	St. Mary's Church, Glens Falls.	A frequently encountered ghost legend in American and European folklore is that the dead sometimes hold religious services at midnight in empty churches. This is one place where mysterious lights and choirs were reportedly observed.
	* The Cloisters, Fort Tryon Park, Manhattan.	This Medieval museum and art gallery consists of the original stones of many European antique buildings reassembled in an impressive wooded setting. The place is rich in atmosphere—even eerie.
	The Dakota, 72nd Street at Central Park West, Manhattan.	This grand apartment building, home of many celebrities, has a darkly ominous group of legends clustered round it. Subject of a recent popular non-fiction work about its colorful history, The Dakota is said to have strongly influenced Ira Levin when he wrote *Rosemary's Baby*.
	12 Gay Street, Manhattan.	Once the townhouse of New York mayor Jimmy Walker, this Greenwich Village house is reputedly haunted by ghosts out-

STATE	LOCATION	NATURE OF HAUNTING
		side and in—passersby have reported seeing an elegantly attired individual emerge from the front steps only to vanish—at least so rumor hath it.
Ohio	Miamisburg cemetery, near Dayton.	A report in the Philadelphia *Press* for March 25, 1884, claims that a huge number of townspersons turned out to "catch" a distaff phantom who promptly appeared each night at 9 P.M. to flit meditatively among the headstones. Billyclubs, brouhaha, even pistol shots merely made the woman vanish—possibly out of indignation?
Pennsylvania	* Loudoun Mansion, 4650 Germantown Avenue, Philadelphia 19144.	A small boy reputedly haunts this restored home of a nineteenth-century merchant, now a museum filled with antiques.
	Millvale Croatian Catholic Church, Millvale (near Pittsburgh).	At least two separate sources report that a painter (variously named Maxo Vanka and Maxim Hvatka) who was commissioned to do religious frescoes in the chapel, often was terrified by the literally chilling presence of a ghostly priest, believed to be a Father Ranzinger, spiritual leader of an earlier church that stood on the same site but burned down.
	Pottstown, near Philadelphia.	Local legend has it that a phantom hitchhiker often thumbs rides on local roads, only to dis-

STATE	LOCATION	NATURE OF HAUNTING
		appear from the back seat while the driver pays attention to the night highway. But in the final chapter of *Things That Go Bump in the Night,* Louis C. Jones points out that oral variations of this scenario may be heard in practically every small town in America—and Europe!
	* The Priestley House, at the juncture of the north and west branches of the Susquehanna River, Northumberland 17857.	Joseph Priestley, freethinker and scientist, settled in a lovely home on the Susquehanna River to be free of religious persecution in his native England. After his death, odd lights were frequently noted by relatives and passersby and one elderly descendant told a reporter several years ago that "Joseph still potters about in his laboratory." When I visited the museum, I noted an extremely friendly "lived-in" atmosphere (see Appendix A).
Tennessee	* Old City Cemetery, Nashville 37202.	An historic and atmospheric graveyard that features a large avenue lit by eerie lamps. Particularly notable is the Ann Rawlings Sanders memorial. This young woman leaped into the nearby Cumberland River after a lovers' quarrel. Her grief-struck boyfriend put up an eternal light on her tomb to quiet her troubled spirit, for she had been afraid of the dark.

STATE	LOCATION	NATURE OF HAUNTING
Texas	"Ghost Light," Chinati Mountain, Highway 90 between Alpine and Marfa.	Locals claim to see a high-up eerie blue light from the highway and attribute it to a ghostly Indian's campfire. Investigations have been fruitless, since the light vanishes when approached.
	* Howard Mansion, South Main Street, Henderson 75652.	James L. Howard built this latter-day museum in 1851. The oldest brick home in town, it was often visited by Sam Houston, a cousin of the Howard clan. The ghost of the original Mrs. Howard is said to have been seen.
Vermont	* Bowman Mansion & Mausoleum, Route 103, near Cuttingsville 05738.	The Haunted Mansion Bookshop is on the premises of a great estate and adjacent to a cemetery once owned by John P. Bowman, a farmer-turned-tanner who left a large will to keep up the grounds and house. Bowman House is said to be a very grim place: footsteps have been heard, a woman's ghost was seen once, and there is an eerie dark spot at the top of a stairway that no one likes to linger by. Once a small girl is supposed to have stuck out her tongue at one of the portraits; several witnesses claimed they saw it fly off the wall and strike her. The bookshop owners allow none to remain on the premises after sundown, and they are quick to depart for the night, as well.

STATE	LOCATION	NATURE OF HAUNTING
Virginia	* Belle Grove, Box 137, Middletown 22645.	This museum nestled in the Shenandoah Mountains was a plantation where a bizarre murder took place. Ghosts still are said to lurk by the smokehouse.
	* Fort Monroe Casemate Museum, Box 341, Fort Monroe 23651 (near Norfolk).	The oldest continually garrisoned fortress in the United States, Fort Monroe boasts at least ten phantoms.
	* Haw Branch Plantation, c/o W. C. McConnaughey, Box 188, Amelia 23002.	Crowds of ghosts are supposed to haunt this 1745 Georgian-Federal residence.
	* Kenmore, c/o Kenmore Assoc., 1201 Washington Avenue, Fredericksburg 22401.	A Georgian mansion, Kenmore is rumored to be haunted by a Revolutionary warrior, Colonel Fielding Lewis, armament manufacturer and organizer of the Virginia Militia.
	* Lee's Boyhood Home, Robert E. Lee House, 607 Oronoco Street, Alexandria 22314.	A small boy haunts the home once owned by Robert E. Lee's father.
	* Ramsay House, c/o Alexandria Tourist Council, 221 King Street, Alexandria 22314.	The Ramsay House was the residence of William Ramsay, a merchant who helped found the city and was its first mayor. His spirit supposedly appears sometimes at an upstairs window.
	* Scotchtown, Route 2, Box 168, Beaverdam 23015.	This venerable mansion was once the home of Dolly Madison, as well as patriot Patrick Henry. One of its legends is that a duel fought in the hall left bloodstains and spectres.

STATE	LOCATION	NATURE OF HAUNTING
	*Shirley Plantation, Route 2, Box 57, Charles City 23030.	Ancestral home of the King Carter family, it is full of architectural and antique treasures. A portrait of an "Aunt Pratt" is said to emit ghostly noises if hung improperly.
	* The Trapezium House, 244 Market Street, Petersburg 23803.	One of America's great architectural oddities, Trapezium House may be the one place to go to be *free* of ghosts! Its builder, Charles O'Hara, had a West Indian servant who convinced him that ghosts and evil spirits inhabit right angles. So the O'Hara home was specially constructed so it would contain *no 90° angles!* The structure has no parallel walls. Dubbed Trapezium Place in the nineteenth century, it is a brick three-story, three-bay, Federal-style building in which every room seems to converge on an imaginary vanishing point. Even windows and doors, mantles and stairs were built to avoid right angles and every floor board was cut on a slant. O'Hara was an eccentric in many ways, but it is true that the house has never had any ghostly legends connected with it. But all that may change: the City of Petersburg acquired the property in 1972 and expects to open it in autumn, 1981, as "The Ghost Story Telling House of Virginia."

STATE	LOCATION	NATURE OF HAUNTING
	* Westover Plantation, c/o Virginia State Travel Service, 6 North Sixth Street, Richmond 23219.	This Georgian home is supposed to harbor the spirit of Evelyn Byrd, who died of grief when her father broke up her engagement to a British nobleman.
	* Wyth House, c/o Director of Travel, Colonial Williamsburg Foundation, Williamsburg 23185.	The Colonial Williamsburg tourist attraction features 160 buildings on 173 acres. One of the restored homes, Wyth House, is supposed to be visited by a ghost in eighteenth-century ball gown, believed to be the spirit of a Lady Skipworth.
Washington	Eagles Gorge, near Seattle.	A story in the January 10, 1892, edition of the Seattle *Press-Times* claims that a phantom train runs along a portion of track at Eagles Gorge on the Northern Pacific line.
West Virginia	Grantsville, some three miles out of town.	A section of Calhoun farm country is said to be haunted by a ghost who will make life unpleasant for anyone living within a rather large radius, not to mention anyone traveling the roads after dark . . . but it *was* a long time ago that the haunting was reported, in the September 30, 1884, edition of the Cincinnati *Enquirer*.

APPENDIX D:

SELECTED BIBLIOGRAPHY

Ghost stories comprise a rich subcategory of fantasy literature, yet first-rate ones are not easy to find. Below is a by-no-means exhaustive list of some of the more interesting supernatural tales and novels, plus a handful of "factual" works on our favorite shivery pastime. Though the quality of writing is quite uneven in the titles selected below, I believe there is something compelling in each for true ghost aficionados to delight in.

It may surprise fantasists to note that several popular authors have been totally omitted—Lovecraft, for instance. But although the old gentleman of Providence has contributed a few gems to weird literature, to call them ghost stories would stretch the term more than I have been willing to do in this collection.

BANGS, JOHN KENDRICK, *The Water Ghost of Harrowby Hall.* One of the few successful humorists in the field, Bangs created several saucy and ingenious phantoms, of which the sopping water-spirit is one of the most amusing.

BENSON, E. F., *The Room in the Tower and Other Stories.* Benson was one of the consummate masters of the form. Every one of his scanty tales in the genre is interesting, but the tale of the awful thing in the tower room, with its hideous recurring nightmares, is one of the most terrifying stories in the English language.

BENSON, ROBERT H., *A Mirror of Shalott,* from which "Father Stein's Tale" was taken, is a rare collection of intellectually provoking ghostly stories, all told by Catholic priests attempting to characterize the invisible world as it relates to their profession.

BULWER-LYTTON, EDWARD, *The House and the Brain,* also known as *The Haunters and the Haunted,* a strong novella of supernatural menace and psychic detecting. The tale has often been reprinted in truncated form, but the full text appears in the Wise-Fraser anthology listed below.

COLLINS, WILKIE, *The Dream Woman,* a nightmarish novella of *déjà vu,* a "future ghost," so to speak. Collins wrote many fine, regrettably obscure ghost stories; though the supernatural may only account for a small portion of some, the keen insight into character makes them worth reading. Especially recommended: *The Haunted Hotel.*

COZZENS, JAMES GOULD, *Castaway.* Author of the best-selling *By Love Possessed,* Cozzens wrote several popular novels, but *Castaway* is little known. An allegory of man's ultimate aloneness in the universe, it is not obviously a ghost tale—yet the enigmatic climax suggests supernatural events, as well as a number of other interpretations. The plot—one man alone in a deserted department store—surely is one of the most unusual in American literature.

CRAWFORD, F. MARION, *The Upper Berth.* A somewhat long, but deservedly famous terror tale of a haunting on board ship. Crawford's ability to create horror through the narrator's sense of touch is remarkable.

DE MAUPASSANT, GUY, "Was It a Dream?" A short-short rich in irony: a mortal witnesses a graveyard of corpses scratch out the lies on their markers. De Maupassant wrote several powerful ghost stories. See also *The Flayed Hand.*

DERLETH, AUGUST, *Mr. George.* A lonely girl is the prey of three unscrupulous relatives, until the spectral protector of the title comes to rescue her. The late proprietor of the all-weird fiction publisher, Arkham House, Derleth wrote vast quantities of ghost stories, many of them depressingly second-rate, just as many unforgettable. *Mr. George* belongs to the latter classification.

DICKENS, CHARLES, *The Signalman,* probably the most famous ghost story by the master, always excepting *A Christmas Carol.* A railroad signalman keeps seeing spirit-world warnings of imminent wrecks that he is powerless to prevent.

DOYLE, ARTHUR CONAN, *The Land of Mist.* The creator of Sherlock Holmes dabbled in weird fiction, too. This novel, more or less forced into the Professor Challenger series, is really a polemic for spiritualism, a movement in which Doyle became greatly involved in his latter years. Though decried for its lack of objectivity, not without cause, it is still well worth reading; Doyle was too consummate a craftsman to write a dull book, and this exploration of the mediumistic profession is more accessible than many texts on the same subject.

DUNNINGER, JOSEPH, *Dunninger's Psychic Revelations.* An important study of fake mediums by the late mentalist.

FAULKNER, WILLIAM, "The Hound." This gritty tale of murder in Yoknapatawpha County comprises a major part of the thrust of *The Mansion,* the final novel in the Snopes trilogy, though the story itself appears in the first volume, *The Hamlet.* It is not generally known that Faulkner rewrote it for the novel; the original is really as much a ghost story as it is a character study, but the weird elements were dispensed with for the book.

GOGOL, NIKOLAI, *Viy,* a powerful novella about vampiric ghosts. The basis for the Karloff segment of the film, *Black Sabbath.*

HARVEY, WILLIAM F., *The Beast with Five Fingers,* a murdered man's severed hand seeks revenge. Basis for a popular Peter Lorre film.

HICHENS, ROBERT, *How Love Came to Professor Guildea,* as sophisticated as an essentially loathsome concept ever can become, an intellectual horror story that may leave many readers lukewarm, and afford some genuine gooseflesh to the judicious few.

HOFFMANN, E. T., *The Entail.* The great fantasist mostly eschewed conventional ghosts, but not in this intricate novella. Though the haunting is misplaced (too near the beginning) and the involved family history cries for editorial compression, *The Entail* has real tragic power, in spite of its narrative flaws.

HOLZER, HANS, *Ghost Hunter, Ghosts I've Met, Yankee Ghosts,* etc. A professional ghost investigator, Holzer has written many popular, easy-to-read recountings of his findings, often in houses not far away from one's home town in the East. The first three titles listed above, though the hardest to find, are probably the best. Whether Holzer is a genuine researcher or a mere opportunist is for the reader to decide . . . but he certainly writes engagingly and briskly. His books are fun to read.

HOUDINI, HARRY, *Houdini's Spirit World.* A classic exposé of charlatanism in the medium business. If one thinks the friendly neighborhood psychic is real, read your Houdini and wonder.

HUNT, LEIGH, "A Tale for a Chimney Corner" is a touching vignette by an author who disapproved of ghost stories. The introduction to the tale is worth the time in itself, as it is a delightfully incisive drubbing of the more meretricious effects achieved by minor fantasists.

JACKSON, SHIRLEY, *The Haunting of Hill House,* though technically a twisted story of haunted people, is generally classed as a ghost story because of its plot: the investigation of an allegedly haunted house by a small team of "sensitives." "Hill House" is probably the finest novel in the genre, certainly the most poetically evocative in style. It has strongly influenced much of its successor ghost novels, esp. Matheson's *Hell House* (Q.V.).

JAMES, HENRY, *The Turn of the Screw.* The ambiguous and well-known story of two possessed children and their heroic-demonic governess, *The Turn of the Screw* is, to my mind, enormously overrated. The pace, even for James, is ponderous. Apologists have tried to liken it to Conrad's *Heart of Darkness* in that both authors attempt to erect a wall of words against the ultimate horror, but the analogy hardly bears up. *The Turn of the Screw* is admittedly a powerful character study, but it hardly occupies the central position in James' philosophy that Conrad's masterpiece did. Henry James wrote many neglected ghost tales, most of them far more readable and psychologically quite as valid as the Quint-Jessel story.

JAMES, M. R., *Oh, Whistle and I'll Come to You, My Lad.* The deservedly famous ghost-story writer, M. R. James, achieved his best effects by understatement and rooting weird events in dry-as-dust scholastic minutiae that nevertheless convinces the reader he is peering into the activities and troubles of real people. Most of James' terror tales are first-rate, but *Oh, Whistle . . .* is certainly the frontrunner.

JONES, LOUIS C., *Things That Go Bump in the Night,* a gracefully written study of the ghostly in American folklore. Jones sent students home during holidays to gather as many oral recountings of neighborhood ghosts as could be gleaned. He then classified them according to type and came up with the surprising fact that ghostly lore tends to follow a relatively small number of recognizable patterns. This lucid and chatty collection is "must" reading for any who profess interest in the supernatural.

KAYE, M., and GODWIN, P., *A Cold Blue Light.* Our forthcoming Berkley novel of a haunted house and its investigators will probe the logical limits of relativism (see Appendix A), though set within the framework of an especially nasty haunting.

KING, STEPHEN, *The Shining,* a much-too-long, redundant novel about a haunted resort hotel. Nevertheless—and in spite of one embarrassingly ludicrous device, a group of animated hedge animals—*The Shining* has many genuinely terrifying moments, believable characters and more strange atmosphere than Kubrick could ever capture in his film version of the book.

KIPLING, RUDYARD, *The Phantom 'Rickshaw.* A memorable *conte cruelle* in which the narrator is haunted by the spurned woman who still adores him. The truly dreadful aspect to the tale is the victim's growing appreciation of his caddish behavior; but though his nature changes, it does him no good at all.

MACARDLE, DOROTHY, *The Uninvited,* the basis for a famous film starring Ray Milland. *The Uninvited* is a gripping novel of an innocent girl who is obsessed with a house she is warned to stay away from, a house haunted by two spectres.

MATHESON, RICHARD, *Hell House.* Luridly written, *Hell House* is as subtle as brass knuckles in tissue-paper gloves. But for pure harrowing fright and ingenuity of plot, it may never be surpassed. Hell House itself is described by one character as the Everest of haunted houses, and it is no hyperbole. The film, though interesting on its own terms, could not recapture one fiftieth of the unrelenting gruesomeness of Matheson's towering nightmare of Belasco House, where there are no gods.

ONIONS, OLIVER, *The Beckoning Fair One* is one of the acknowledged handful of masterpieces in ghost fiction. The lure and appeal of a spirit *sans merci* captivates a sensitive artist, but to tell more would neither enlighten nor even hint at the uniquely haunting tone of this obsessive novella.

PRICE, HARRY, *The Most Haunted House in England* is an engrossing and unfortunately scarce non-fiction book on the lively hauntings observed at Borley Rectory before it burned down. Though Price came under serious adverse scrutiny by British parapsychologists, his book is enjoyable what-if reading, as is its equally scarce sequel, *The End of Borley Rectory,* in which ghostly doings were allegedly observed in the ruins of the old pile.

STOKER, BRAM, "The Judge's House," a suspenseful short story about the phantom of an evil judge; written by the author of *Dracula.*

STRAUB, PETER, *Ghost Story.* A popular but thin novel of reincarnative revenge. Straub's evocative prose and gift for characterization creates a haunting, dreamlike atmosphere that might have been memorable if he hadn't adopted a tortuously convoluted structure (flashbacks within flashbacks, including a shameful rural knockoff of *The Turn of the Screw*) that attenuates the suspense until the reader is left with a perfectly predictable plotline hundreds of pages before the end. Straub has been compared to Faulkner, which is neither stylistically accurate nor fair to Straub. It is a colossal insult to Faulkner.

WISE, H., and FRASER, P., *Great Tales of Terror and the Supernatural,* an indispensable anthology for every library. Published by Modern Library, this large tome contains several of the items listed above.